JUST ROLL WITH IT

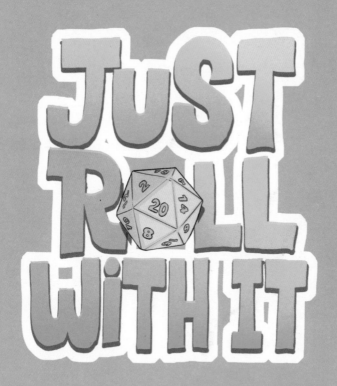

JUST ROLL WITH IT

WRITTEN BY LEE DURFEY-LAVOIE
ILLUSTRATED BY VERONICA AGARWAL

RH GRAPHIC

NEW YORK

Just Roll with It was thumbnailed with a 1.5 Faber-Castell pen and then penciled, inked, and colored digitally using a Cintiq 13HD and Adobe Photoshop CS5.1.

Text copyright © 2021 by Lee Durfey-Lavoie
Cover art and interior illustrations copyright © 2021 by Veronica Agarwal

All rights reserved. Published in the United States by RH Graphic, an imprint of Random House Children's Books, a division of Penguin Random House LLC, New York.

RH Graphic with the book design is a trademark of Penguin Random House LLC.

Visit us on the web! RHKidsGraphic.com • @RHKidsGraphic

Educators and librarians, for a variety of teaching tools, visit us at RHTeachersLibrarians.com

Library of Congress Cataloging-in-Publication Data is available upon request.
ISBN 978-0-593-12541-0 (hardcover) — ISBN 978-1-9848-9700-8 (library binding)
ISBN 978-1-9848-9699-5 (paperback) — ISBN 978-1-9848-9701-5 (ebook)

Designed by Patrick Crotty

MANUFACTURED IN CHINA
10 9 8 7 6 5 4 3 2
First Edition

A comic on every bookshelf.

To our family and friends, and my therapist. It's with your support, patience, love, and guidance that I'm able to become a better version of myself every day.
—V.A.

To everybody who needs to know they're not alone.
—L.D.-L.

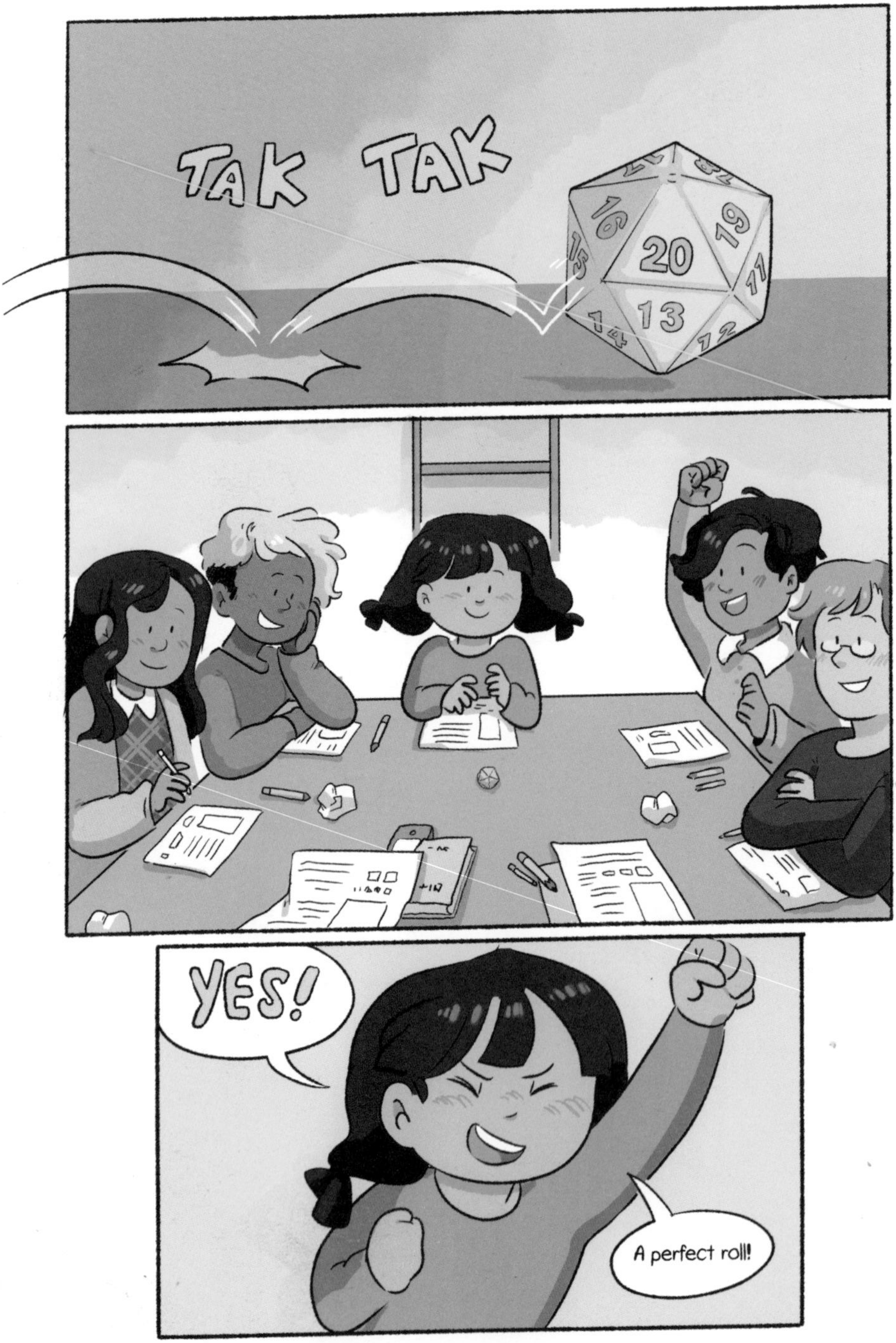
TAK TAK
YES!
A perfect roll!

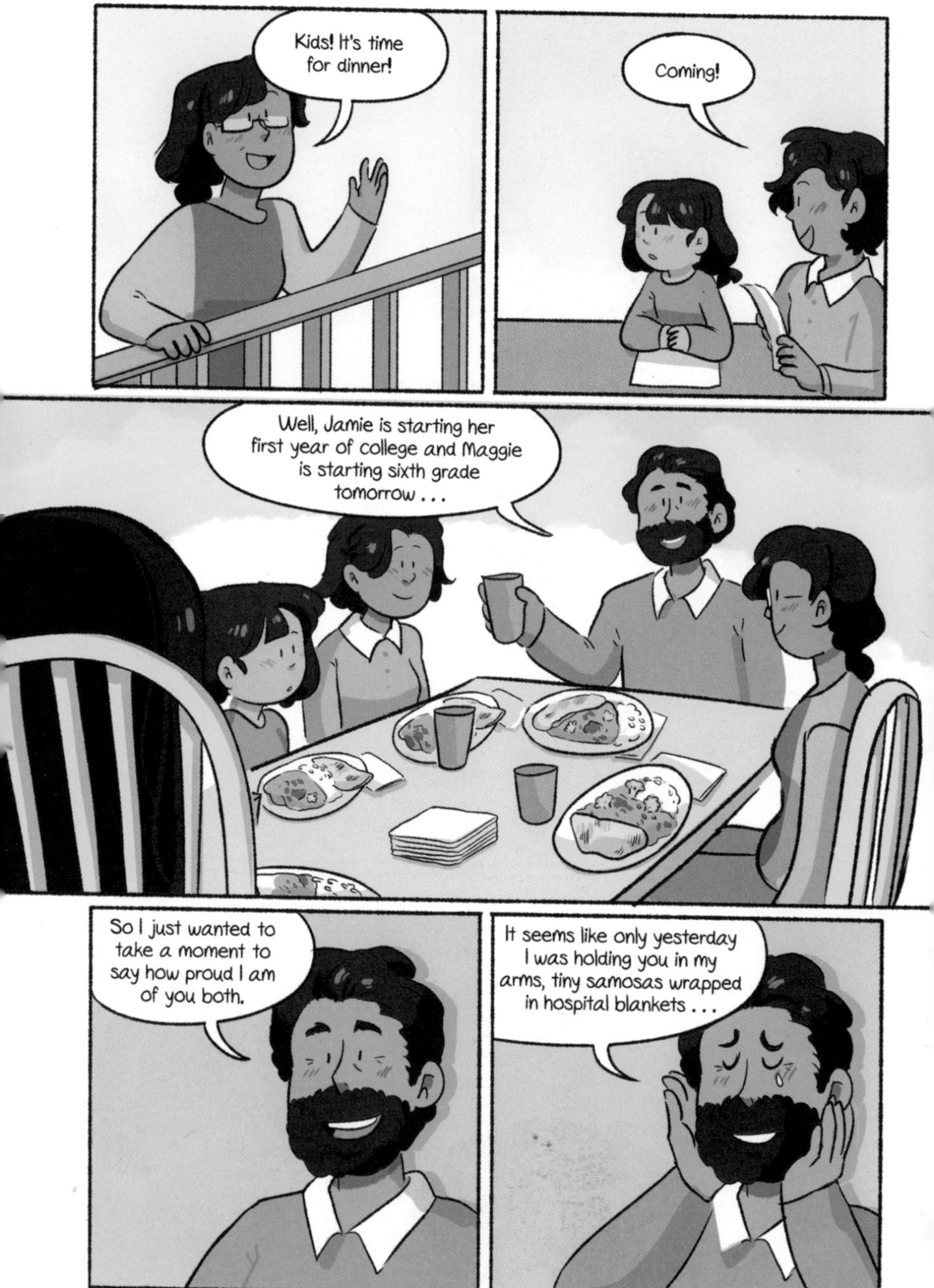
Kids! It's time for dinner!
Coming!
Well, Jamie is starting her first year of college and Maggie is starting sixth grade tomorrow . . .
So I just wanted to take a moment to say how proud I am of you both.
It seems like only yesterday I was holding you in my arms, tiny samosas wrapped in hospital blankets . . .

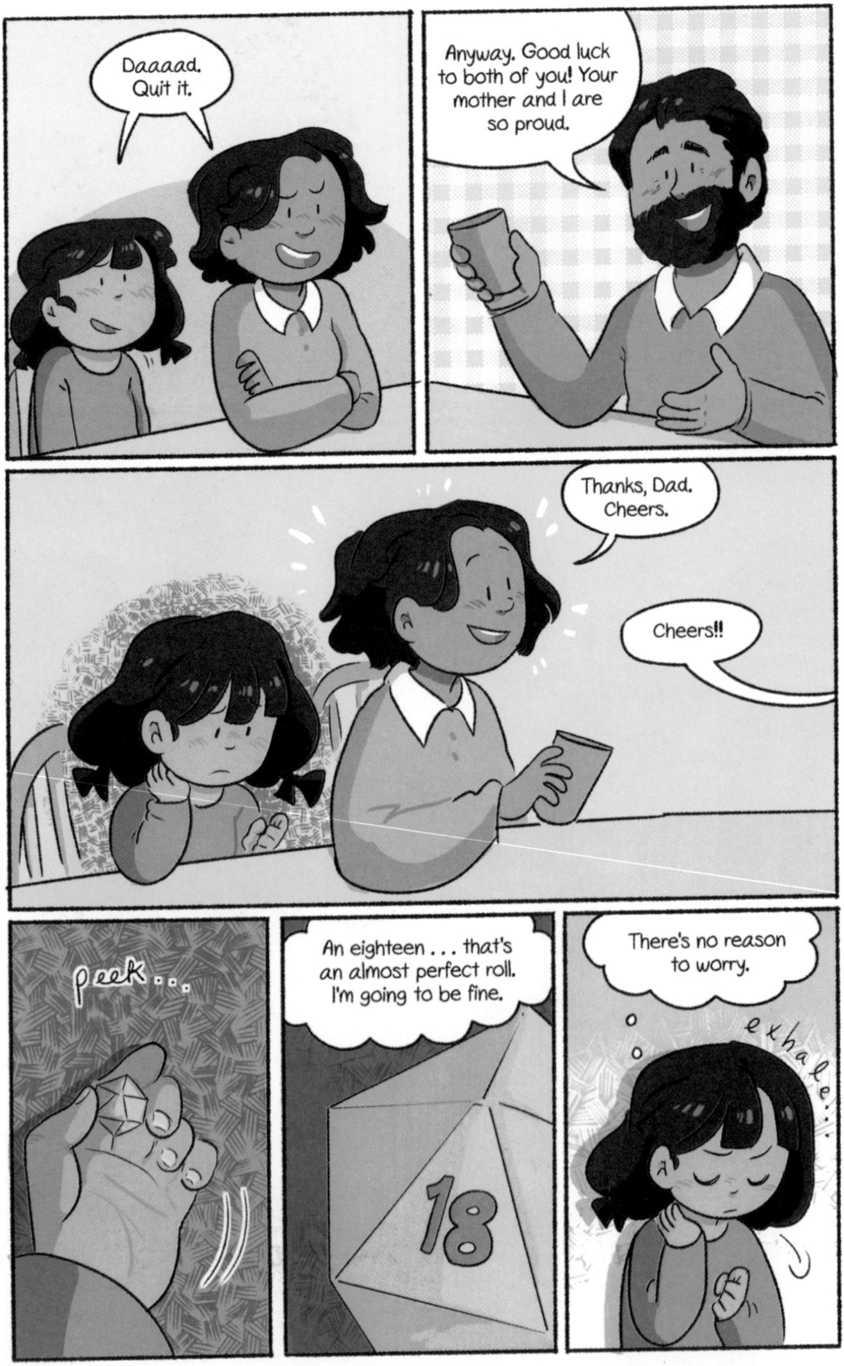
Daaaad. Quit it.
Anyway. Good luck to both of you! Your mother and I are so proud.
Thanks, Dad. Cheers.
Cheers!!
peek . . .
An eighteen . . . that's an almost perfect roll. I'm going to be fine.
18
There's no reason to worry.
exhale . . .

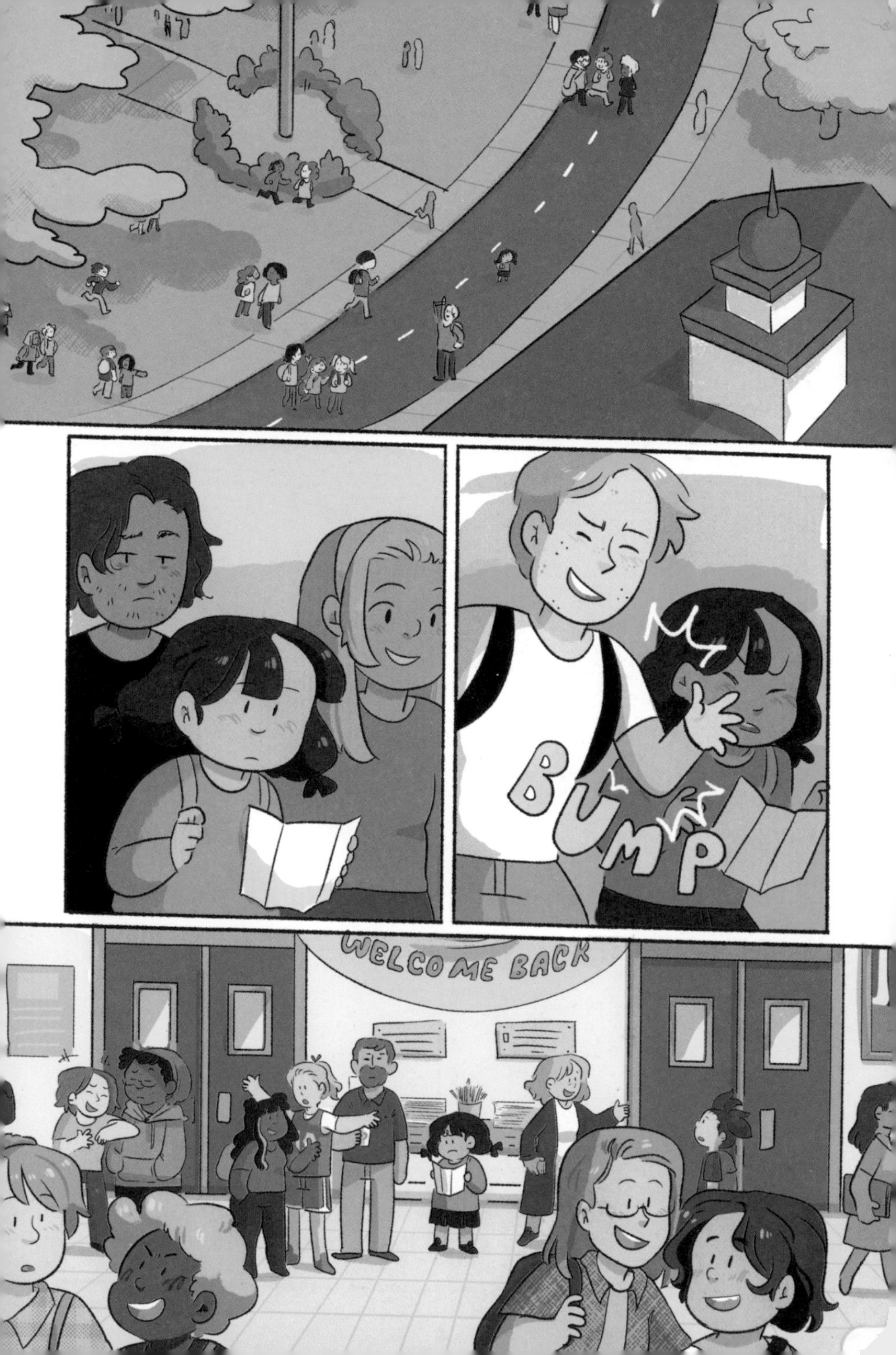
BUMP
WELCOME BACK

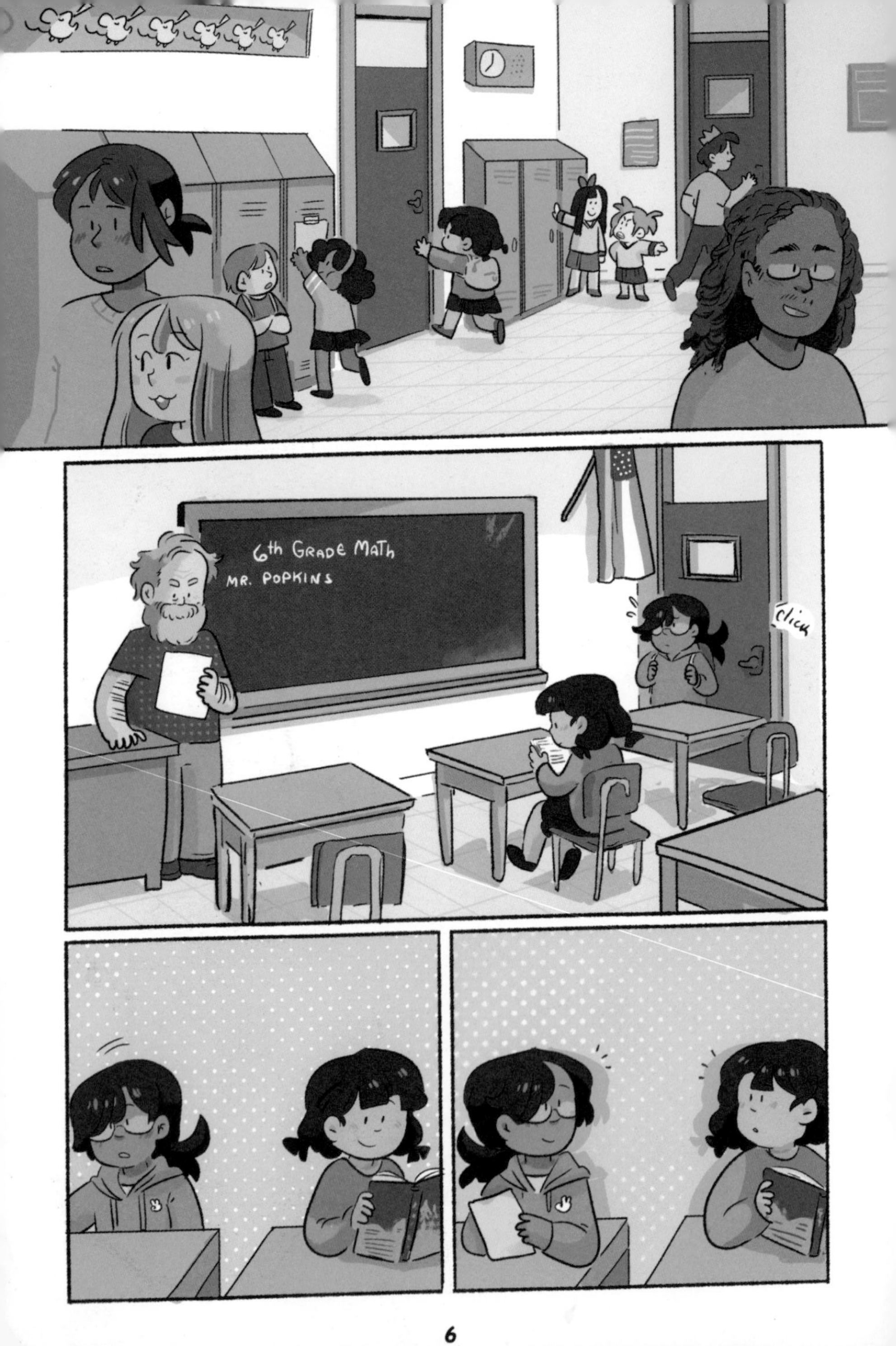
6th GRADE MATH
MR. POPKINS
click

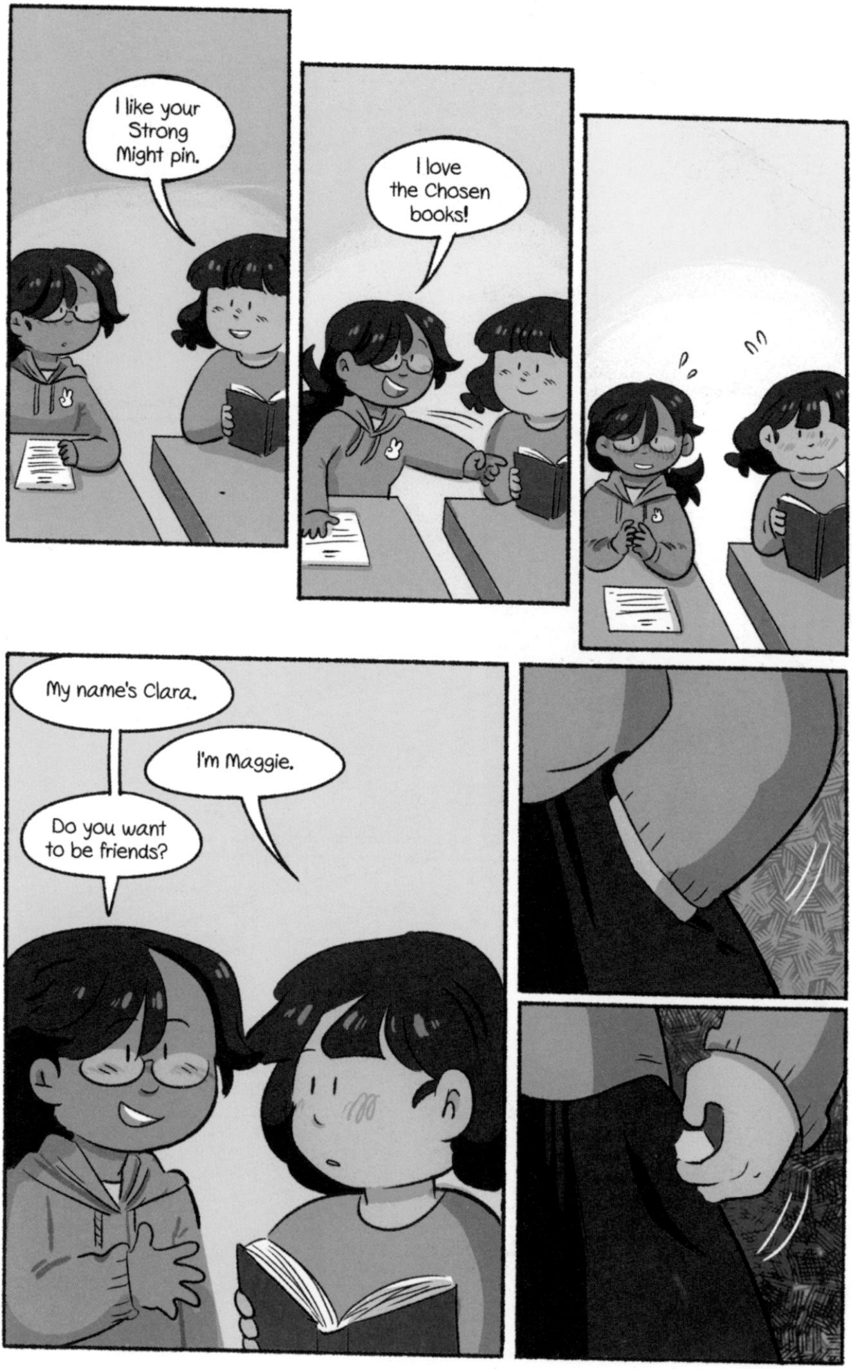

I like your Strong Might pin.
I love the Chosen books!
My name's Clara.
I'm Maggie.
Do you want to be friends?

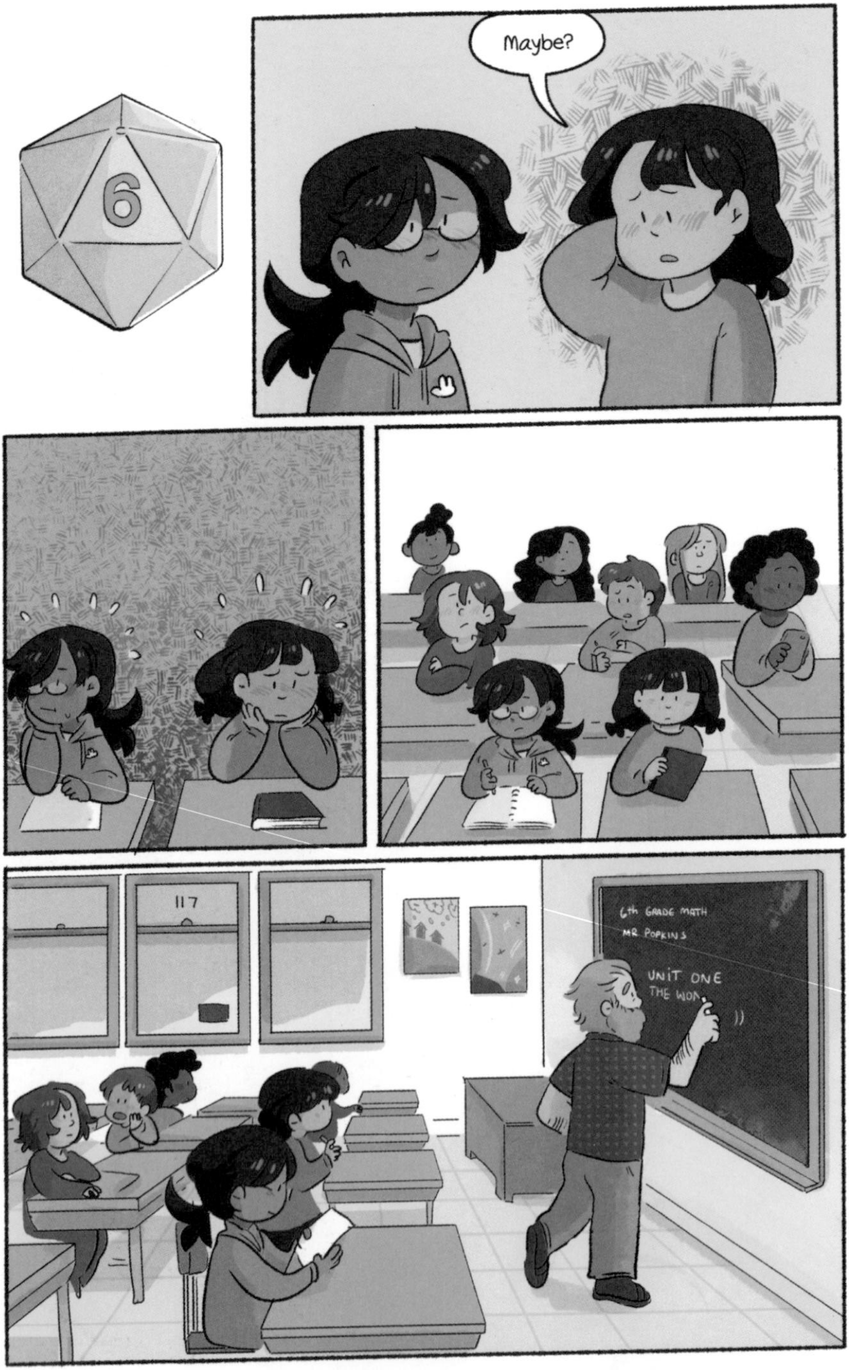
6
Maybe?
117
6th GRADE MATH
MR POPKINS
UNIT ONE

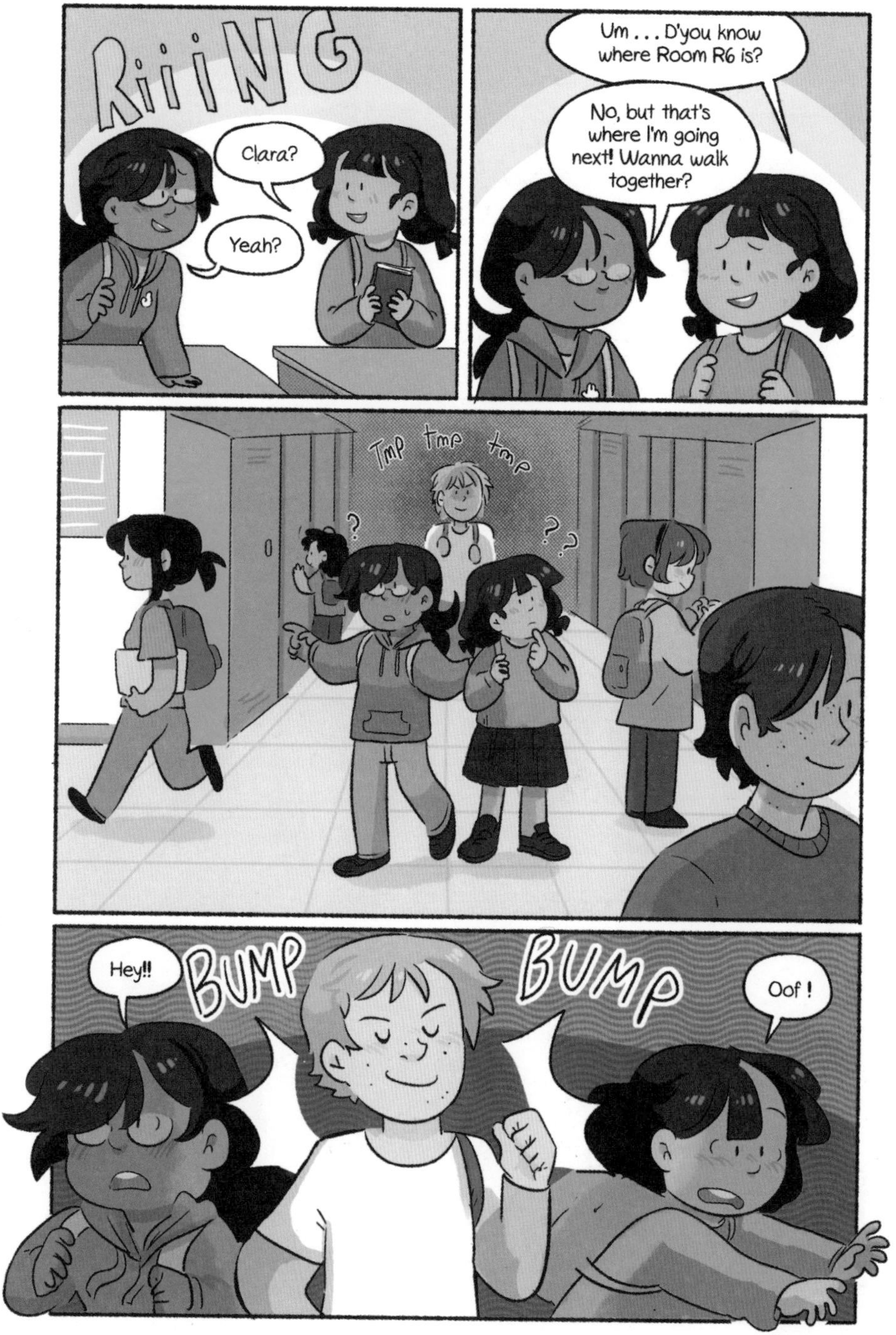
RiiiNG
Clara?
Yeah?
Um . . . D'you know where Room R6 is?
No, but that's where I'm going next! Wanna walk together?
Tmp tmp tmp
?
??
Hey!!
BUMP
BUMP
Oof !

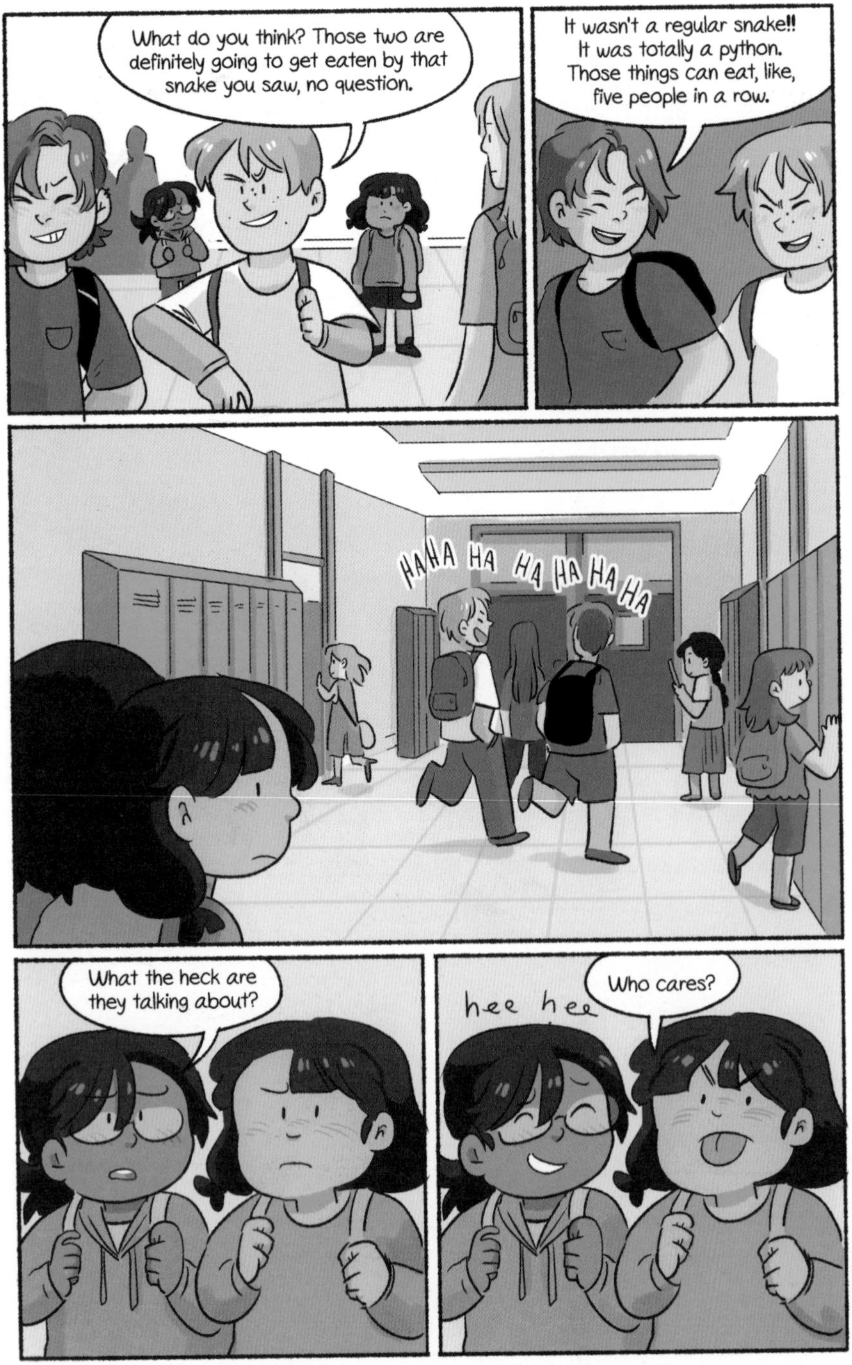
What do you think? Those two are definitely going to get eaten by that snake you saw, no question.
It wasn't a regular snake!! It was totally a python. Those things can eat, like, five people in a row.
HAHA HA HA HA HA HA
What the heck are they talking about?
hee hee
Who cares?

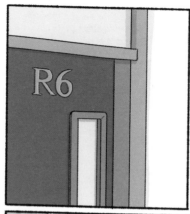

That guy was so rude.

I bet he's an eighth grader and thinks he can do whatever he wants because he'll be going to high school next year.

Yeah, I bet. Too bad eighth graders are at the bottom of the high school food chain.

ha ha ha

That's true!! I guess he'll get his next year, huh?

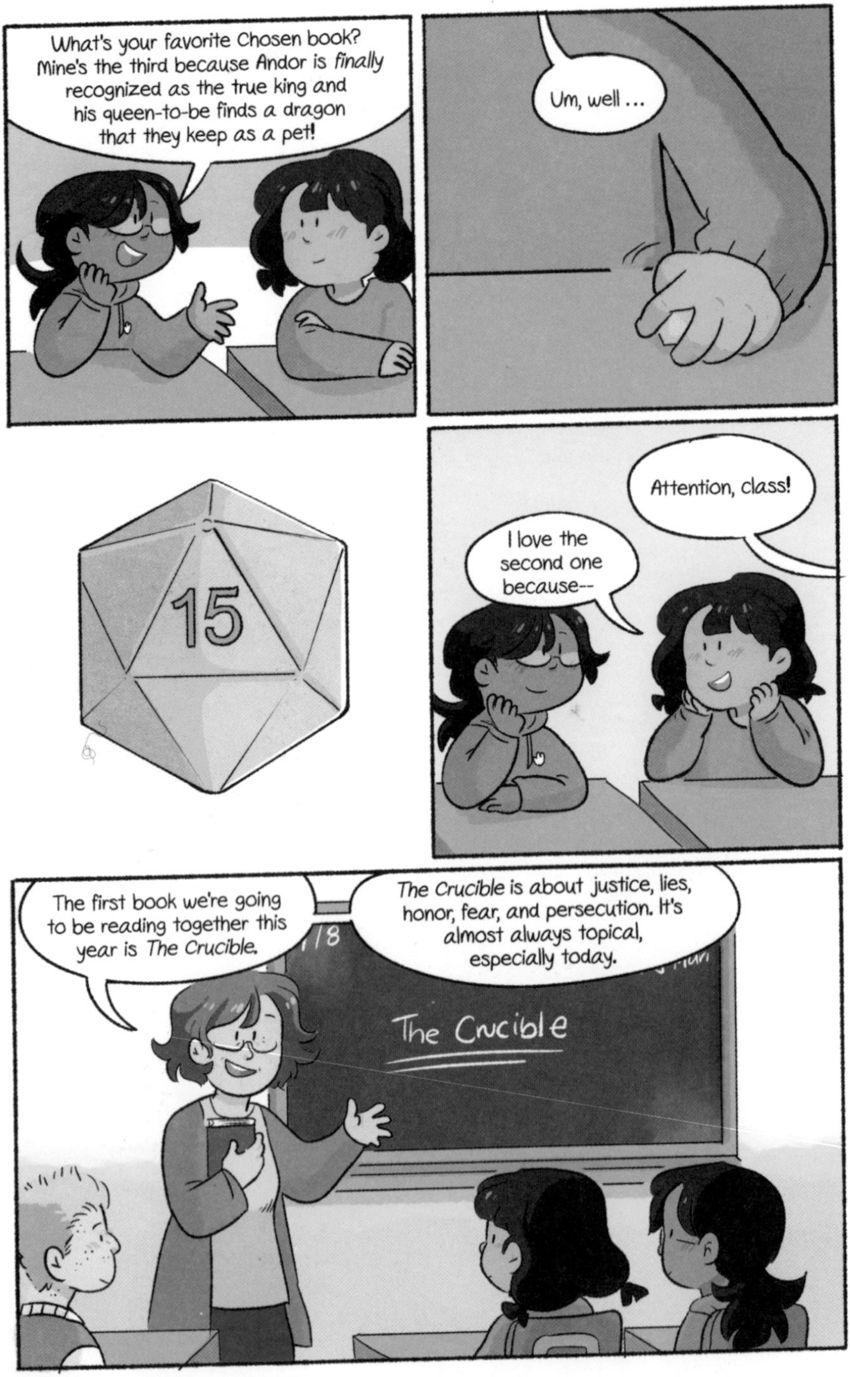
What's your favorite Chosen book? Mine's the third because Andor is *finally* recognized as the true king and his queen-to-be finds a dragon that they keep as a pet!
Um, well ...
15
I love the second one because--
Attention, class!
The first book we're going to be reading together this year is *The Crucible*.
The Crucible is about justice, lies, honor, fear, and persecution. It's almost always topical, especially today.
The Crucible

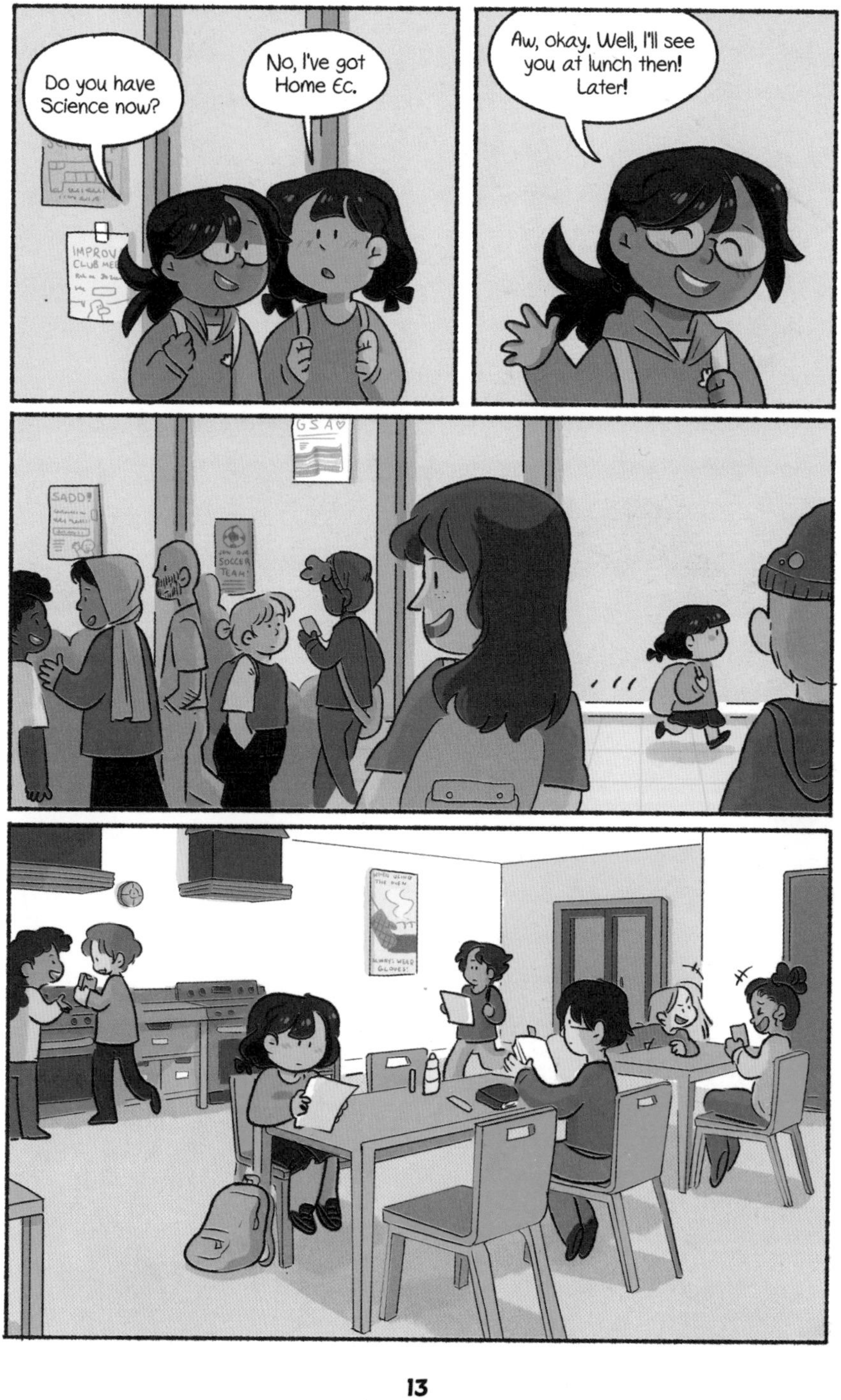
Do you have Science now?
No, I've got Home Ec.
Aw, okay. Well, I'll see you at lunch then! Later!
GSA
SADD!
SOCCER TEAM!

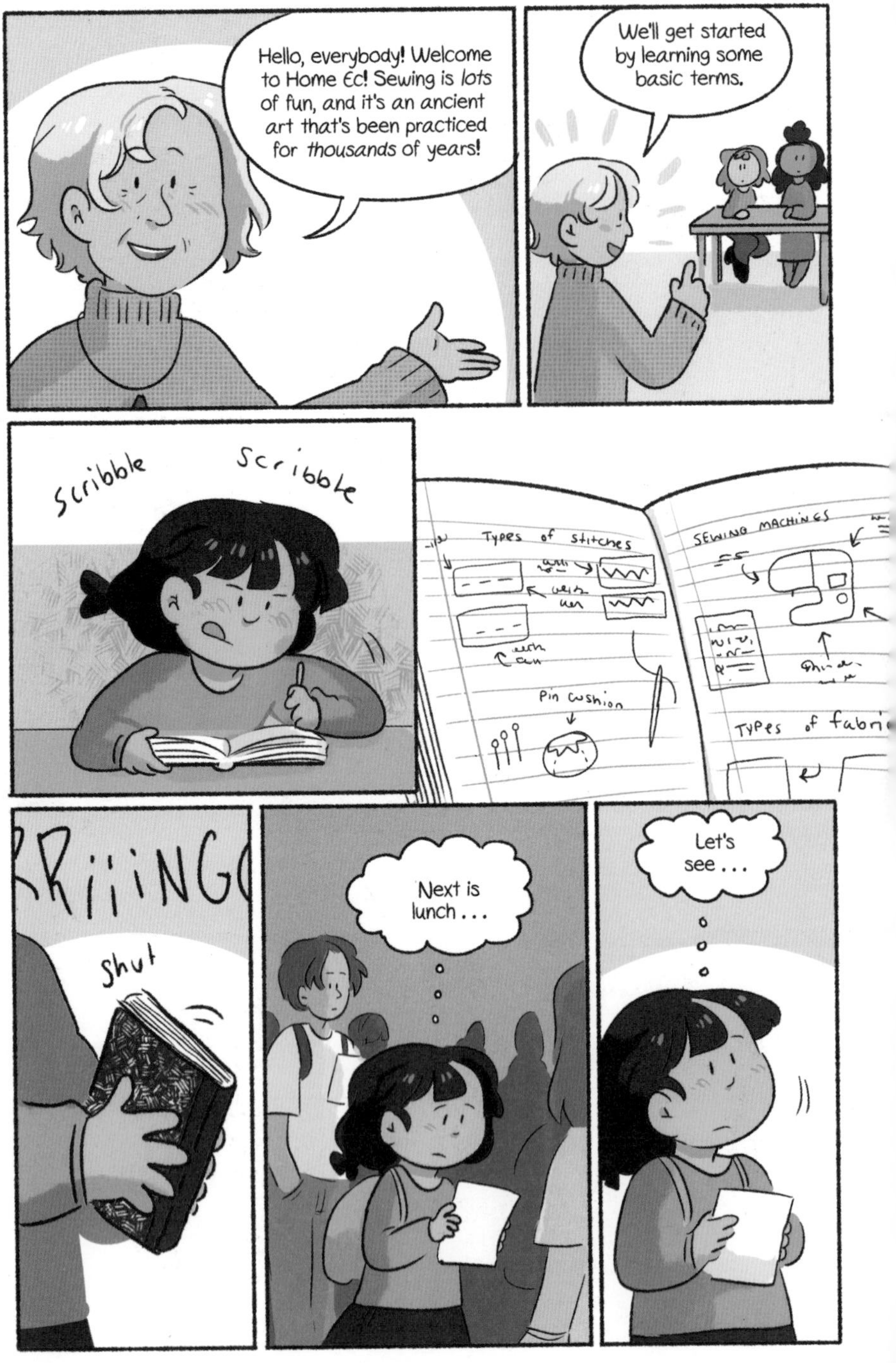
Hello, everybody! Welcome to Home Ec! Sewing is *lots* of fun, and it's an ancient art that's been practiced for *thousands* of years!
We'll get started by learning some basic terms.
Scribble
Scribble
Types of stitches
Pin cushion
SEWING MACHINES
Types of fabri
RRIIING
Shut
Next is lunch . . .
Let's see . . .

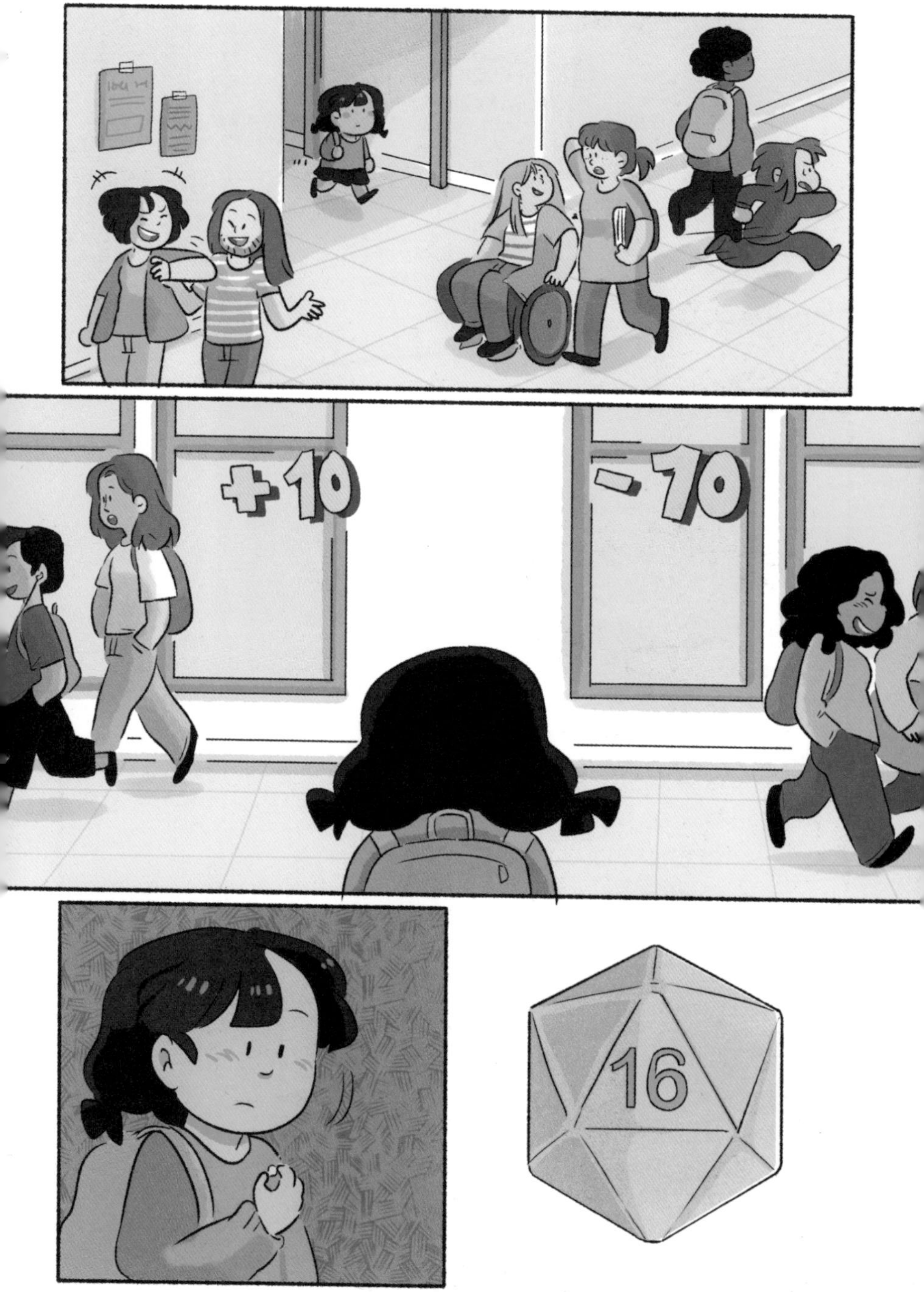
+10
-10
16

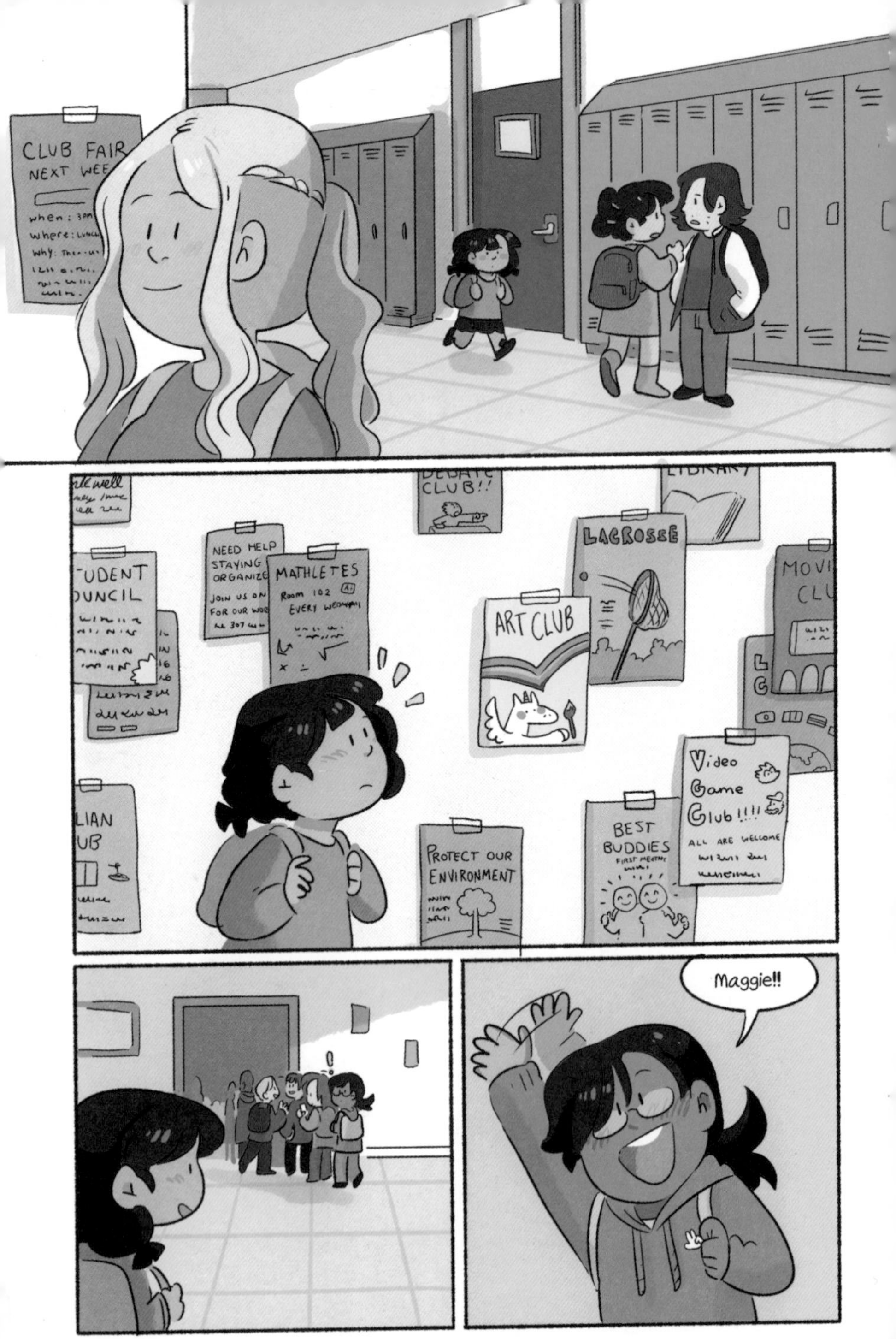
CLUB FAIR
NEXT WEE
when:
where:
why:
CLUB!!
LACROSSE
NEED HELP
STAYING
ORGANIZE
MATHLETES
Room 102
ART CLUB
MOVI
CLU
Video
Game
Club!!!!
ALL ARE WELCOME
BEST
BUDDIES
FIRST MEETING
PROTECT OUR
ENVIRONMENT
Maggie!!

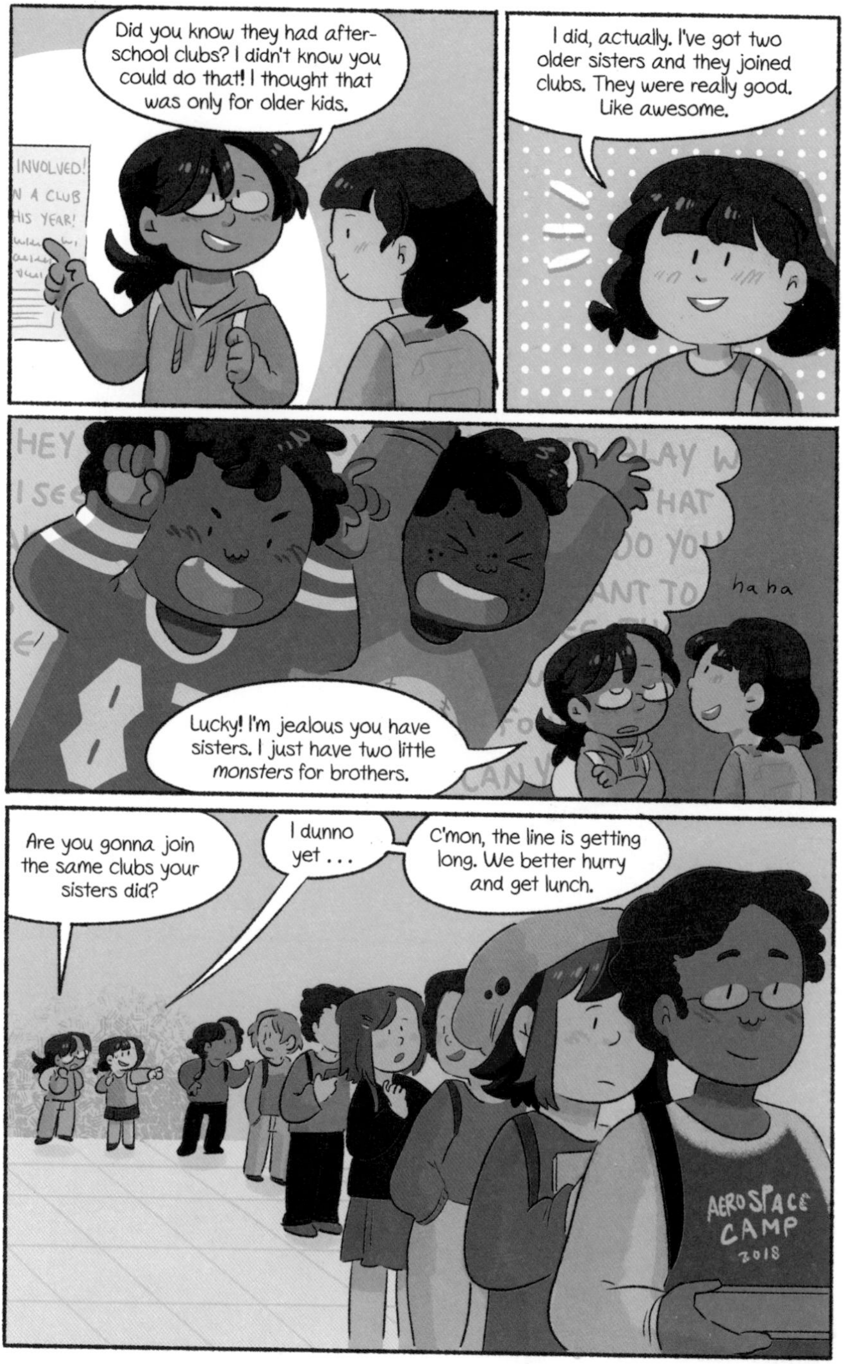
INVOLVED!
Did you know they had after-school clubs? I didn't know you could do that! I thought that was only for older kids.
I did, actually. I've got two older sisters and they joined clubs. They were really good. Like awesome.
ha ha
Lucky! I'm jealous you have sisters. I just have two little *monsters* for brothers.
Are you gonna join the same clubs your sisters did?
I dunno yet . . .
C'mon, the line is getting long. We better hurry and get lunch.
AEROSPACE CAMP 2018

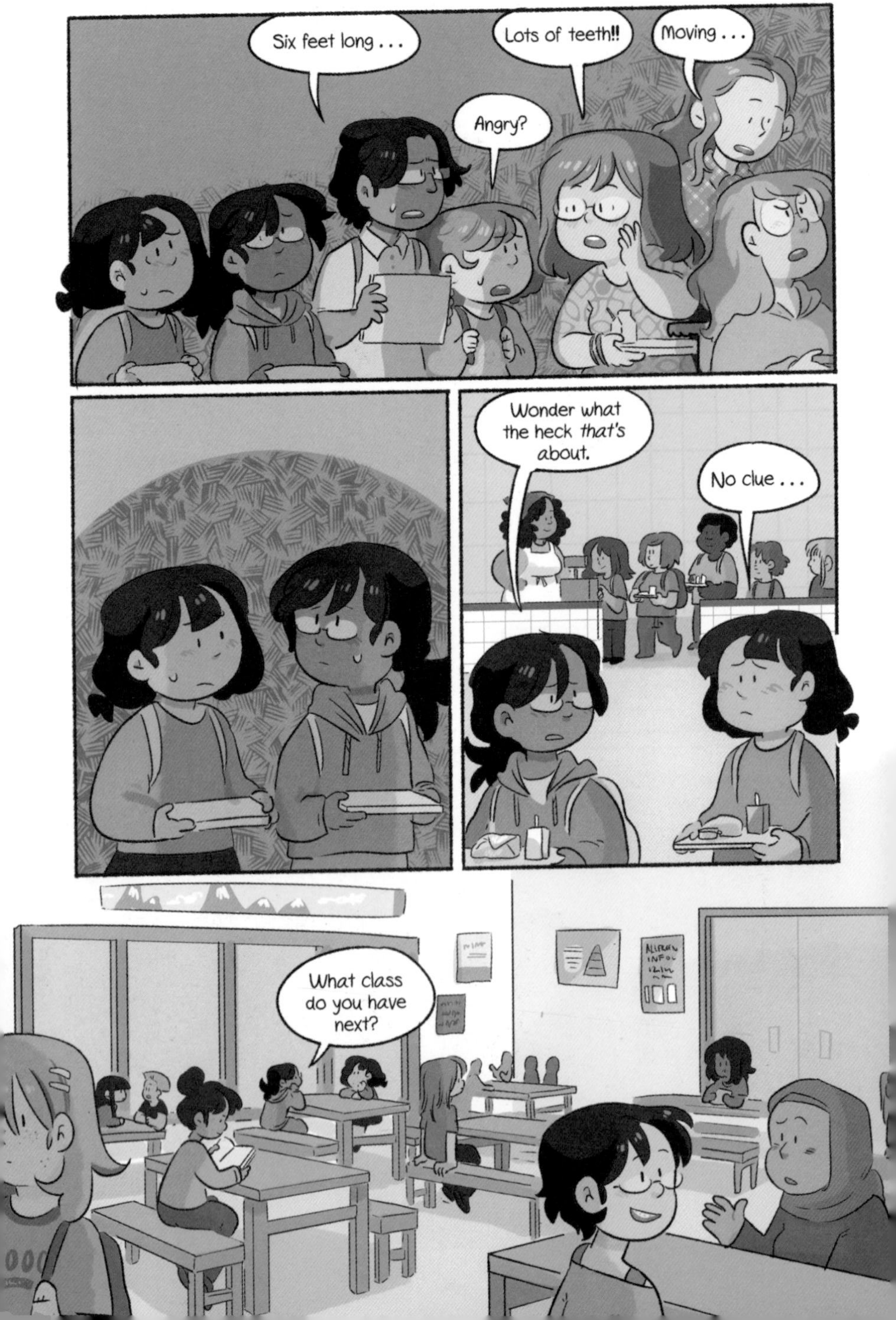
Six feet long . . .
Angry?
Lots of teeth!!
Moving . . .
Wonder what the heck *that's* about.
No clue . . .
What class do you have next?

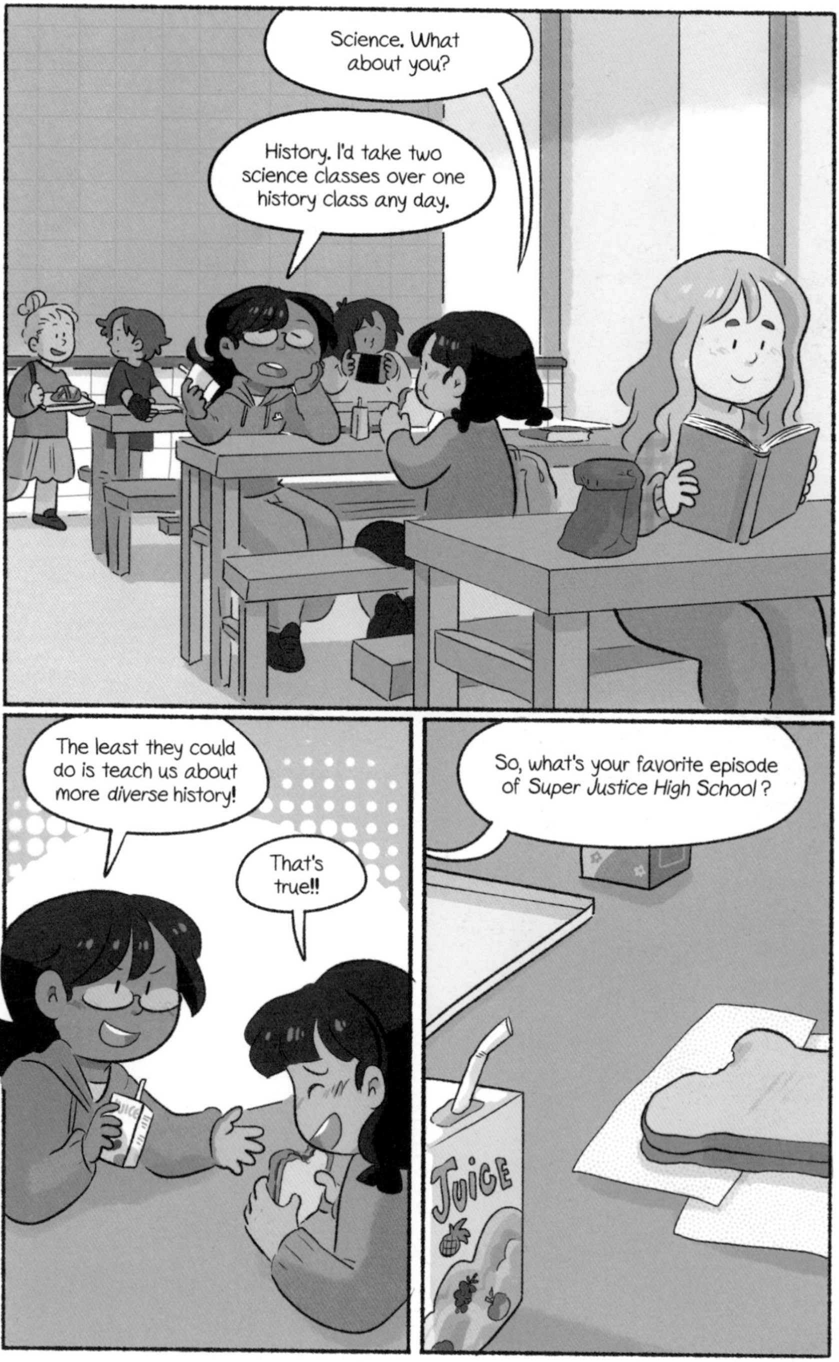
Science. What about you?
History. I'd take two science classes over one history class any day.
The least they could do is teach us about more *diverse* history!
That's true!!
So, what's your favorite episode of *Super Justice High School*?
JUICE

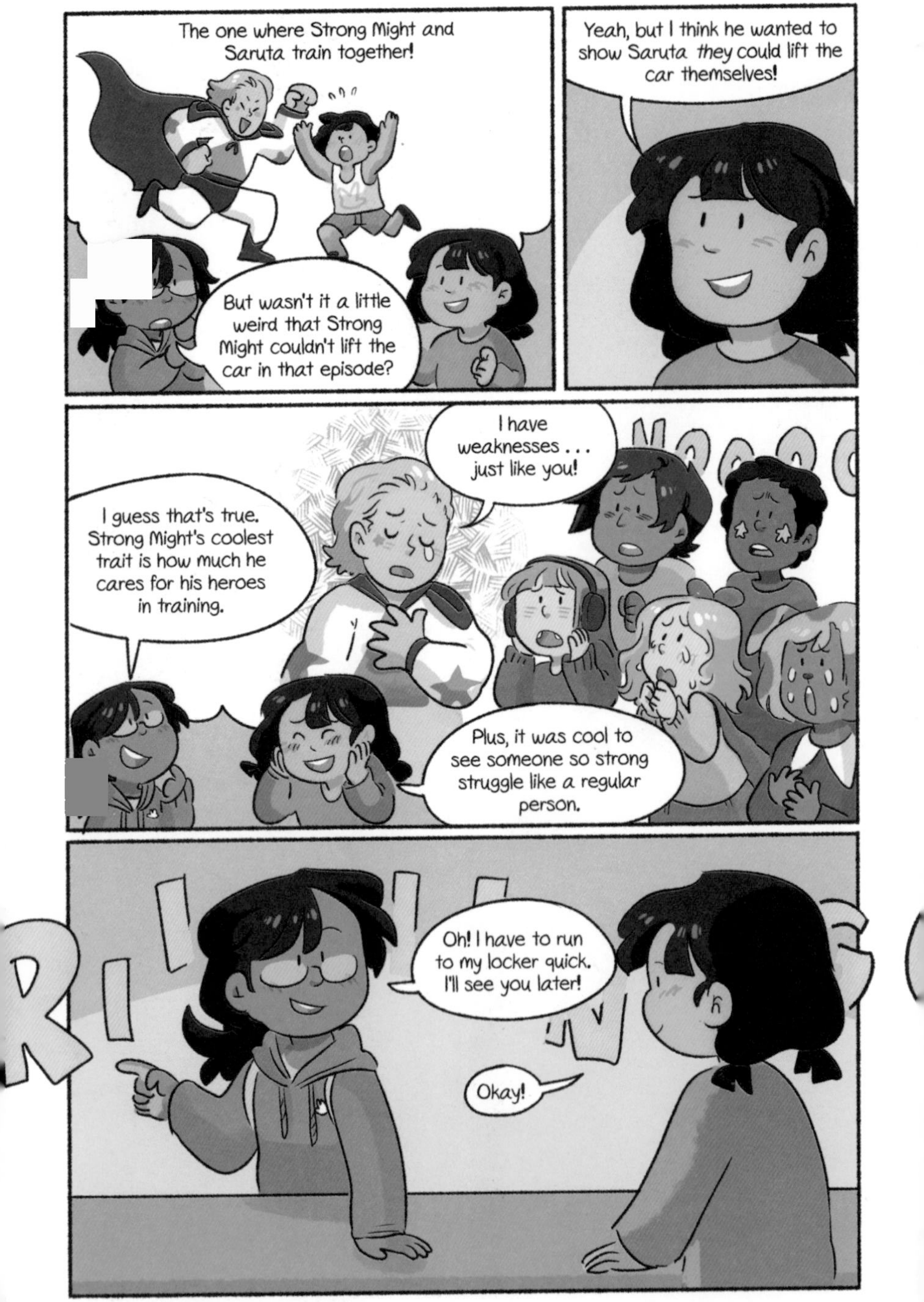
The one where Strong Might and Saruta train together!
But wasn't it a little weird that Strong Might couldn't lift the car in that episode?
Yeah, but I think he wanted to show Saruta *they* could lift the car themselves!
I guess that's true. Strong Might's coolest trait is how much he cares for his heroes in training.
I have weaknesses . . . just like you!
Plus, it was cool to see someone so strong struggle like a regular person.
Oh! I have to run to my locker quick. I'll see you later!
Okay!

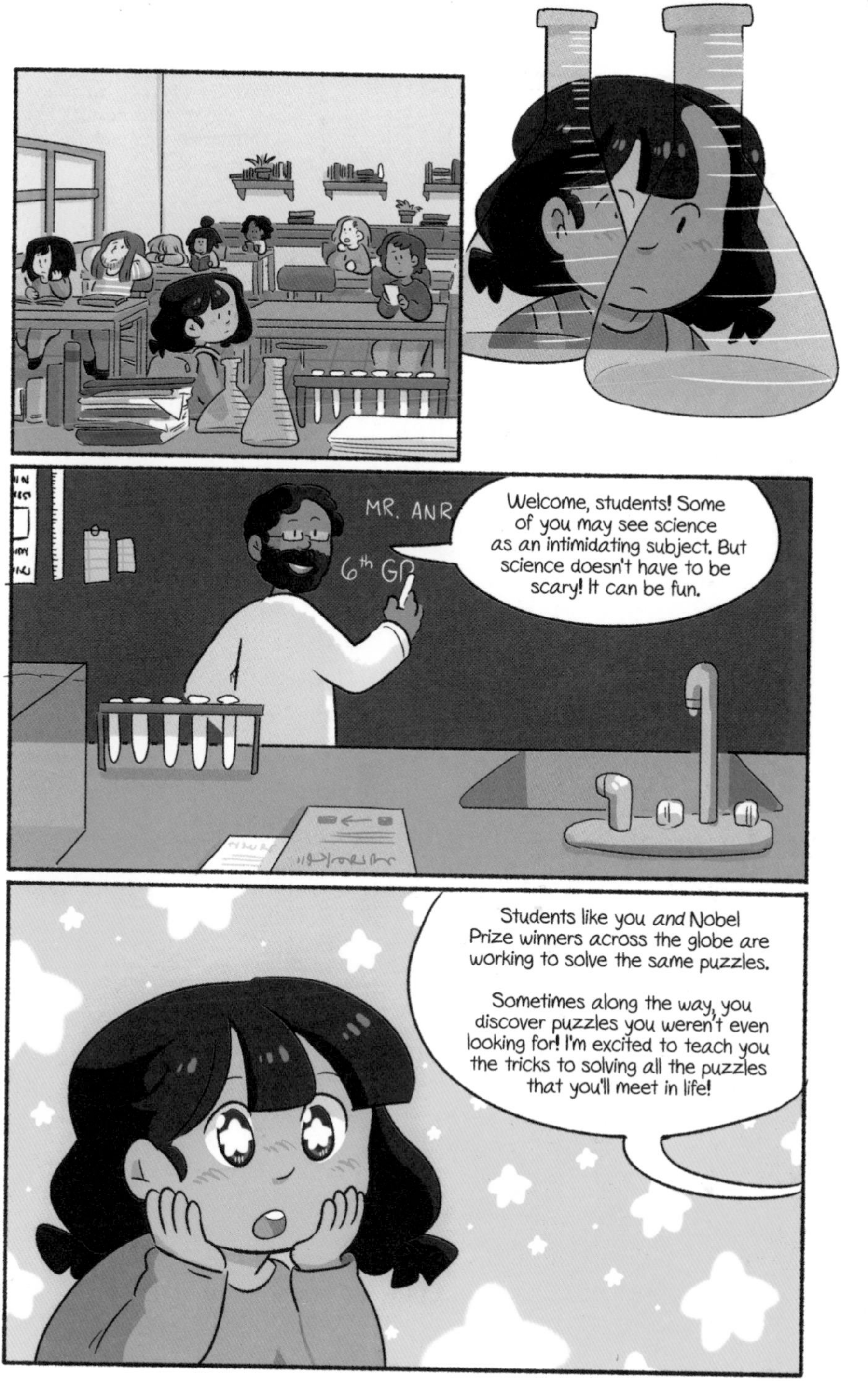
MR. ANR
Welcome, students! Some of you may see science as an intimidating subject. But science doesn't have to be scary! It can be fun.
Students like you *and* Nobel Prize winners across the globe are working to solve the same puzzles.
Sometimes along the way, you discover puzzles you weren't even looking for! I'm excited to teach you the tricks to solving all the puzzles that you'll meet in life!

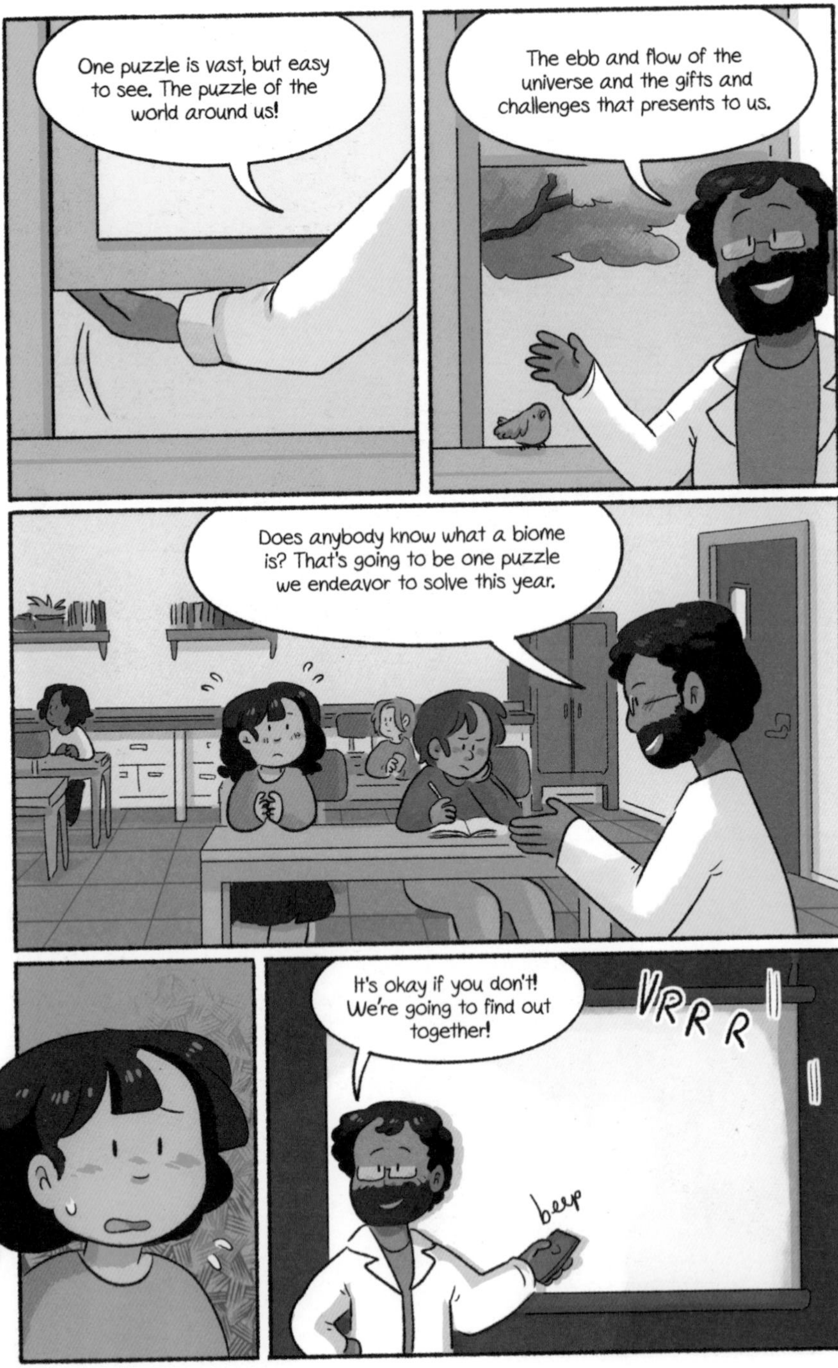
One puzzle is vast, but easy to see. The puzzle of the world around us!
The ebb and flow of the universe and the gifts and challenges that presents to us.
Does anybody know what a biome is? That's going to be one puzzle we endeavor to solve this year.
It's okay if you don't! We're going to find out together!
VRRR R
beep

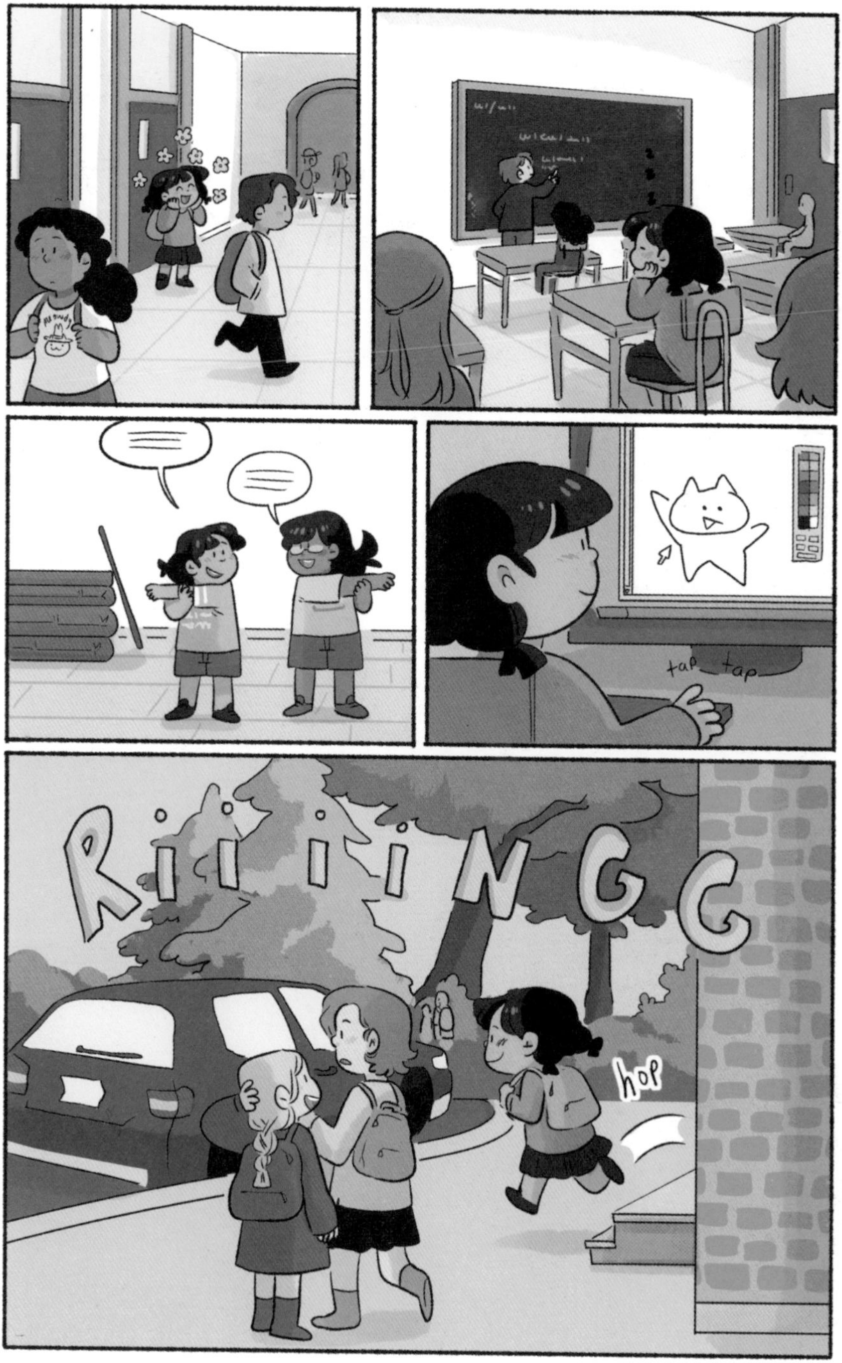
tap tap
RIIING
hop

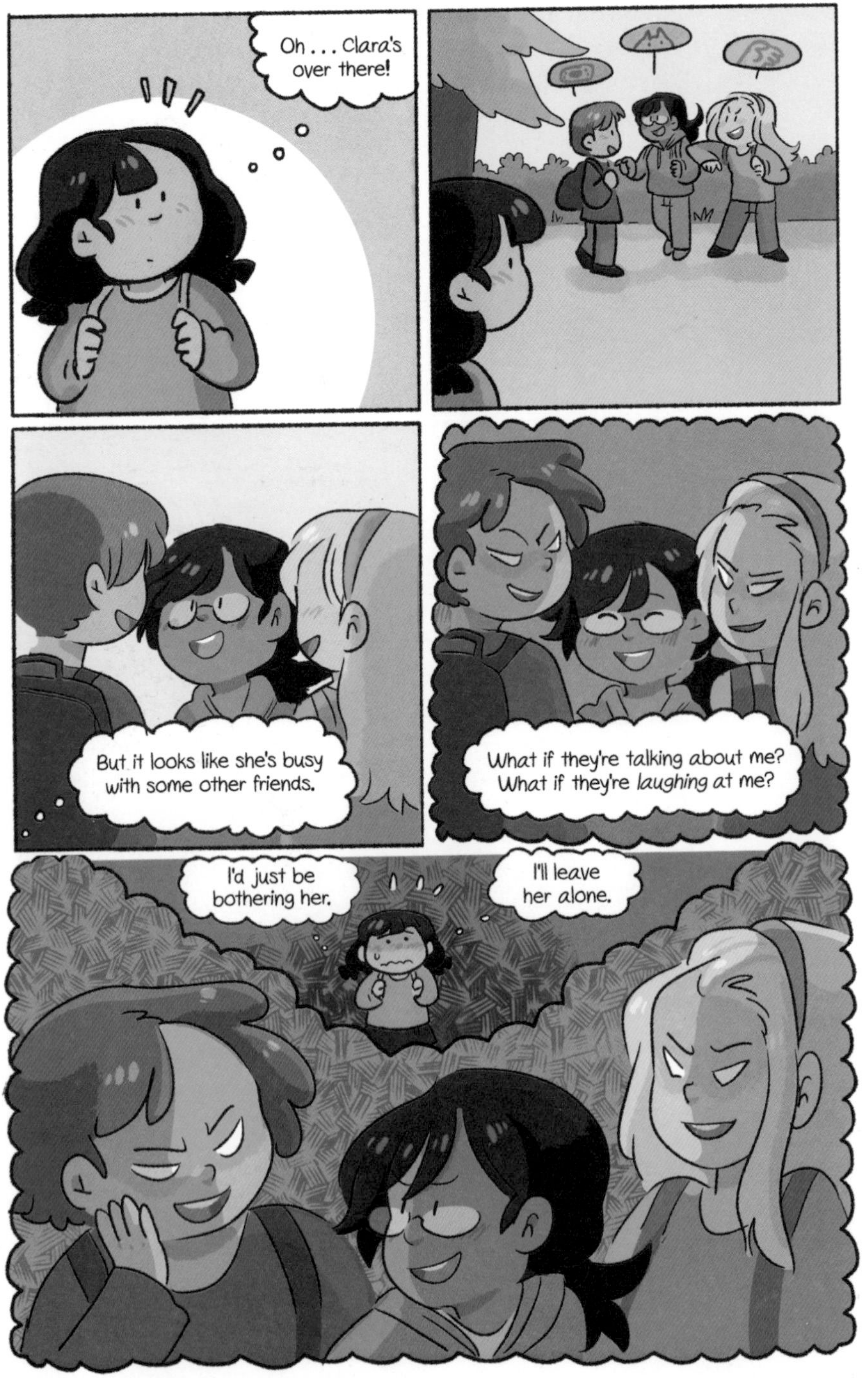
Oh . . . Clara's over there!
But it looks like she's busy with some other friends.
What if they're talking about me? What if they're *laughing* at me?
I'd just be bothering her.
I'll leave her alone.

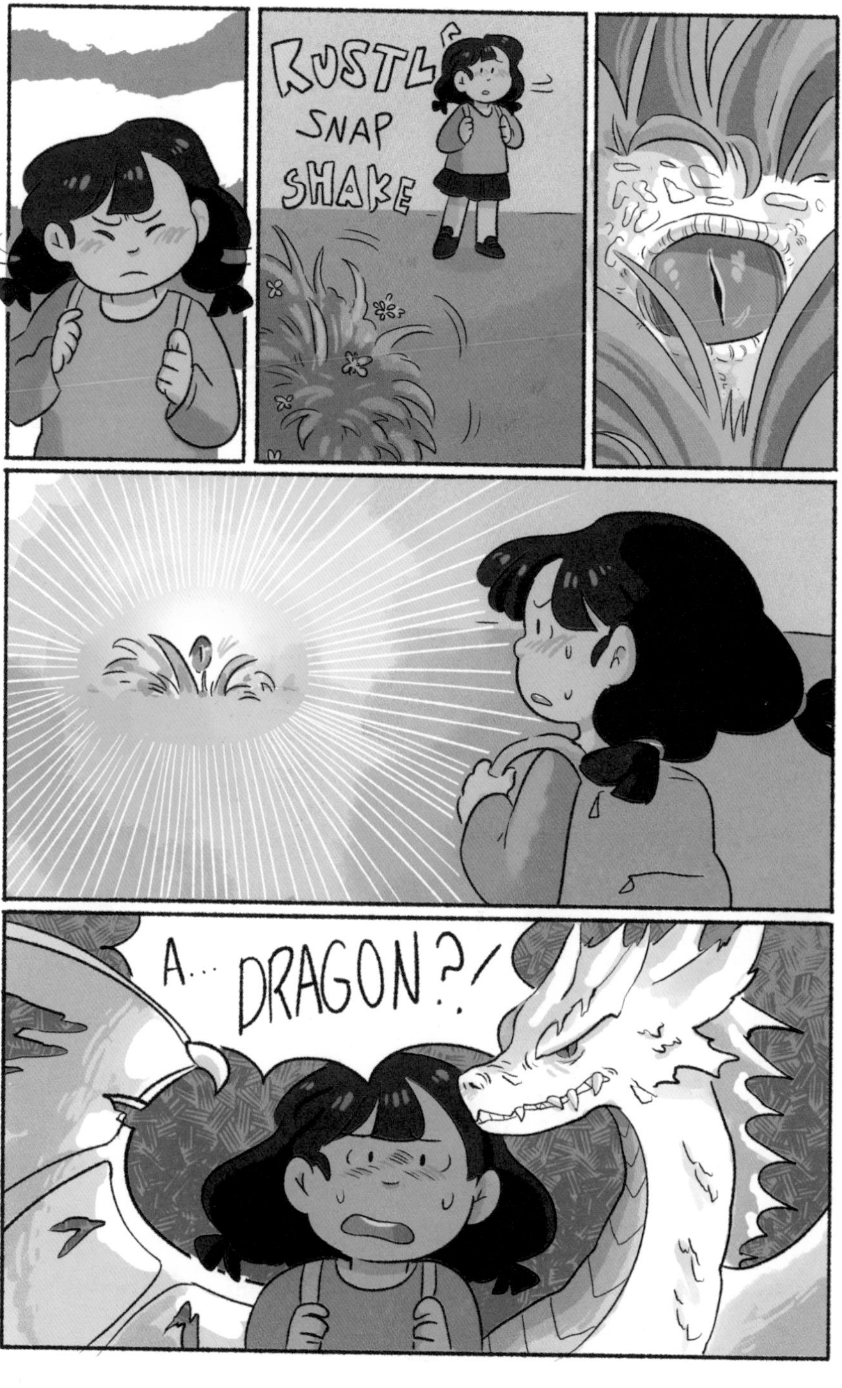
RUSTLE
SNAP
SHAKE
A... DRAGON?!

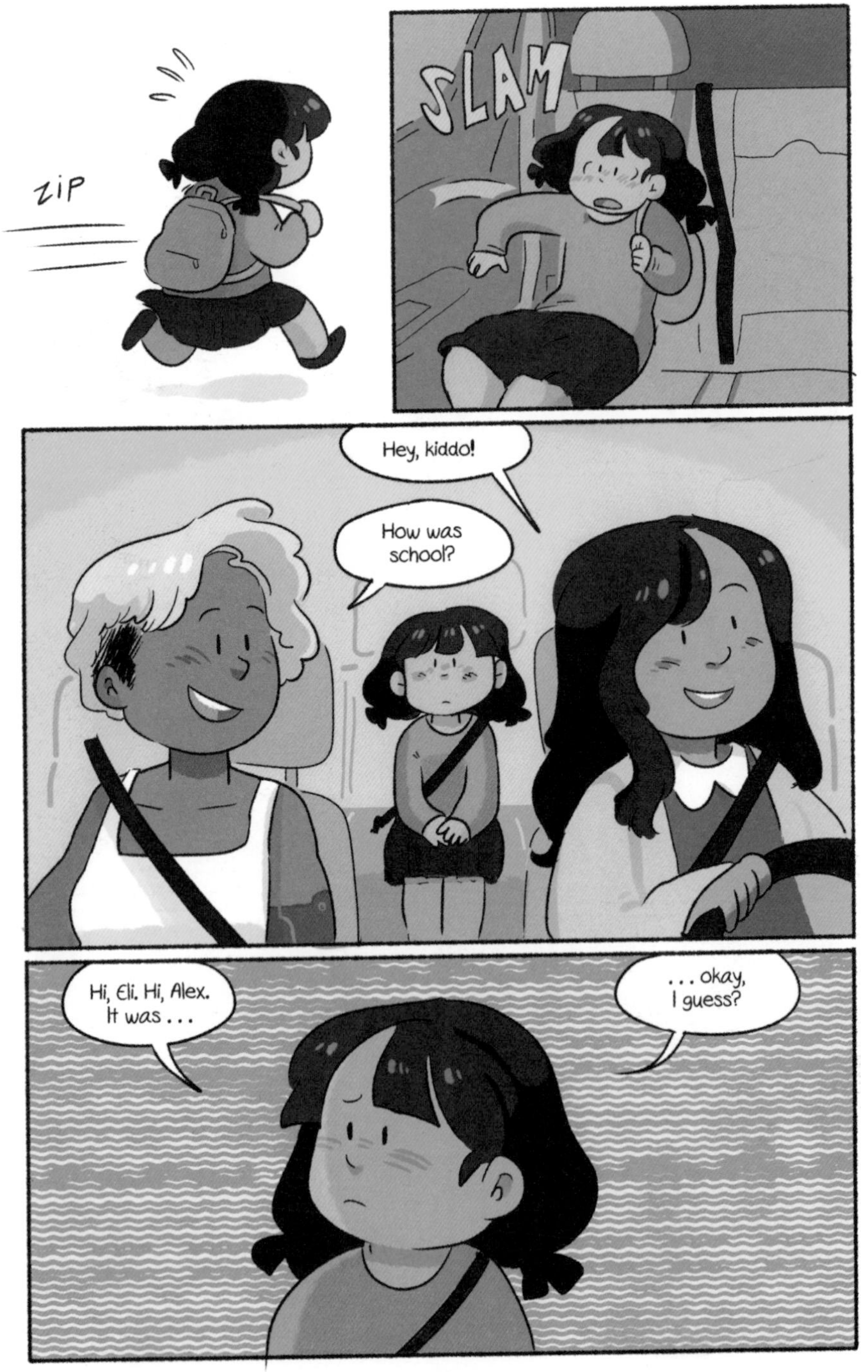
ZIP
SLAM
Hey, kiddo!
How was school?
Hi, Eli. Hi, Alex. It was . . .
. . . okay, I guess?

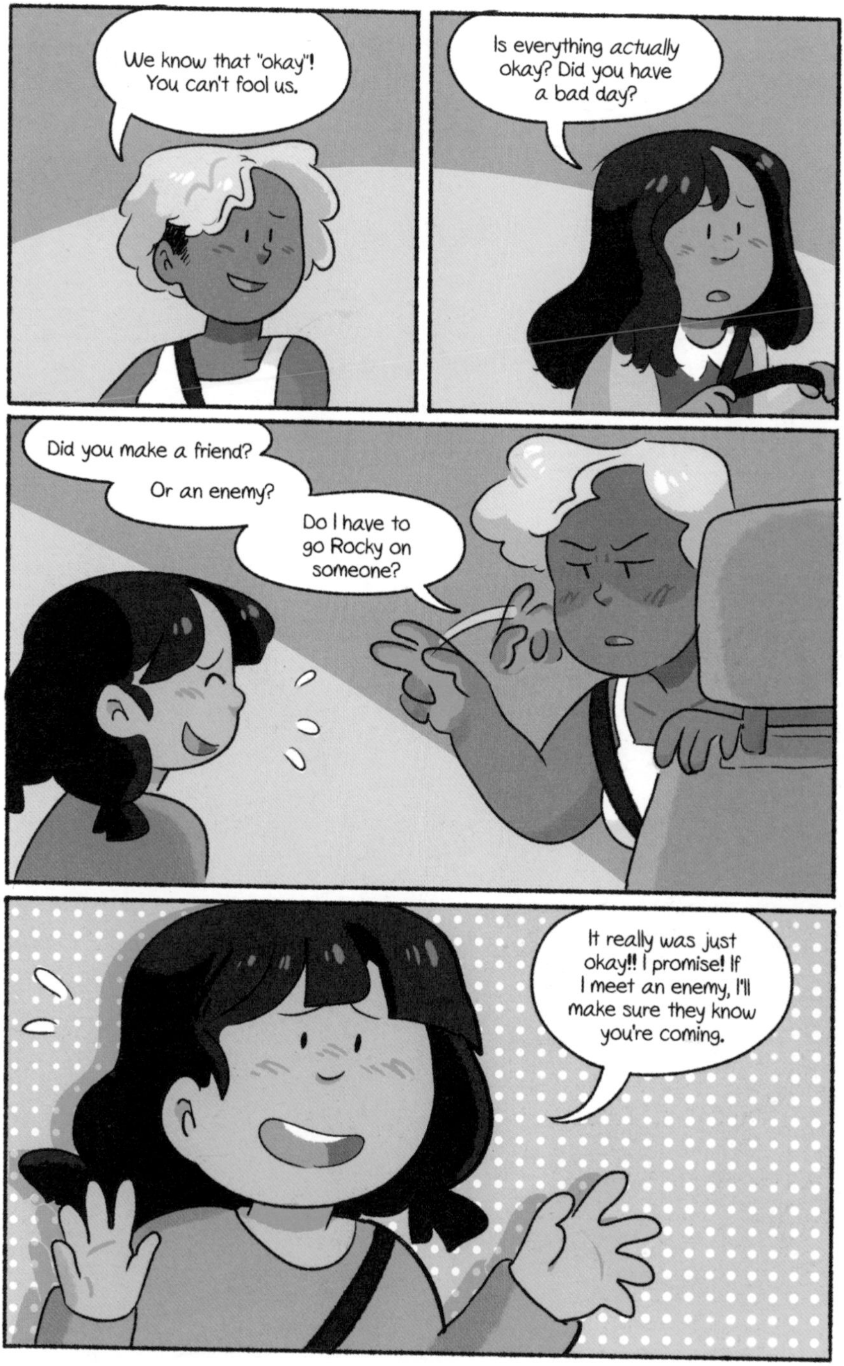
We know that "okay"! You can't fool us.
Is everything *actually* okay? Did you have a bad day?
Did you make a friend?
Or an enemy?
Do I have to go Rocky on someone?
It really was just okay!! I promise! If I meet an enemy, I'll make sure they know you're coming.

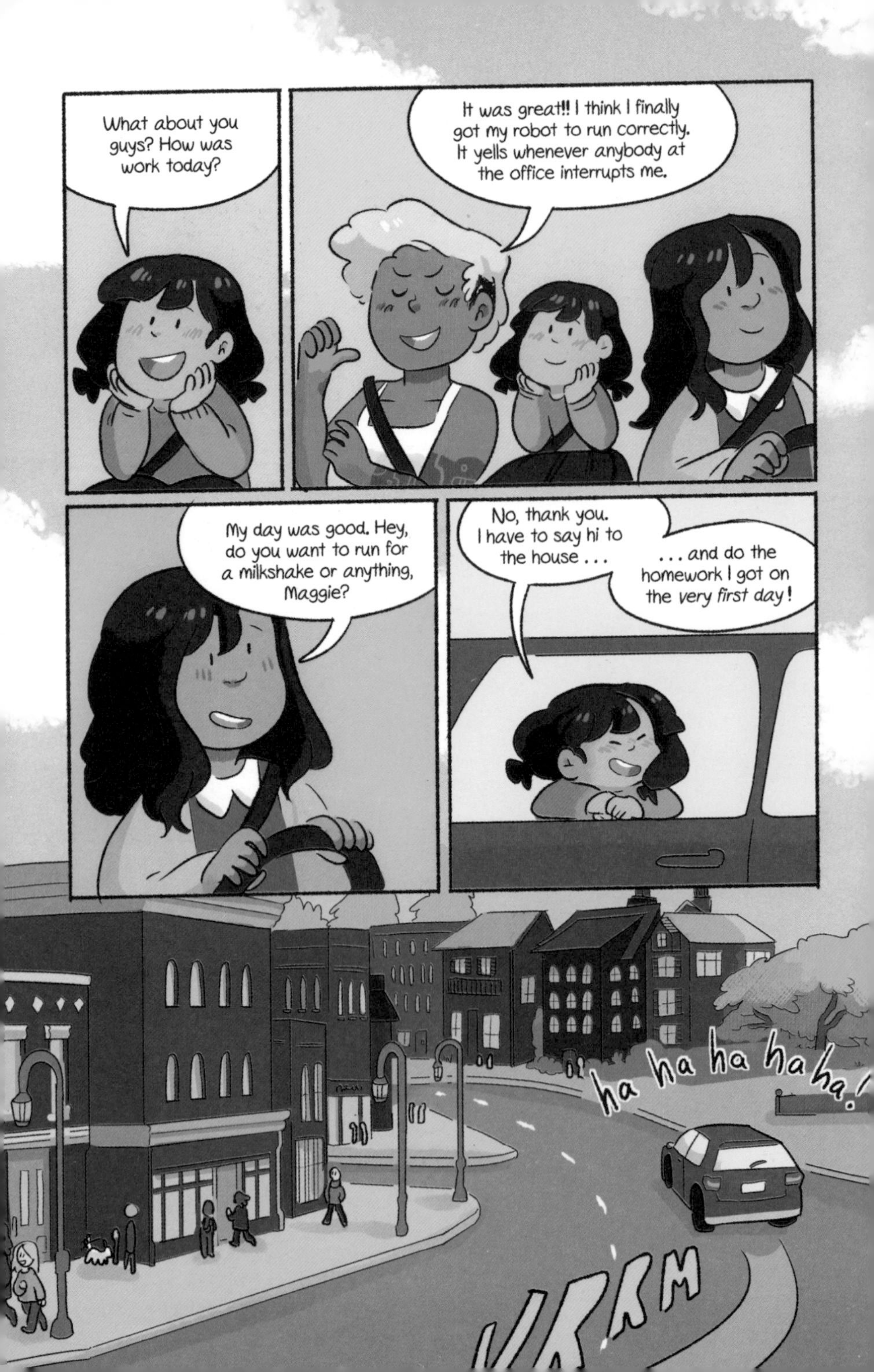
What about you guys? How was work today?
It was great!! I think I finally got my robot to run correctly. It yells whenever anybody at the office interrupts me.
My day was good. Hey, do you want to run for a milkshake or anything, Maggie?
No, thank you. I have to say hi to the house . . .
. . . and do the homework I got on the *very first day*!
ha ha ha ha ha!
VRRM

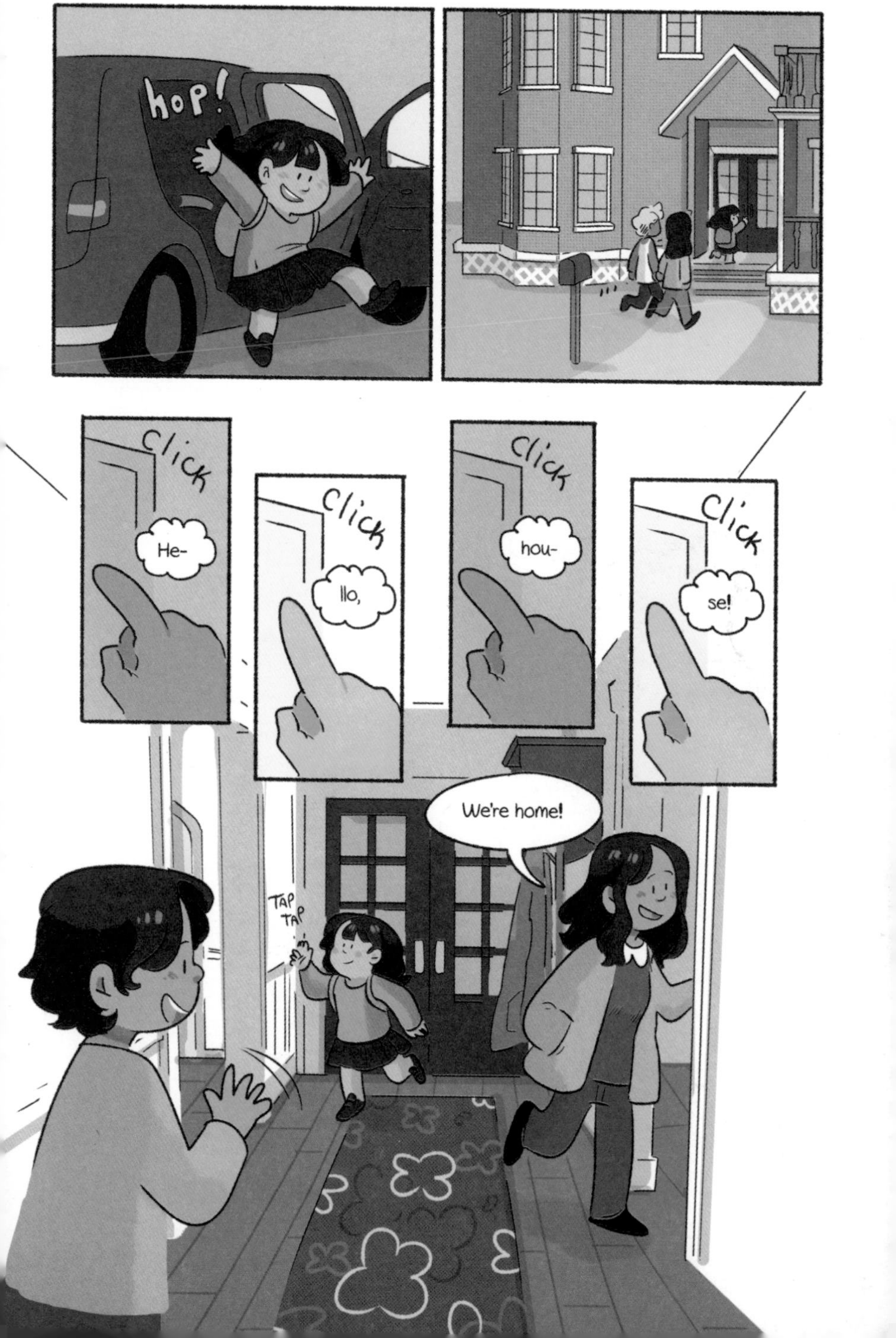
hop!
Click
He-
Click
llo,
Click
hou-
Click
se!
We're home!
TAP
TAP

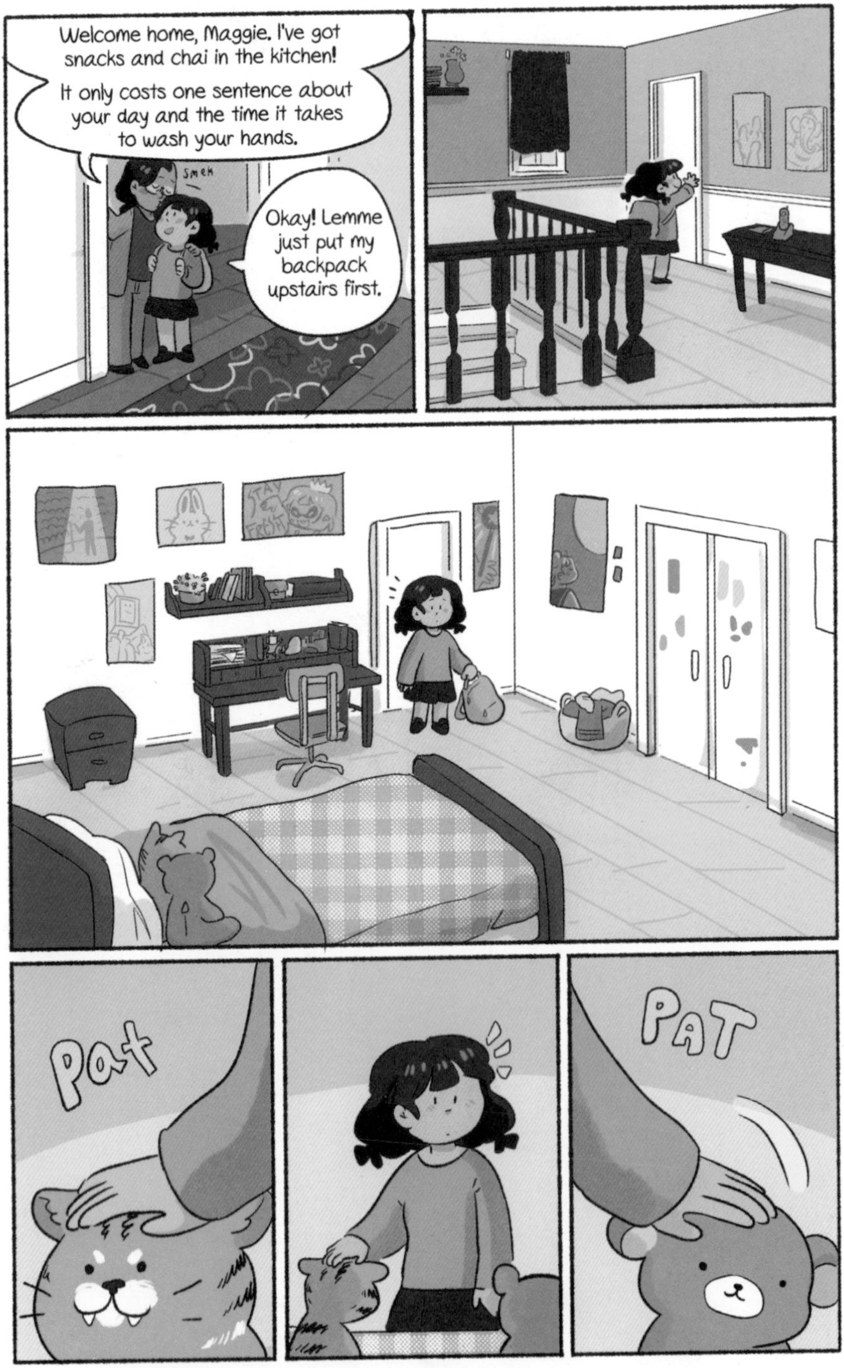
Welcome home, Maggie. I've got snacks and chai in the kitchen!
It only costs one sentence about your day and the time it takes to wash your hands.
SMEK
Okay! Lemme just put my backpack upstairs first.
STAY FRESH
Pat
PAT

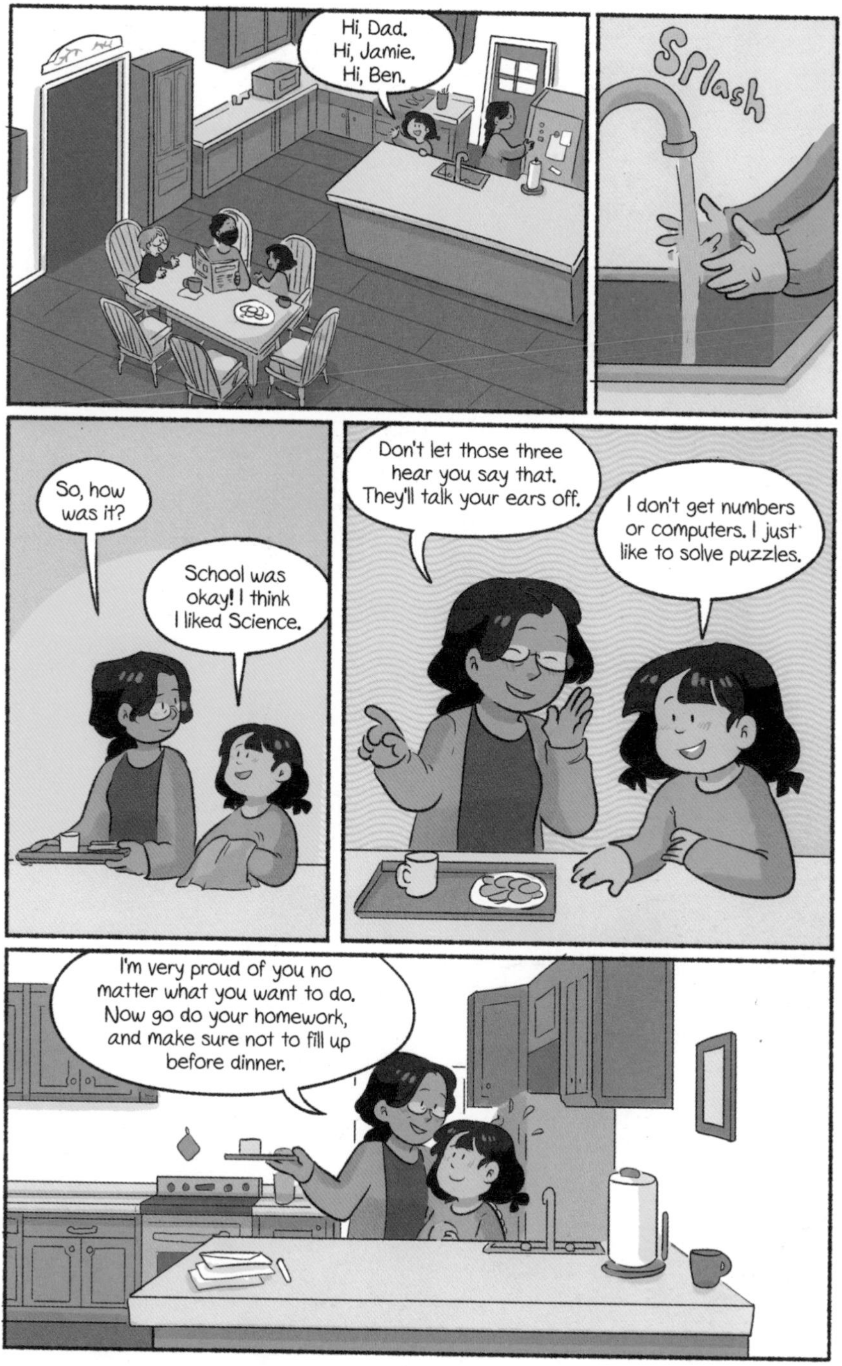
Hi, Dad.
Hi, Jamie.
Hi, Ben.
Splash
So, how was it?
School was okay! I think I liked Science.
Don't let those three hear you say that. They'll talk your ears off.
I don't get numbers or computers. I just like to solve puzzles.
I'm very proud of you no matter what you want to do. Now go do your homework, and make sure not to fill up before dinner.

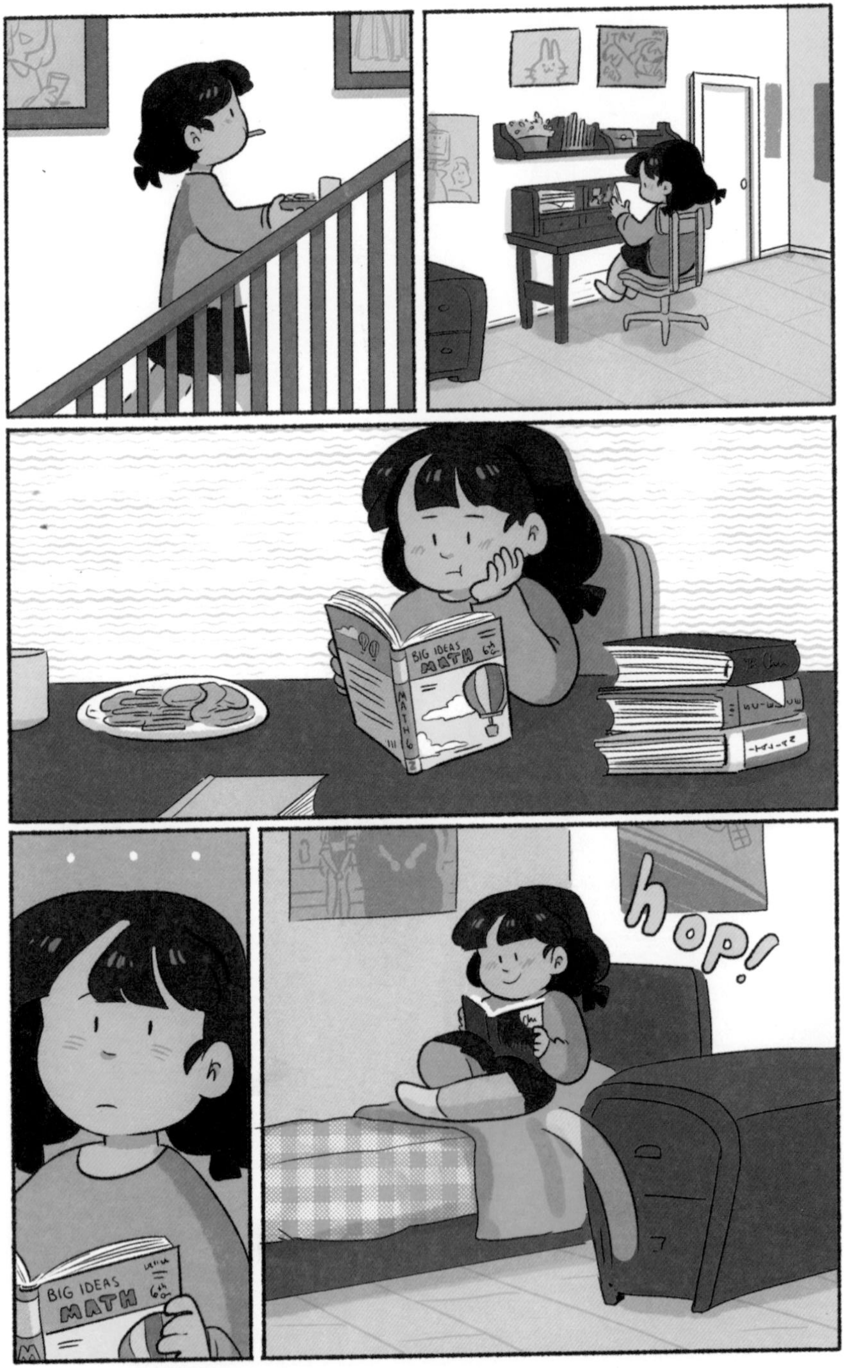
BIG IDEAS MATH 6th
MATH 6
BIG IDEAS MATH 6th
hop!

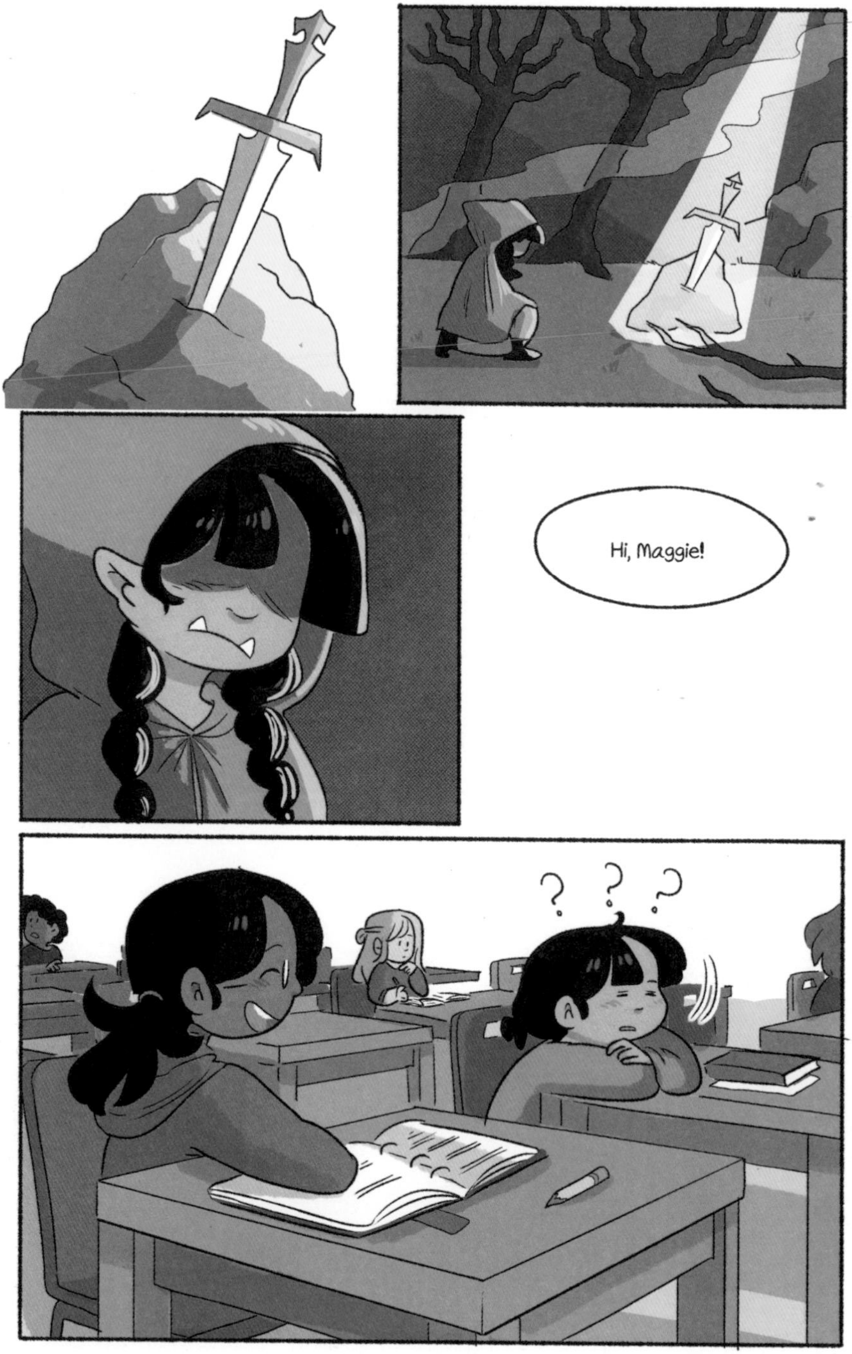
Hi, Maggie!
? ? ?

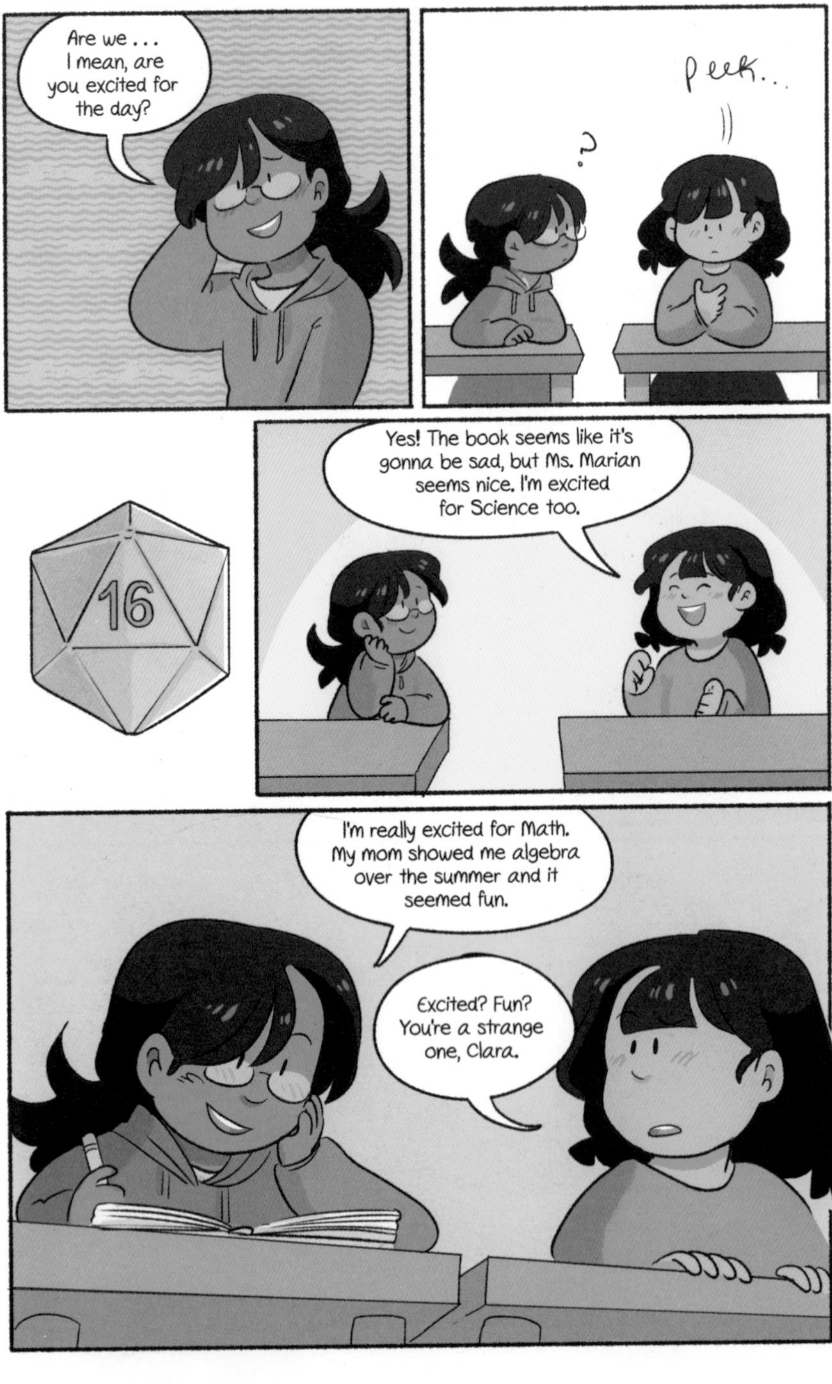
Are we . . .
I mean, are you excited for the day?
?
peek...
Yes! The book seems like it's gonna be sad, but Ms. Marian seems nice. I'm excited for Science too.
16
I'm really excited for Math. My mom showed me algebra over the summer and it seemed fun.
Excited? Fun? You're a strange one, Clara.

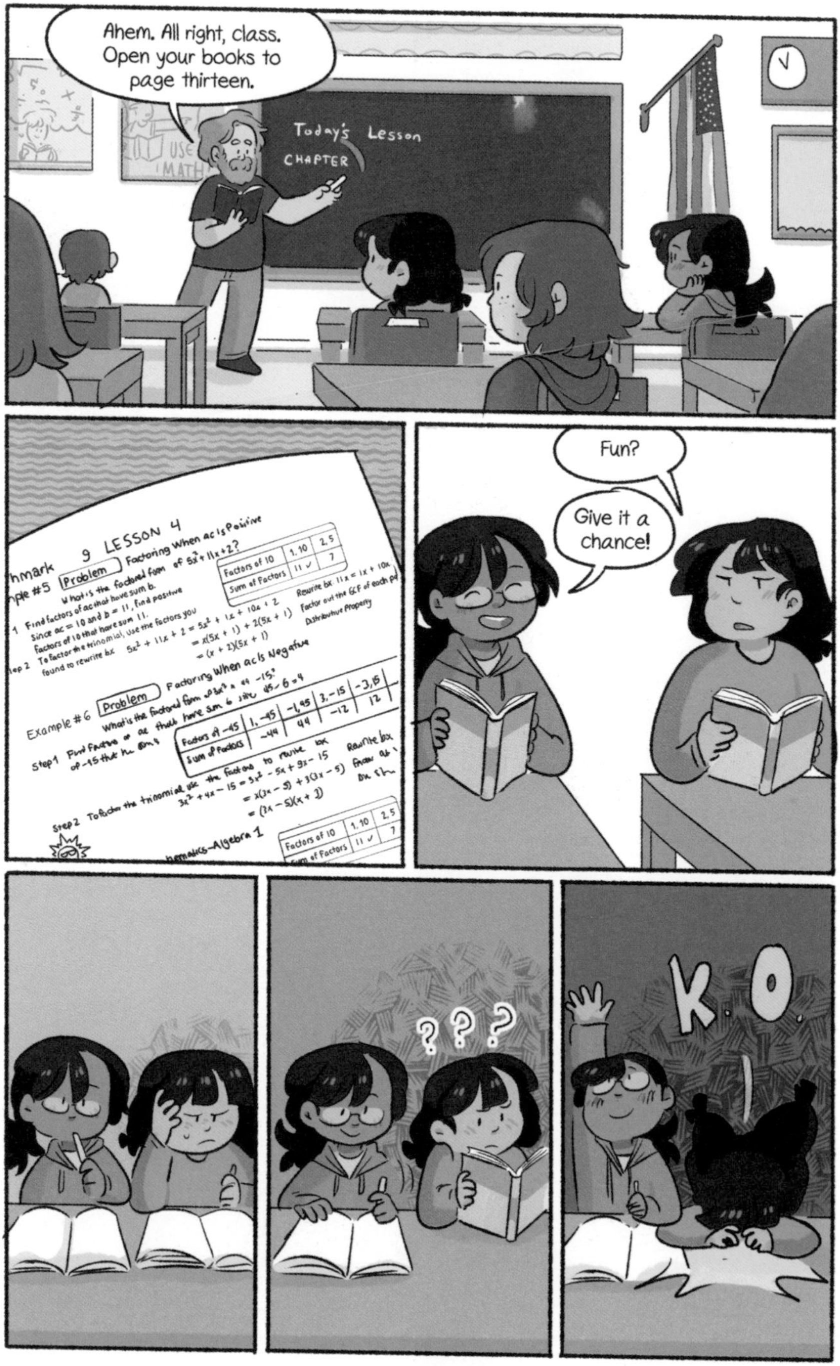
Ahem. All right, class. Open your books to page thirteen.
USE MATH
Today's Lesson
CHAPTER
LESSON 4
Factoring When ac Is Positive
Problem
Factors of 10
Sum of Factors
Factoring When ac Is Negative
Example #6
Problem
Step 1
Step 2
Fun?
Give it a chance!
???
K.O.

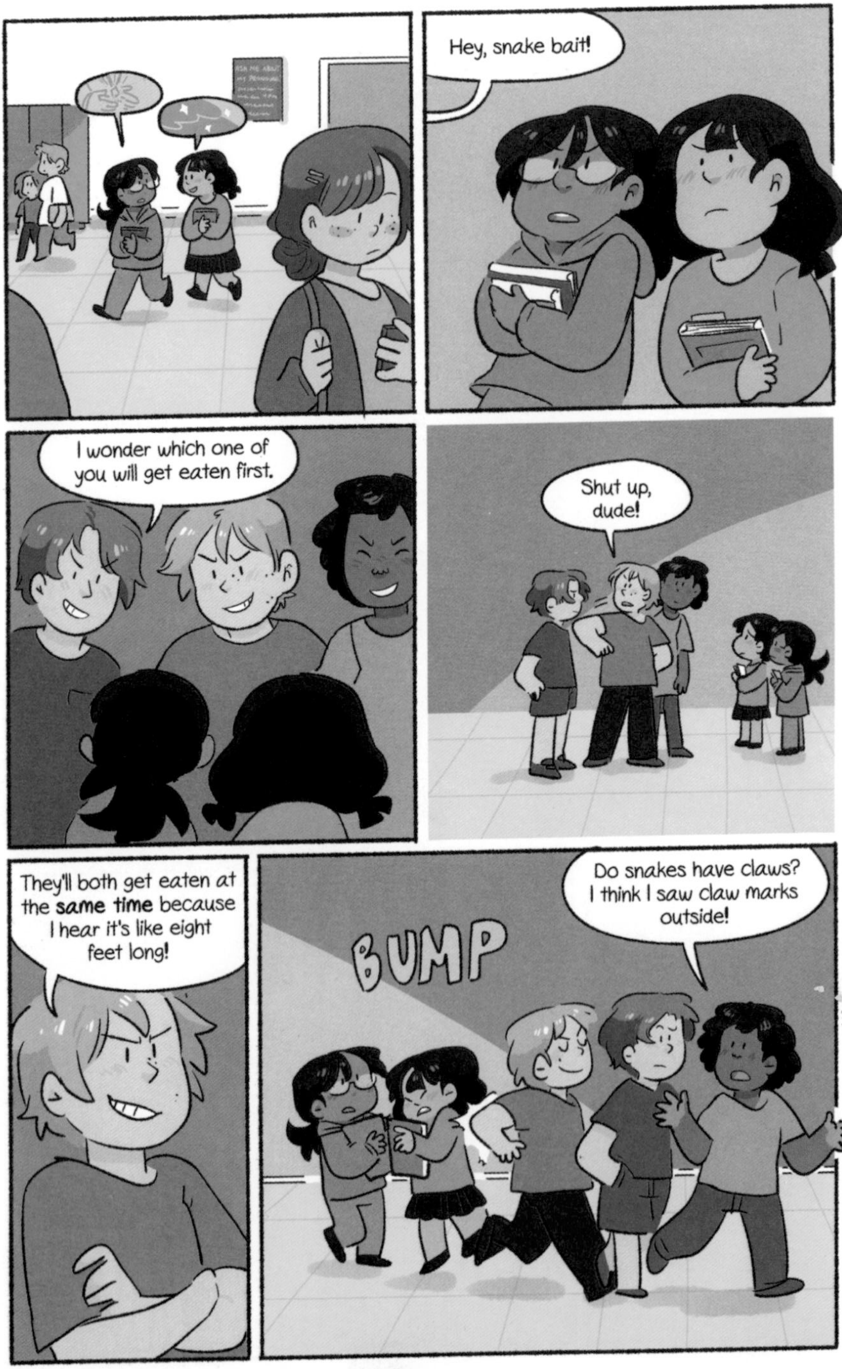
Hey, snake bait!
I wonder which one of you will get eaten first.
Shut up, dude!
They'll both get eaten at the same time because I hear it's like eight feet long!
BUMP
Do snakes have claws? I think I saw claw marks outside!

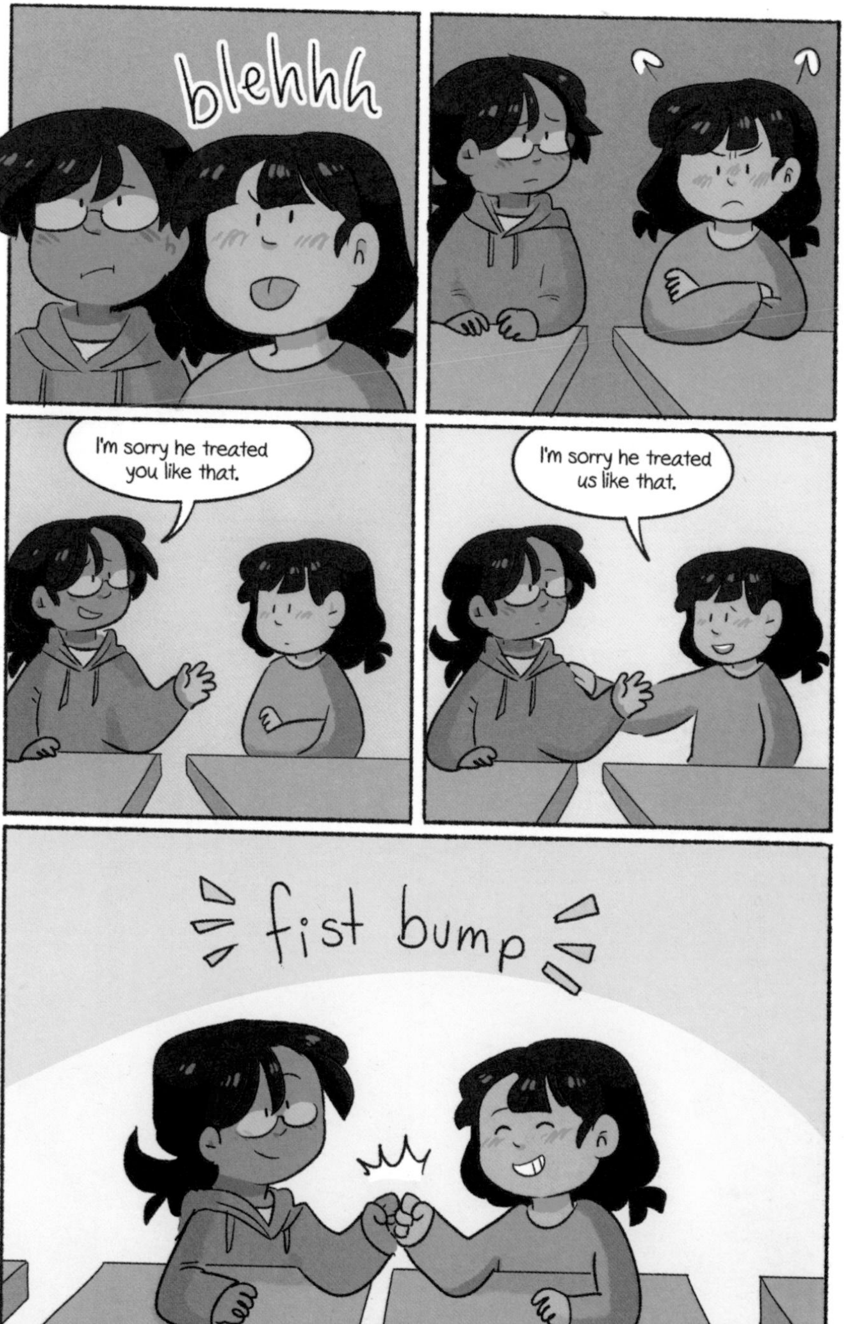
blehhh
I'm sorry he treated you like that.
I'm sorry he treated us like that.
fist bump

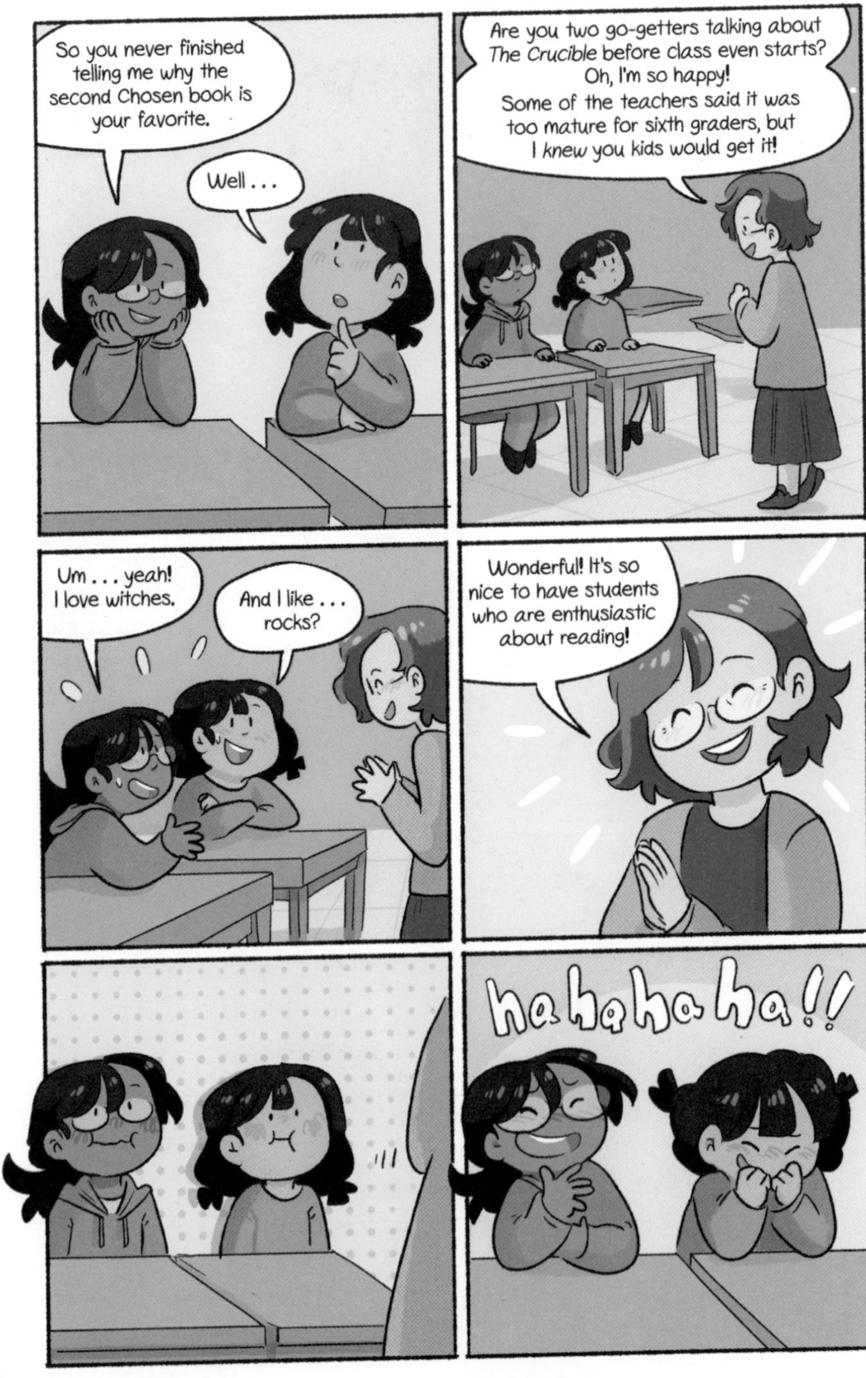
So you never finished telling me why the second Chosen book is your favorite.
Well . . .
Are you two go-getters talking about *The Crucible* before class even starts? Oh, I'm so happy! Some of the teachers said it was too mature for sixth graders, but I *knew* you kids would get it!
Um . . . yeah! I love witches.
And I like . . . rocks?
Wonderful! It's so nice to have students who are enthusiastic about reading!
hahahaha!!

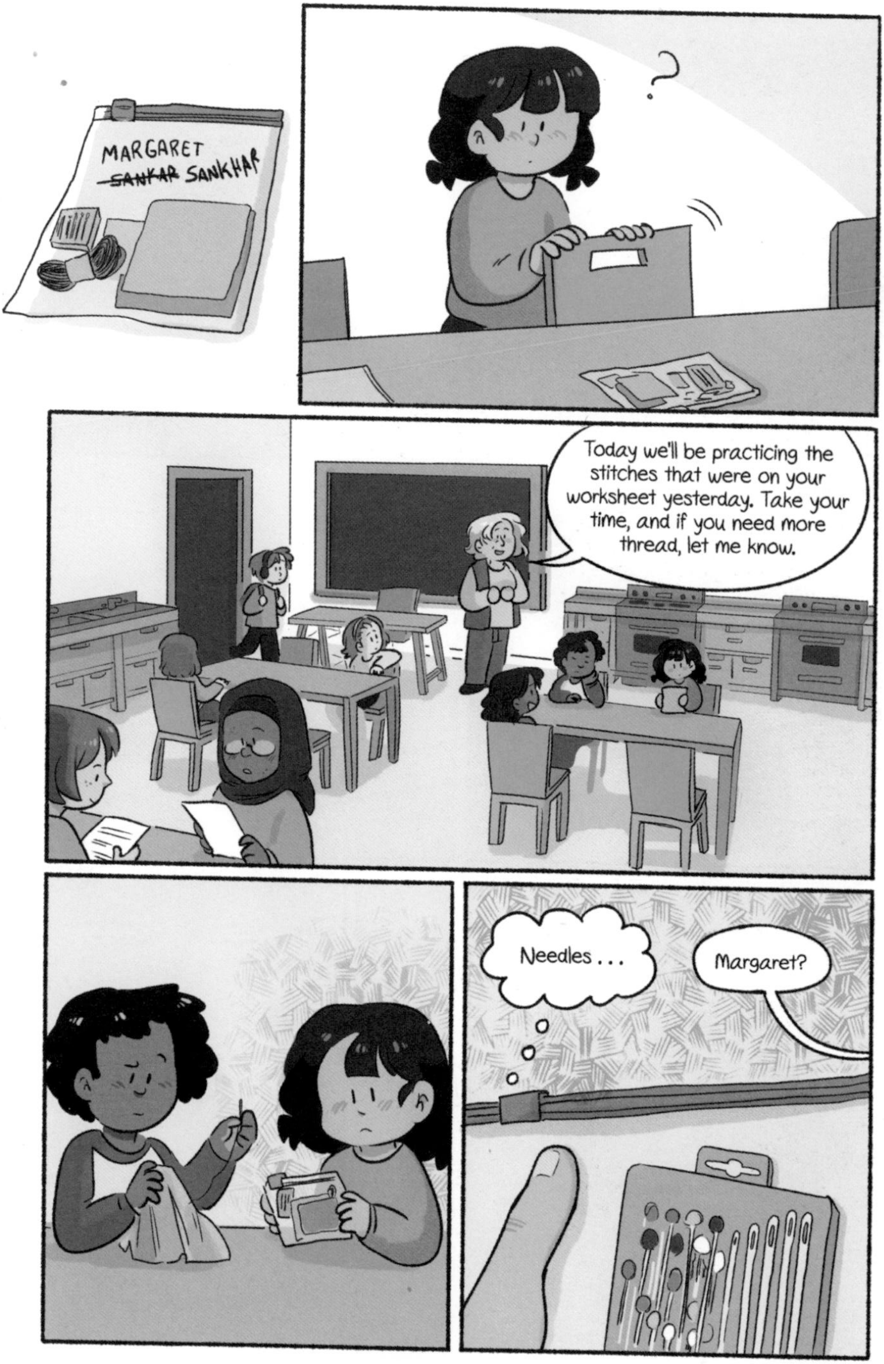
MARGARET
SANKAR SANKHAR
Today we'll be practicing the stitches that were on your worksheet yesterday. Take your time, and if you need more thread, let me know.
Needles . . .
Margaret?

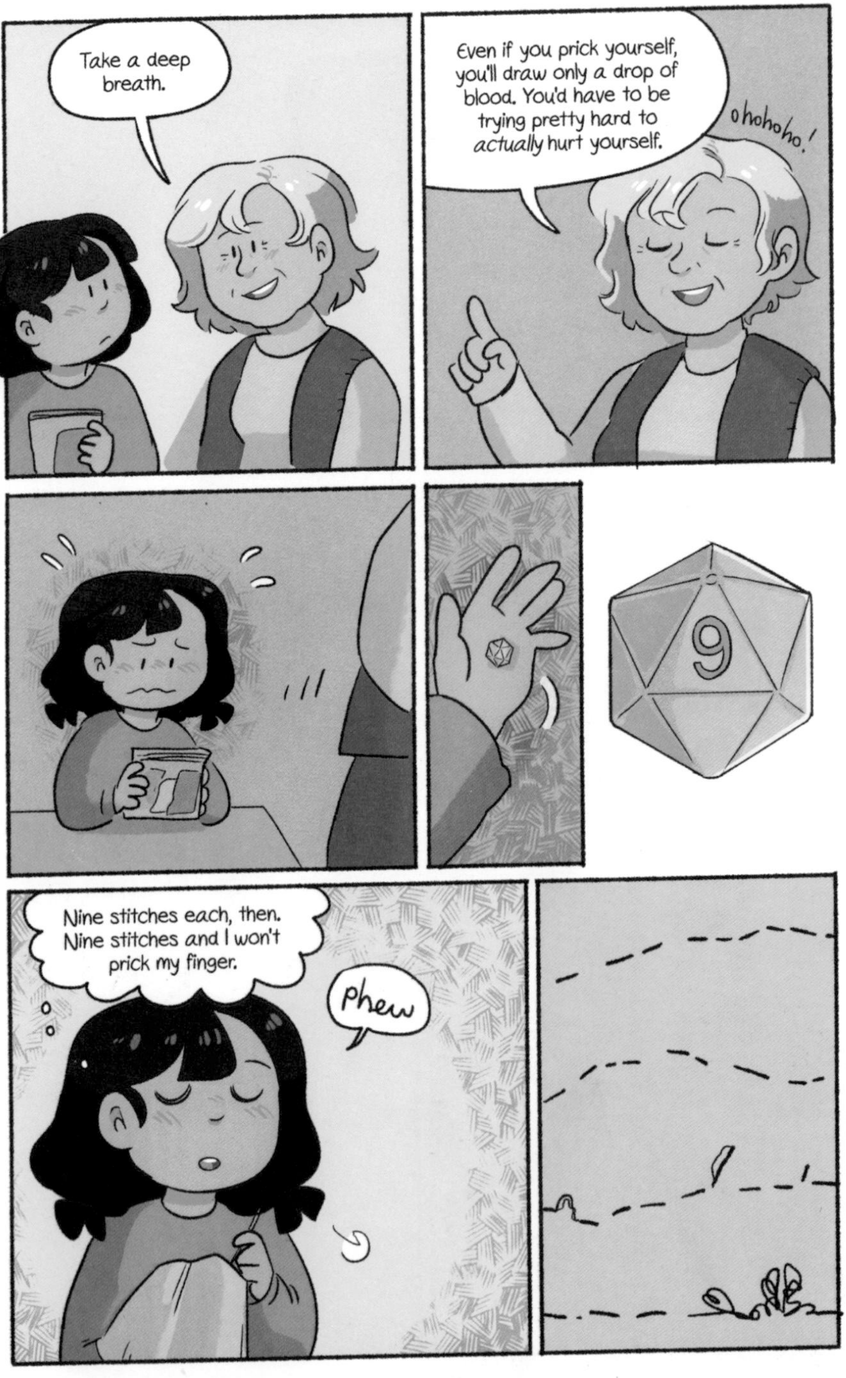

Take a deep breath.
Even if you prick yourself, you'll draw only a drop of blood. You'd have to be trying pretty hard to *actually* hurt yourself.
ohohoho!
9
Nine stitches each, then. Nine stitches and I won't prick my finger.
phew

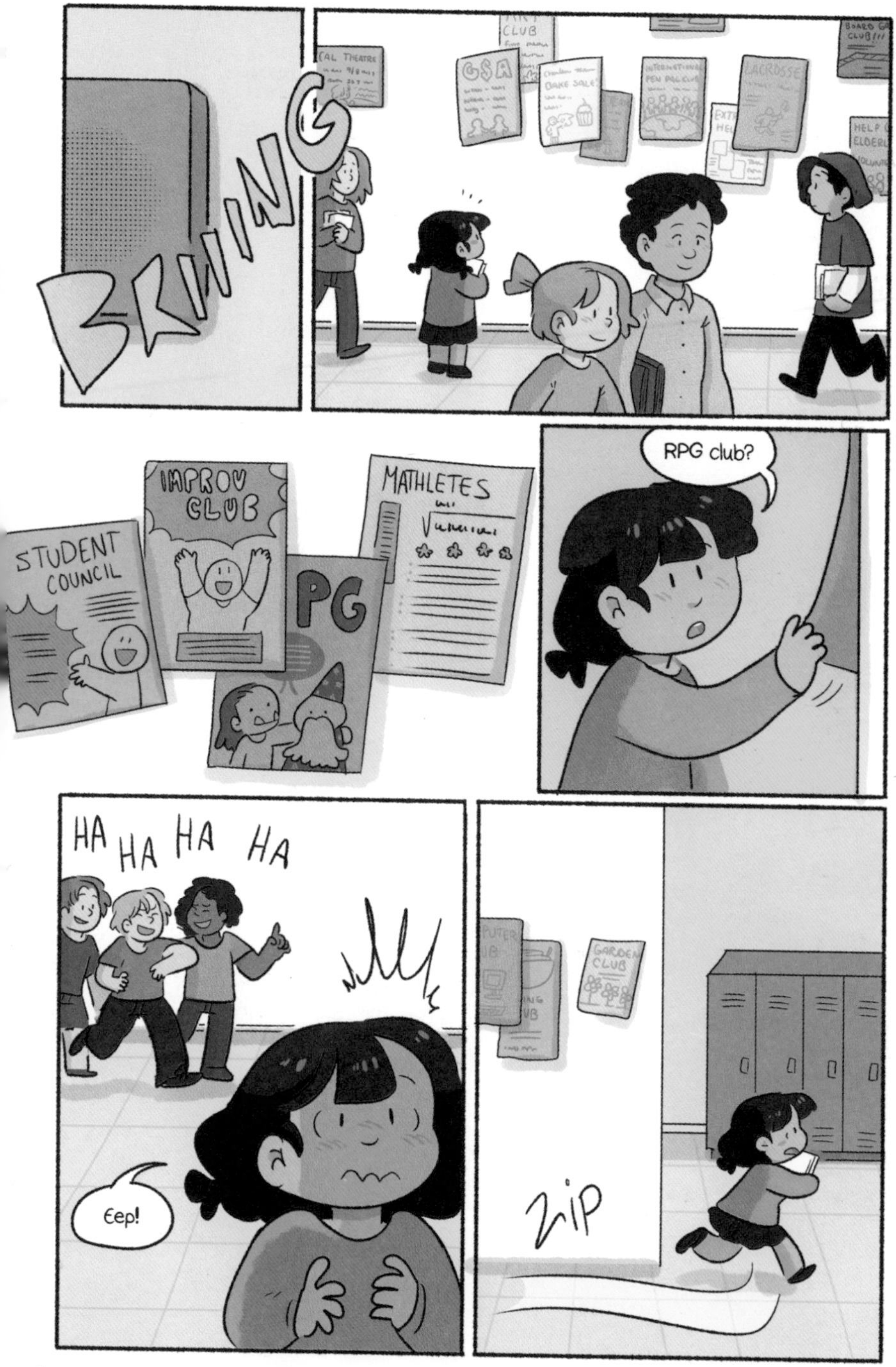
BRIIING
RPG club?
HA HA HA HA
Eep!
ZIP

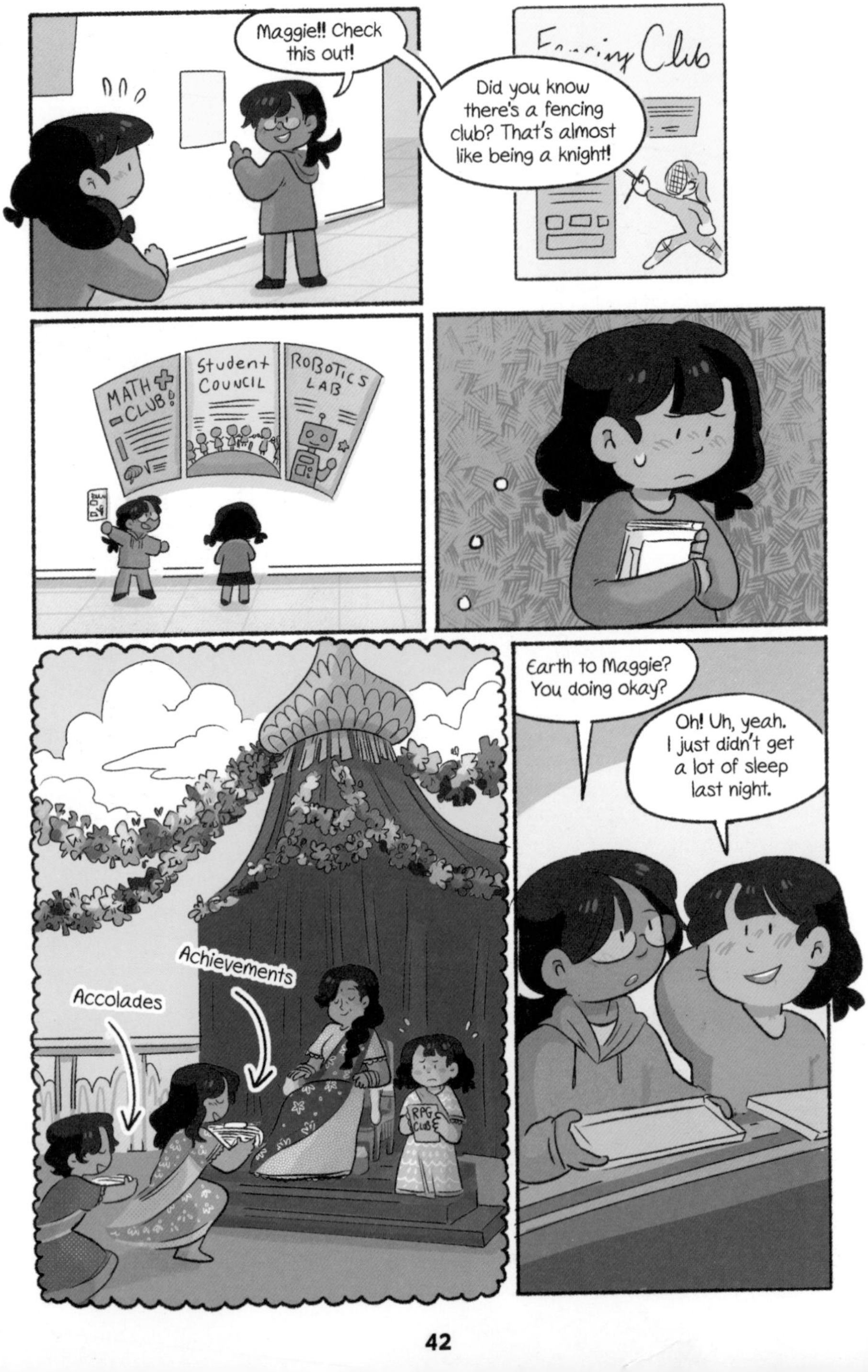

Maggie!! Check this out!
Did you know there's a fencing club? That's almost like being a knight!
Fencing Club
MATH CLUB
Student Council
RoBoTICS LAB
Achievements
Accolades
RPG CLUB
Earth to Maggie? You doing okay?
Oh! Uh, yeah. I just didn't get a lot of sleep last night.

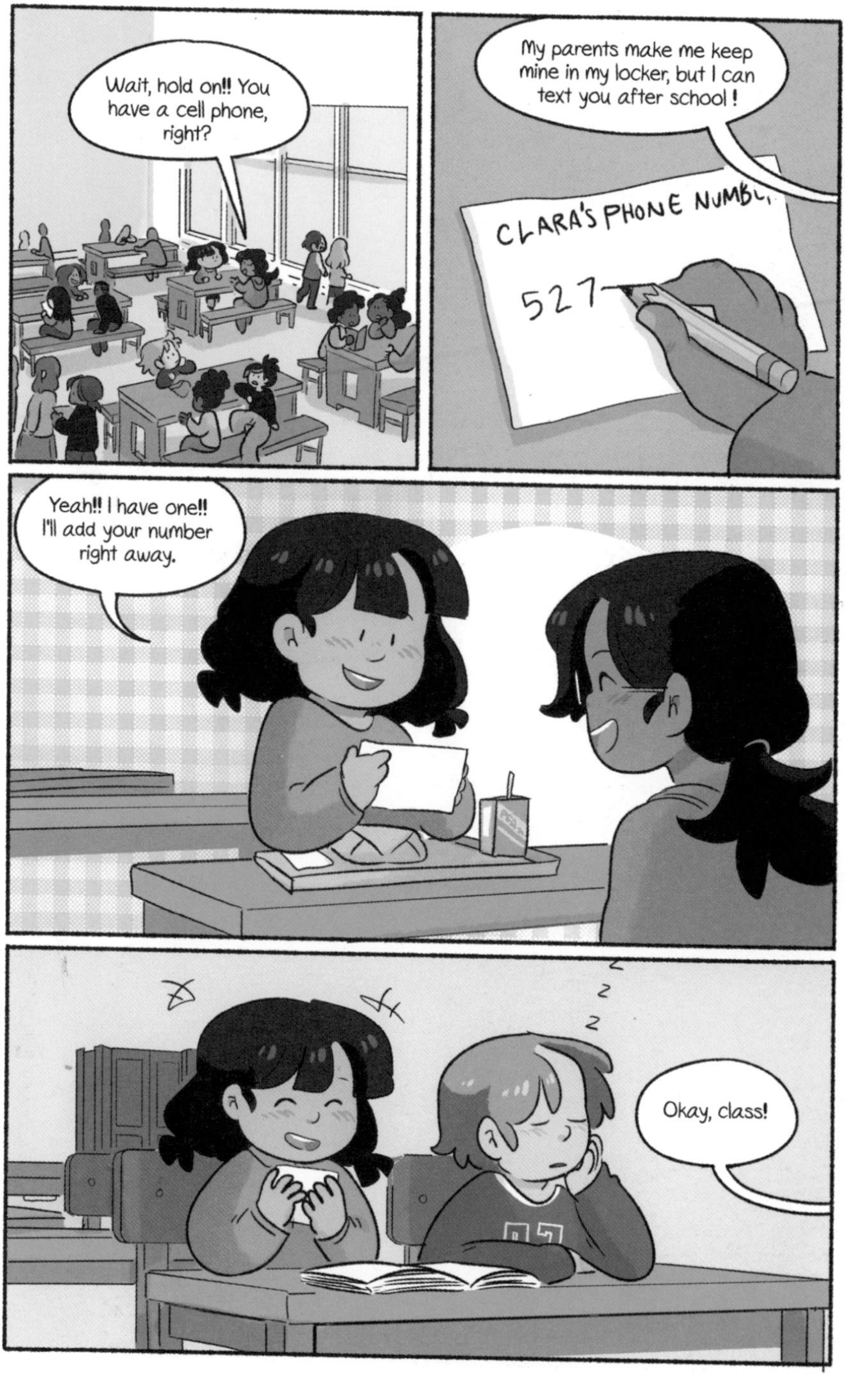
Wait, hold on!! You have a cell phone, right?
My parents make me keep mine in my locker, but I can text you after school!
CLARA'S PHONE NUMB
527-
Yeah!! I have one!! I'll add your number right away.
Okay, class!

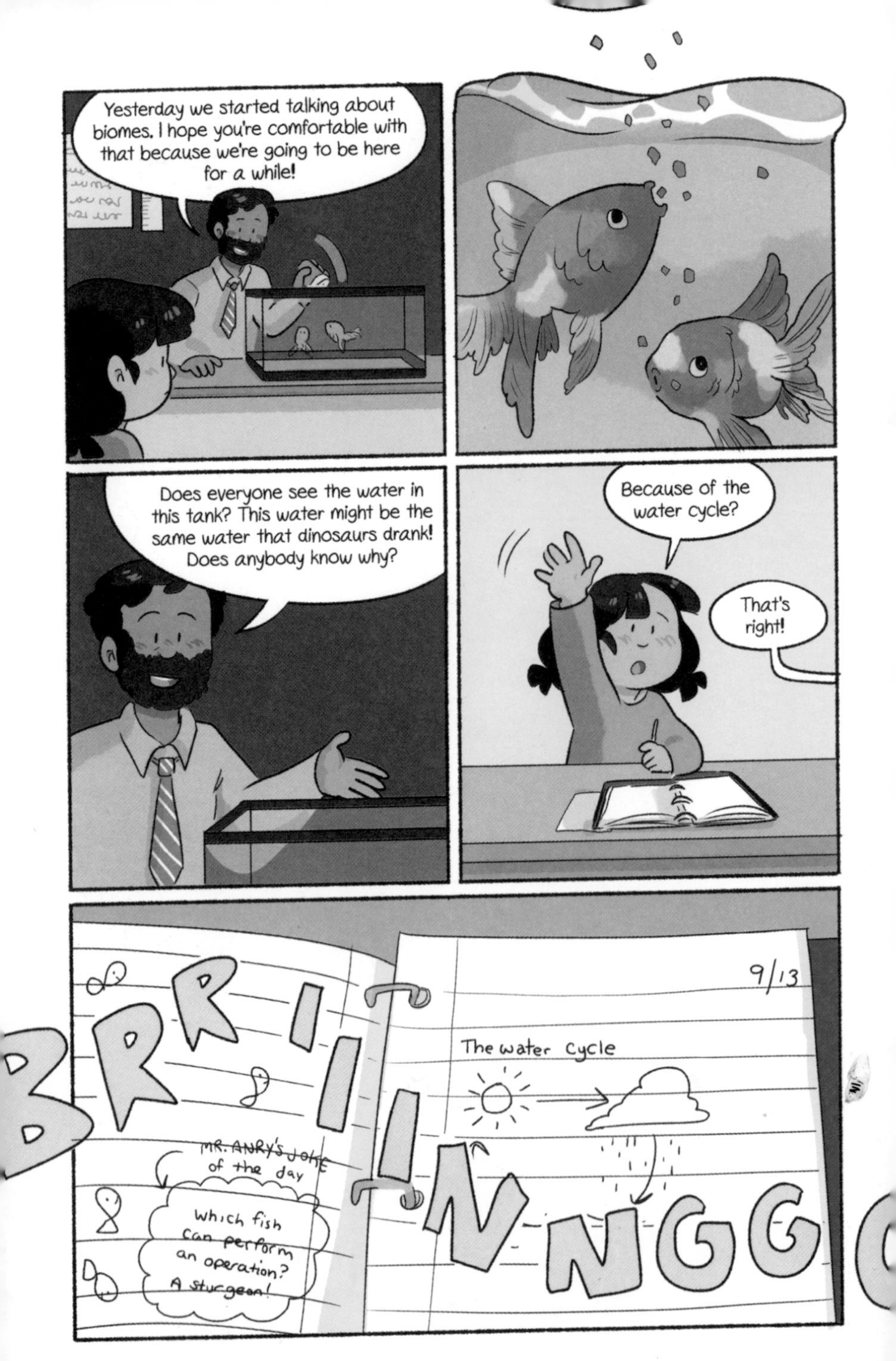

Yesterday we started talking about biomes. I hope you're comfortable with that because we're going to be here for a while!
Does everyone see the water in this tank? This water might be the same water that dinosaurs drank! Does anybody know why?
Because of the water cycle?
That's right!
9/13
The water cycle
MR. ANRY'S JOKE of the day
Which fish can perform an operation? A sturgeon!
BRRIIINNGGG

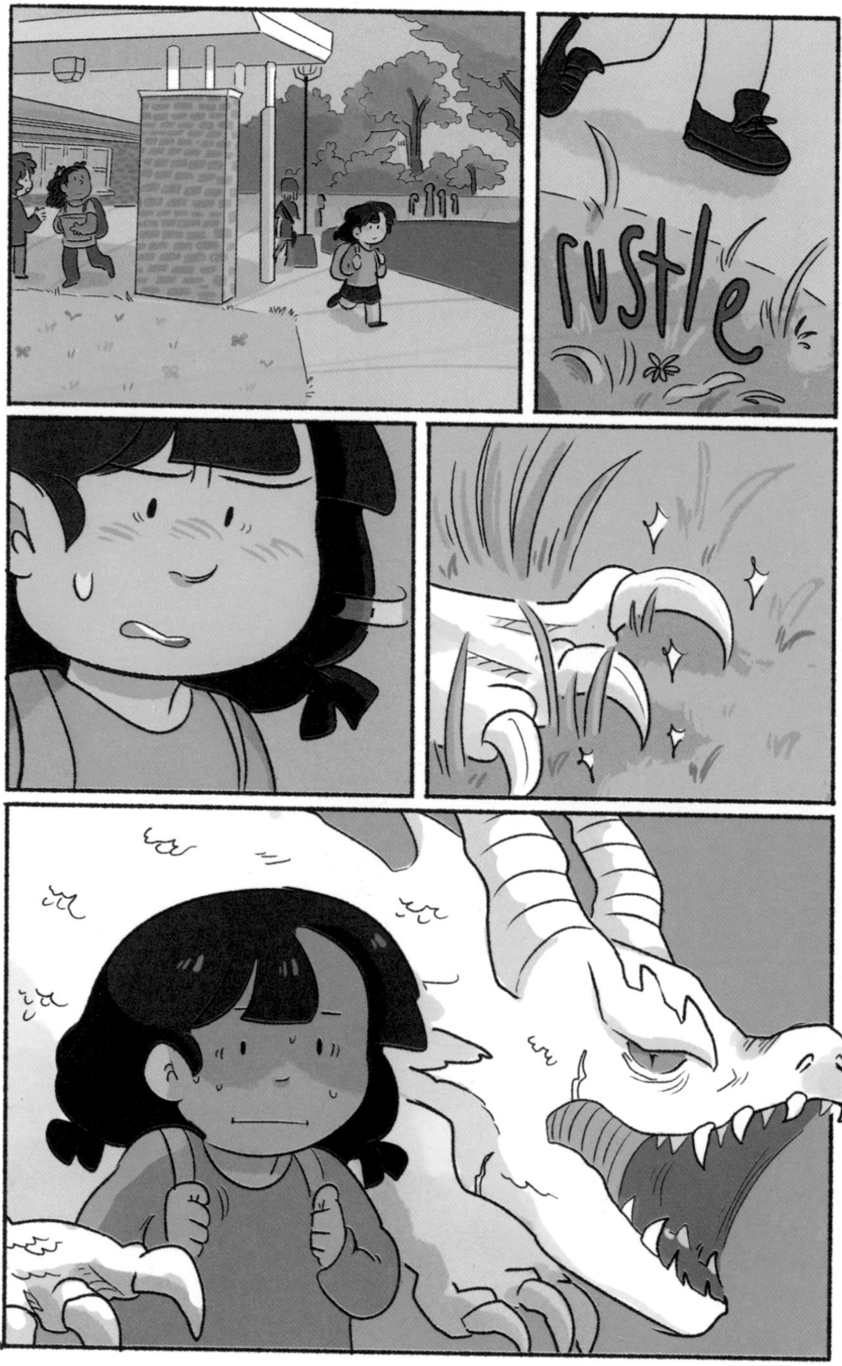
rustle

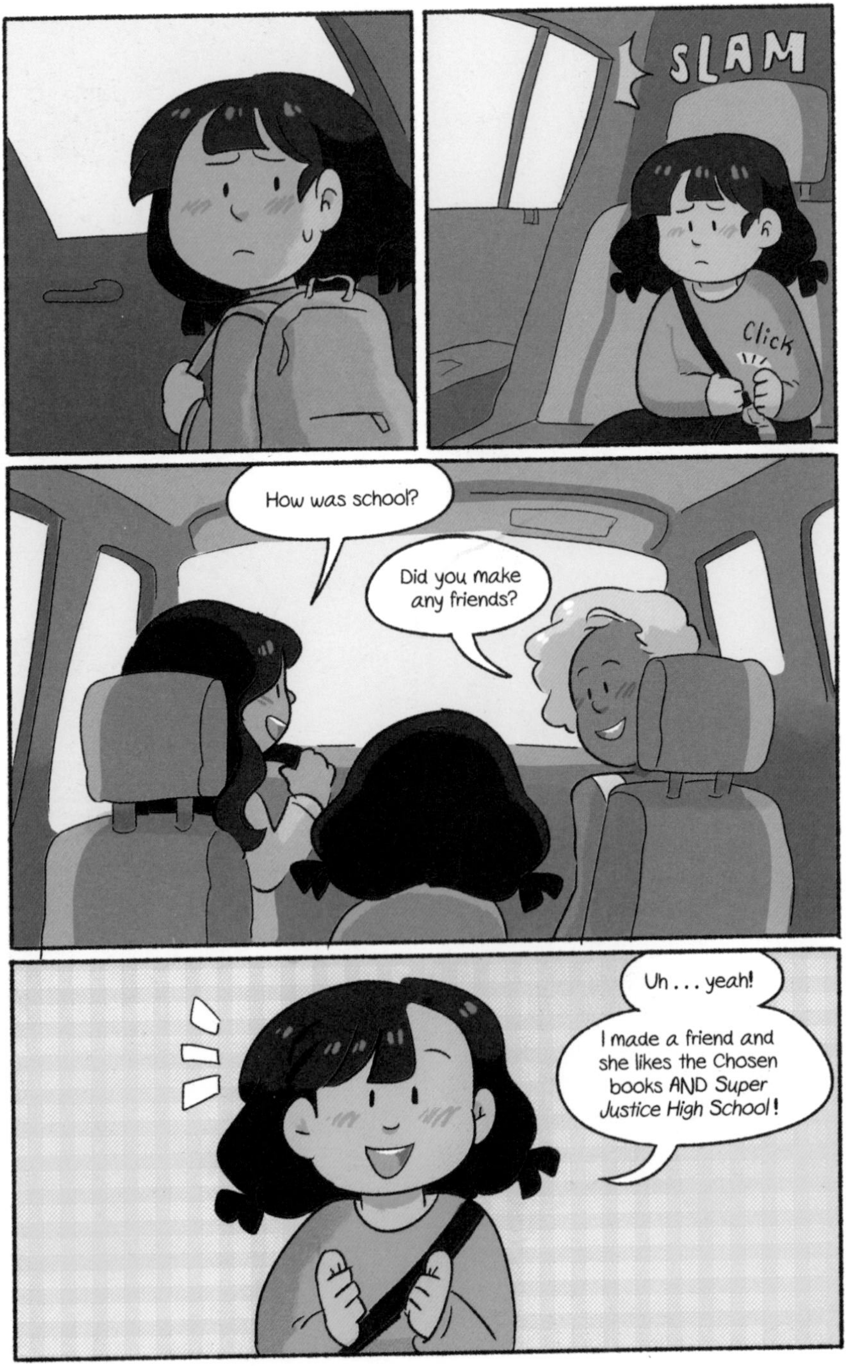
SLAM
Click
How was school?
Did you make any friends?
Uh . . . yeah!
I made a friend and she likes the Chosen books AND *Super Justice High School*!

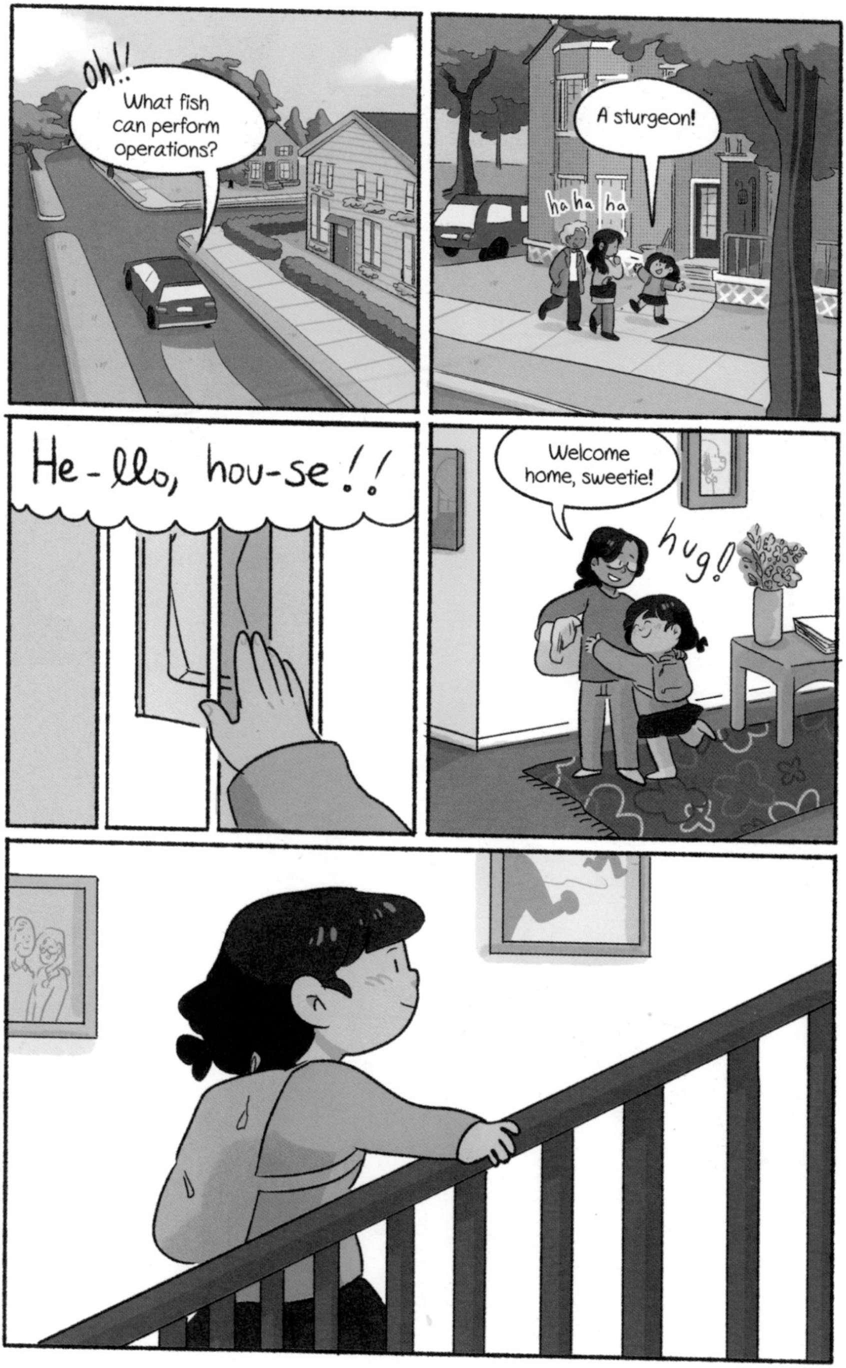

oh!!
What fish can perform operations?
A sturgeon!
ha ha ha
He-llo, hou-se!!
Welcome home, sweetie!
hug!

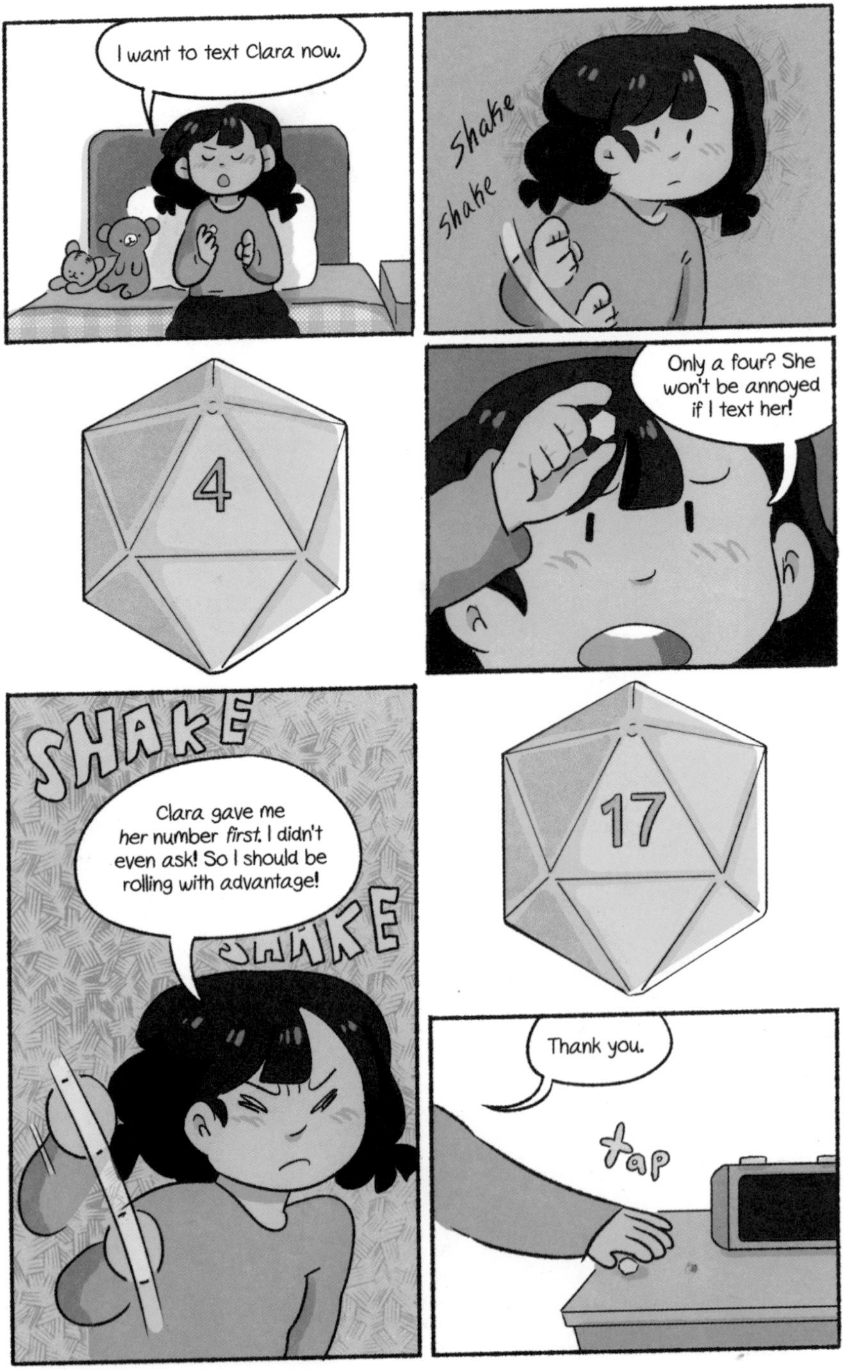
I want to text Clara now.
shake
shake
4
Only a four? She won't be annoyed if I text her!
SHAKE
Clara gave me her number *first*. I didn't even ask! So I should be rolling with advantage!
SHAKE
17
Thank you.
tap

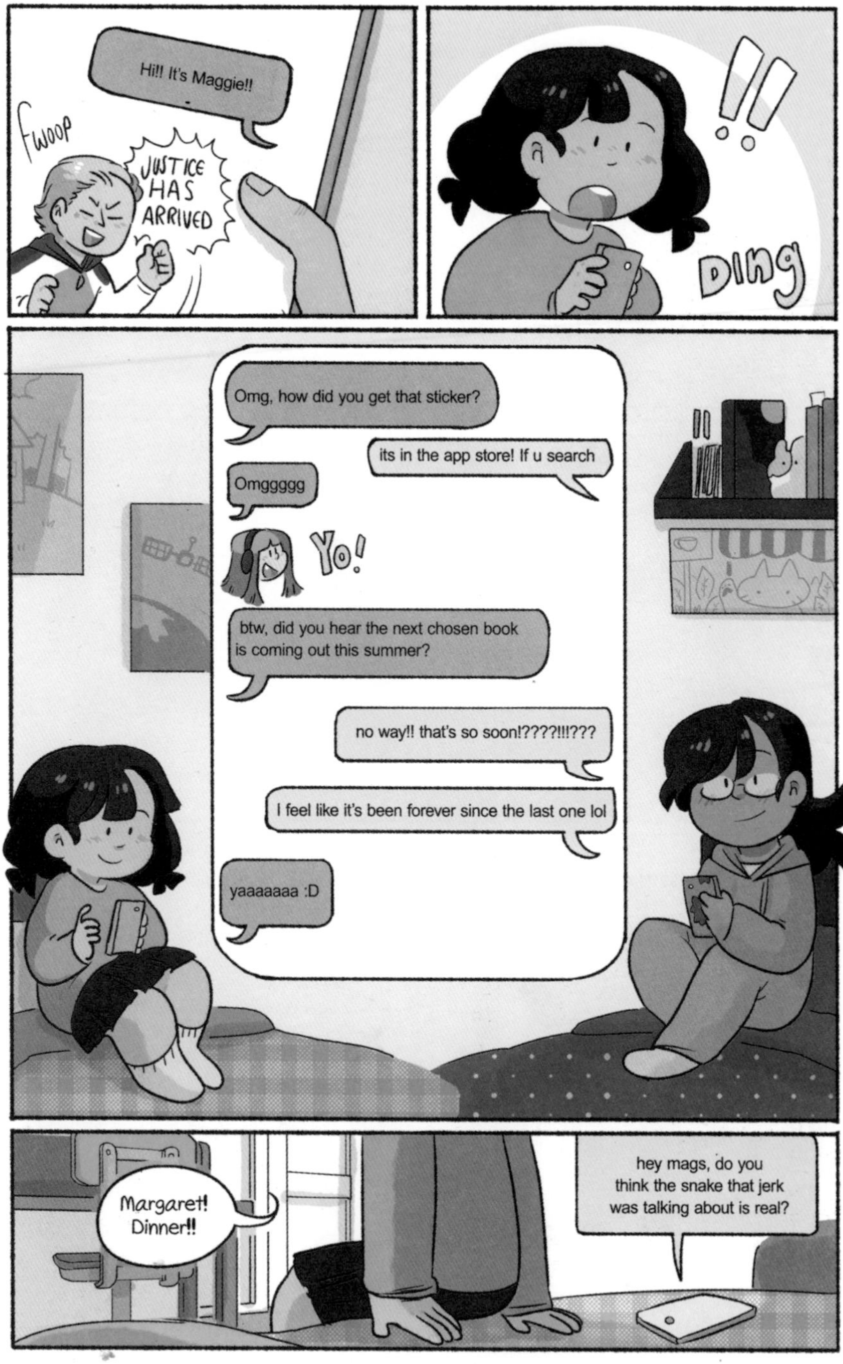

Hi!! It's Maggie!!
fwoop
JUSTICE HAS ARRIVED
!!
DING
Omg, how did you get that sticker?
its in the app store! If u search
Omgggggg
Yo!
btw, did you hear the next chosen book is coming out this summer?
no way!! that's so soon!????!!!???
I feel like it's been forever since the last one lol
yaaaaaaa :D
Margaret! Dinner!!
hey mags, do you think the snake that jerk was talking about is real?

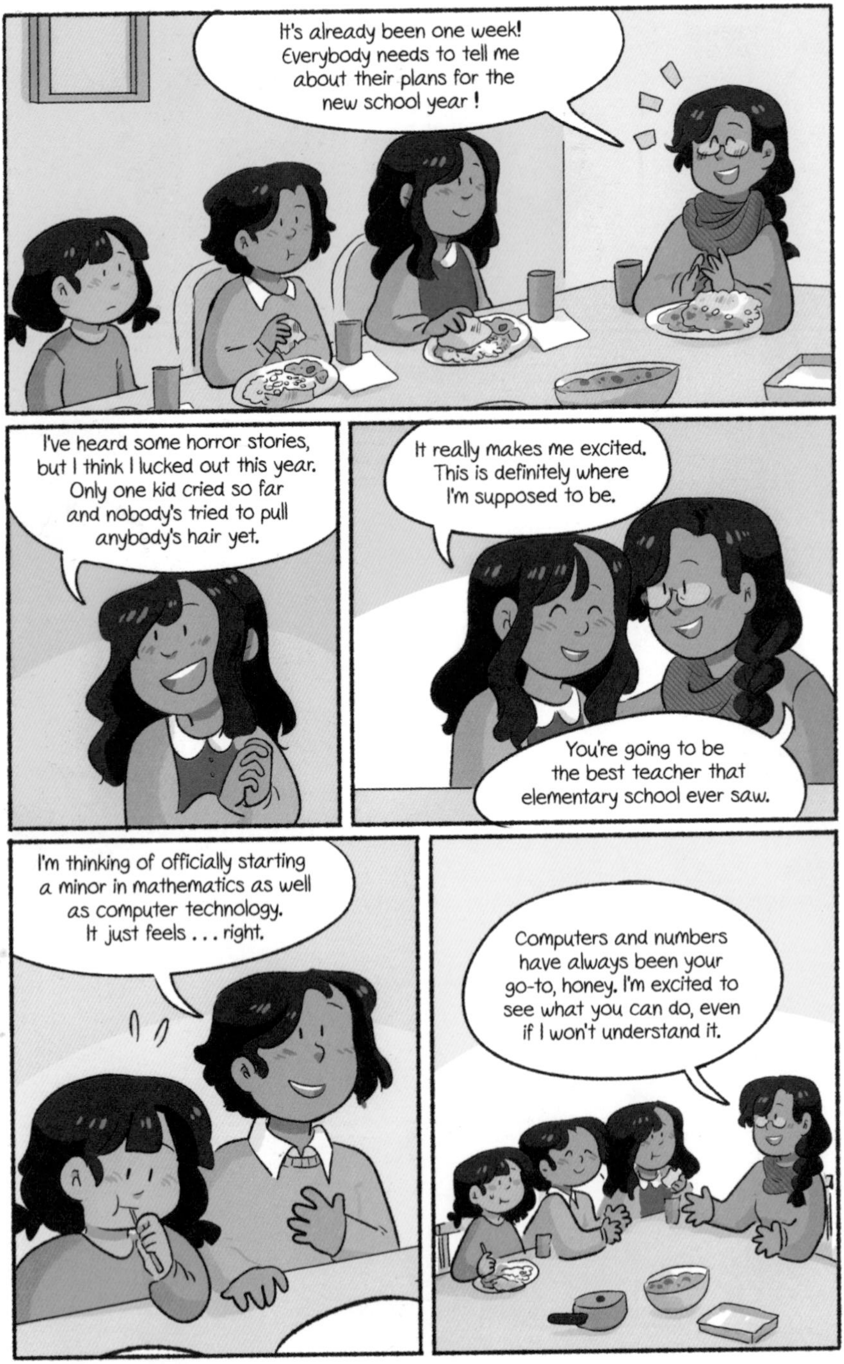

It's already been one week! Everybody needs to tell me about their plans for the new school year!
I've heard some horror stories, but I think I lucked out this year. Only one kid cried so far and nobody's tried to pull anybody's hair yet.
It really makes me excited. This is definitely where I'm supposed to be.
You're going to be the best teacher that elementary school ever saw.
I'm thinking of officially starting a minor in mathematics as well as computer technology. It just feels . . . right.
Computers and numbers have always been your go-to, honey. I'm excited to see what you can do, even if I won't understand it.

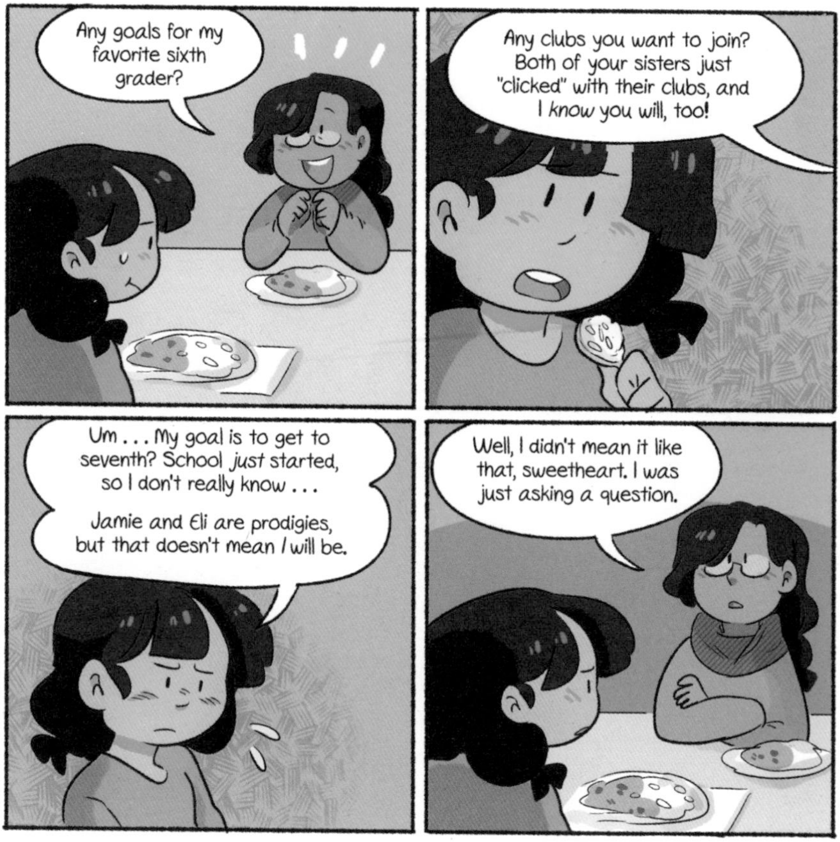
Any goals for my favorite sixth grader?
Any clubs you want to join? Both of your sisters just "clicked" with their clubs, and I *know* you will, too!
Um . . . My goal is to get to seventh? School *just* started, so I don't really know . . .
Jamie and Eli are prodigies, but that doesn't mean *I* will be.
Well, I didn't mean it like that, sweetheart. I was just asking a question.

• • •

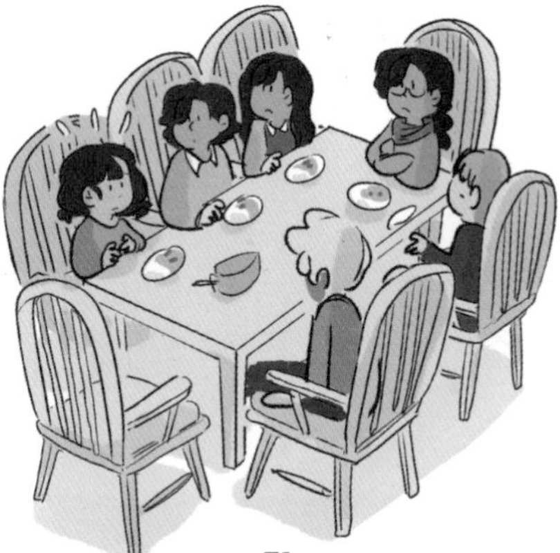

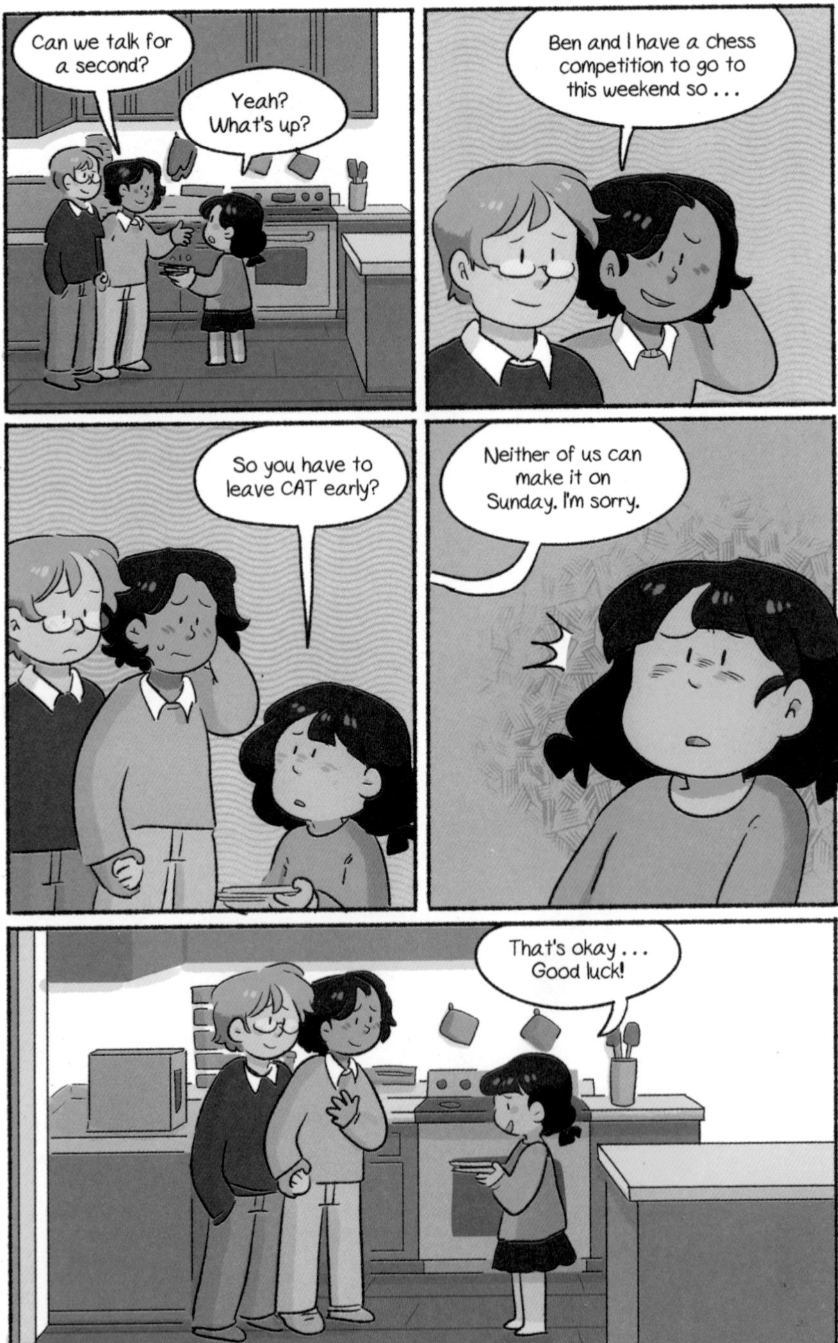
Can we talk for a second?
Yeah? What's up?
Ben and I have a chess competition to go to this weekend so . . .
So you have to leave CAT early?
Neither of us can make it on Sunday. I'm sorry.
That's okay . . . Good luck!

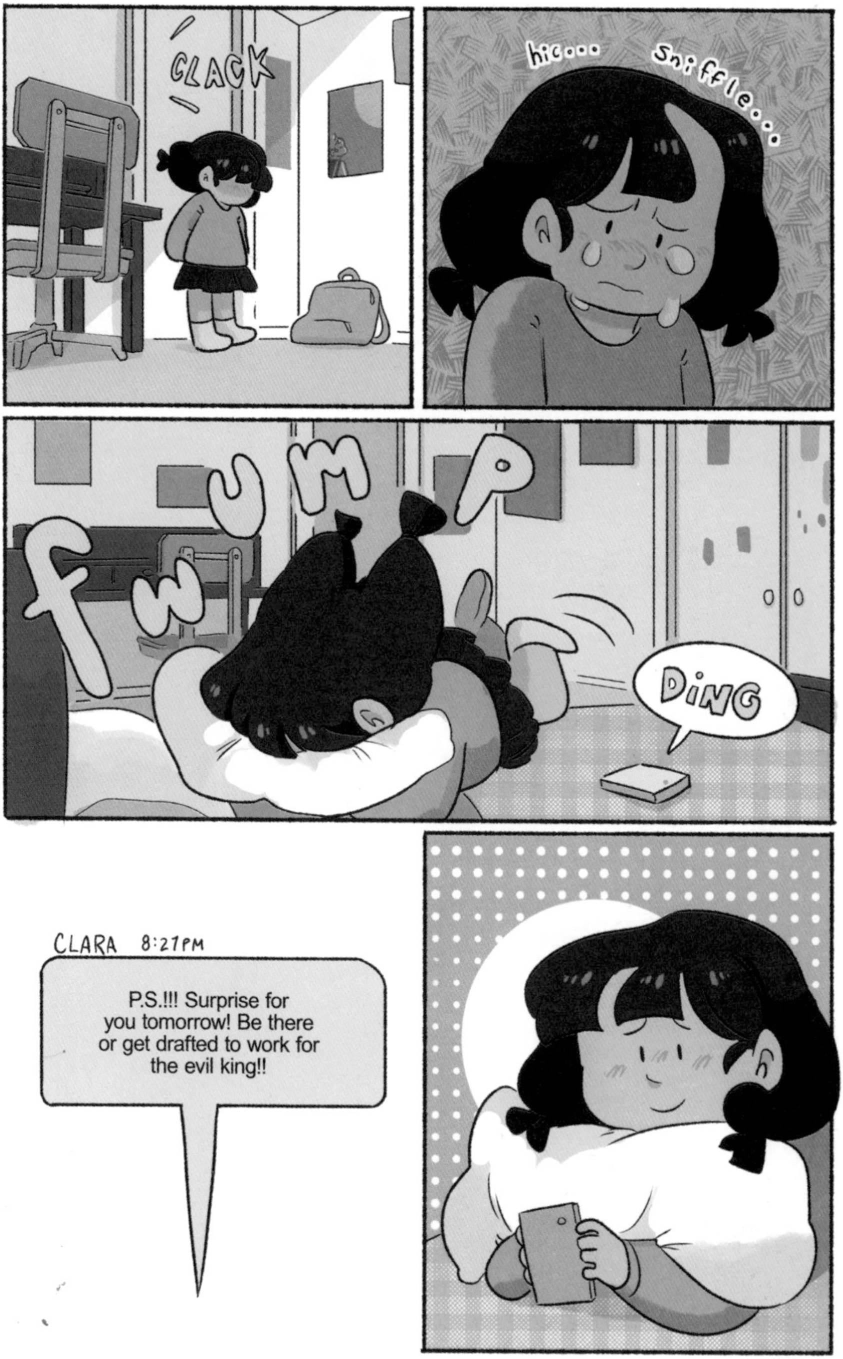
CLACK
hic...
Sniffle...
fwump
DiNG
CLARA 8:27PM
P.S.!!! Surprise for you tomorrow! Be there or get drafted to work for the evil king!!

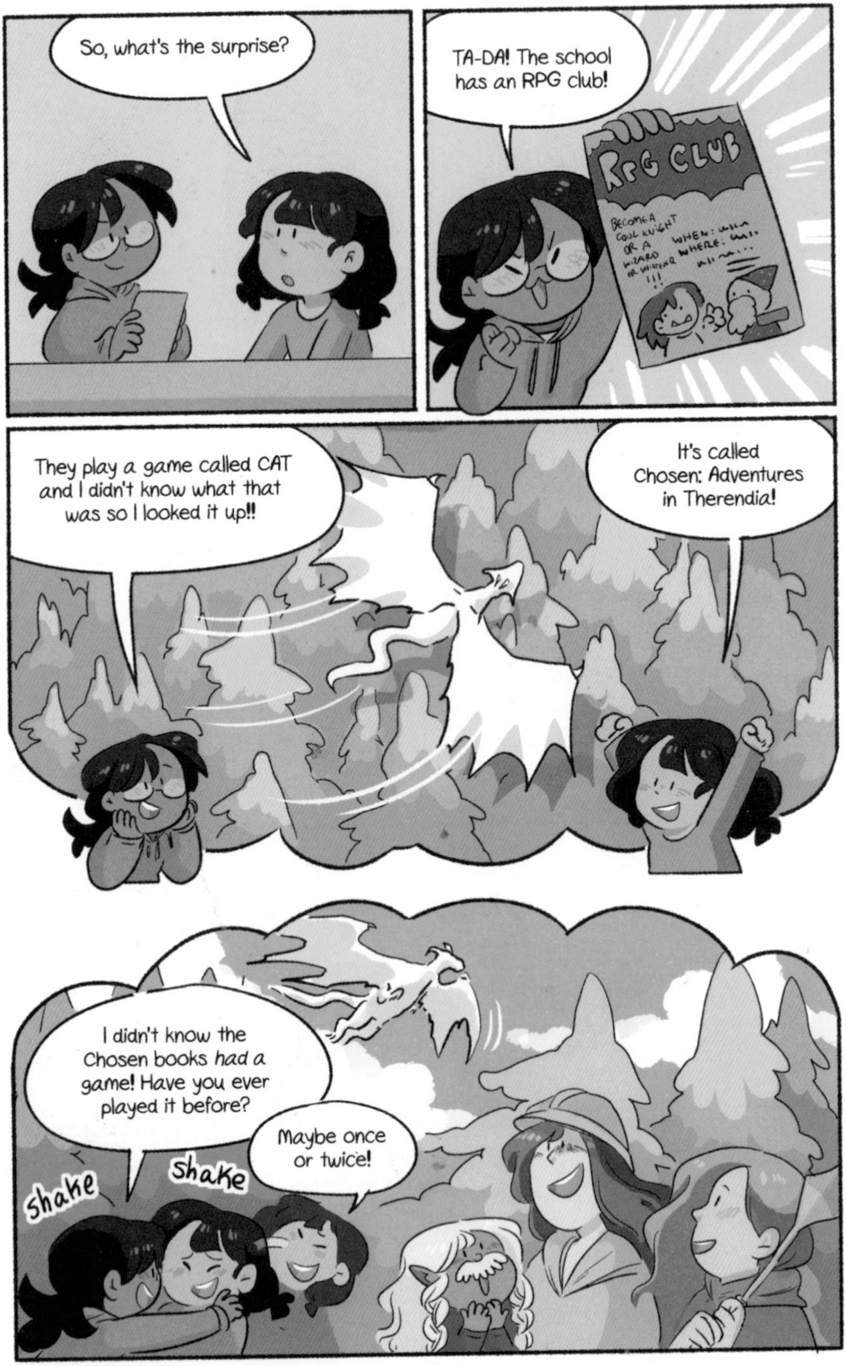
So, what's the surprise?
TA-DA! The school has an RPG club!
RPG CLUB
They play a game called CAT and I didn't know what that was so I looked it up!!
It's called Chosen: Adventures in Therendia!
I didn't know the Chosen books *had* a game! Have you ever played it before?
Maybe once or twice!
shake
shake

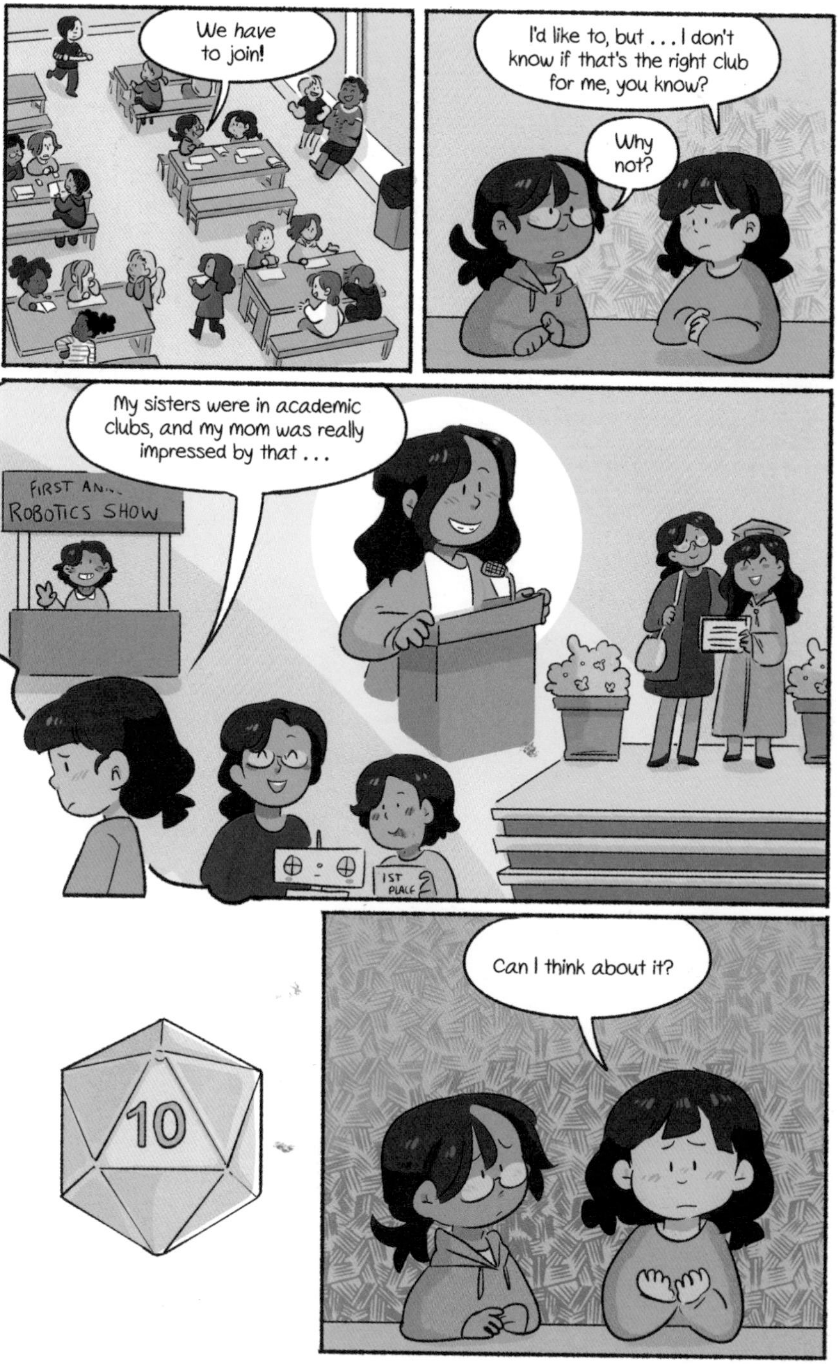
We have to join!
I'd like to, but . . . I don't know if that's the right club for me, you know?
Why not?
My sisters were in academic clubs, and my mom was really impressed by that . . .
FIRST AN...
ROBOTICS SHOW
1ST PLACE
10
Can I think about it?

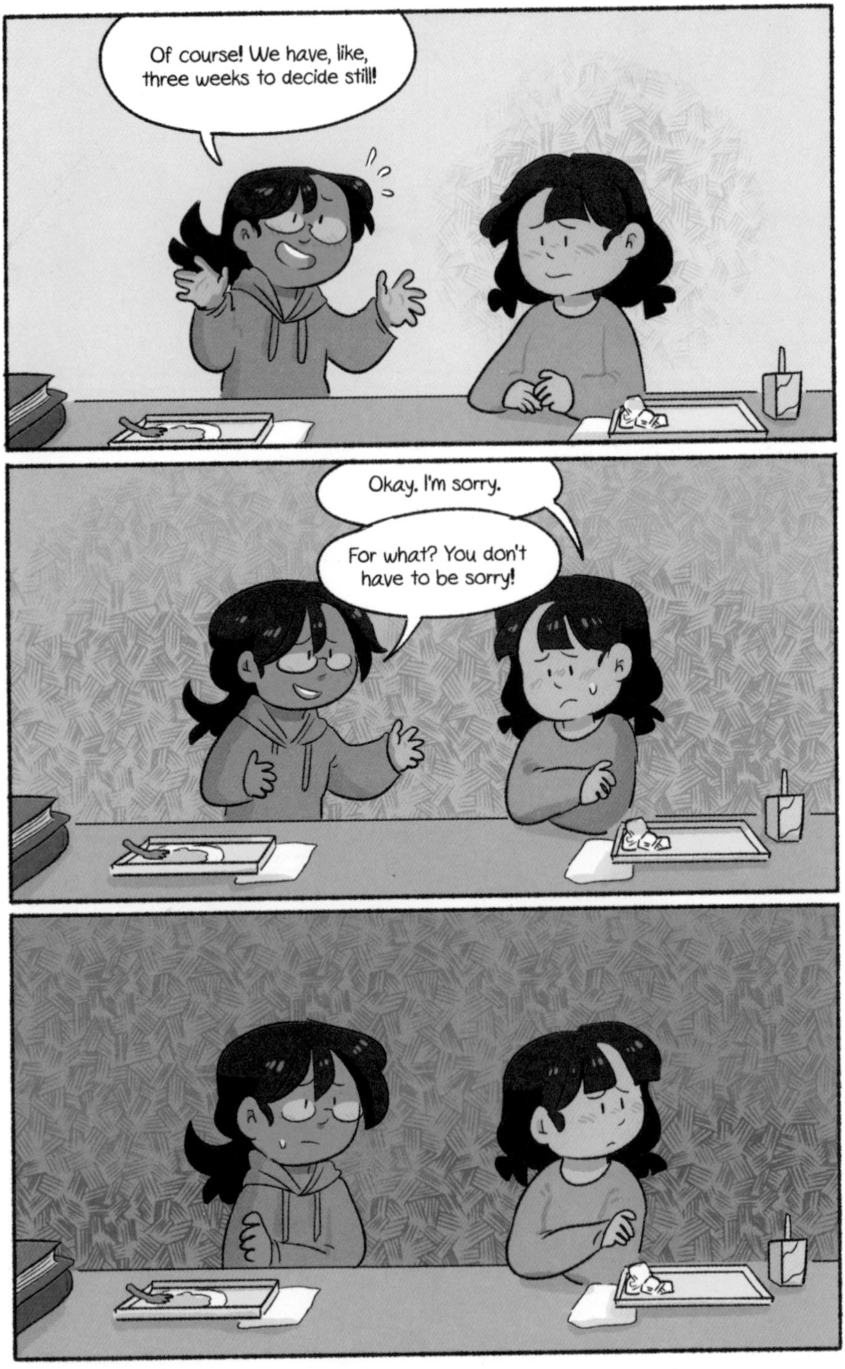
Of course! We have, like, three weeks to decide still!
Okay. I'm sorry.
For what? You don't have to be sorry!

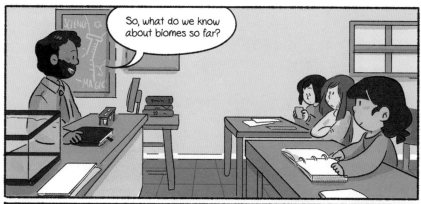

So, what do we know about biomes so far?

Anybody?

17

Biomes are sections of the earth, but divided up into groups. The type of biome tells you what sort of things can live there, along with the temperature and stuff.

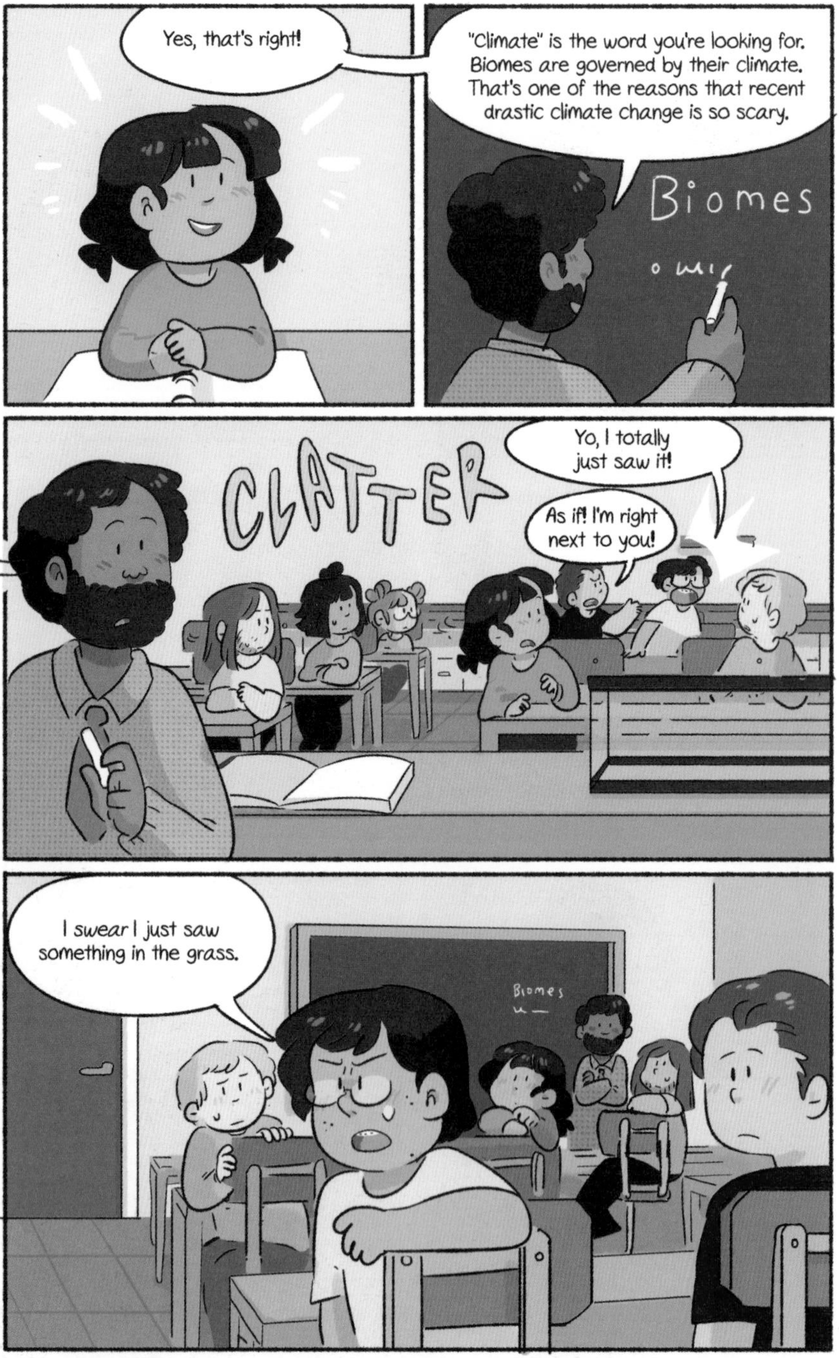
Yes, that's right!
"Climate" is the word you're looking for. Biomes are governed by their climate. That's one of the reasons that recent drastic climate change is so scary.
Biomes
CLATTER
Yo, I totally just saw it!
As if! I'm right next to you!
I *swear* I just saw something in the grass.

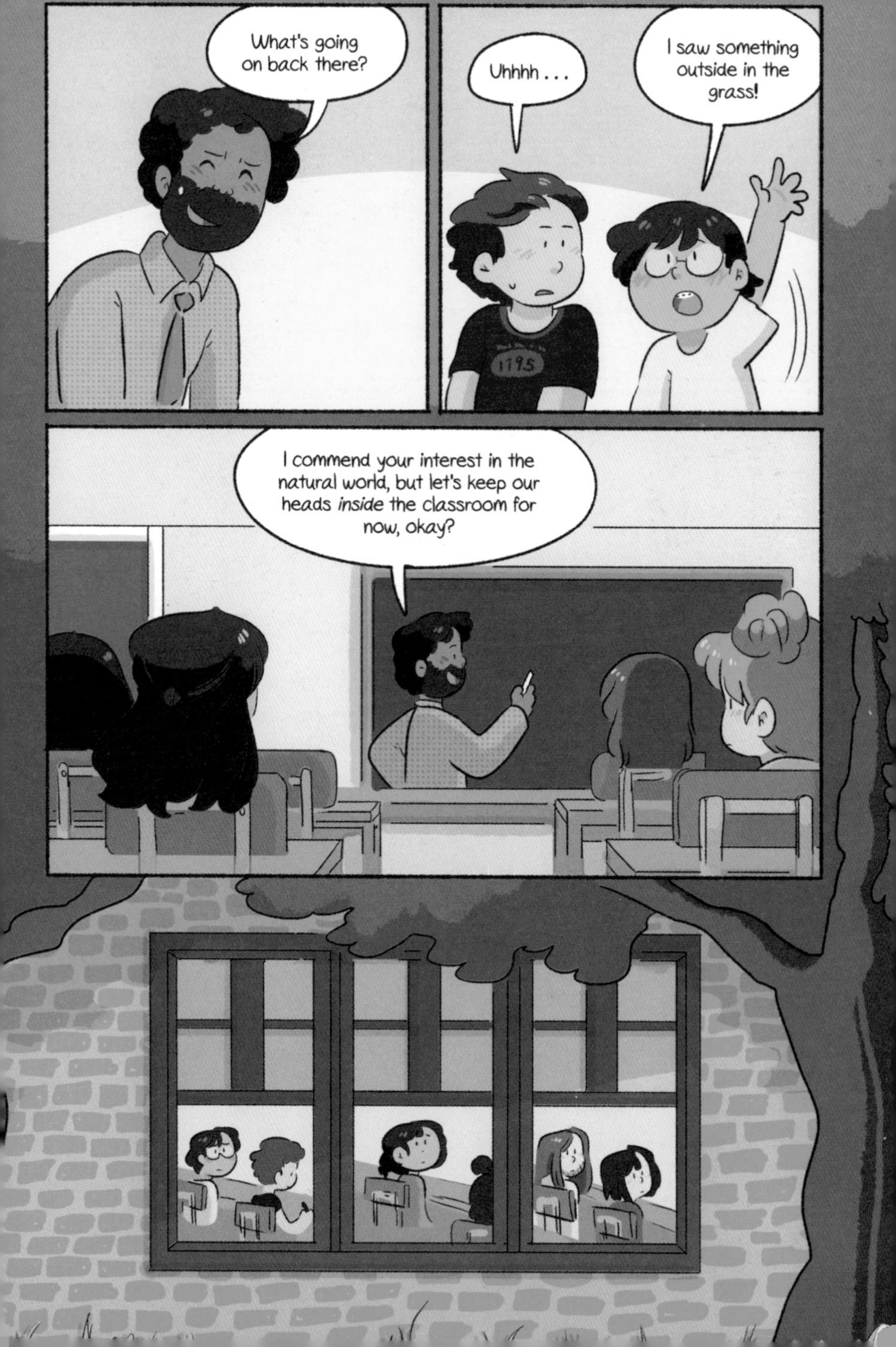
What's going on back there?
Uhhhh . . .
I saw something outside in the grass!
1795
I commend your interest in the natural world, but let's keep our heads *inside* the classroom for now, okay?

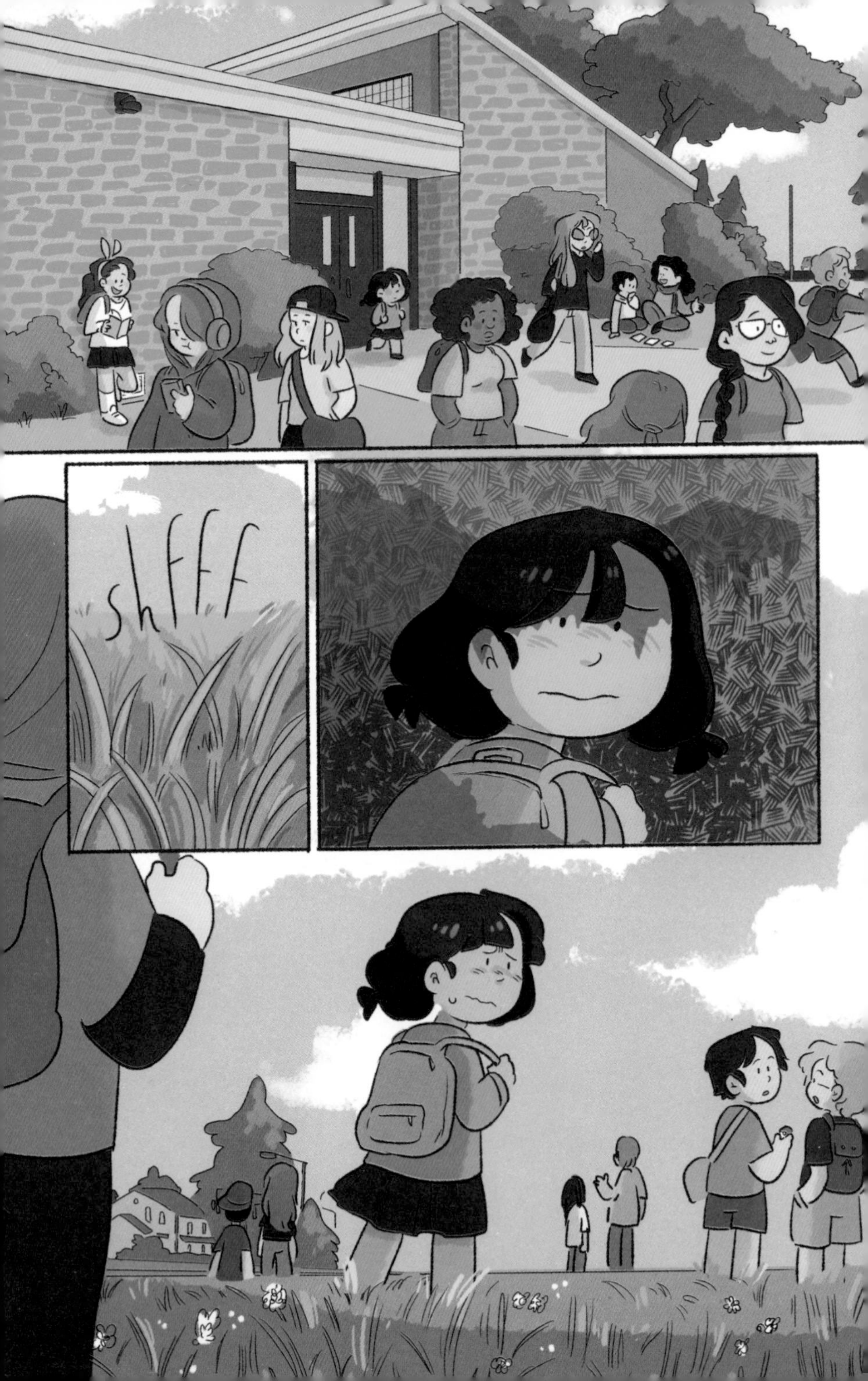
shfff

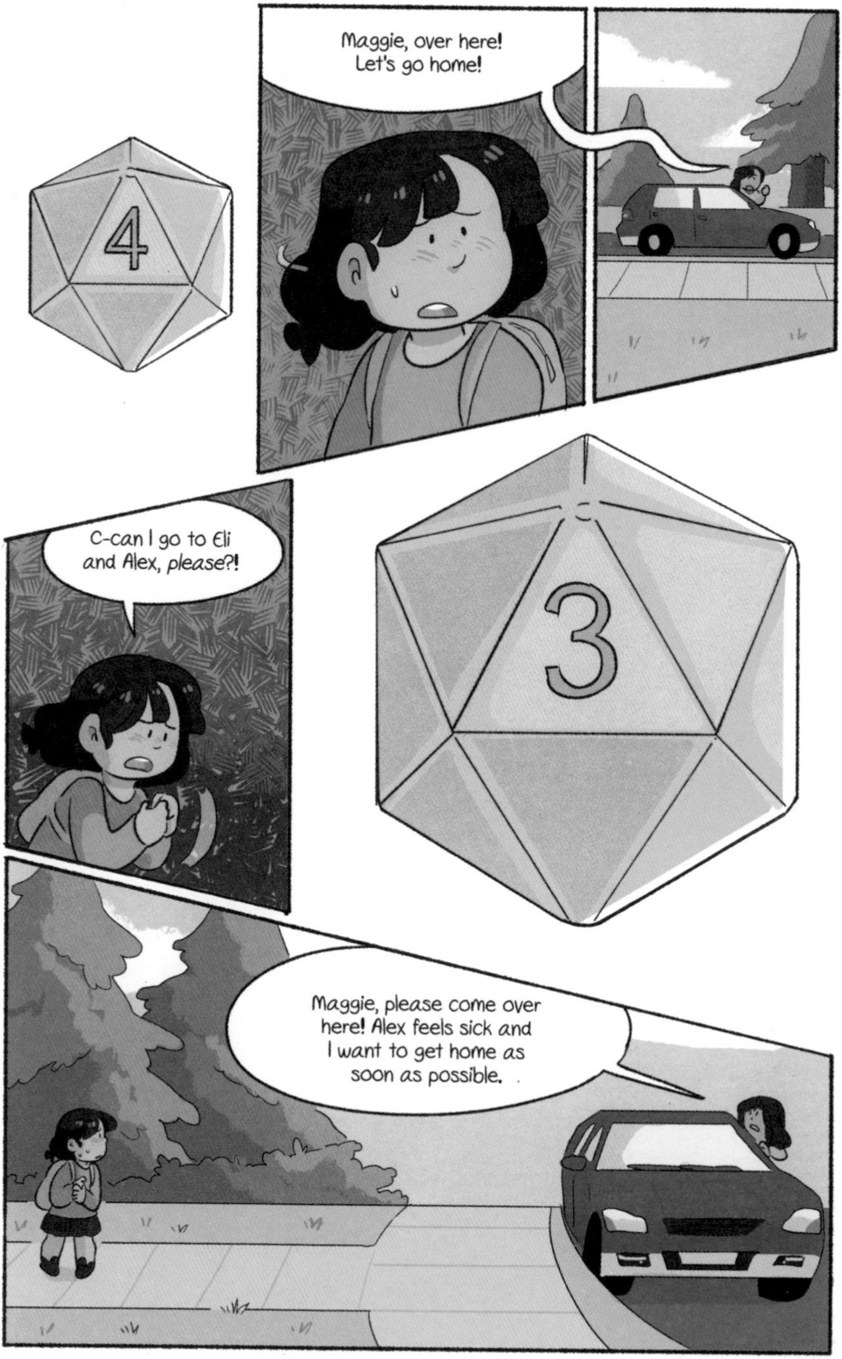
4
Maggie, over here!
Let's go home!
C-can I go to Eli and Alex, *please*?!
3
Maggie, please come over here! Alex feels sick and I want to get home as soon as possible.

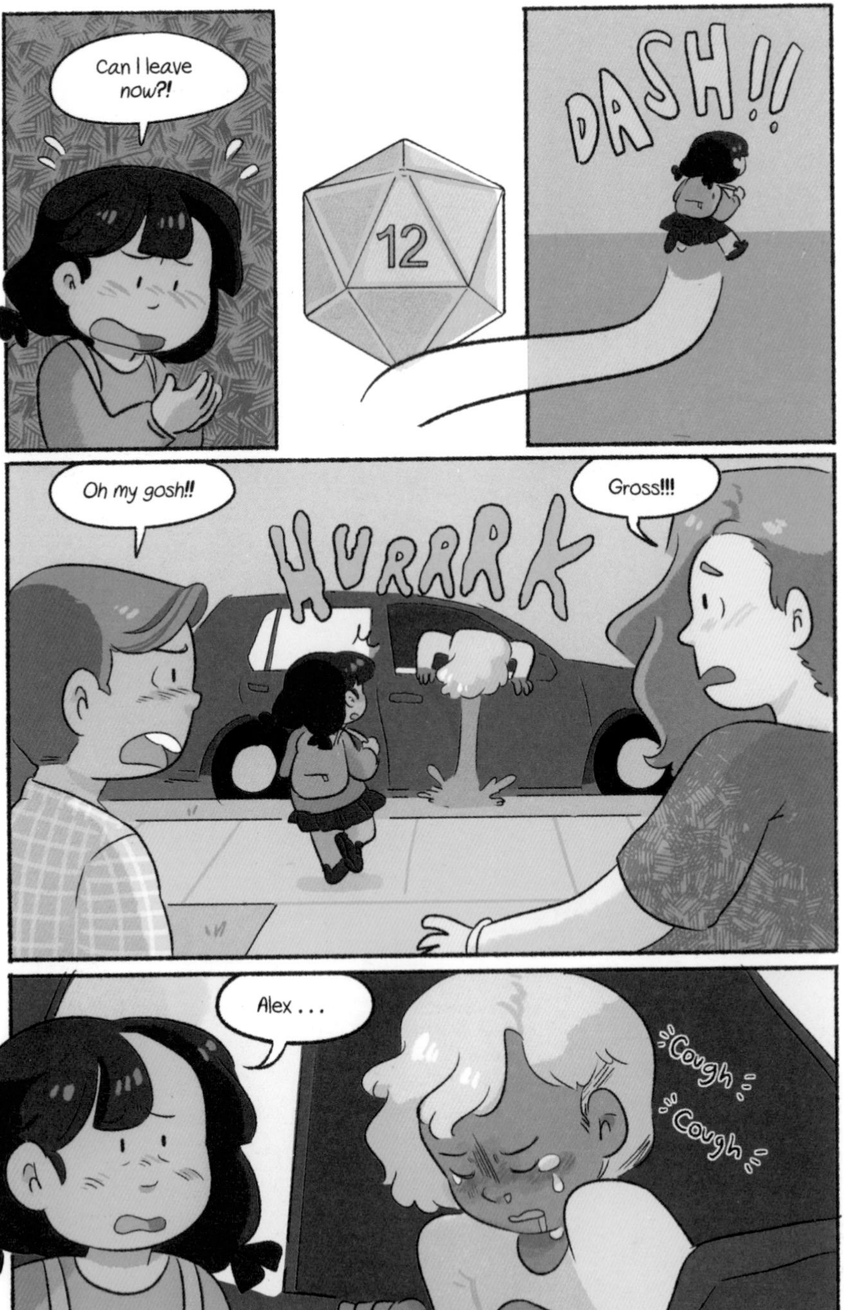

Can I leave now?!
12
DASH!!
Oh my gosh!!
HURRRK
Gross!!!
Alex . . .
Cough
Cough

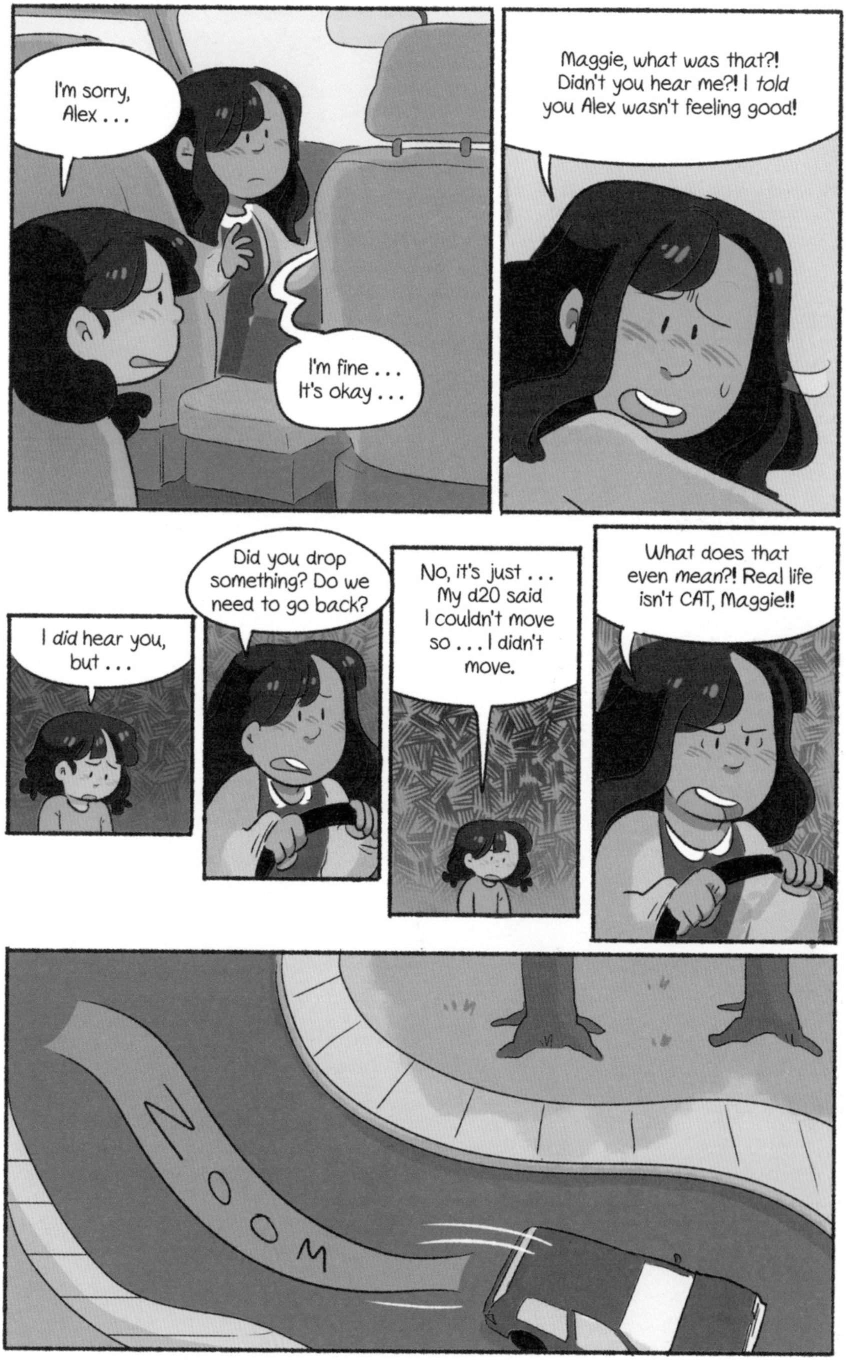
I'm sorry, Alex . . .
I'm fine . . . It's okay . . .
Maggie, what was that?! Didn't you hear me?! I *told* you Alex wasn't feeling good!
I *did* hear you, but . . .
Did you drop something? Do we need to go back?
No, it's just . . . My d20 said I couldn't move so . . . I didn't move.
What does that even *mean*?! Real life isn't CAT, Maggie!!
ZOOM

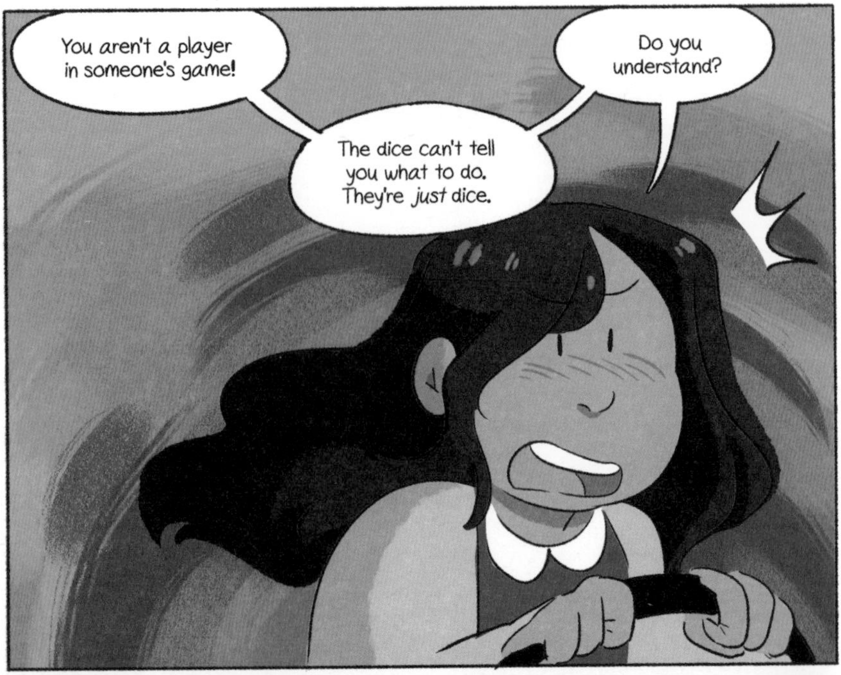
You aren't a player in someone's game!
The dice can't tell you what to do. They're *just* dice.
Do you understand?

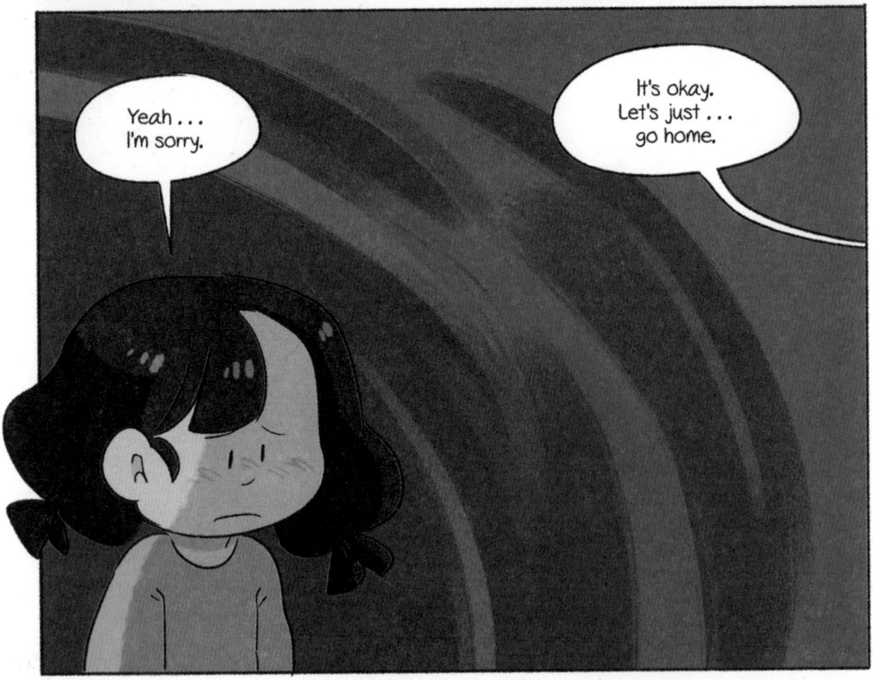
Yeah . . . I'm sorry.
It's okay. Let's just . . . go home.

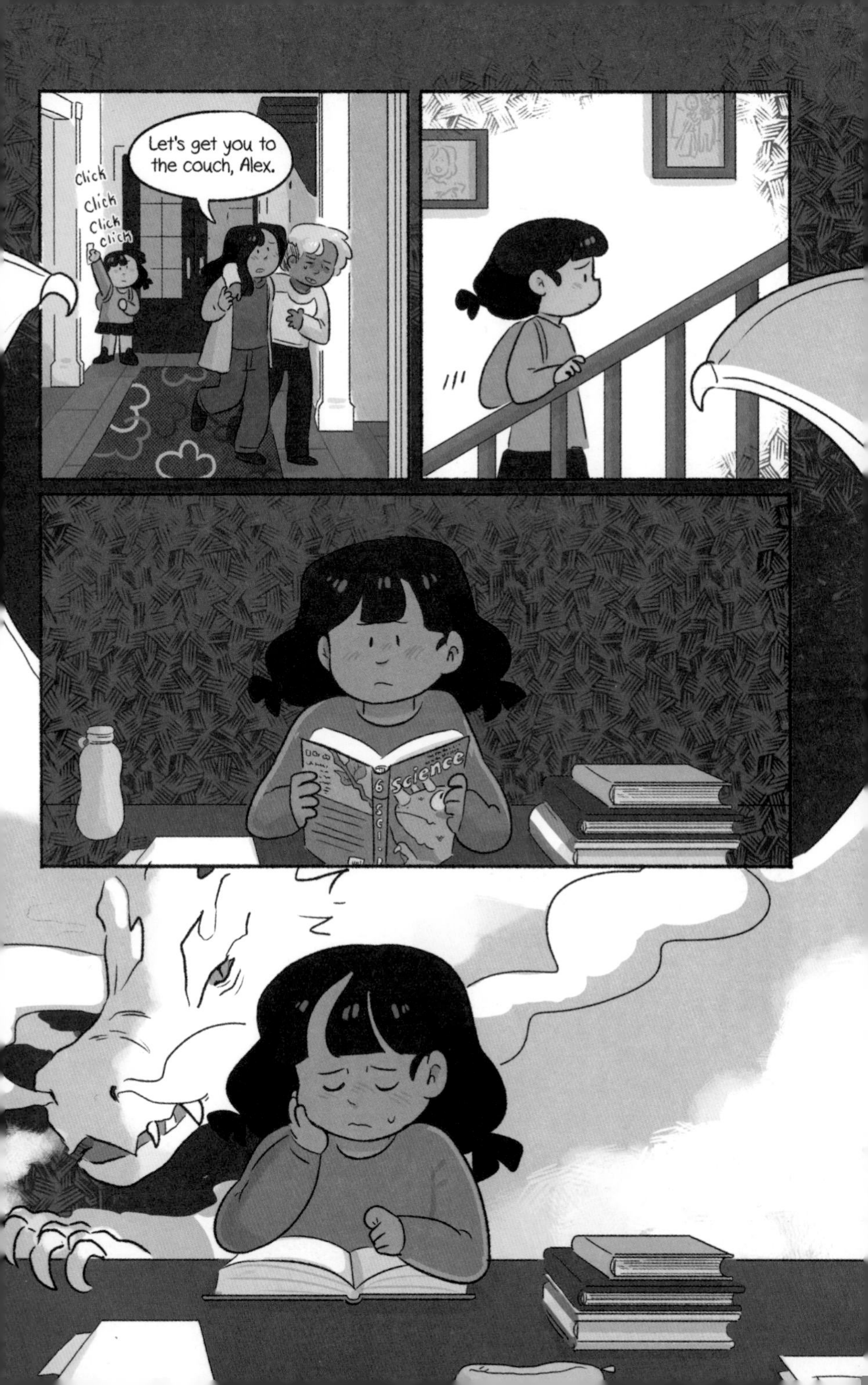
click
click
click
click
Let's get you to the couch, Alex.
science

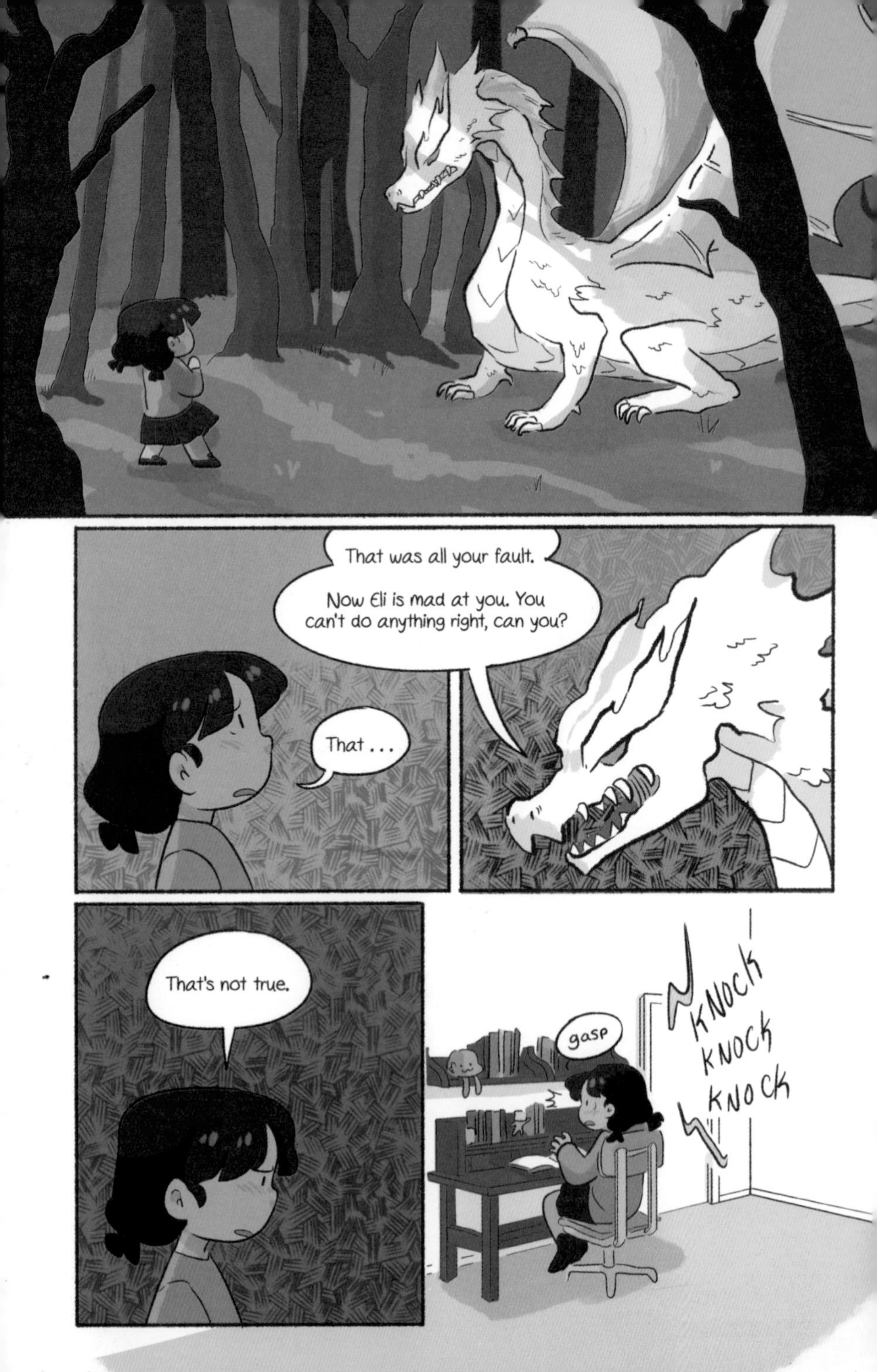
That was all your fault.
Now Eli is mad at you. You can't do anything right, can you?
That . . .
That's not true.
gasp
KNOCK KNOCK KNOCK

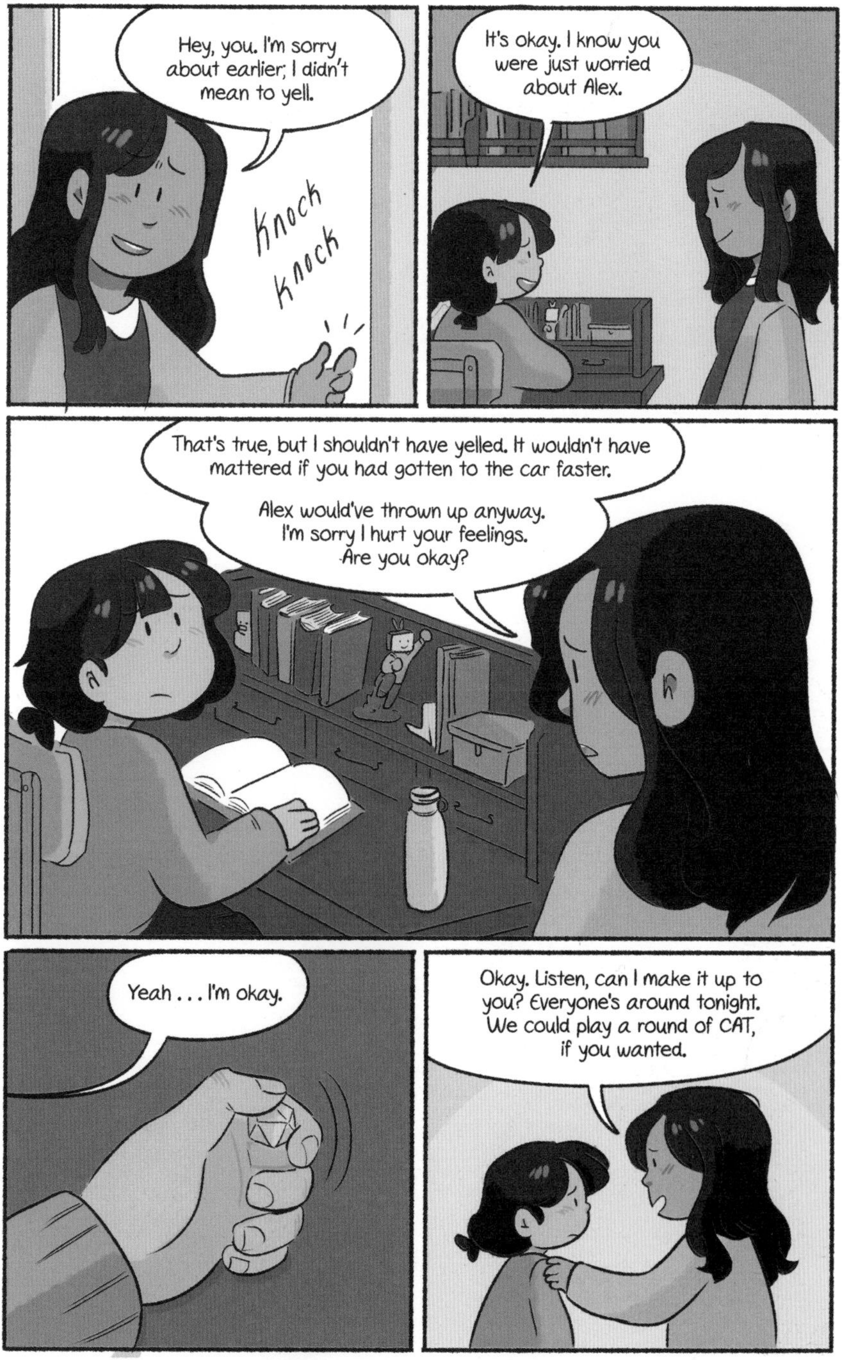
Hey, you. I'm sorry about earlier; I didn't mean to yell.
Knock knock
It's okay. I know you were just worried about Alex.
That's true, but I shouldn't have yelled. It wouldn't have mattered if you had gotten to the car faster.
Alex would've thrown up anyway. I'm sorry I hurt your feelings. Are you okay?
Yeah . . . I'm okay.
Okay. Listen, can I make it up to you? Everyone's around tonight. We could play a round of CAT, if you wanted.

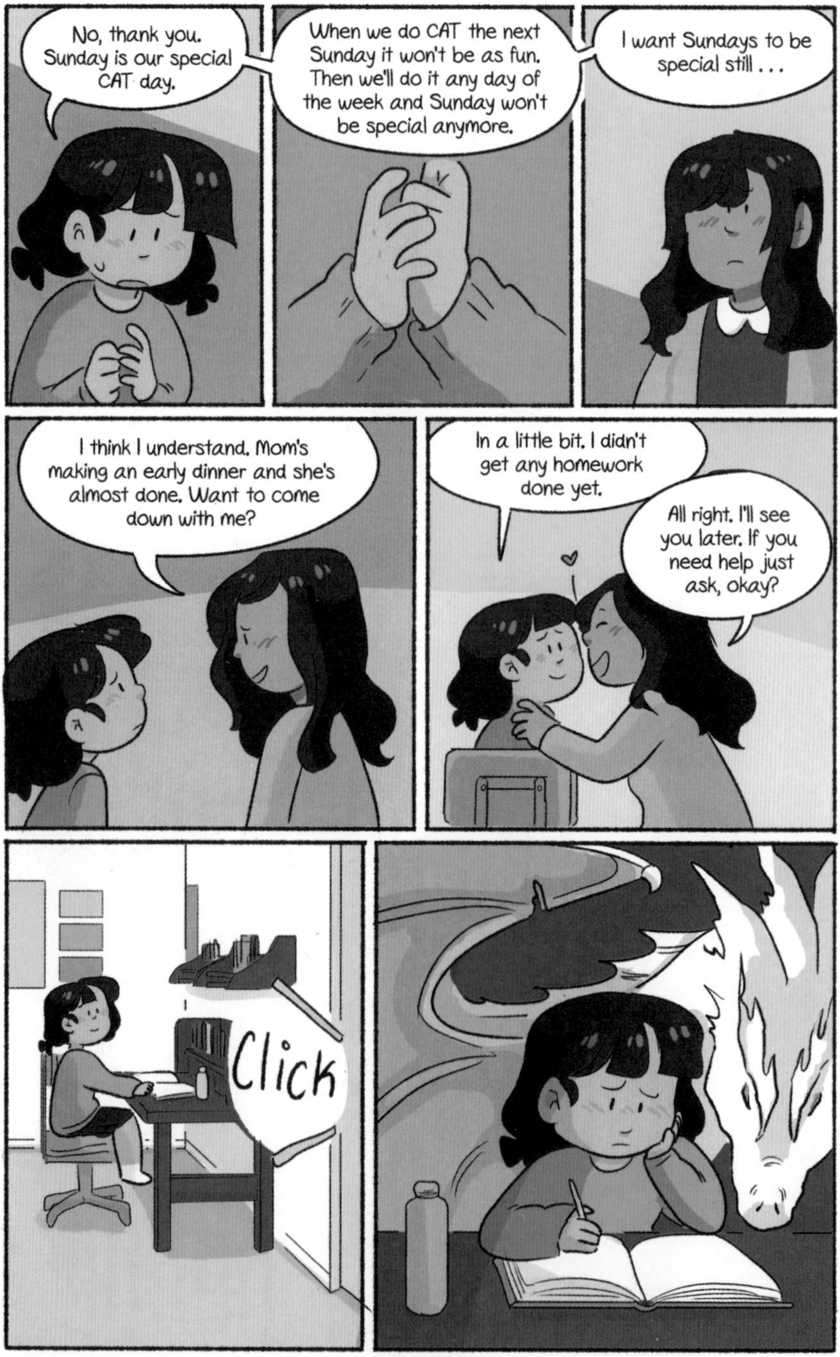
No, thank you. Sunday is our special CAT day.
When we do CAT the next Sunday it won't be as fun. Then we'll do it any day of the week and Sunday won't be special anymore.
I want Sundays to be special still . . .
I think I understand. Mom's making an early dinner and she's almost done. Want to come down with me?
In a little bit. I didn't get any homework done yet.
All right. I'll see you later. If you need help just ask, okay?
Click

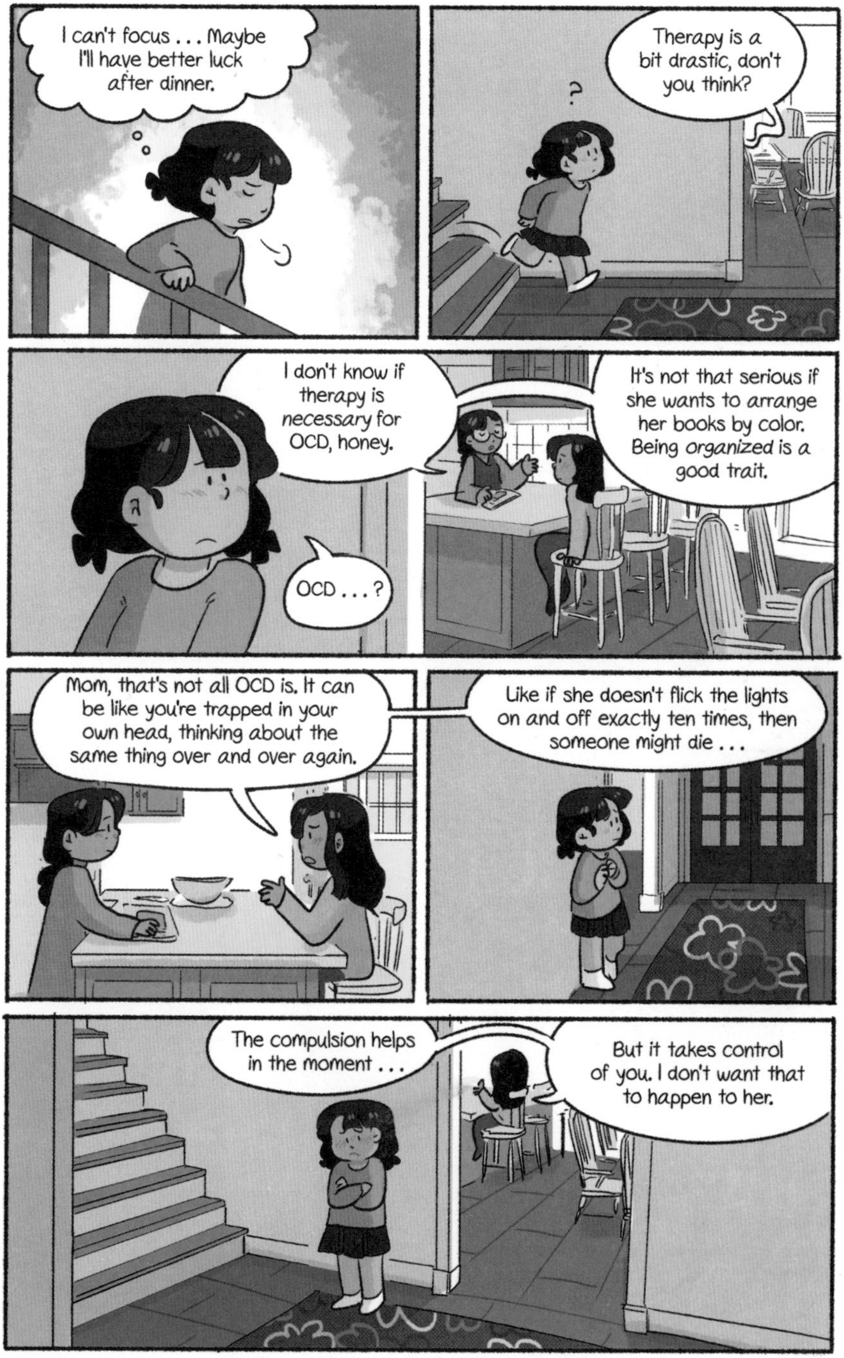
I can't focus . . . Maybe I'll have better luck after dinner.
Therapy is a bit drastic, don't you think?
?
I don't know if therapy is *necessary* for OCD, honey.
It's not that serious if she wants to *arrange* her books by color. Being *organized* is a good trait.
OCD . . . ?
Mom, that's not all OCD is. It can be like you're trapped in your own head, thinking about the same thing over and over again.
Like if she doesn't flick the lights on and off exactly ten times, then someone might die . . .
The compulsion helps in the moment . . .
But it takes control of you. I don't want that to happen to her.

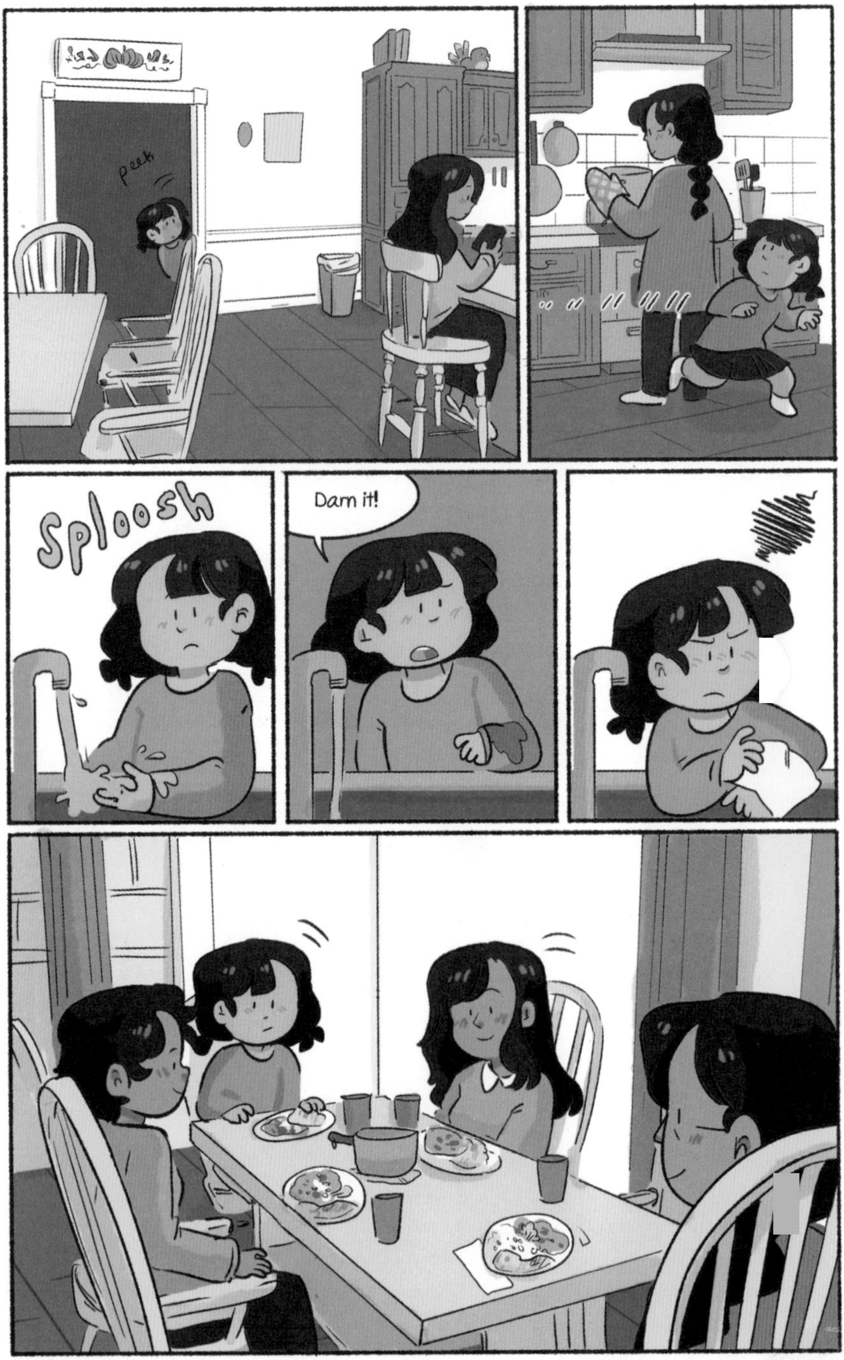
peek
Sploosh
Darn it!

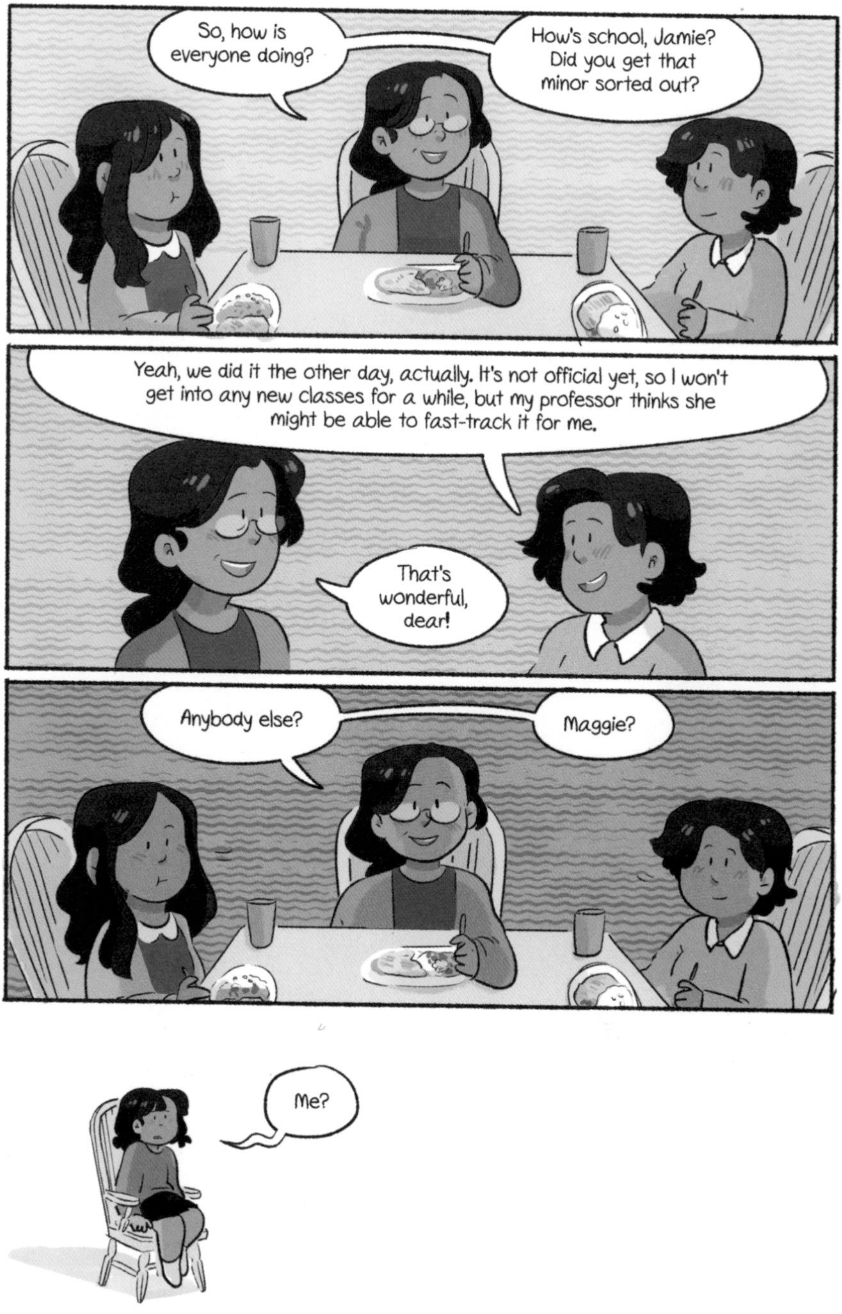
So, how is everyone doing?
How's school, Jamie? Did you get that minor sorted out?
Yeah, we did it the other day, actually. It's not official yet, so I won't get into any new classes for a while, but my professor thinks she might be able to fast-track it for me.
That's wonderful, dear!
Anybody else?
Maggie?
Me?

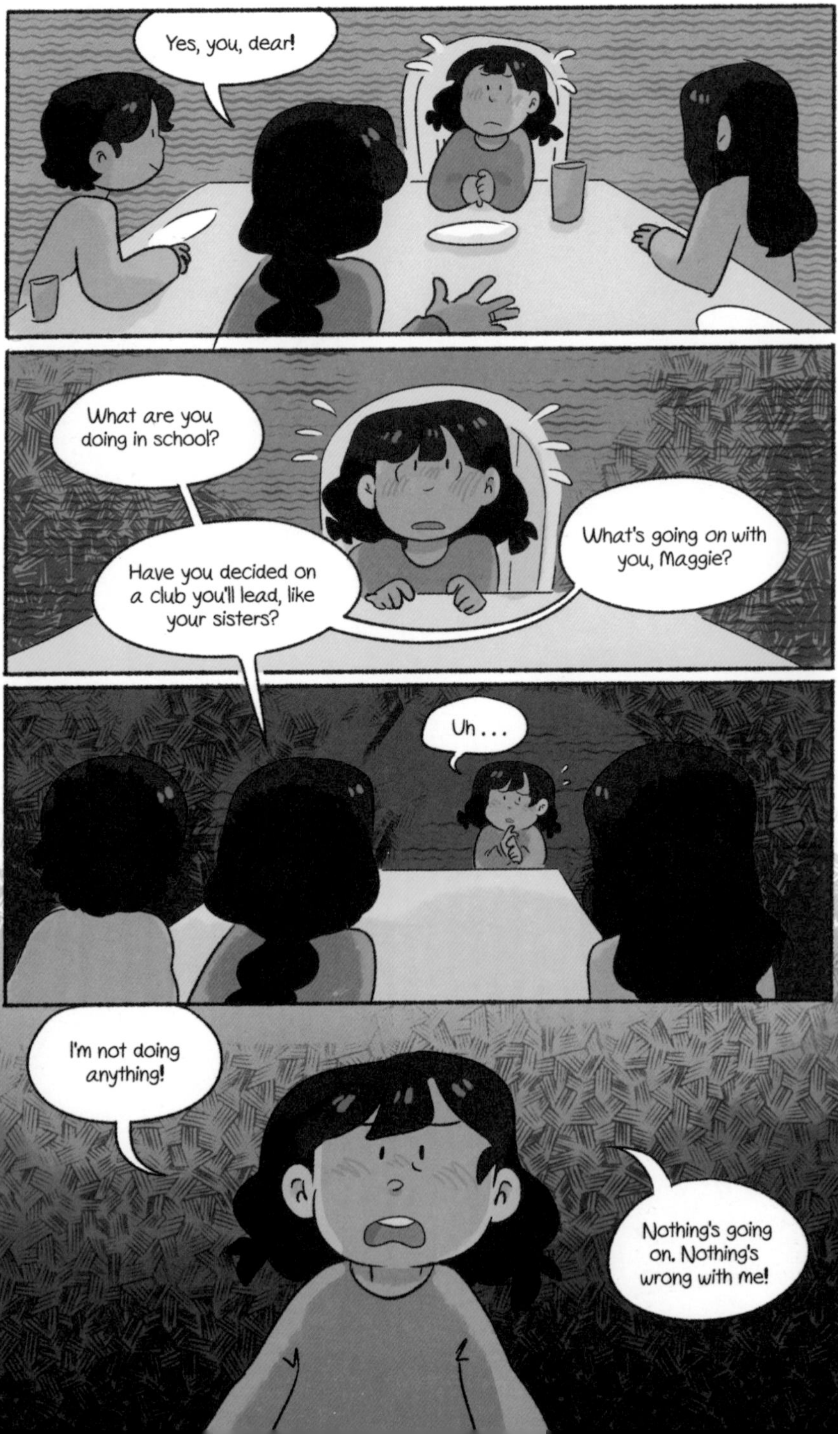

Yes, you, dear!
What are you doing in school?
Have you decided on a club you'll lead, like your sisters?
What's going on with you, Maggie?
Uh . . .
I'm not doing anything!
Nothing's going on. Nothing's wrong with me!

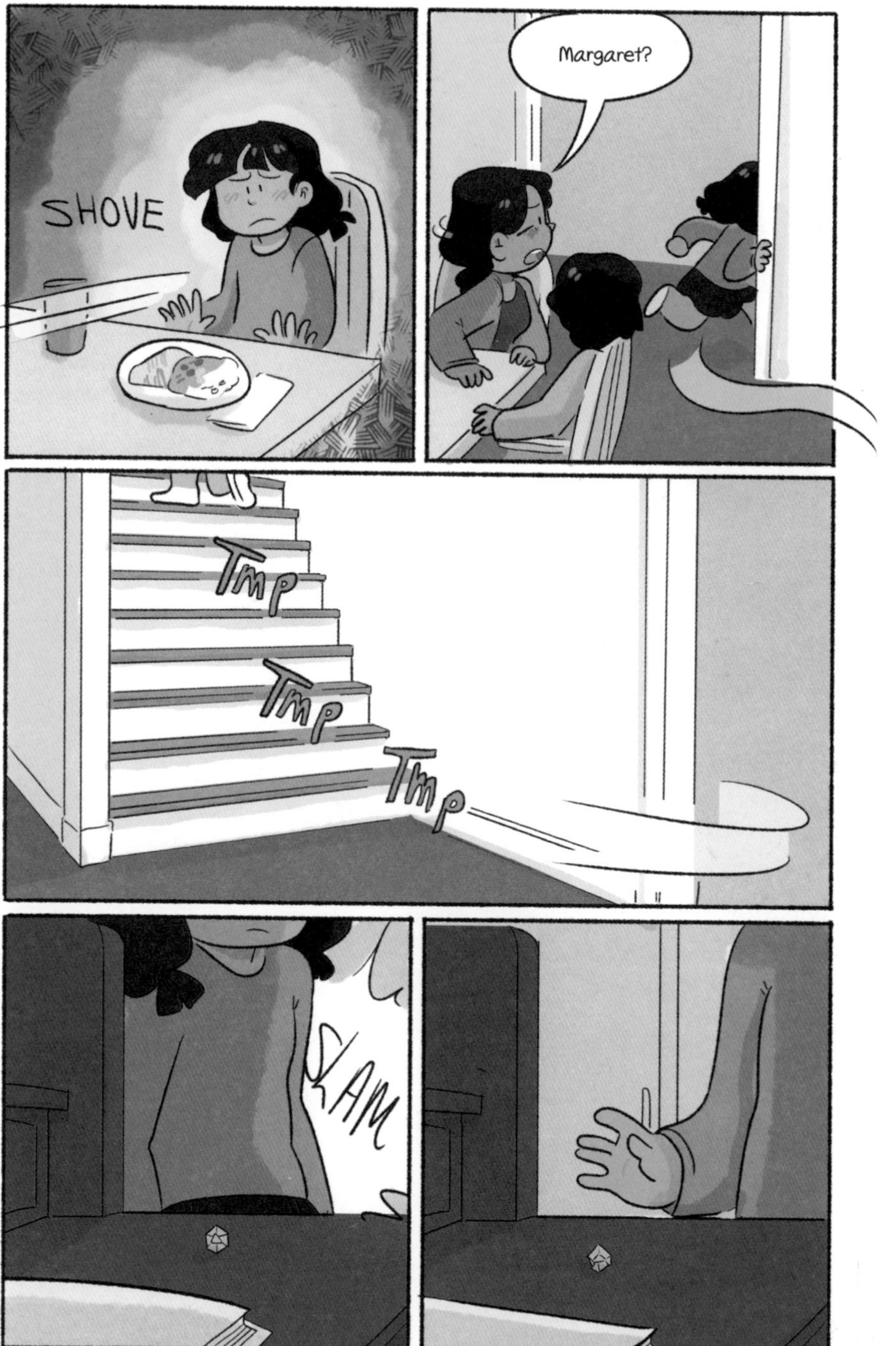
SHOVE
Margaret?
Tmp
Tmp
Tmp
SLAM

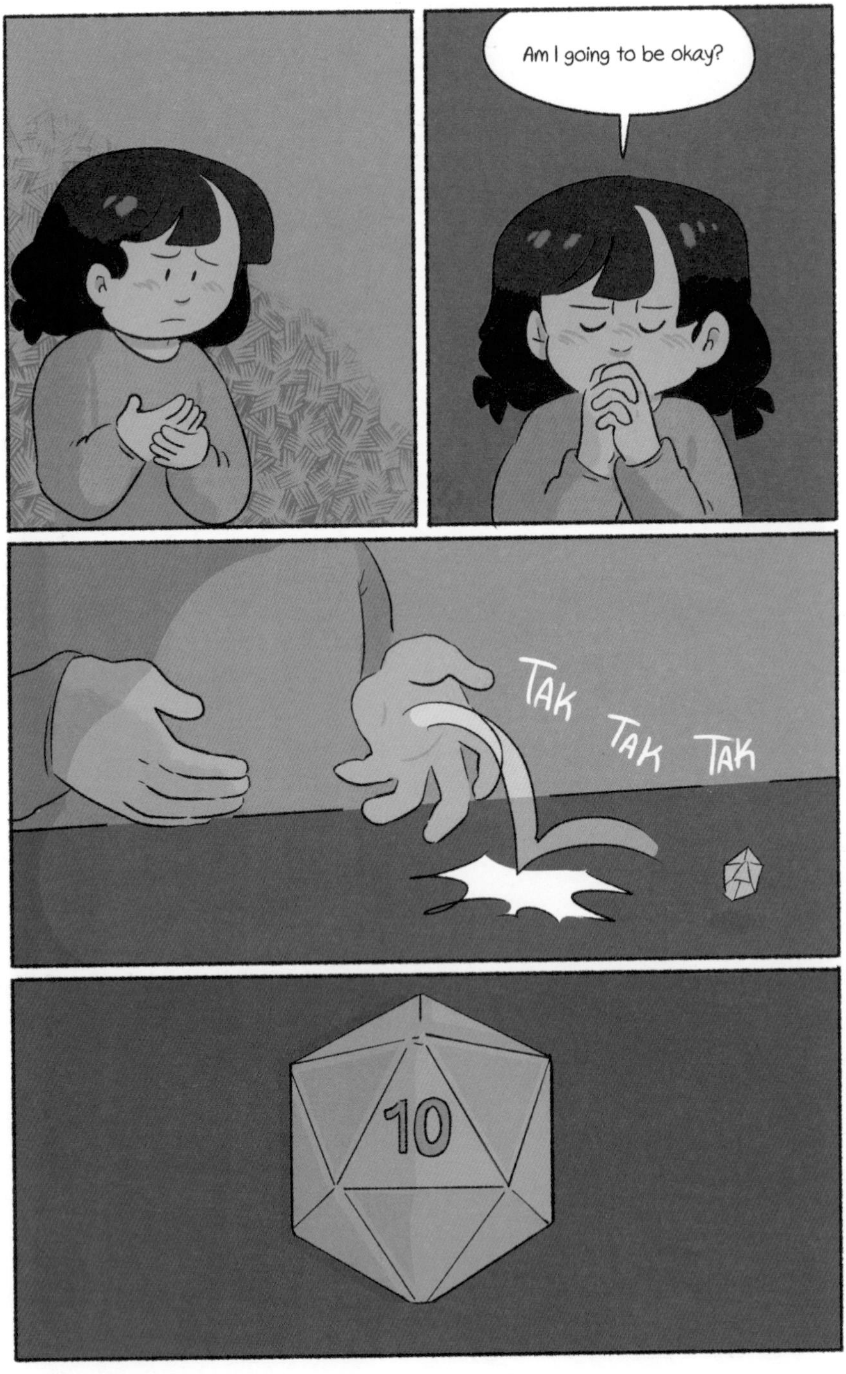
Am I going to be okay?
TAK TAK TAK
10

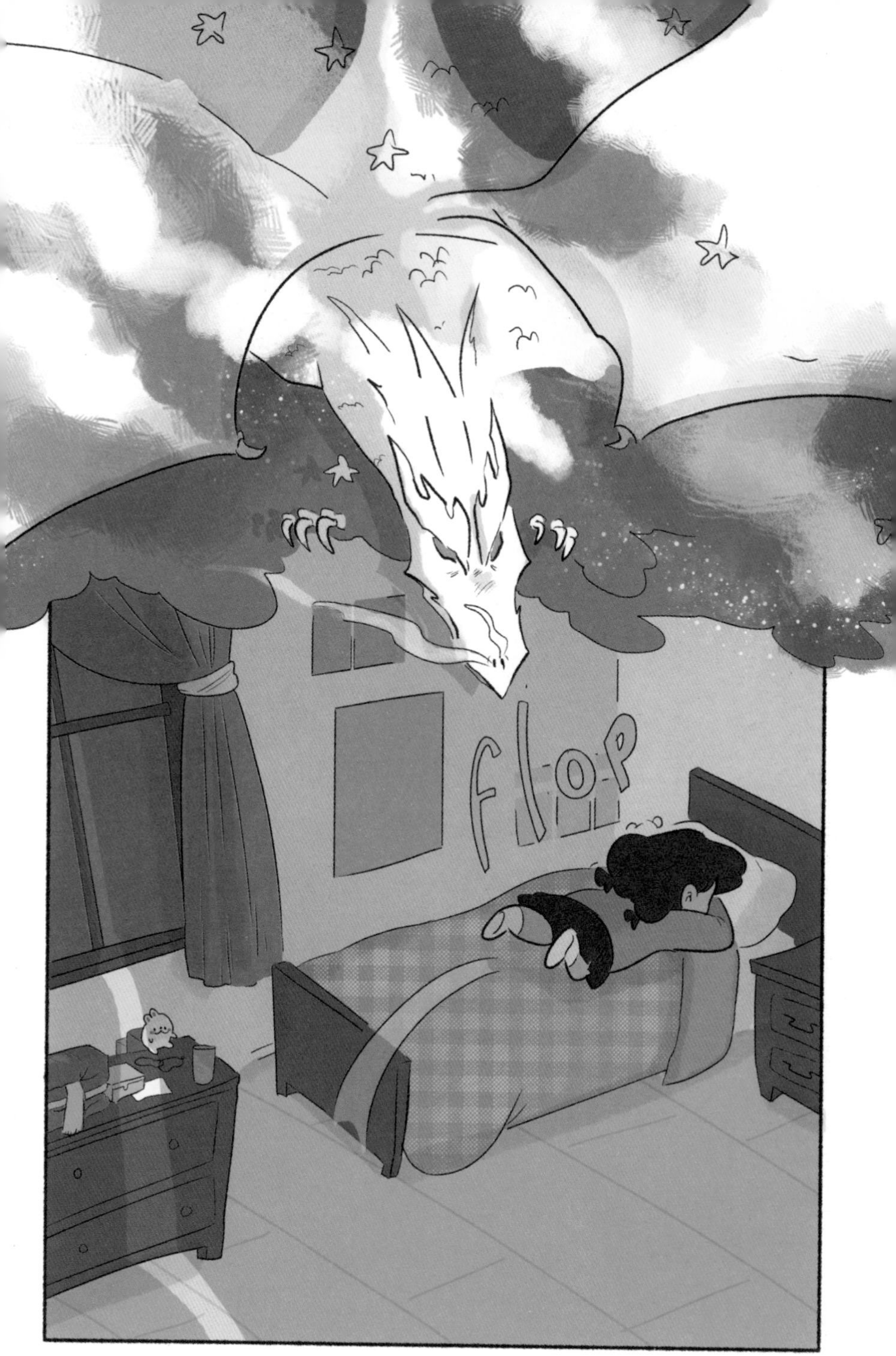
flop

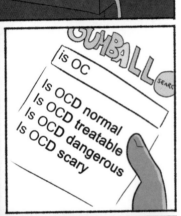

is OC

Is OCD normal
Is OCD treatable
Is OCD dangerous
Is OCD scary

tap tap tap

RETURN

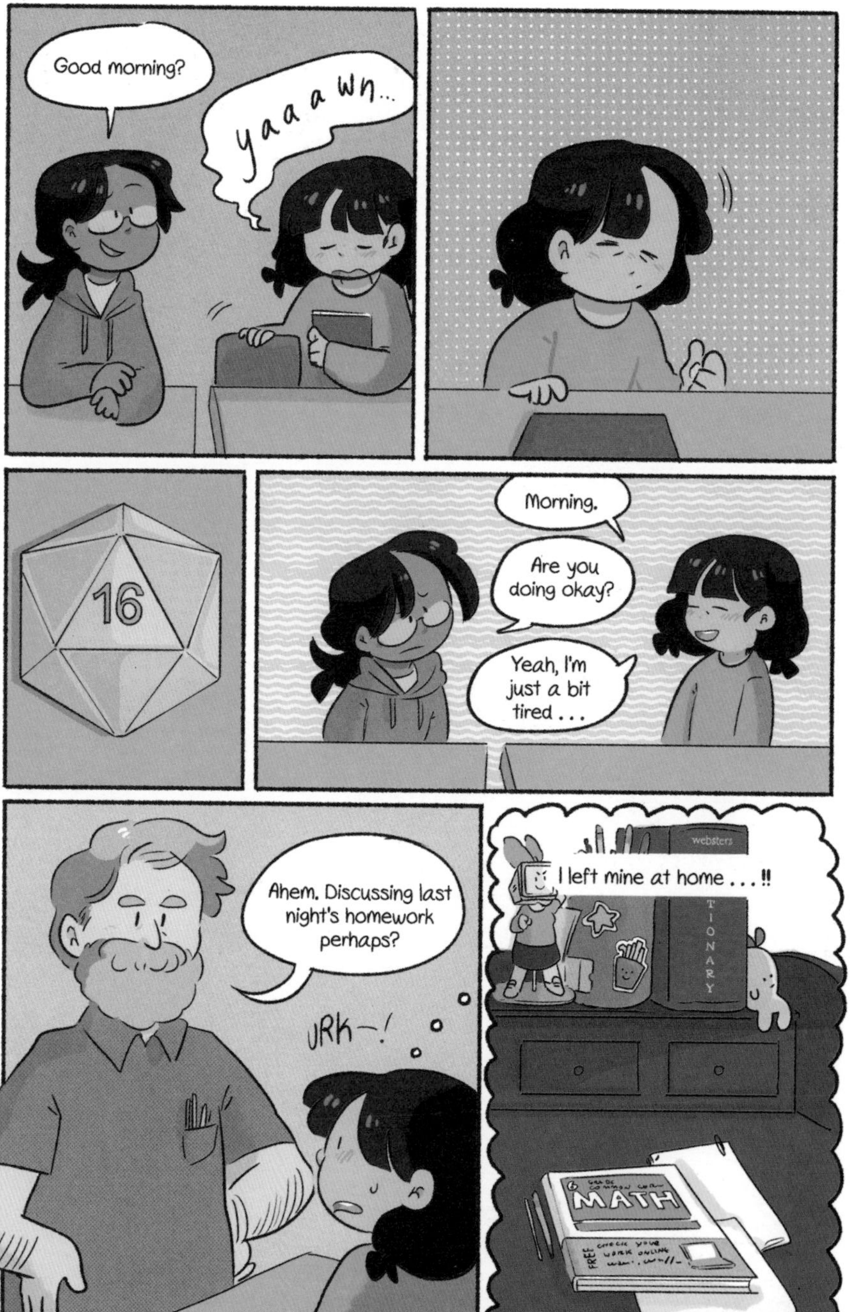
Good morning?
yaaawn...
16
Morning.
Are you doing okay?
Yeah, I'm just a bit tired . . .
Ahem. Discussing last night's homework perhaps?
URK—!
websters
I left mine at home . . . !!
TIONARY
MATH

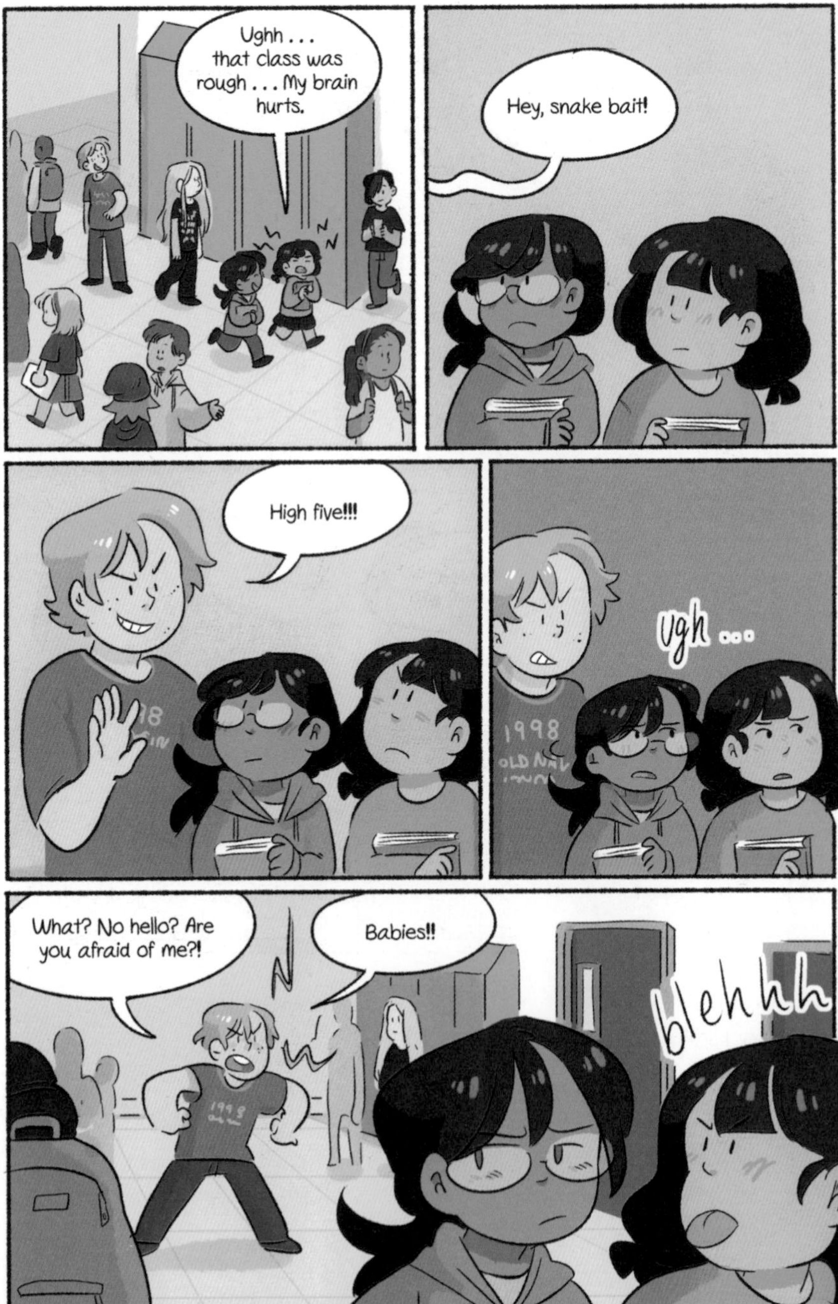

Ughh . . . that class was rough . . . My brain hurts.
Hey, snake bait!
High five!!!
ugh . . .
What? No hello? Are you afraid of me?!
Babies!!
blehhh

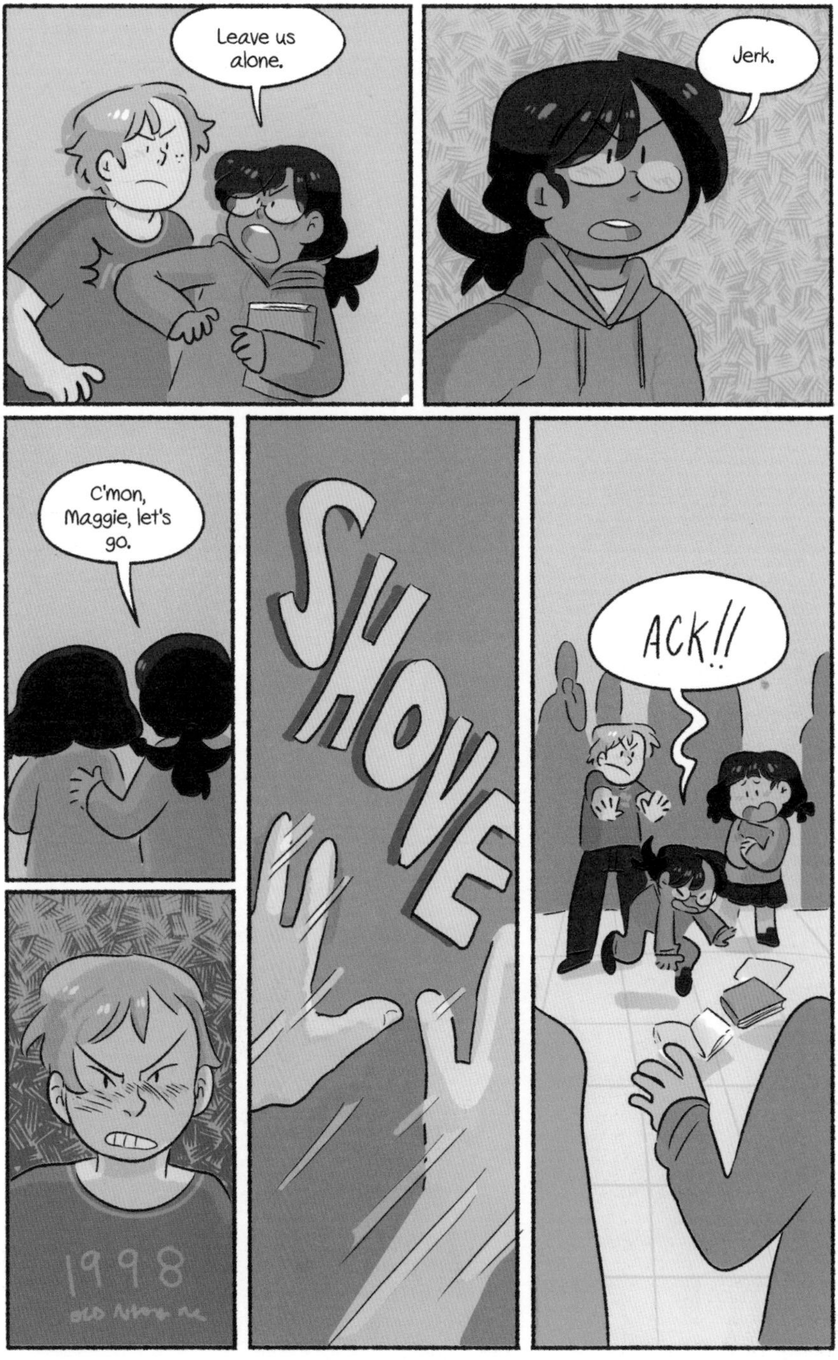
Leave us alone.
Jerk.
C'mon, Maggie, let's go.
1998
SHOVE
ACK!!

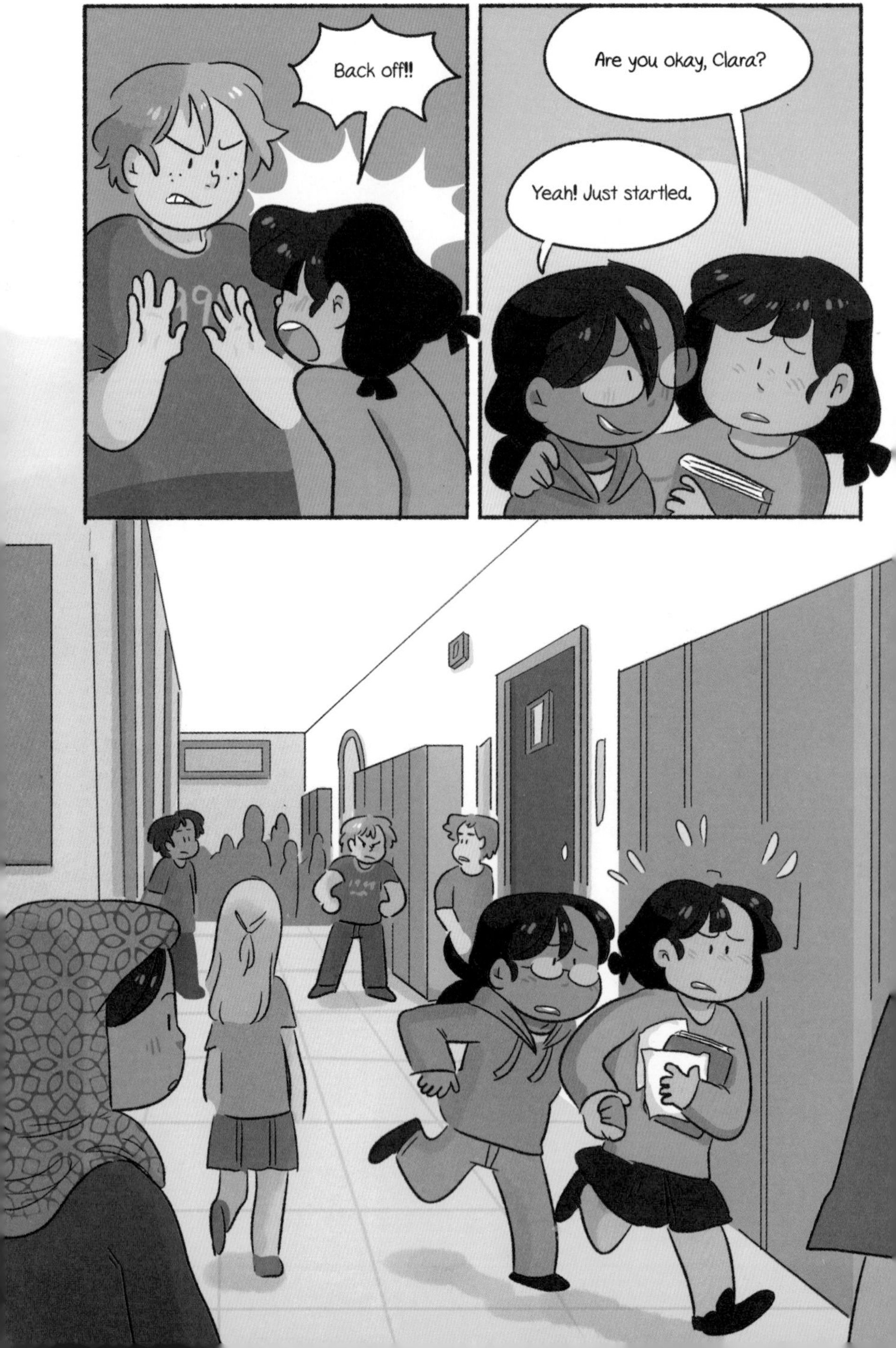
Back off!!
Are you okay, Clara?
Yeah! Just startled.

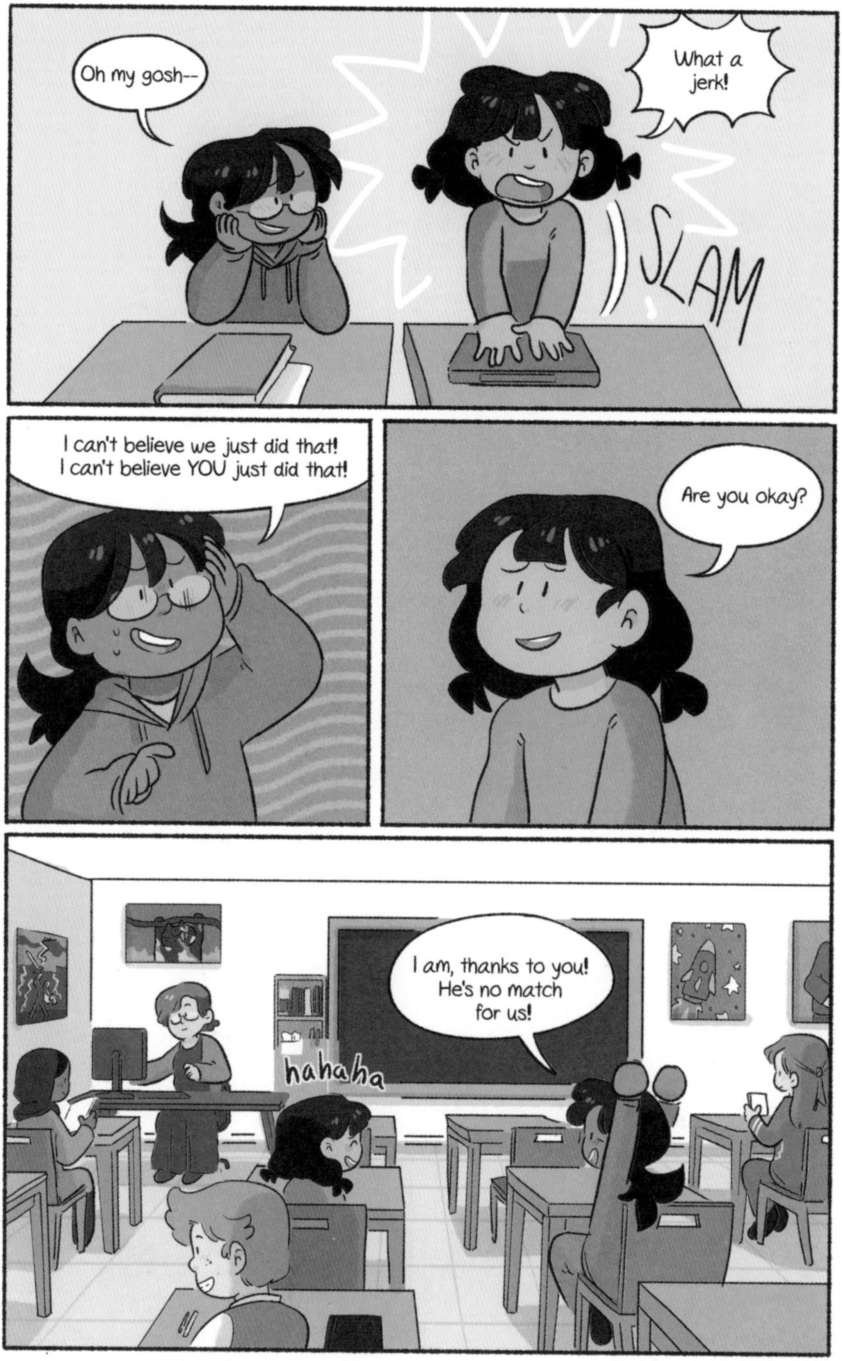
Oh my gosh--
What a jerk!
SLAM
I can't believe we just did that!
I can't believe YOU just did that!
Are you okay?
I am, thanks to you!
He's no match
for us!
hahaha

heh...

So, how does everyone feel about Sarah Good?

In the story, Sarah's community turns on her.

What do you think we can learn from this? How do you think Sarah must be feeling?

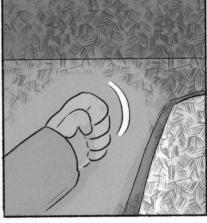

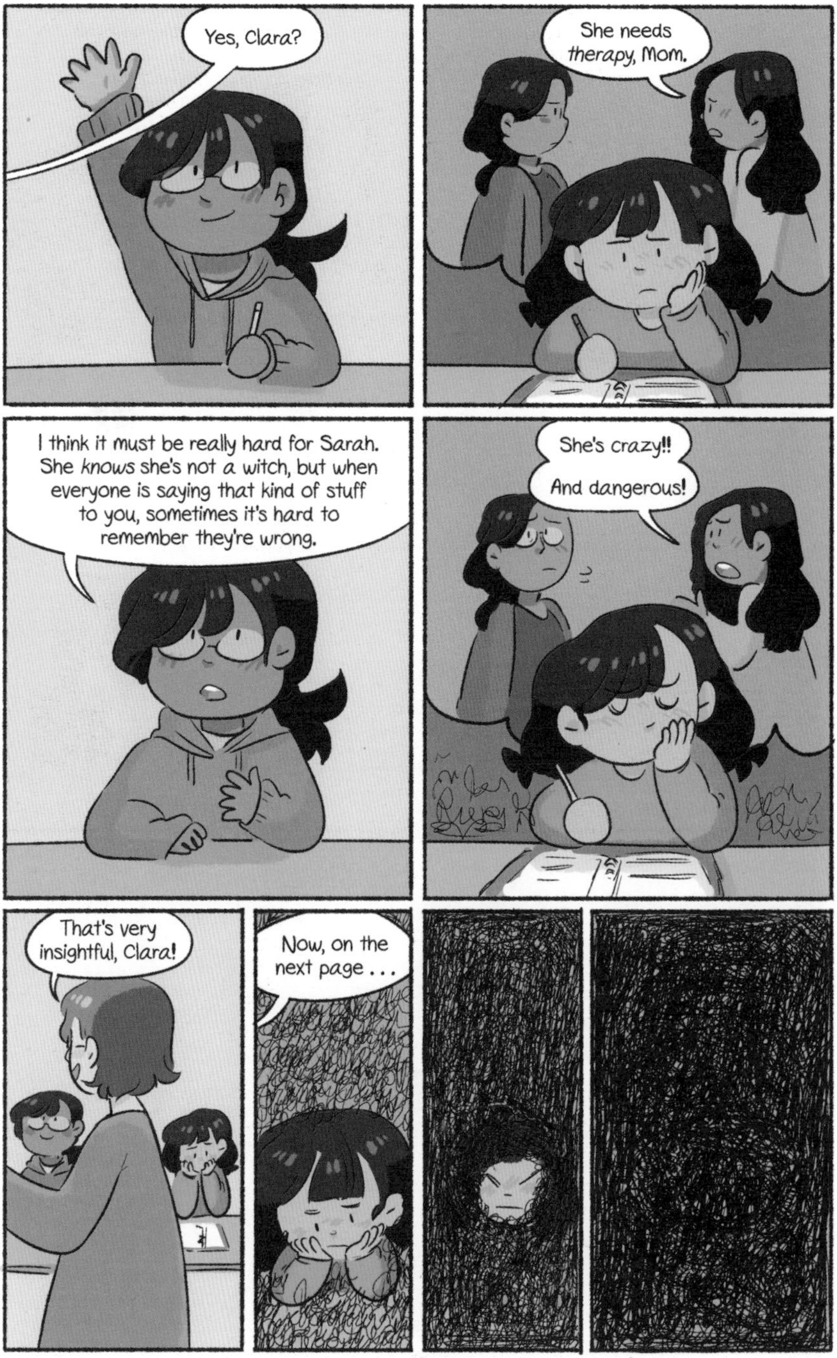
Yes, Clara?
She needs *therapy*, Mom.
I think it must be really hard for Sarah. She *knows* she's not a witch, but when everyone is saying that kind of stuff to you, sometimes it's hard to remember they're wrong.
She's crazy!!
And dangerous!
That's very insightful, Clara!
Now, on the next page . . .

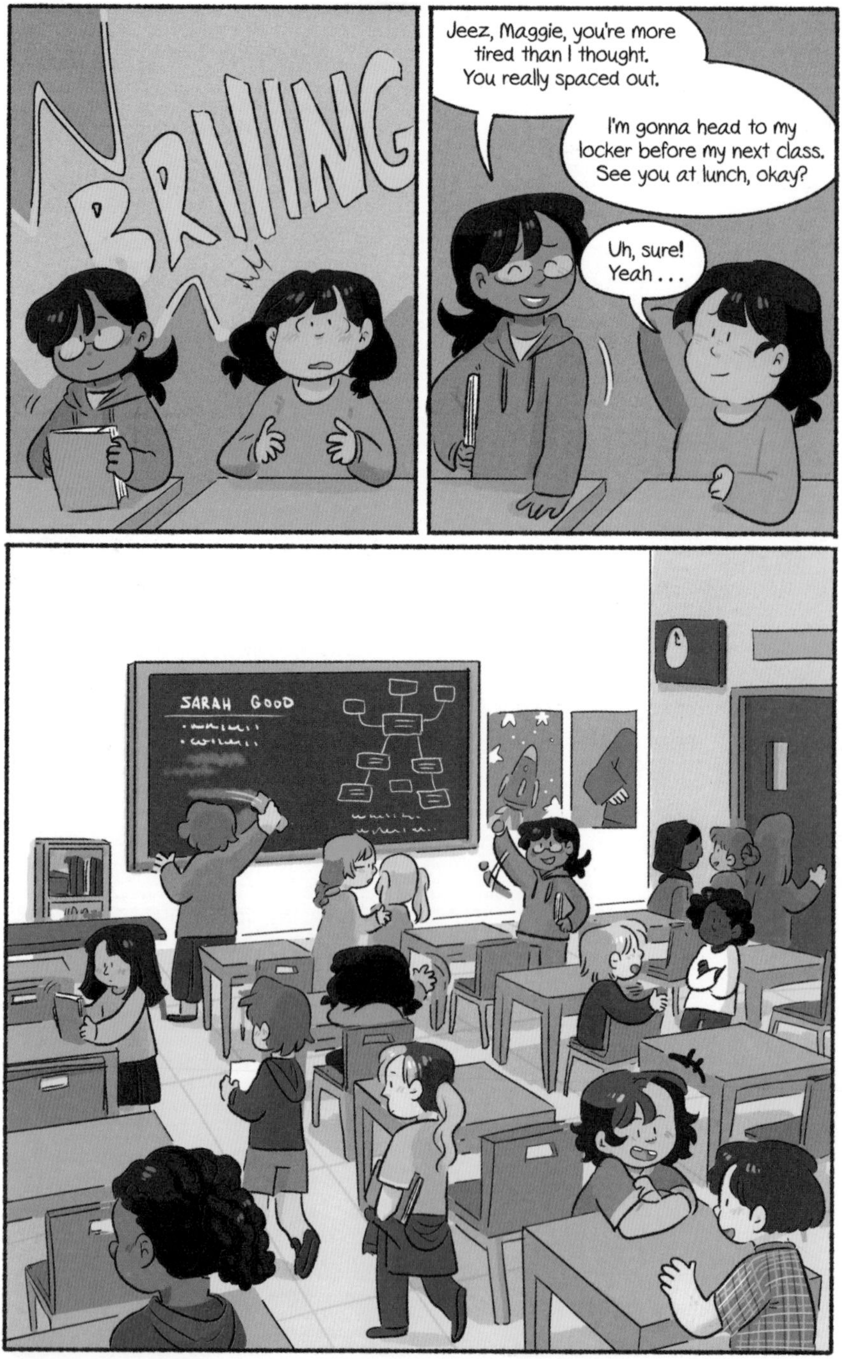
BRIIING
Jeez, Maggie, you're more tired than I thought. You really spaced out.
I'm gonna head to my locker before my next class. See you at lunch, okay?
Uh, sure! Yeah . . .
SARAH GOOD

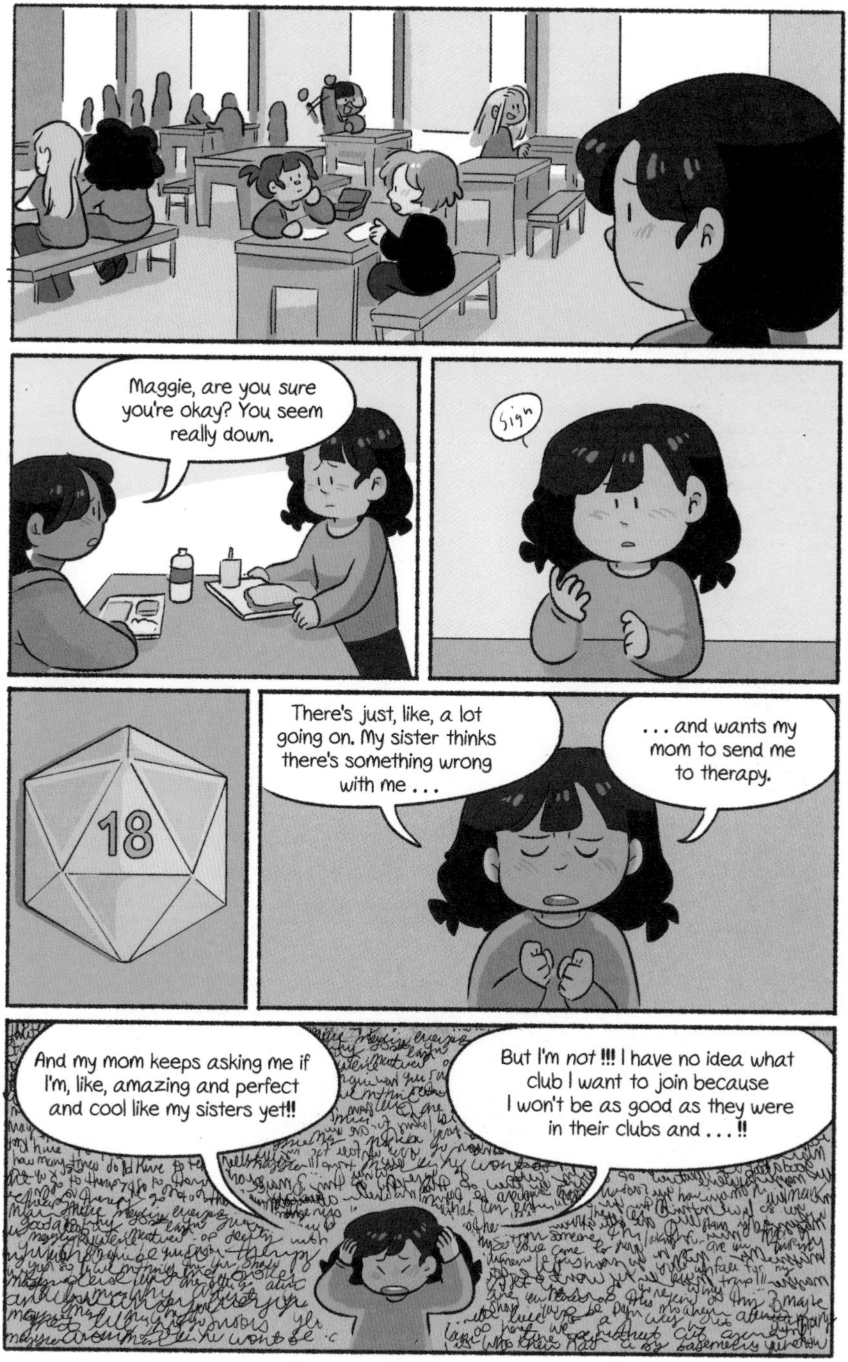

Maggie, are you sure you're okay? You seem really down.
Sigh
There's just, like, a lot going on. My sister thinks there's something wrong with me . . .
. . . and wants my mom to send me to therapy.
18
And my mom keeps asking me if I'm, like, amazing and perfect and cool like my sisters yet!!
But I'm not !!! I have no idea what club I want to join because I won't be as good as they were in their clubs and . . . !!

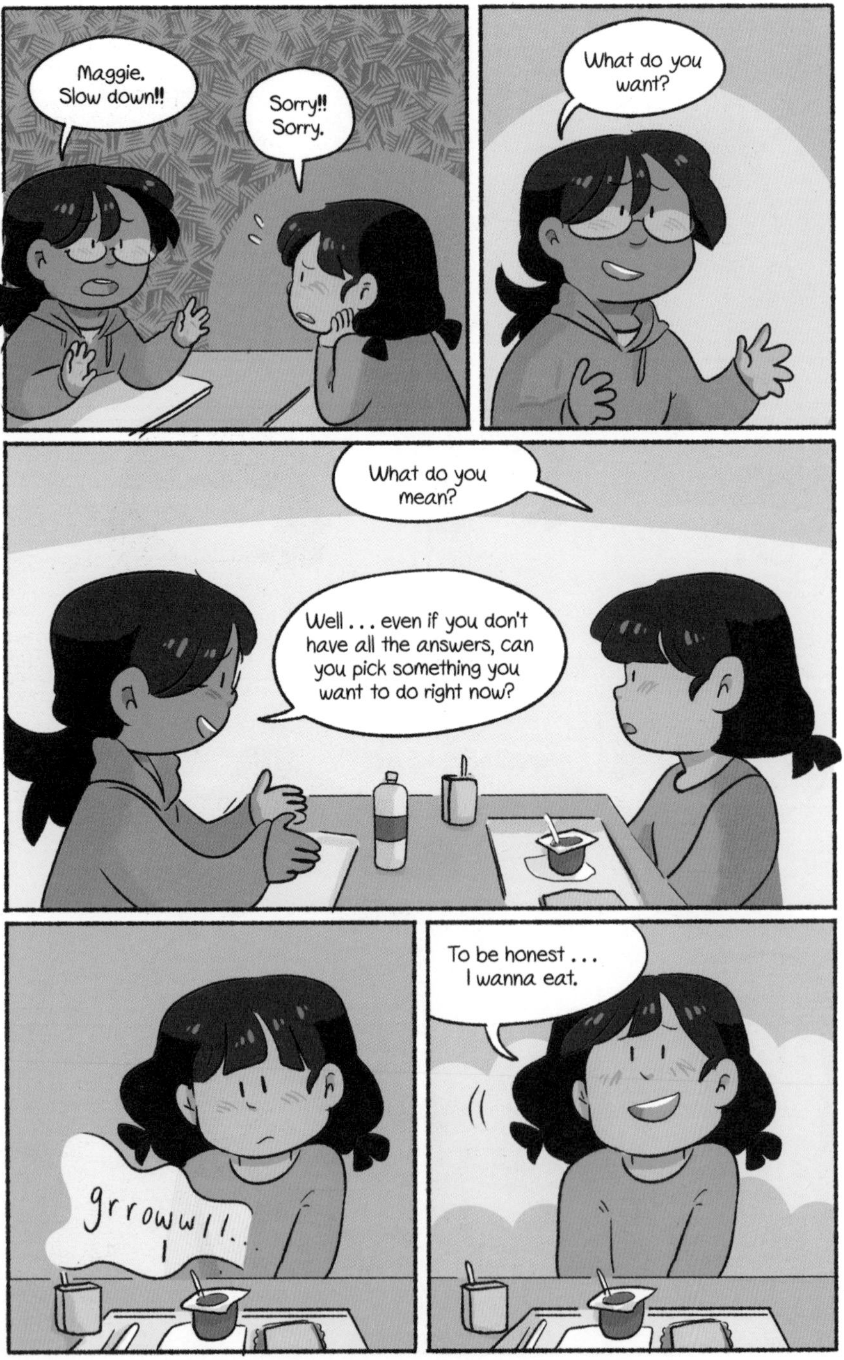
Maggie.
Slow down!!
Sorry!!
Sorry.
What do you want?
What do you mean?
Well . . . even if you don't have all the answers, can you pick something you want to do right now?
grrowwll...
To be honest . . . I wanna eat.

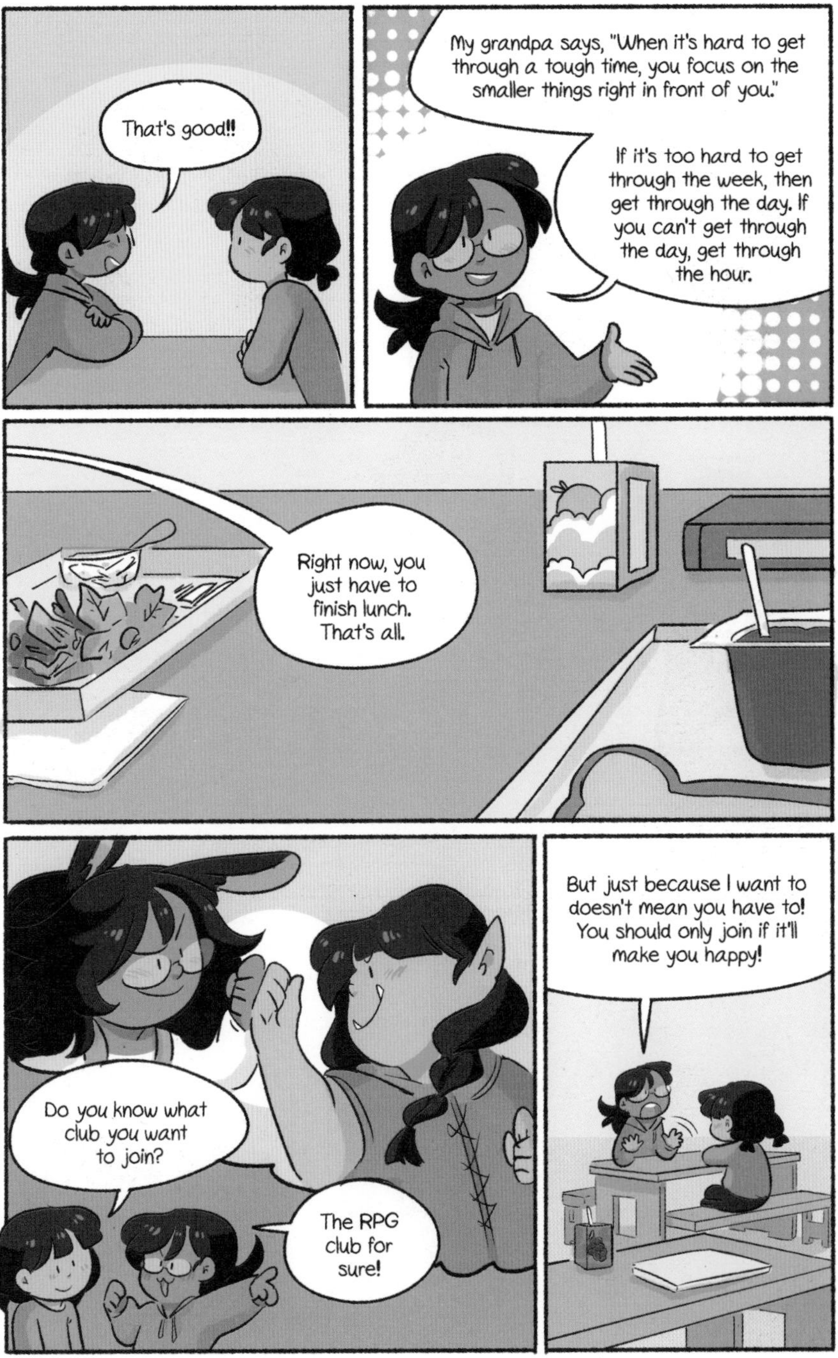
That's good!!
My grandpa says, "When it's hard to get through a tough time, you focus on the smaller things right in front of you."
If it's too hard to get through the week, then get through the day. If you can't get through the day, get through the hour.
Right now, you just have to finish lunch. That's all.
Do you know what club you want to join?
The RPG club for sure!
But just because I want to doesn't mean you have to! You should only join if it'll make you happy!

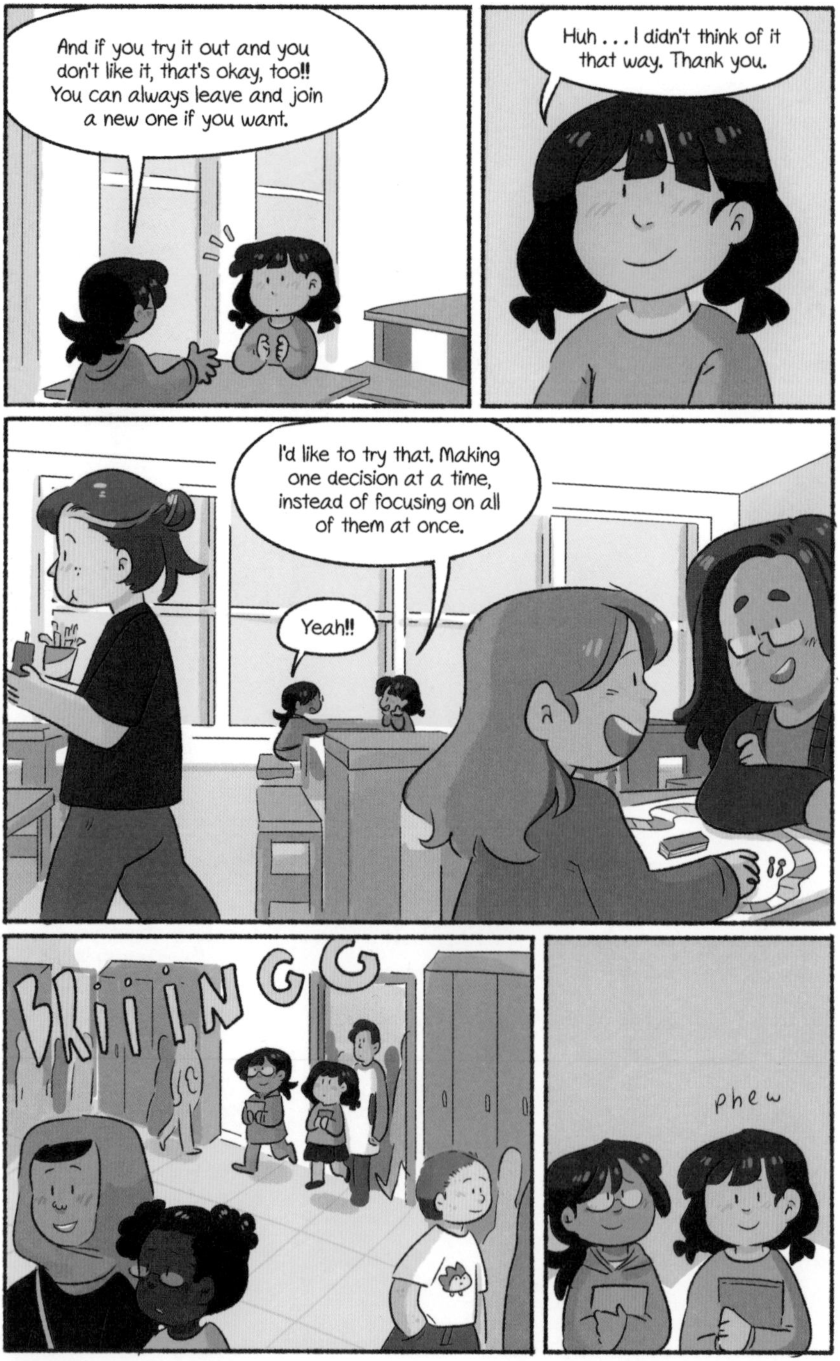
And if you try it out and you don't like it, that's okay, too!! You can always leave and join a new one if you want.
Huh . . . I didn't think of it that way. Thank you.
I'd like to try that. Making one decision at a time, instead of focusing on all of them at once.
Yeah!!
BRIIING
phew

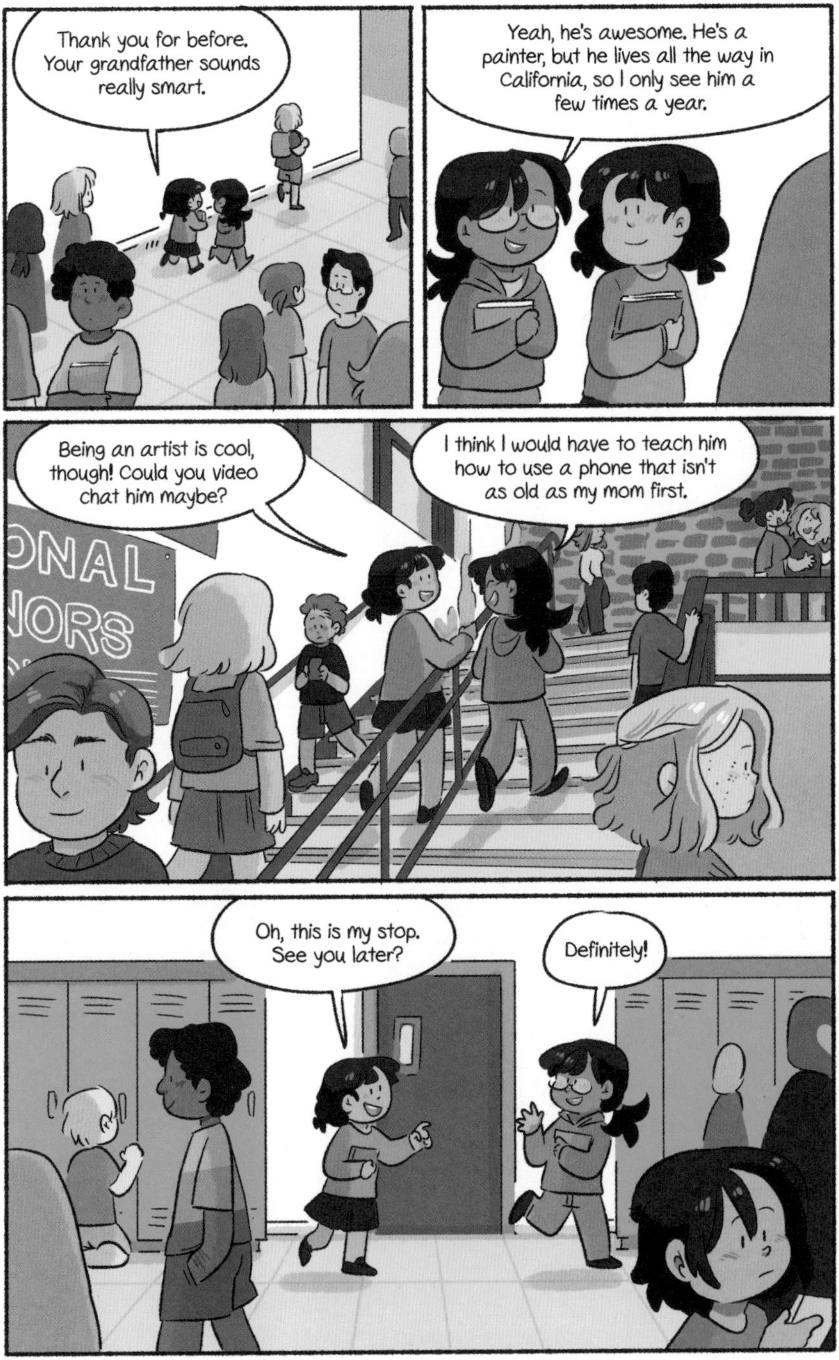
Thank you for before. Your grandfather sounds really smart.
Yeah, he's awesome. He's a painter, but he lives all the way in California, so I only see him a few times a year.
Being an artist is cool, though! Could you video chat him maybe?
I think I would have to teach him how to use a phone that isn't as old as my mom first.
Oh, this is my stop. See you later?
Definitely!

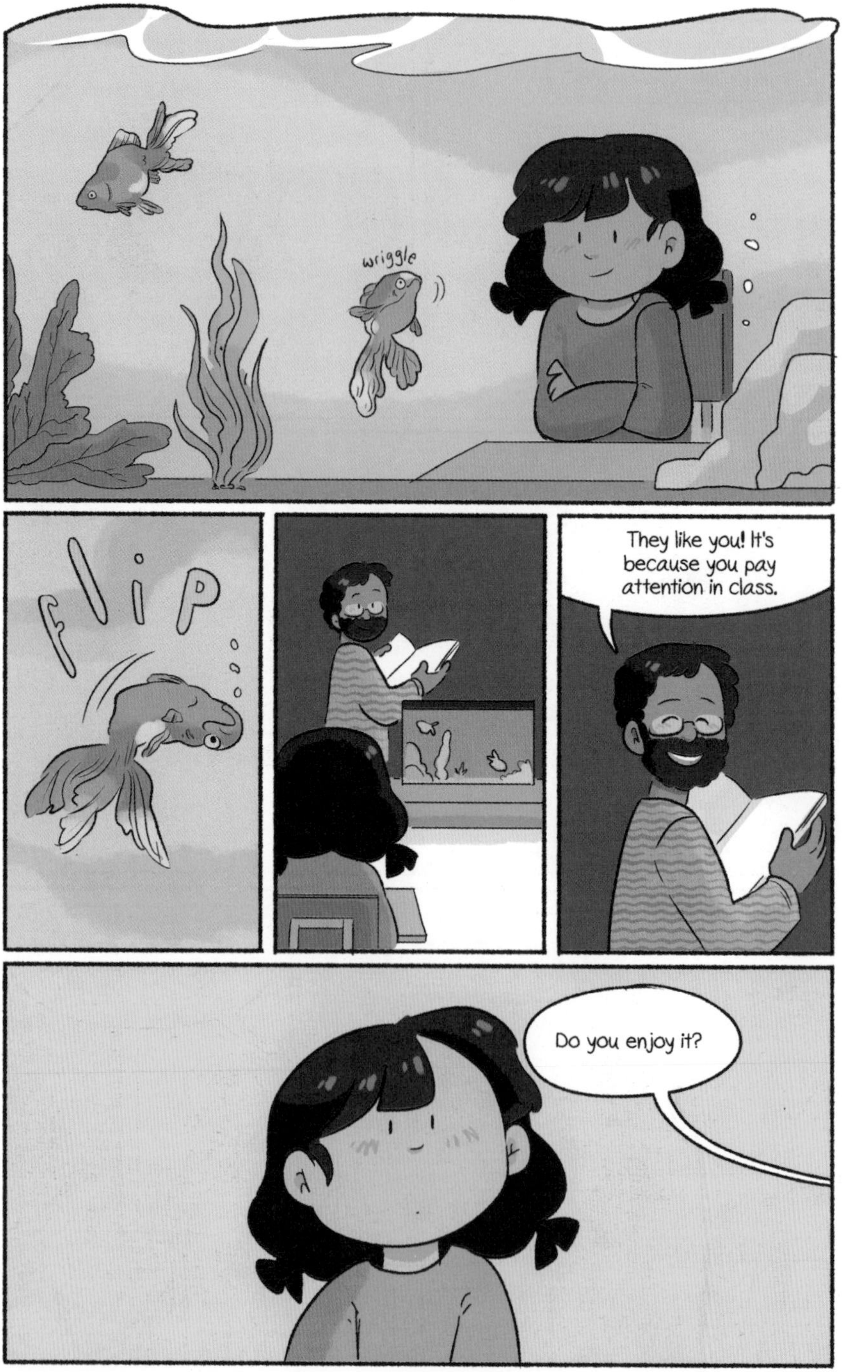
wriggle
FLIP
They like you! It's because you pay attention in class.
Do you enjoy it?

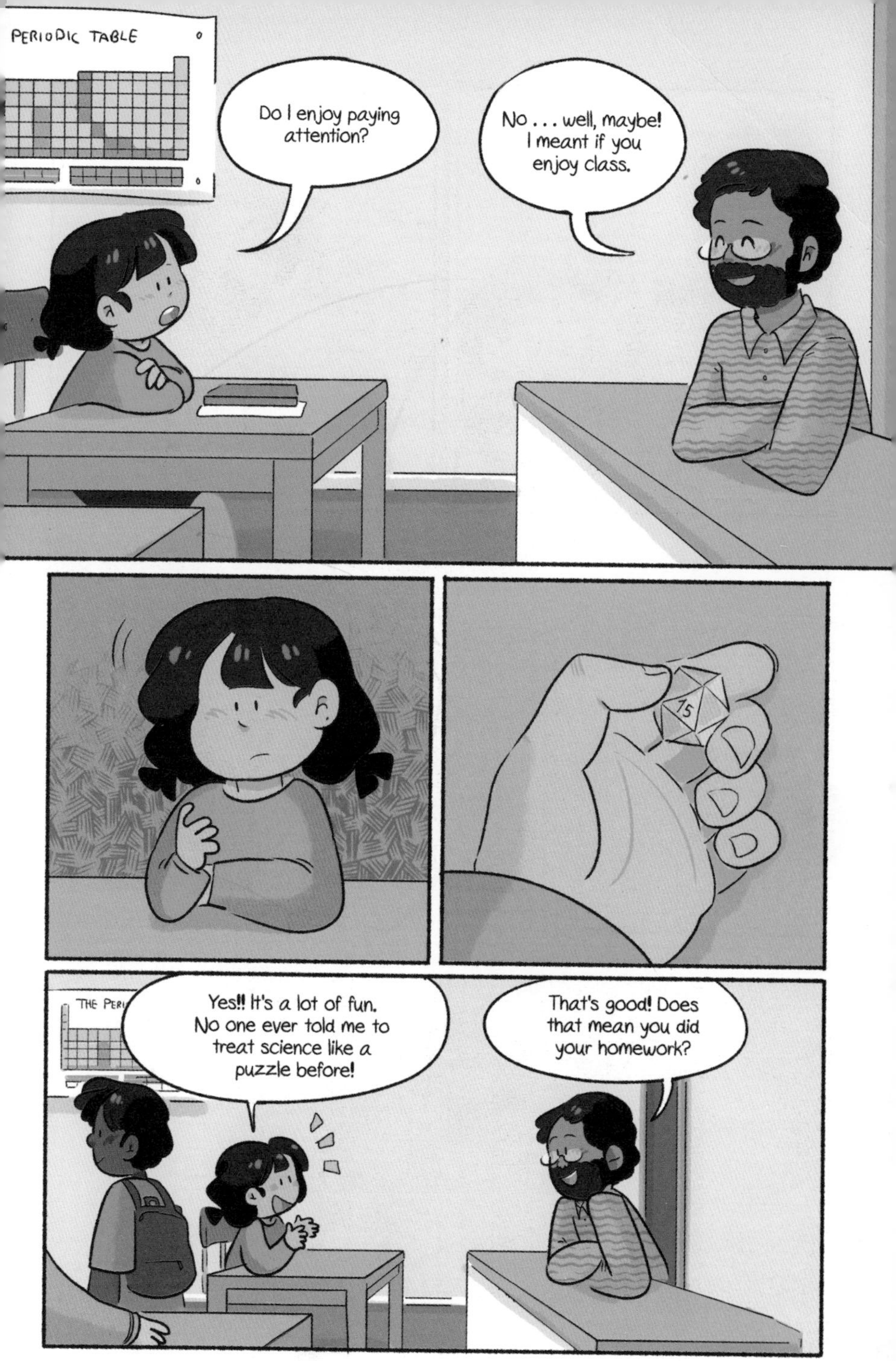
PERIODIC TABLE
Do I enjoy paying attention?
No . . . well, maybe! I meant if you enjoy class.
15
Yes!! It's a lot of fun. No one ever told me to treat science like a puzzle before!
That's good! Does that mean you did your homework?

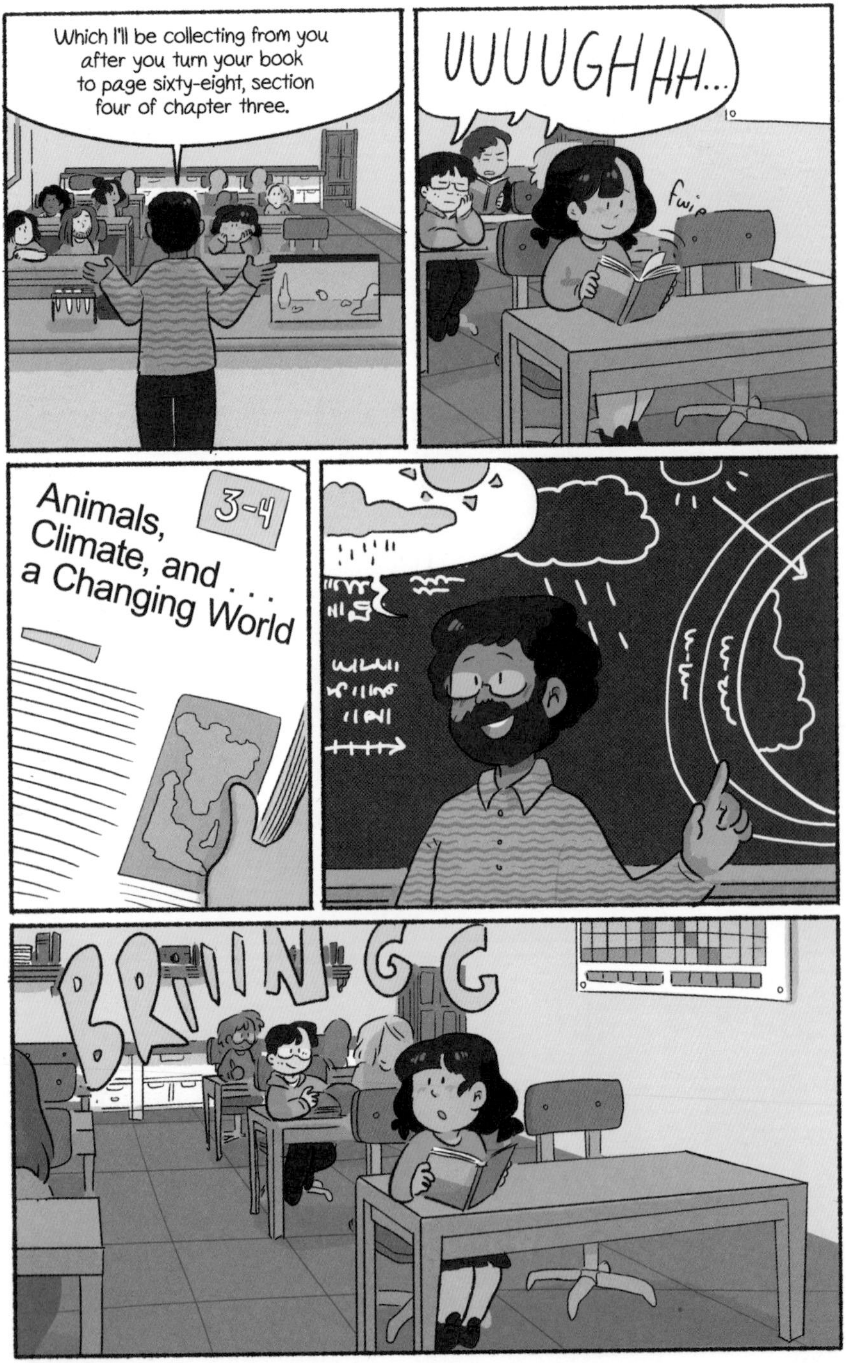
Which I'll be collecting from you after you turn your book to page sixty-eight, section four of chapter three.
UUUUGHHH...
fwip
3-4
Animals, Climate, and . . . a Changing World
BRIIINGG

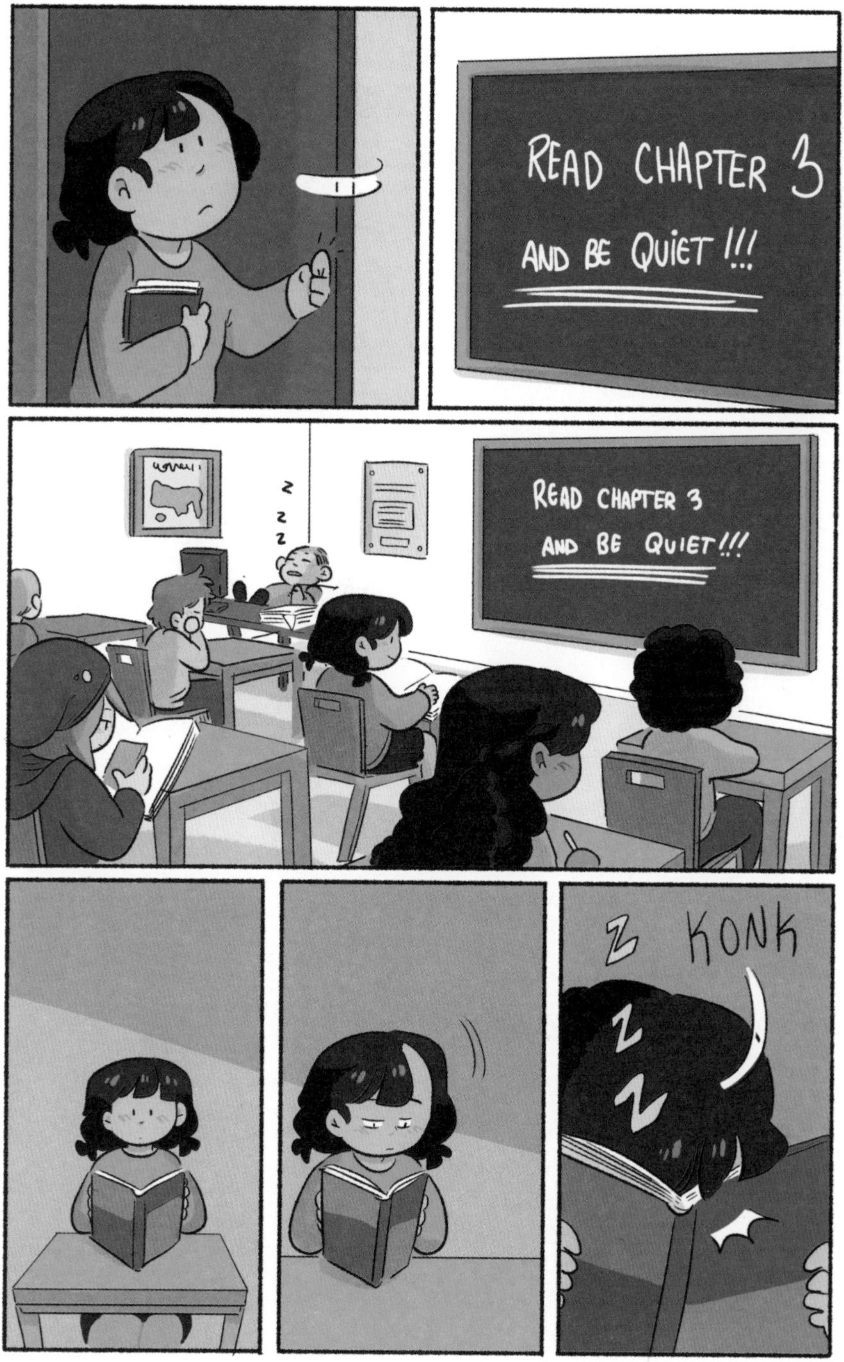
READ CHAPTER 3
AND BE QUIET!!!
READ CHAPTER 3
AND BE QUIET!!!
Z Z Z
Z
KONK
Z
Z

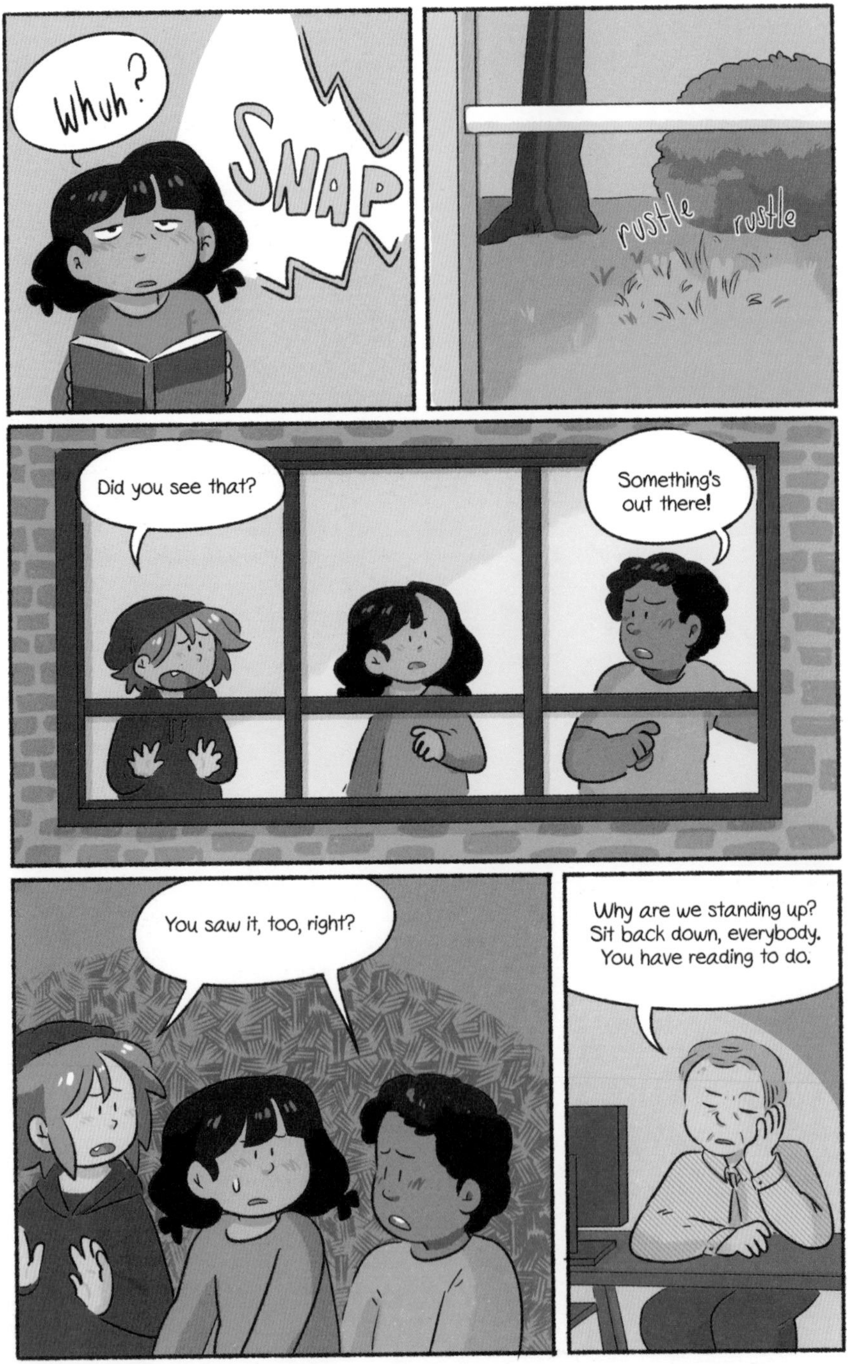
Whuh?
SNAP
rustle
rustle
Did you see that?
Something's out there!
You saw it, too, right?
Why are we standing up? Sit back down, everybody. You have reading to do.

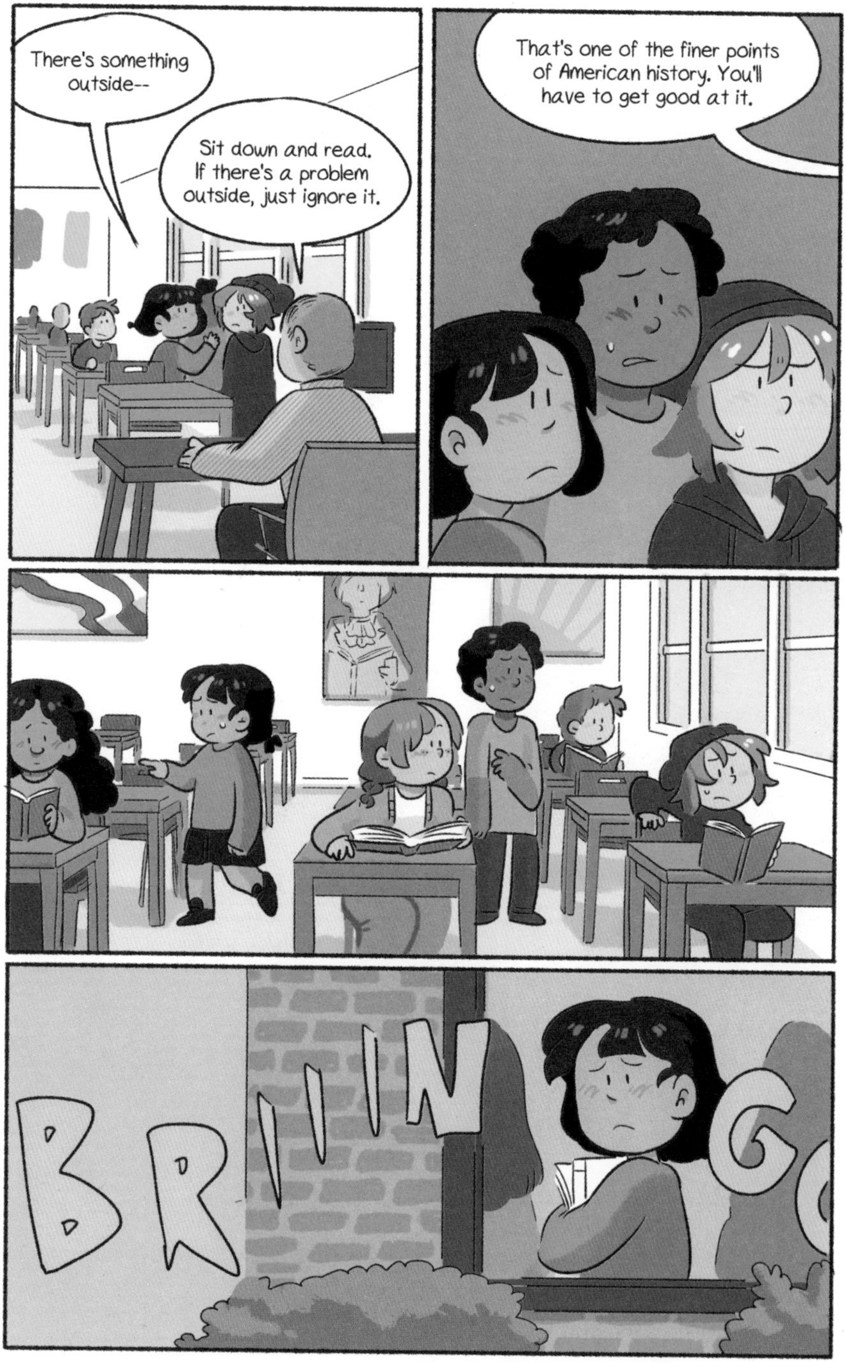
There's something outside--
Sit down and read. If there's a problem outside, just ignore it.
That's one of the finer points of American history. You'll have to get good at it.
BRIIING

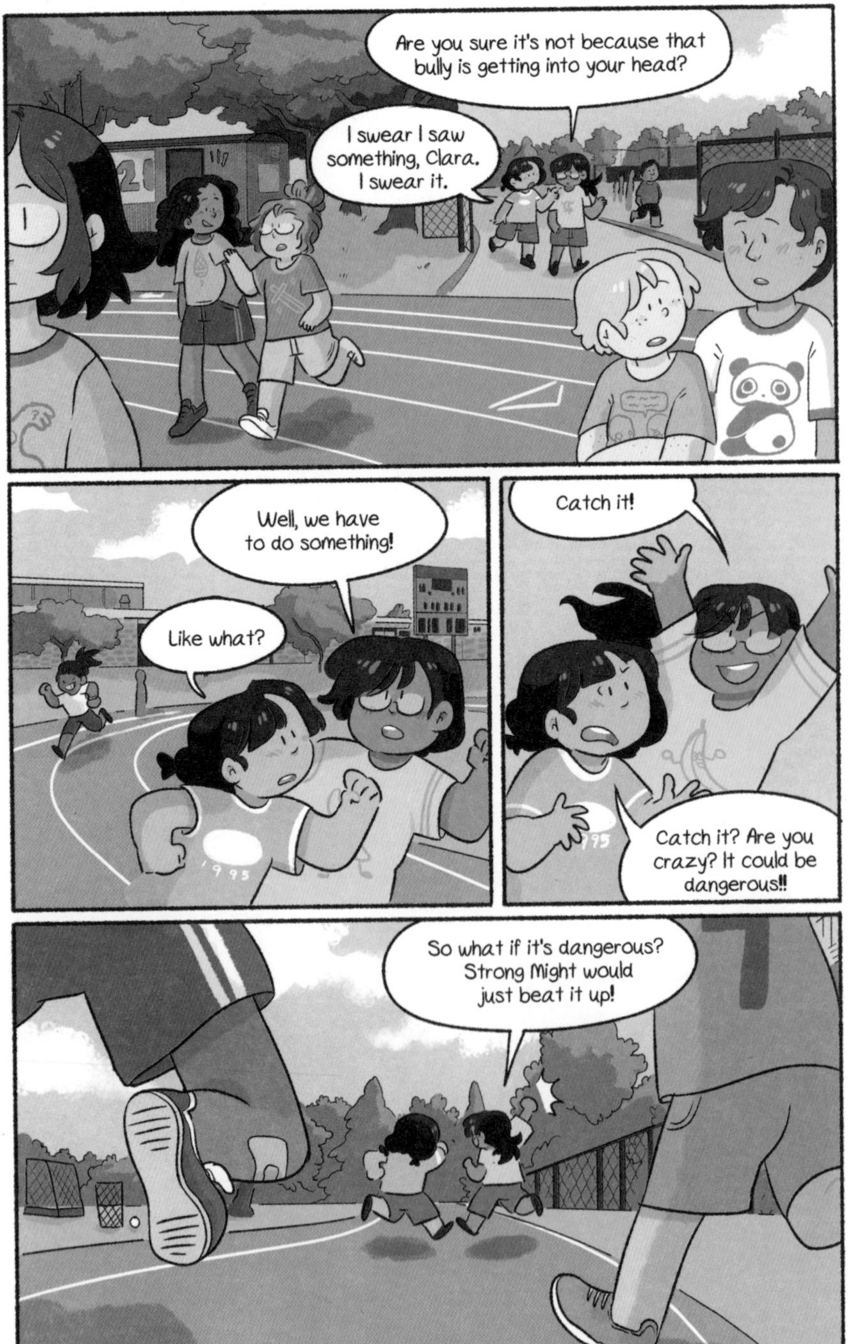
Are you sure it's not because that bully is getting into your head?
I swear I saw something, Clara. I swear it.
Well, we have to do something!
Like what?
Catch it!
Catch it? Are you crazy? It could be dangerous!!
So what if it's dangerous? Strong Might would just beat it up!

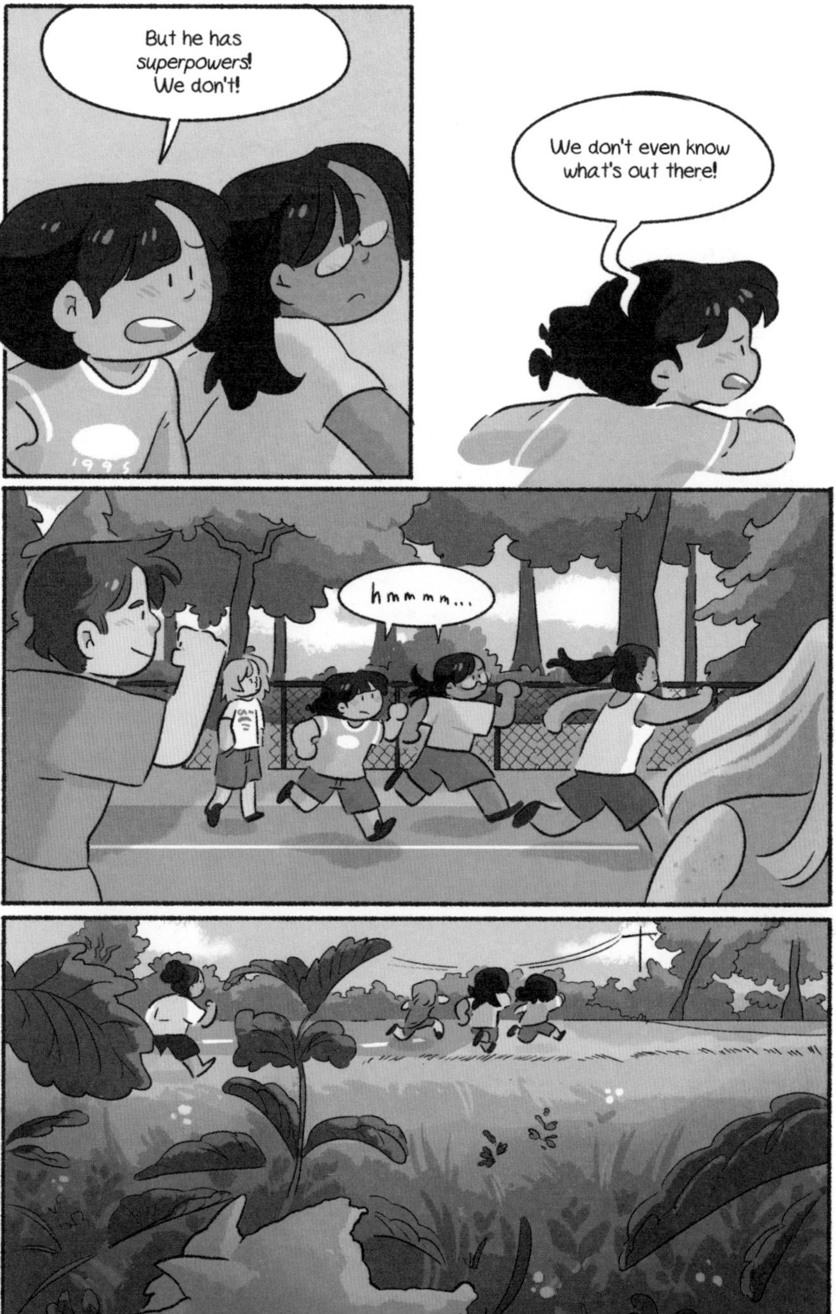
But he has superpowers! We don't!
We don't even know what's out there!
hmmmm...

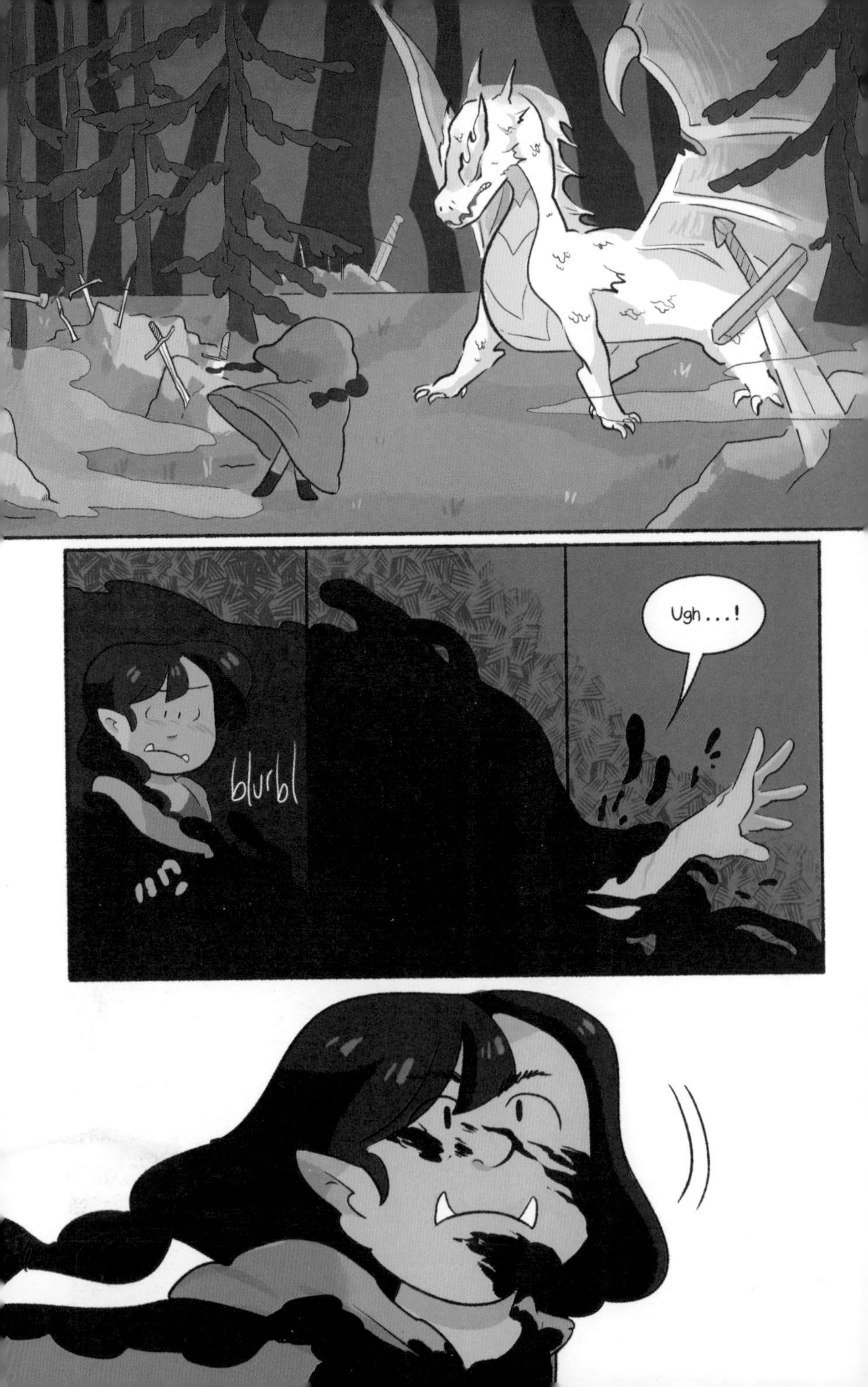
blurbl
Ugh...!

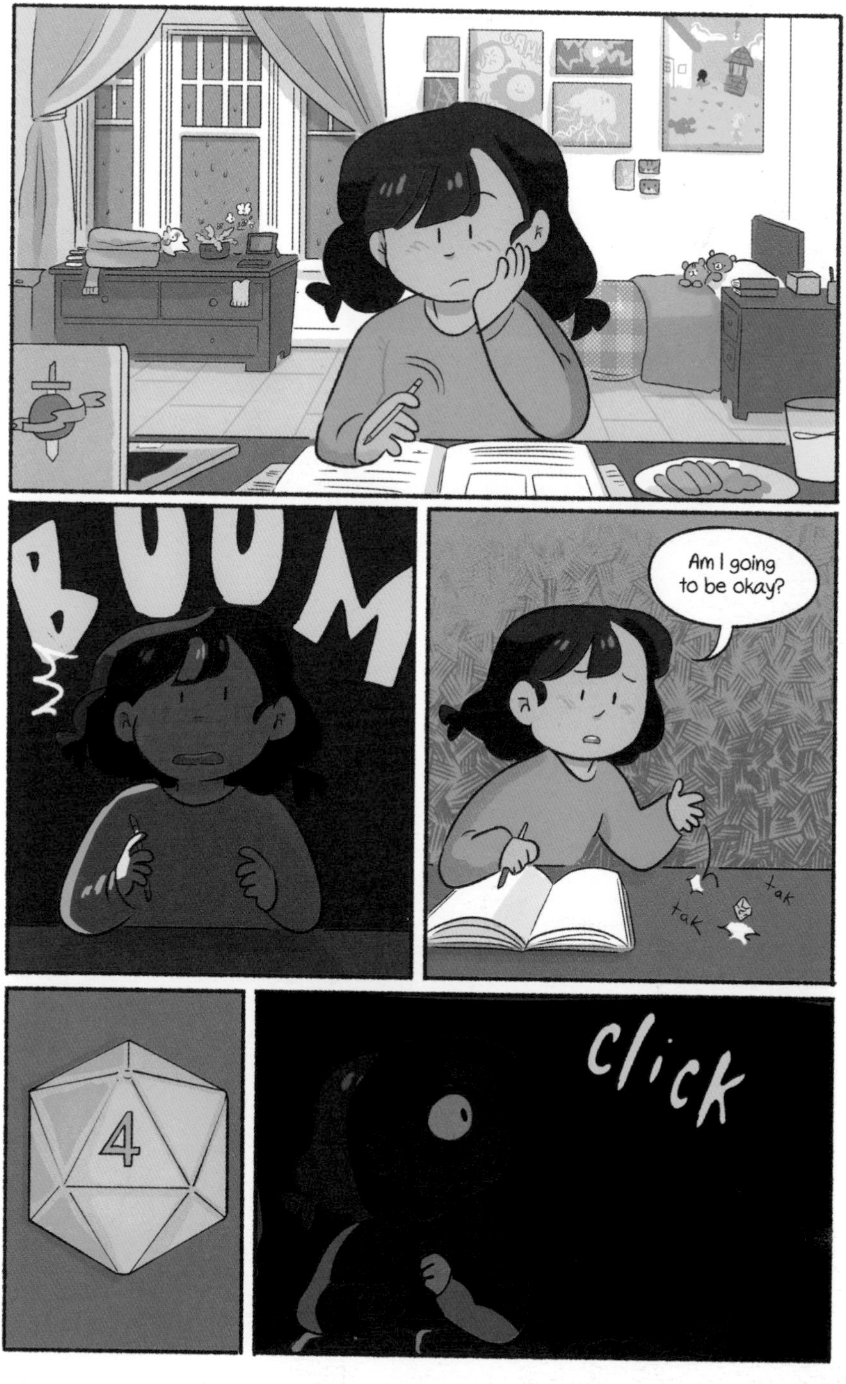
BOOM
Am I going to be okay?
tak
tak
click

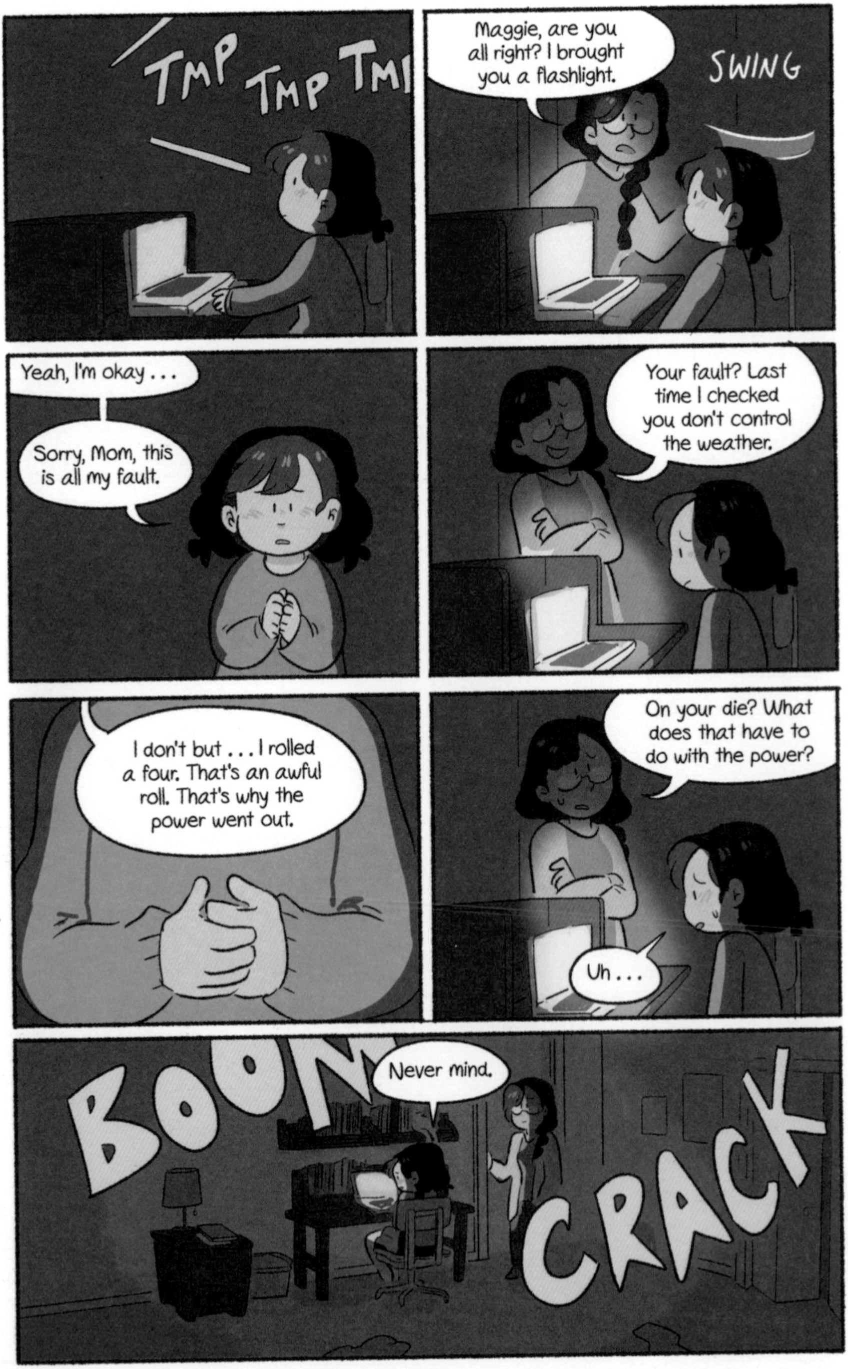
TMP TMP TMI
Maggie, are you all right? I brought you a flashlight.
SWING
Yeah, I'm okay . . .
Sorry, Mom, this is all my fault.
Your fault? Last time I checked you don't control the weather.
I don't but . . . I rolled a four. That's an awful roll. That's why the power went out.
On your die? What does that have to do with the power?
Uh . . .
BOOM
Never mind.
CRACK

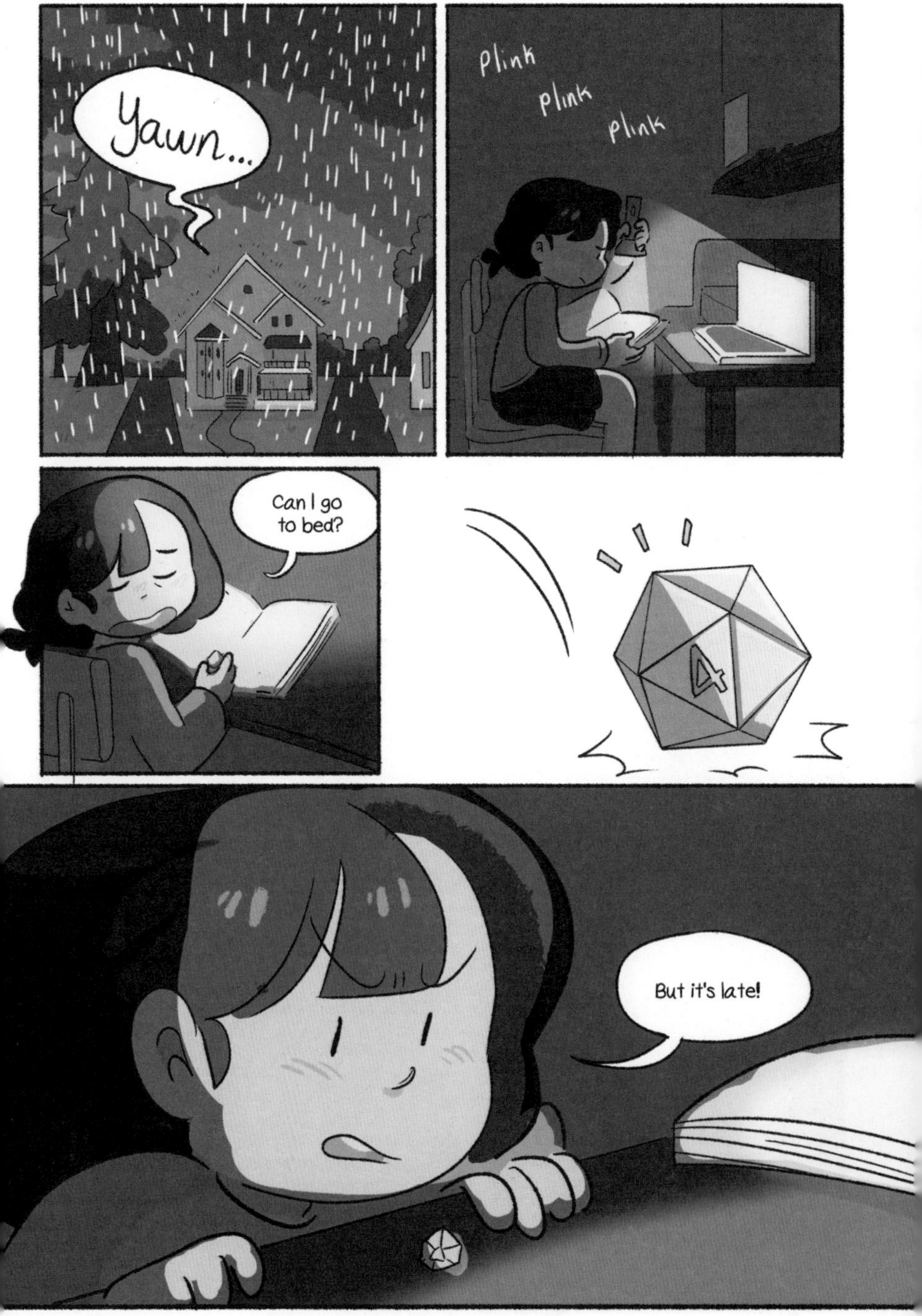
Yawn...
plink
plink
plink
Can I go to bed?
4
But it's late!

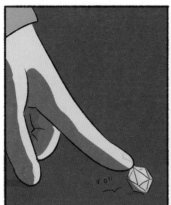

Split down the middle . . .

Oh! I'll take that as plus two advantage.

Click

Thanks, house!

SHUT

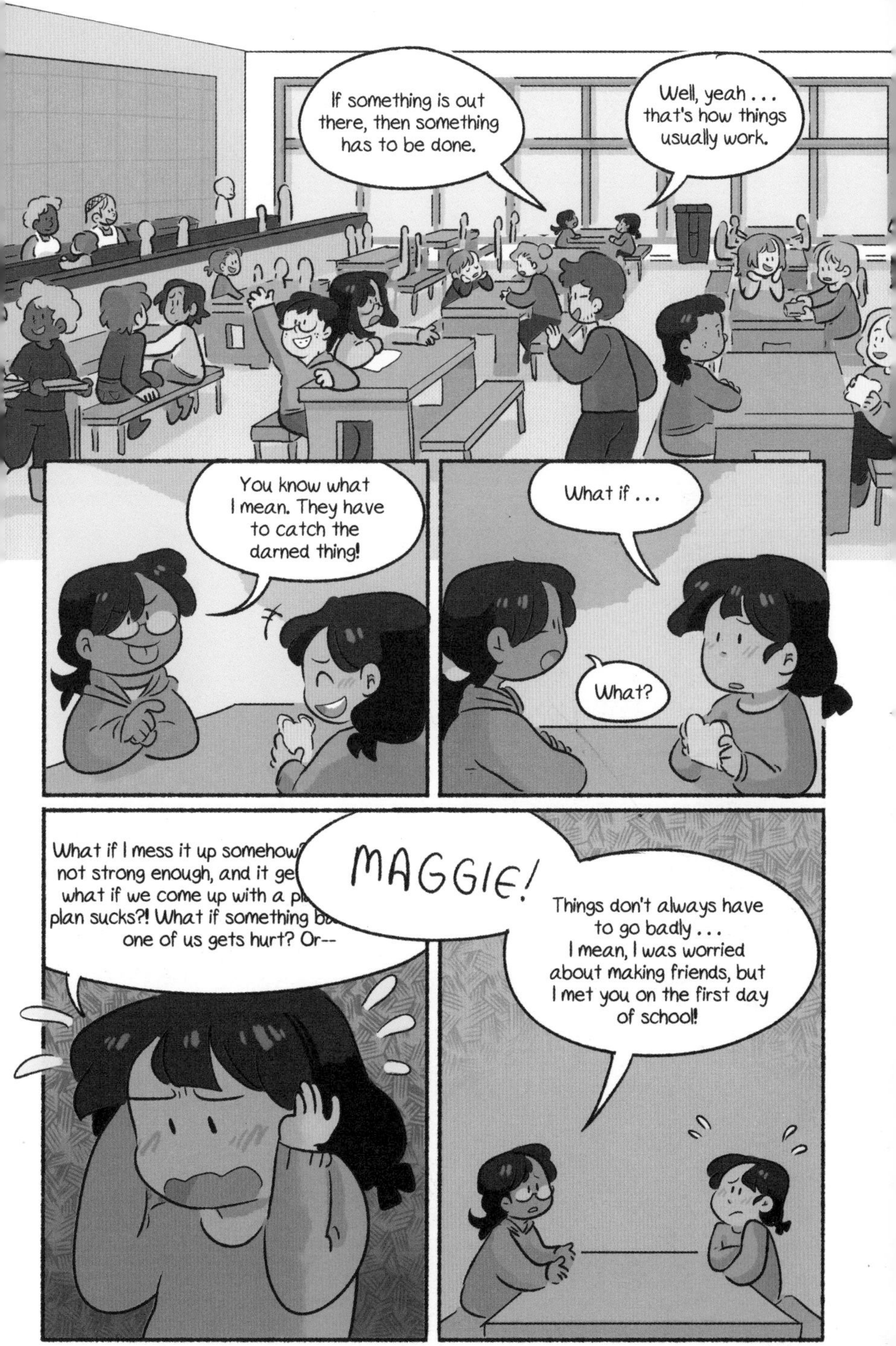
If something is out there, then something has to be done.
Well, yeah . . . that's how things usually work.
You know what I mean. They have to catch the darned thing!
What if . . .
What?
What if I mess it up somehow? not strong enough, and it ge what if we come up with a pl plan sucks?! What if something ba one of us gets hurt? Or--
MAGGIE!
Things don't always have to go badly . . . I mean, I was worried about making friends, but I met you on the first day of school!

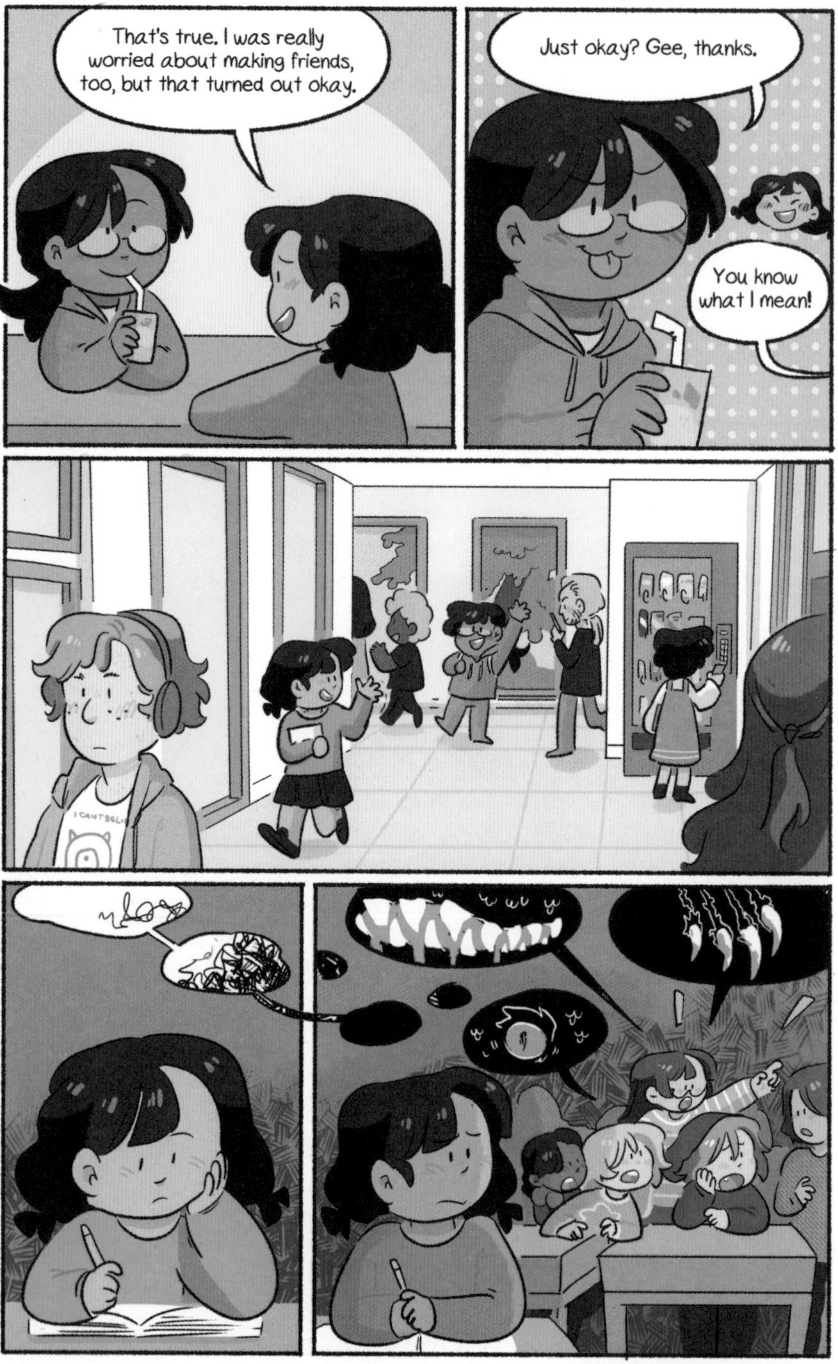
That's true. I was really worried about making friends, too, but that turned out okay.
Just okay? Gee, thanks.
You know what I mean!
I CANT BELI

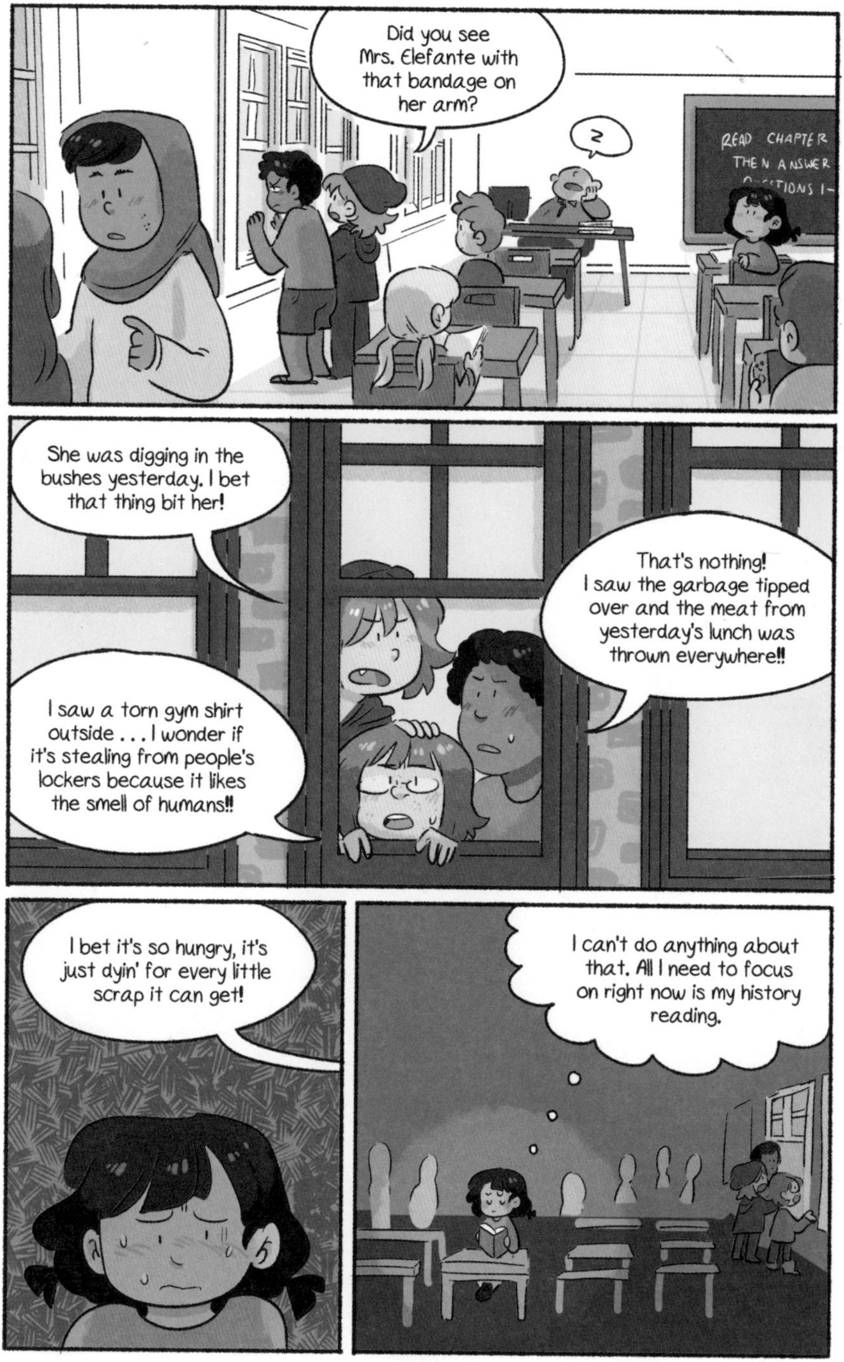
Did you see Mrs. Elefante with that bandage on her arm?
Z
READ CHAPTER
THEN ANSWER
She was digging in the bushes yesterday. I bet that thing bit her!
That's nothing! I saw the garbage tipped over and the meat from yesterday's lunch was thrown everywhere!!
I saw a torn gym shirt outside . . . I wonder if it's stealing from people's lockers because it likes the smell of humans!!
I bet it's so hungry, it's just dyin' for every little scrap it can get!
I can't do anything about that. All I need to focus on right now is my history reading.

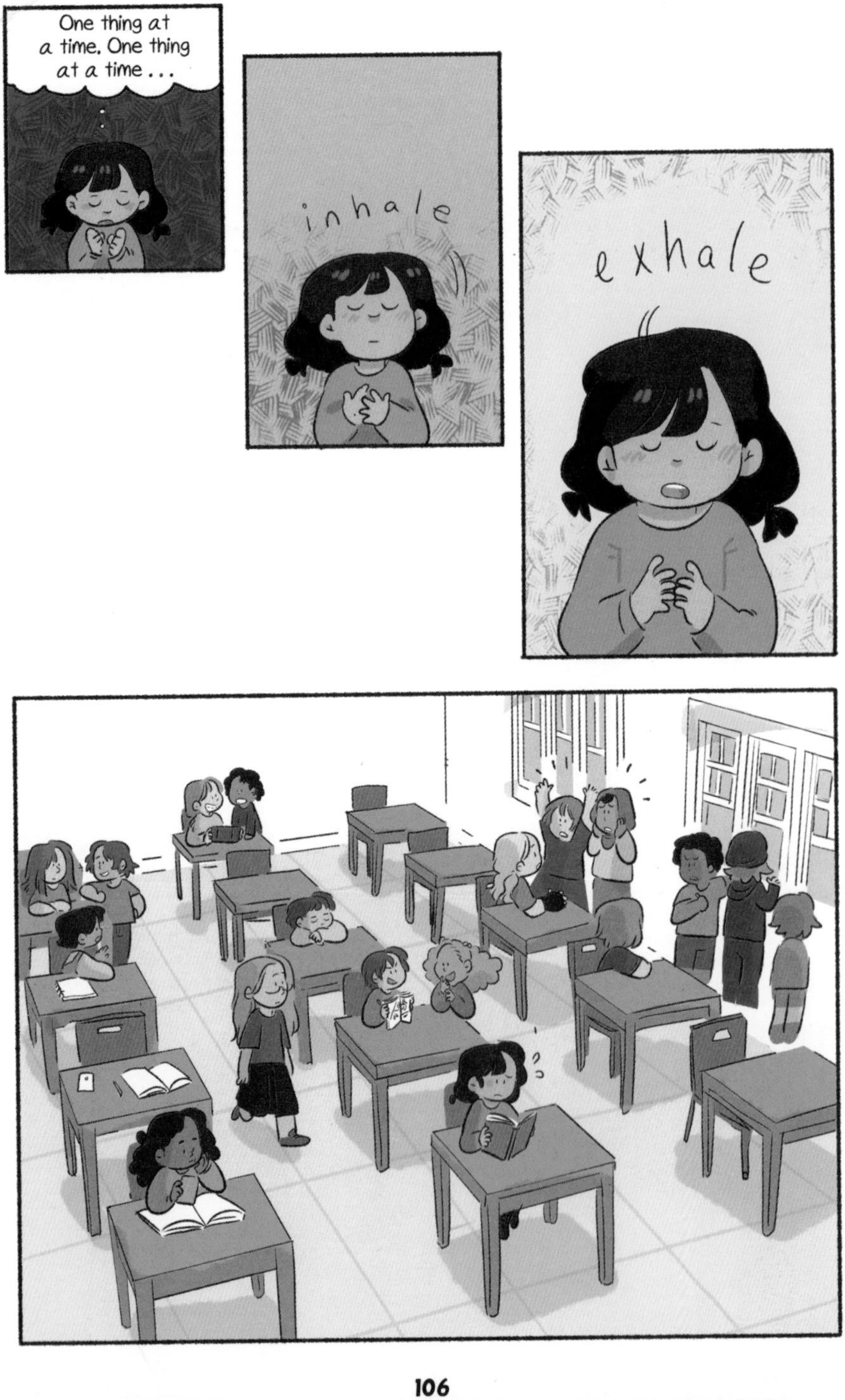
One thing at a time. One thing at a time . . .
inhale
exhale

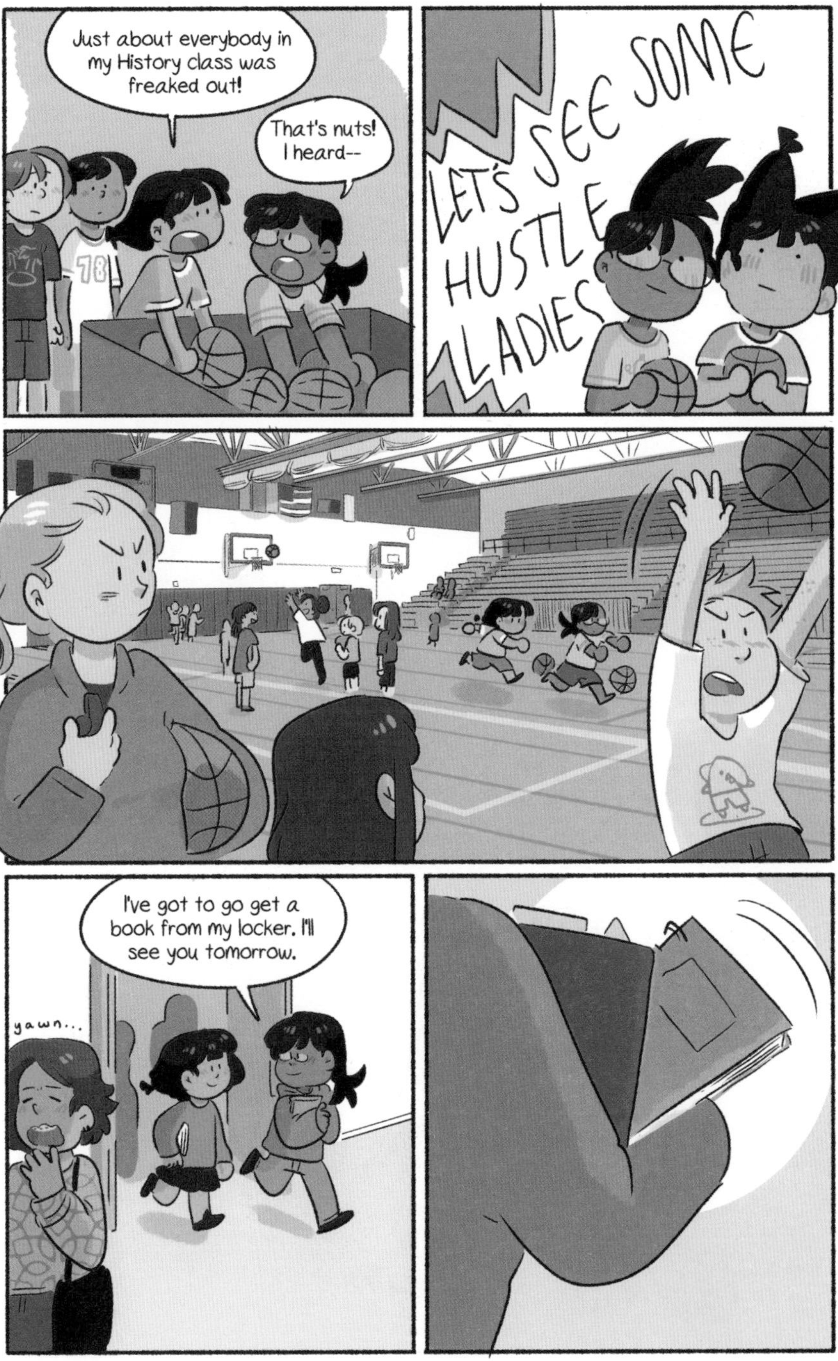
Just about everybody in my History class was freaked out!
That's nuts! I heard--
LET'S SEE SOME HUSTLE LADIES
I've got to go get a book from my locker. I'll see you tomorrow.
yawn...

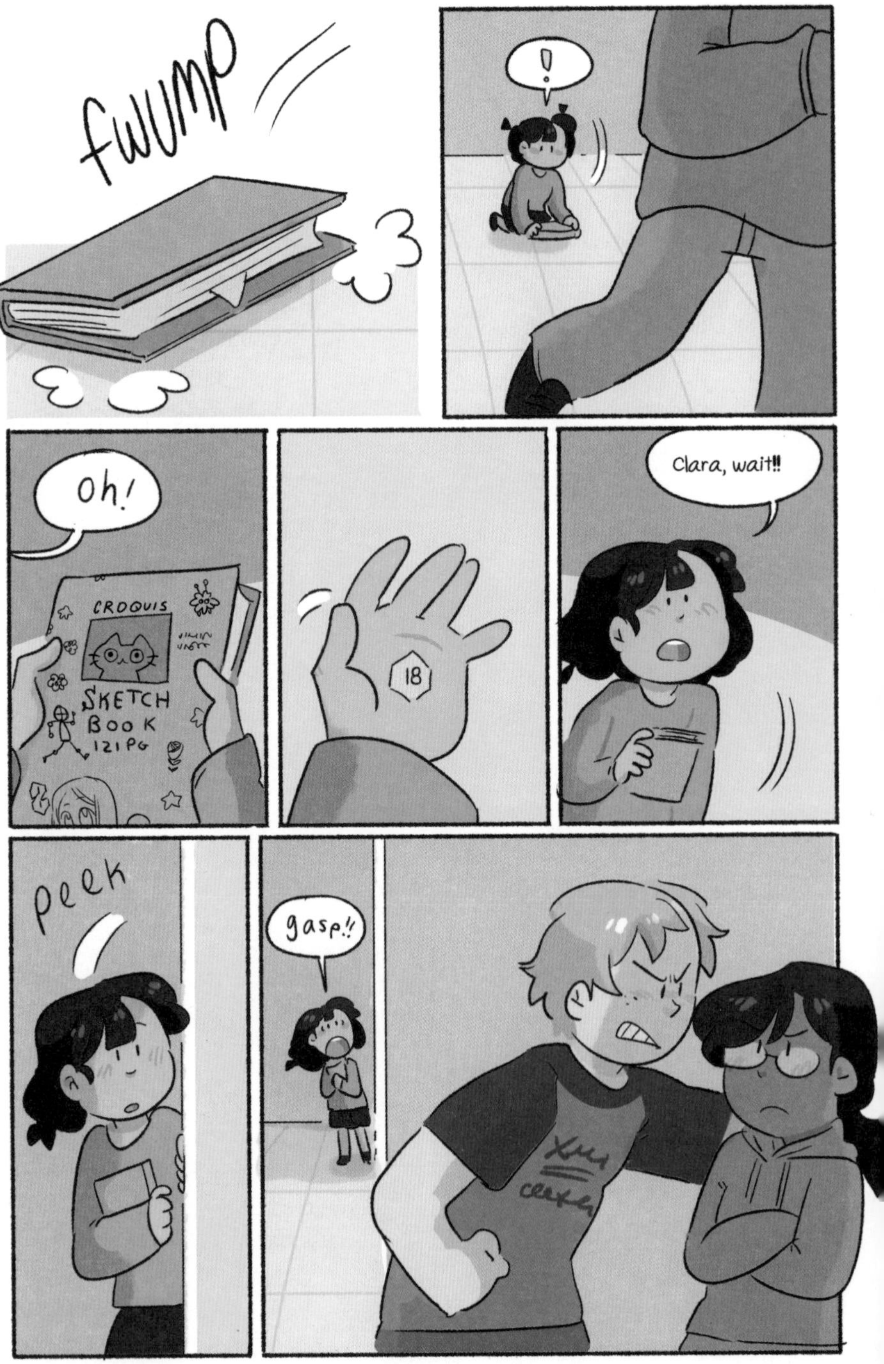
FWUMP
!
Oh!
CROQUIS
SKETCH BOOK
121 PG
18
Clara, wait!!
peek
gasp!!

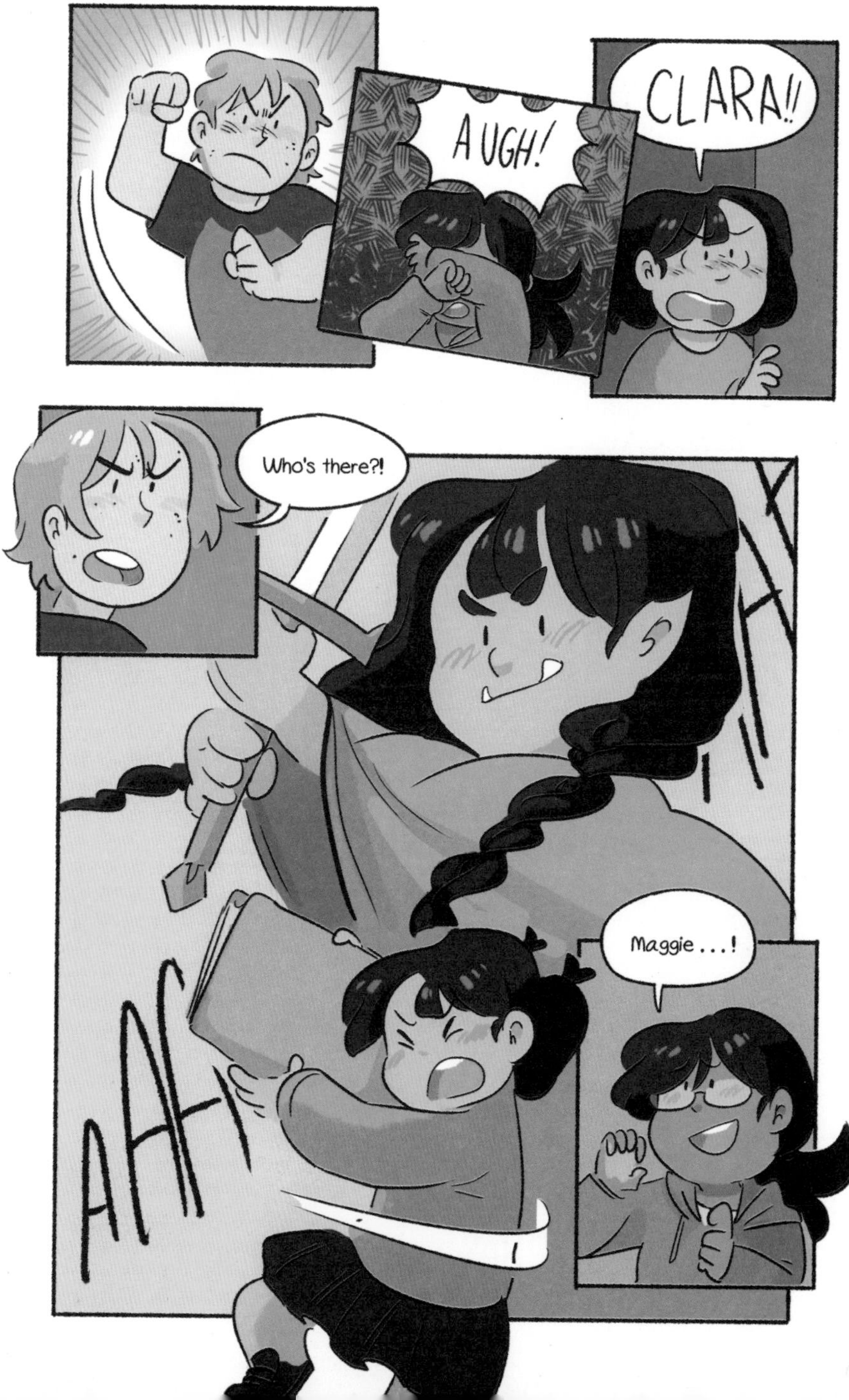
AUGH!
CLARA!!
Who's there?!
AAH!
Maggie . . . !

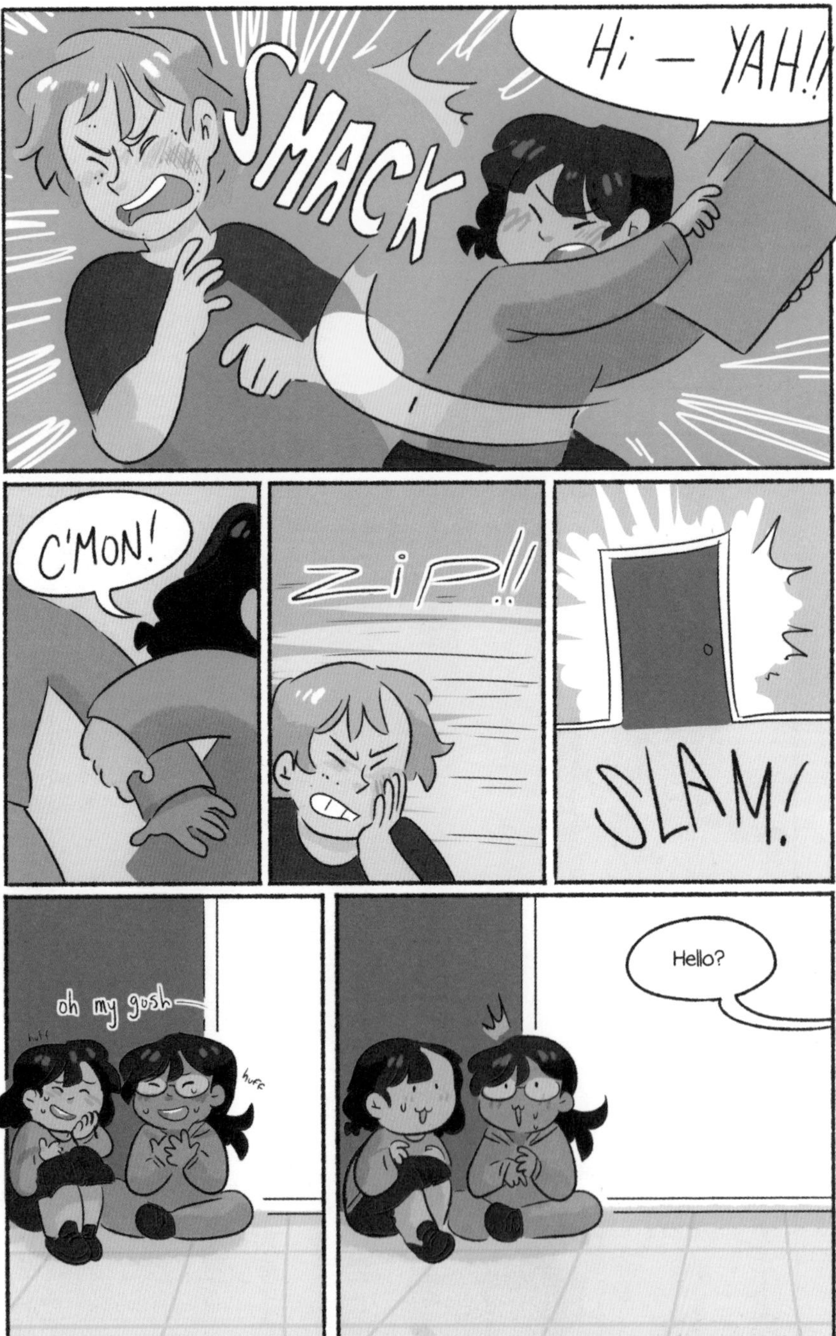
SMACK
Hi — YAH!!
C'MON!
ZiP!!
SLAM!
oh my gosh—
huff
huff
Hello?

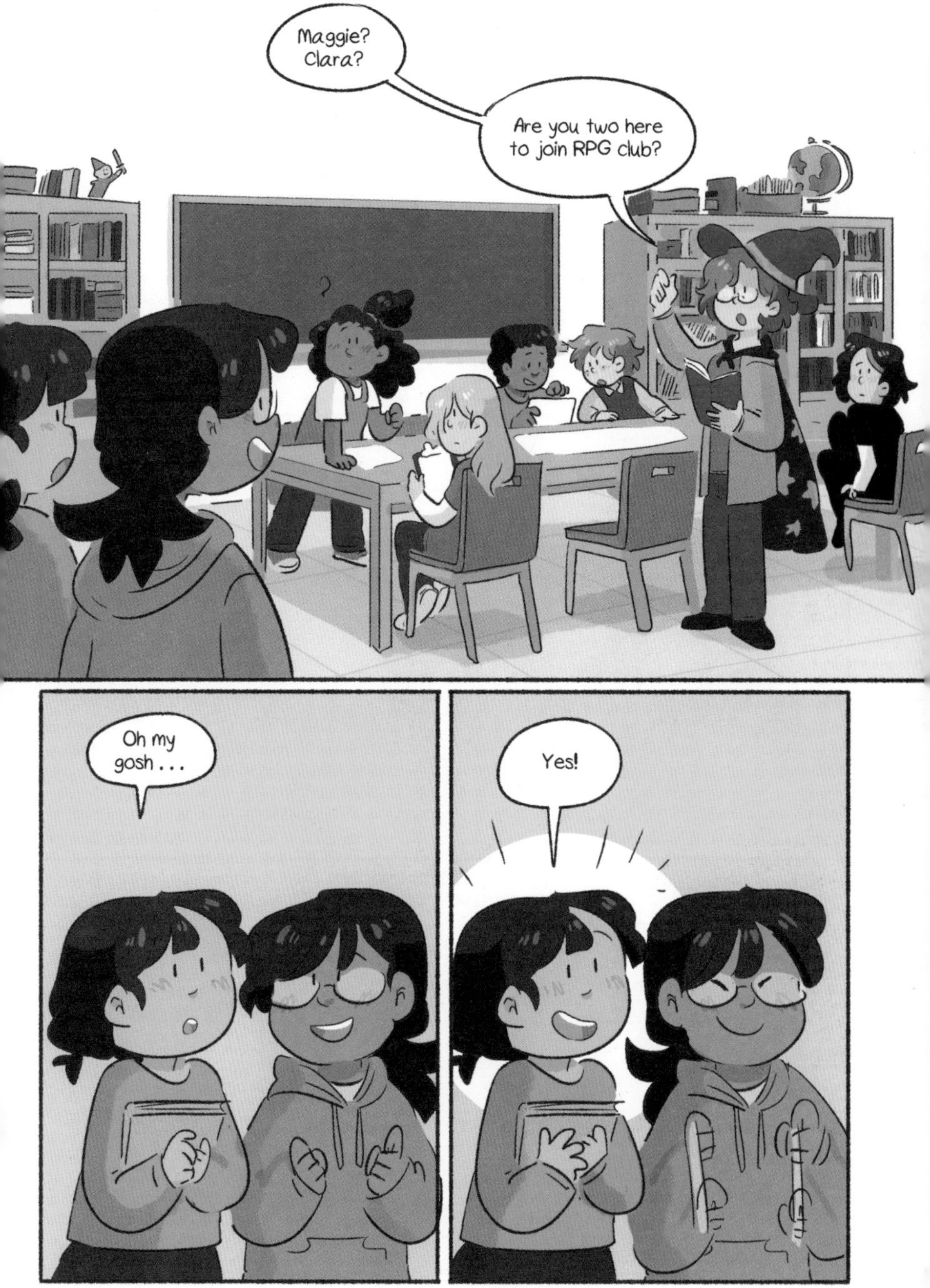

Maggie?
Clara?
Are you two here to join RPG club?
Oh my gosh . . .
Yes!

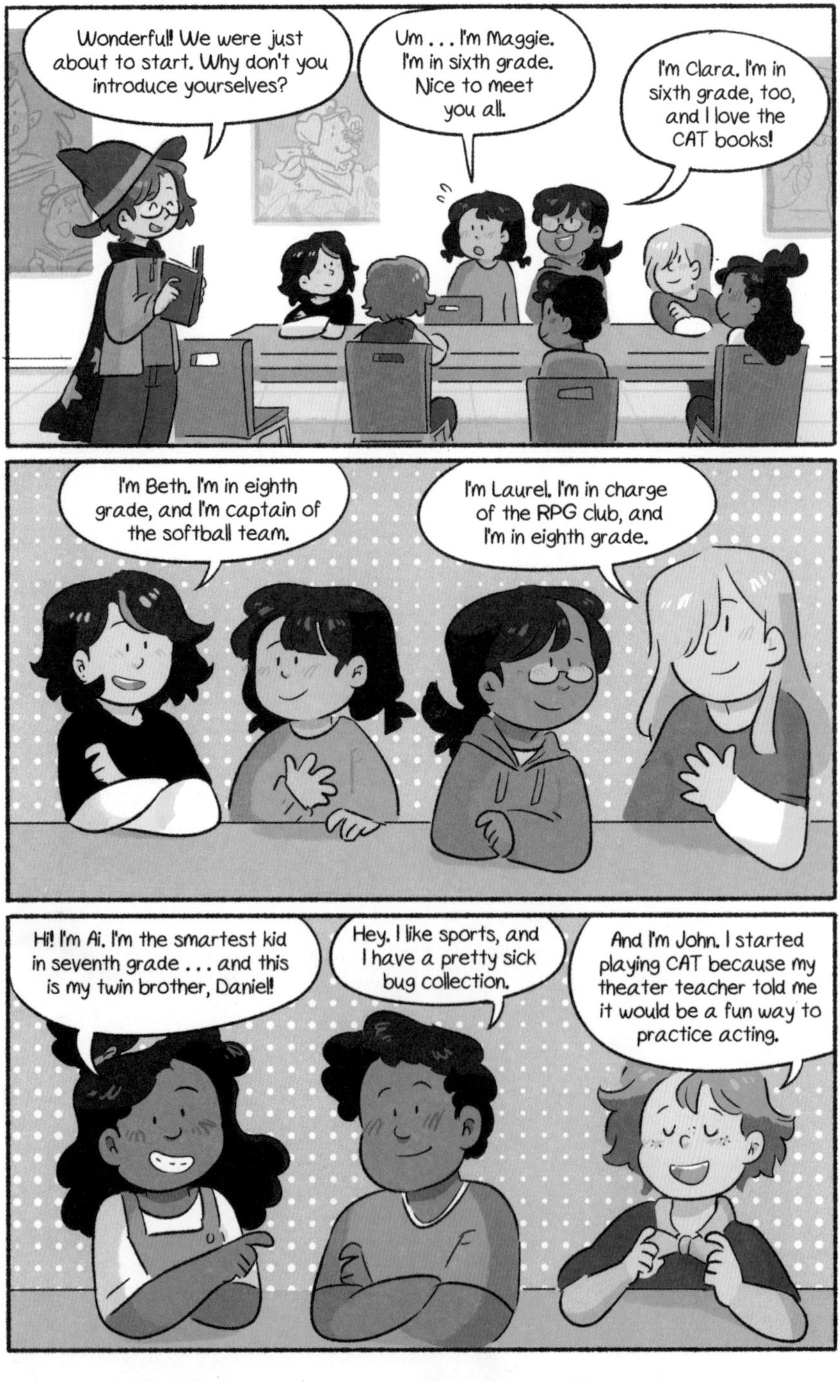
Wonderful! We were just about to start. Why don't you introduce yourselves?
Um . . . I'm Maggie. I'm in sixth grade. Nice to meet you all.
I'm Clara. I'm in sixth grade, too, and I love the CAT books!
I'm Beth. I'm in eighth grade, and I'm captain of the softball team.
I'm Laurel. I'm in charge of the RPG club, and I'm in eighth grade.
Hi! I'm Ai. I'm the smartest kid in seventh grade . . . and this is my twin brother, Daniel!
Hey. I like sports, and I have a pretty sick bug collection.
And I'm John. I started playing CAT because my theater teacher told me it would be a fun way to practice acting.

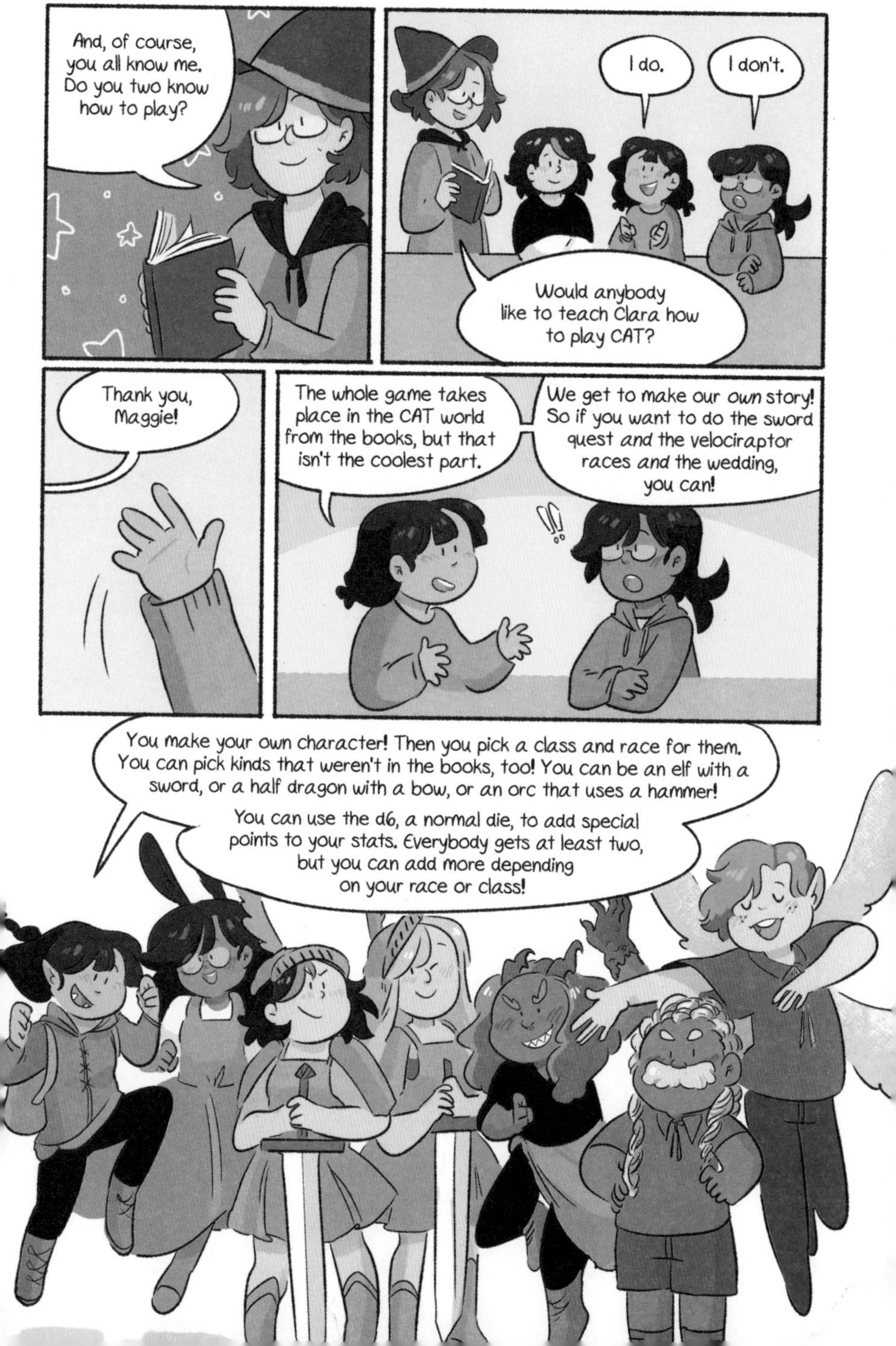
And, of course, you all know me. Do you two know how to play?
I do.
I don't.
Would anybody like to teach Clara how to play CAT?
Thank you, Maggie!
The whole game takes place in the CAT world from the books, but that isn't the coolest part.
We get to make our *own* story! So if you want to do the sword quest *and* the velociraptor races *and* the wedding, you can!
!!
You make your own character! Then you pick a class and race for them. You can pick kinds that weren't in the books, too! You can be an elf with a sword, or a half dragon with a bow, or an orc that uses a hammer!
You can use the d6, a normal die, to add special points to your stats. Everybody gets at least two, but you can add more depending on your race or class!

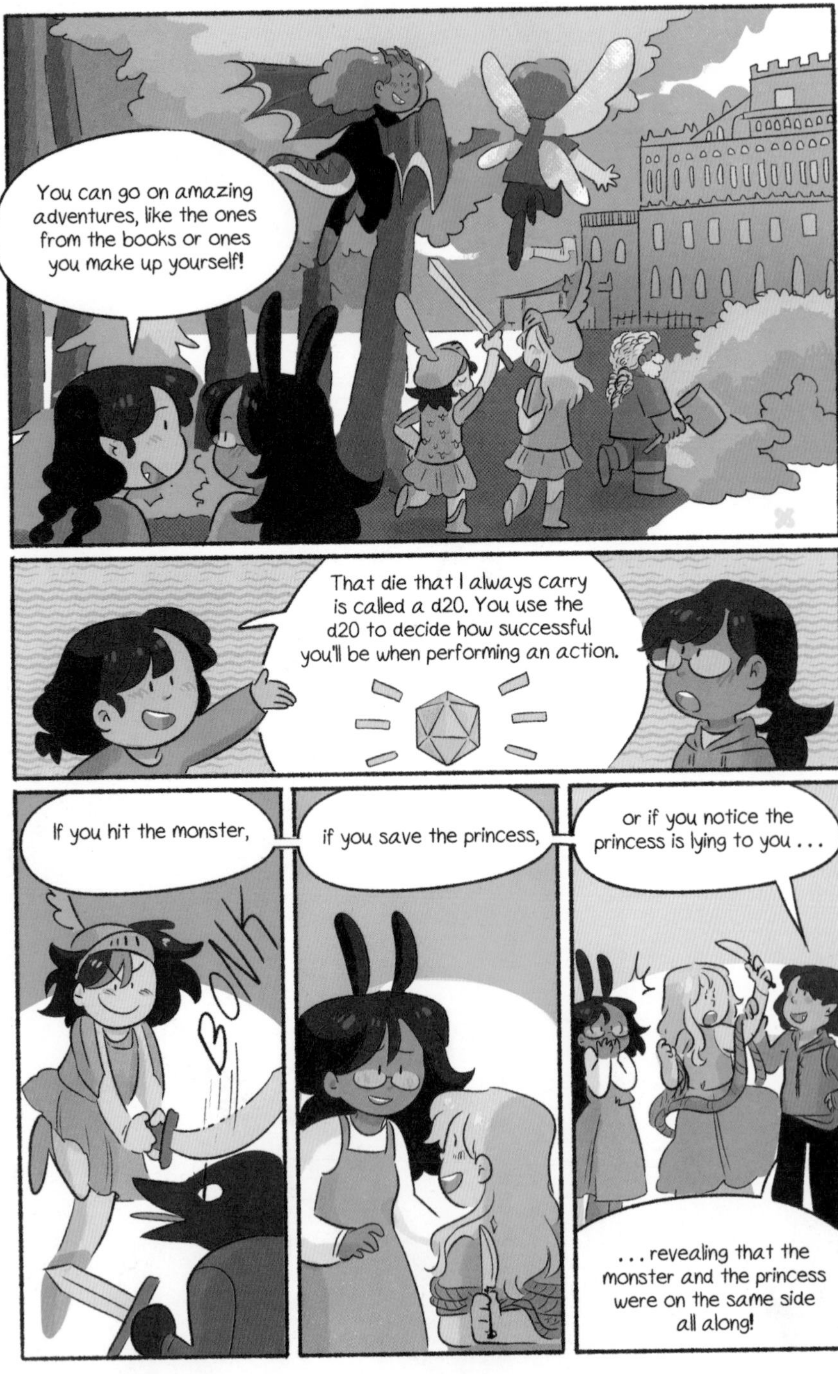
You can go on amazing adventures, like the ones from the books or ones you make up yourself!
That die that I always carry is called a d20. You use the d20 to decide how successful you'll be when performing an action.
If you hit the monster,
BONK
if you save the princess,
or if you notice the princess is lying to you . . .
. . . revealing that the monster and the princess were on the same side all along!

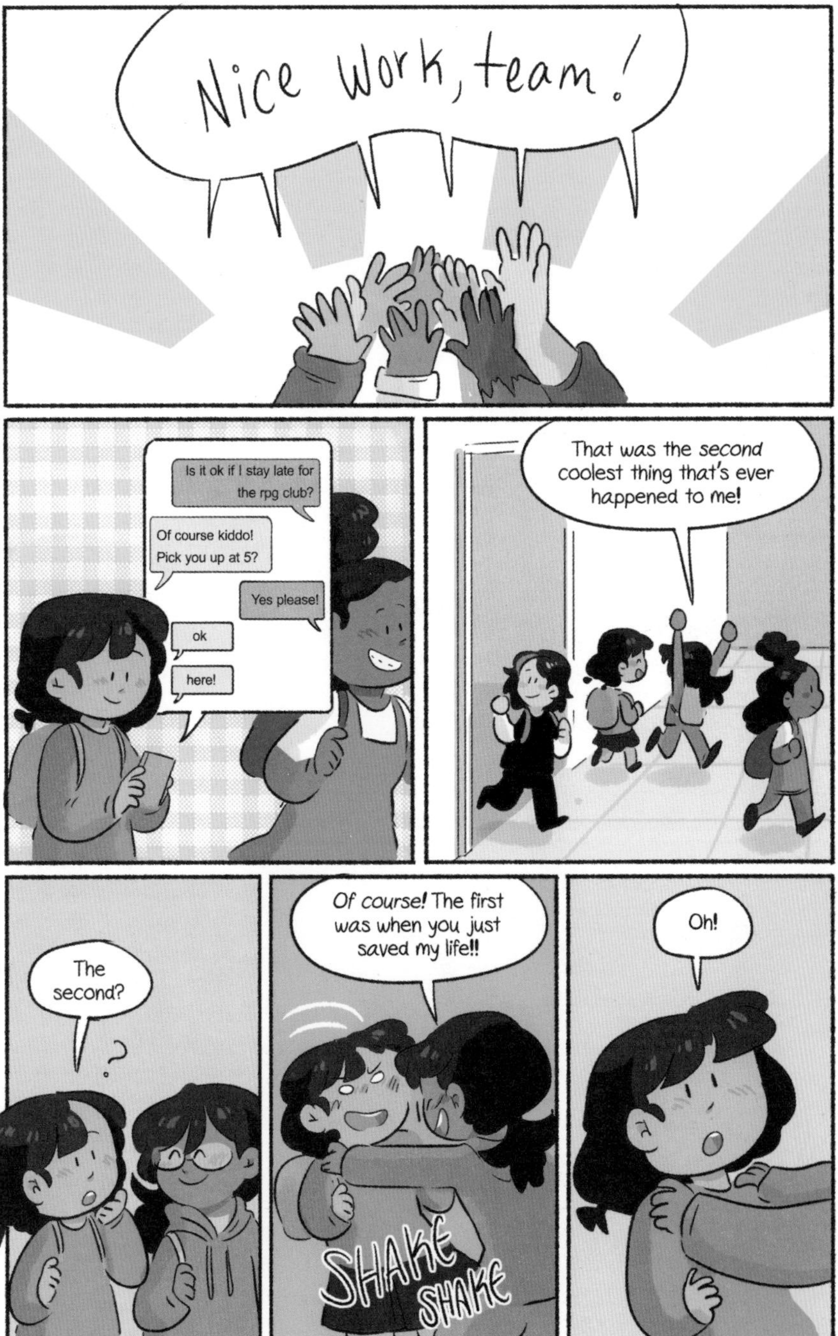
Nice work, team!
Is it ok if I stay late for the rpg club?
Of course kiddo! Pick you up at 5?
Yes please!
ok
here!
That was the *second* coolest thing that's ever happened to me!
The second?
Of course! The first was when you just saved my life!!
SHAKE
SHAKE
Oh!

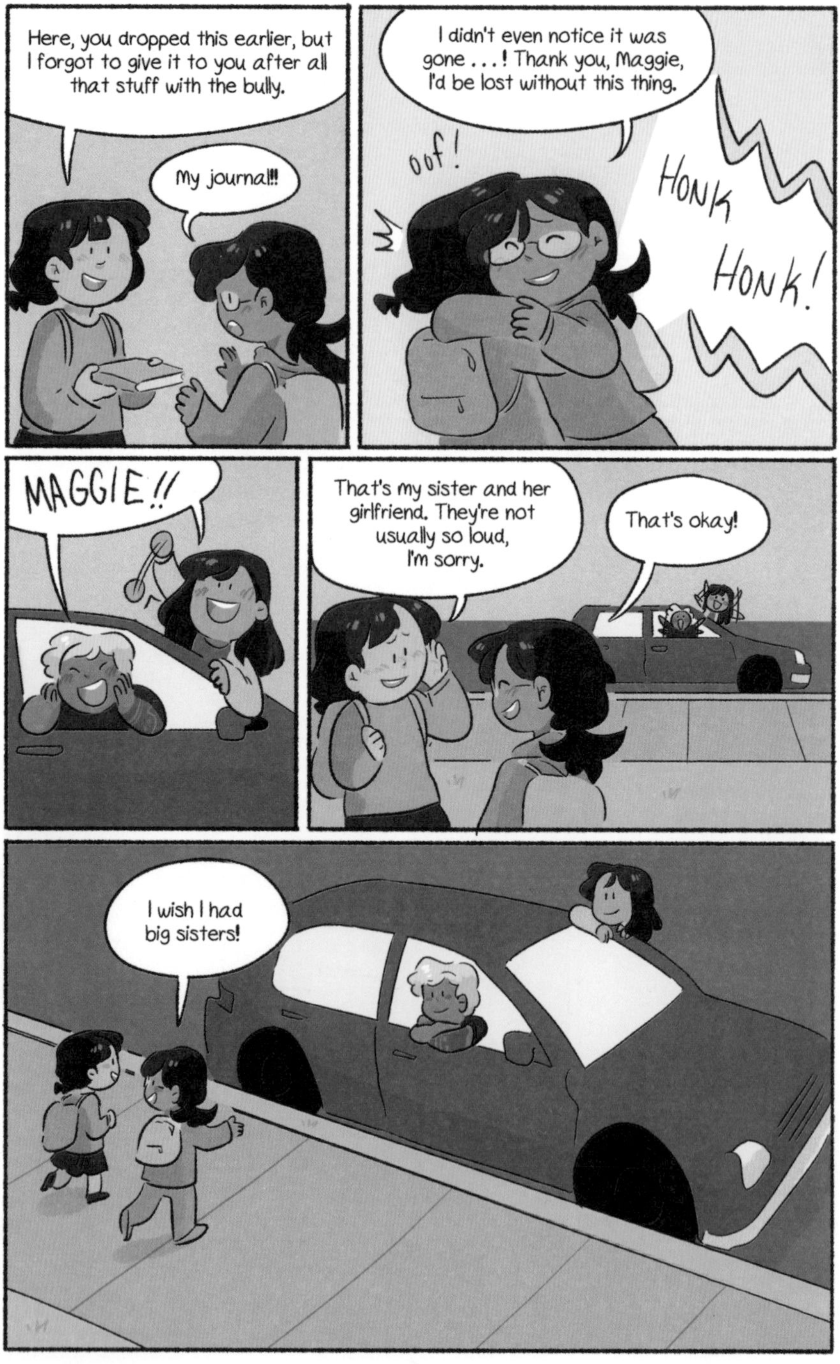
Here, you dropped this earlier, but I forgot to give it to you after all that stuff with the bully.
My journal!!
I didn't even notice it was gone . . . ! Thank you, Maggie, I'd be lost without this thing.
oof!
HONK
HONK!
MAGGIE!!
That's my sister and her girlfriend. They're not usually so loud, I'm sorry.
That's okay!
I wish I had big sisters!

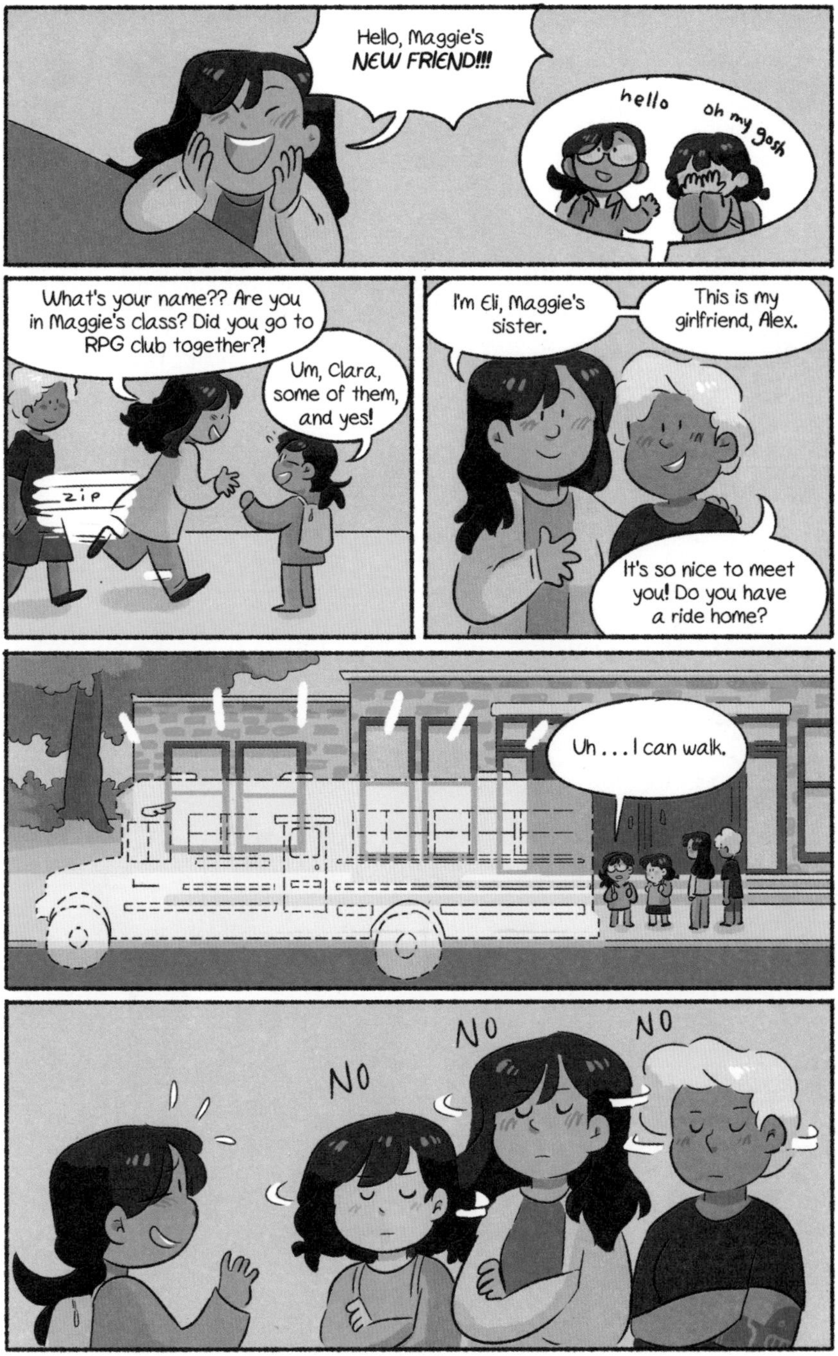
Hello, Maggie's NEW FRIEND!!!
hello
oh my gosh
What's your name?? Are you in Maggie's class? Did you go to RPG club together?!
zip
Um, Clara, some of them, and yes!
I'm Eli, Maggie's sister.
This is my girlfriend, Alex.
It's so nice to meet you! Do you have a ride home?
Uh . . . I can walk.
NO
NO
NO

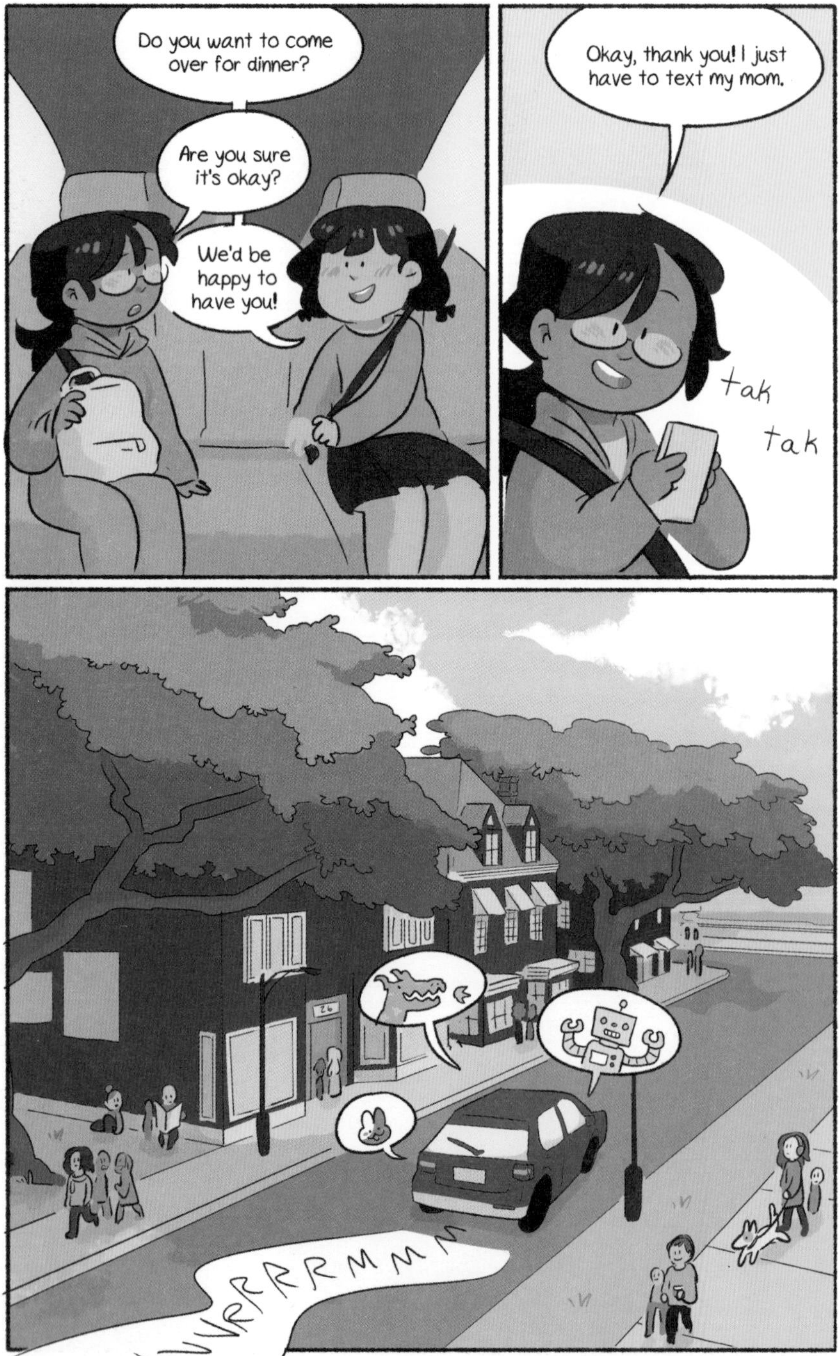
Do you want to come over for dinner?
Are you sure it's okay?
We'd be happy to have you!
Okay, thank you! I just have to text my mom.
tak
tak
26
VVVRRRRMMM

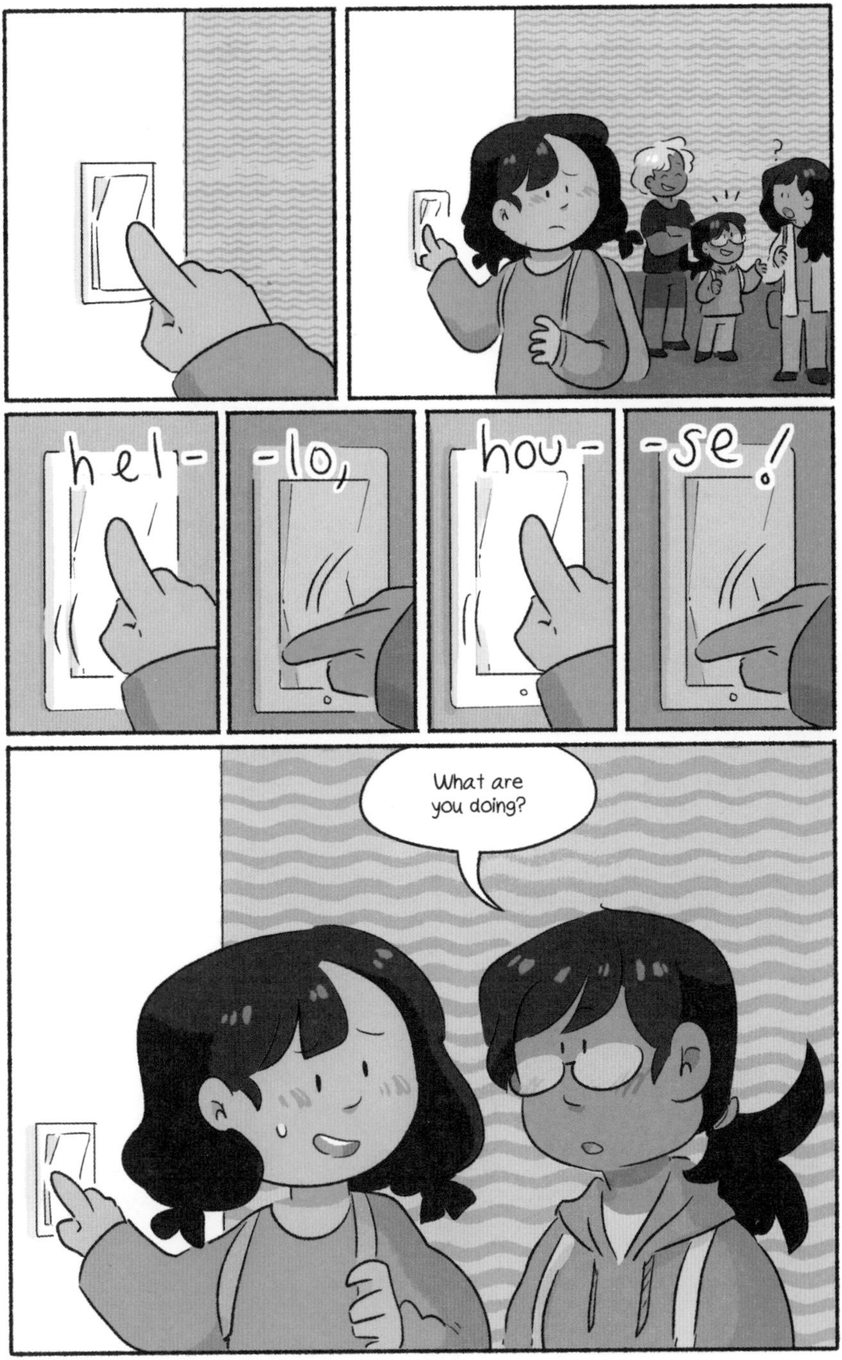

hel-
-lo,
hou-
-se!
What are you doing?

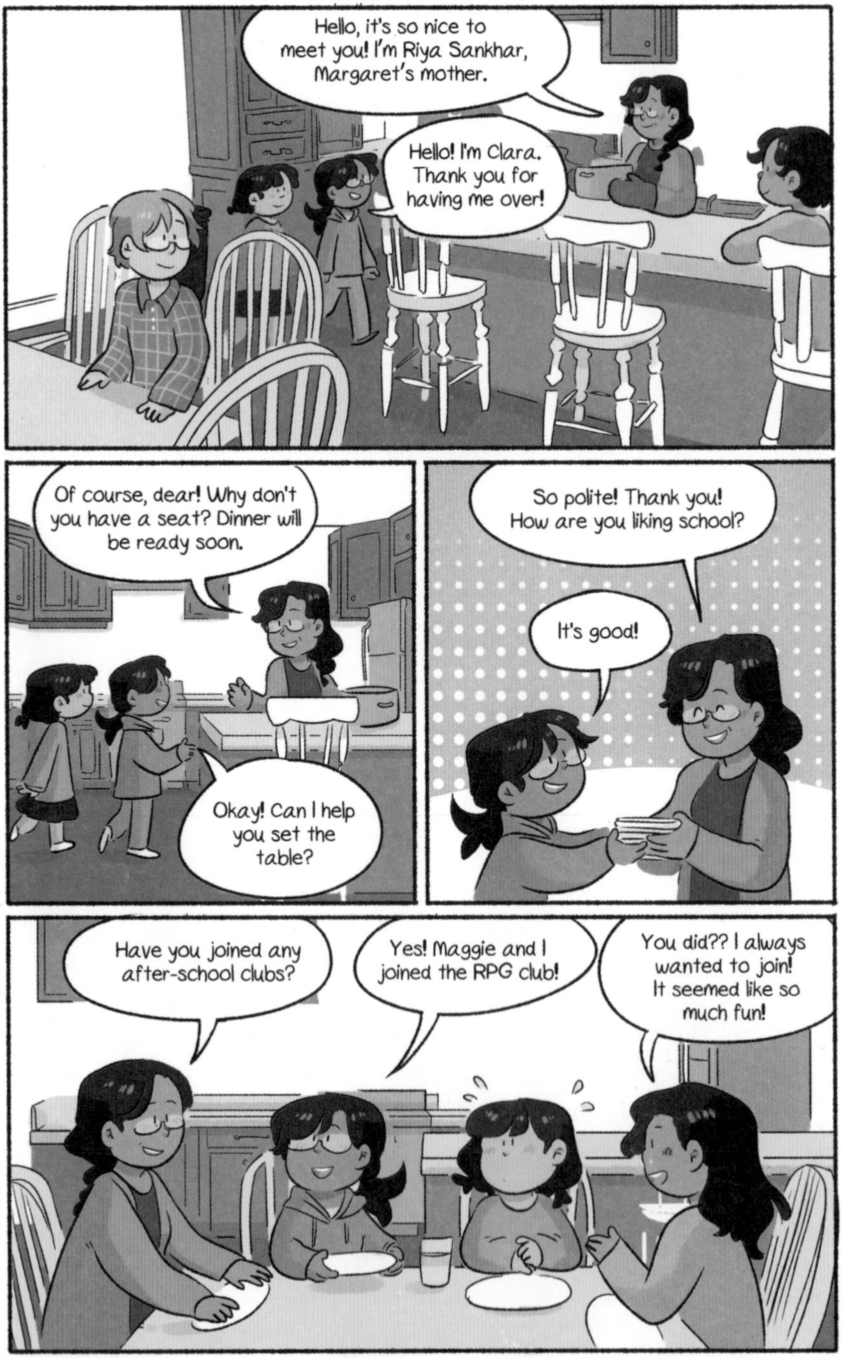
Hello, it's so nice to meet you! I'm Riya Sankhar, Margaret's mother.
Hello! I'm Clara. Thank you for having me over!
Of course, dear! Why don't you have a seat? Dinner will be ready soon.
Okay! Can I help you set the table?
So polite! Thank you! How are you liking school?
It's good!
Have you joined any after-school clubs?
Yes! Maggie and I joined the RPG club!
You did?? I always wanted to join! It seemed like so much fun!

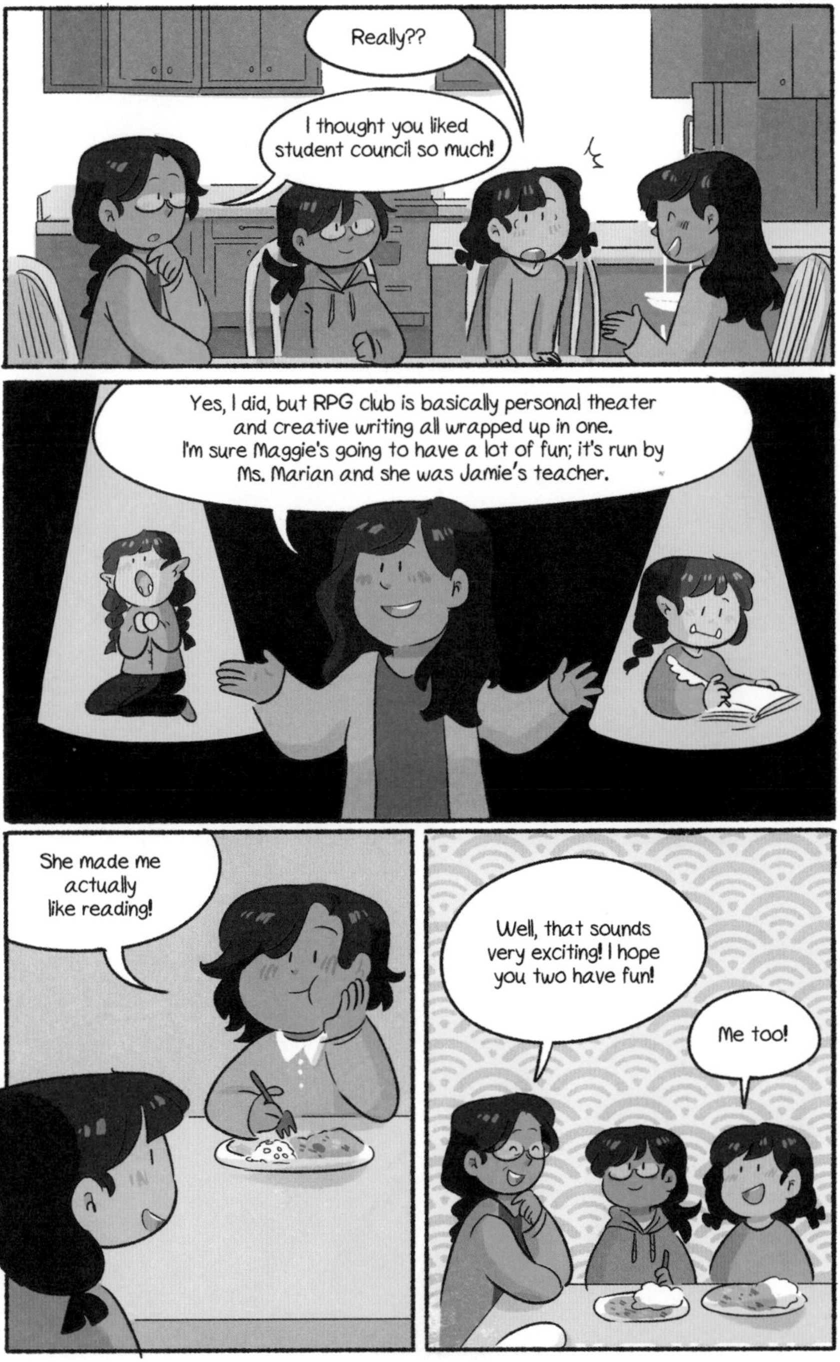
Really??
I thought you liked student council so much!
Yes, I did, but RPG club is basically personal theater and creative writing all wrapped up in one. I'm sure Maggie's going to have a lot of fun; it's run by Ms. Marian and she was Jamie's teacher.
She made me actually like reading!
Well, that sounds very exciting! I hope you two have fun!
Me too!

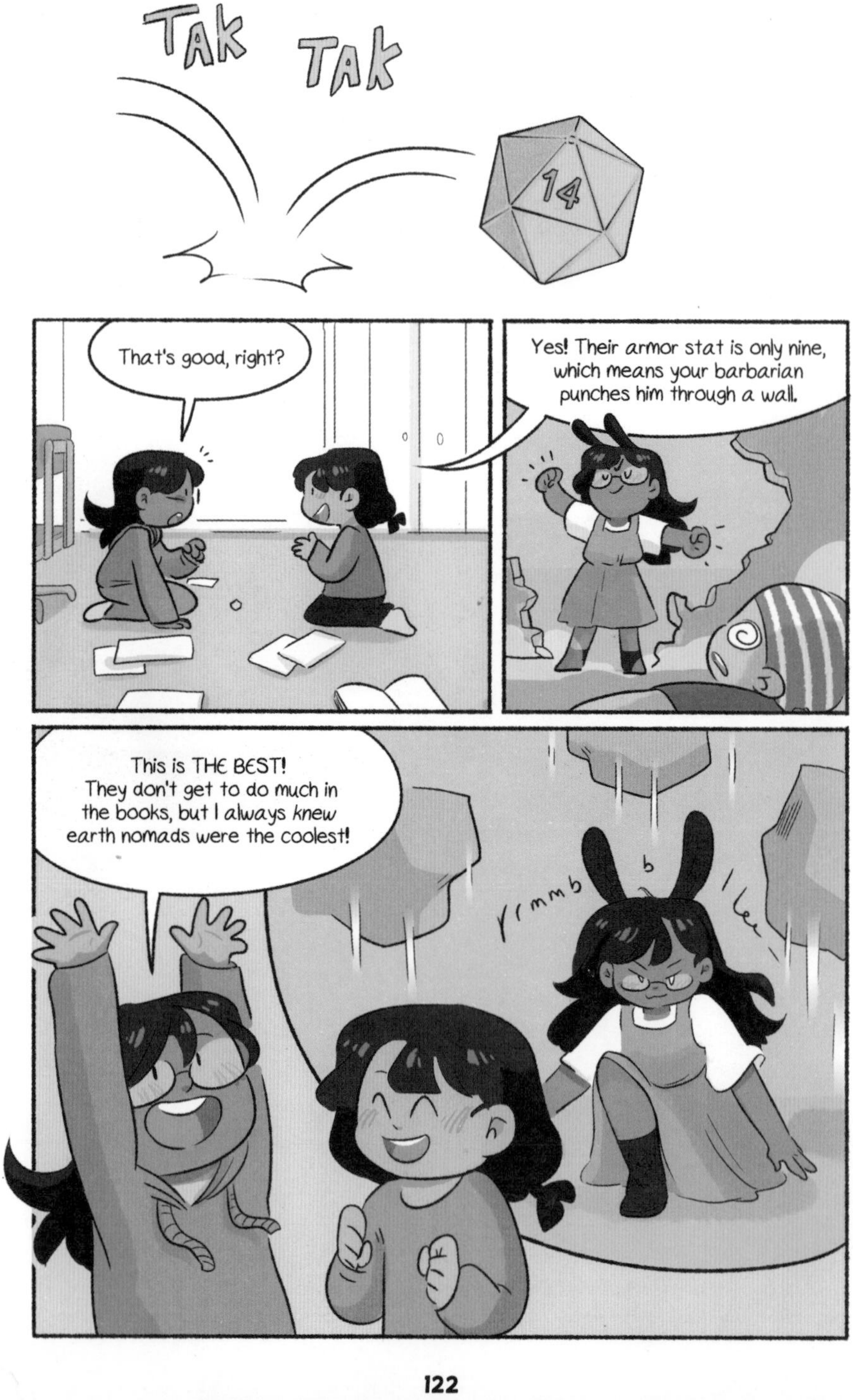
TAK TAK
14
That's good, right?
Yes! Their armor stat is only nine, which means your barbarian punches him through a wall.
This is THE BEST! They don't get to do much in the books, but I always *knew* earth nomads were the coolest!

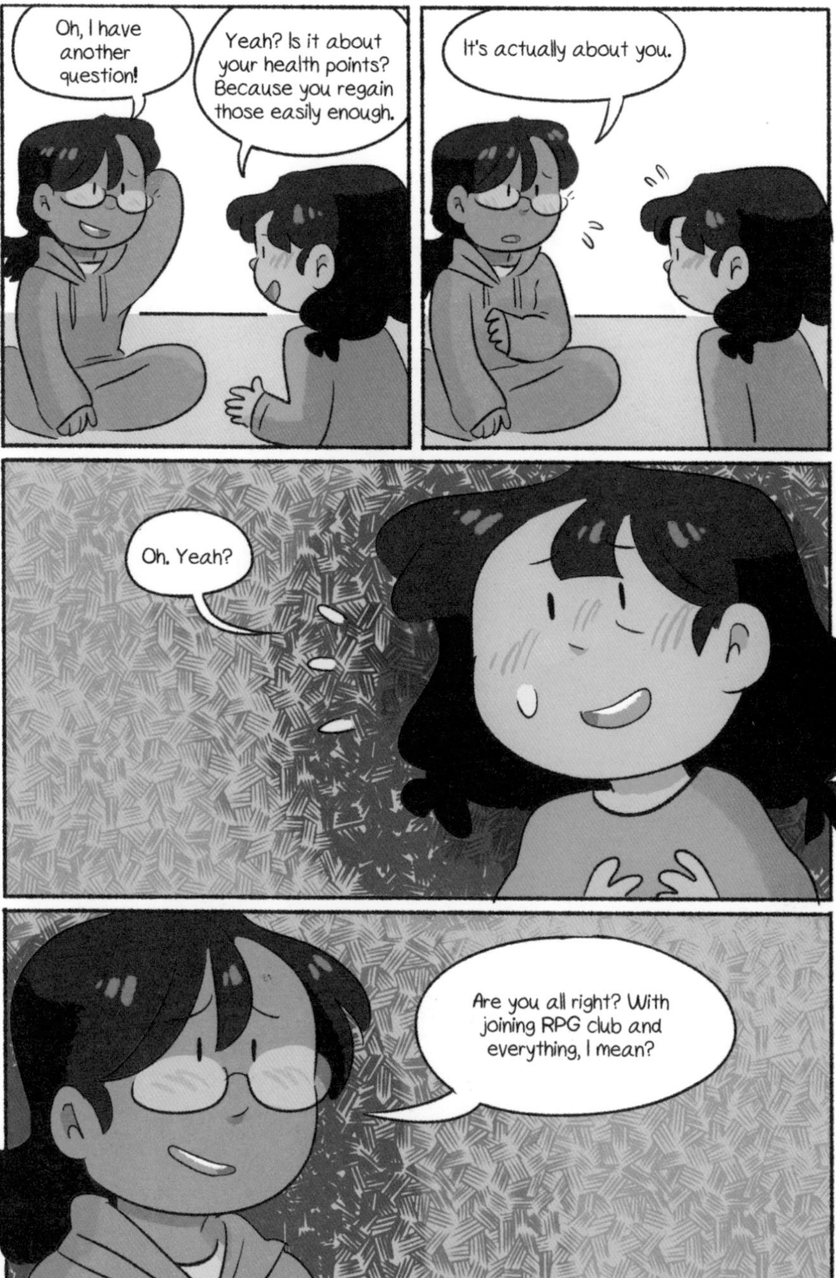
Oh, I have another question!
Yeah? Is it about your health points? Because you regain those easily enough.
It's actually about you.
Oh. Yeah?
Are you all right? With joining RPG club and everything, I mean?

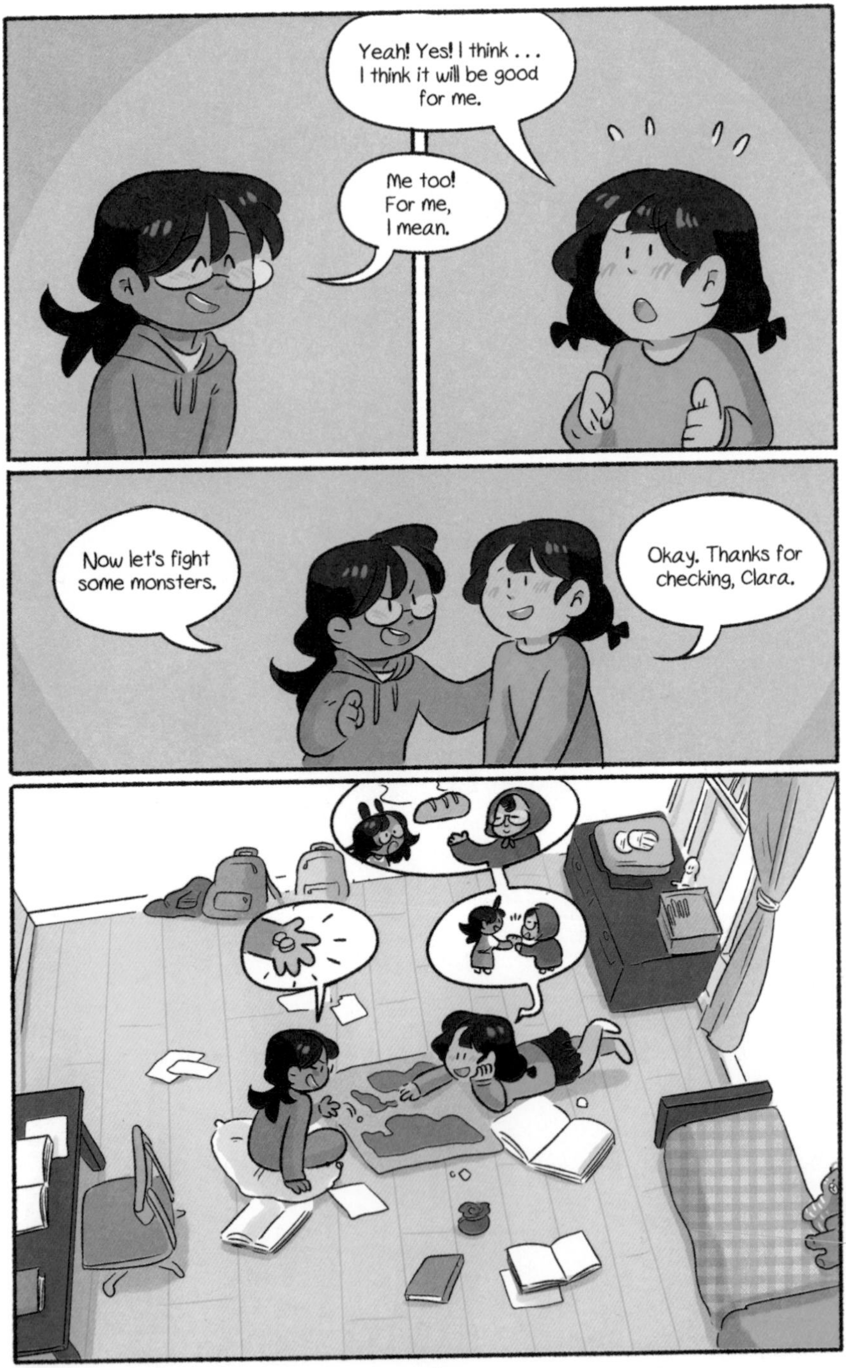
Yeah! Yes! I think . . . I think it will be good for me.
Me too! For me, I mean.
Now let's fight some monsters.
Okay. Thanks for checking, Clara.

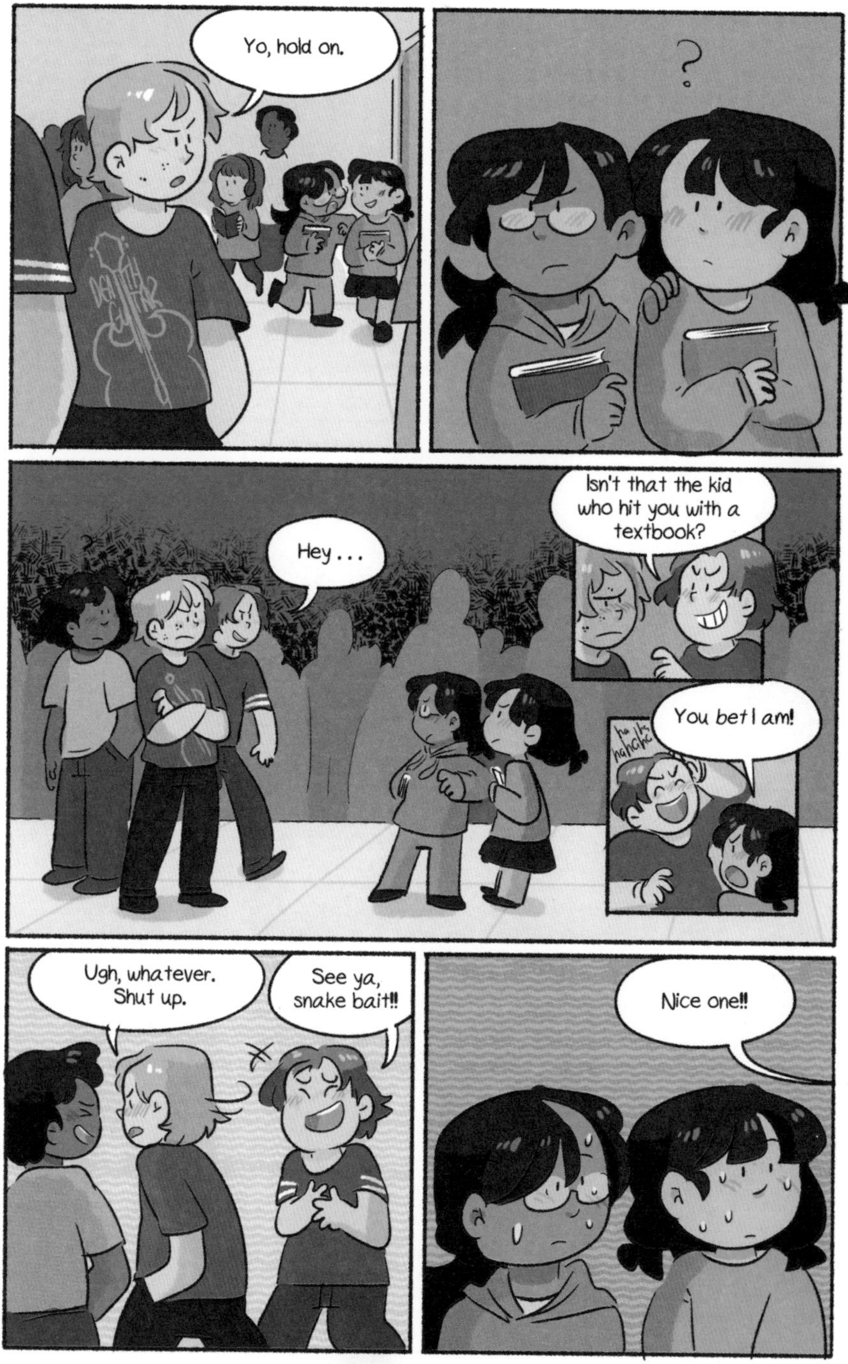
Yo, hold on.
?
Hey . . .
Isn't that the kid who hit you with a textbook?
haha hahaha
You bet I am!
Ugh, whatever. Shut up.
See ya, snake bait!!
Nice one!!

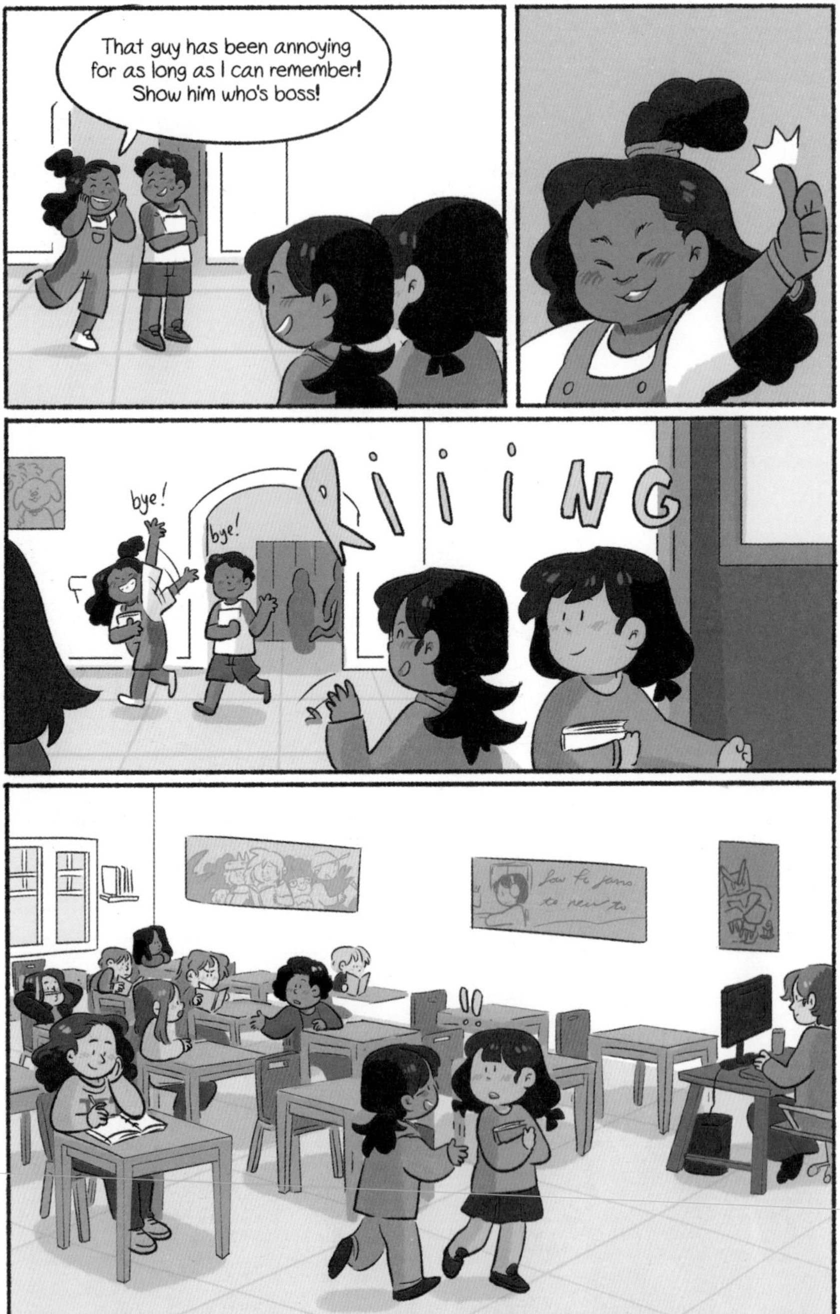
That guy has been annoying for as long as I can remember! Show him who's boss!
bye!
bye!
RIIING

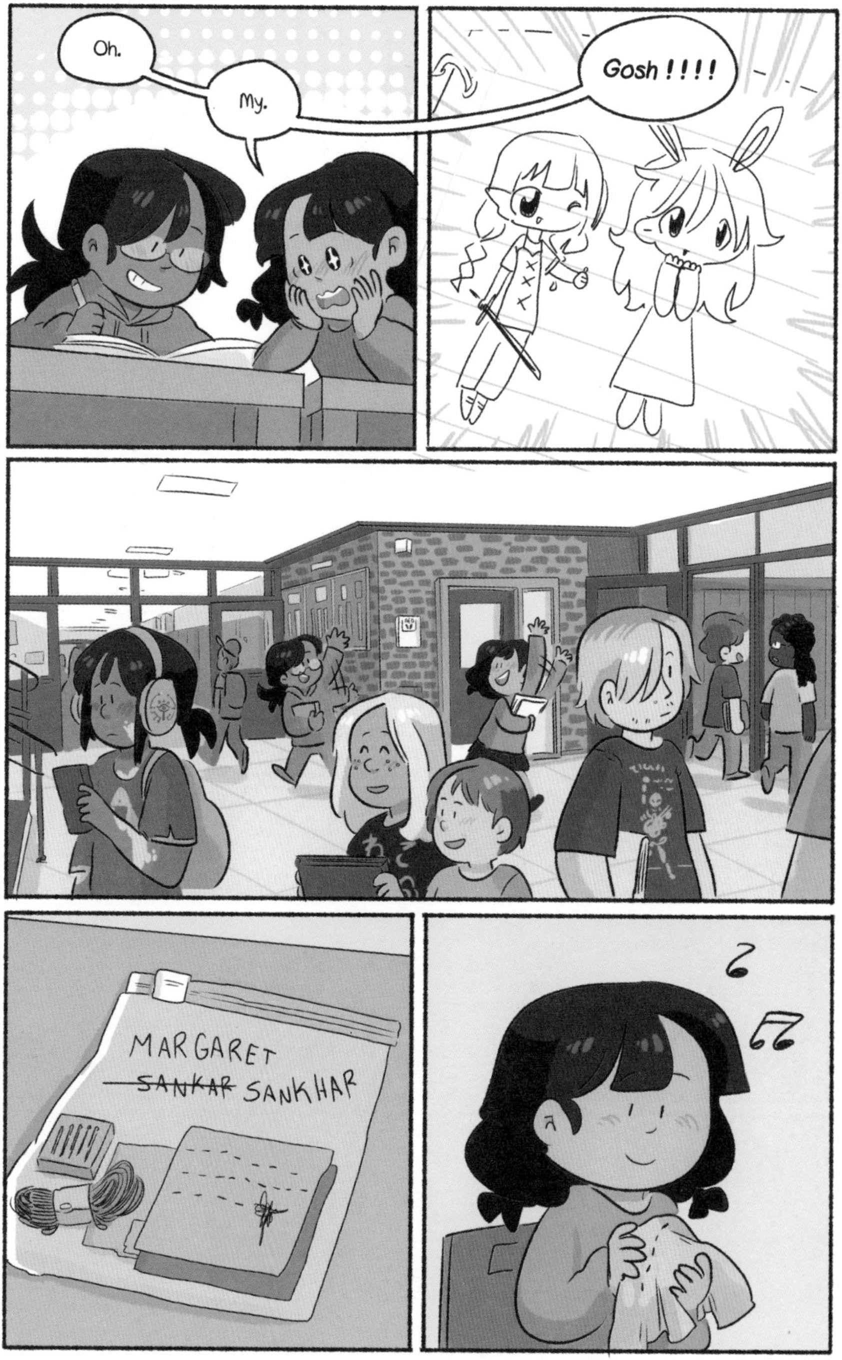
Oh.
My.
Gosh !!!!
MARGARET
SANKAR SANKHAR

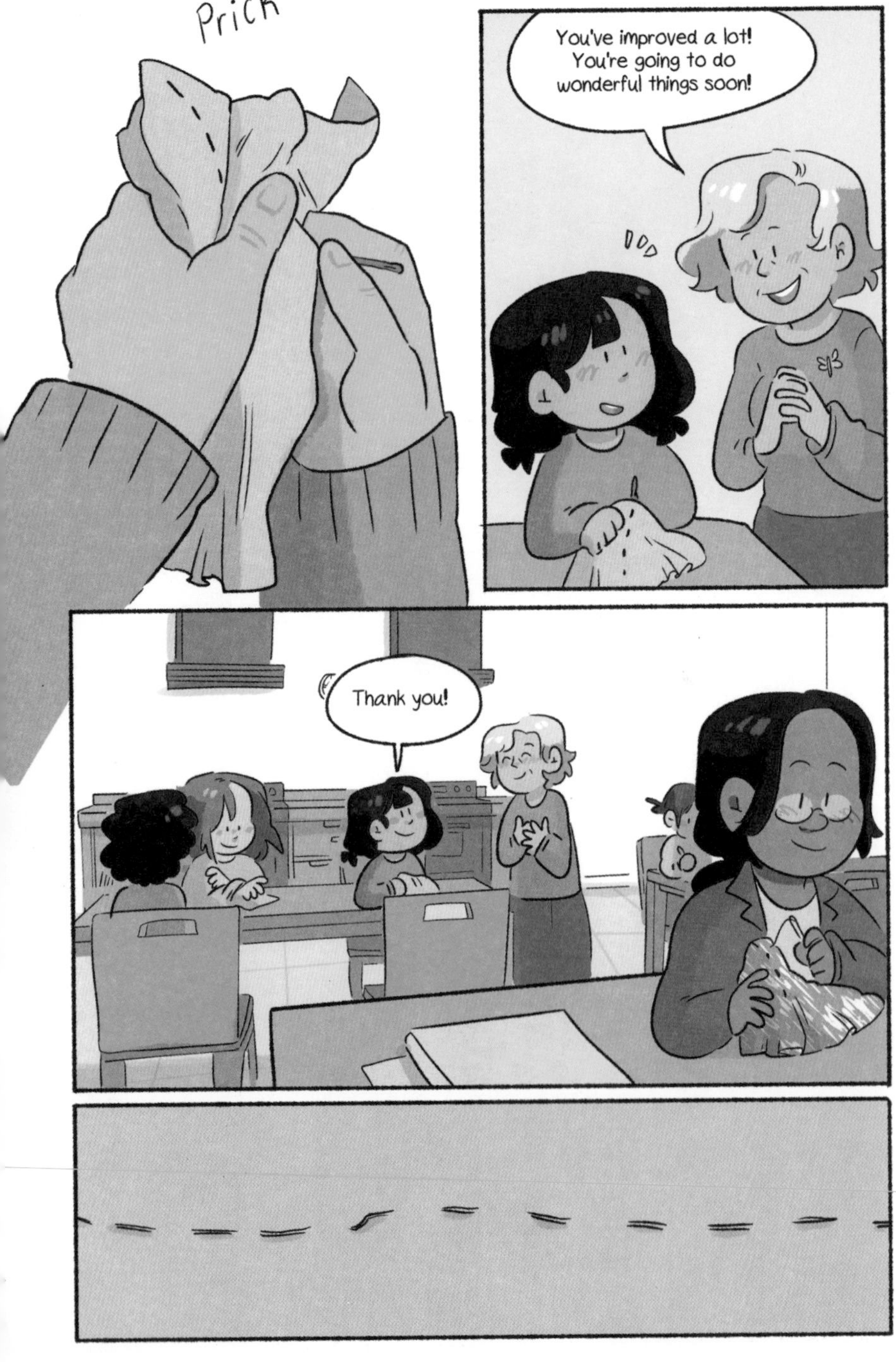
Prick
You've improved a lot! You're going to do wonderful things soon!
Thank you!

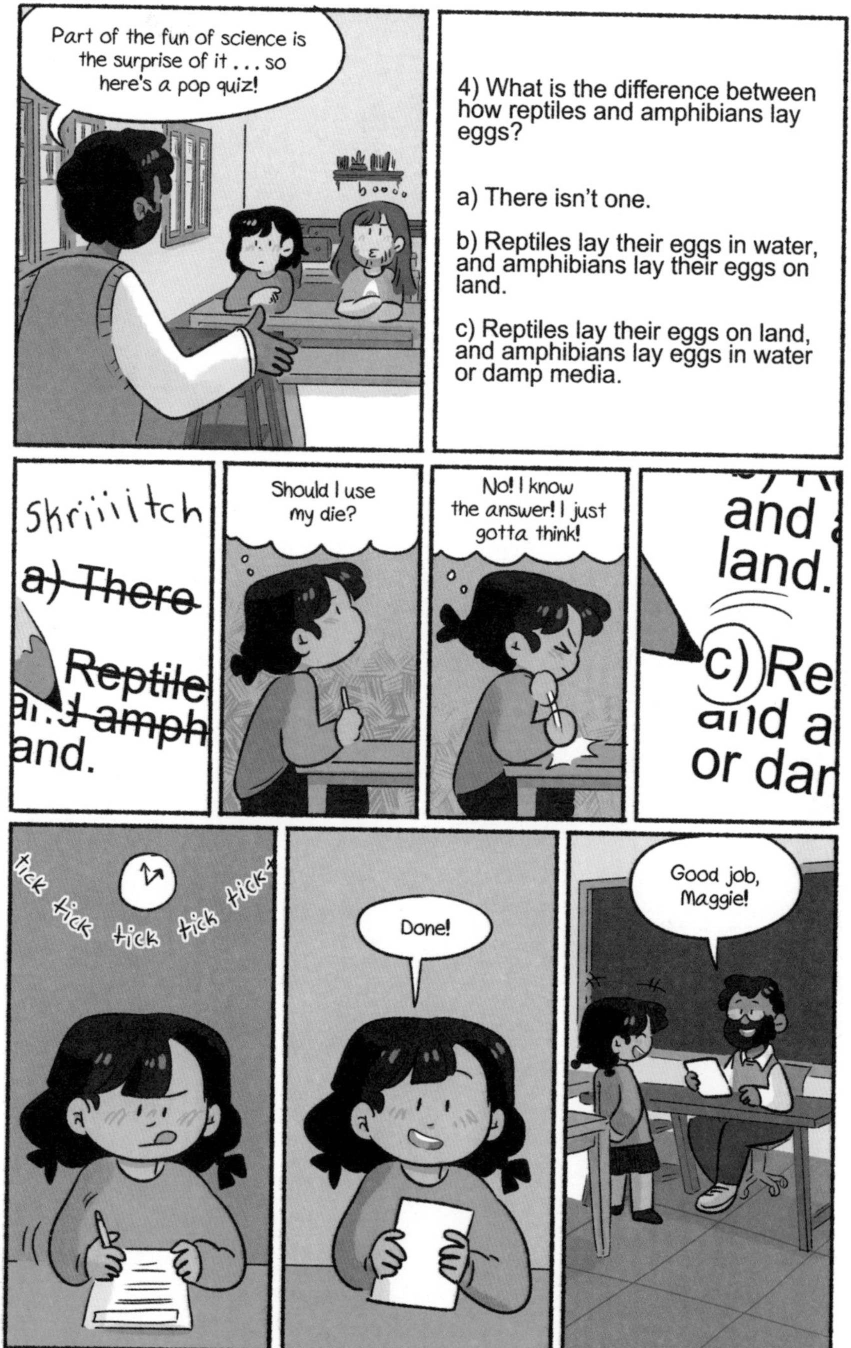
Part of the fun of science is the surprise of it . . . so here's a pop quiz!
boooo
4) What is the difference between how reptiles and amphibians lay eggs?
a) There isn't one.
b) Reptiles lay their eggs in water, and amphibians lay their eggs on land.
c) Reptiles lay their eggs on land, and amphibians lay eggs in water or damp media.
Skriiiitch
a) There
Reptile
and amph
and.
Should I use my die?
No! I know the answer! I just gotta think!
and
land.
c) Re
and a
or dar
tick tick tick tick tick
Done!
Good job, Maggie!

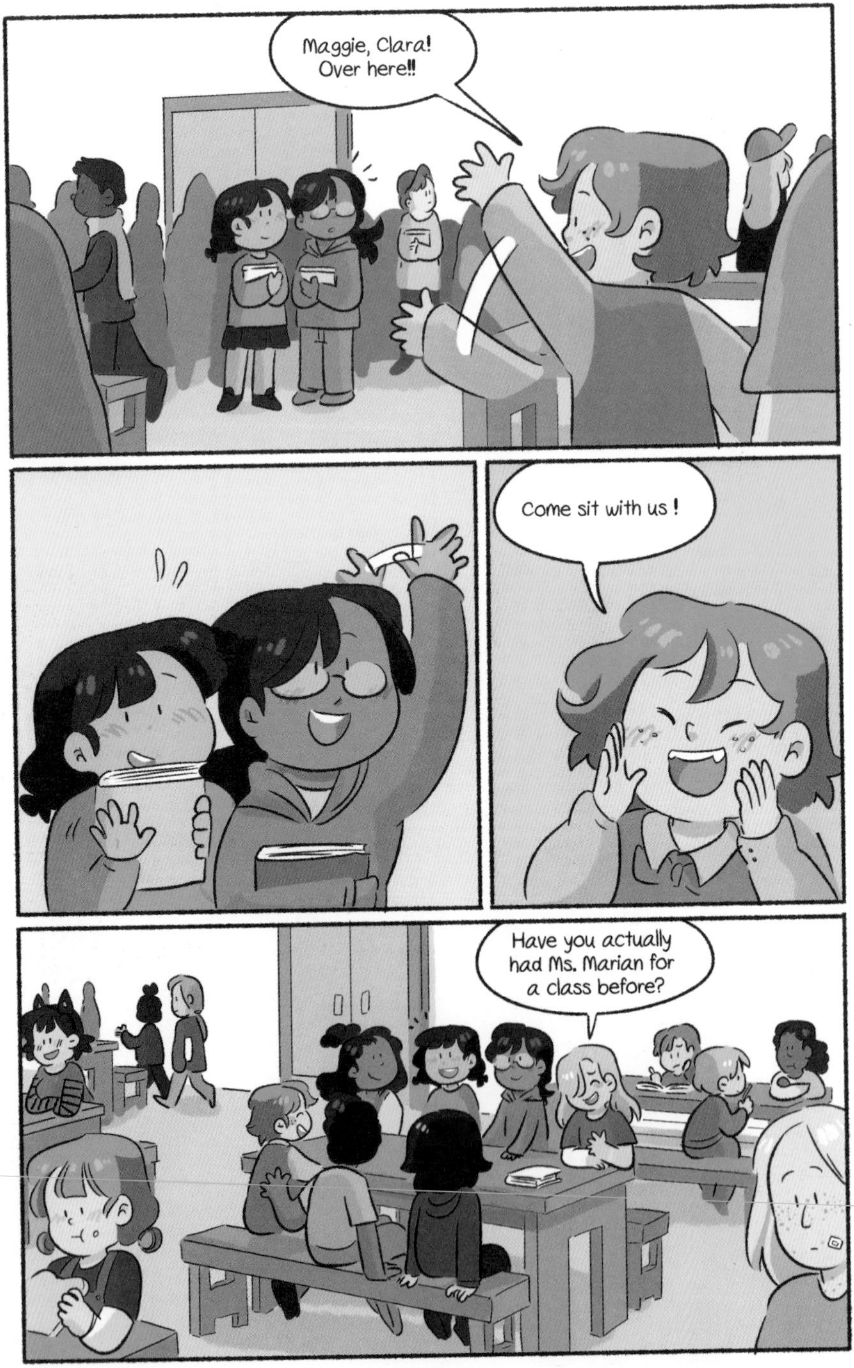
Maggie, Clara! Over here!!
Come sit with us!
Have you actually had Ms. Marian for a class before?

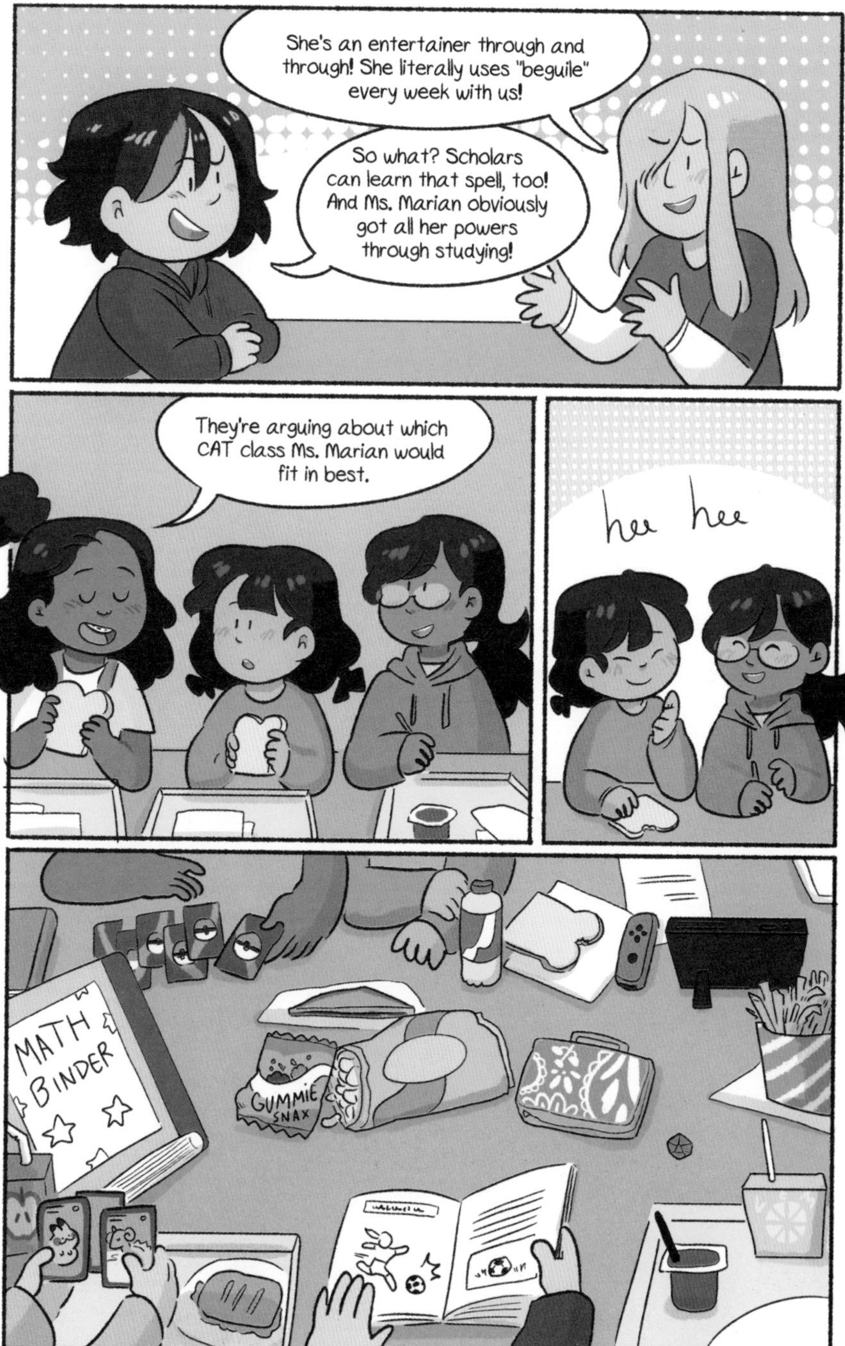
She's an entertainer through and through! She literally uses "beguile" every week with us!
So what? Scholars can learn that spell, too! And Ms. Marian obviously got all her powers through studying!
They're arguing about which CAT class Ms. Marian would fit in best.
hee hee
MATH BINDER
GUMMIE SNAX

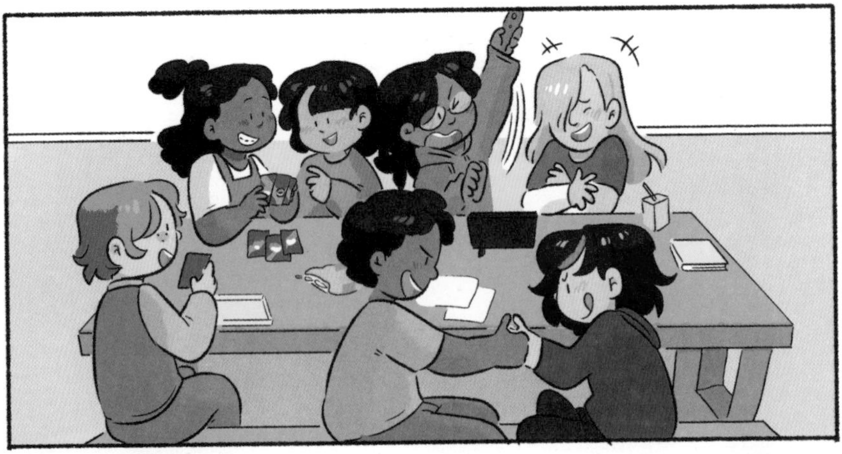

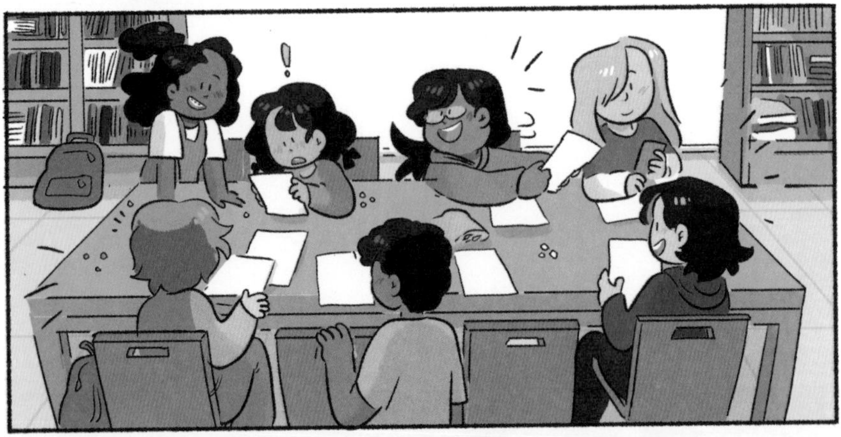

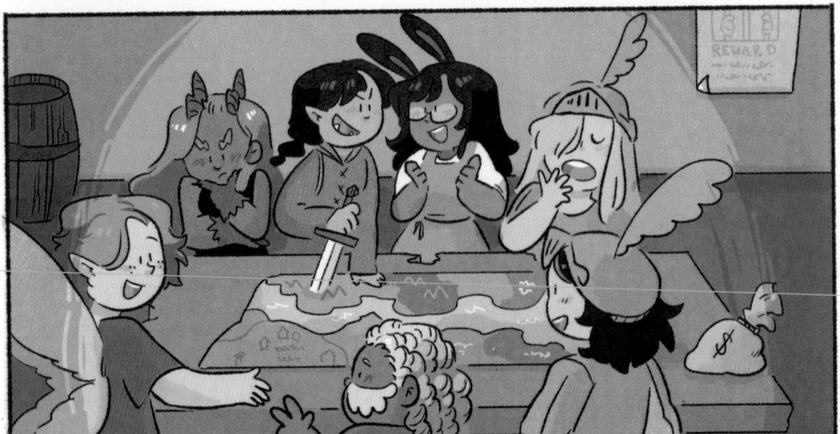
REWARD

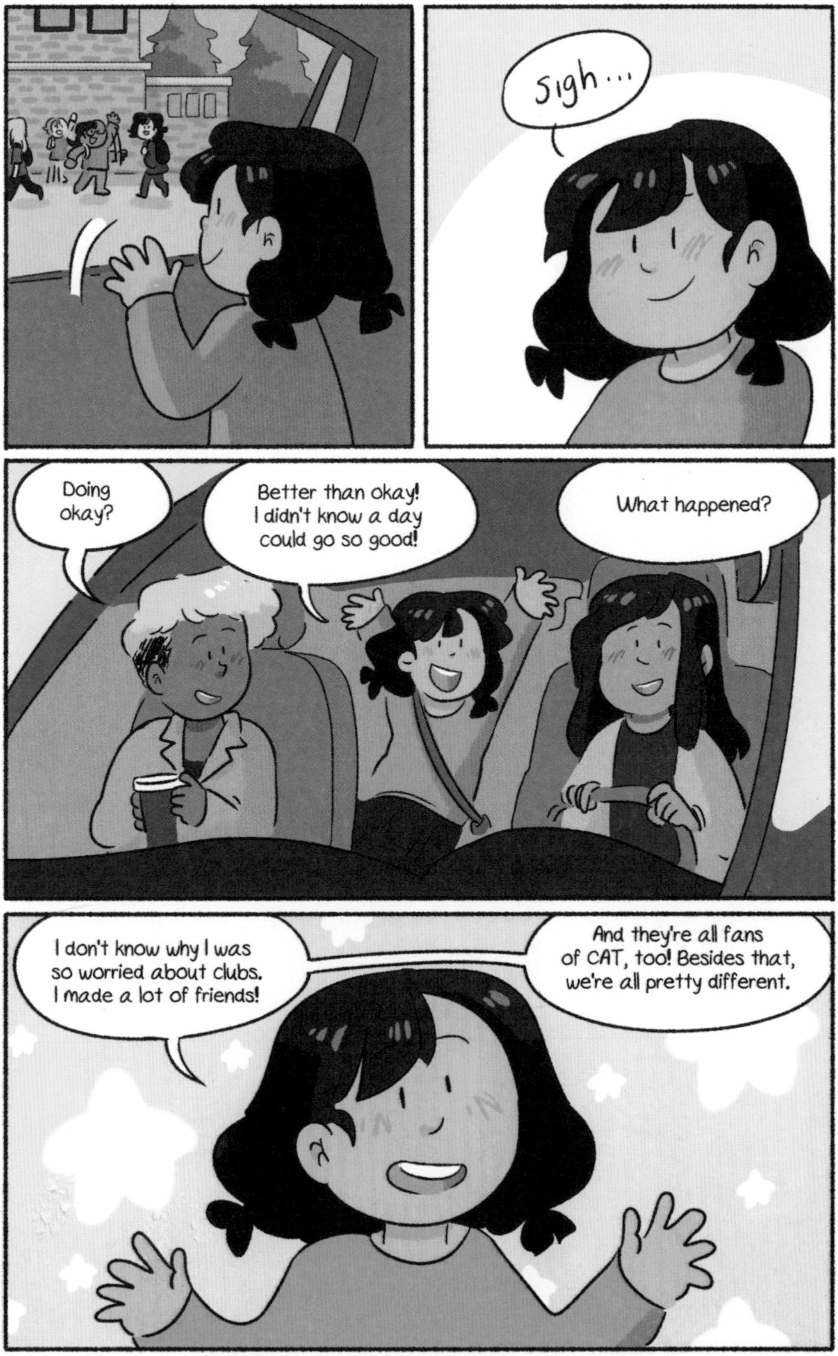
Sigh...
Doing okay?
Better than okay! I didn't know a day could go so good!
What happened?
I don't know why I was so worried about clubs. I made a lot of friends!
And they're all fans of CAT, too! Besides that, we're all pretty different.

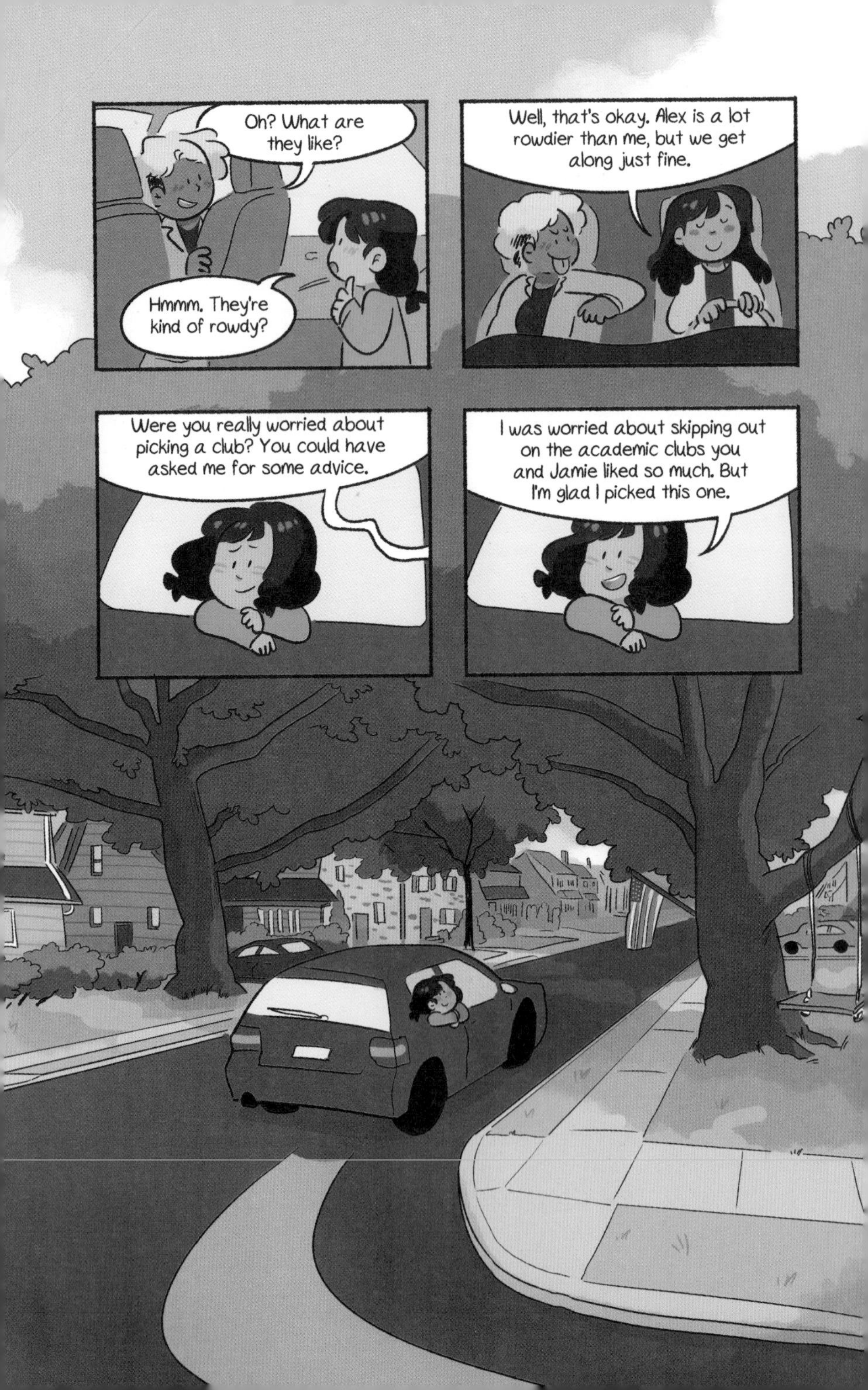
Oh? What are they like?
Hmmm. They're kind of rowdy?
Well, that's okay. Alex is a lot rowdier than me, but we get along just fine.
Were you really worried about picking a club? You could have asked me for some advice.
I was worried about skipping out on the academic clubs you and Jamie liked so much. But I'm glad I picked this one.

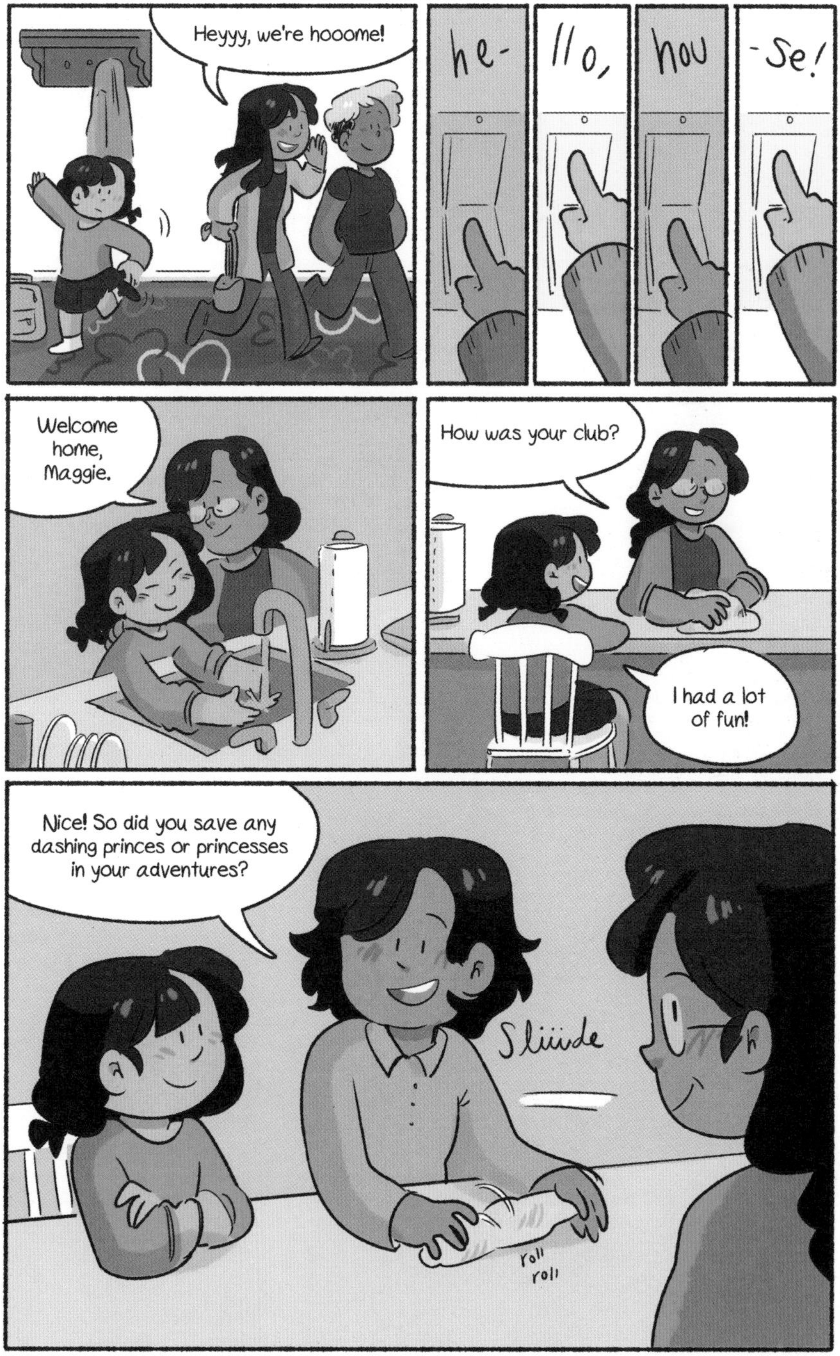
Heyyy, we're hooome!
he-
llo,
hou
-se!
Welcome home, Maggie.
How was your club?
I had a lot of fun!
Nice! So did you save any dashing princes or princesses in your adventures?
Sliiide
roll roll

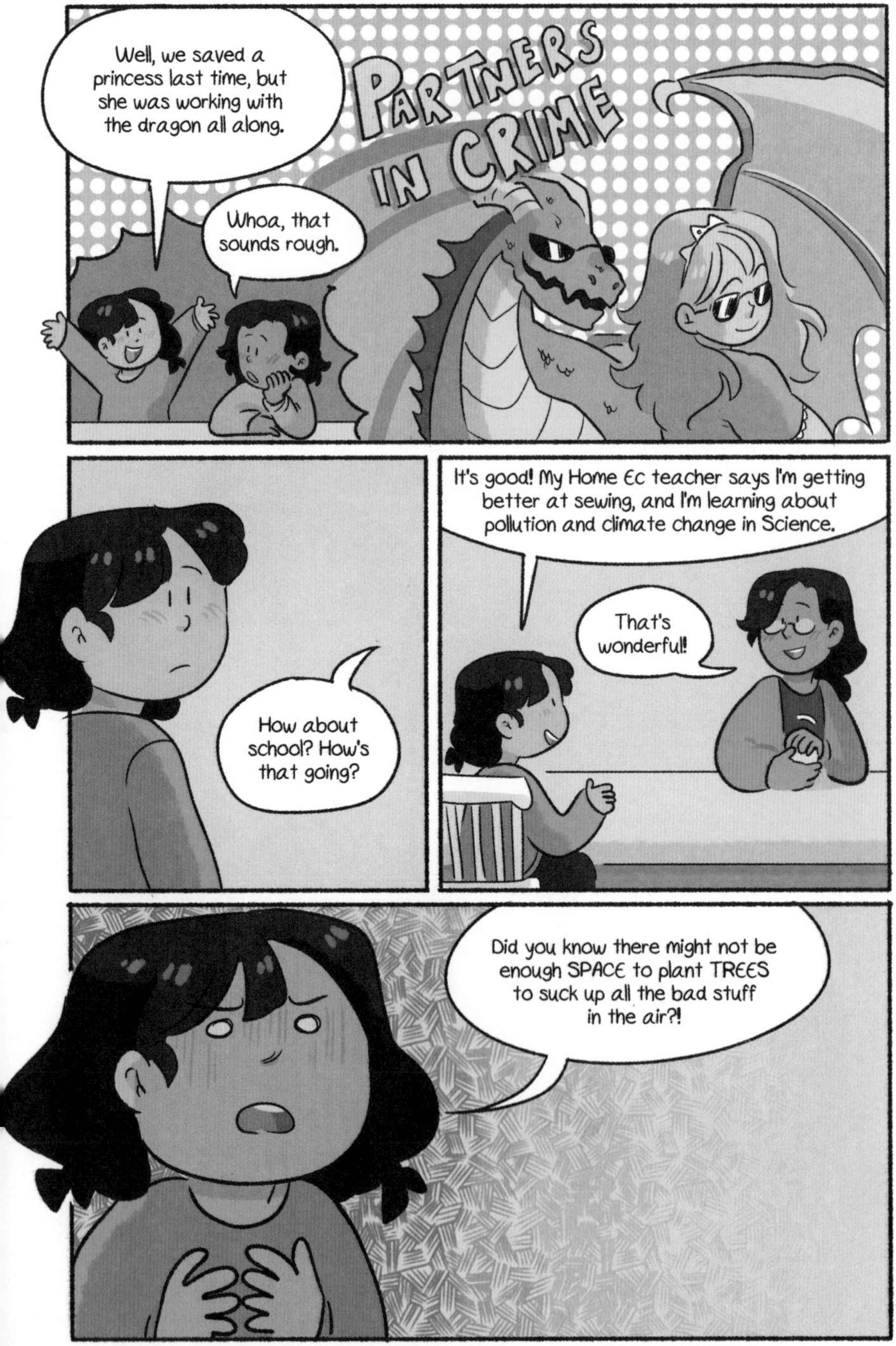
Well, we saved a princess last time, but she was working with the dragon all along.
PARTNERS IN CRIME
Whoa, that sounds rough.
How about school? How's that going?
It's good! My Home Ec teacher says I'm getting better at sewing, and I'm learning about pollution and climate change in Science.
That's wonderful!
Did you know there might not be enough SPACE to plant TREES to suck up all the bad stuff in the air?!

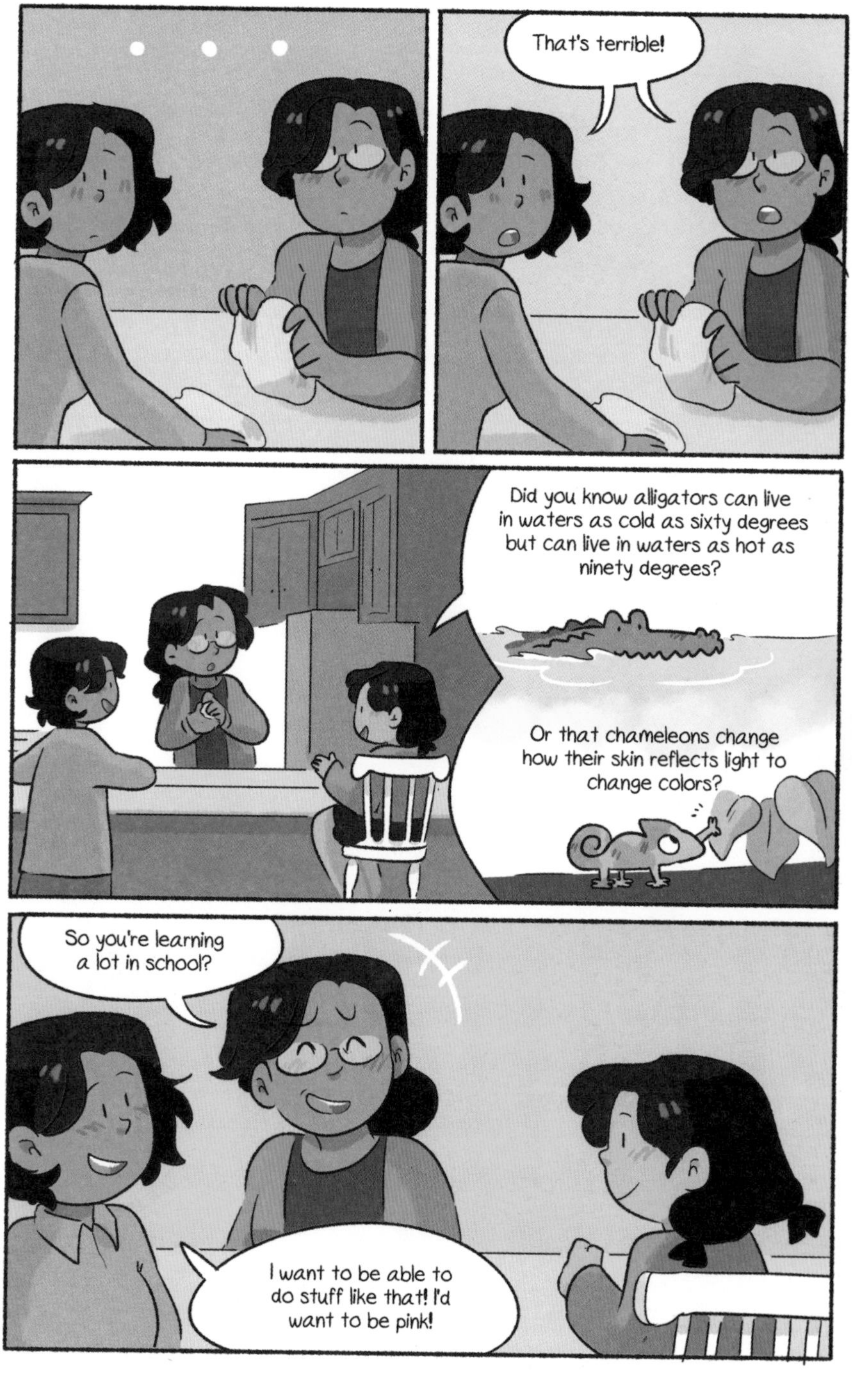
That's terrible!
Did you know alligators can live in waters as cold as sixty degrees but can live in waters as hot as ninety degrees?
Or that chameleons change how their skin reflects light to change colors?
So you're learning a lot in school?
I want to be able to do stuff like that! I'd want to be pink!

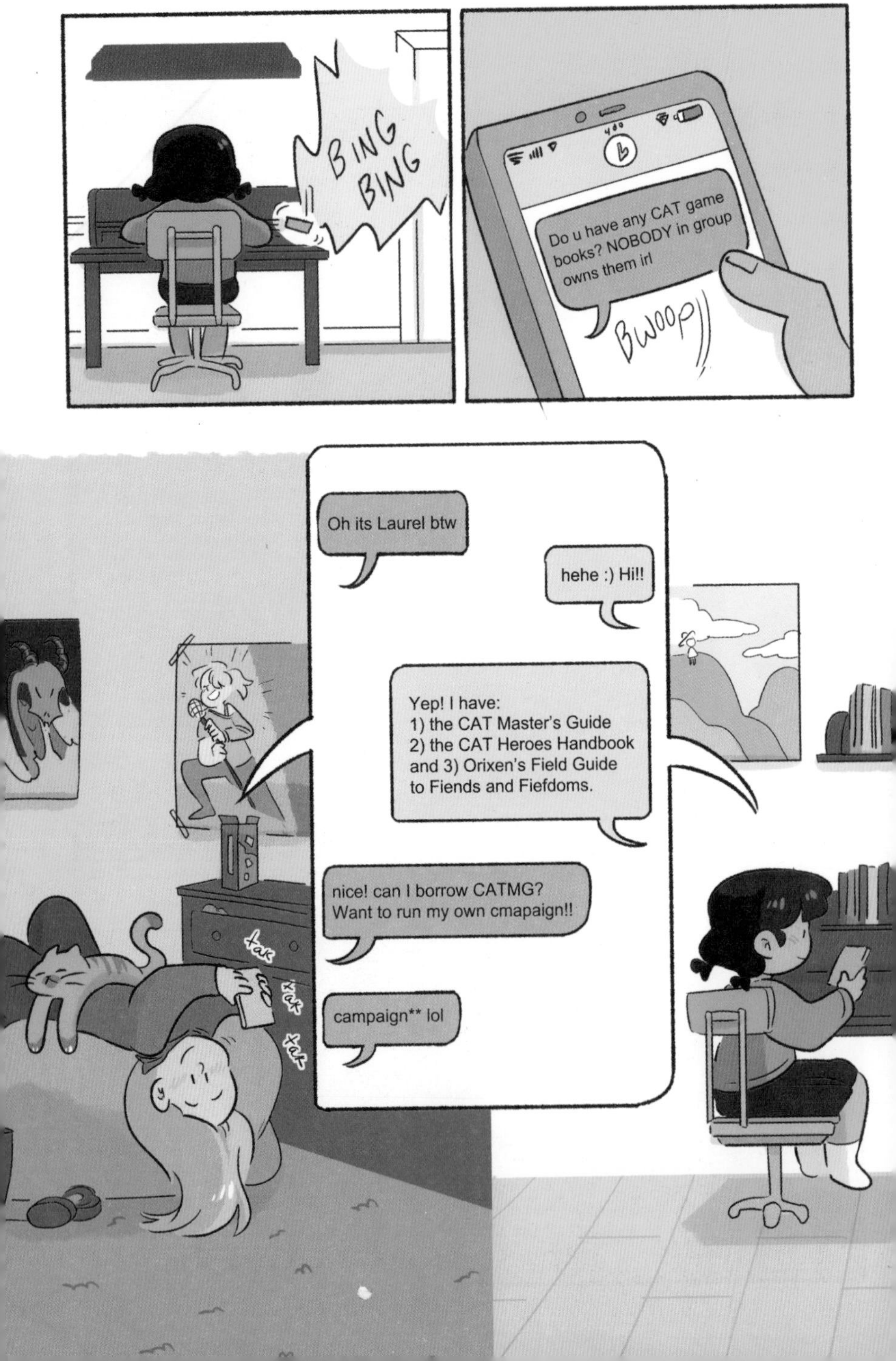
BING
BING
Do u have any CAT game books? NOBODY in group owns them irl
BWOOP
Oh its Laurel btw
hehe :) Hi!!
Yep! I have:
1) the CAT Master's Guide
2) the CAT Heroes Handbook
and 3) Orixen's Field Guide to Fiends and Fiefdoms.
nice! can I borrow CATMG? Want to run my own cmapaign!!
tak tak tak
campaign** lol

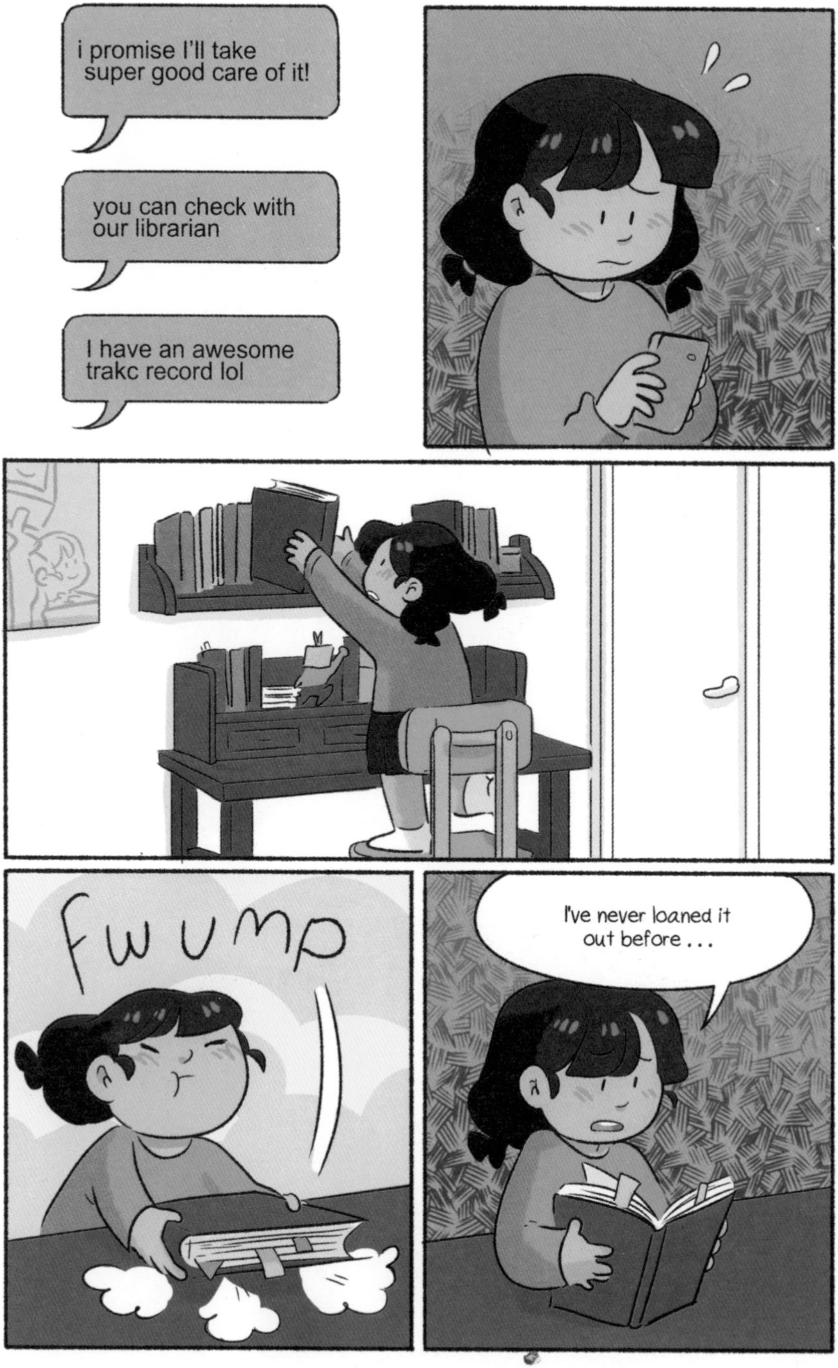
i promise I'll take super good care of it!
you can check with our librarian
I have an awesome trakc record lol
FWUMP
I've never loaned it out before . . .

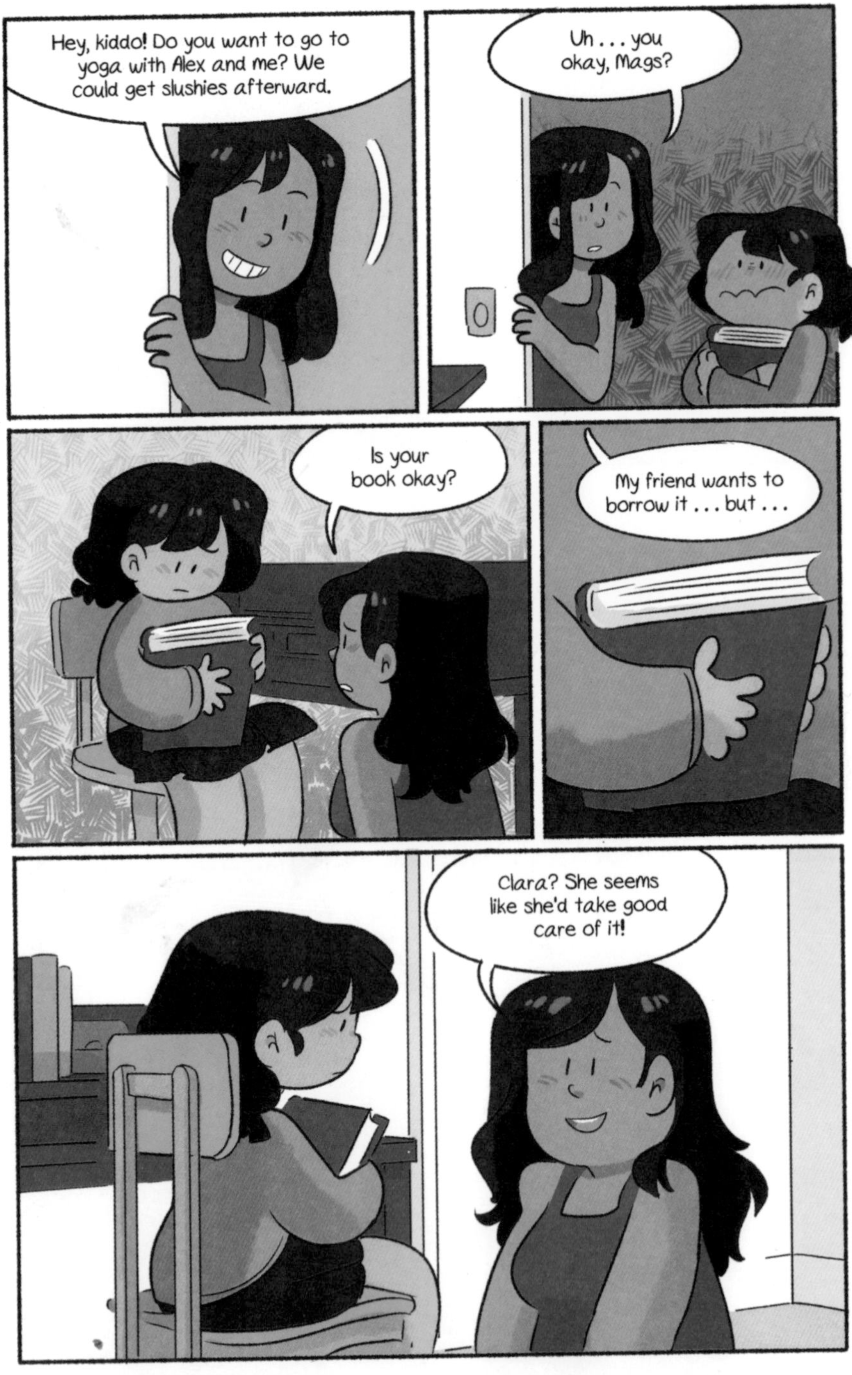

Hey, kiddo! Do you want to go to yoga with Alex and me? We could get slushies afterward.
Uh . . . you okay, Mags?
Is your book okay?
My friend wants to borrow it . . . but . . .
Clara? She seems like she'd take good care of it!

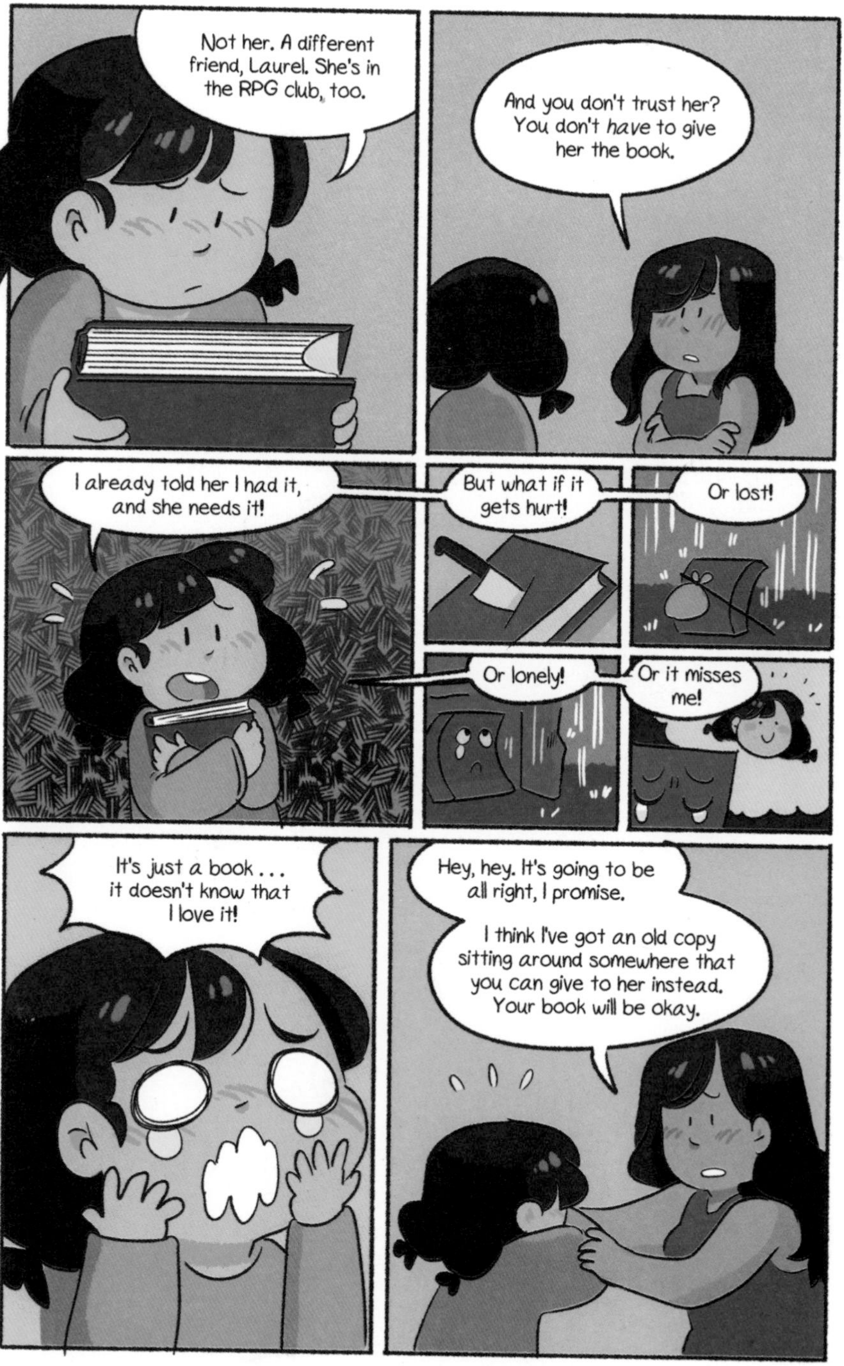
Not her. A different friend, Laurel. She's in the RPG club, too.
And you don't trust her? You don't *have* to give her the book.
I already told her I had it, and she needs it!
But what if it gets hurt!
Or lost!
Or lonely!
Or it misses me!
It's just a book . . . it doesn't know that I love it!
Hey, hey. It's going to be all right, I promise.
I think I've got an old copy sitting around somewhere that you can give to her instead. Your book will be okay.

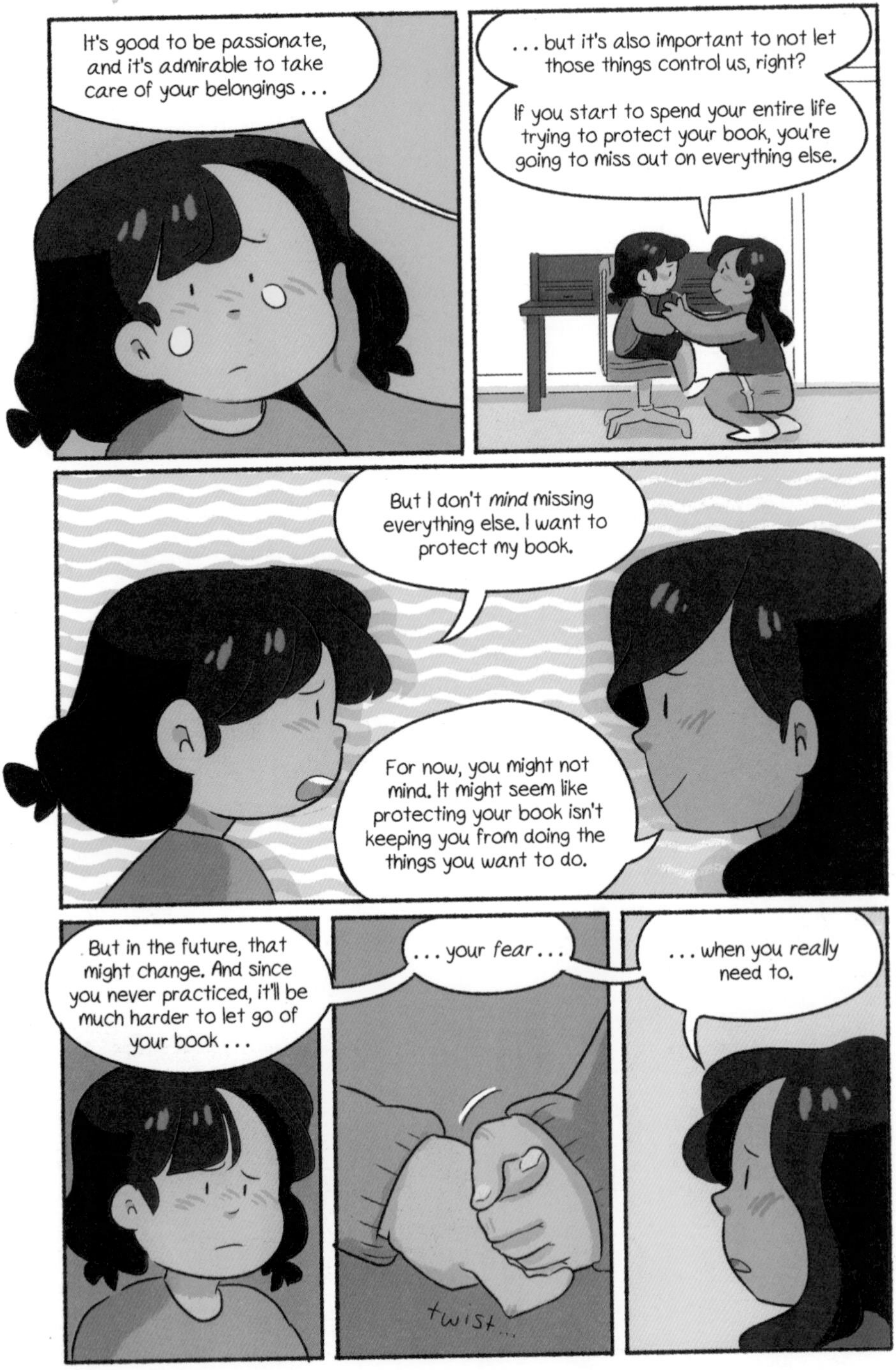
It's good to be passionate, and it's admirable to take care of your belongings . . .
. . . but it's also important to not let those things control us, right?
If you start to spend your entire life trying to protect your book, you're going to miss out on everything else.
But I don't *mind* missing everything else. I want to protect my book.
For now, you might not mind. It might seem like protecting your book isn't keeping you from doing the things you want to do.
But in the future, that might change. And since you never practiced, it'll be much harder to let go of your book . . .
. . . your *fear* . . .
. . . when you *really* need to.
twist . . .

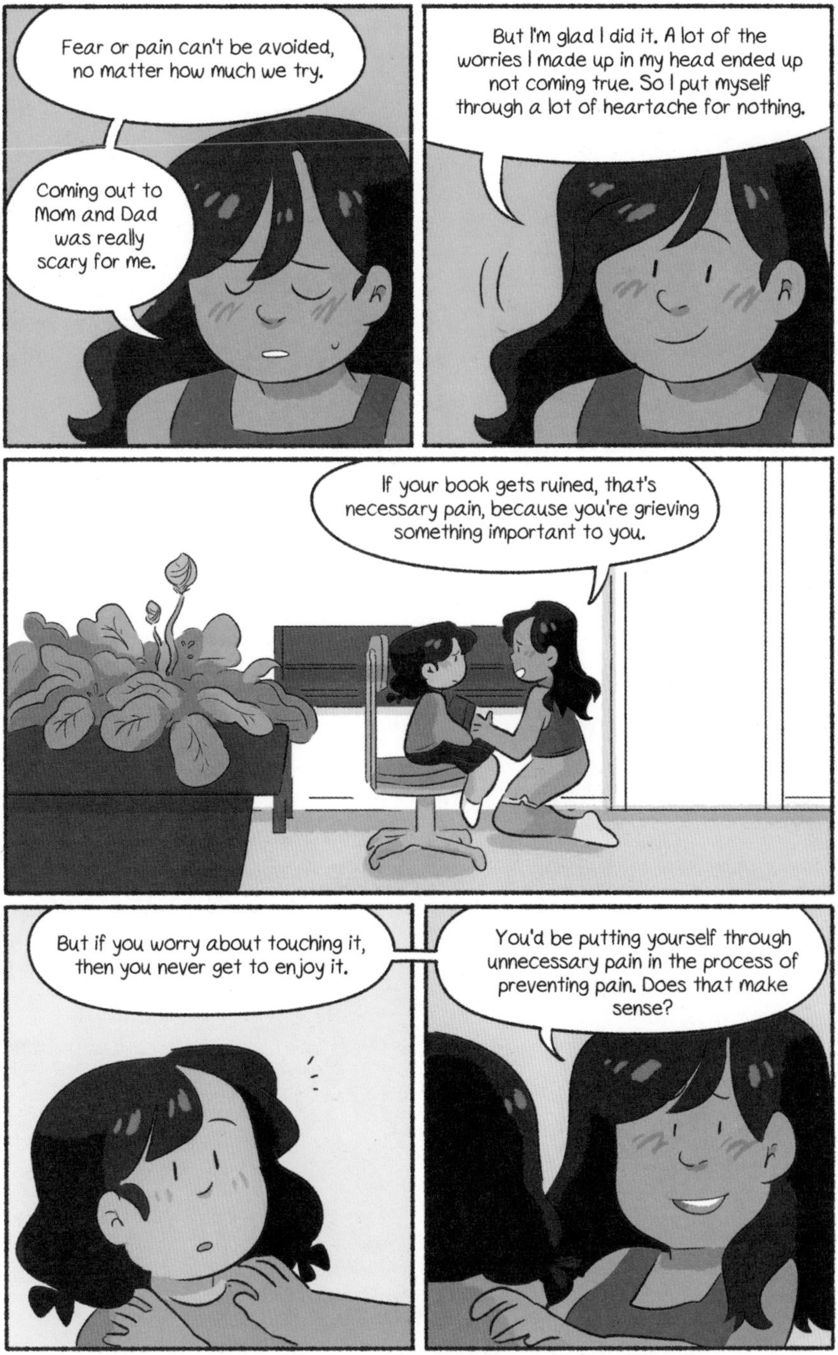
Fear or pain can't be avoided, no matter how much we try.
Coming out to Mom and Dad was really scary for me.
But I'm glad I did it. A lot of the worries I made up in my head ended up not coming true. So I put myself through a lot of heartache for nothing.
If your book gets ruined, that's necessary pain, because you're grieving something important to you.
But if you worry about touching it, then you never get to enjoy it.
You'd be putting yourself through unnecessary pain in the process of preventing pain. Does that make sense?

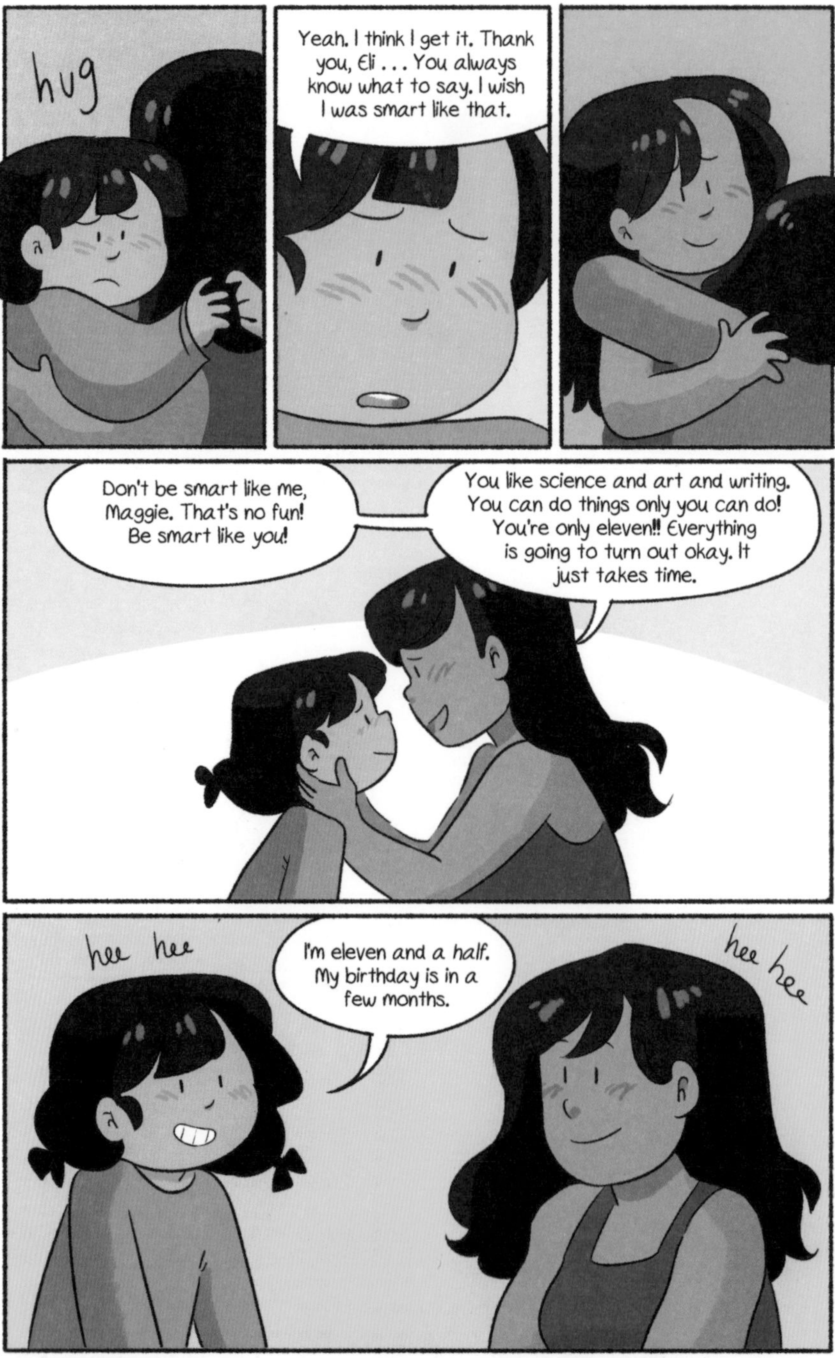
hug
Yeah. I think I get it. Thank you, Eli . . . You always know what to say. I wish I was smart like that.
Don't be smart like me, Maggie. That's no fun! Be smart like you!
You like science and art and writing. You can do things only you can do! You're only eleven!! Everything is going to turn out okay. It just takes time.
hee hee
I'm eleven and a half. My birthday is in a few months.
hee hee

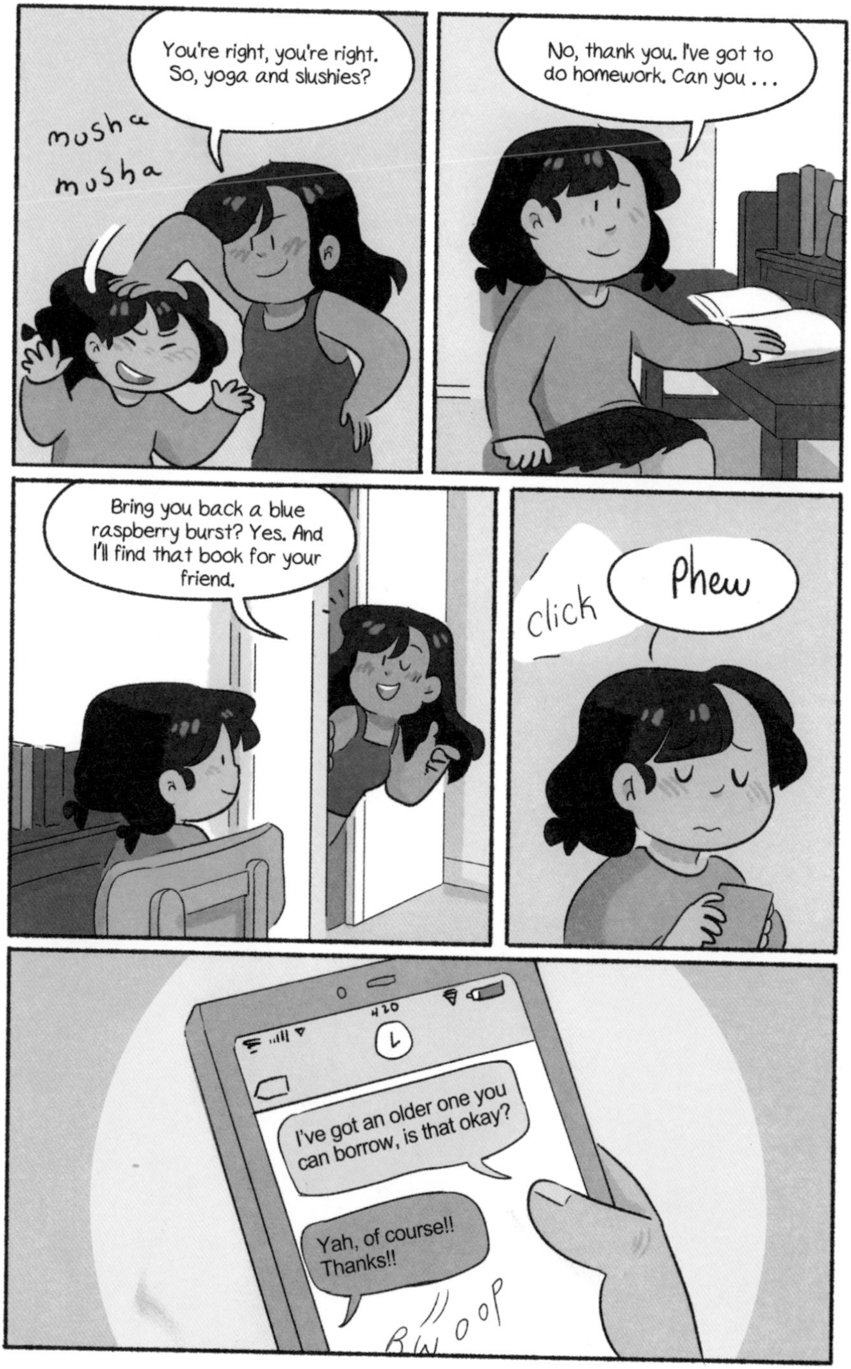
You're right, you're right. So, yoga and slushies?
musha musha
No, thank you. I've got to do homework. Can you . . .
Bring you back a blue raspberry burst? Yes. And I'll find that book for your friend.
click
Phew
I've got an older one you can borrow, is that okay?
Yah, of course!! Thanks!!
BWOOP

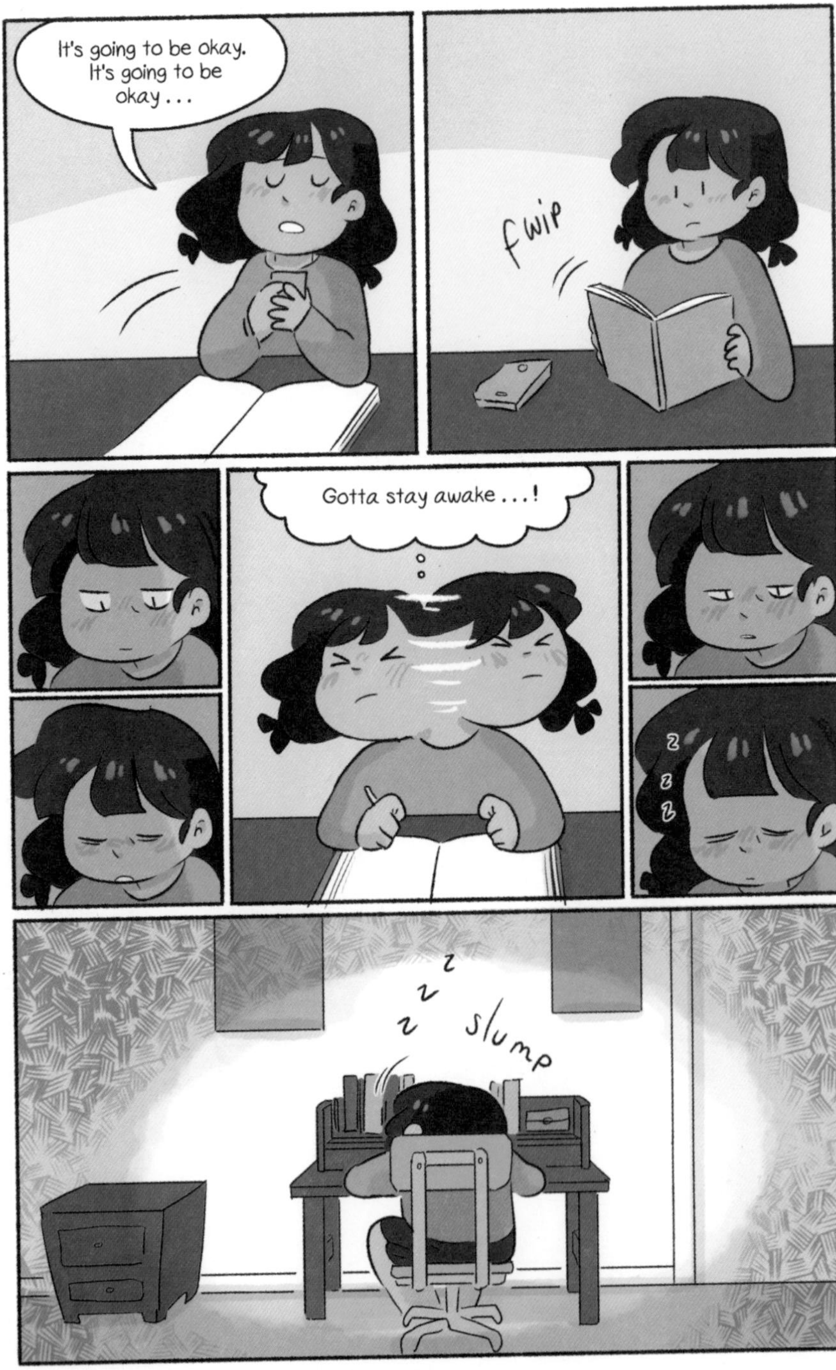
It's going to be okay. It's going to be okay...
fwip
Gotta stay awake...!
z
z
z
z
z
z
slump

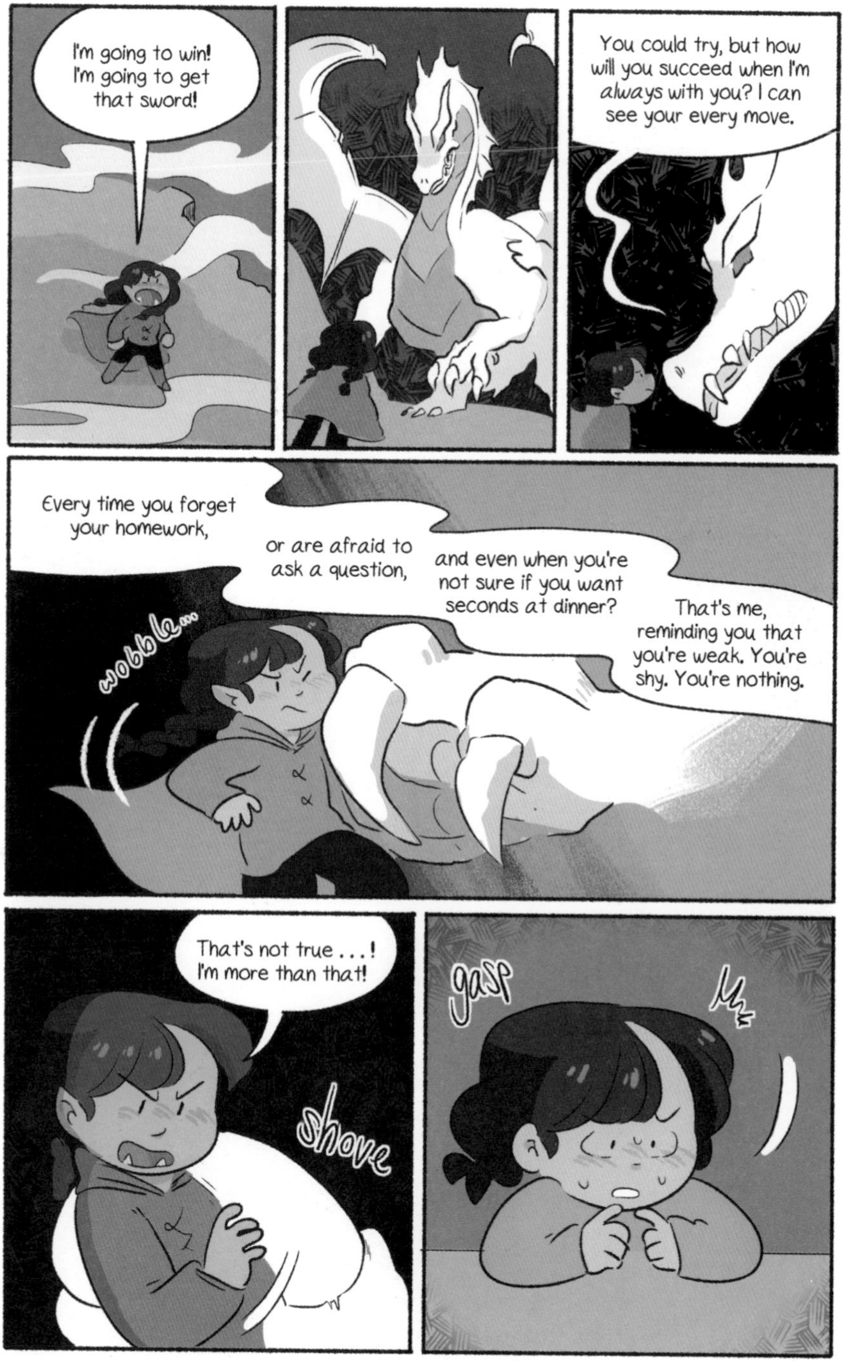
I'm going to win! I'm going to get that sword!
You could try, but how will you succeed when I'm *always* with you? I can see your every move.
Every time you forget your homework,
or are afraid to ask a question,
and even when you're not sure if you want seconds at dinner?
That's me, reminding you that you're weak. You're shy. You're nothing.
wobble...
That's not true . . . ! I'm more than that!
shove
gasp

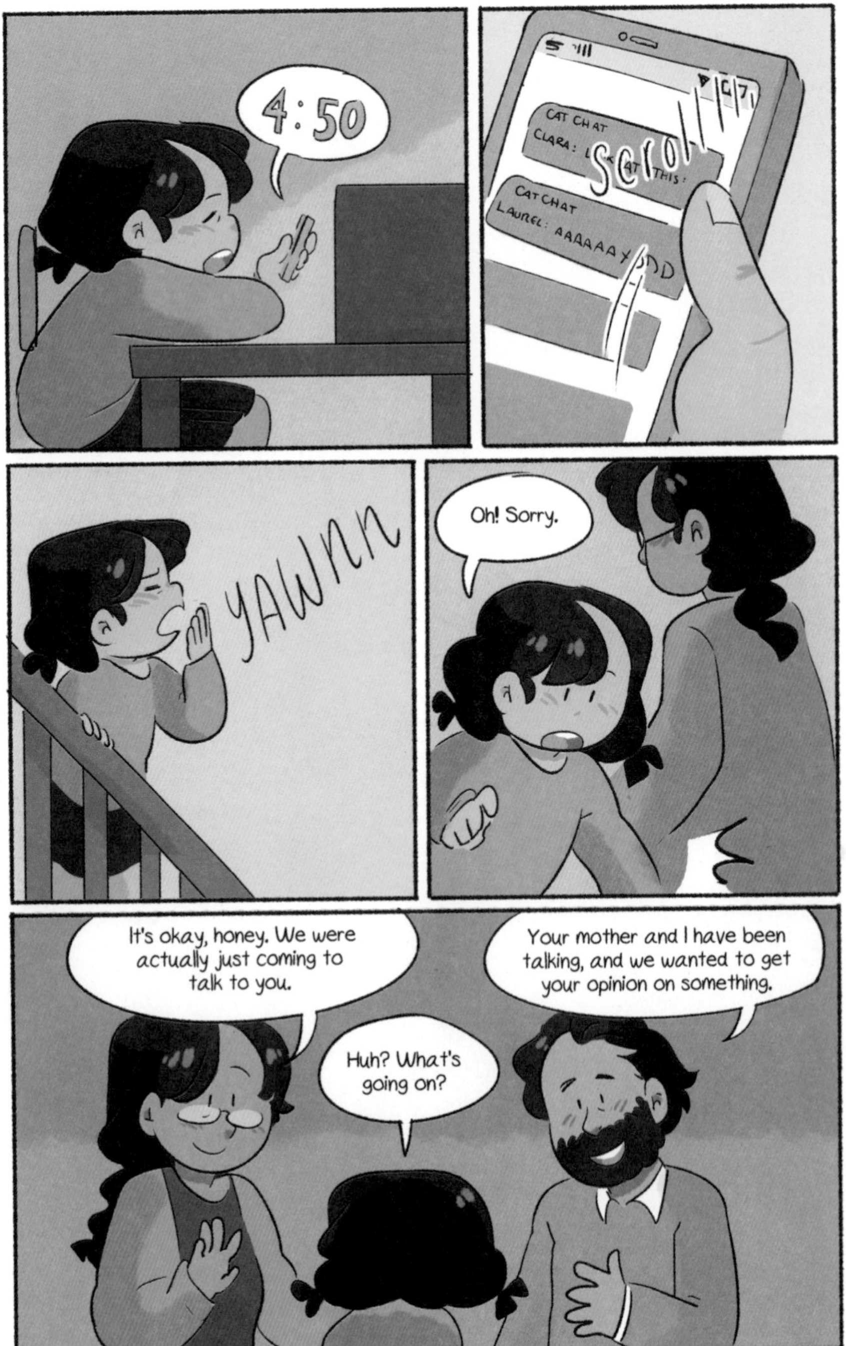
4:50
CAT CHAT
CLARA:
THIS!
SCROLL
CAT CHAT
LAUREL: AAAAAAY
YAWNN
Oh! Sorry.
It's okay, honey. We were actually just coming to talk to you.
Your mother and I have been talking, and we wanted to get your opinion on something.
Huh? What's going on?

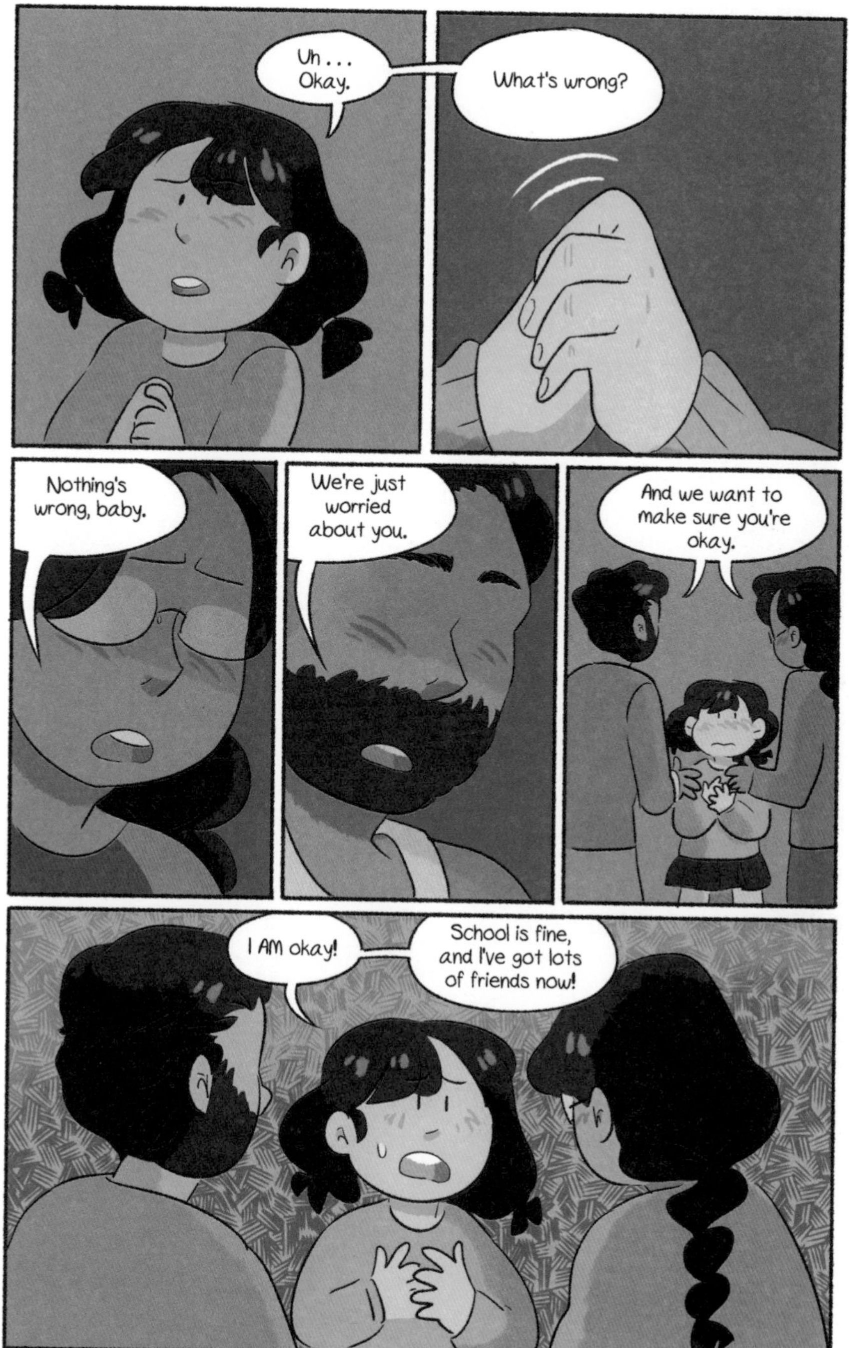
Uh . . .
Okay.
What's wrong?
Nothing's wrong, baby.
We're just worried about you.
And we want to make sure you're okay.
I AM okay!
School is fine, and I've got lots of friends now!

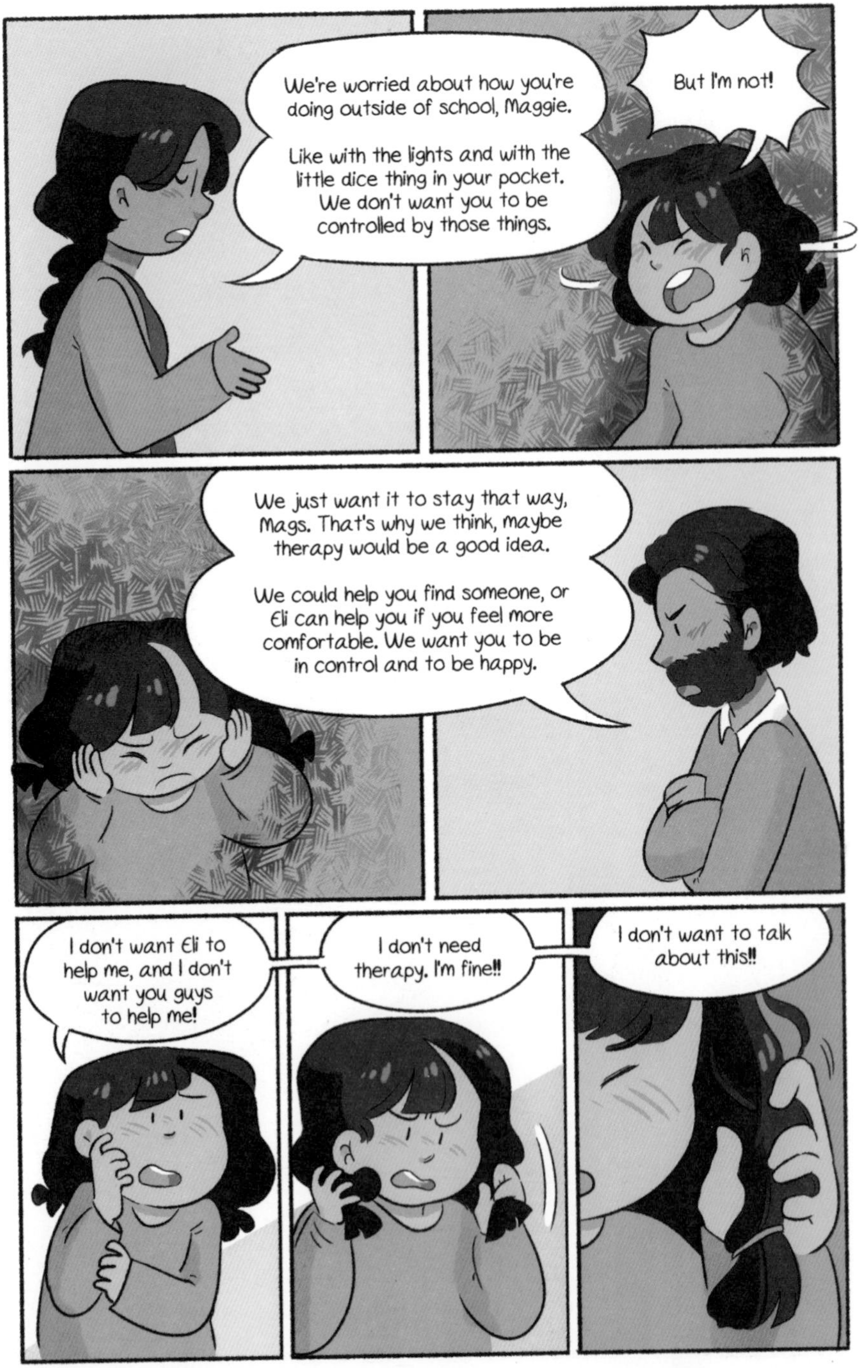
We're worried about how you're doing outside of school, Maggie.
Like with the lights and with the little dice thing in your pocket. We don't want you to be controlled by those things.
But I'm not!
We just want it to stay that way, Mags. That's why we think, maybe therapy would be a good idea.
We could help you find someone, or Eli can help you if you feel more comfortable. We want you to be in control and to be happy.
I don't want Eli to help me, and I don't want you guys to help me!
I don't need therapy. I'm fine!!
I don't want to talk about this!!

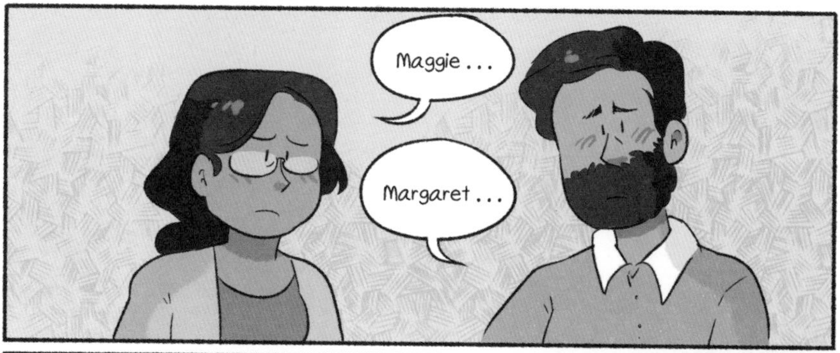
Maggie . . .
Margaret . . .

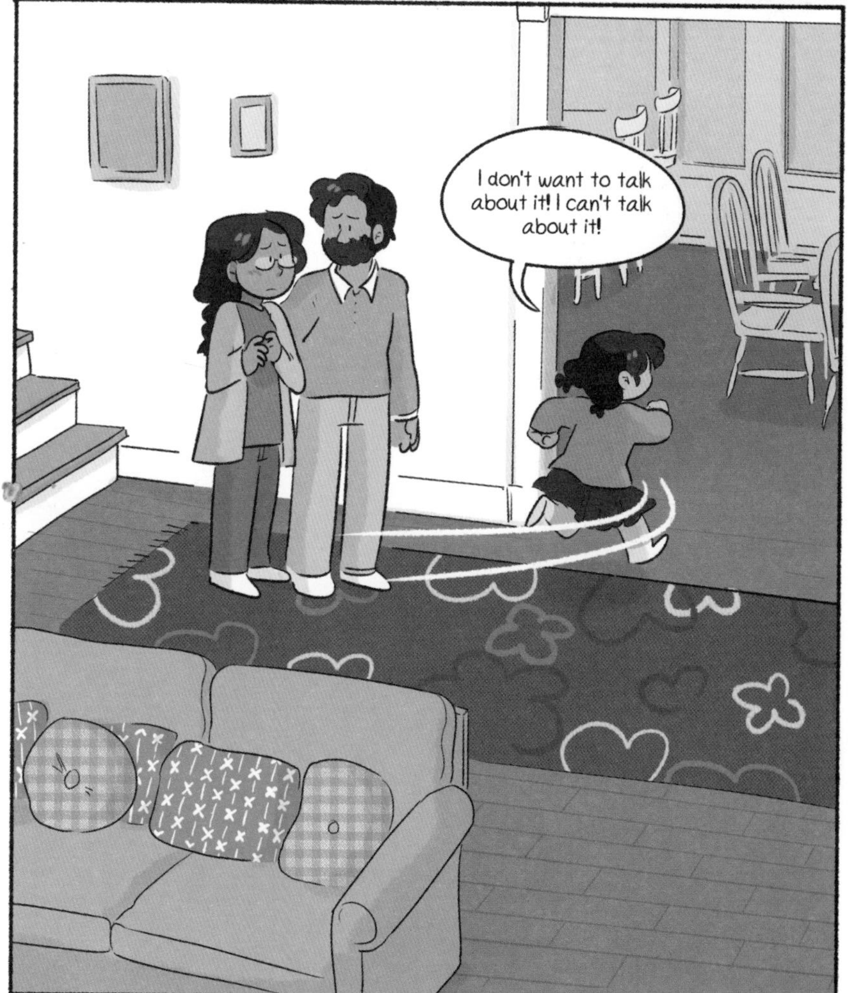
I don't want to talk about it! I can't talk about it!

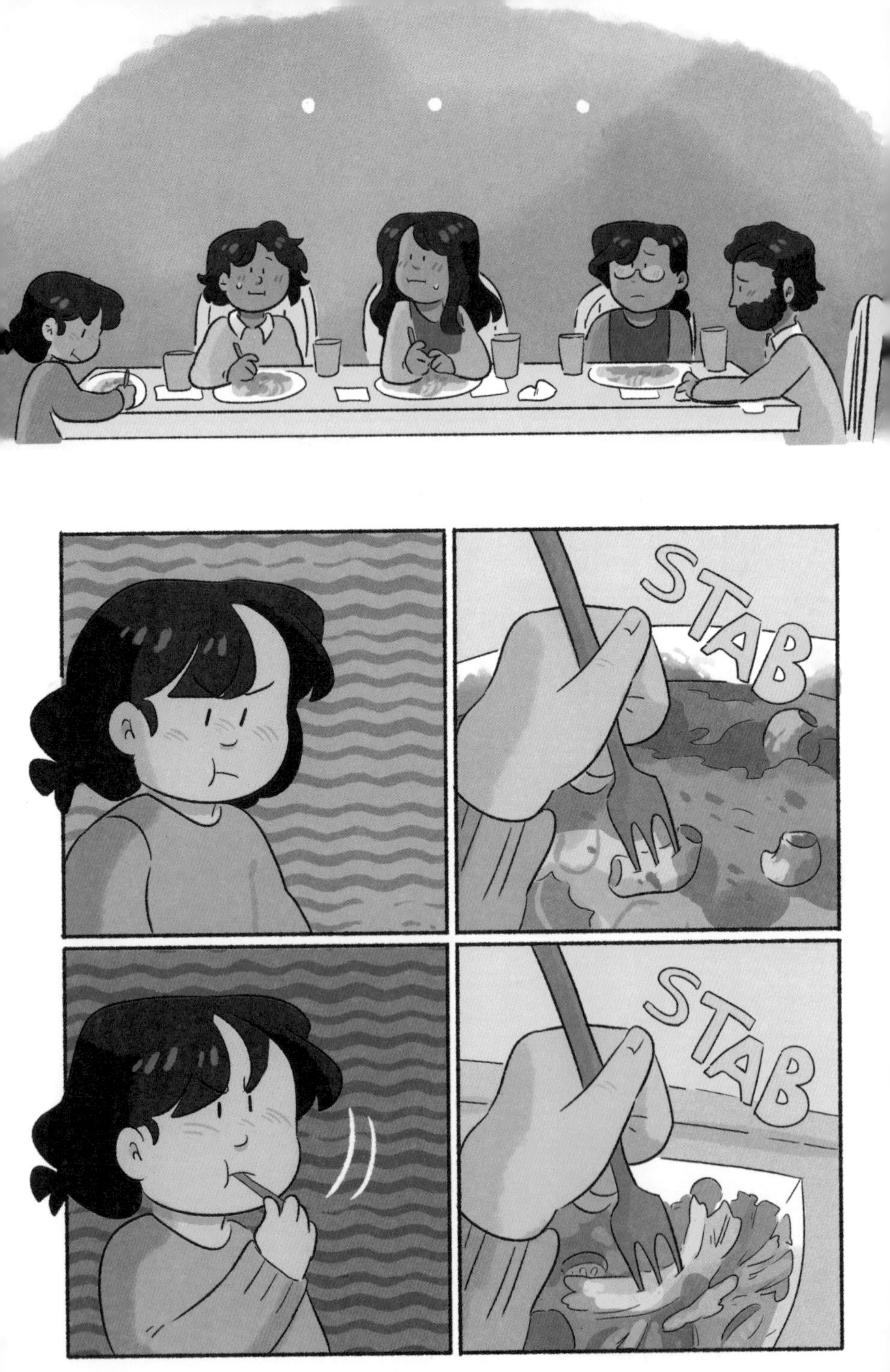
STAB
STAB

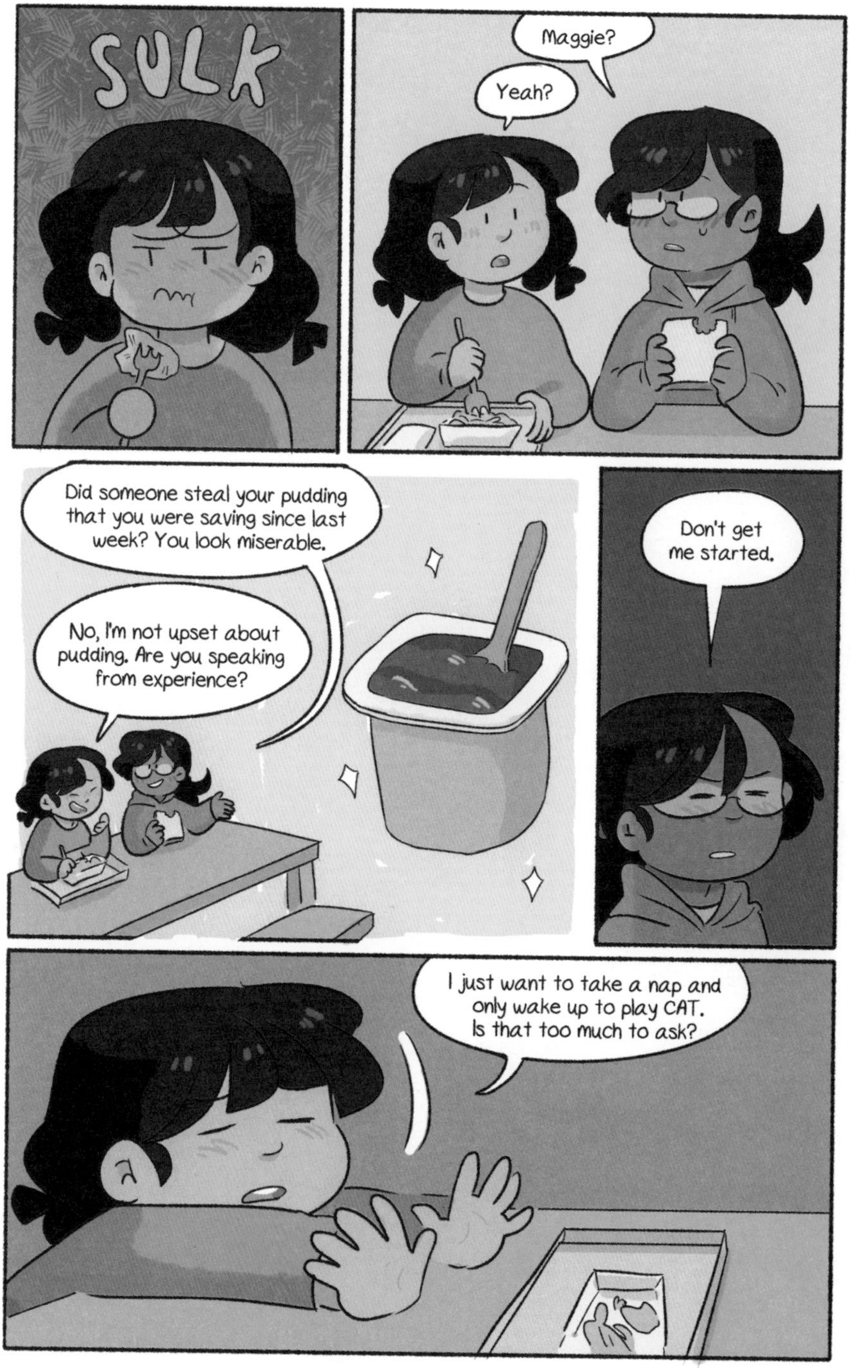
SULK
Maggie?
Yeah?
Did someone steal your pudding that you were saving since last week? You look miserable.
No, I'm not upset about pudding. Are you speaking from experience?
Don't get me started.
I just want to take a nap and only wake up to play CAT. Is that too much to ask?

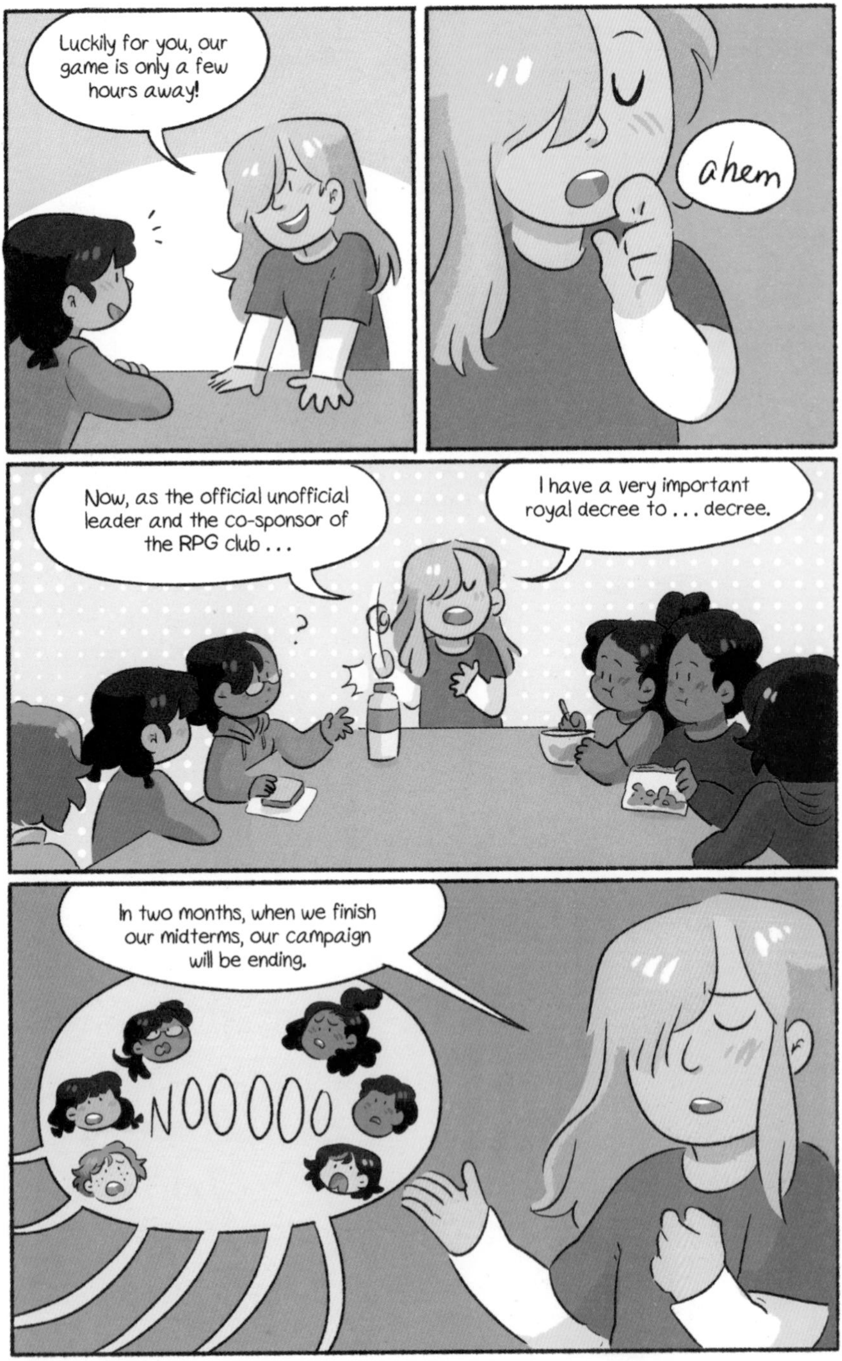
Luckily for you, our game is only a few hours away!
ahem
Now, as the official unofficial leader and the co-sponsor of the RPG club . . .
I have a very important royal decree to . . . decree.
In two months, when we finish our midterms, our campaign will be ending.
NOOOOO

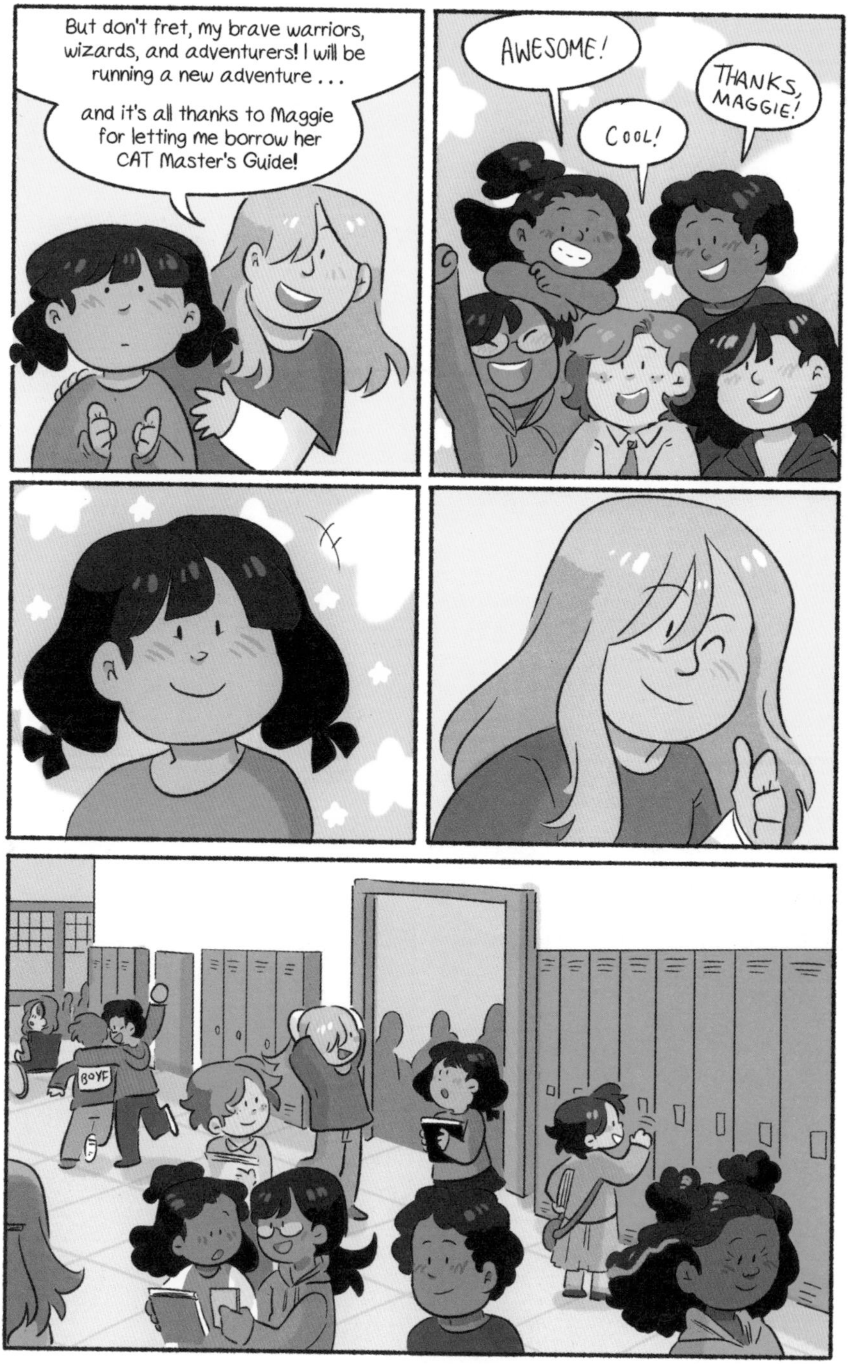
But don't fret, my brave warriors, wizards, and adventurers! I will be running a new adventure . . .
and it's all thanks to Maggie for letting me borrow her CAT Master's Guide!
AWESOME!
COOL!
THANKS, MAGGIE!
BOYF

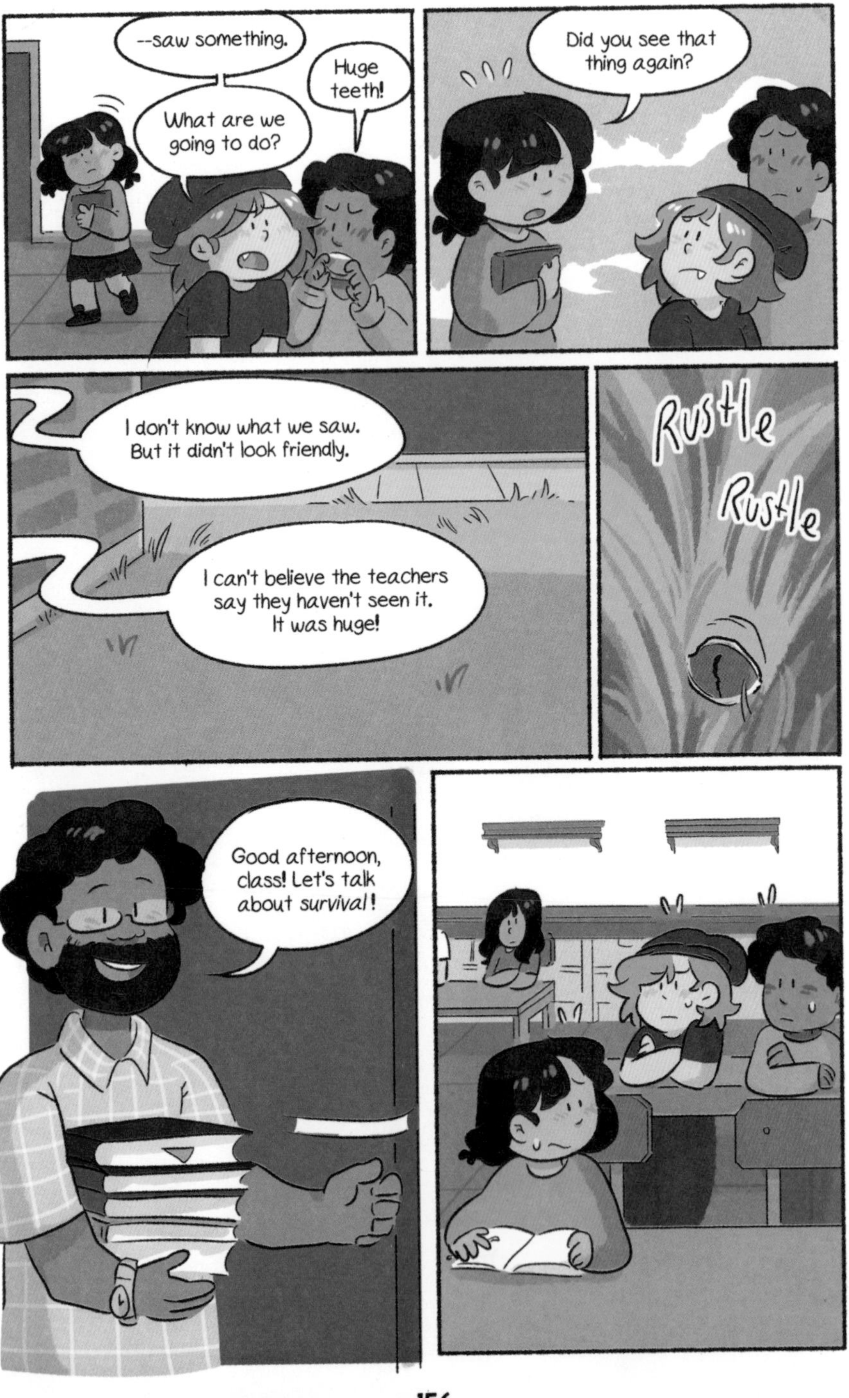

--saw something.
What are we going to do?
Huge teeth!
Did you see that thing again?
I don't know what we saw. But it didn't look friendly.
I can't believe the teachers say they haven't seen it. It was huge!
Rustle
Rustle
Good afternoon, class! Let's talk about *survival*!

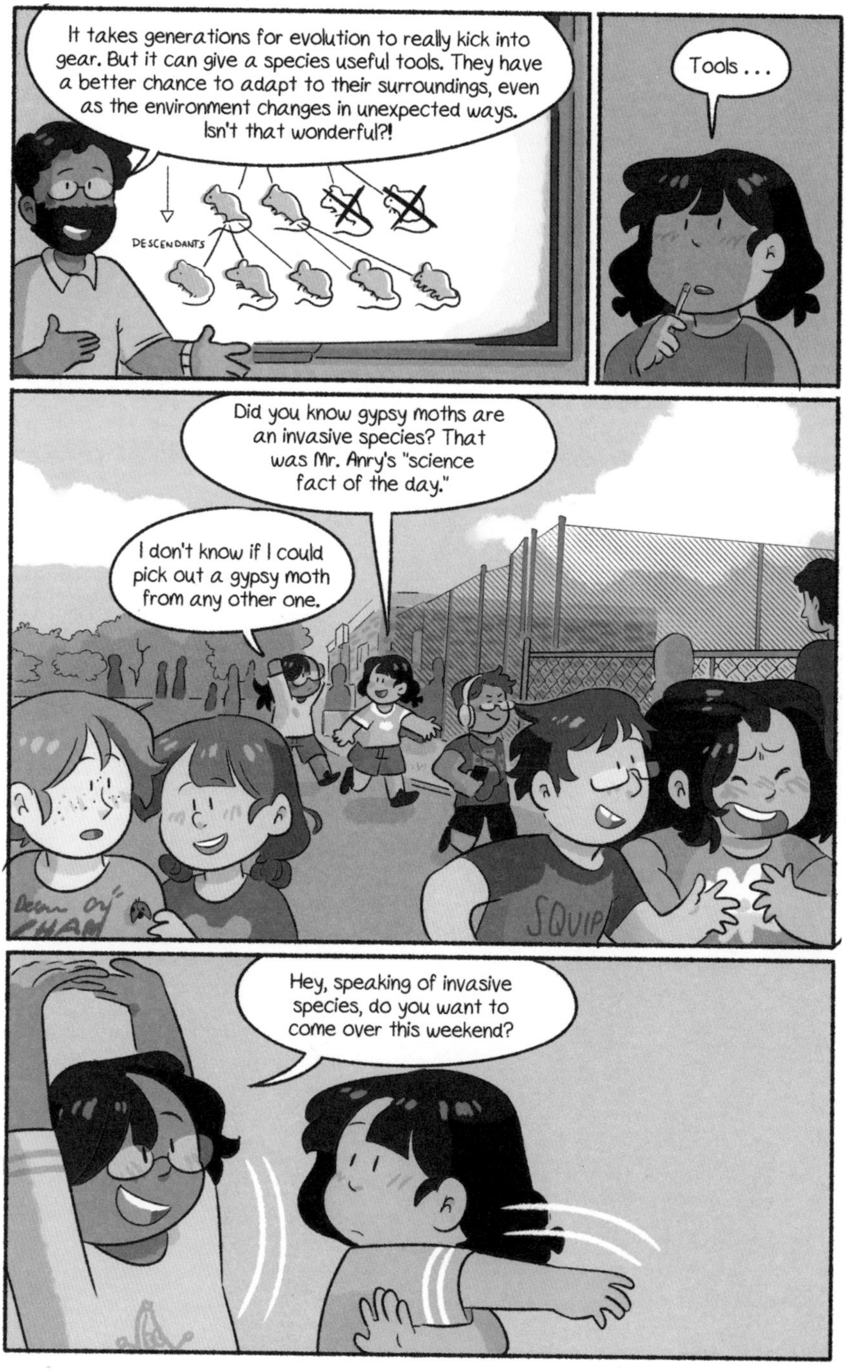
It takes generations for evolution to really kick into gear. But it can give a species useful tools. They have a better chance to adapt to their surroundings, even as the environment changes in unexpected ways. Isn't that wonderful?!
DESCENDANTS
Tools . . .
Did you know gypsy moths are an invasive species? That was Mr. Anry's "science fact of the day."
I don't know if I could pick out a gypsy moth from any other one.
SQUIP
Hey, speaking of invasive species, do you want to come over this weekend?

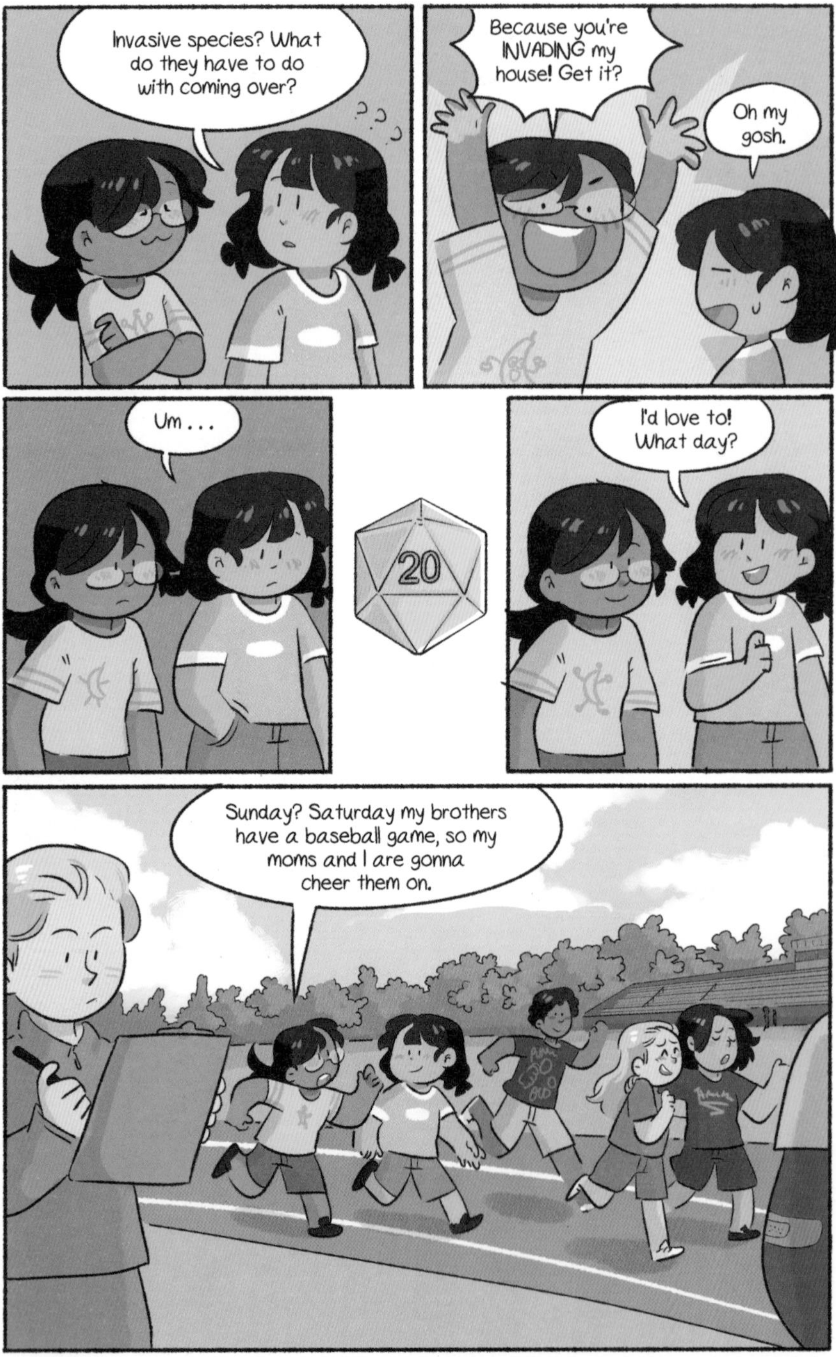
Invasive species? What do they have to do with coming over?
Because you're INVADING my house! Get it?
Oh my gosh.
Um . . .
20
I'd love to! What day?
Sunday? Saturday my brothers have a baseball game, so my moms and I are gonna cheer them on.

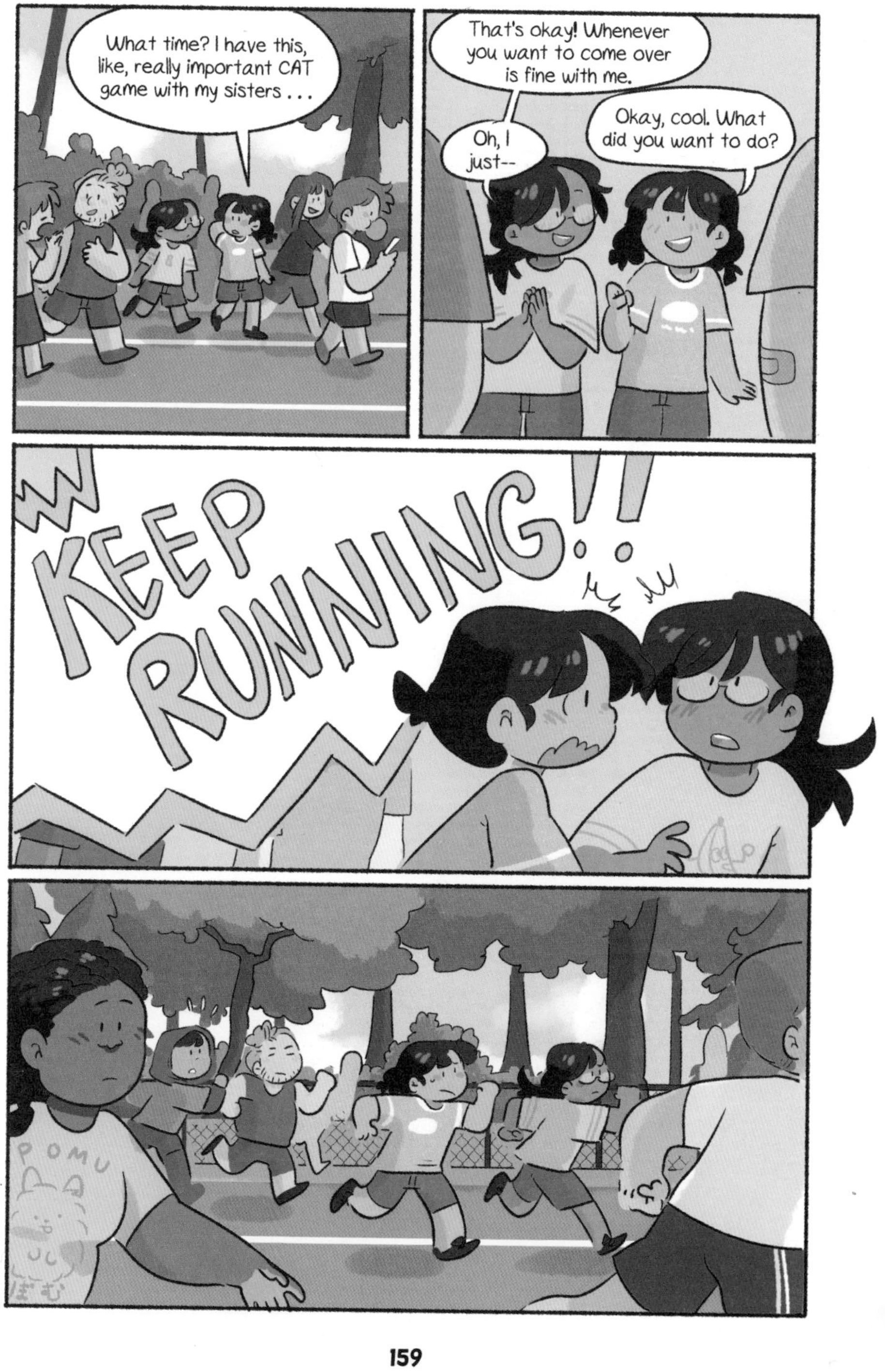
What time? I have this, like, really important CAT game with my sisters . . .
That's okay! Whenever you want to come over is fine with me.
Oh, I just--
Okay, cool. What did you want to do?
KEEP RUNNING!!
POMU
ぽむ

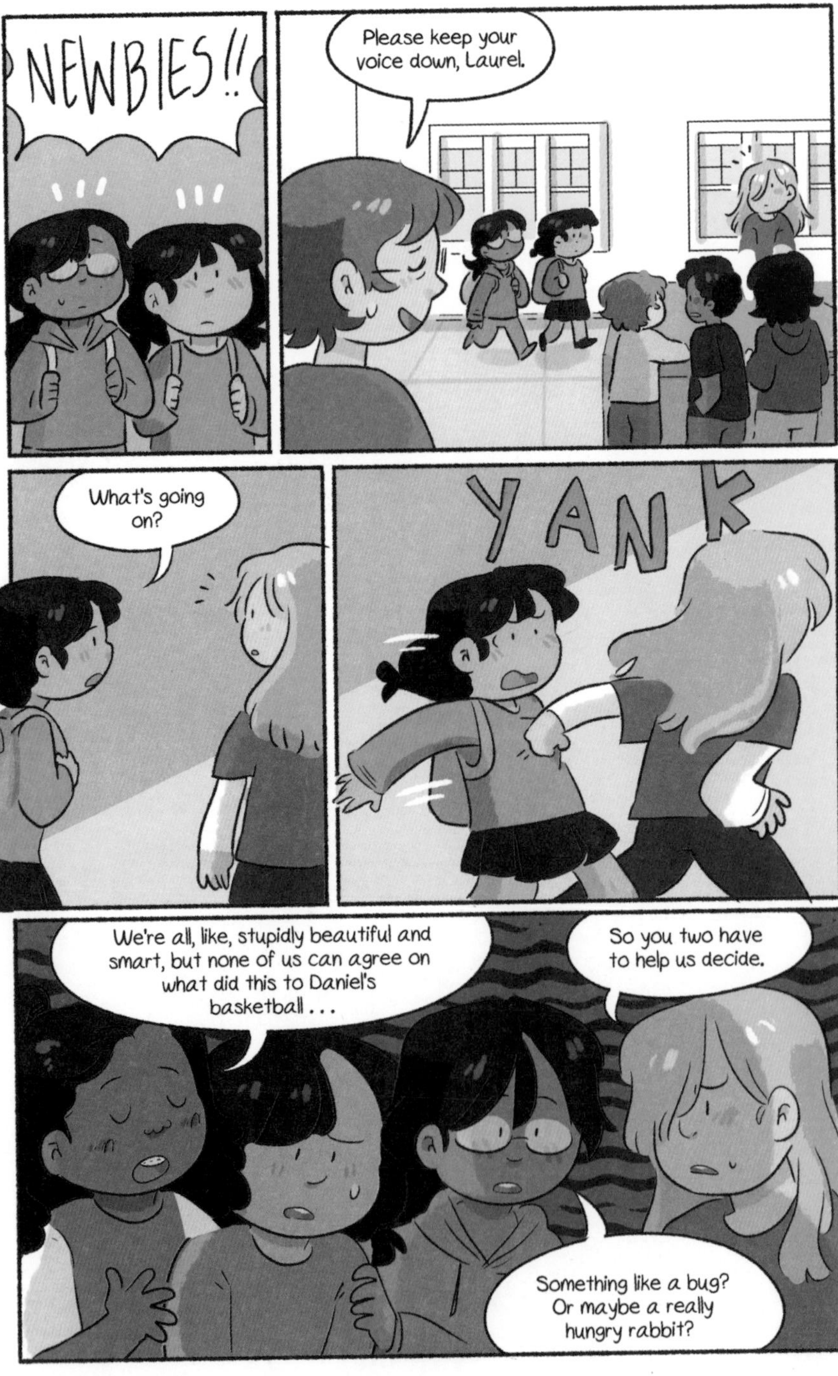
NEWBIES!!
Please keep your voice down, Laurel.
What's going on?
YANK
We're all, like, stupidly beautiful and smart, but none of us can agree on what did this to Daniel's basketball . . .
So you two have to help us decide.
Something like a bug? Or maybe a really hungry rabbit?

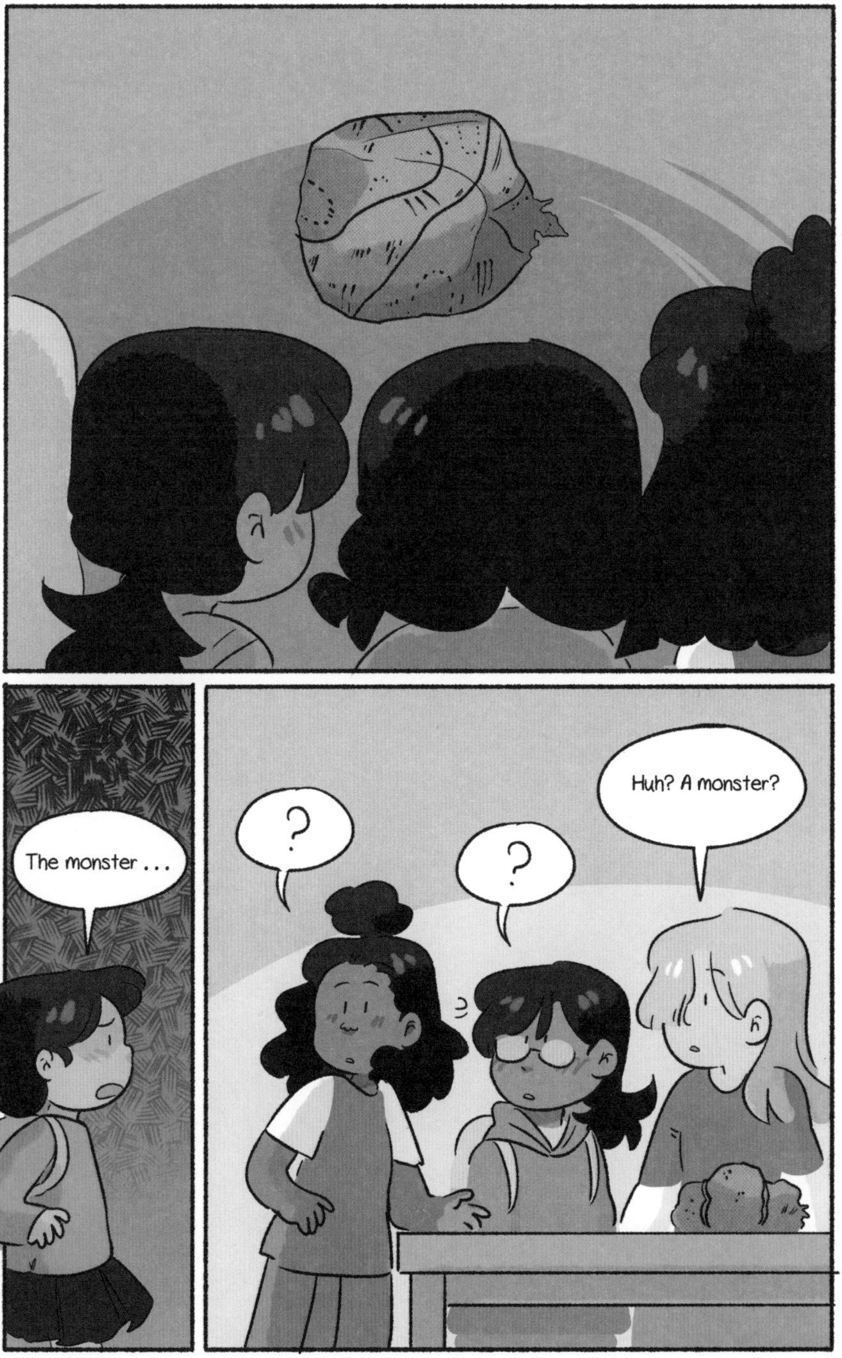
The monster . . .
?
?
Huh? A monster?

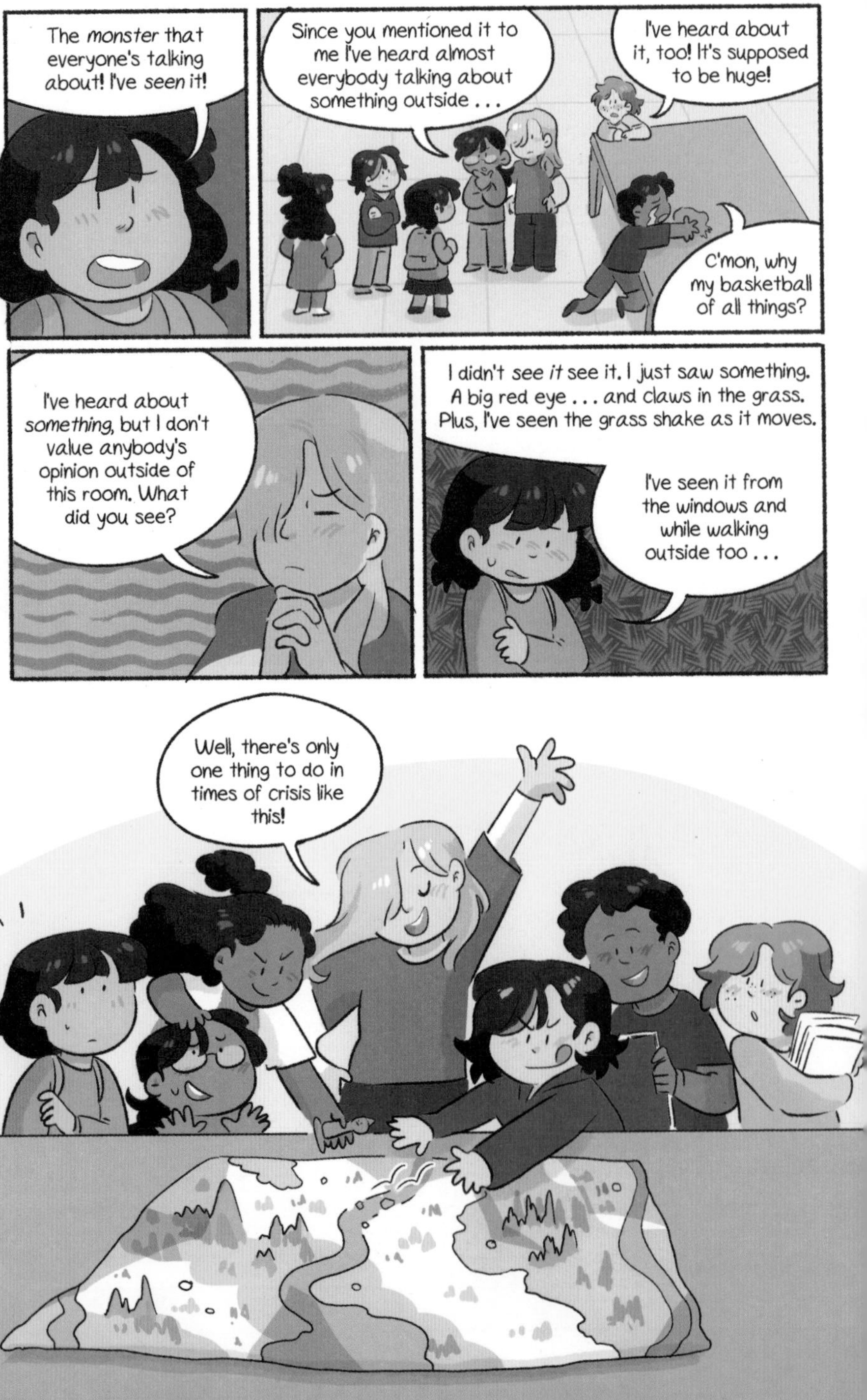
The *monster* that everyone's talking about! I've *seen* it!
Since you mentioned it to me I've heard almost everybody talking about something outside . . .
I've heard about it, too! It's supposed to be huge!
C'mon, why my basketball of all things?
I've heard about *something*, but I don't value anybody's opinion outside of this room. What did you see?
I didn't *see it* see it. I just saw something. A big red eye . . . and claws in the grass. Plus, I've seen the grass shake as it moves.
I've seen it from the windows and while walking outside too . . .
Well, there's only one thing to do in times of crisis like this!

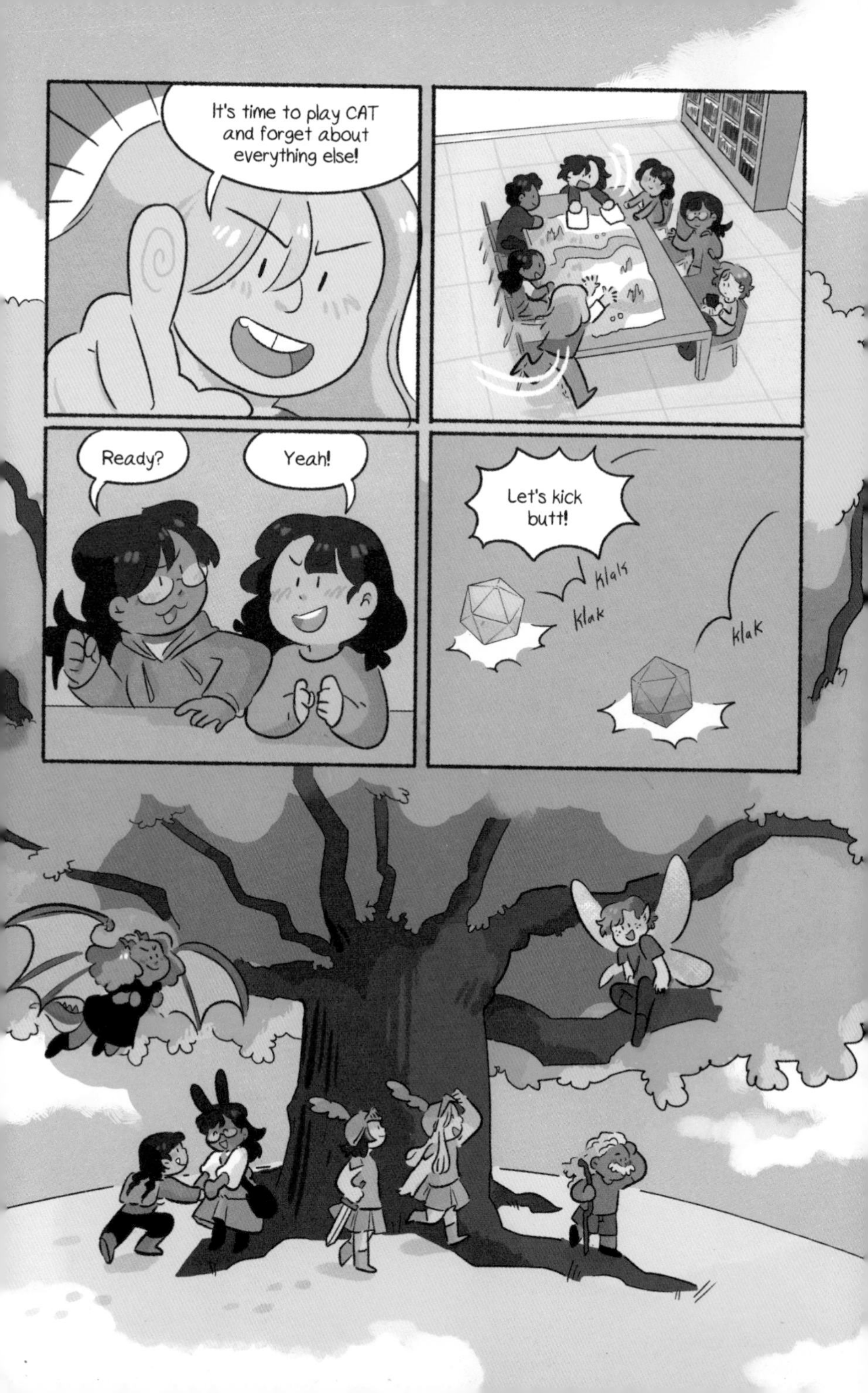
It's time to play CAT and forget about everything else!
Ready?
Yeah!
Let's kick butt!
klak
klak
klak

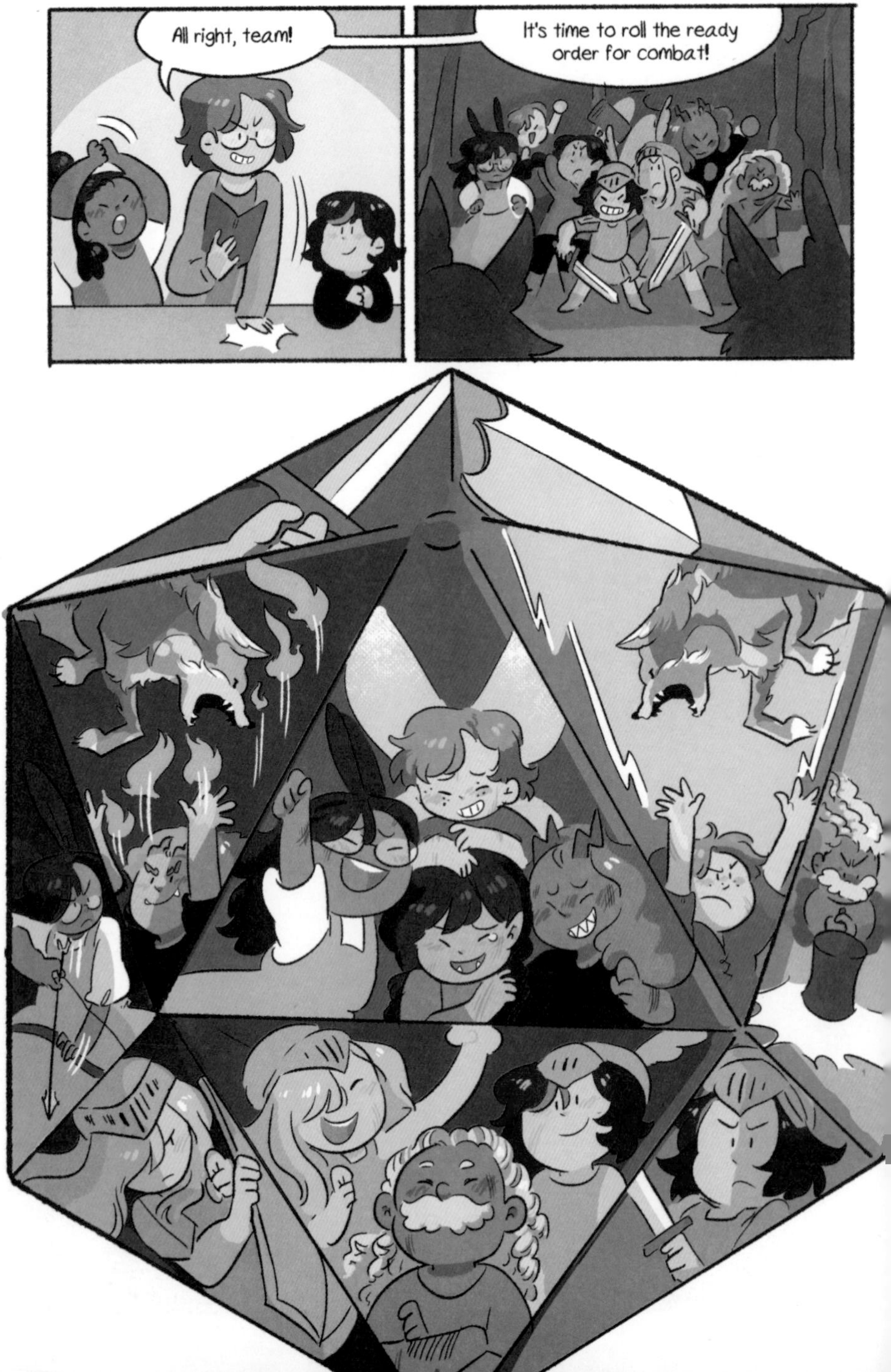
All right, team!
It's time to roll the ready order for combat!

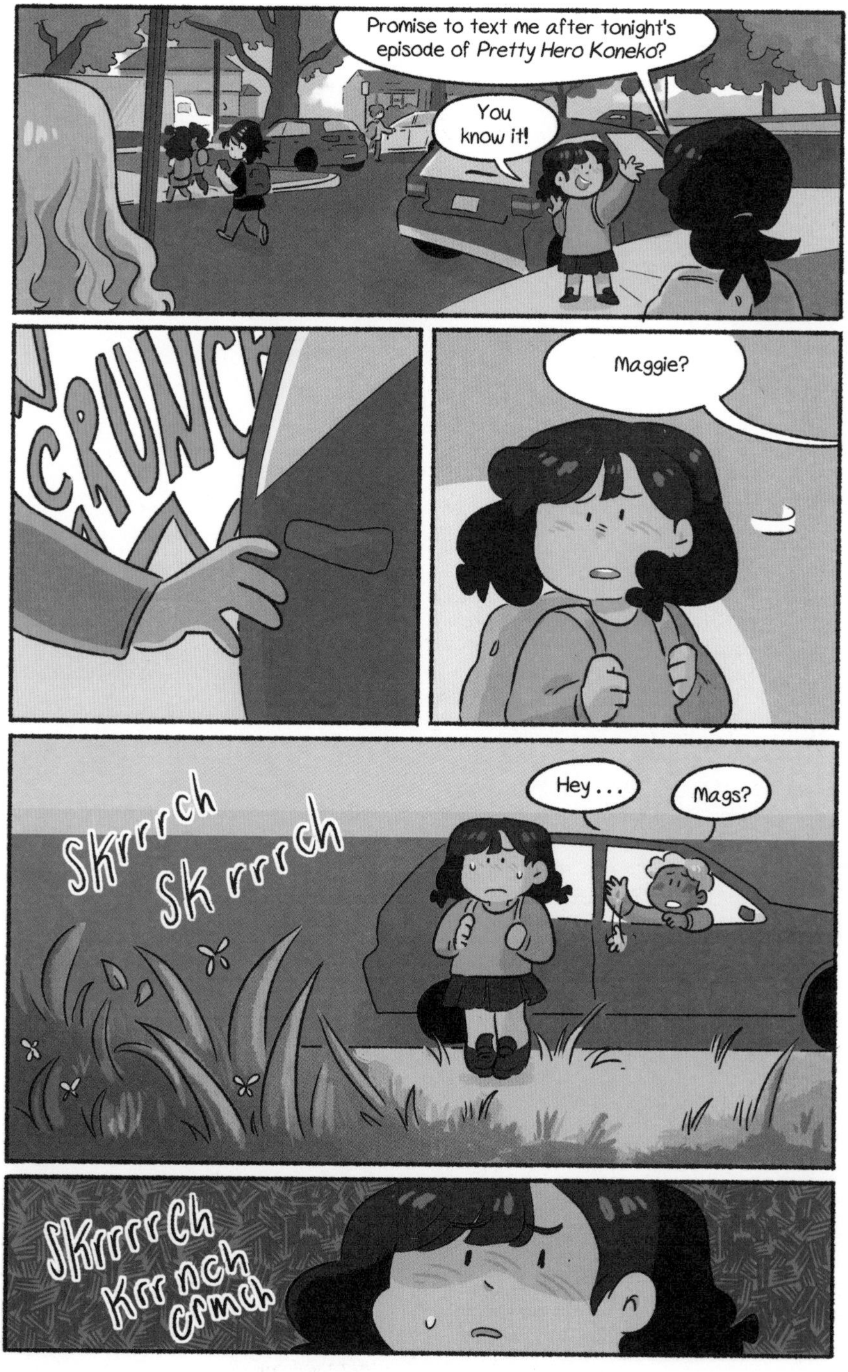

Promise to text me after tonight's episode of *Pretty Hero Koneko*?
You know it!
CRUNCH
Maggie?
Hey . . .
Mags?
SKrrrch
SK rrrch
SKrrrrCh
Krr nch
crmch

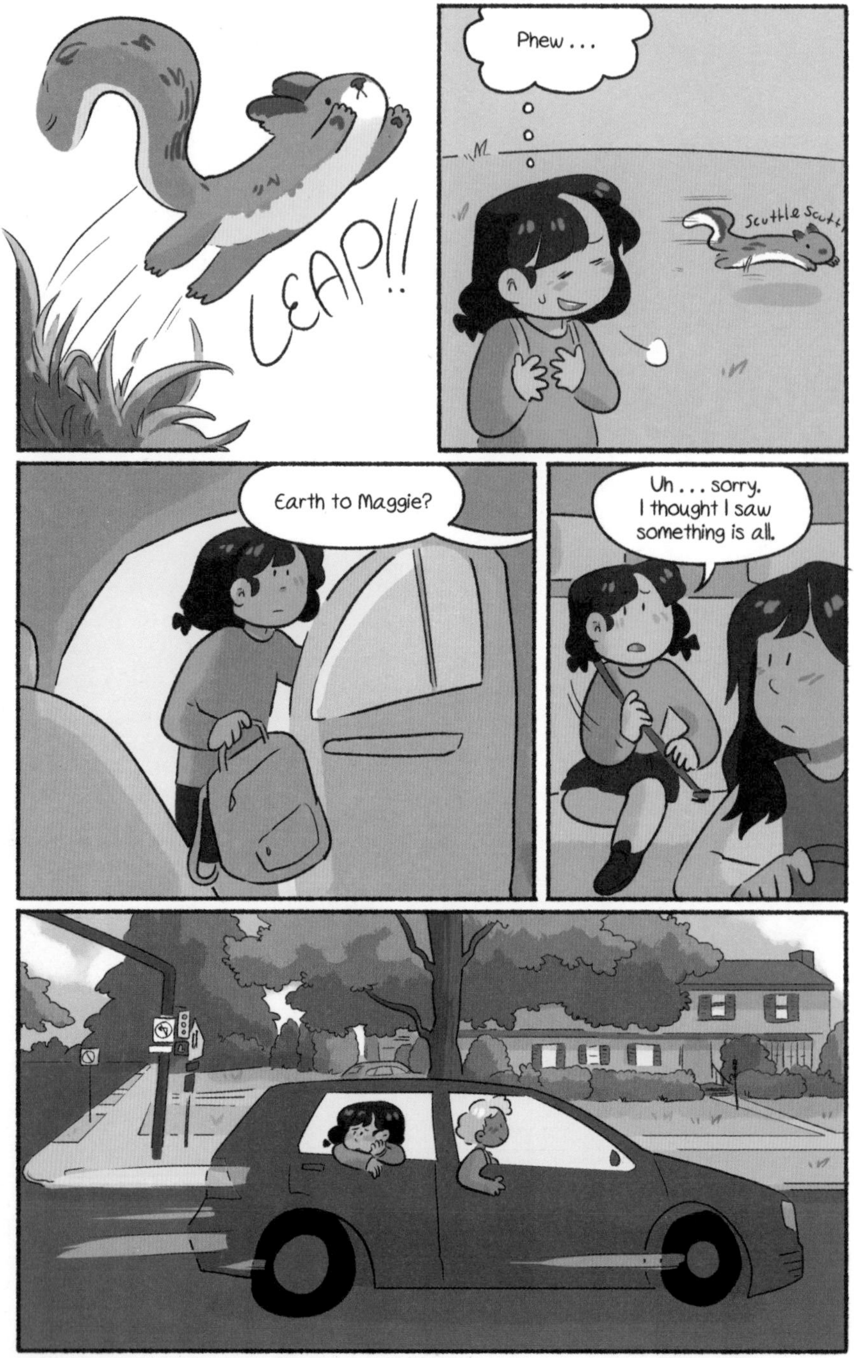
LEAP!!
Phew . . .
Scuttle Scutt
Earth to Maggie?
Uh . . . sorry.
I thought I saw
something is all.

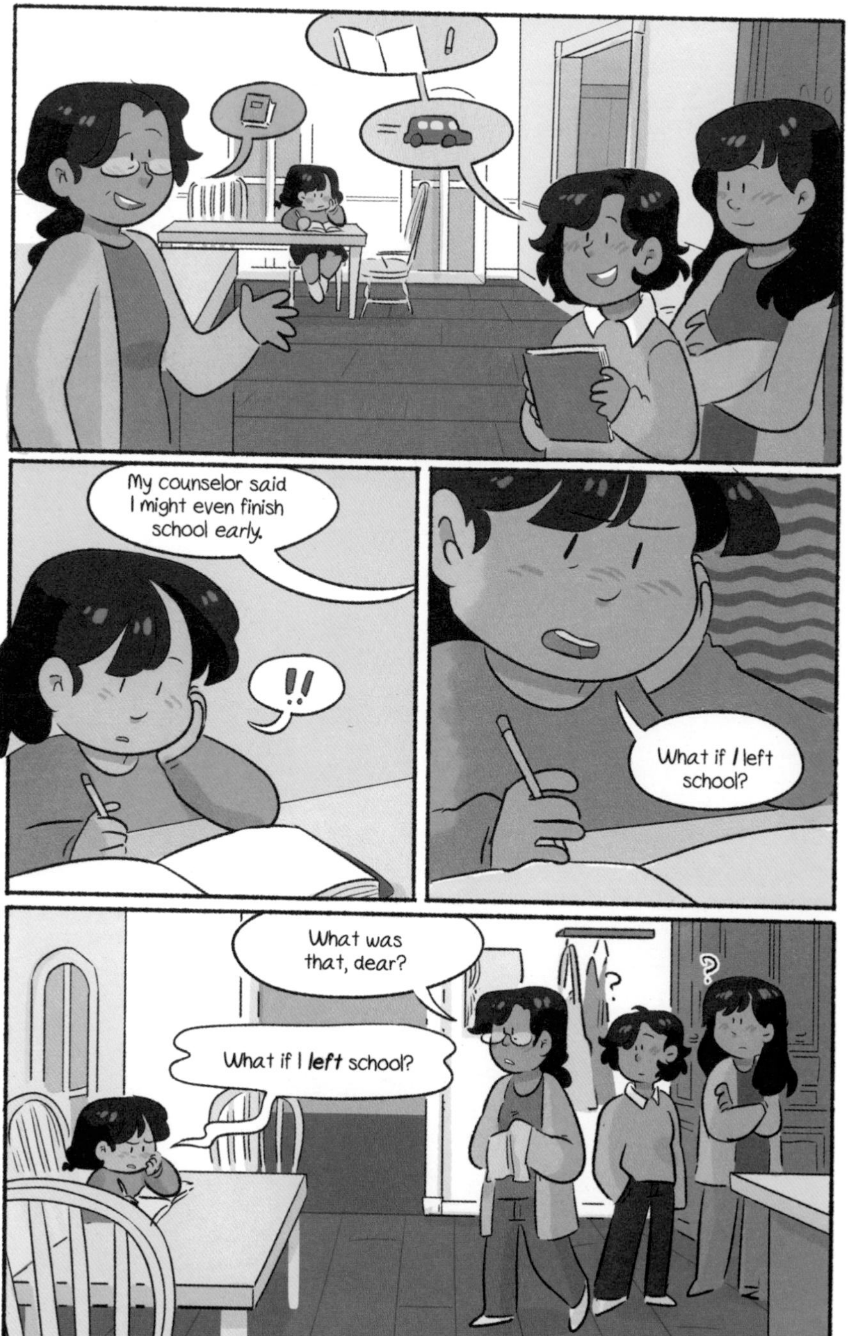
My counselor said I might even finish school *early.*
!!
What if I left school?
What was that, dear?
What if I **left** school?
?
?

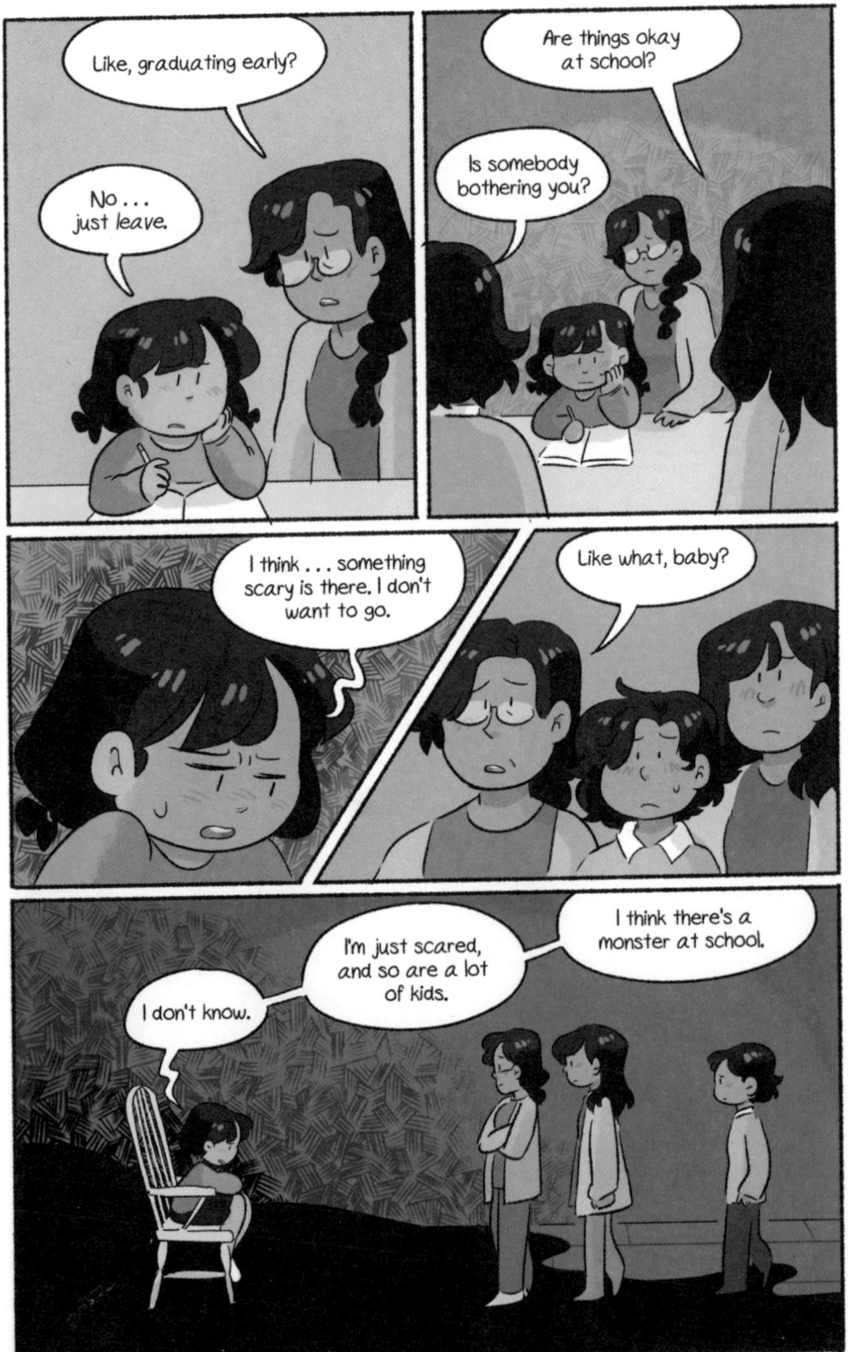
Like, graduating early?
No . . . just leave.
Are things okay at school?
Is somebody bothering you?
I think . . . something scary is there. I don't want to go.
Like what, baby?
I think there's a monster at school.
I'm just scared, and so are a lot of kids.
I don't know.

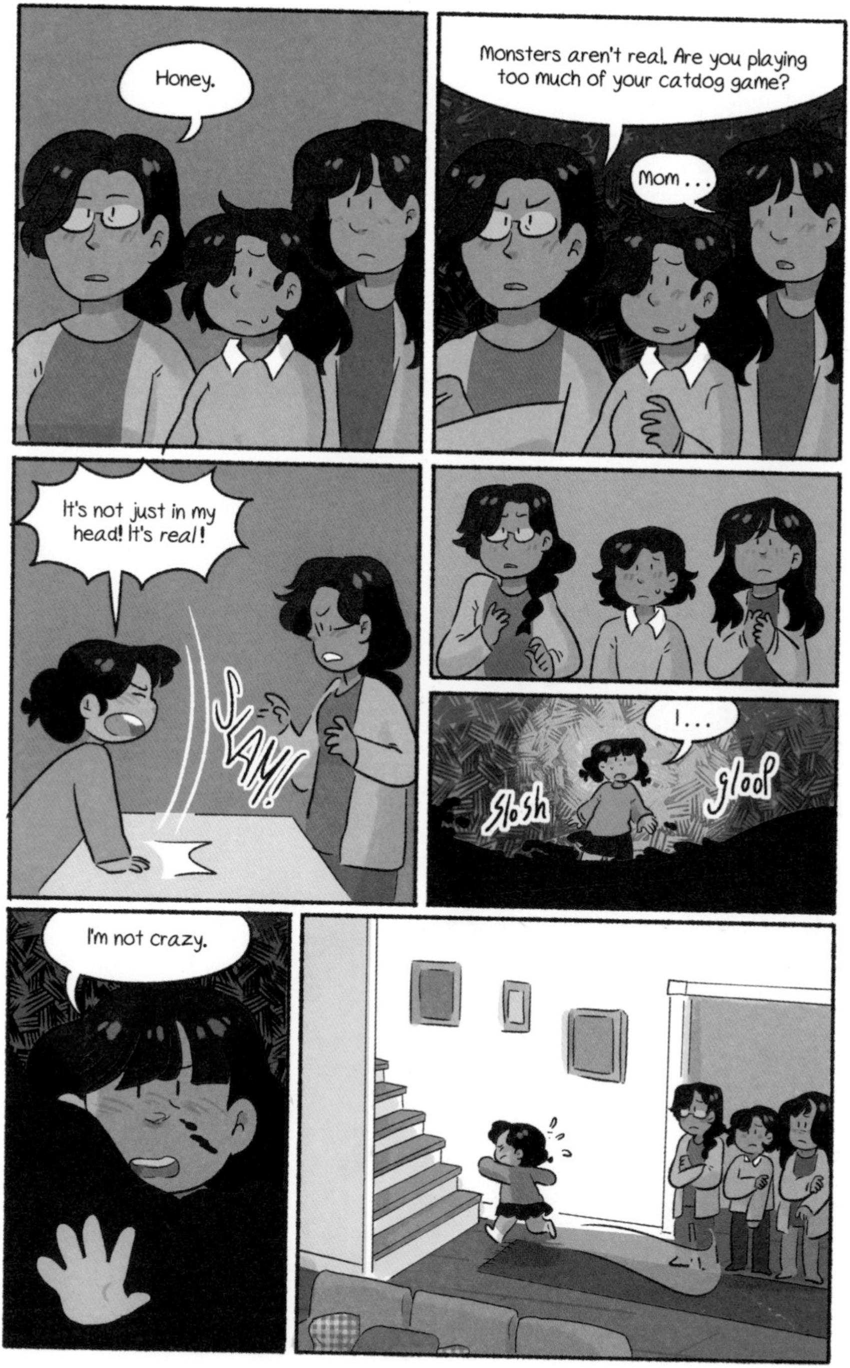
Honey.
Monsters aren't real. Are you playing too much of your catdog game?
Mom . . .
It's not just in my head! It's *real*!
SLAM!
I . . .
Slosh
gloop
I'm not crazy.

roll roll

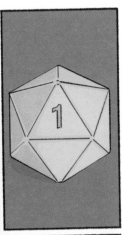

THUNK

Can I text Clara?

Im worried.
I think there's a
dragon.

A realnone
real one*

How do we fight a
real dragon?????

TAK
TAK TAK

170

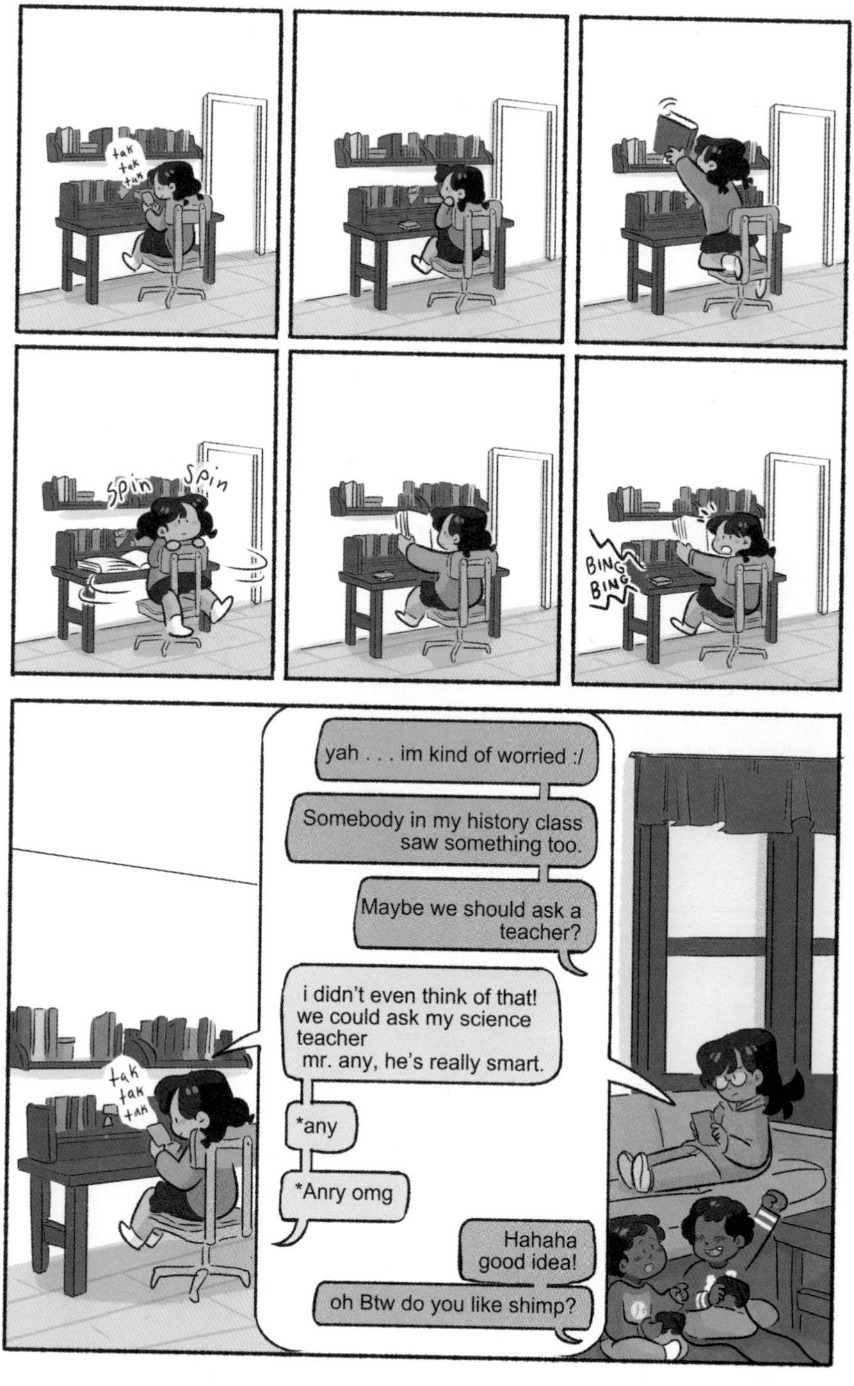
tak
tak
tak
spin
spin
BING
BING
yah . . . im kind of worried :/
Somebody in my history class saw something too.
Maybe we should ask a teacher?
tak
tak
tak
i didn't even think of that! we could ask my science teacher mr. any, he's really smart.
*any
*Anry omg
Hahaha good idea!
oh Btw do you like shimp?

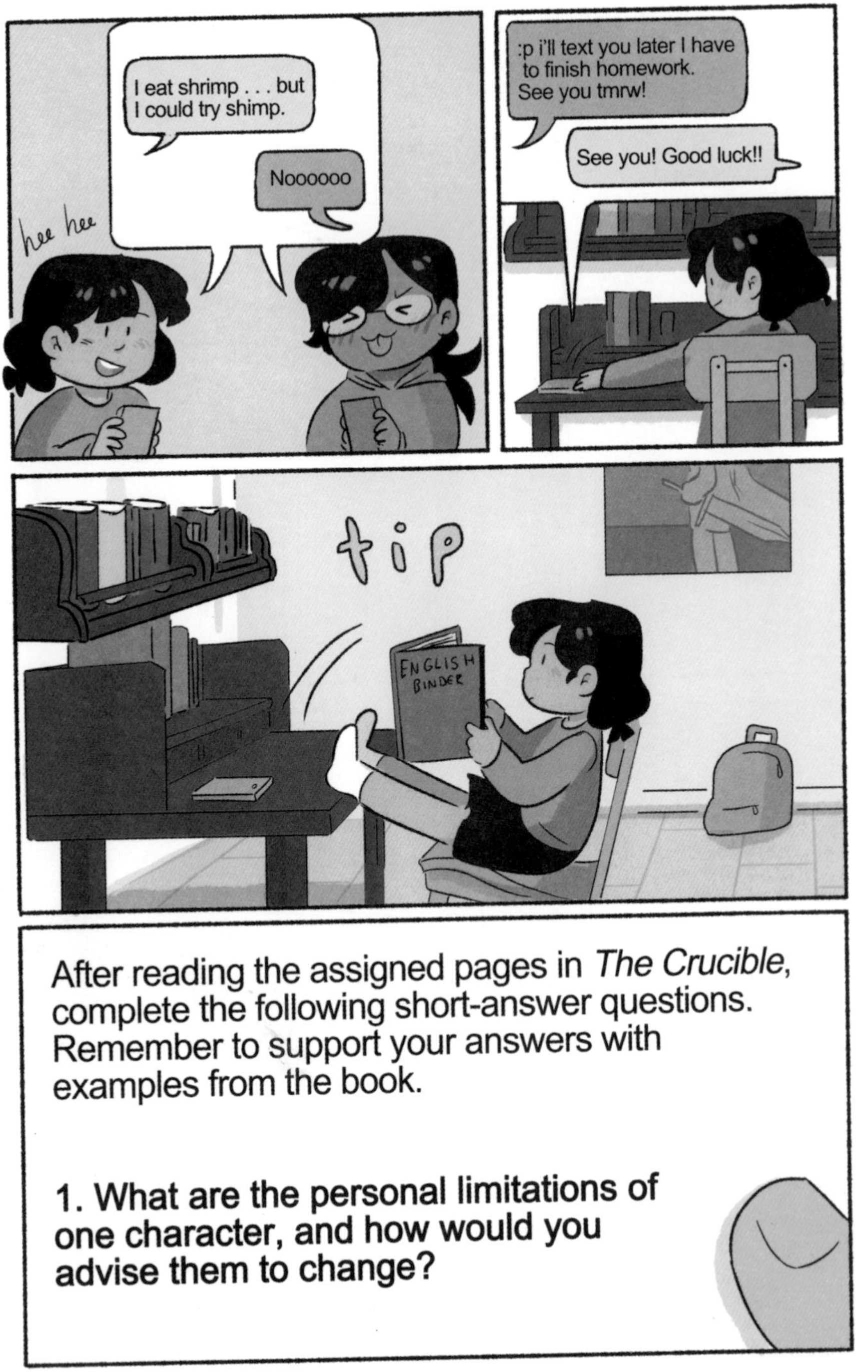
hee hee
I eat shrimp . . . but I could try shimp.
Noooooo
:p i'll text you later I have to finish homework. See you tmrw!
See you! Good luck!!
tip
ENGLISH BINDER
After reading the assigned pages in *The Crucible*, complete the following short-answer questions. Remember to support your answers with examples from the book.
1. What are the personal limitations of one character, and how would you advise them to change?

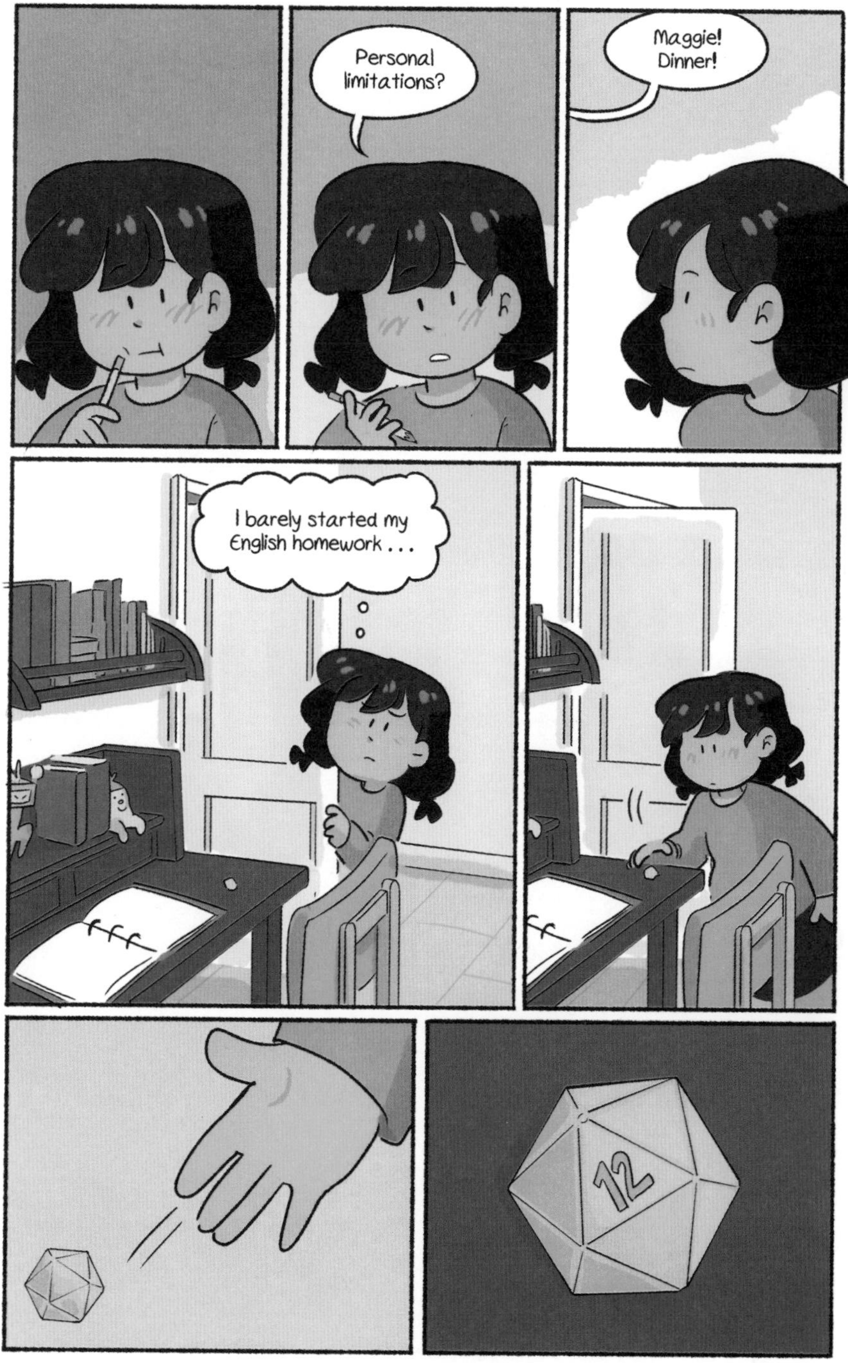

Personal limitations?
Maggie! Dinner!
I barely started my English homework . . .
12

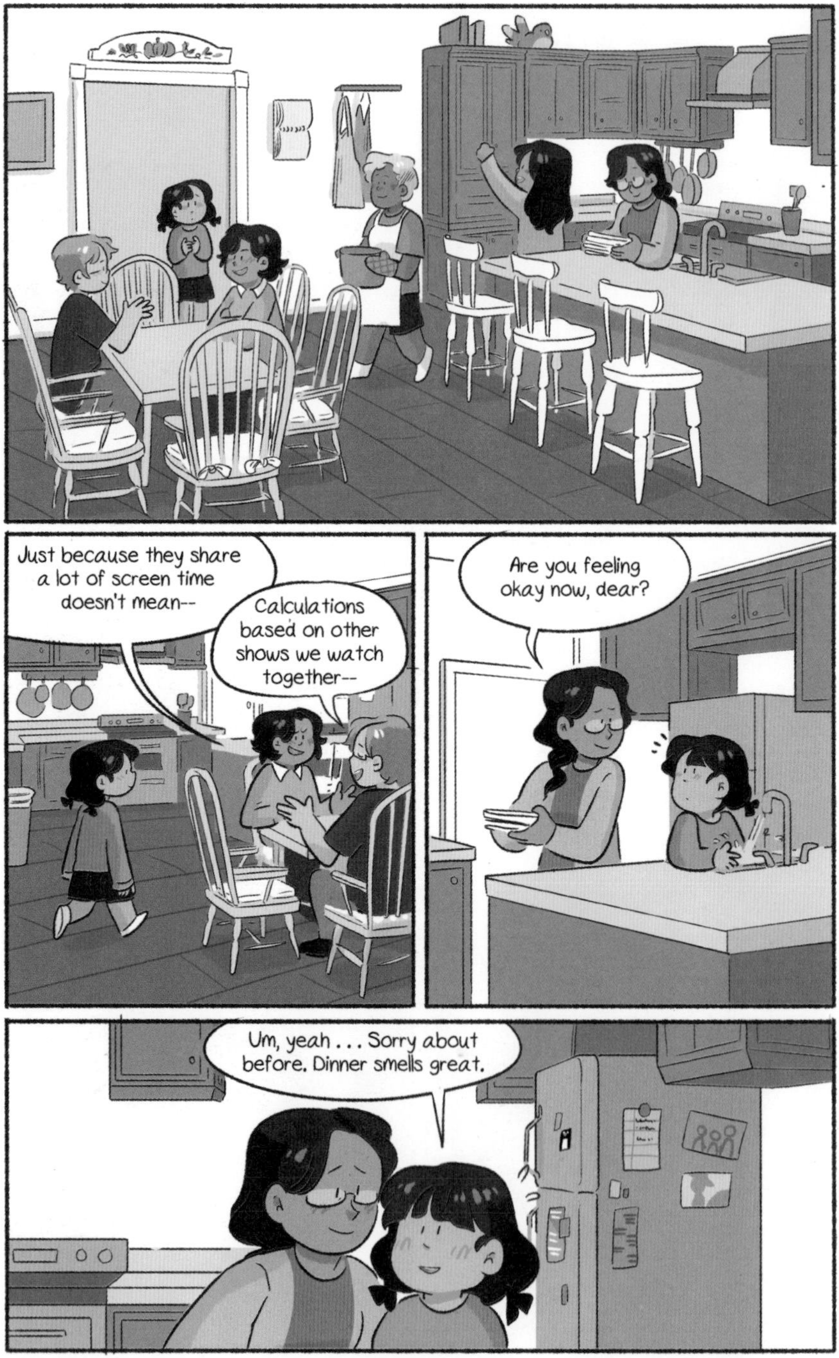
Just because they share a lot of screen time doesn't mean--
Calculations based on other shows we watch together--
Are you feeling okay now, dear?
Um, yeah . . . Sorry about before. Dinner smells great.

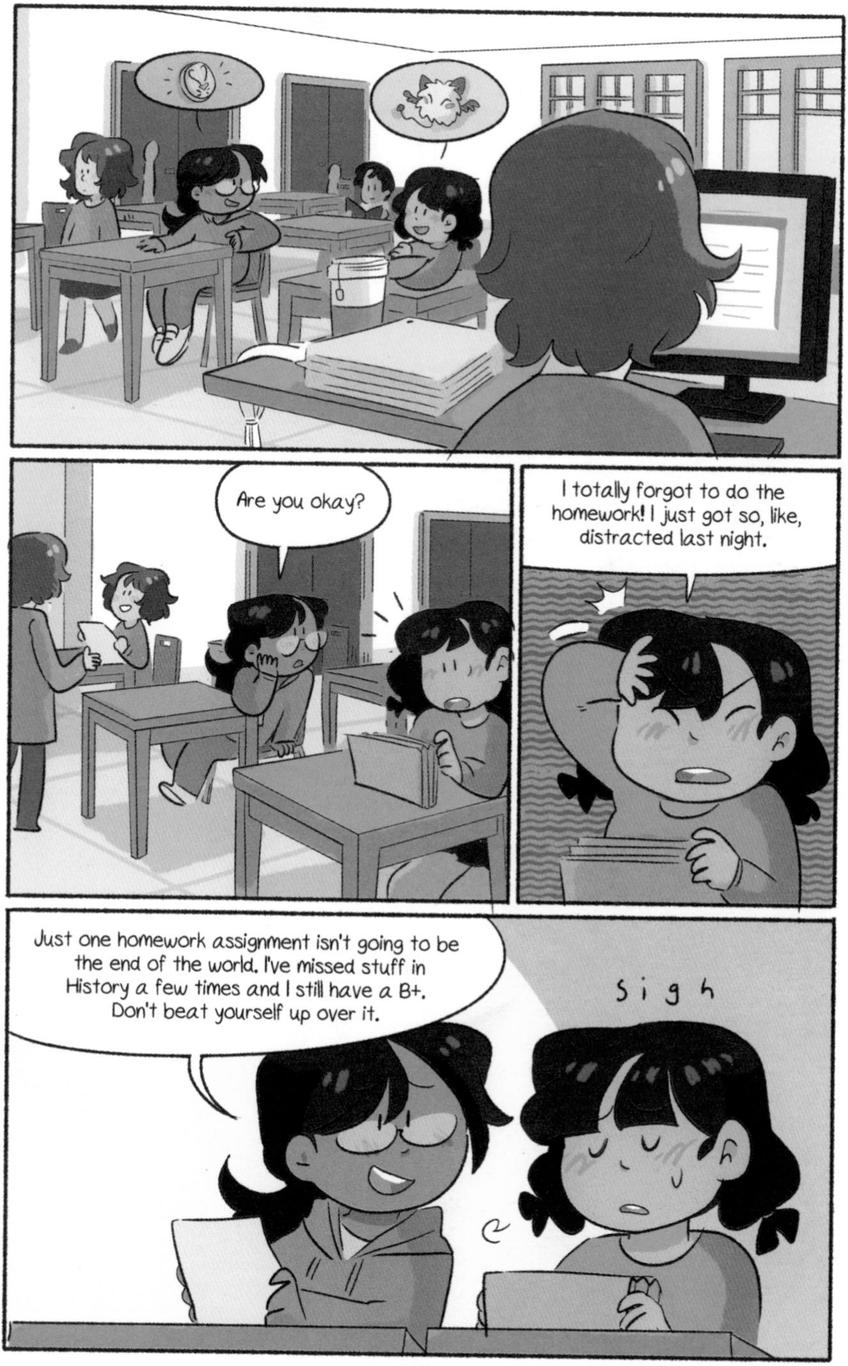
Are you okay?
I totally forgot to do the homework! I just got so, like, distracted last night.
Just one homework assignment isn't going to be the end of the world. I've missed stuff in History a few times and I still have a B+. Don't beat yourself up over it.
Sigh

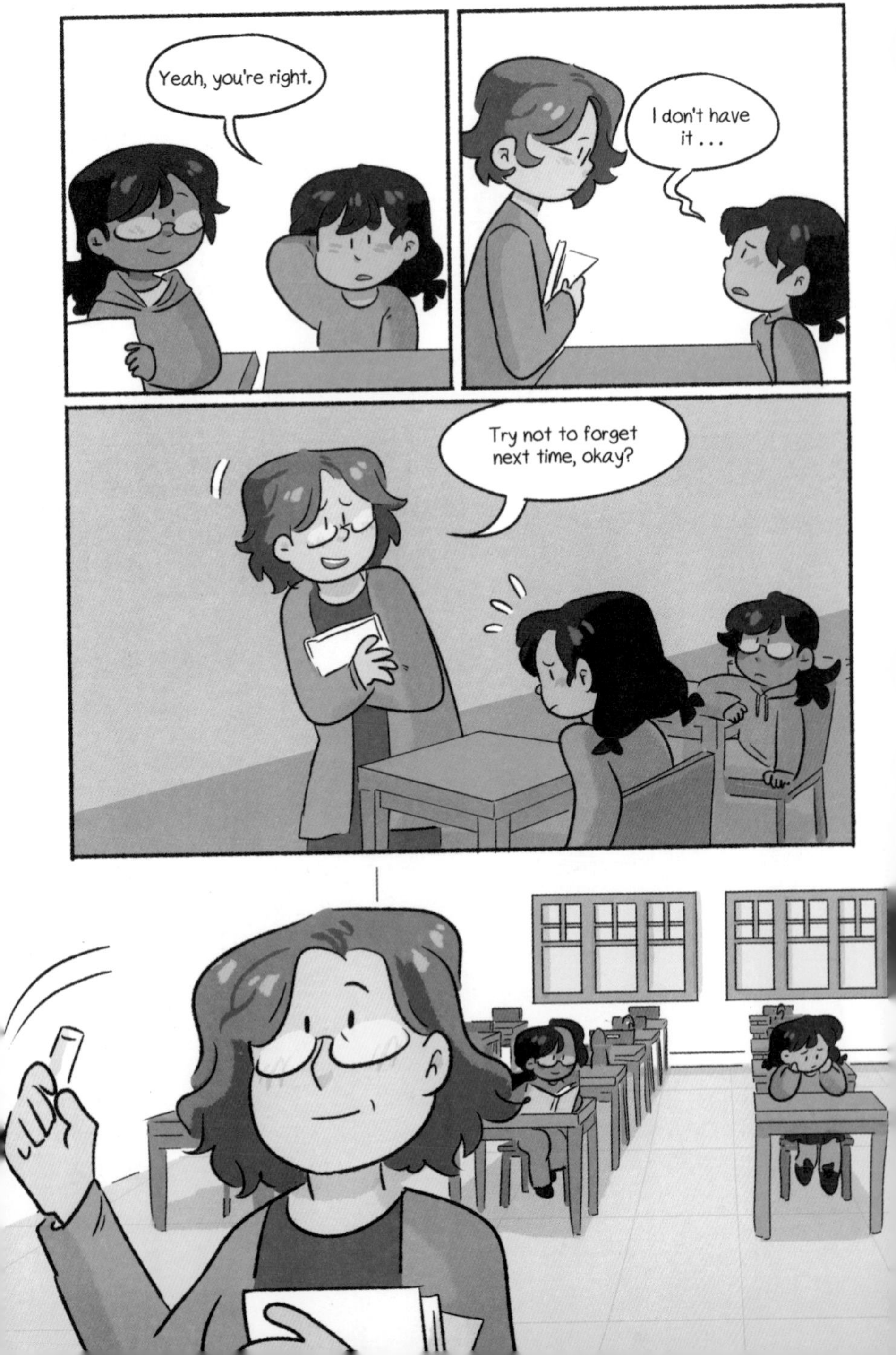
Yeah, you're right.
I don't have it . . .
Try not to forget next time, okay?

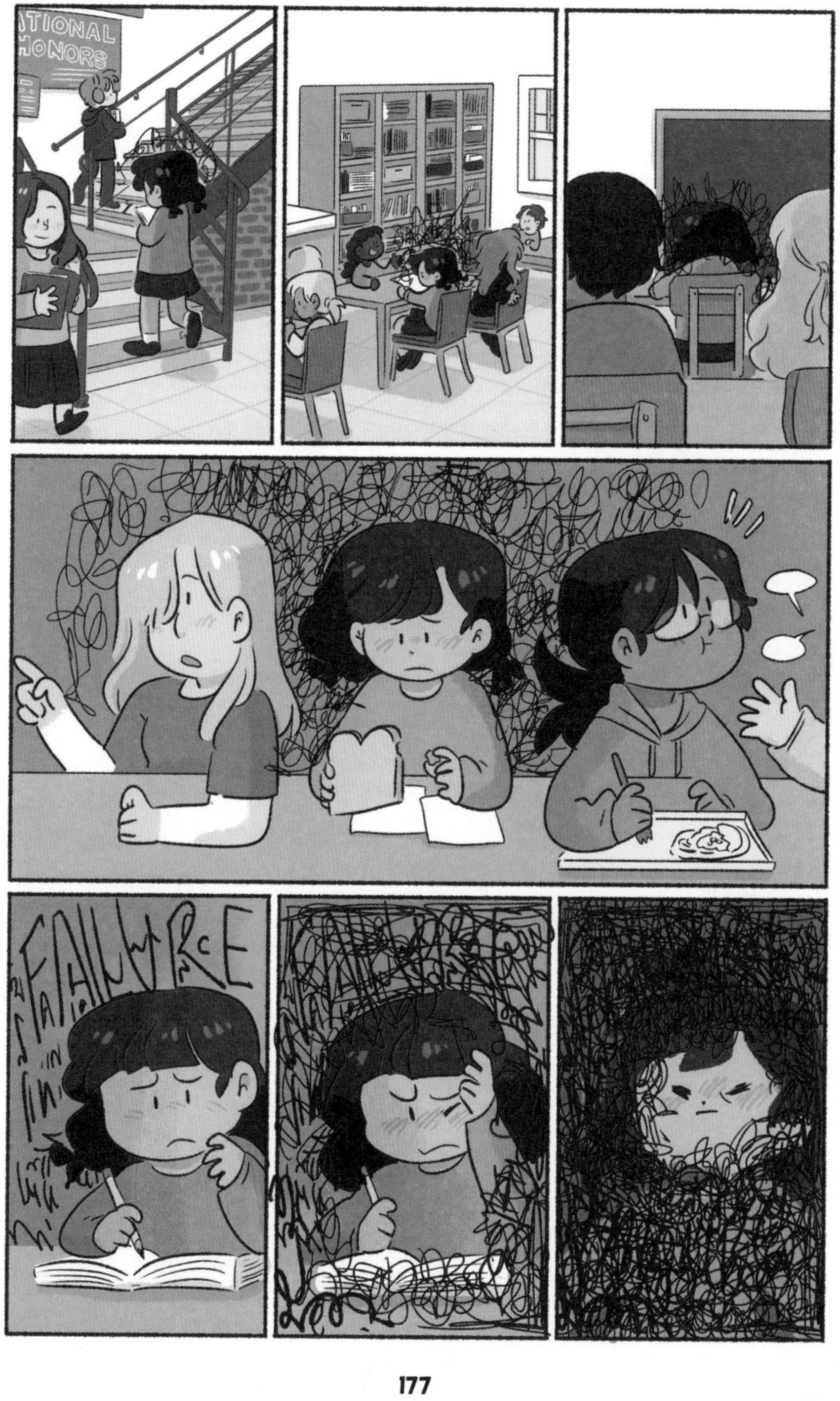
TIONAL
HONORS
FAILURE

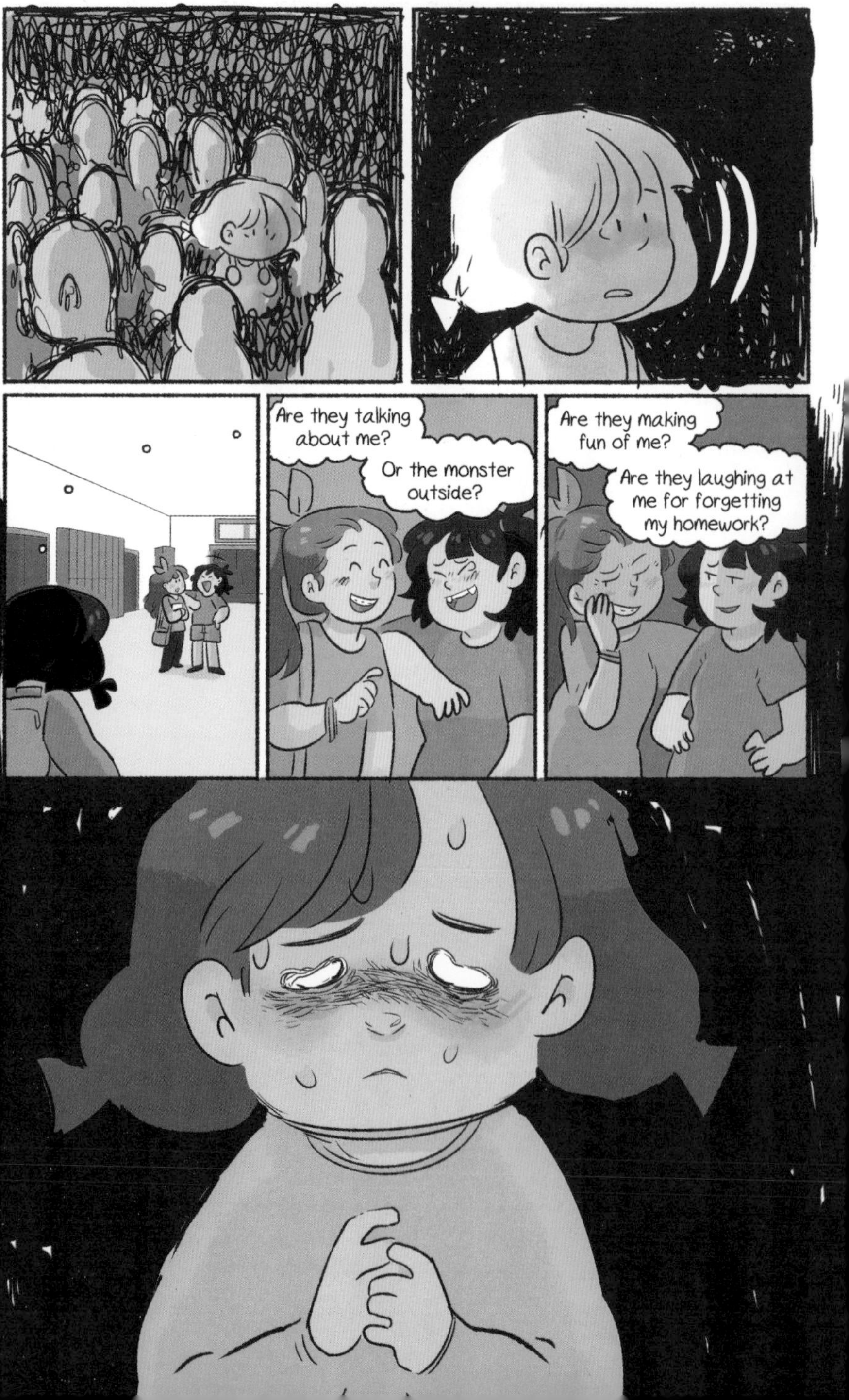
Are they talking about me?
Or the monster outside?
Are they making fun of me?
Are they laughing at me for forgetting my homework?

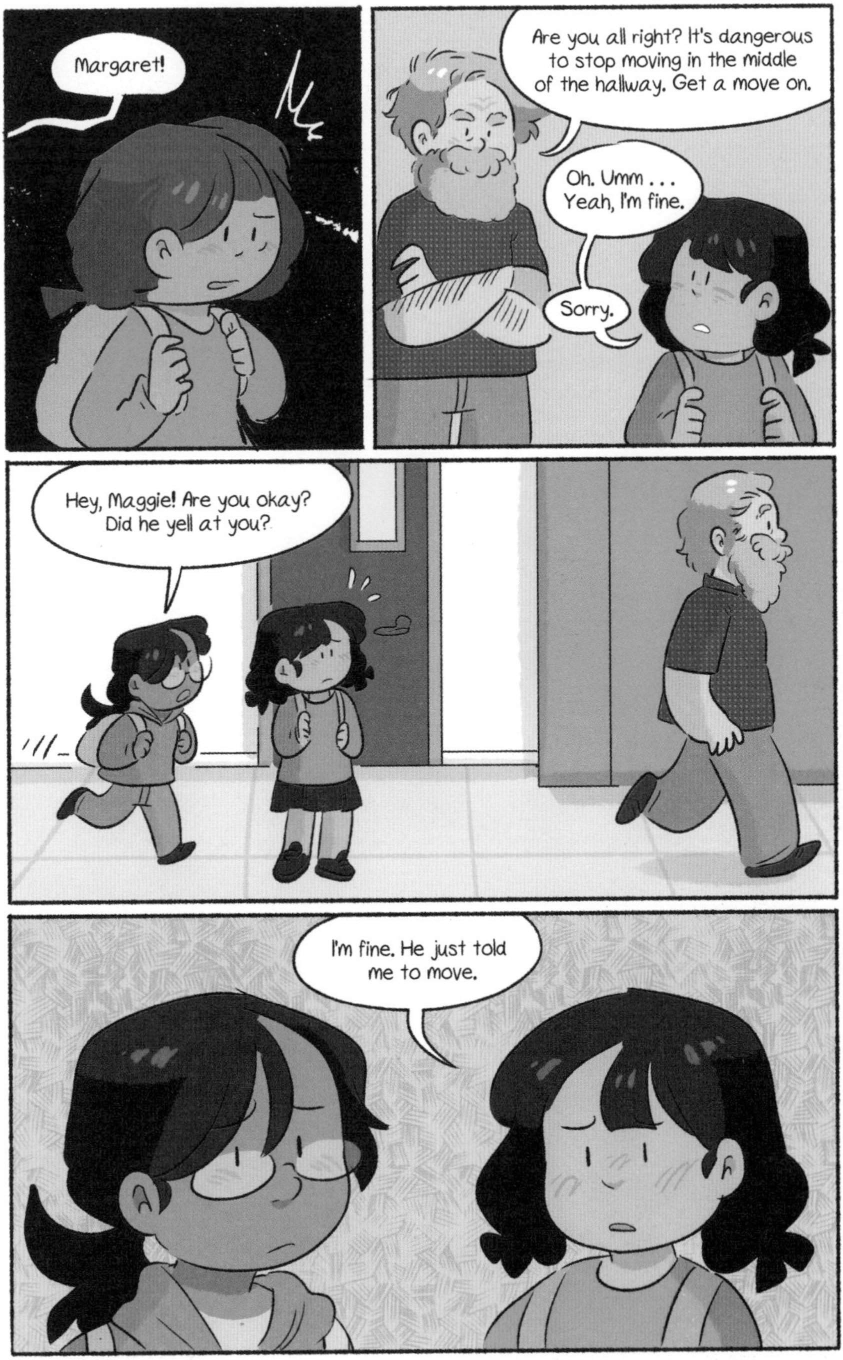
Margaret!
Are you all right? It's dangerous to stop moving in the middle of the hallway. Get a move on.
Oh. Umm . . . Yeah, I'm fine.
Sorry.
Hey, Maggie! Are you okay? Did he yell at you?
I'm fine. He just told me to move.

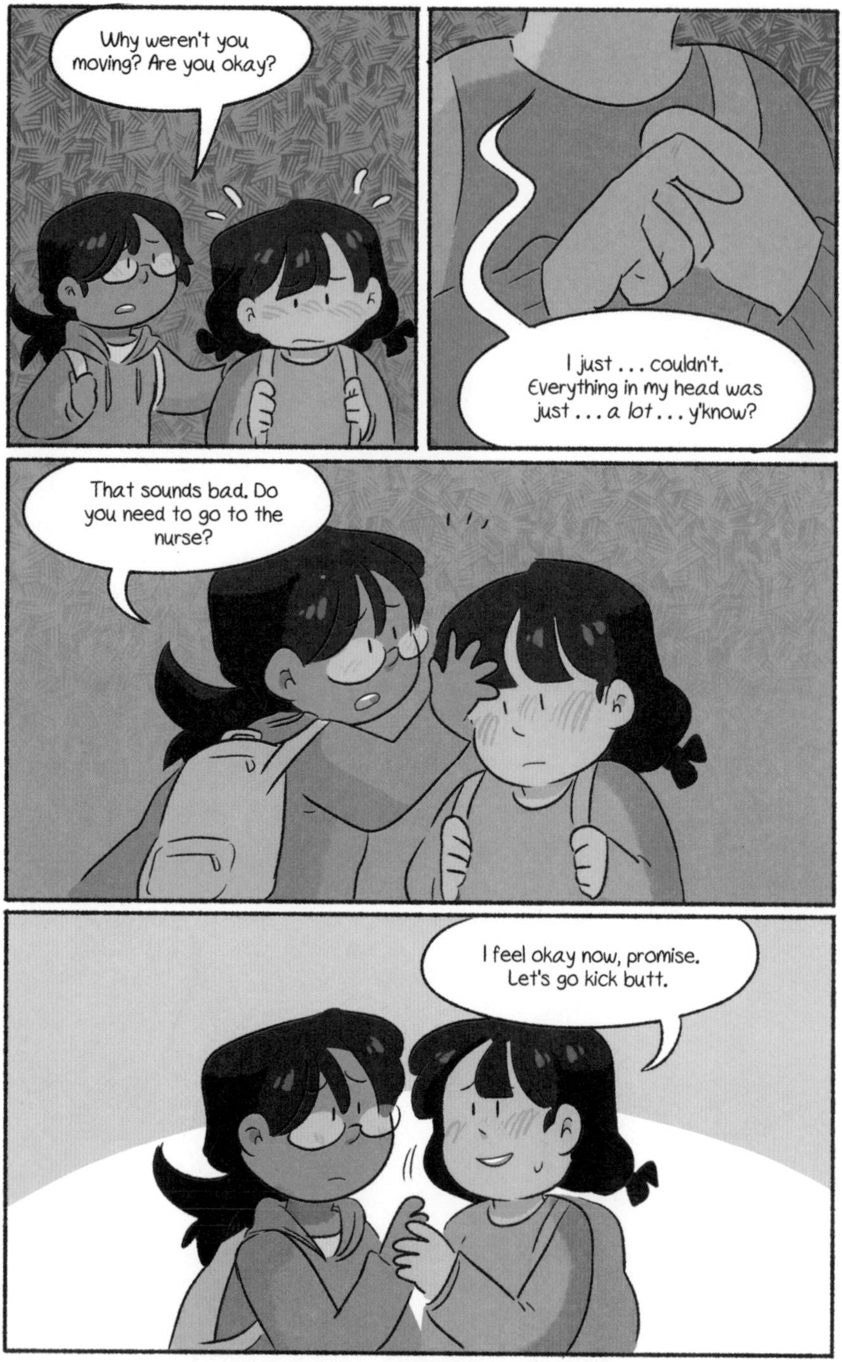
Why weren't you moving? Are you okay?
I just . . . couldn't. Everything in my head was just . . . a lot . . . y'know?
That sounds bad. Do you need to go to the nurse?
I feel okay now, promise. Let's go kick butt.

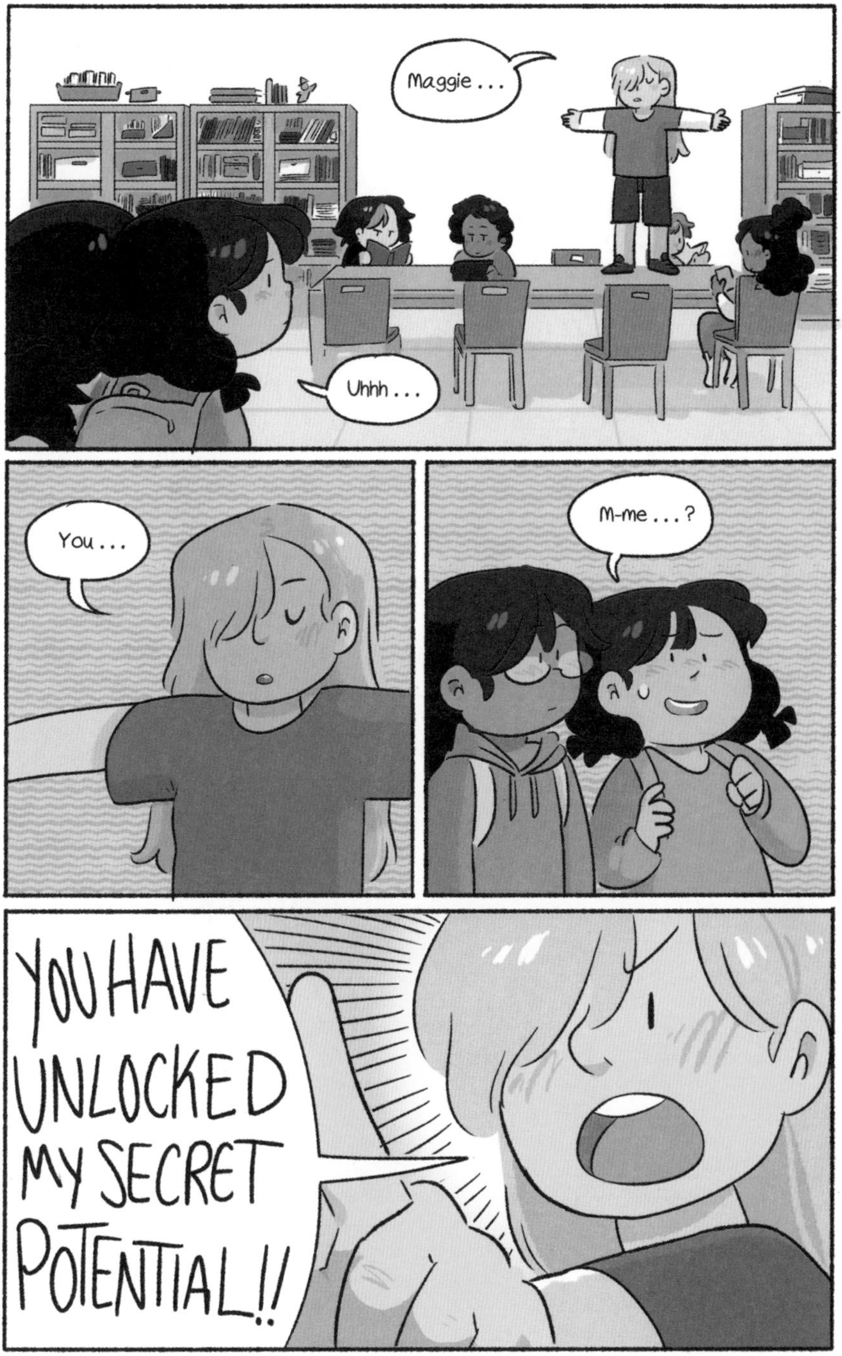
Maggie . . .
Uhhh . . .
You . . .
M-me . . . ?
YOU HAVE UNLOCKED MY SECRET POTENTIAL!!

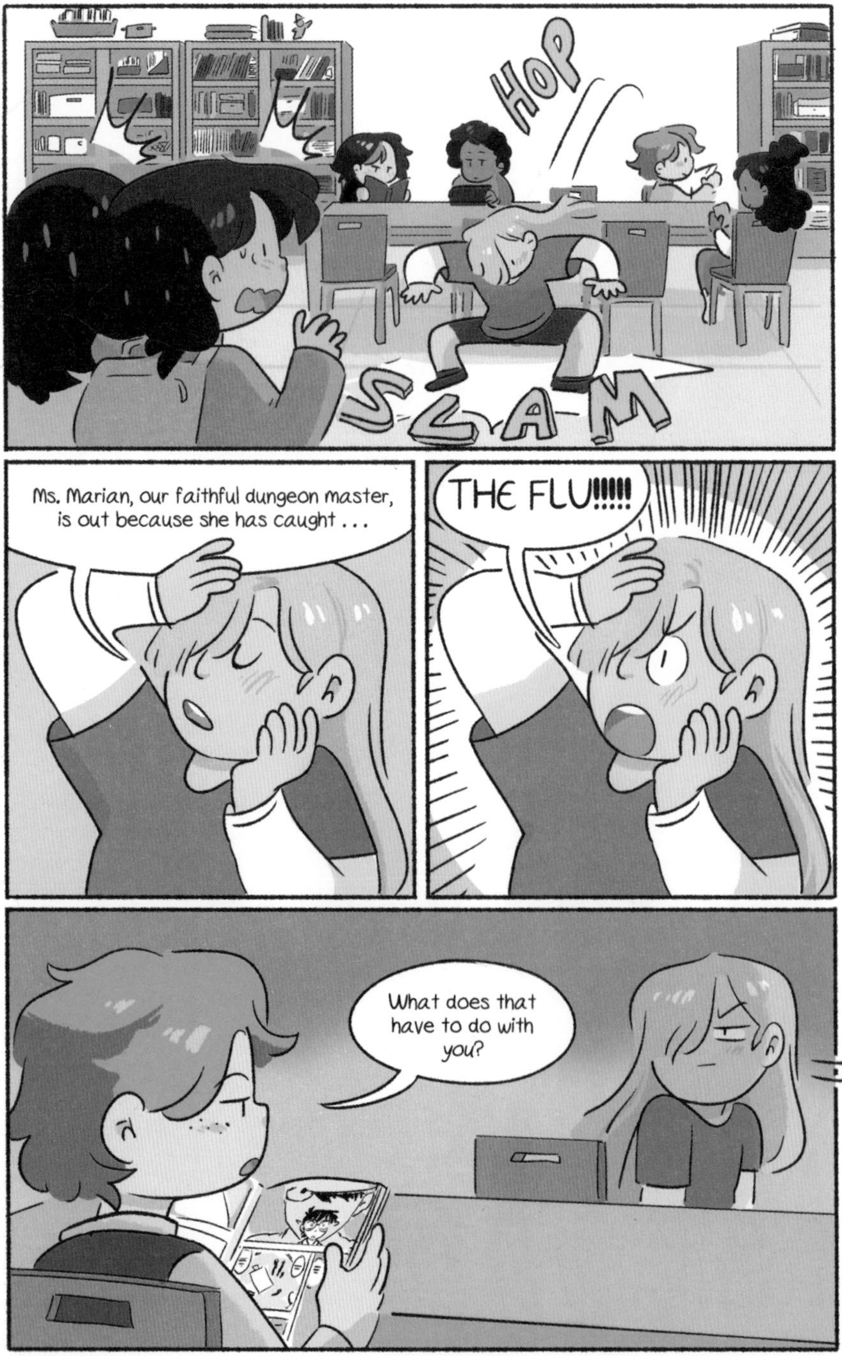
HOP
SLAM
Ms. Marian, our faithful dungeon master, is out because she has caught . . .
THE FLU!!!!!!
What does that have to do with you?

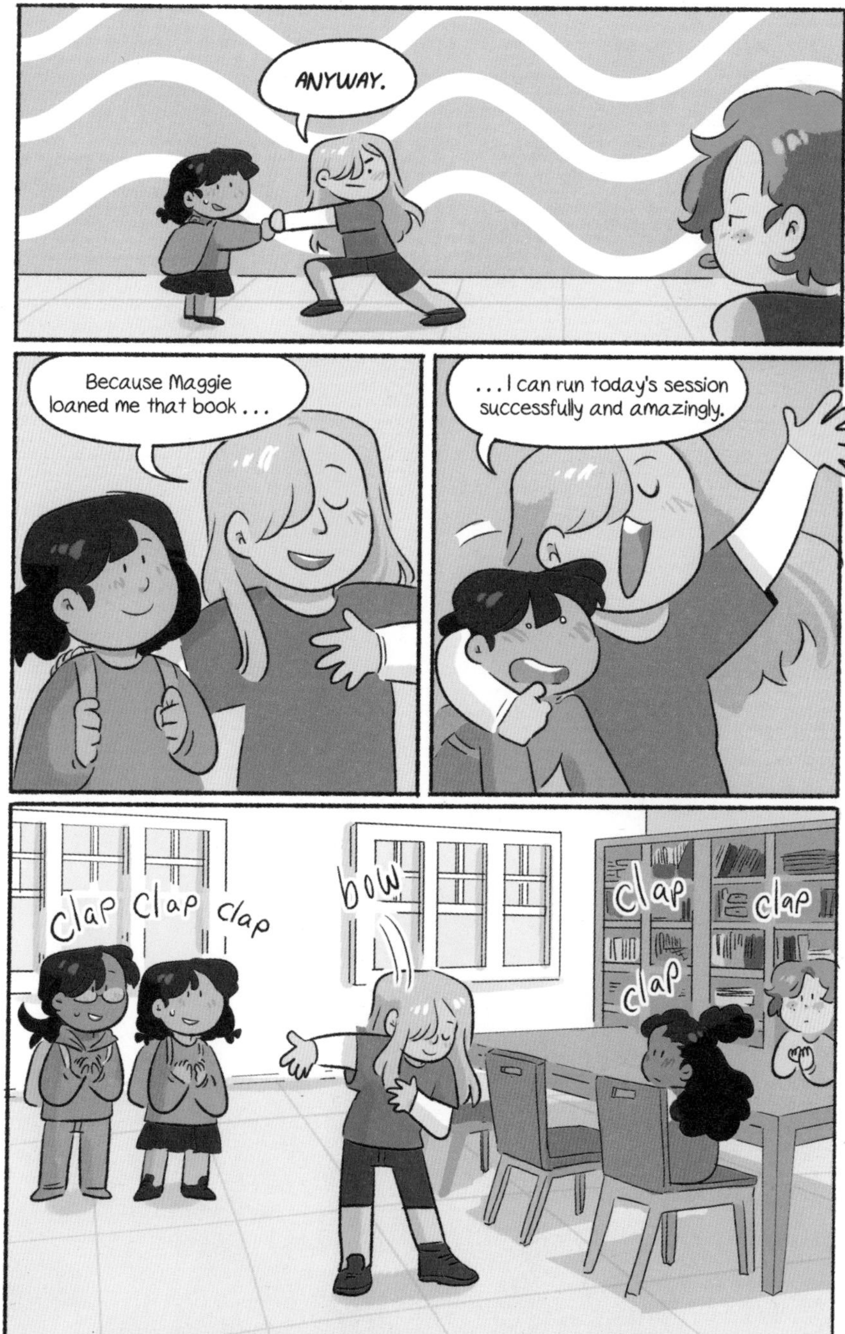
ANYWAY.
Because Maggie loaned me that book . . .
. . . I can run today's session successfully and amazingly.
clap clap clap
bow
clap
clap
clap

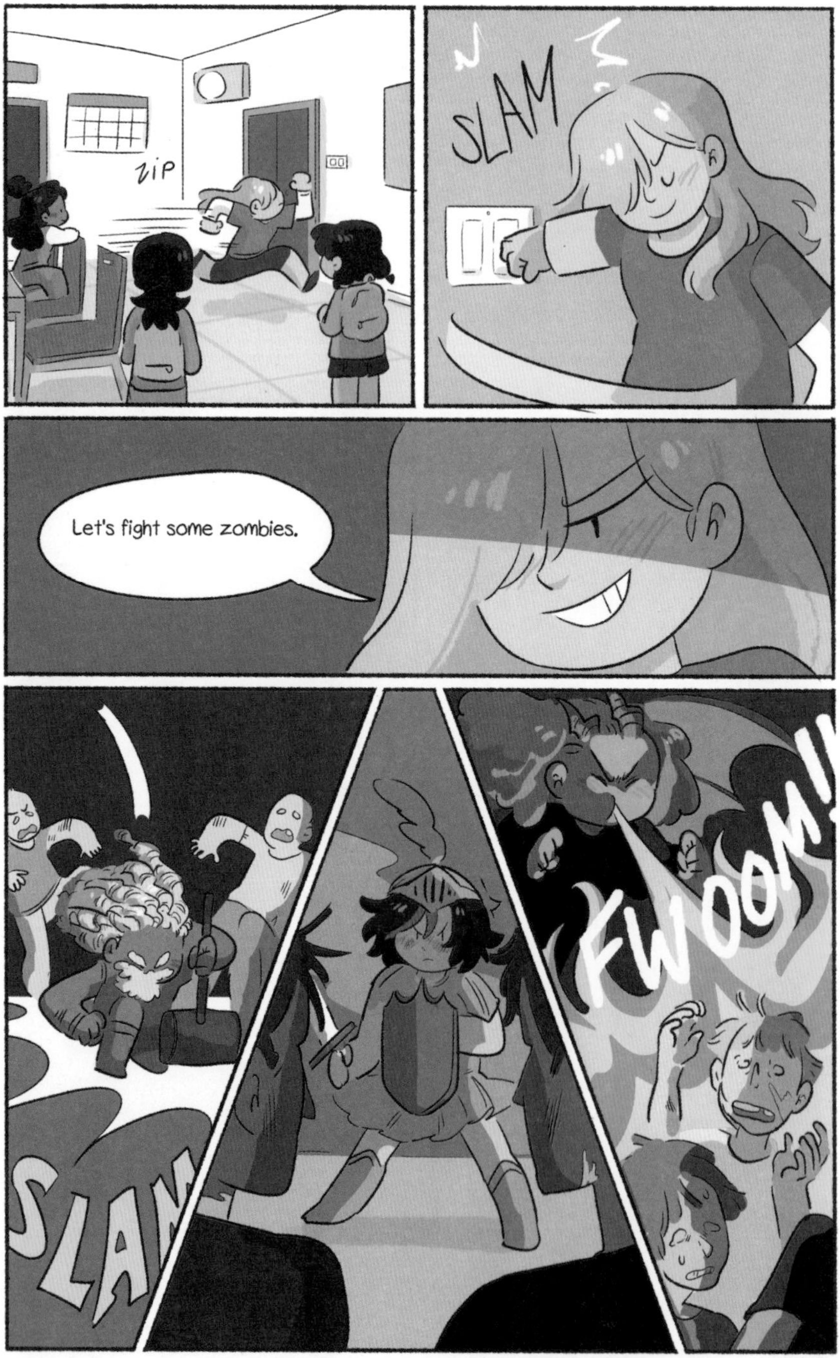
ZIP
SLAM
Let's fight some zombies.
SLAM
FWOOM!!

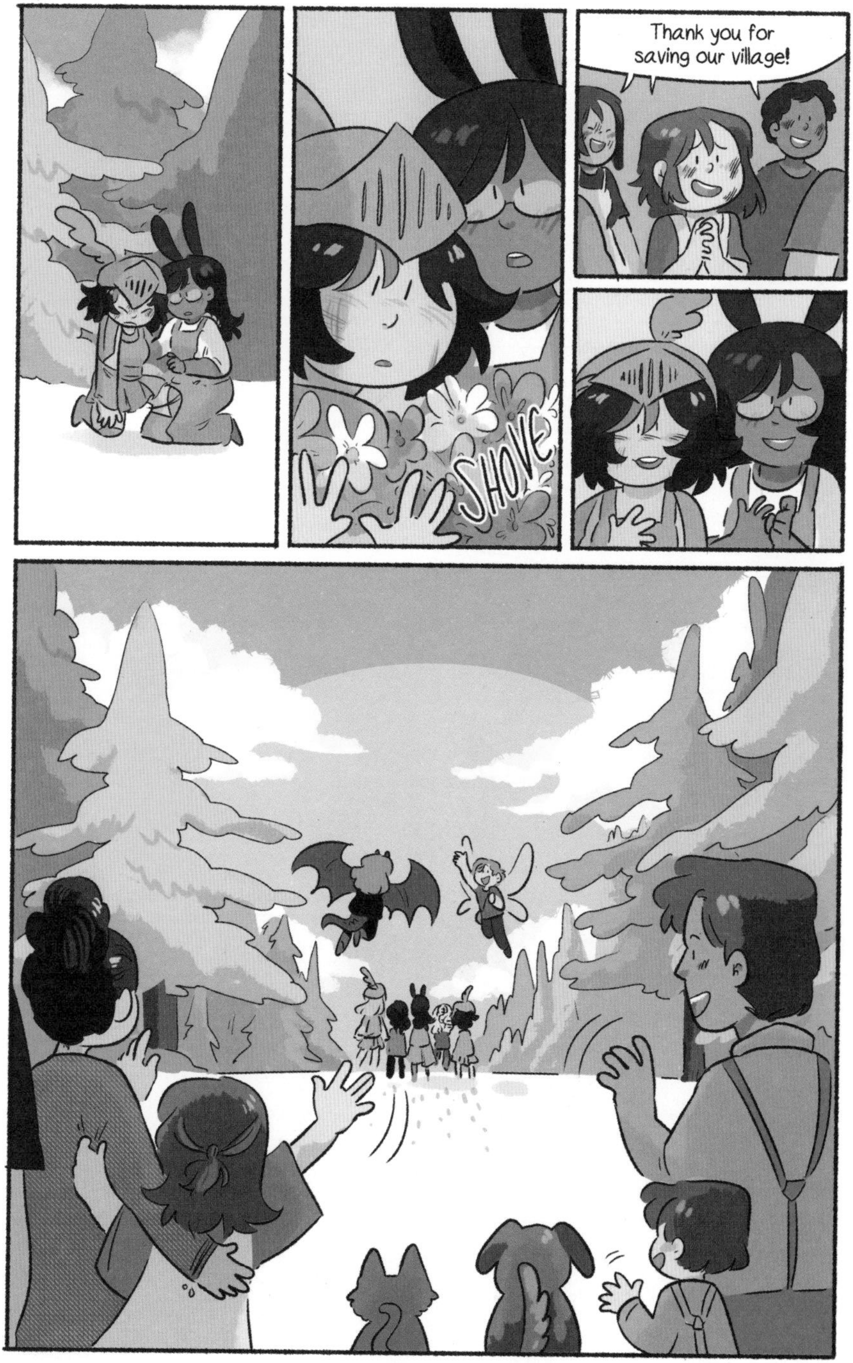
SHOVE
Thank you for saving our village!

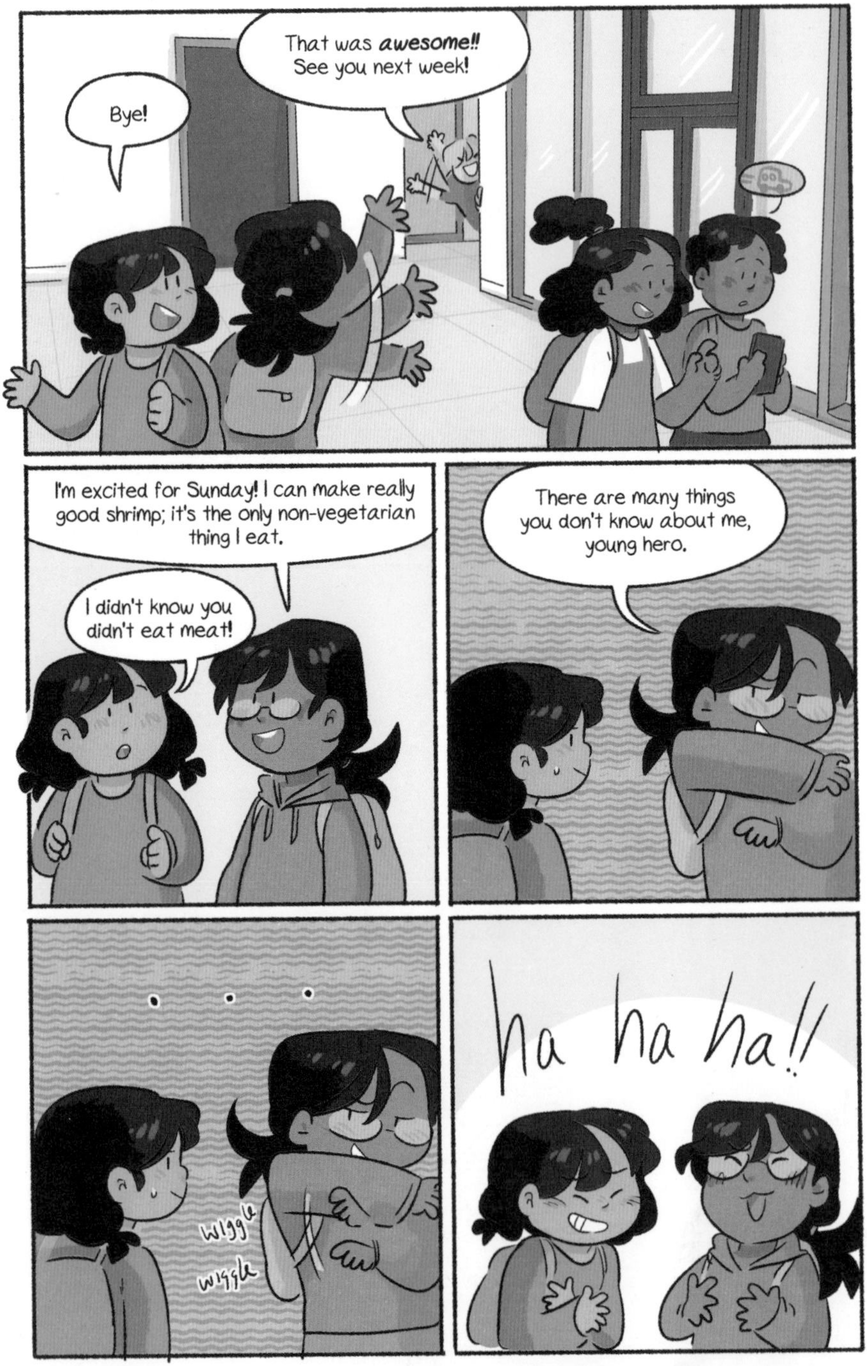
That was **awesome!!** See you next week!
Bye!
I'm excited for Sunday! I can make really good shrimp; it's the only non-vegetarian thing I eat.
I didn't know you didn't eat meat!
There are many things you don't know about me, young hero.
. . .
wiggle
wiggle
ha ha ha!!

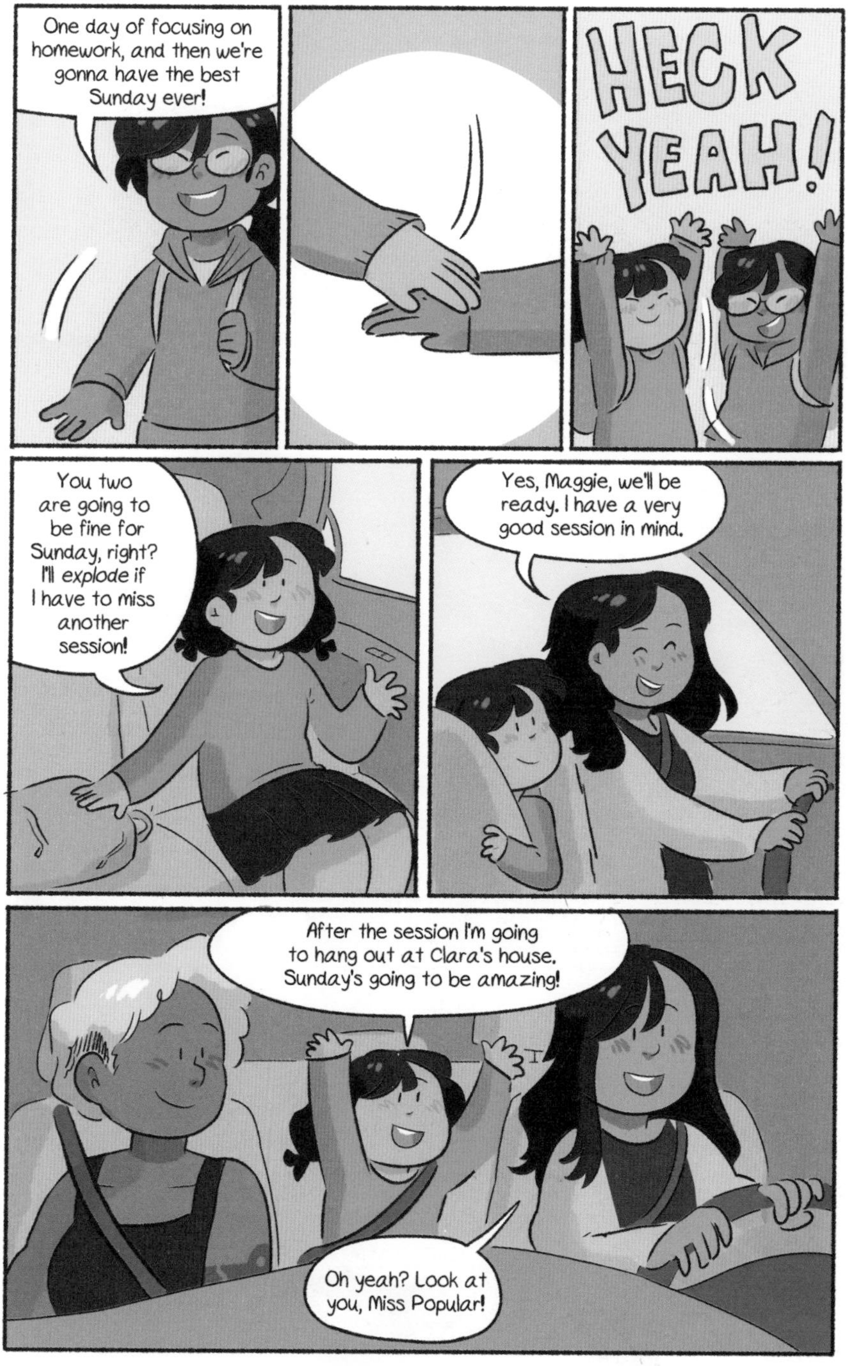
One day of focusing on homework, and then we're gonna have the best Sunday ever!
HECK YEAH!
You two are going to be fine for Sunday, right? I'll *explode* if I have to miss another session!
Yes, Maggie, we'll be ready. I have a very good session in mind.
After the session I'm going to hang out at Clara's house. Sunday's going to be *amazing*!
Oh yeah? Look at you, Miss Popular!

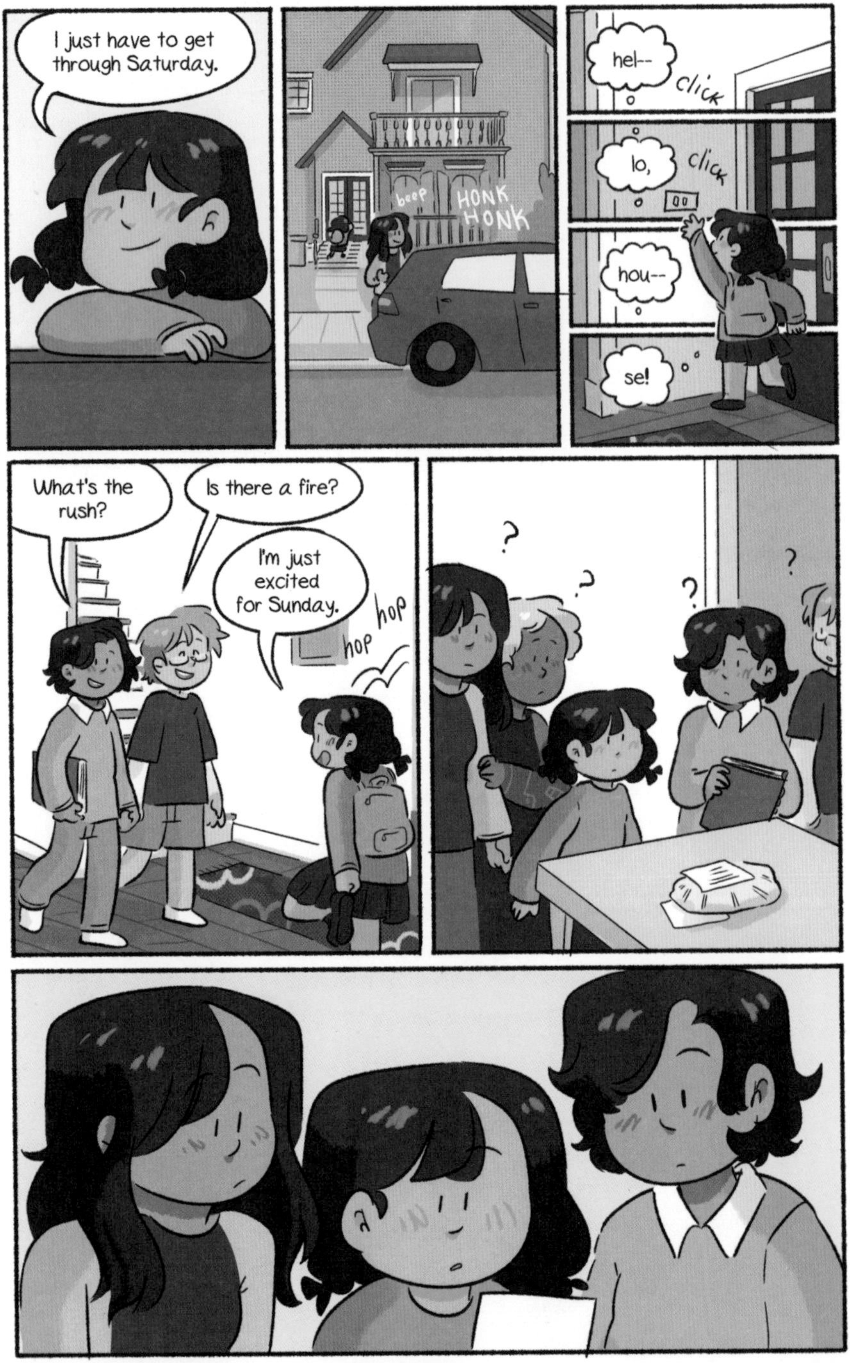
I just have to get through Saturday.
beep
HONK HONK
hel--
click
lo,
click
hou--
se!
What's the rush?
Is there a fire?
I'm just excited for Sunday.
hop
hop
?
?
?
?

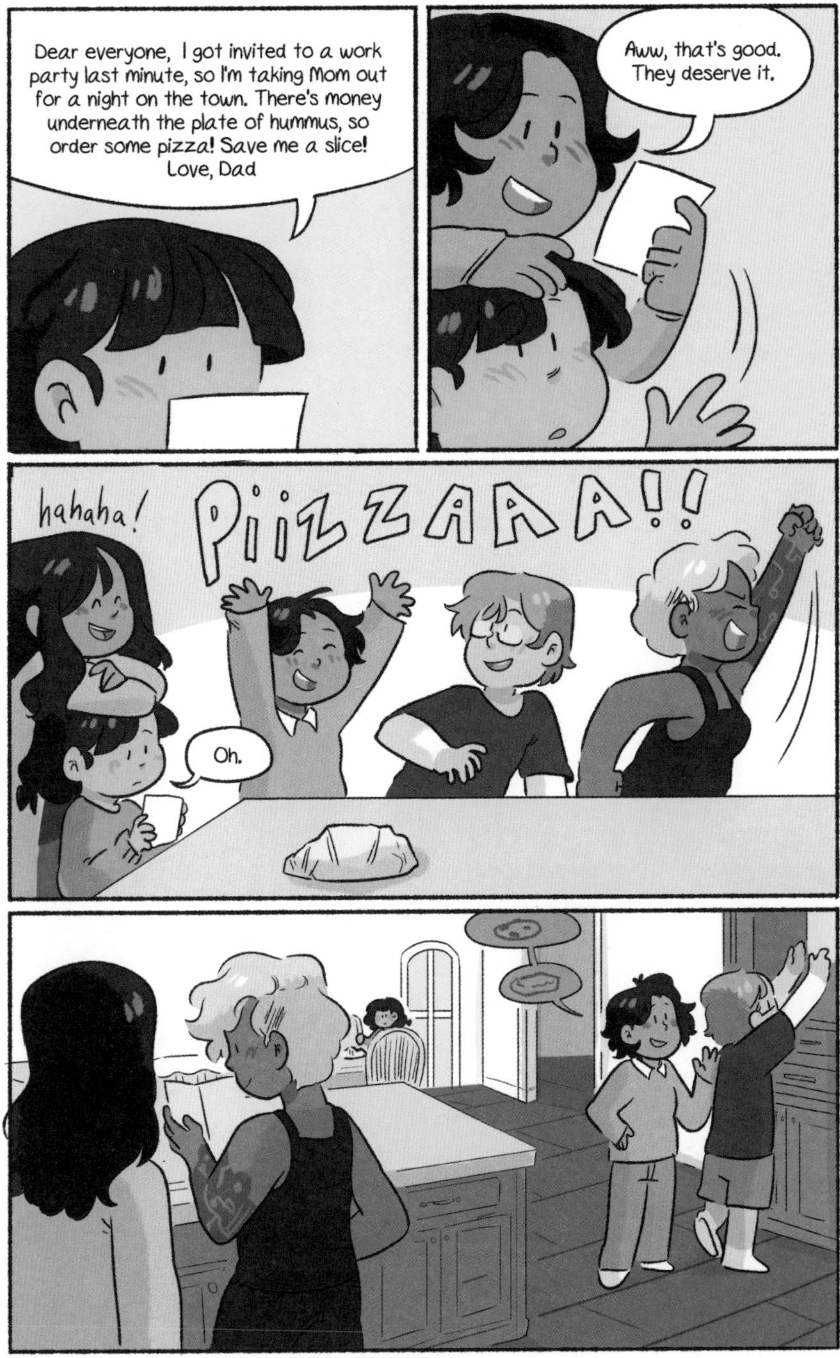
Dear everyone, I got invited to a work party last minute, so I'm taking Mom out for a night on the town. There's money underneath the plate of hummus, so order some pizza! Save me a slice! Love, Dad
Aww, that's good. They deserve it.
hahaha!
PIIZZAAA!!
Oh.

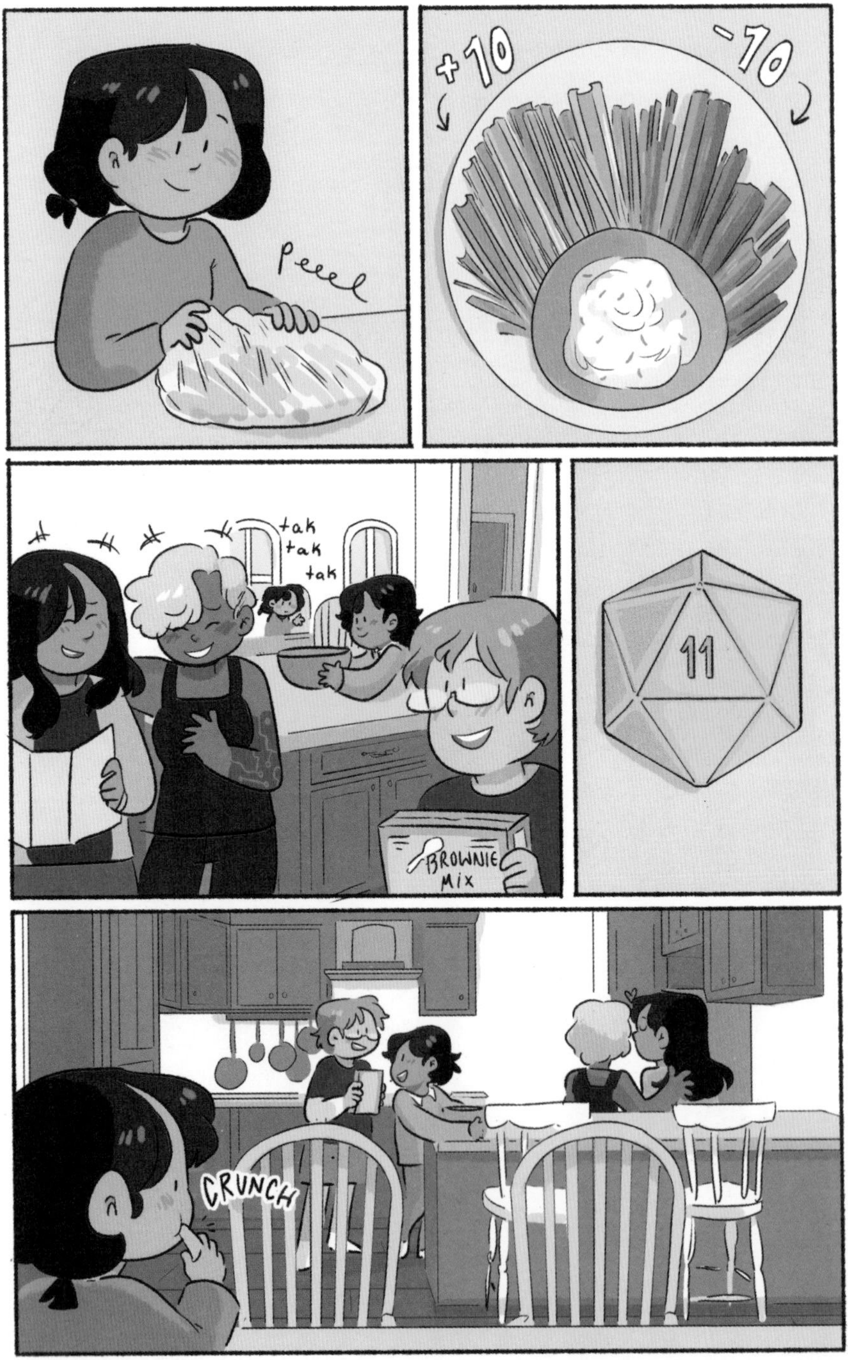
peeel
+10
-10
tak
tak
tak
BROWNIE MIX
11
CRUNCH

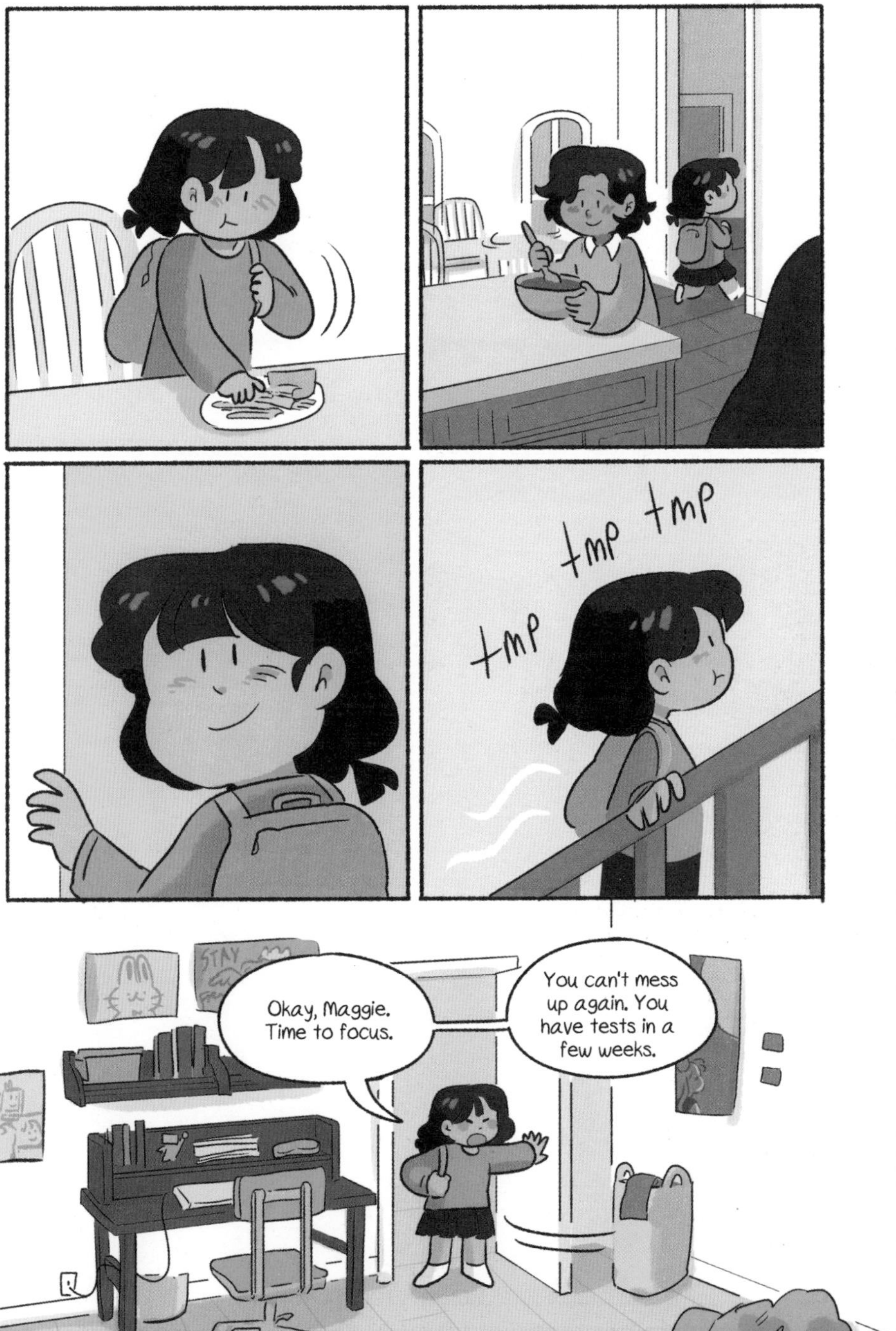
tmp
tmp
tmp
Okay, Maggie. Time to focus.
You can't mess up again. You have tests in a few weeks.

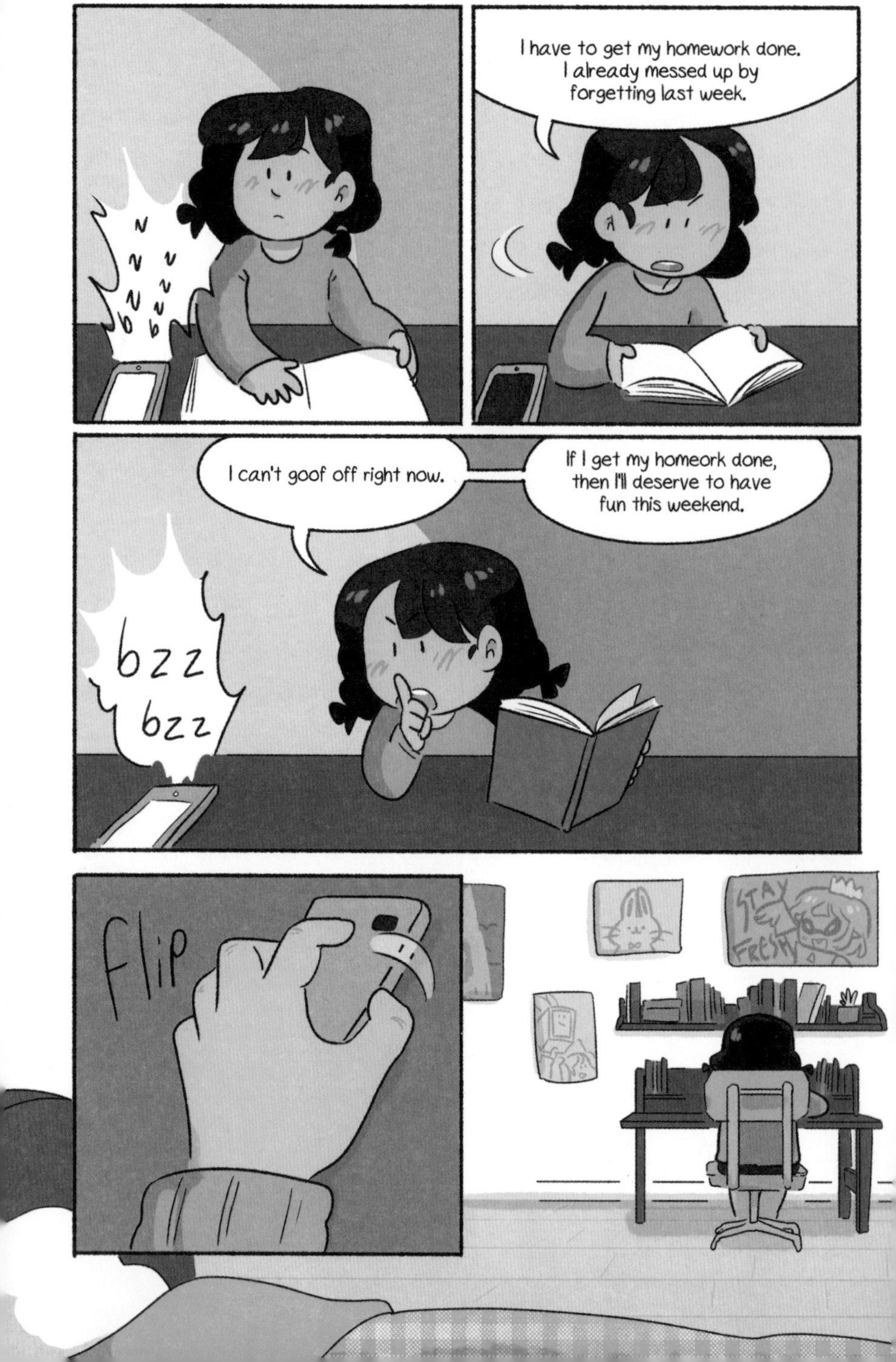
bzz bzz
I have to get my homework done. I already messed up by forgetting last week.
I can't goof off right now.
If I get my homeork done, then I'll deserve to have fun this weekend.
bzz bzz
flip
STAY FRESH

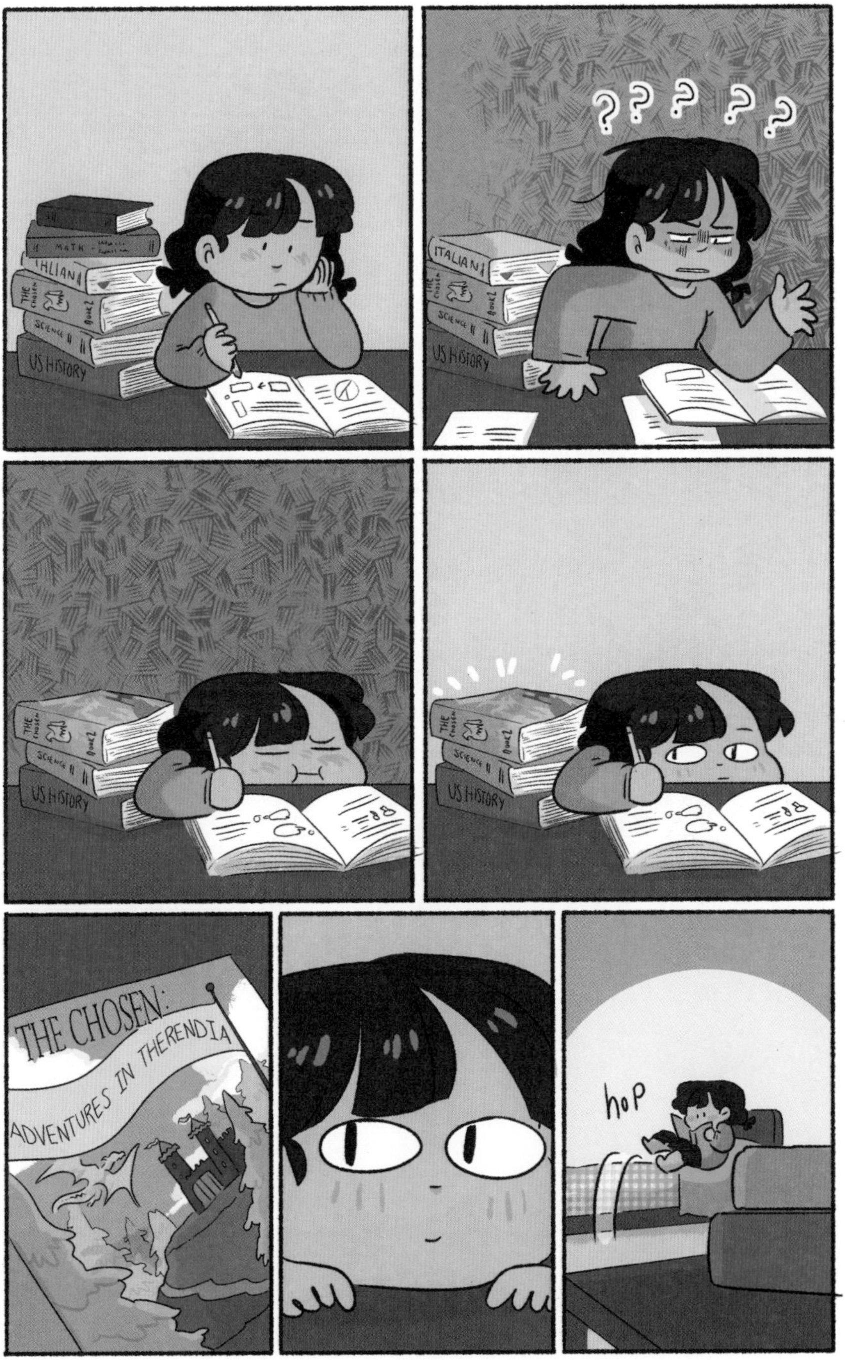
MATH
ITALIAN 1
THE CHOSEN
BOOK 2
SCIENCE II
US HISTORY
???
ITALIAN 1
THE CHOSEN
SCIENCE II
US HISTORY
THE CHOSEN
SCIENCE II
US HISTORY
THE CHOSEN
SCIENCE II
US HISTORY
THE CHOSEN:
ADVENTURES IN THERENDIA
hop

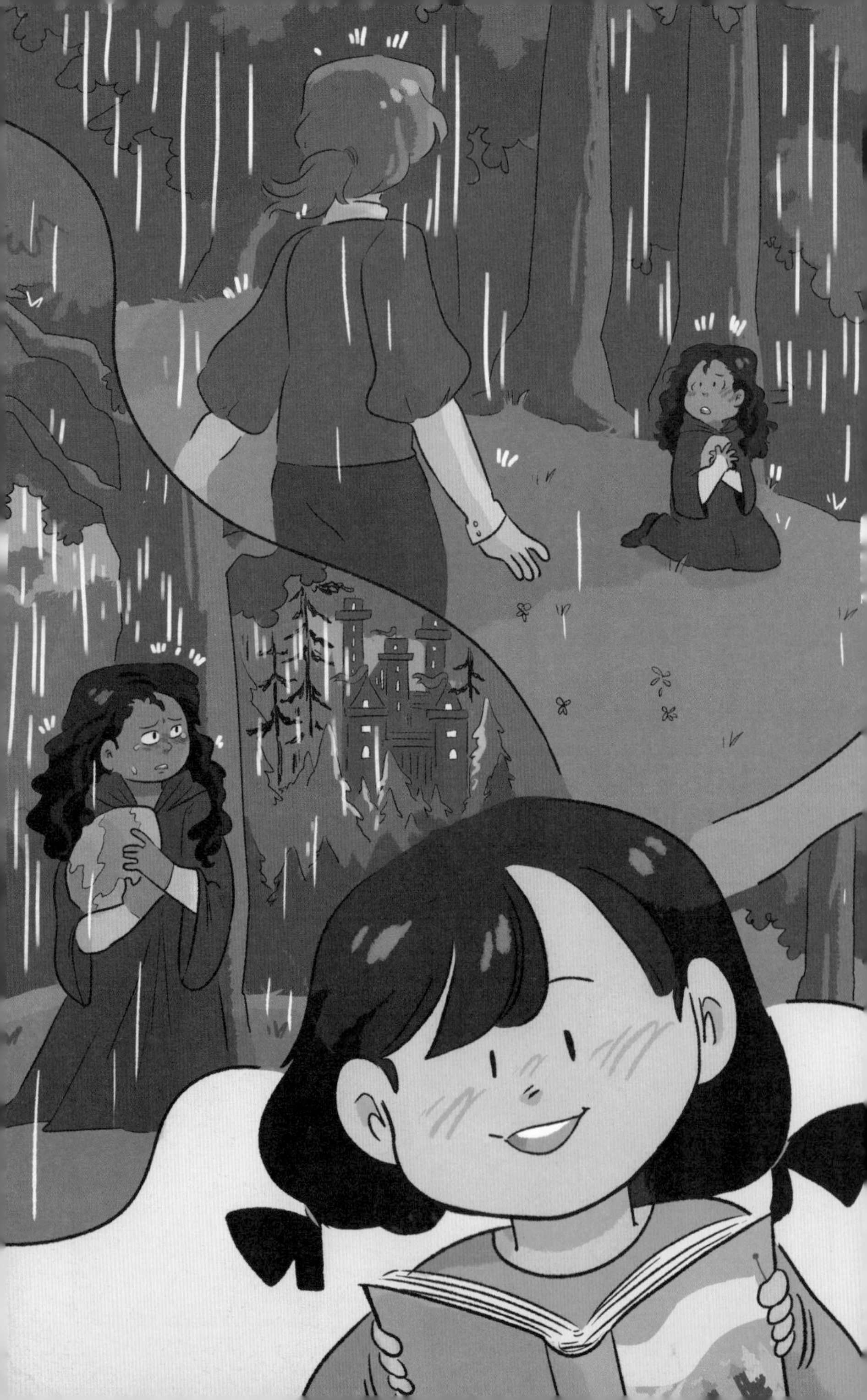

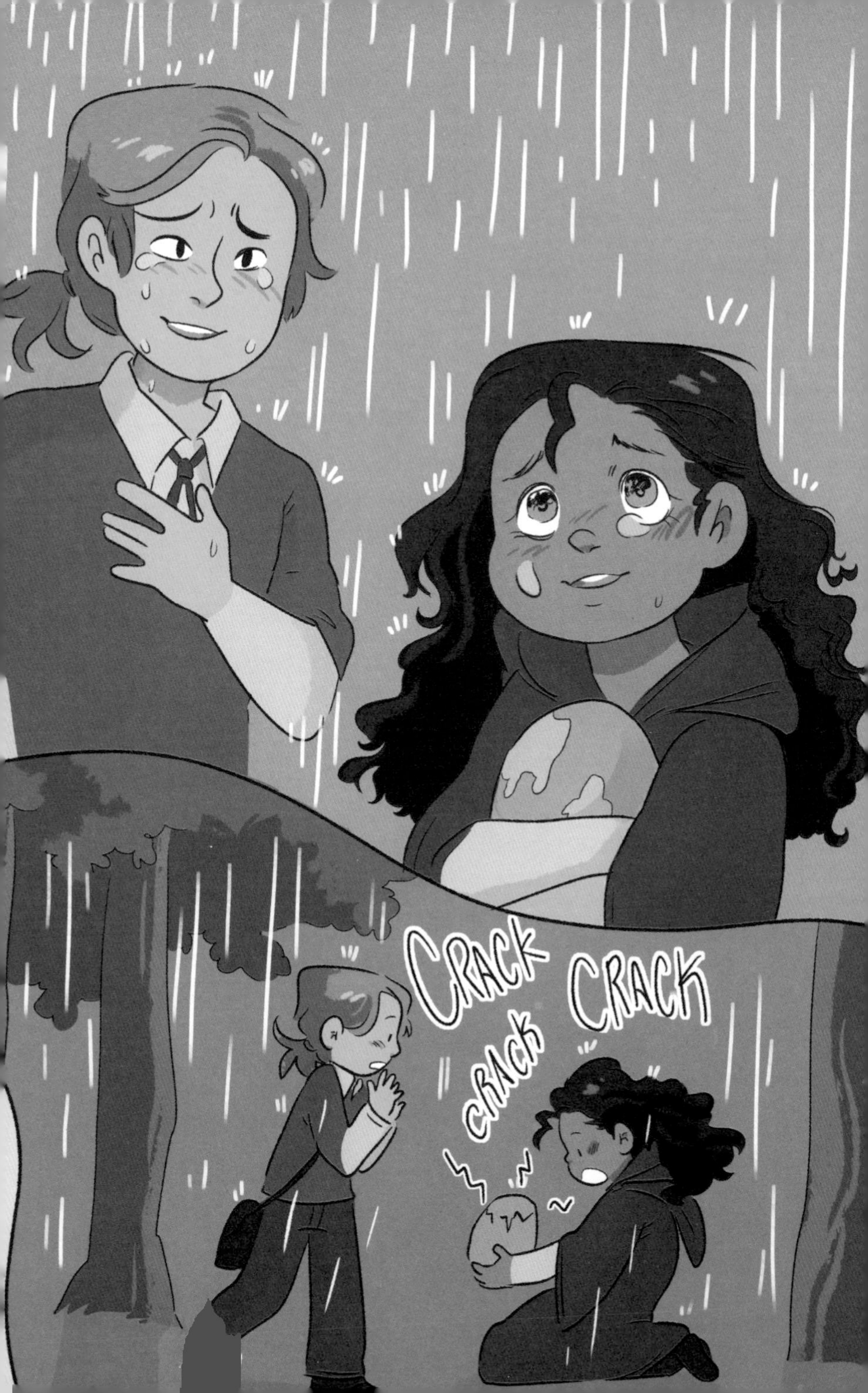
CRACK
CRACK
CRACK

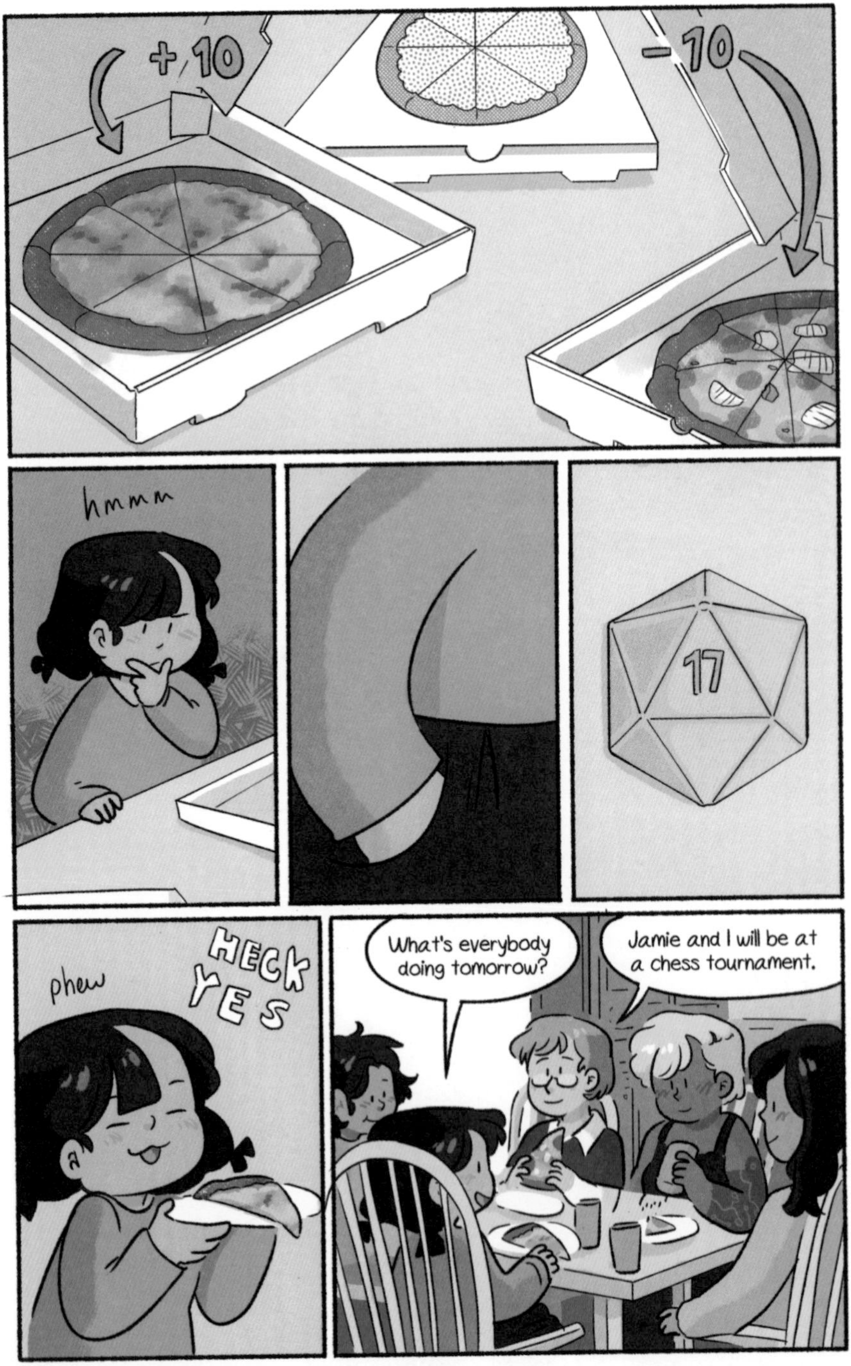
+10
-10
hmmm
17
phew
HECK YES
What's everybody doing tomorrow?
Jamie and I will be at a chess tournament.

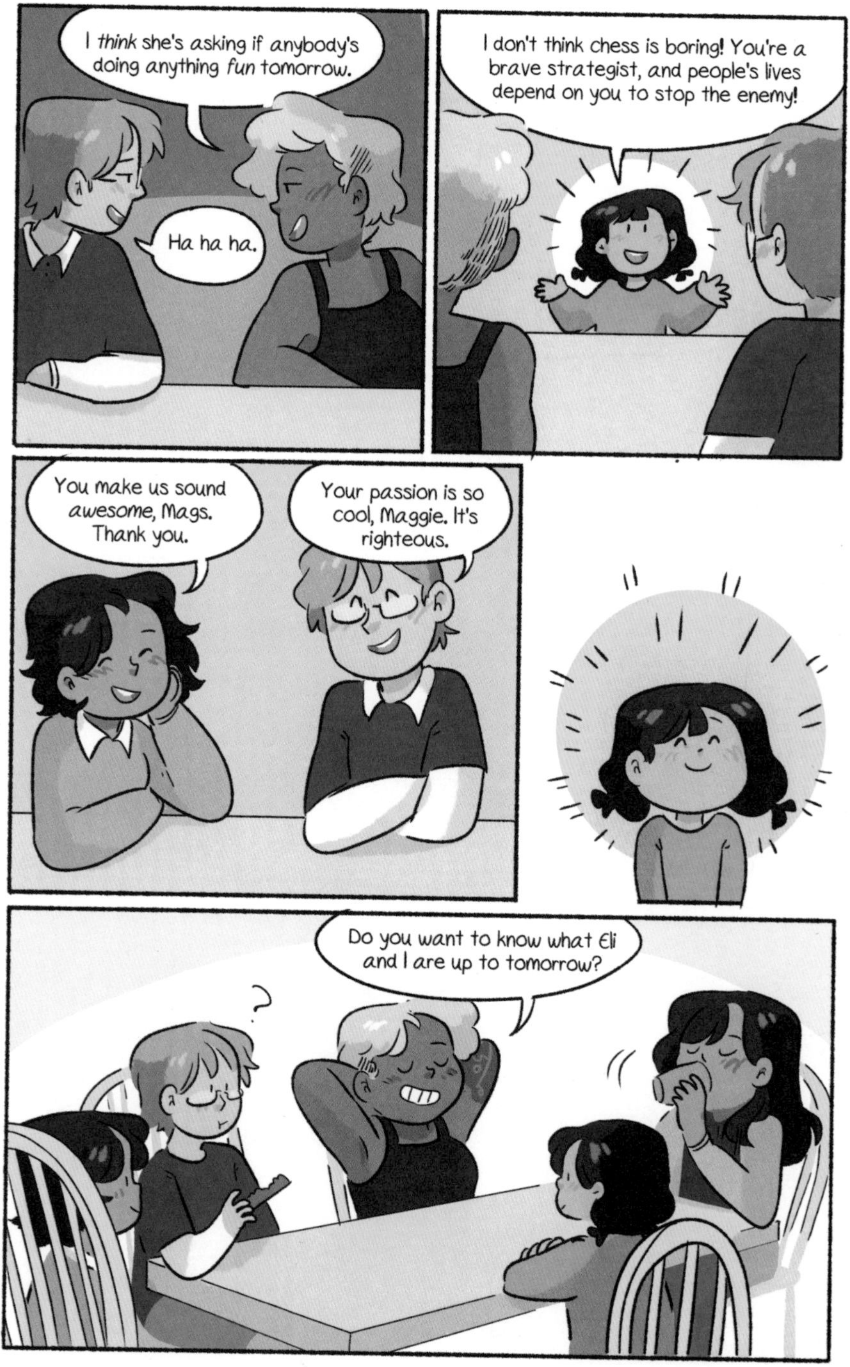
I think she's asking if anybody's doing anything fun tomorrow.
Ha ha ha.
I don't think chess is boring! You're a brave strategist, and people's lives depend on you to stop the enemy!
You make us sound awesome, Mags. Thank you.
Your passion is so cool, Maggie. It's righteous.
Do you want to know what Eli and I are up to tomorrow?
?

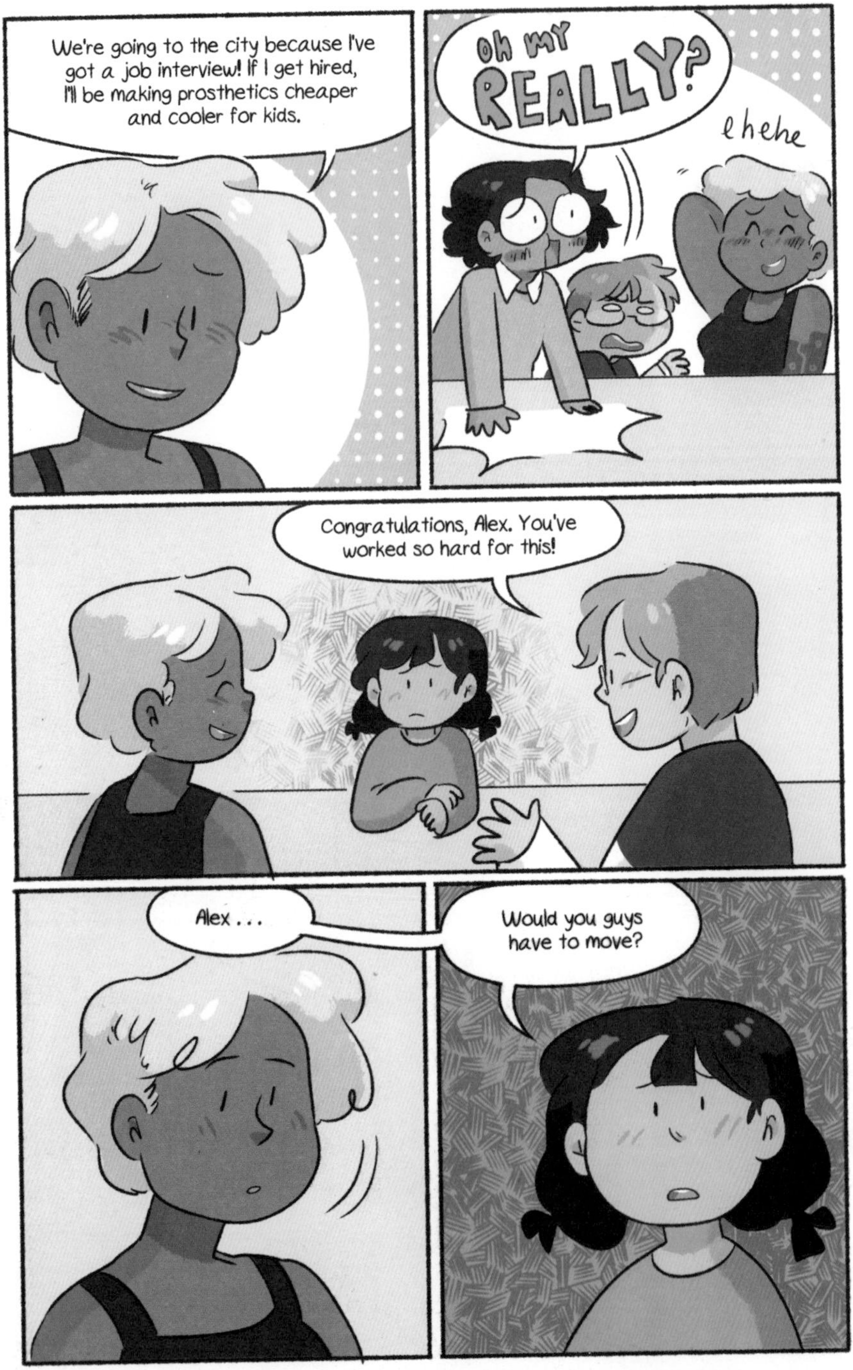
We're going to the city because I've got a job interview! If I get hired, I'll be making prosthetics cheaper and cooler for kids.
OH MY REALLY?
ehehe
Congratulations, Alex. You've worked so hard for this!
Alex . . .
Would you guys have to move?

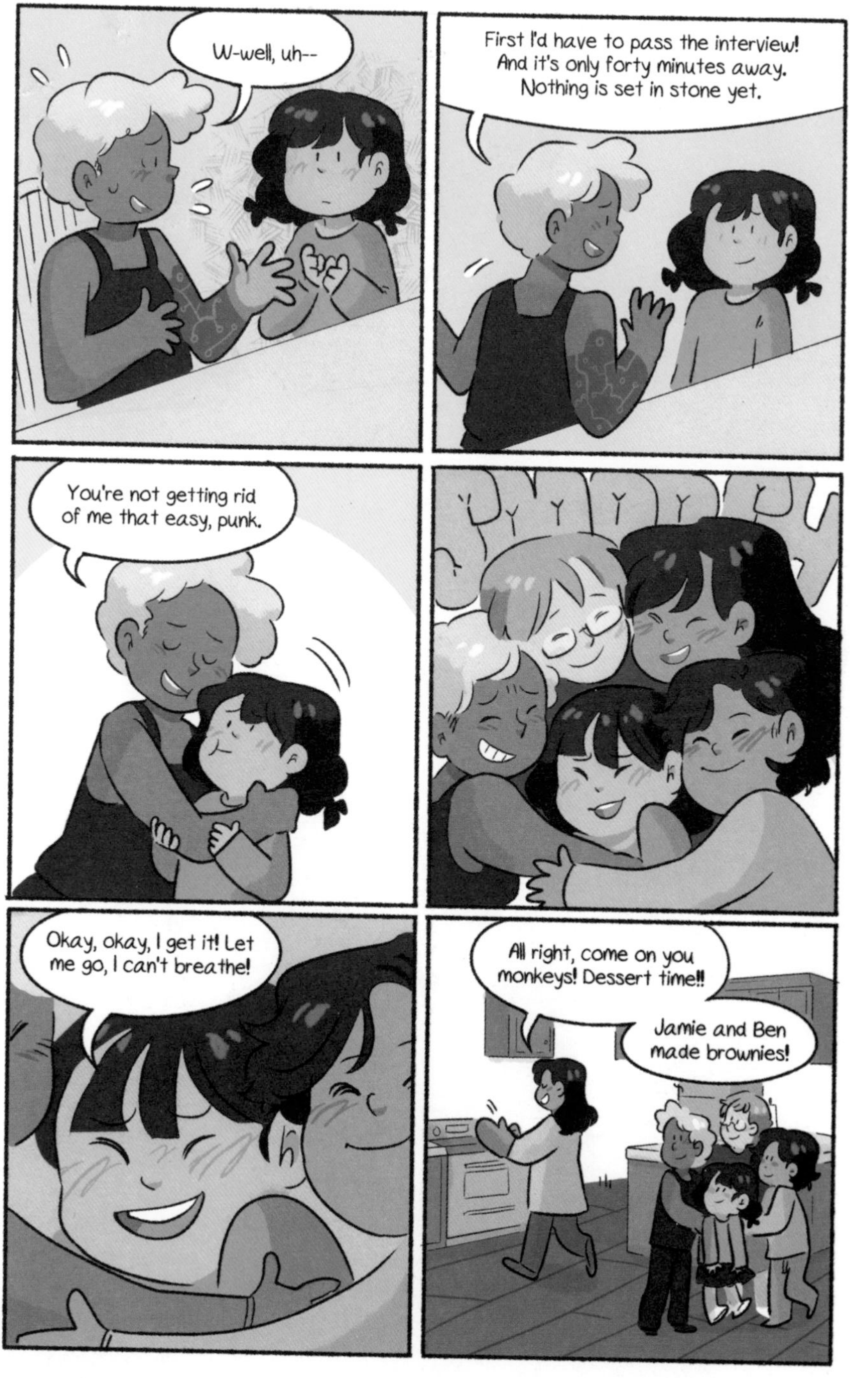
W-well, uh--
First I'd have to pass the interview! And it's only forty minutes away. Nothing is set in stone yet.
You're not getting rid of me that easy, punk.
Okay, okay, I get it! Let me go, I can't breathe!
All right, come on you monkeys! Dessert time!!
Jamie and Ben made brownies!

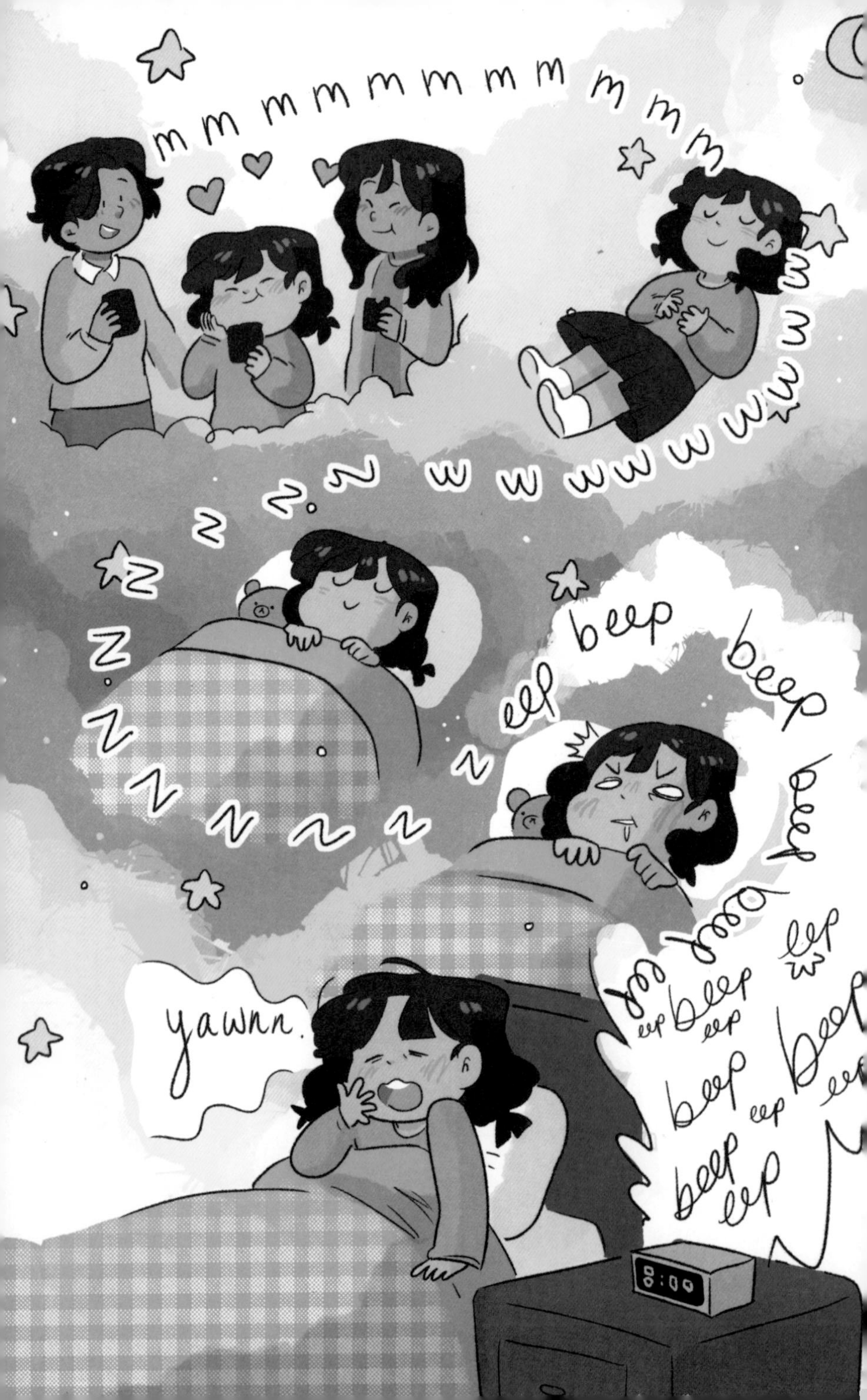

m m m m m m m m m m m m m
w w w w w w w w
z z z z z z z z z z z
beep
beep
beep
beep
yawnn.
beep beep beep beep beep

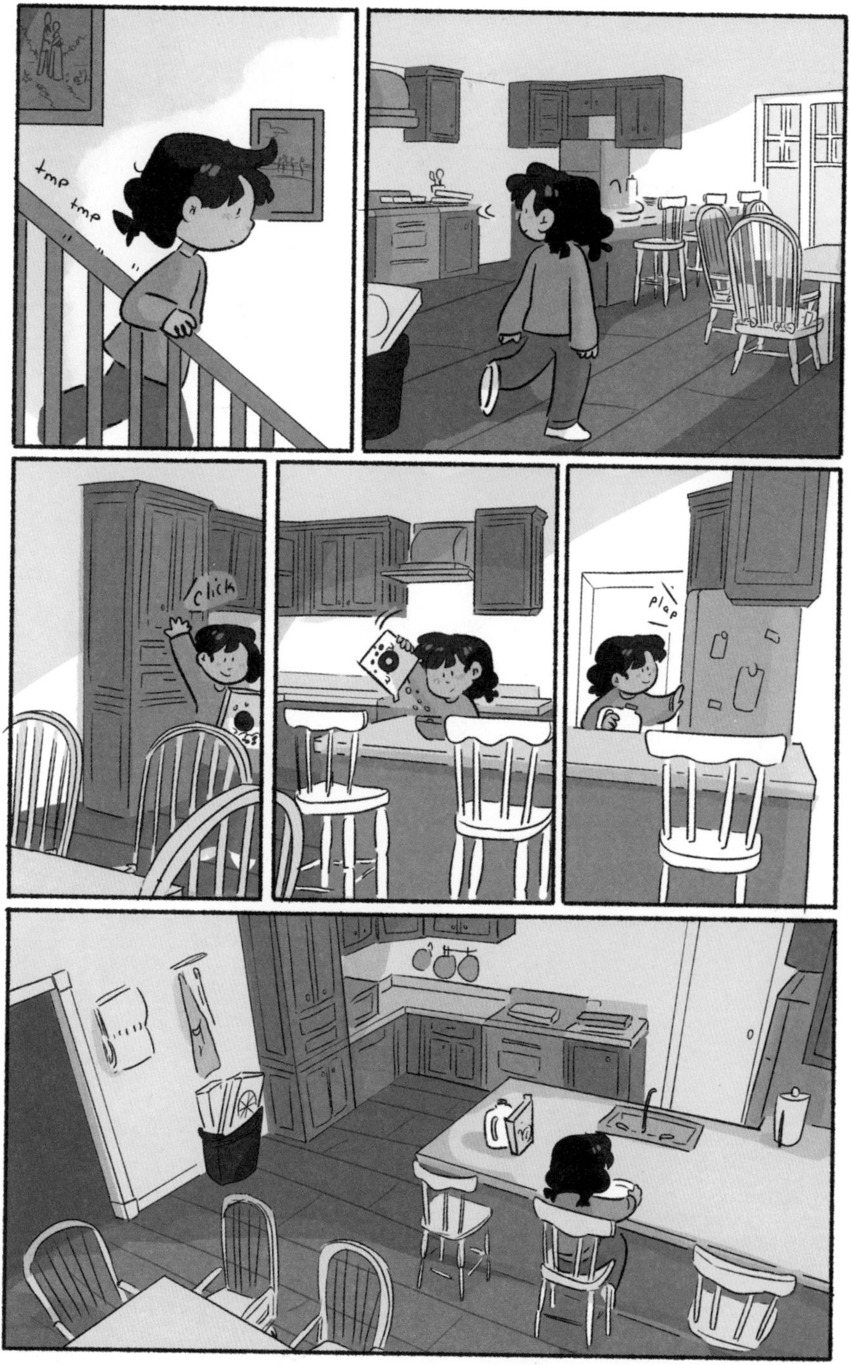
tmp tmp
click
plap

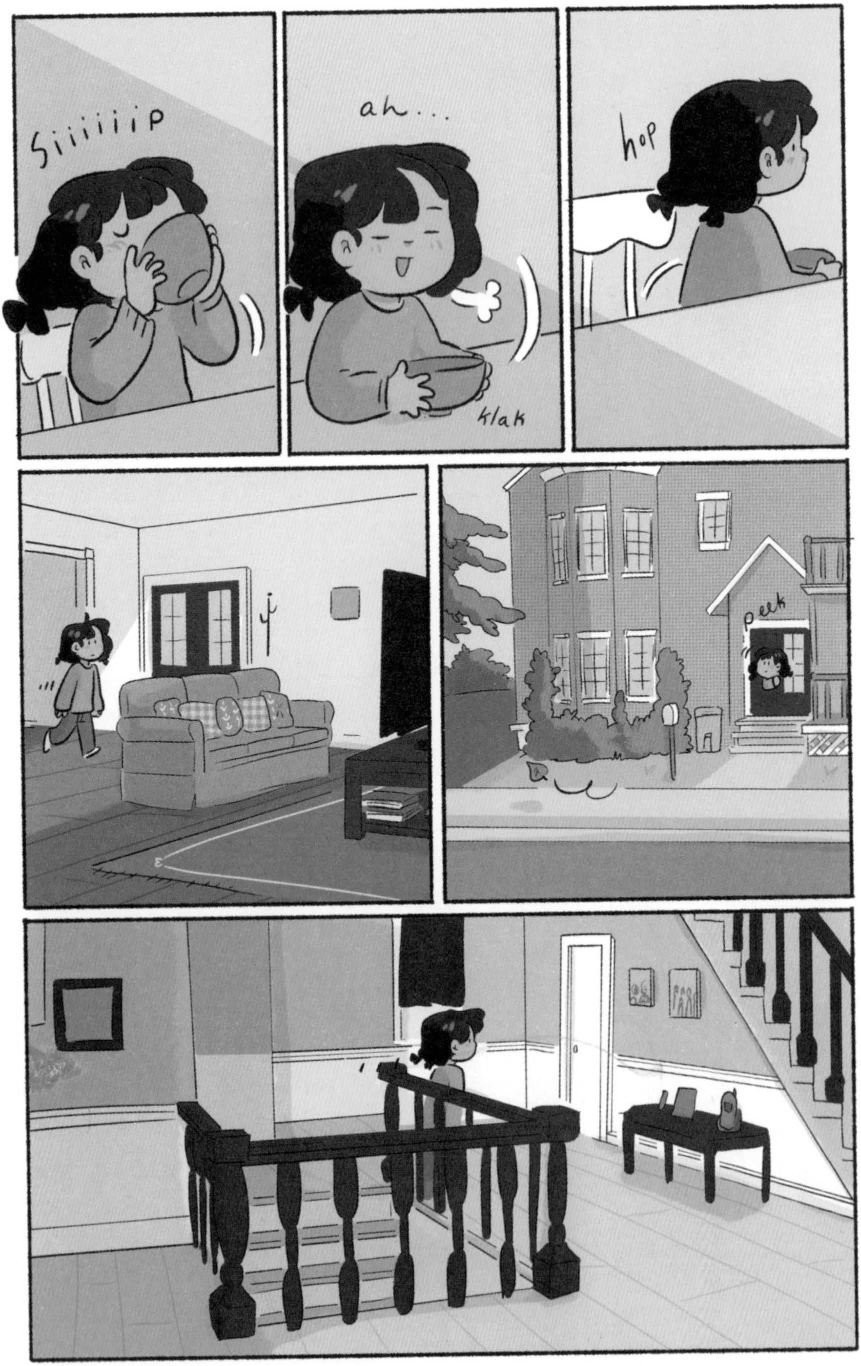

Siiiiiip
ah...
klak
hop
peek

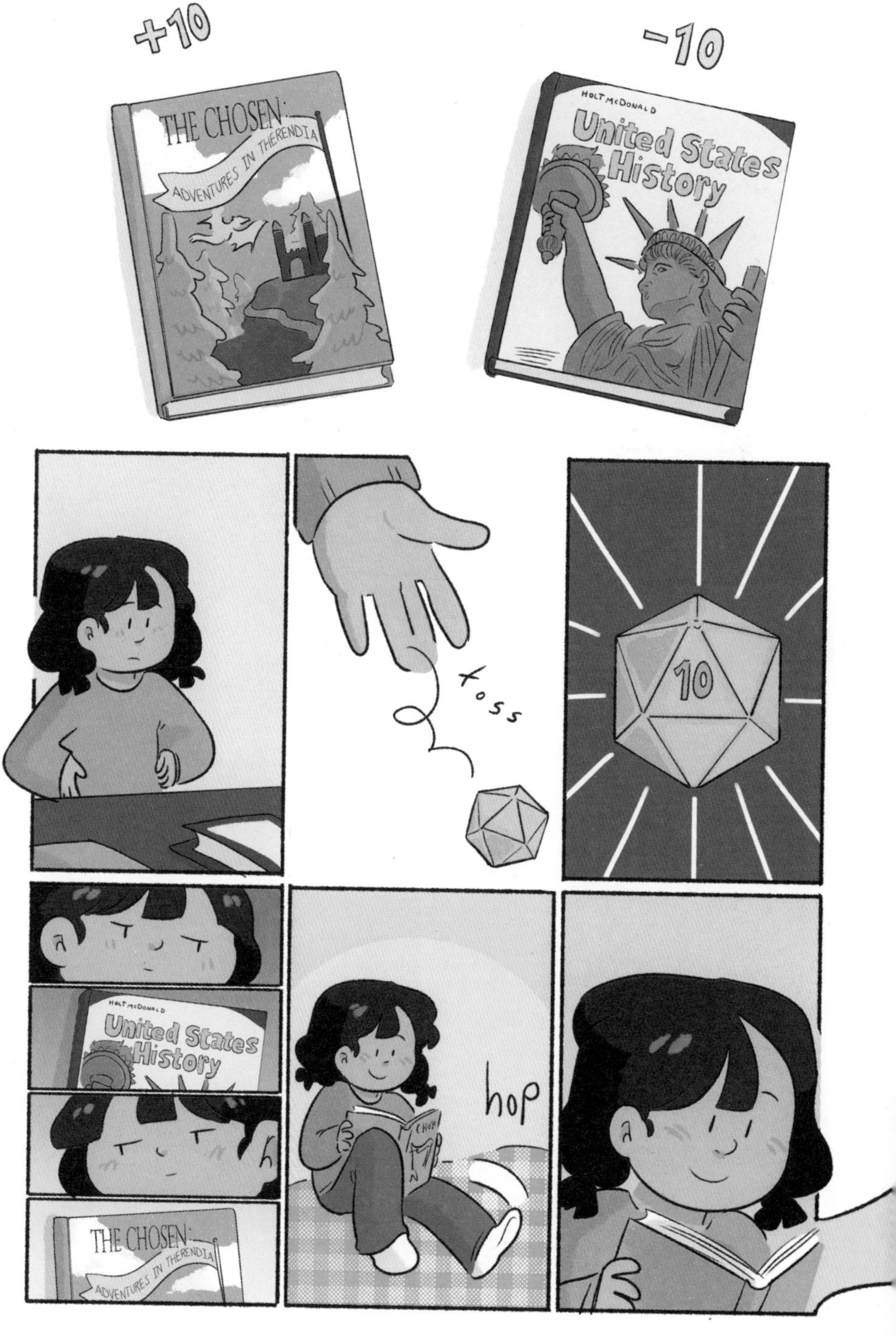
+10
-10
THE CHOSEN:
ADVENTURES IN THERENDIA
HOLT McDONALD
United States History
toss
10
HOLT McDONALD
United States History
THE CHOSEN:
ADVENTURES IN THERENDIA
hop

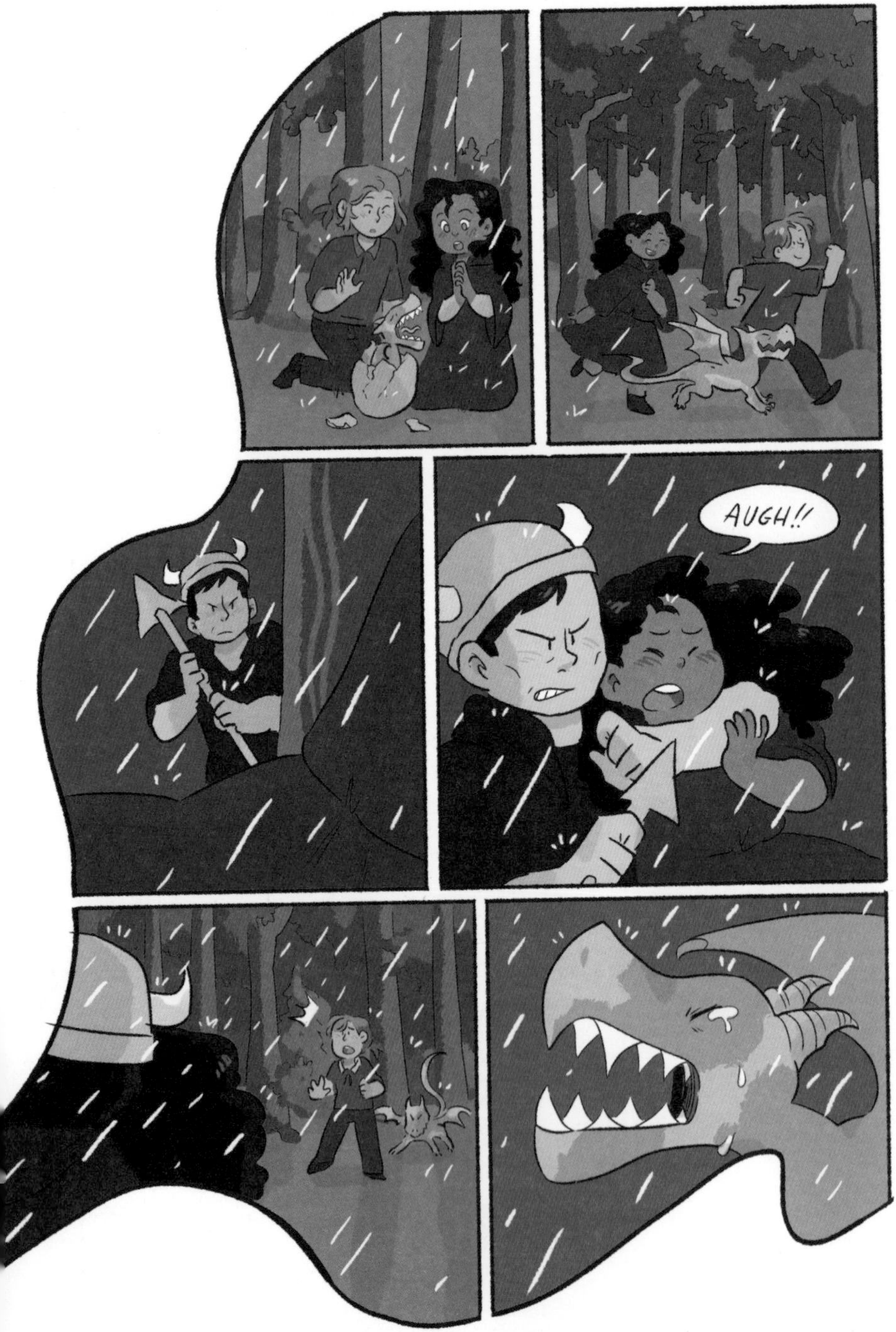
AUGH!!

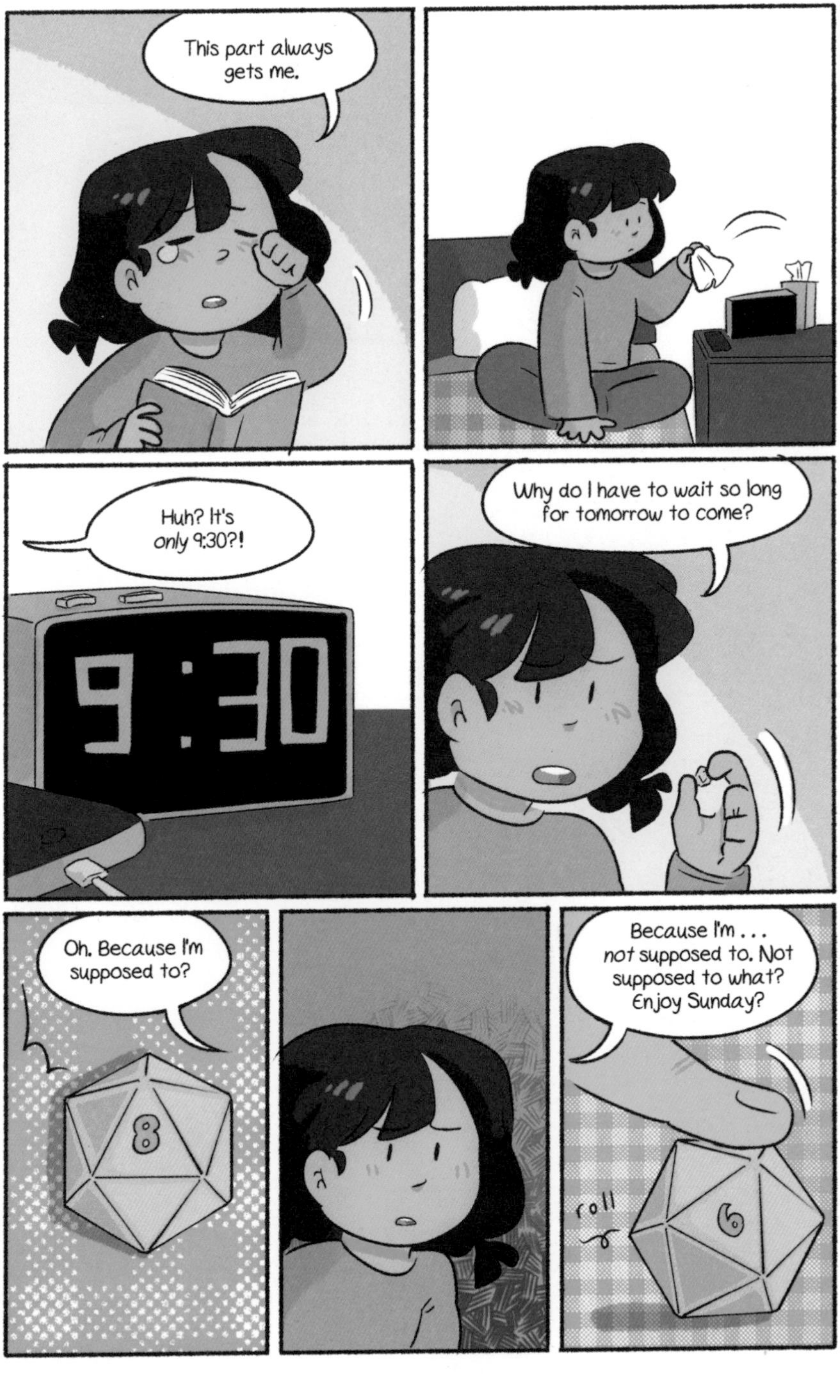
This part always gets me.
Huh? It's *only* 9:30?!
9:30
Why do I have to wait so long for tomorrow to come?
Oh. Because I'm supposed to?
8
Because I'm . . . *not* supposed to. Not supposed to what? Enjoy Sunday?
roll
6

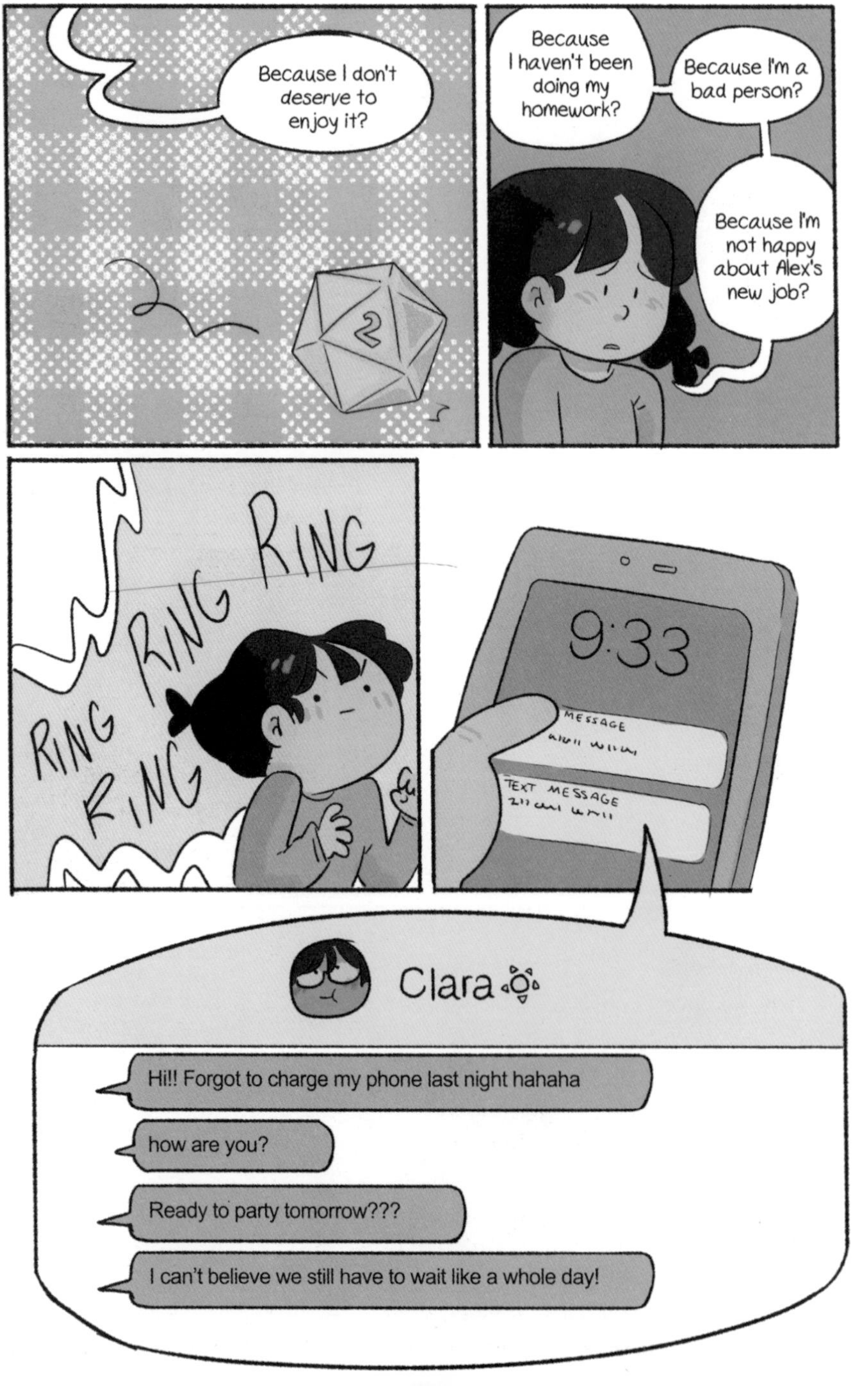
Because I don't deserve to enjoy it?
Because I haven't been doing my homework?
Because I'm a bad person?
Because I'm not happy about Alex's new job?
2
RING RING RING RING
9:33
MESSAGE
TEXT MESSAGE
Clara
Hi!! Forgot to charge my phone last night hahaha
how are you?
Ready to party tomorrow???
I can't believe we still have to wait like a whole day!

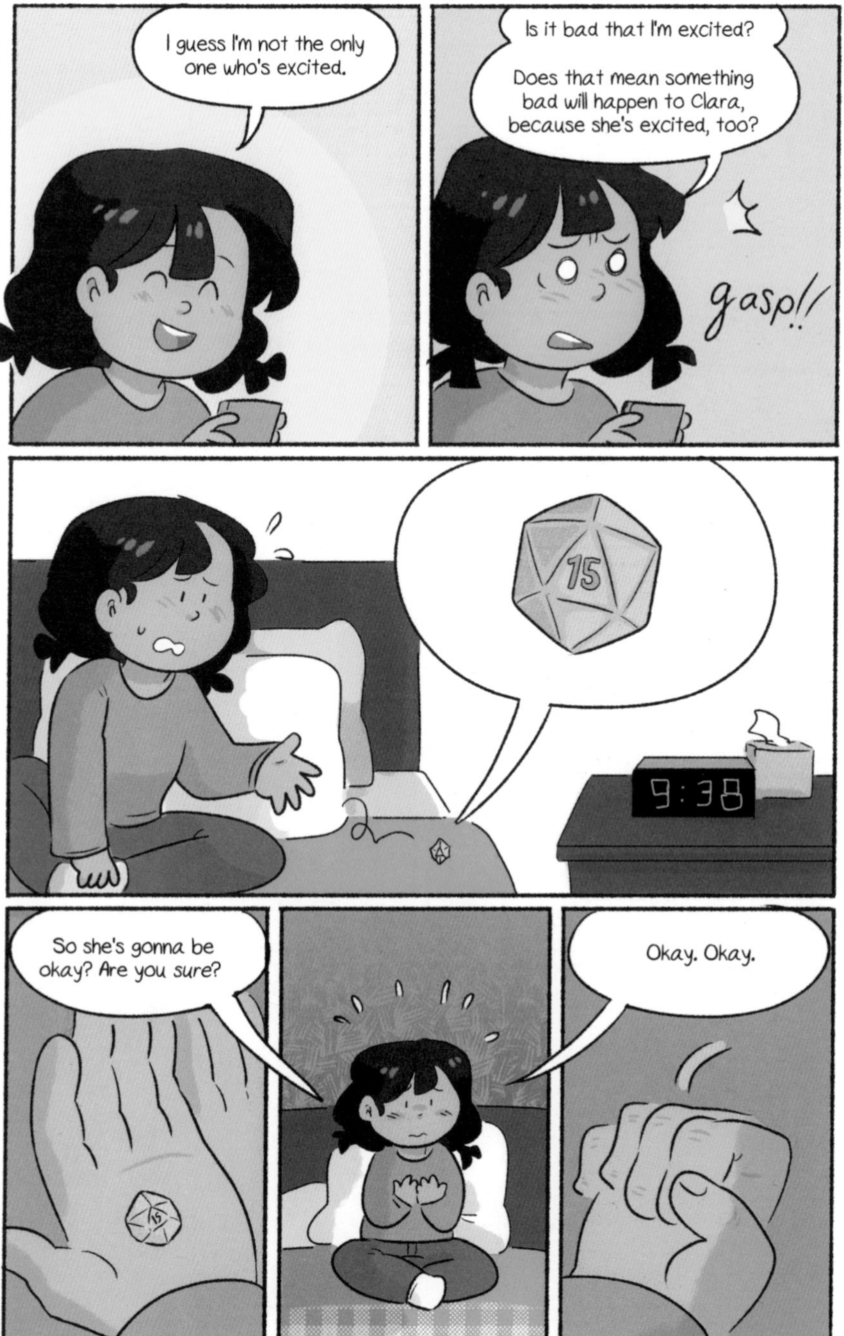
I guess I'm not the only one who's excited.
Is it bad that I'm excited?
Does that mean something bad will happen to Clara, because she's excited, too?
gasp!!
15
9:38
So she's gonna be okay? Are you sure?
Okay. Okay.

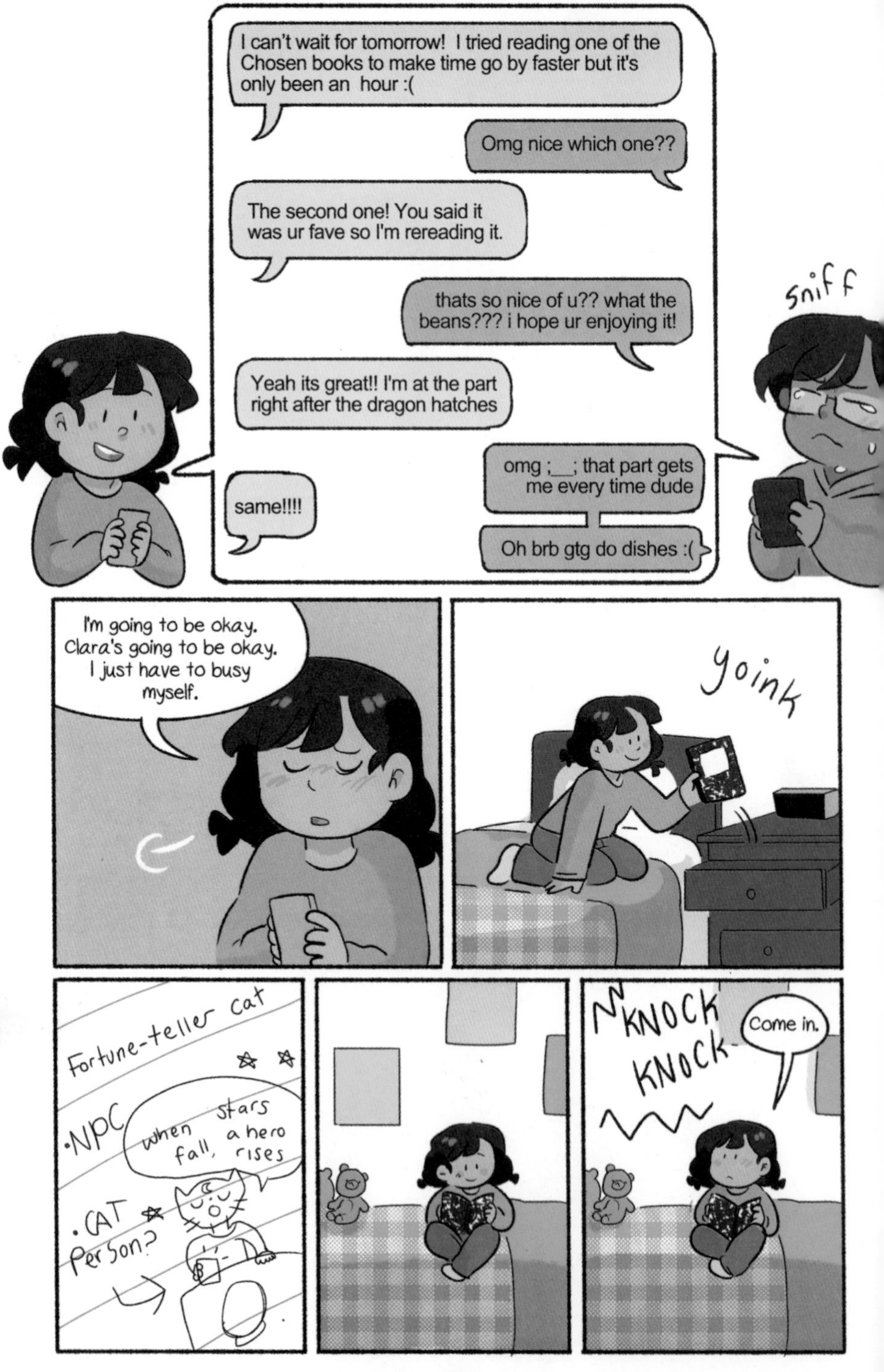

I can't wait for tomorrow! I tried reading one of the Chosen books to make time go by faster but it's only been an hour :(
Omg nice which one??
The second one! You said it was ur fave so I'm rereading it.
thats so nice of u?? what the beans??? i hope ur enjoying it!
Yeah its great!! I'm at the part right after the dragon hatches
omg ;__; that part gets me every time dude
same!!!!
Oh brb gtg do dishes :(
sniff
I'm going to be okay. Clara's going to be okay. I just have to busy myself.
yoink
Fortune-teller cat
•NPC
when stars fall, a hero rises
•CAT person?
KNOCK KNOCK
Come in.

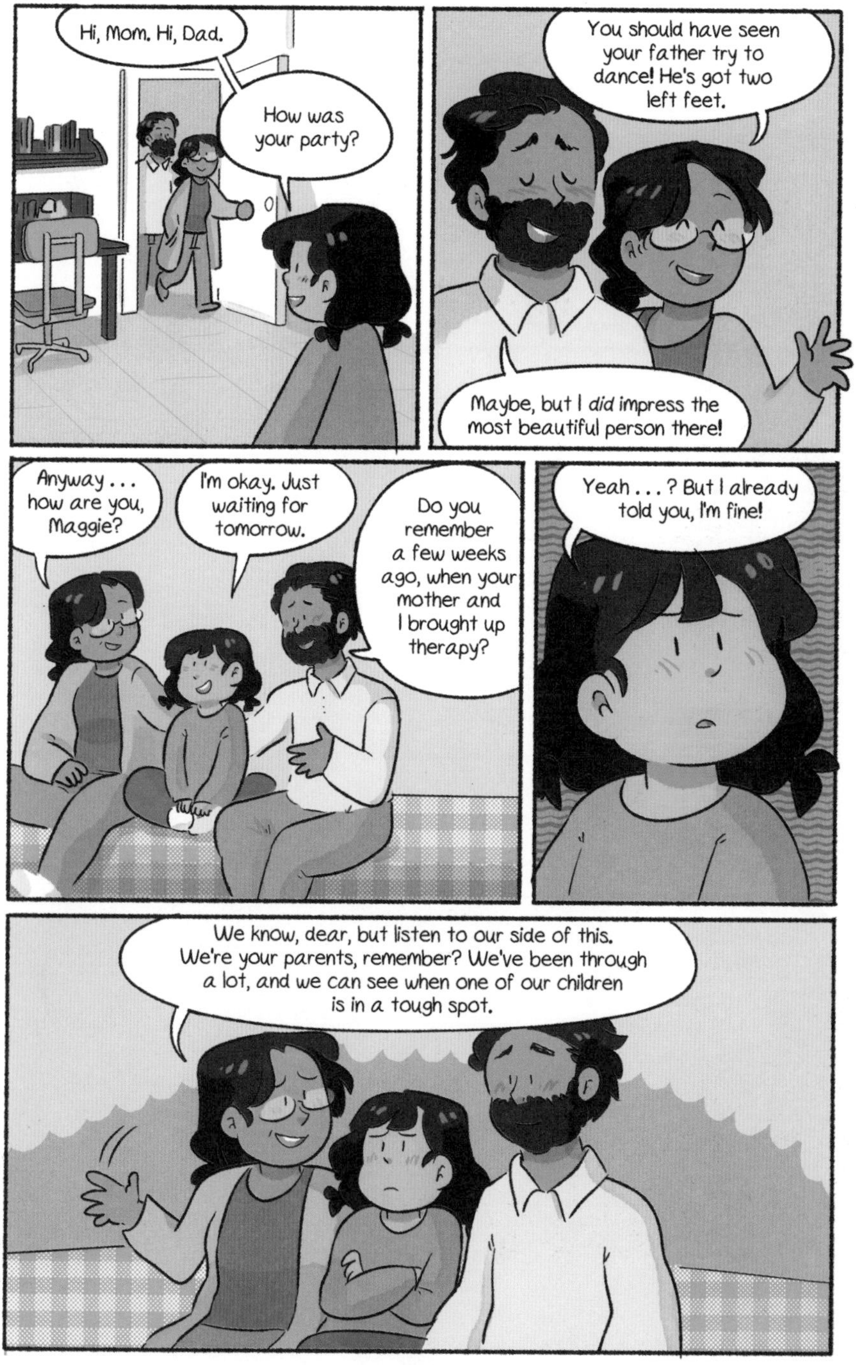
Hi, Mom. Hi, Dad.
How was your party?
You should have seen your father try to dance! He's got two left feet.
Maybe, but I *did* impress the most beautiful person there!
Anyway . . . how are you, Maggie?
I'm okay. Just waiting for tomorrow.
Do you remember a few weeks ago, when your mother and I brought up therapy?
Yeah . . . ? But I already told you, I'm fine!
We know, dear, but listen to our side of this. We're your parents, remember? We've been through a lot, and we can see when one of our children is in a tough spot.

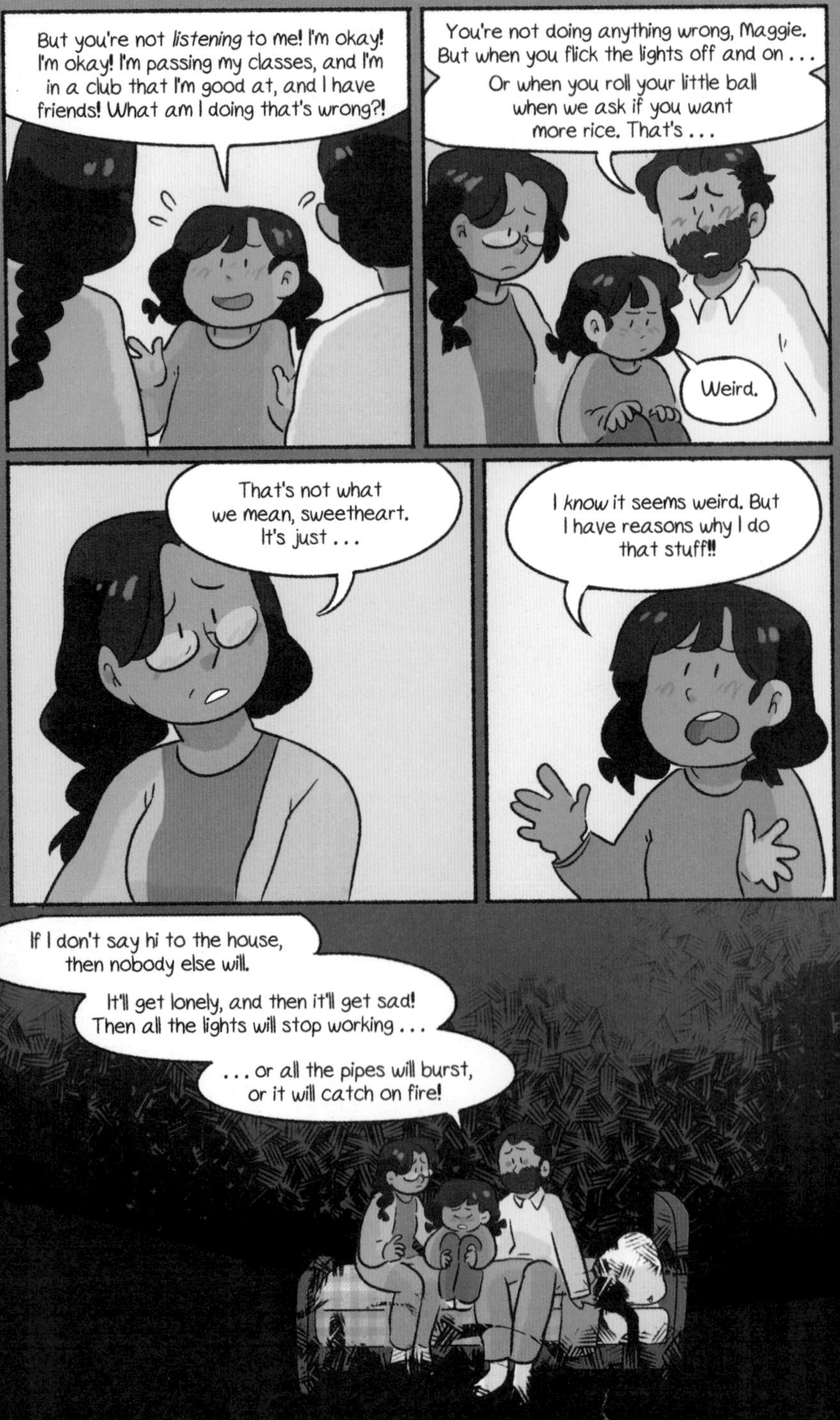

But you're not *listening* to me! I'm okay! I'm okay! I'm passing my classes, and I'm in a club that I'm good at, and I have friends! What am I doing that's wrong?!
You're not doing anything wrong, Maggie. But when you flick the lights off and on . . .
Or when you roll your little ball when we ask if you want more rice. That's . . .
Weird.
That's not what we mean, sweetheart. It's just . . .
I *know* it seems weird. But I have reasons why I do that stuff!!
If I don't say hi to the house, then nobody else will.
It'll get lonely, and then it'll get sad! Then all the lights will stop working . . .
. . . or all the pipes will burst, or it will catch on fire!

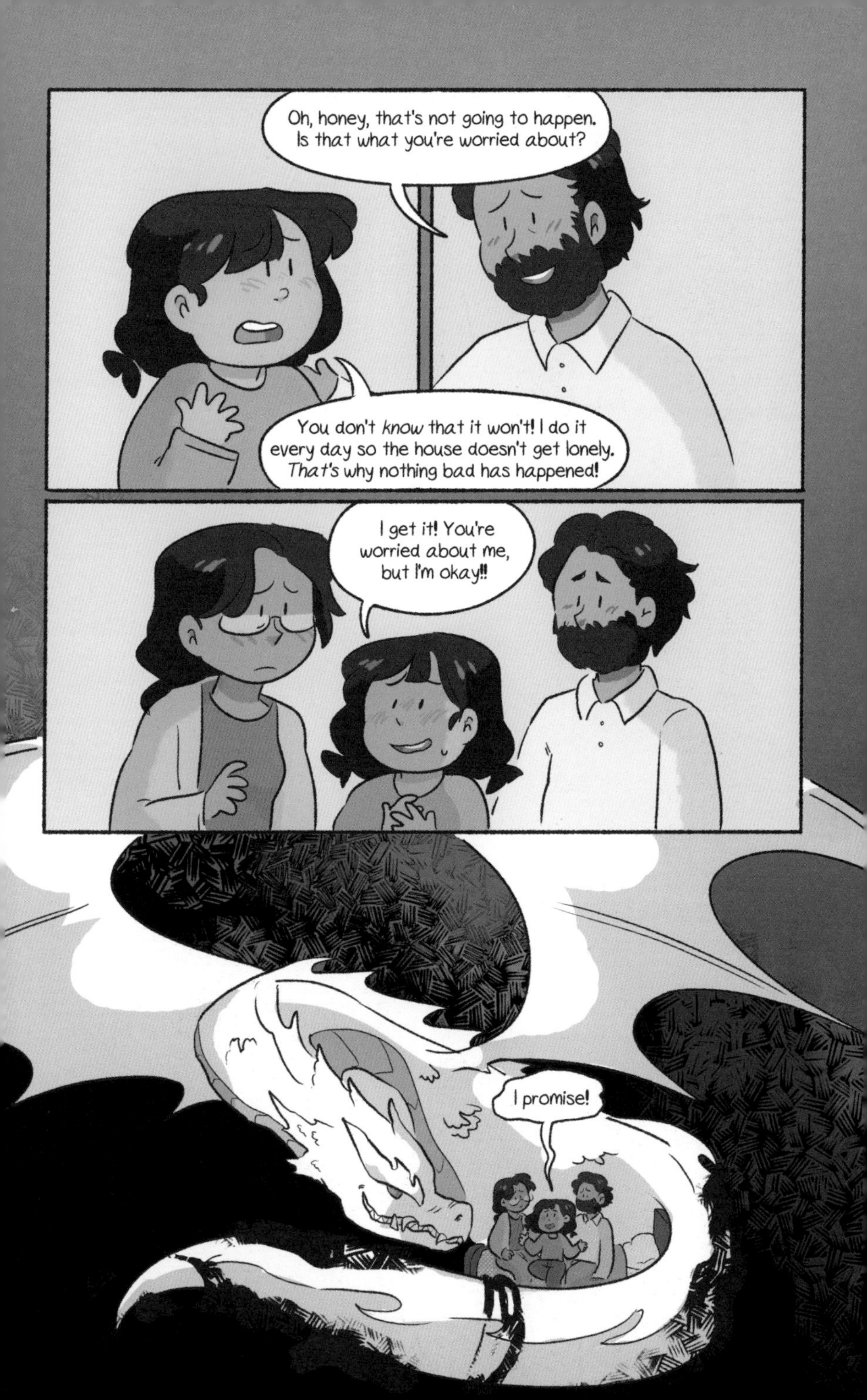
Oh, honey, that's not going to happen. Is that what you're worried about?
You don't *know* that it won't! I do it every day so the house doesn't get lonely. *That's* why nothing bad has happened!
I get it! You're worried about me, but I'm okay!!
I promise!

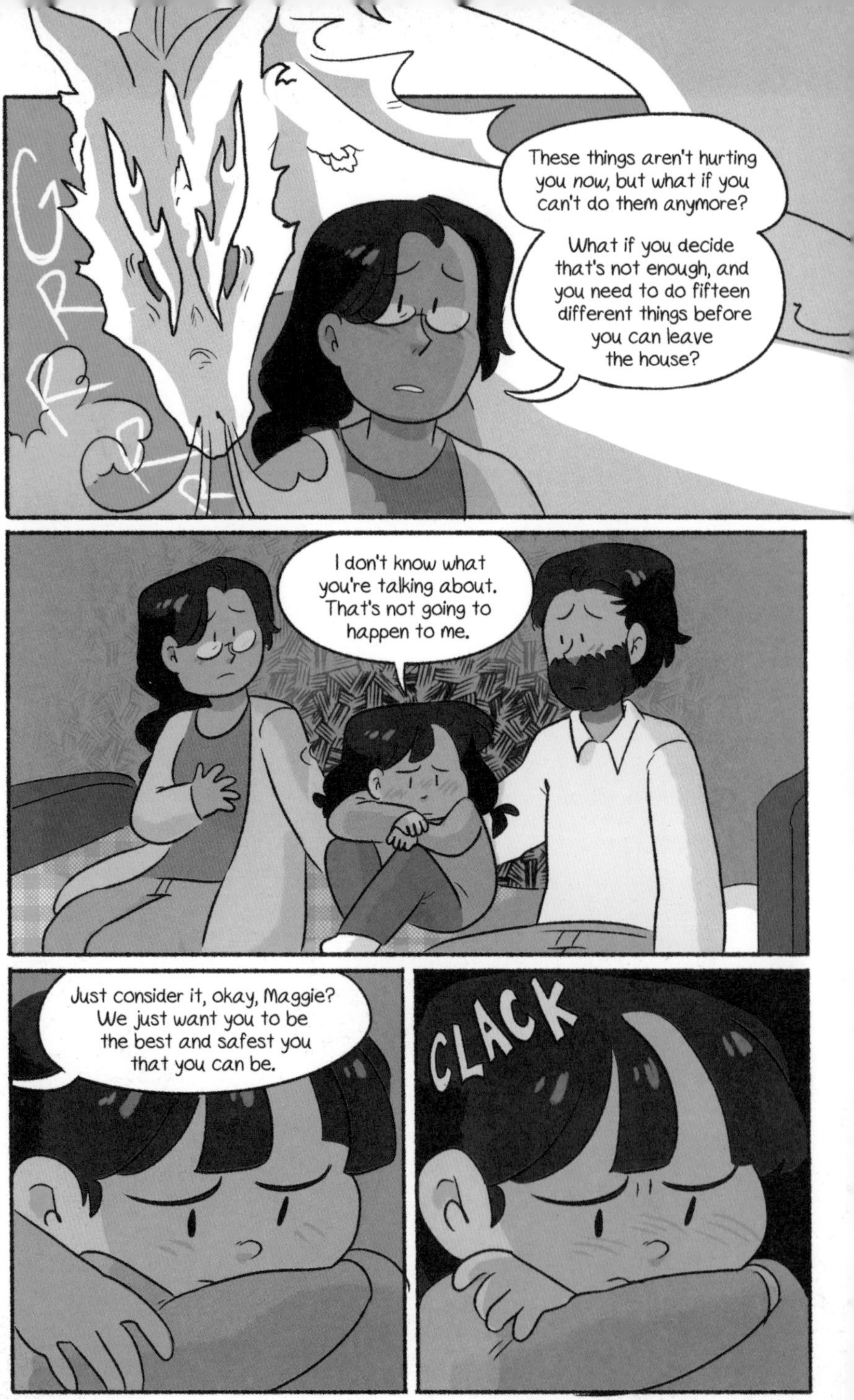
GRRR
These things aren't hurting you now, but what if you can't do them anymore?
What if you decide that's not enough, and you need to do fifteen different things before you can leave the house?
I don't know what you're talking about. That's not going to happen to me.
Just consider it, okay, Maggie? We just want you to be the best and safest you that you can be.
CLACK

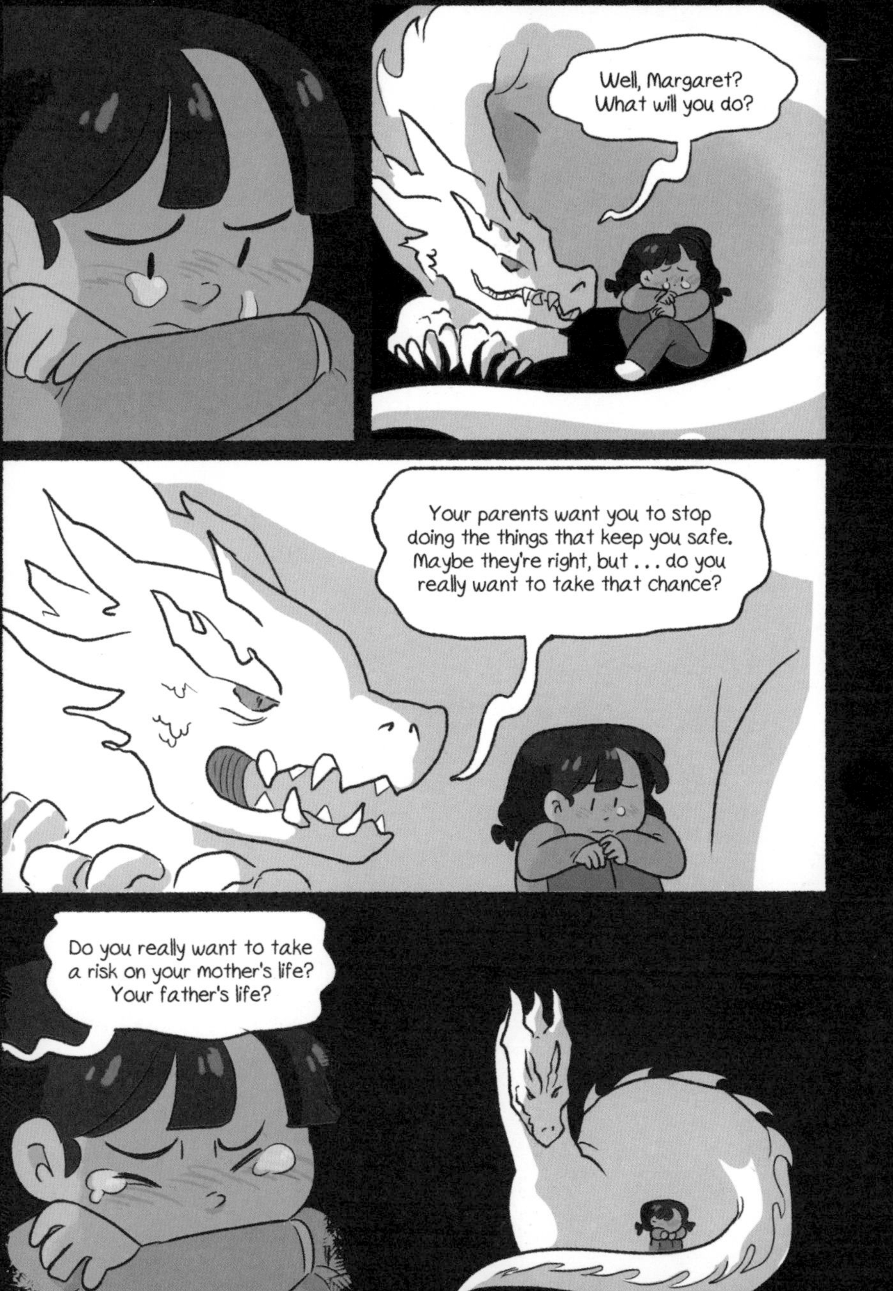
Well, Margaret? What will you do?
Your parents want you to stop doing the things that keep you safe. Maybe they're right, but . . . do you really want to take that chance?
Do you really want to take a risk on your mother's life? Your father's life?

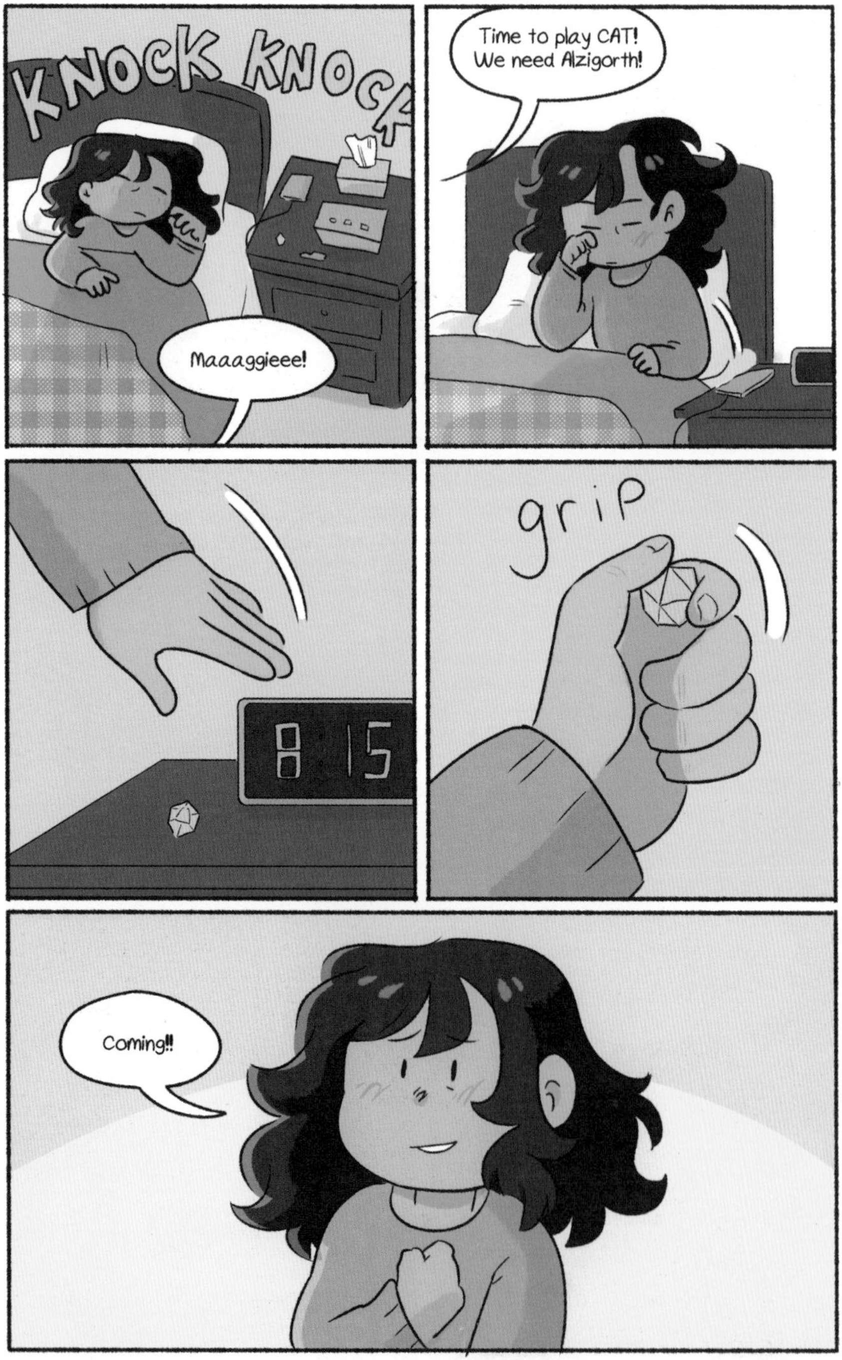
KNOCK KNOCK
Maaaggieee!
Time to play CAT!
We need Alzigorth!
grip
Coming!!

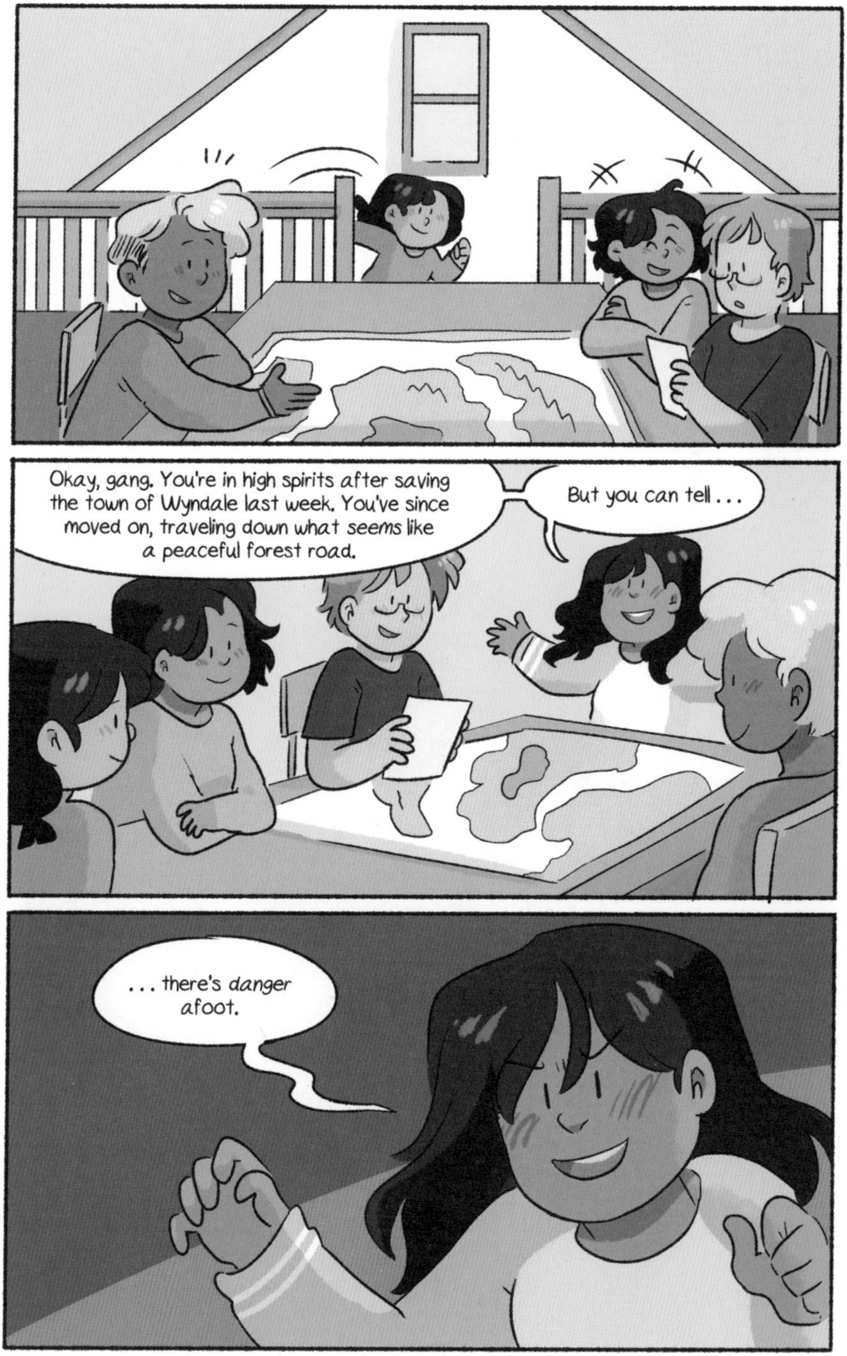
Okay, gang. You're in high spirits after saving the town of Wyndale last week. You've since moved on, traveling down what seems like a peaceful forest road.
But you can tell . . .
. . . there's danger afoot.

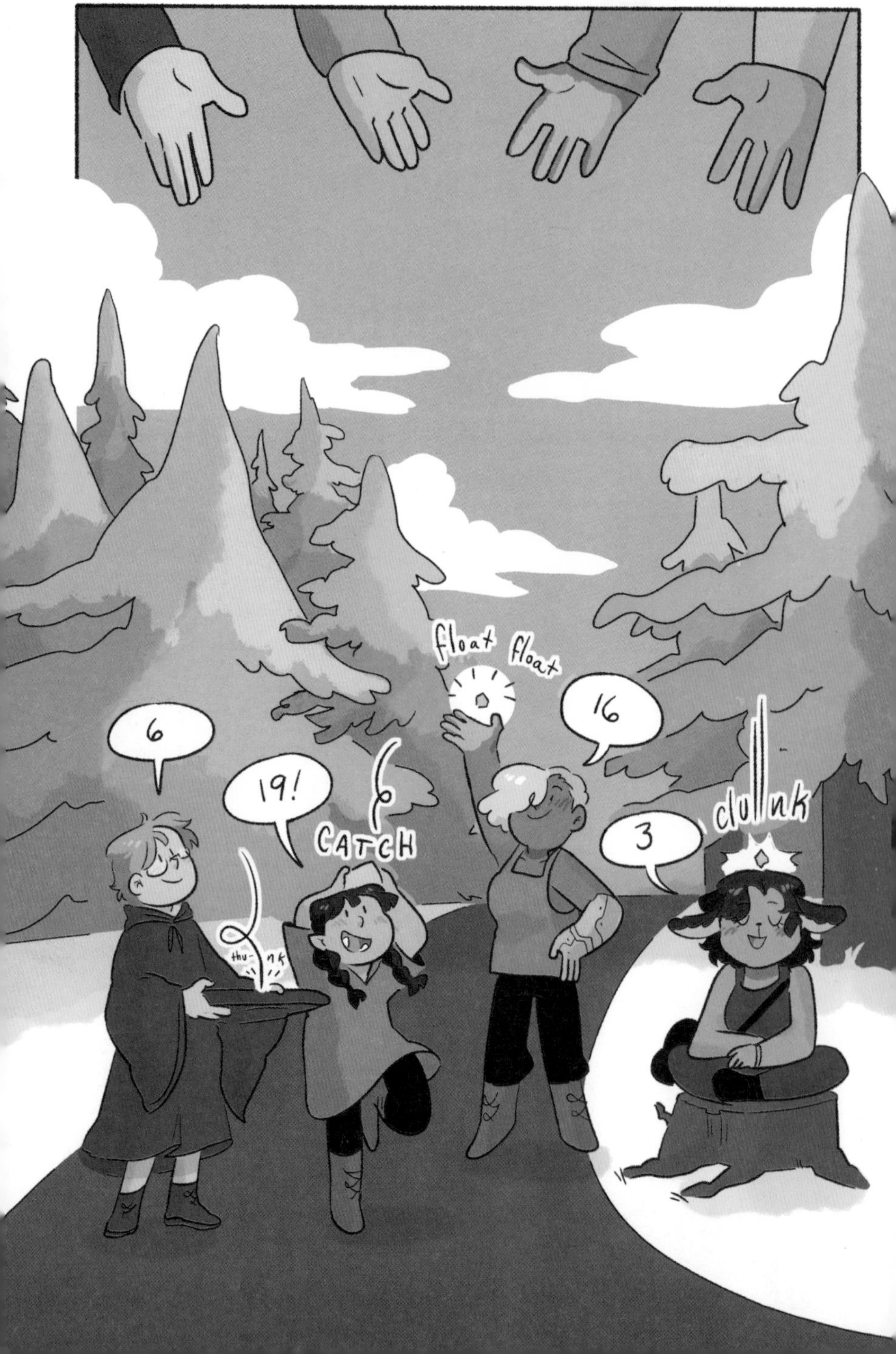
float float
16
6
19!
CATCH
thu-nk
3
clunk

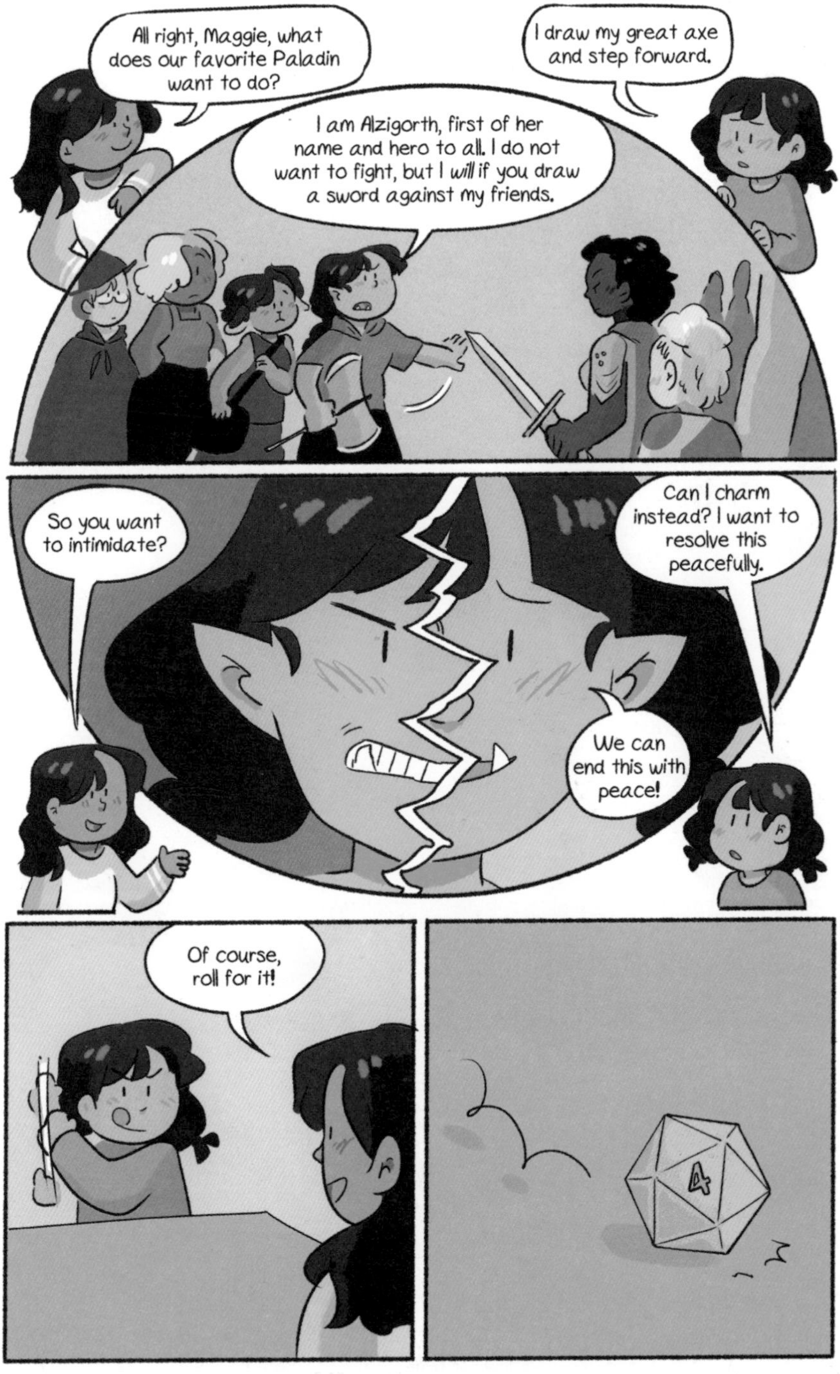
All right, Maggie, what does our favorite Paladin want to do?
I draw my great axe and step forward.
I am Alzigorth, first of her name and hero to all. I do not want to fight, but I *will* if you draw a sword against my friends.
So you want to intimidate?
Can I charm instead? I want to resolve this peacefully.
We can end this with peace!
Of course, roll for it!
4

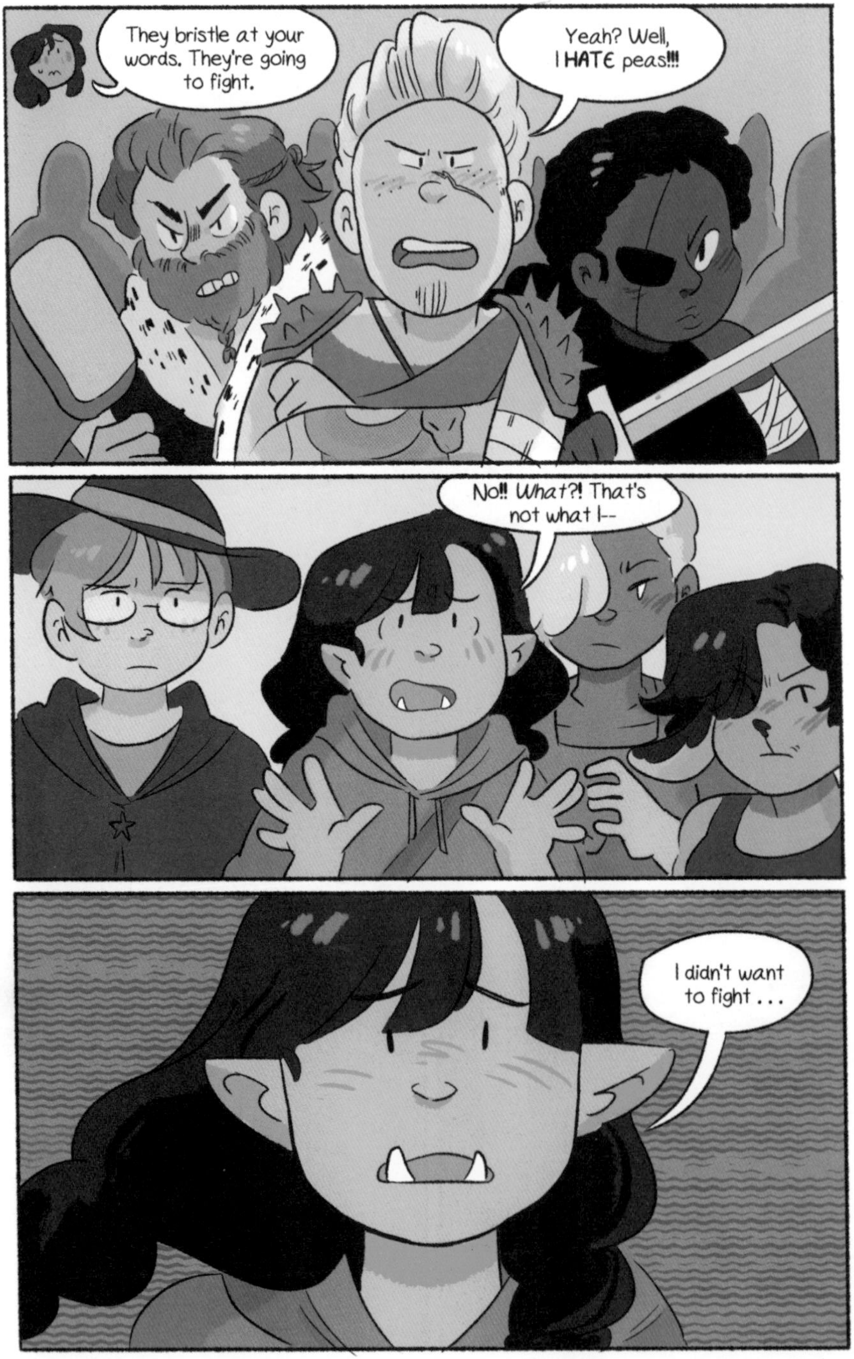
They bristle at your words. They're going to fight.
Yeah? Well, I HATE peas!!!
No!! What?! That's not what I--
I didn't want to fight . . .

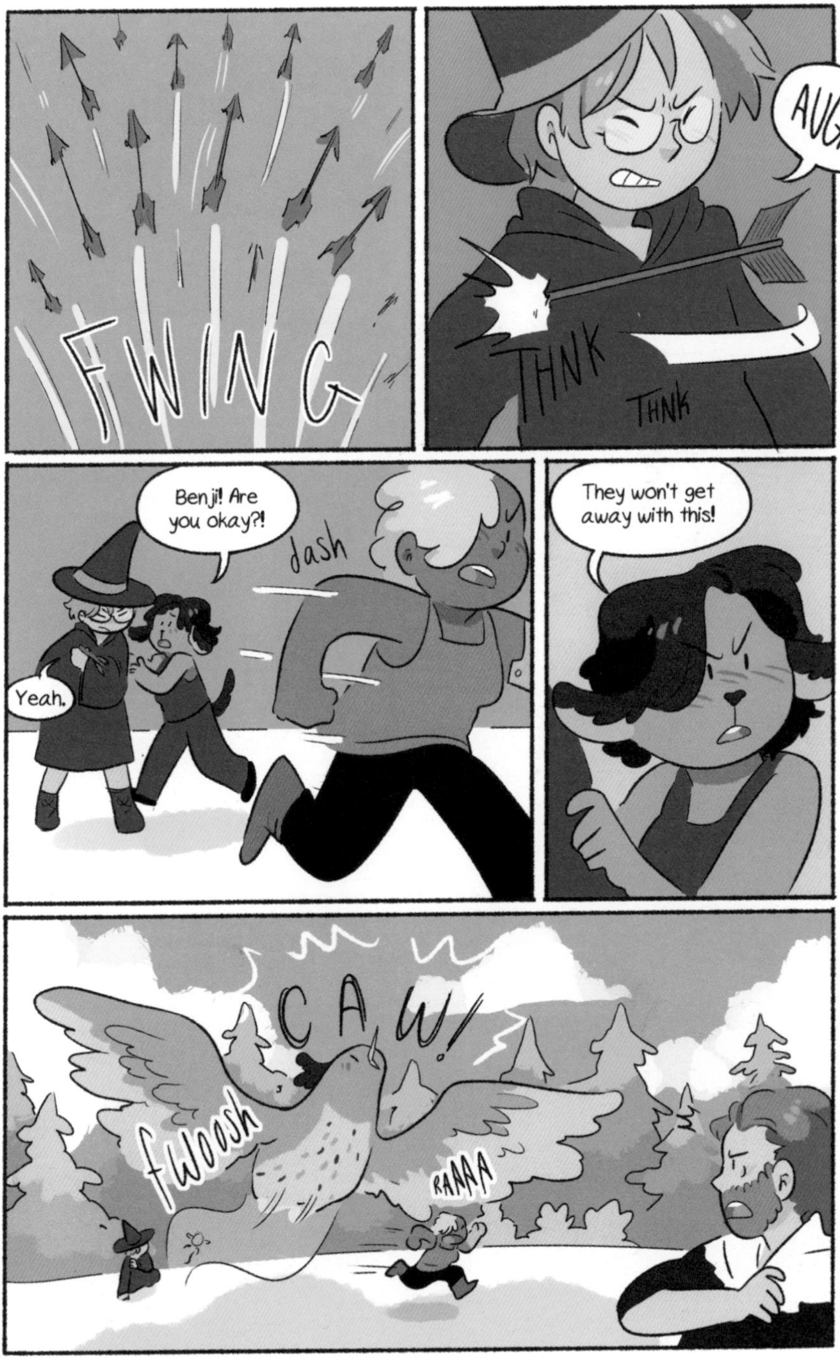
FWING
AUGH!!
THNK
THNK
Benji! Are you okay?!
dash
Yeah.
They won't get away with this!
CAW!
fWOOSH
RAAAA

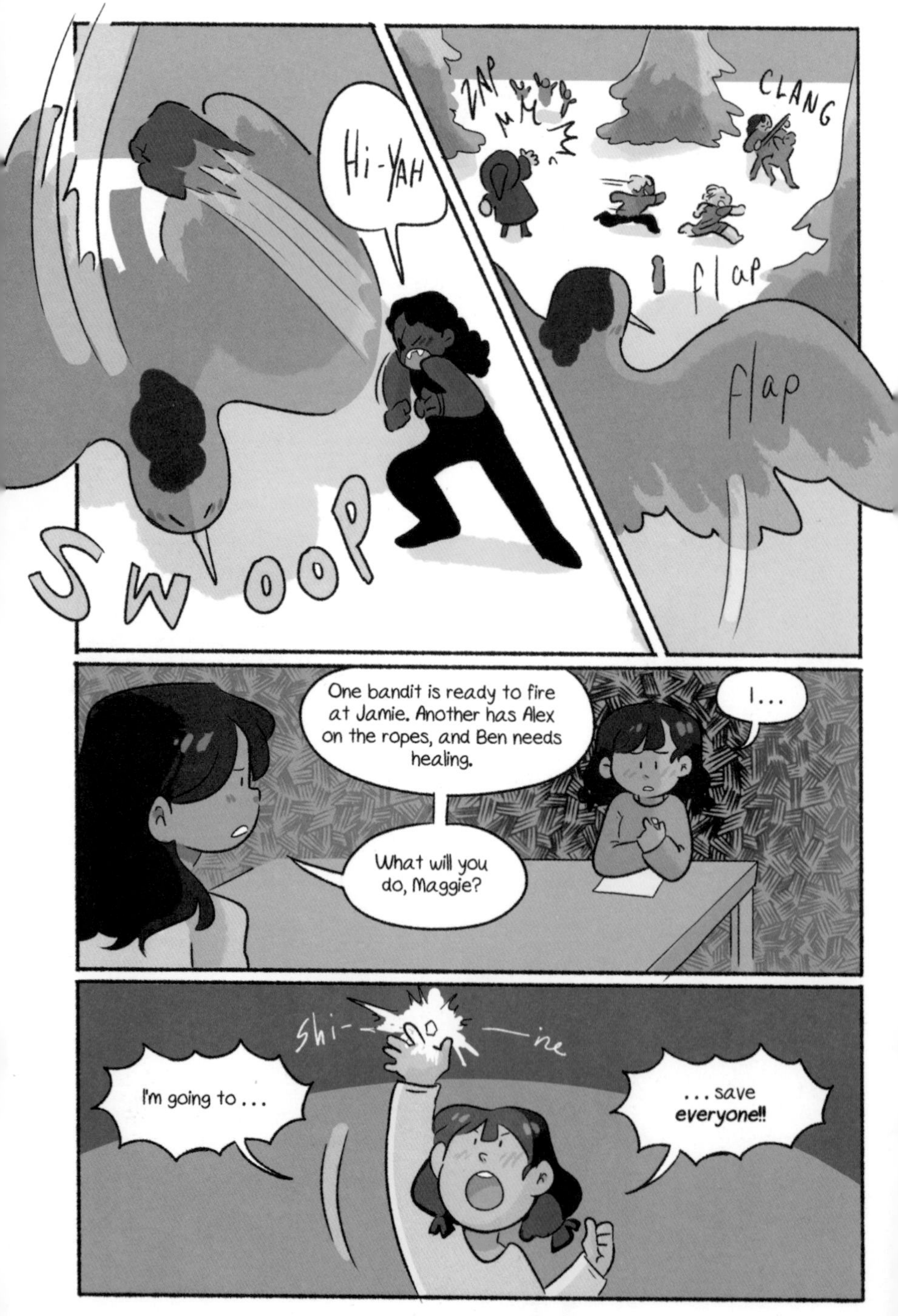
Hi-YAH
SWOOP
ZAP
CLANG
flap
flap
One bandit is ready to fire at Jamie. Another has Alex on the ropes, and Ben needs healing.
What will you do, Maggie?
I...
Shi-ne
I'm going to...
...save everyone!!

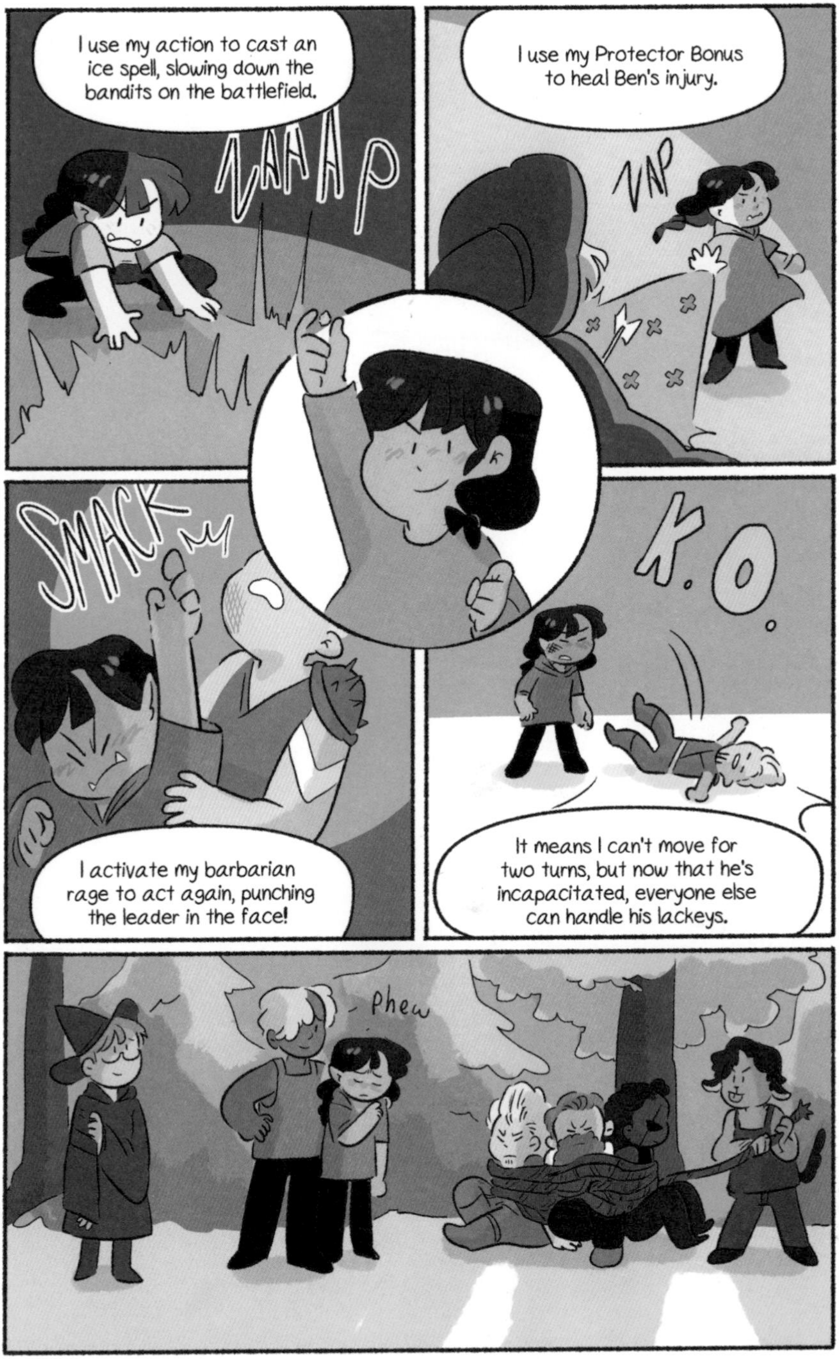
I use my action to cast an ice spell, slowing down the bandits on the battlefield.
ZAAAP
I use my Protector Bonus to heal Ben's injury.
ZAP
SMACK
I activate my barbarian rage to act again, punching the leader in the face!
K.O.
It means I can't move for two turns, but now that he's incapacitated, everyone else can handle his lackeys.
phew

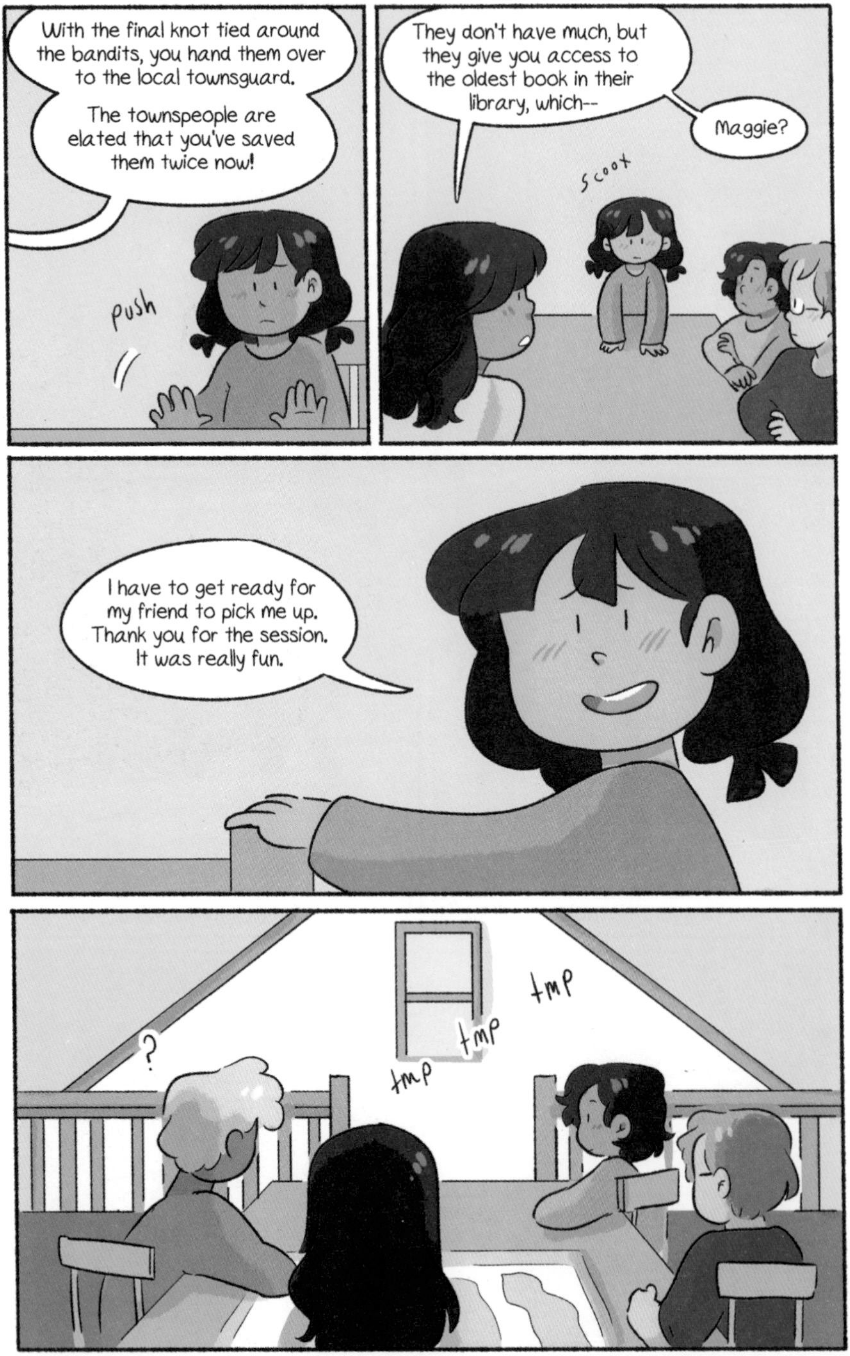
With the final knot tied around the bandits, you hand them over to the local townsguard.
The townspeople are elated that you've saved them twice now!
push
They don't have much, but they give you access to the oldest book in their library, which--
Maggie?
scoot
I have to get ready for my friend to pick me up. Thank you for the session. It was really fun.
?
tmp
tmp
tmp

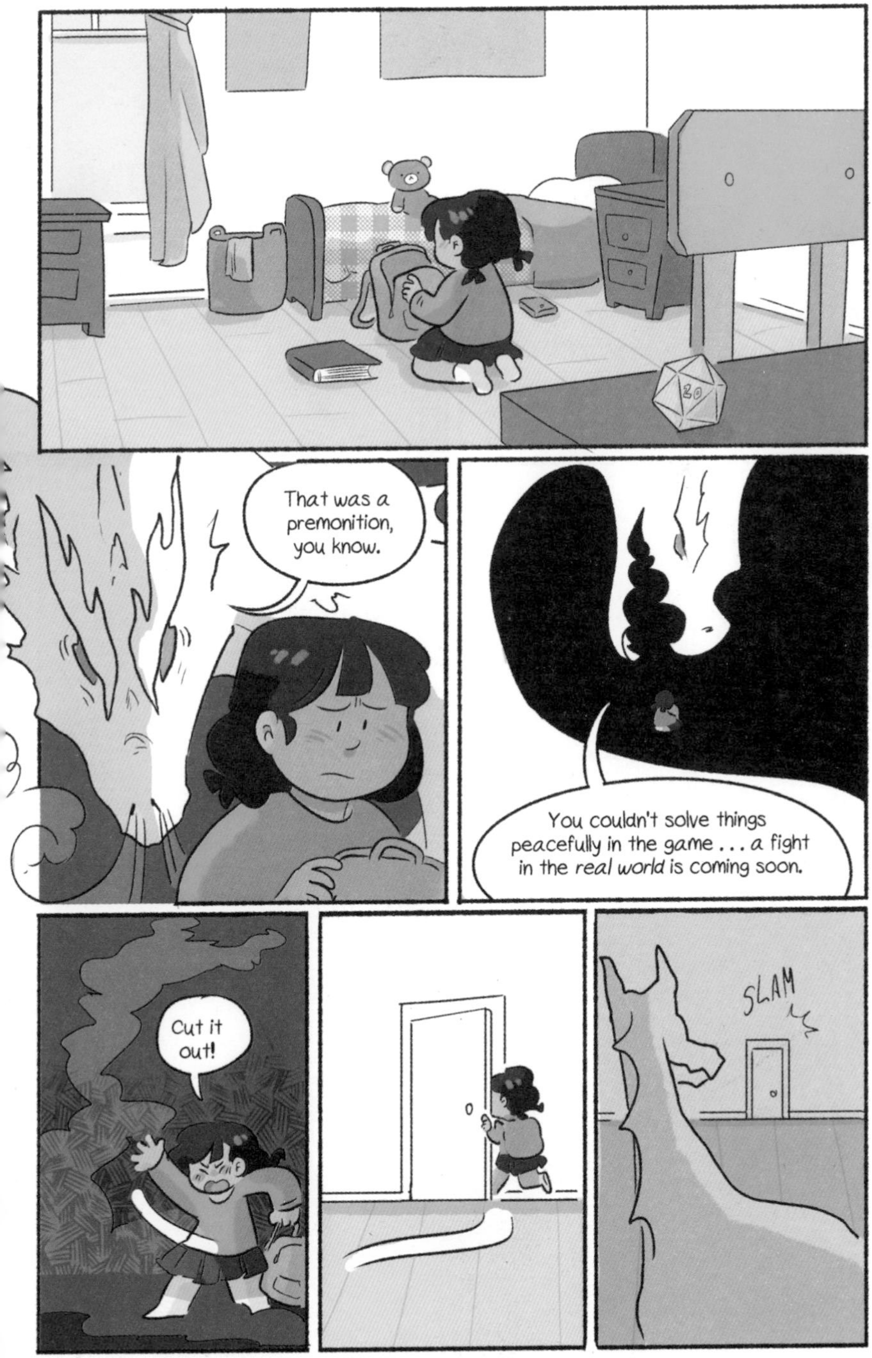
That was a premonition, you know.
You couldn't solve things peacefully in the game . . . a fight in the *real world* is coming soon.
Cut it out!
SLAM

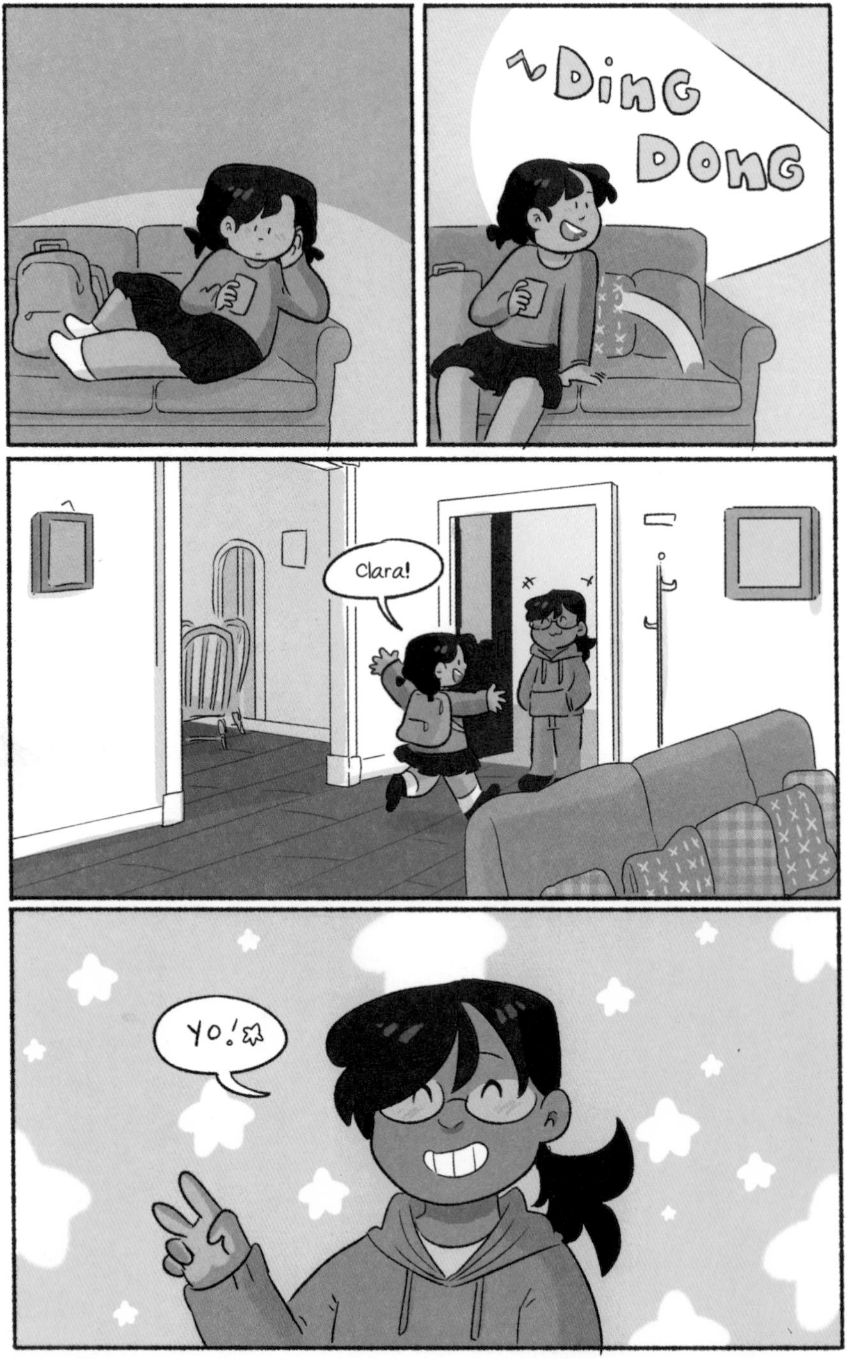
DING
DONG
Clara!
YO!

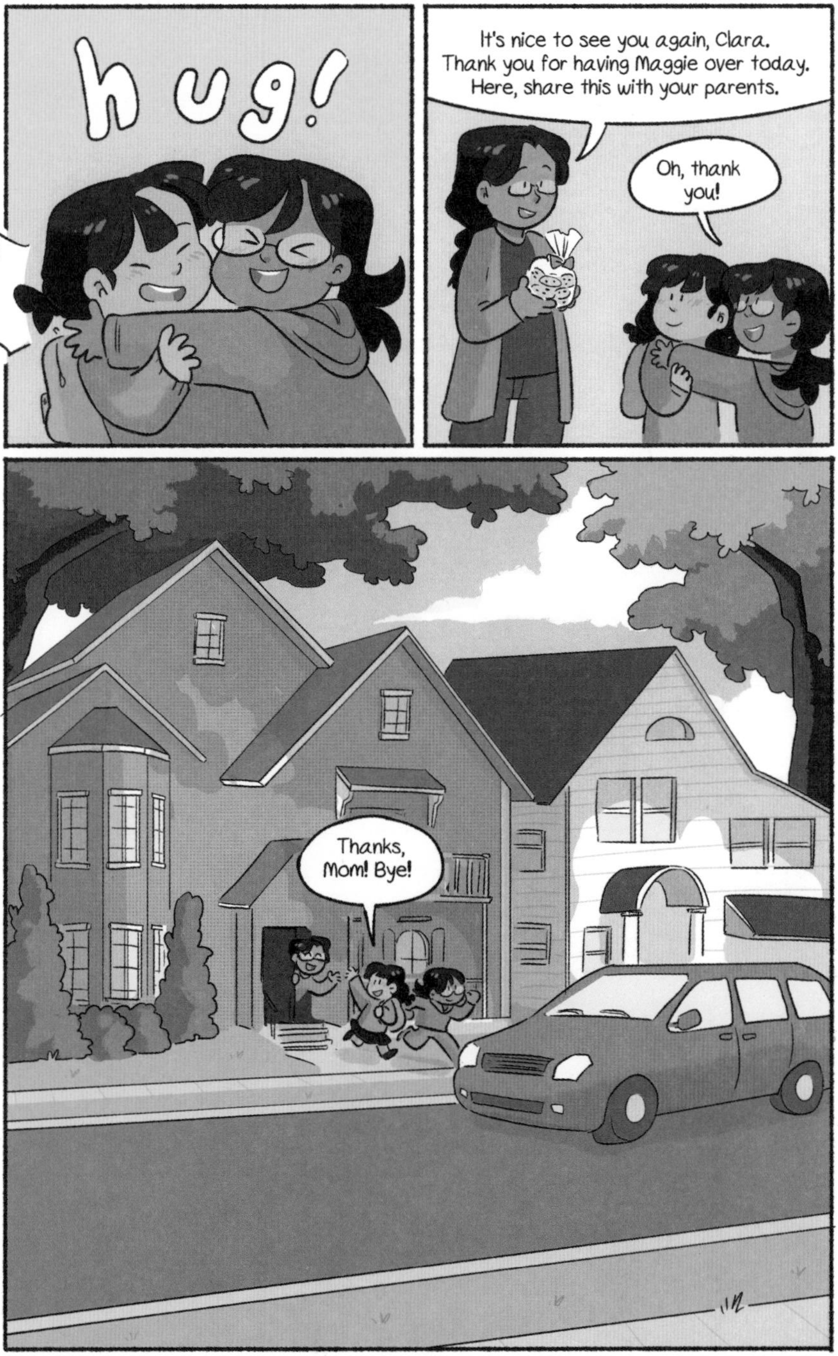
hug!
It's nice to see you again, Clara. Thank you for having Maggie over today. Here, share this with your parents.
Oh, thank you!
Thanks, Mom! Bye!

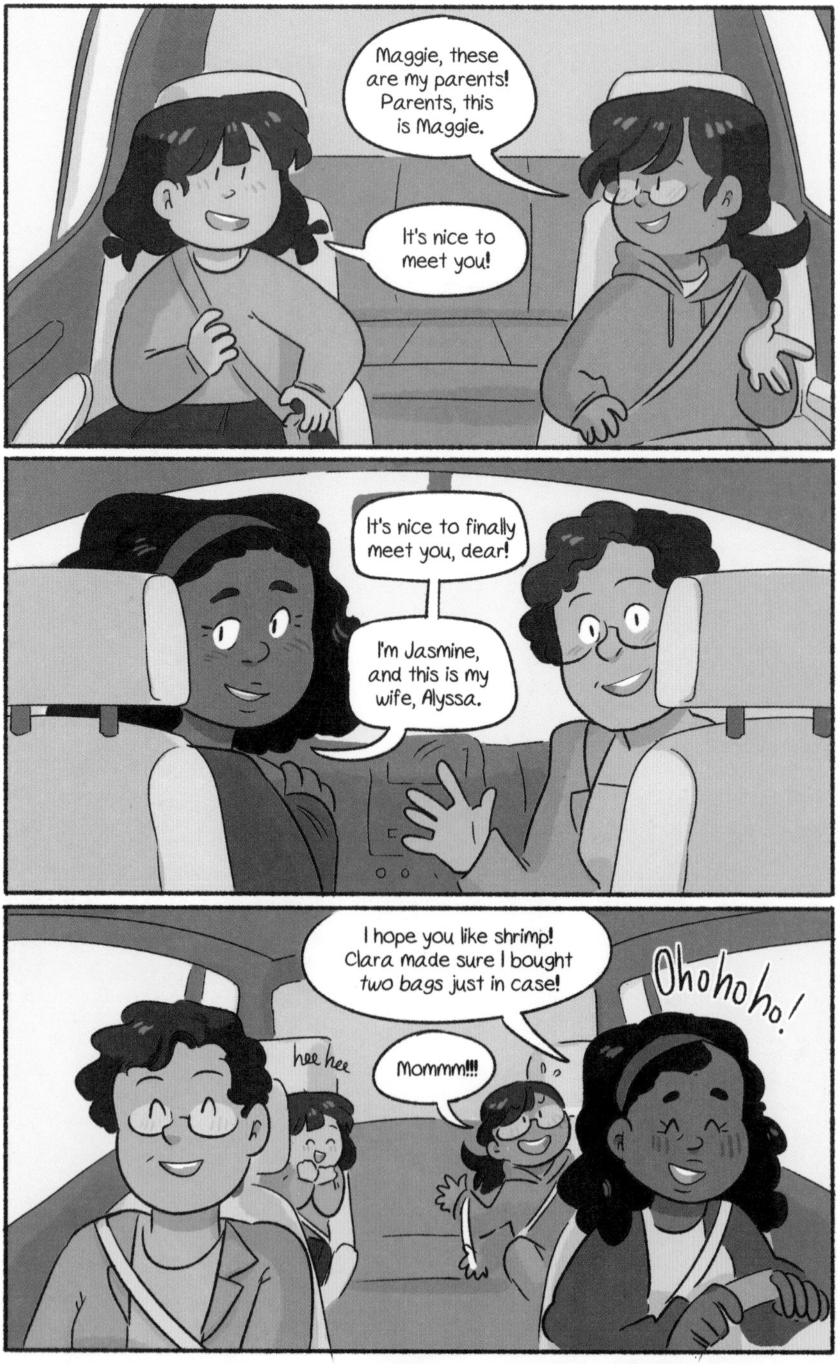
Maggie, these are my parents! Parents, this is Maggie.
It's nice to meet you!
It's nice to finally meet you, dear!
I'm Jasmine, and this is my wife, Alyssa.
I hope you like shrimp! Clara made sure I bought two bags just in case!
Ohohoho!
hee hee
Mommm!!!

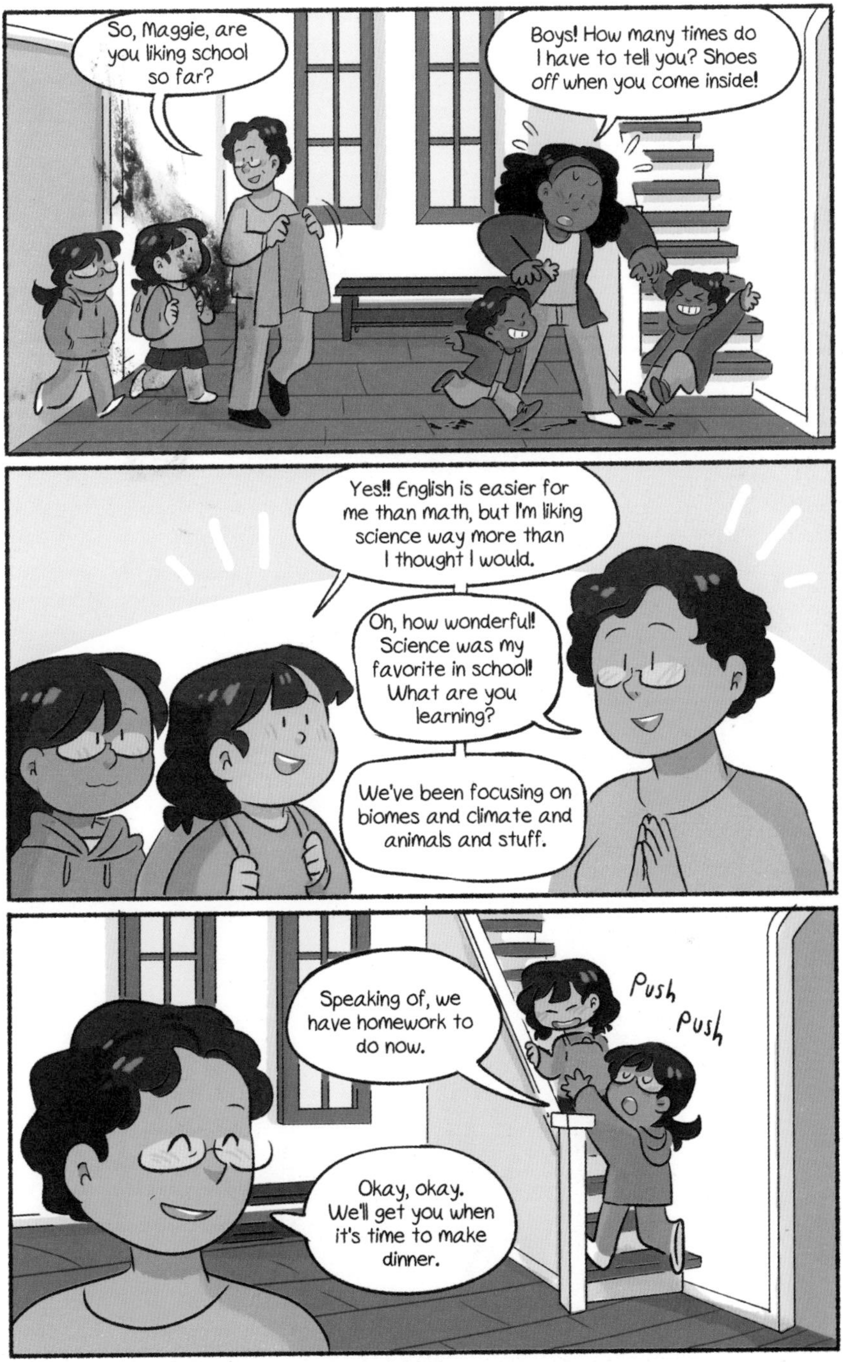
So, Maggie, are you liking school so far?
Boys! How many times do I have to tell you? Shoes *off* when you come inside!
Yes!! English is easier for me than math, but I'm liking science way more than I thought I would.
Oh, how wonderful! Science was my favorite in school! What are you learning?
We've been focusing on biomes and climate and animals and stuff.
Speaking of, we have homework to do now.
Push
Push
Okay, okay. We'll get you when it's time to make dinner.

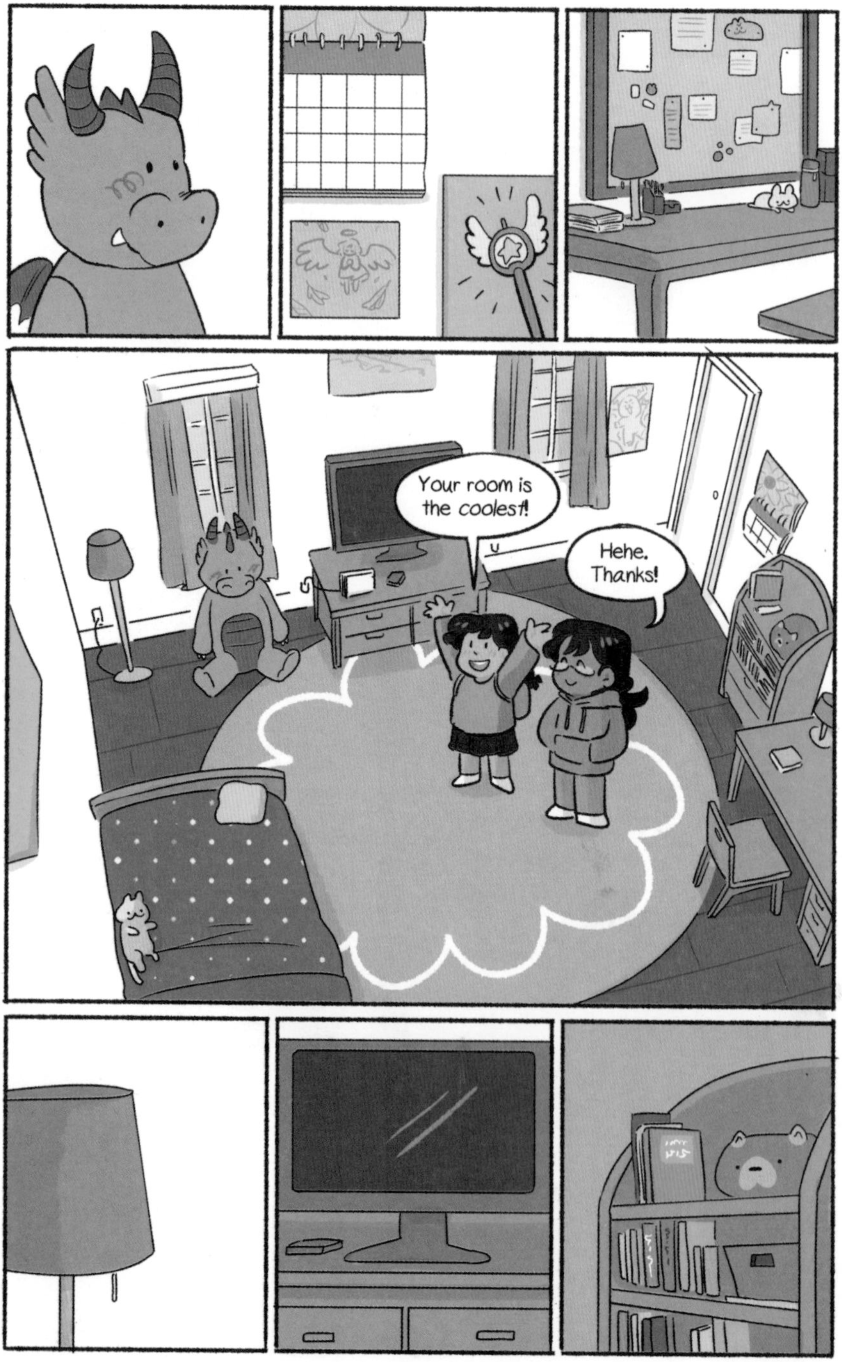
Your room is the *coolest*!
Hehe. Thanks!

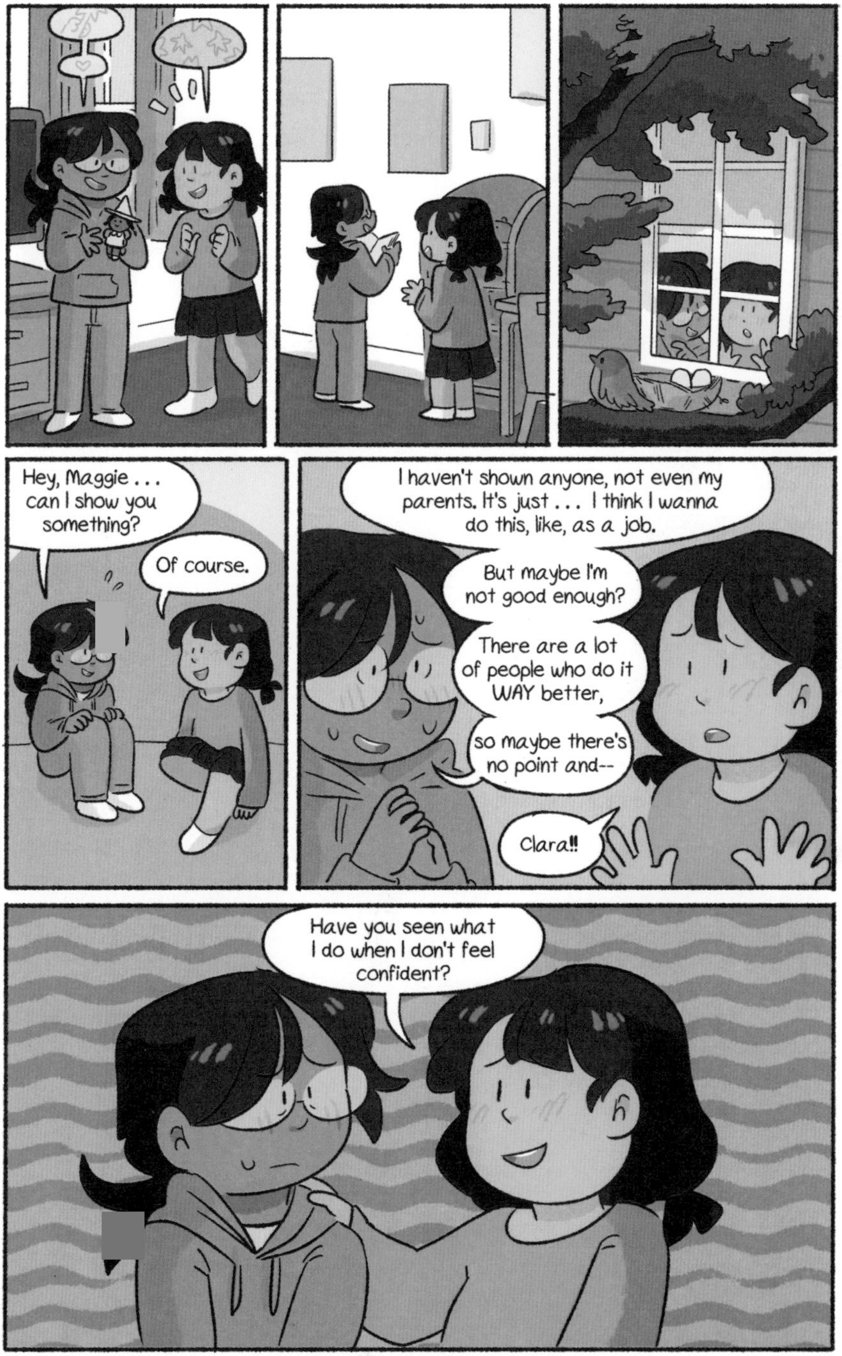
Hey, Maggie . . . can I show you something?
Of course.
I haven't shown anyone, not even my parents. It's just . . . I think I wanna do this, like, as a job.
But maybe I'm not good enough?
There are a lot of people who do it WAY better,
so maybe there's no point and--
Clara!!
Have you seen what I do when I don't feel confident?

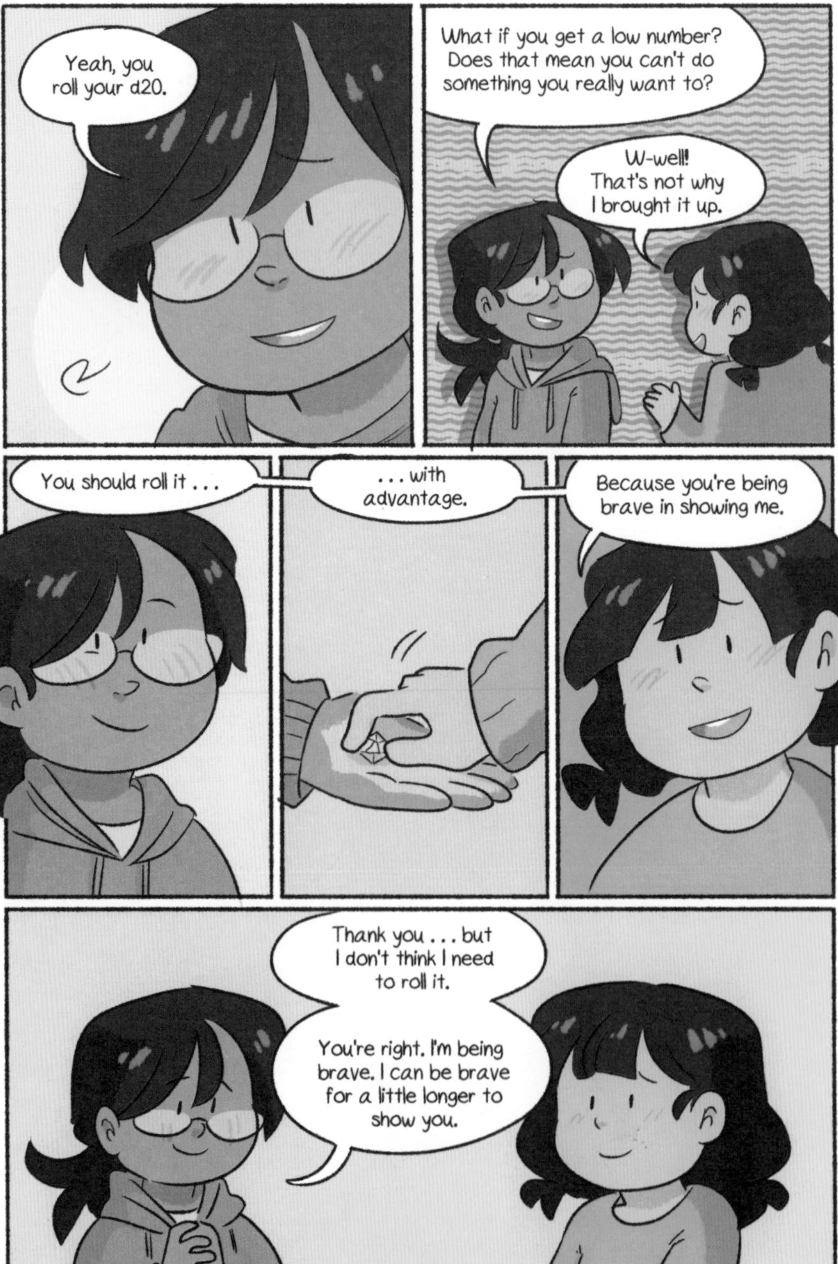
Yeah, you roll your d20.
What if you get a low number? Does that mean you can't do something you really want to?
W-well! That's not why I brought it up.
You should roll it . . .
. . . with advantage.
Because you're being brave in showing me.
Thank you . . . but I don't think I need to roll it.
You're right. I'm being brave. I can be brave for a little longer to show you.

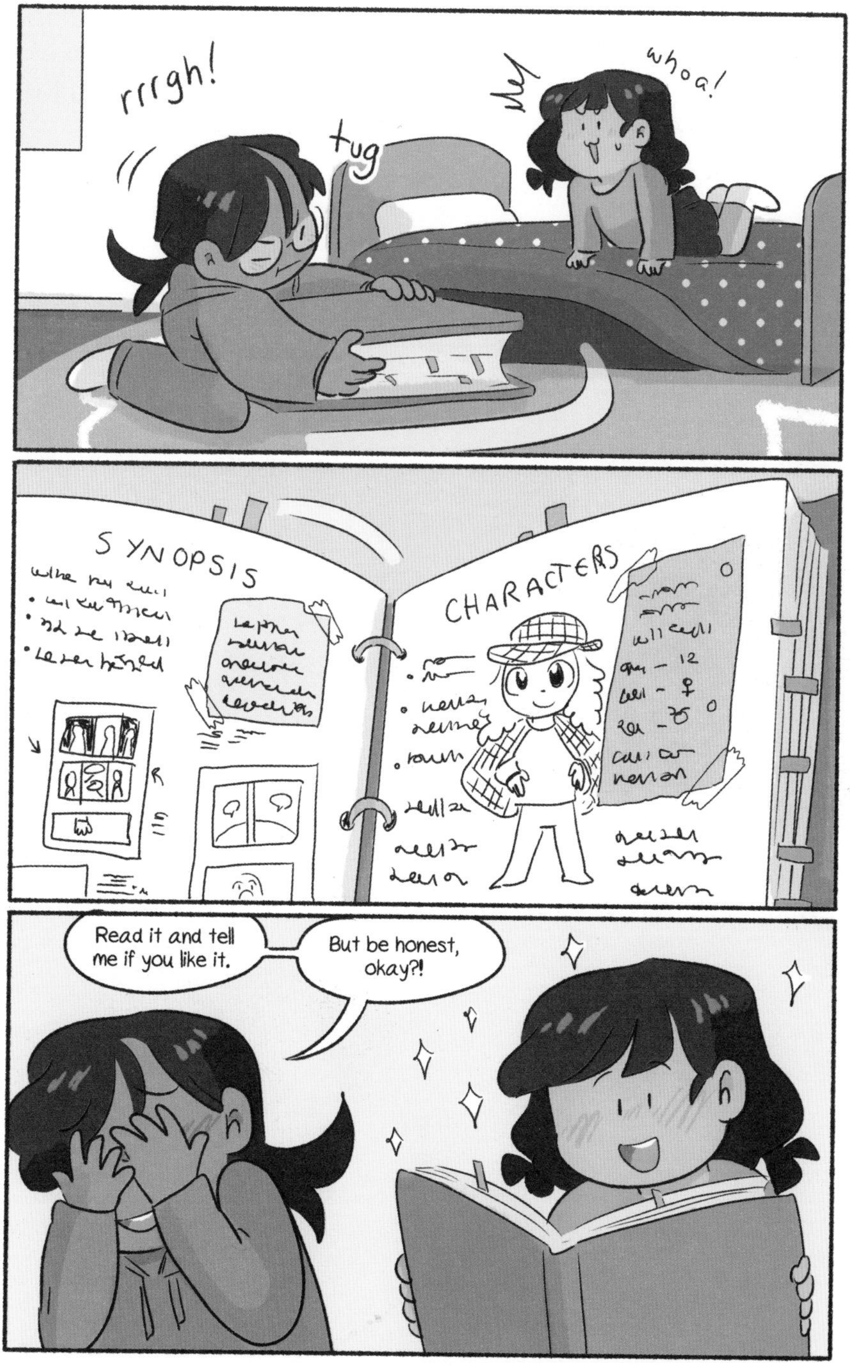
rrrgh!
tug
whoa!
SYNOPSIS
CHARACTERS
Read it and tell me if you like it.
But be honest, okay?!

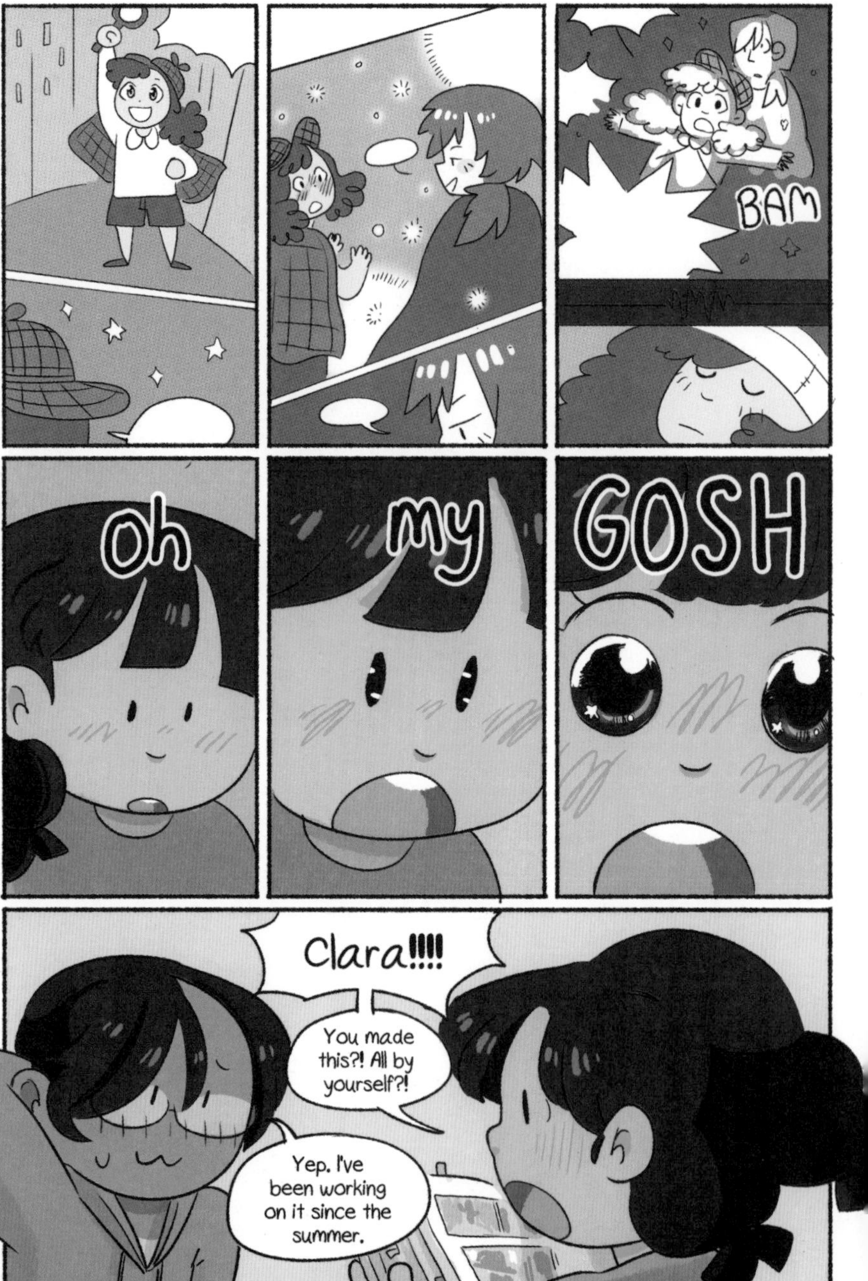
BAM
Oh
my
GOSH
Clara!!!!
You made this?! All by yourself?!
Yep. I've been working on it since the summer.

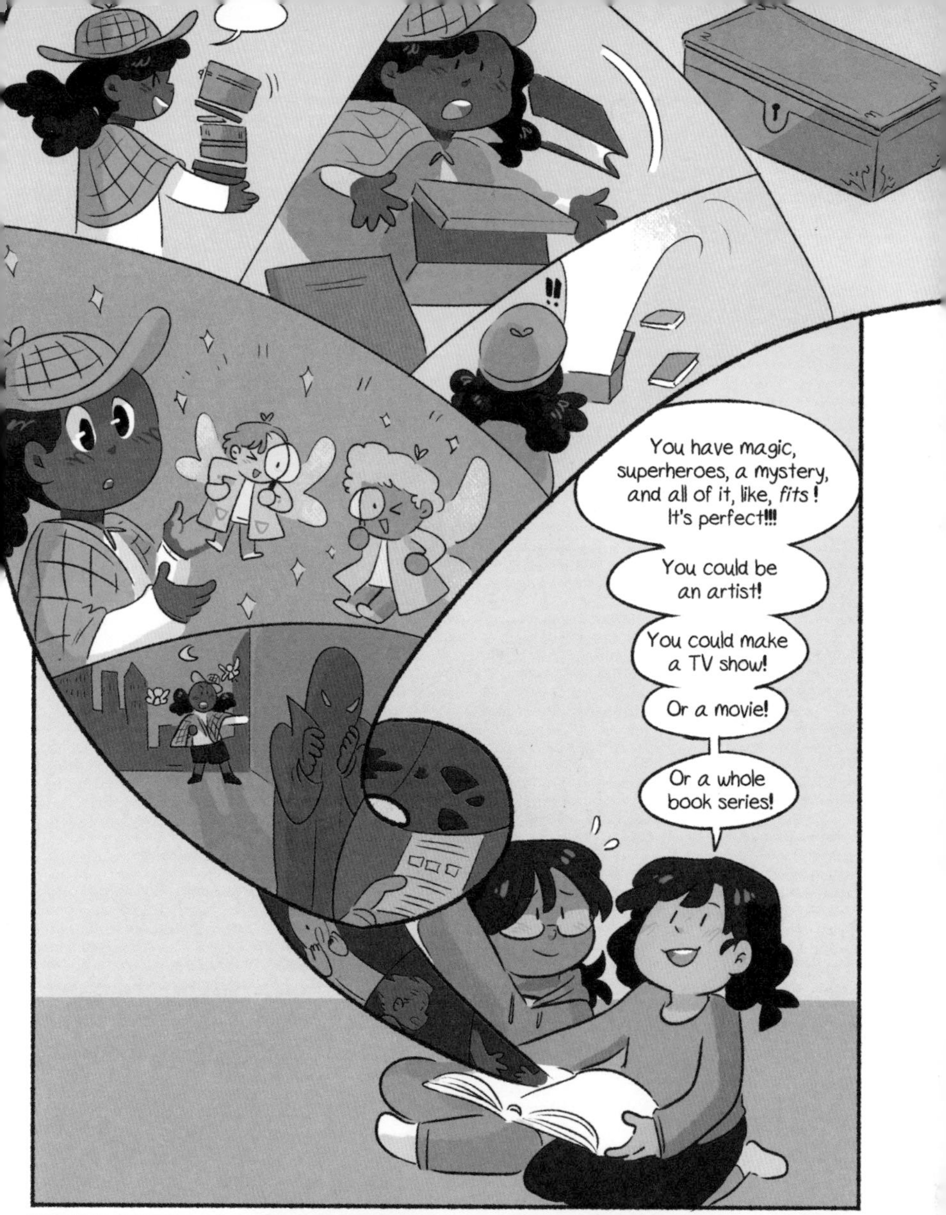

!!
You have magic, superheroes, a mystery, and all of it, like, *fits*! It's perfect!!!
You could be an artist!
You could make a TV show!
Or a movie!
Or a whole book series!

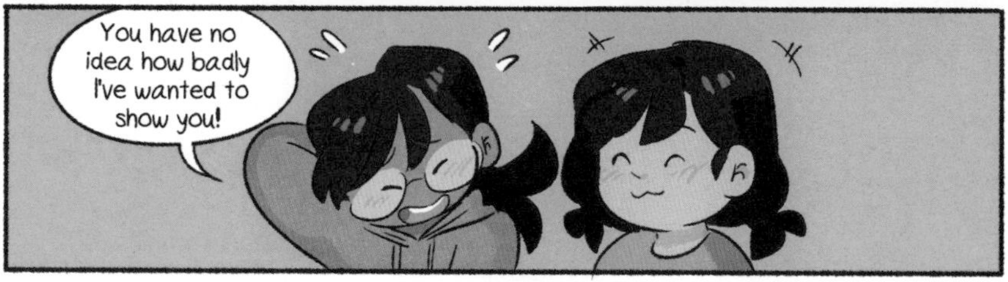

You have no idea how badly I've wanted to show you!

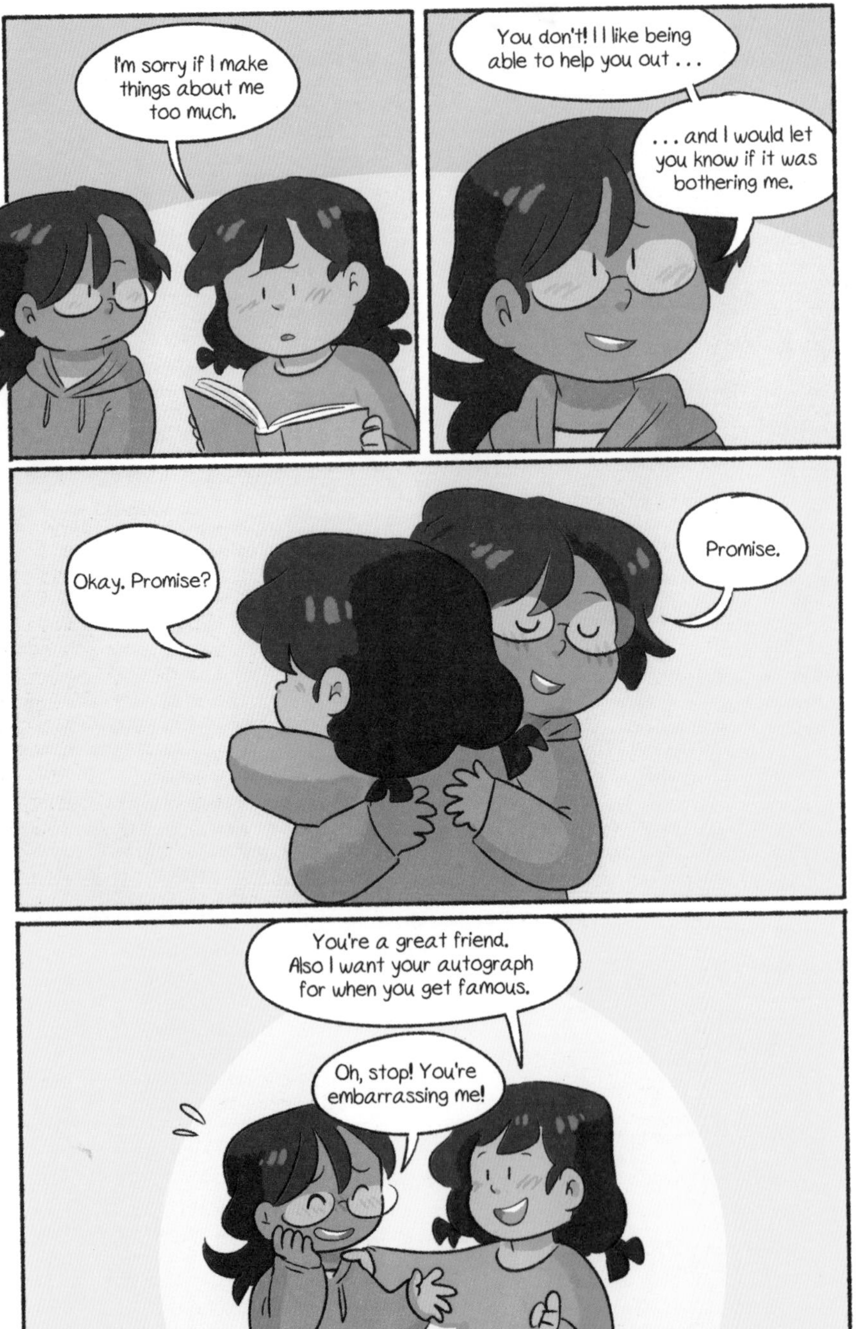
I'm sorry if I make things about me too much.
You don't! I I like being able to help you out . . .
. . . and I would let you know if it was bothering me.
Okay. Promise?
Promise.
You're a great friend. Also I want your autograph for when you get famous.
Oh, stop! You're embarrassing me!

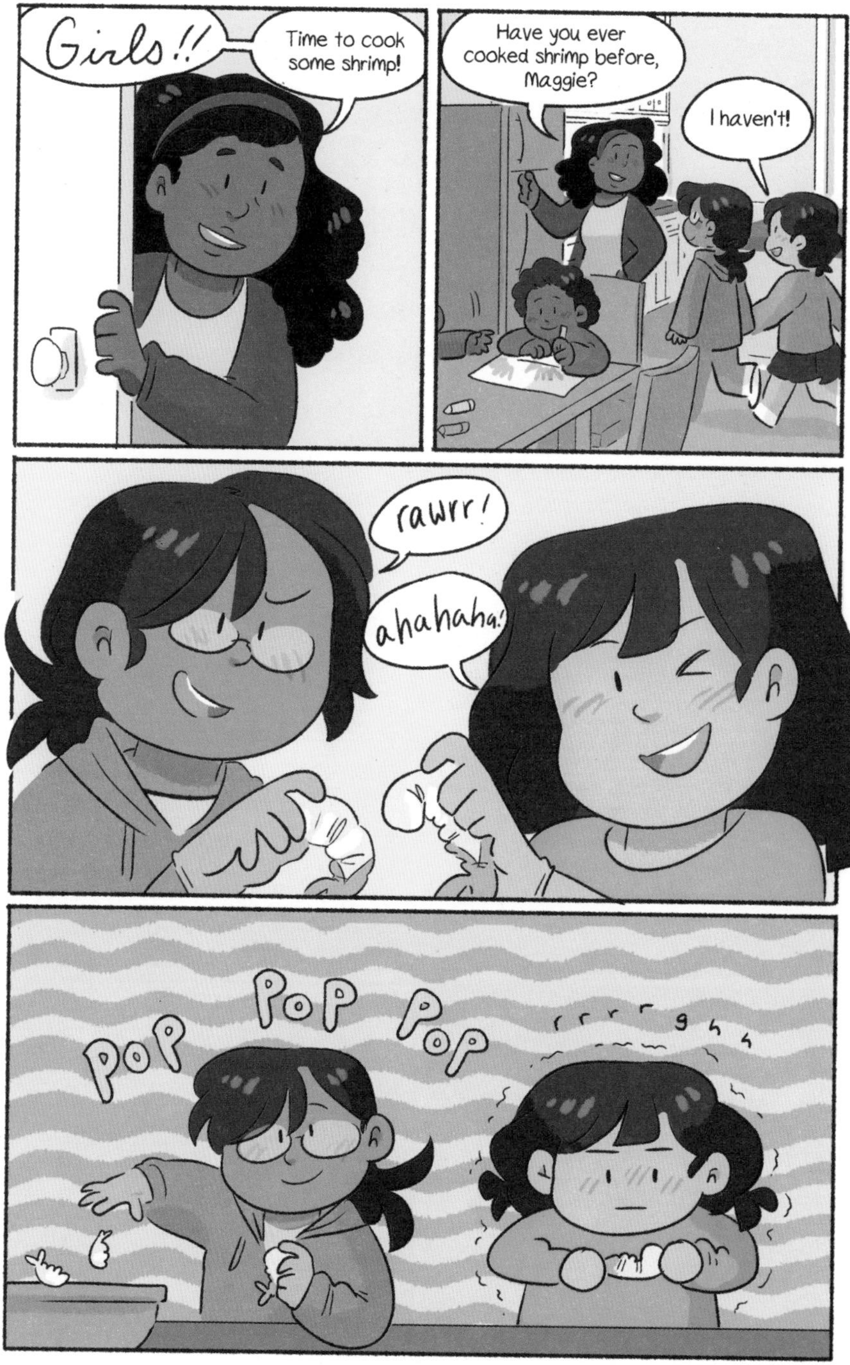
Girls!!
Time to cook some shrimp!
Have you ever cooked shrimp before, Maggie?
I haven't!
rawrr!
ahahaha!
POP
POP
POP
POP
rrrrghh

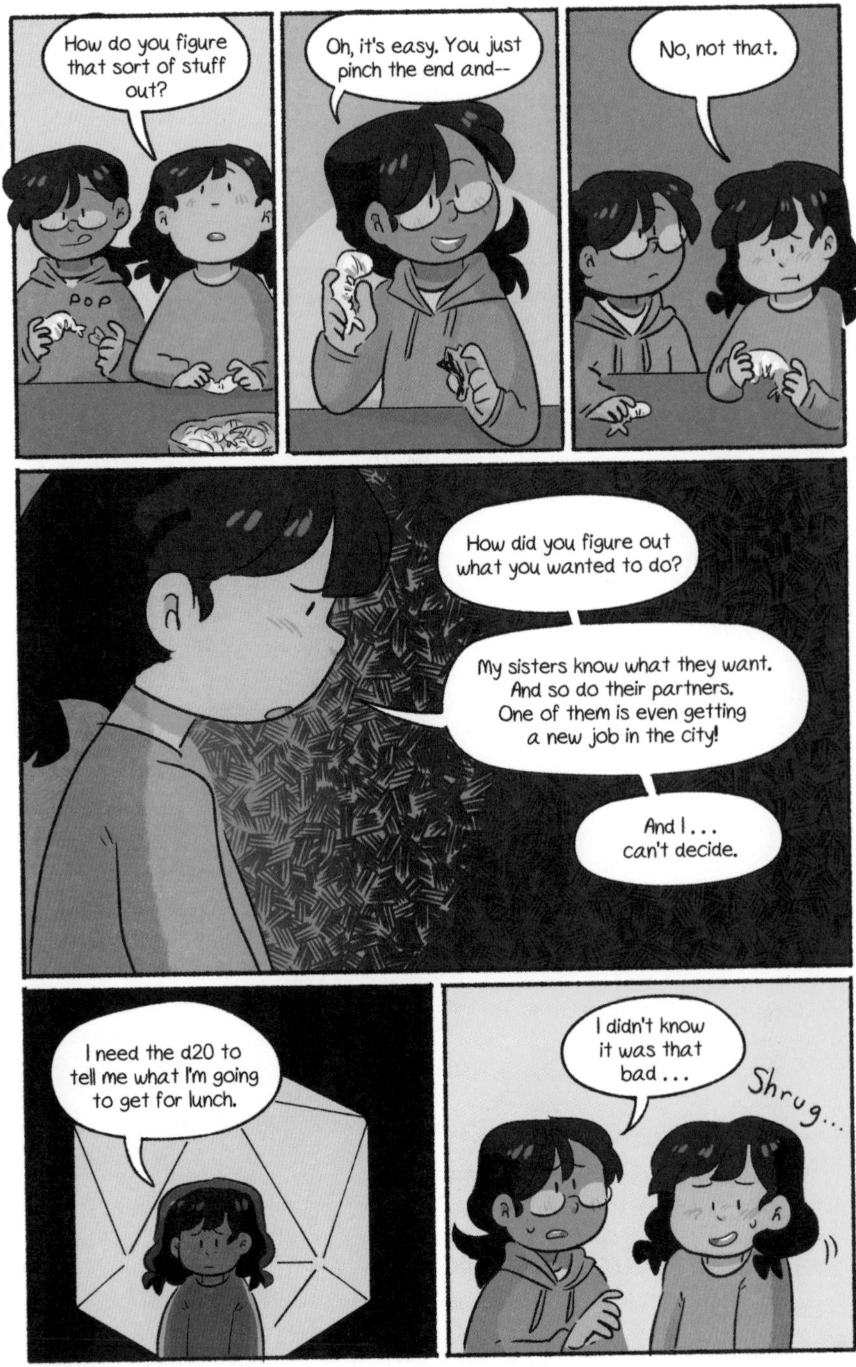
How do you figure that sort of stuff out?
POP
Oh, it's easy. You just pinch the end and--
No, not that.
How did you figure out what you wanted to do?
My sisters know what they want. And so do their partners. One of them is even getting a new job in the city!
And I . . . can't decide.
I need the d20 to tell me what I'm going to get for lunch.
I didn't know it was that bad . . .
Shrug...

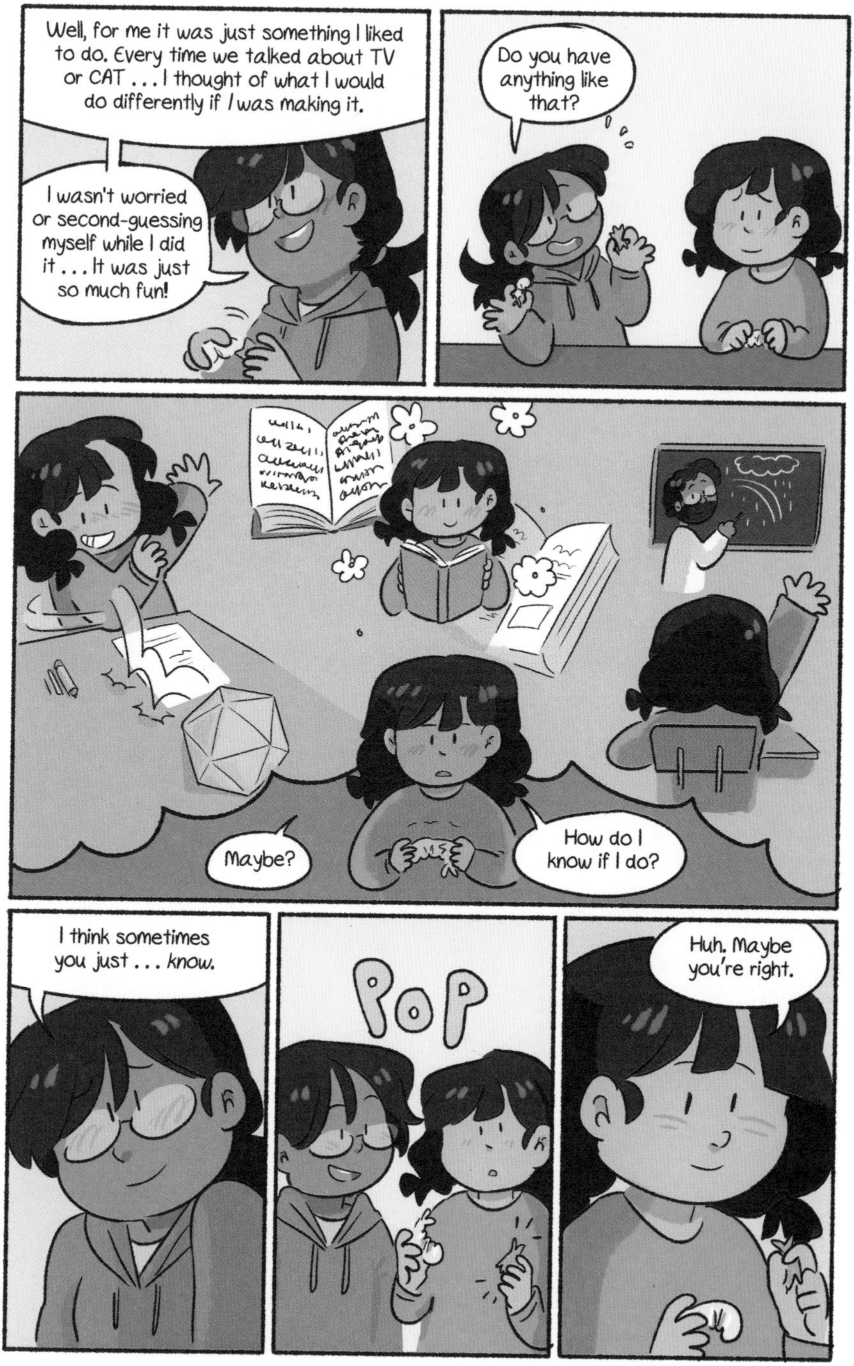
Well, for me it was just something I liked to do. Every time we talked about TV or CAT . . . I thought of what I would do differently if I was making it.
I wasn't worried or second-guessing myself while I did it . . . It was just so much fun!
Do you have anything like that?
Maybe?
How do I know if I do?
I think sometimes you just . . . know.
POP
Huh. Maybe you're right.

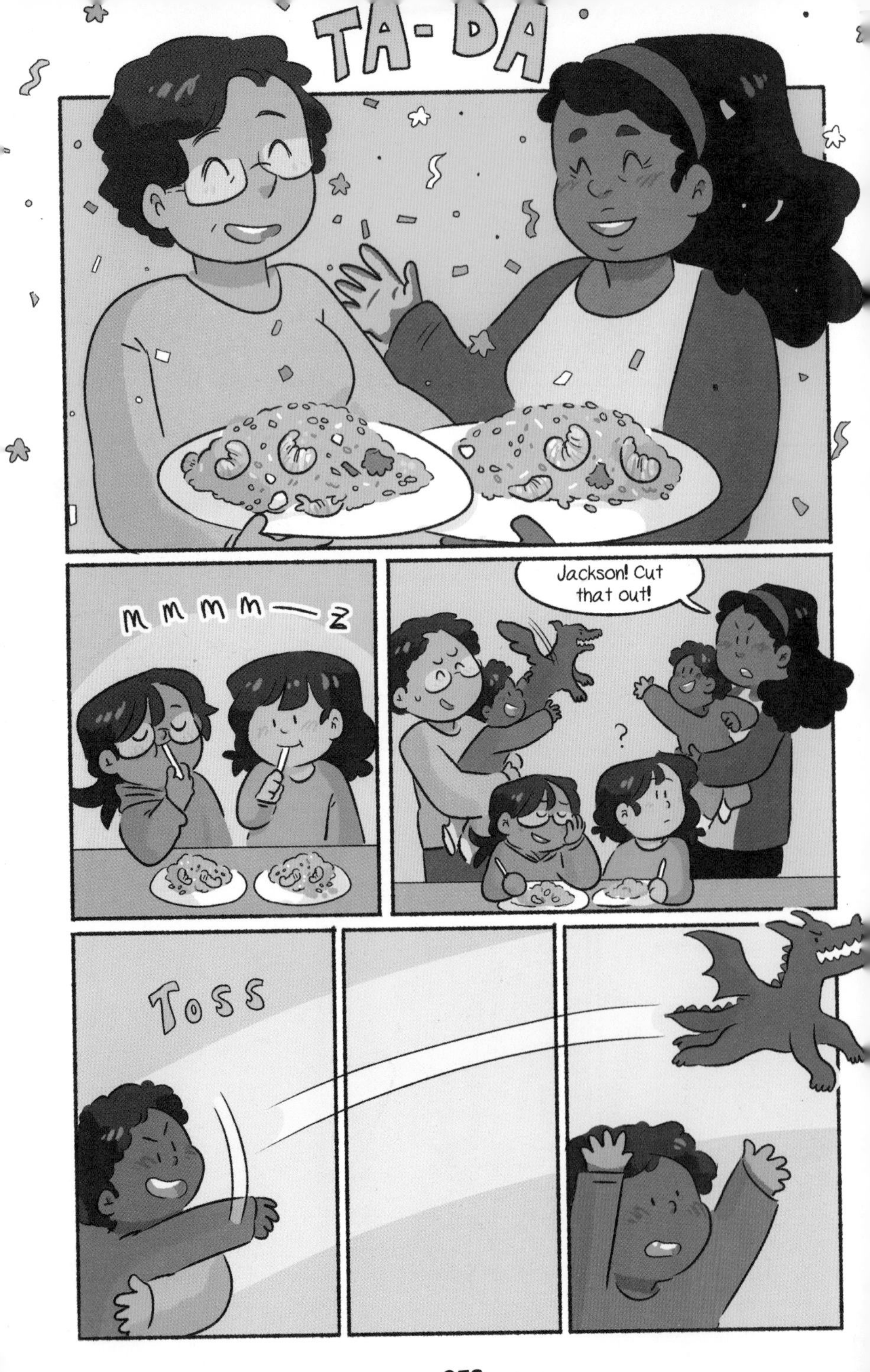
TA-DA
MMMM—Z
Jackson! Cut that out!
?
TOSS

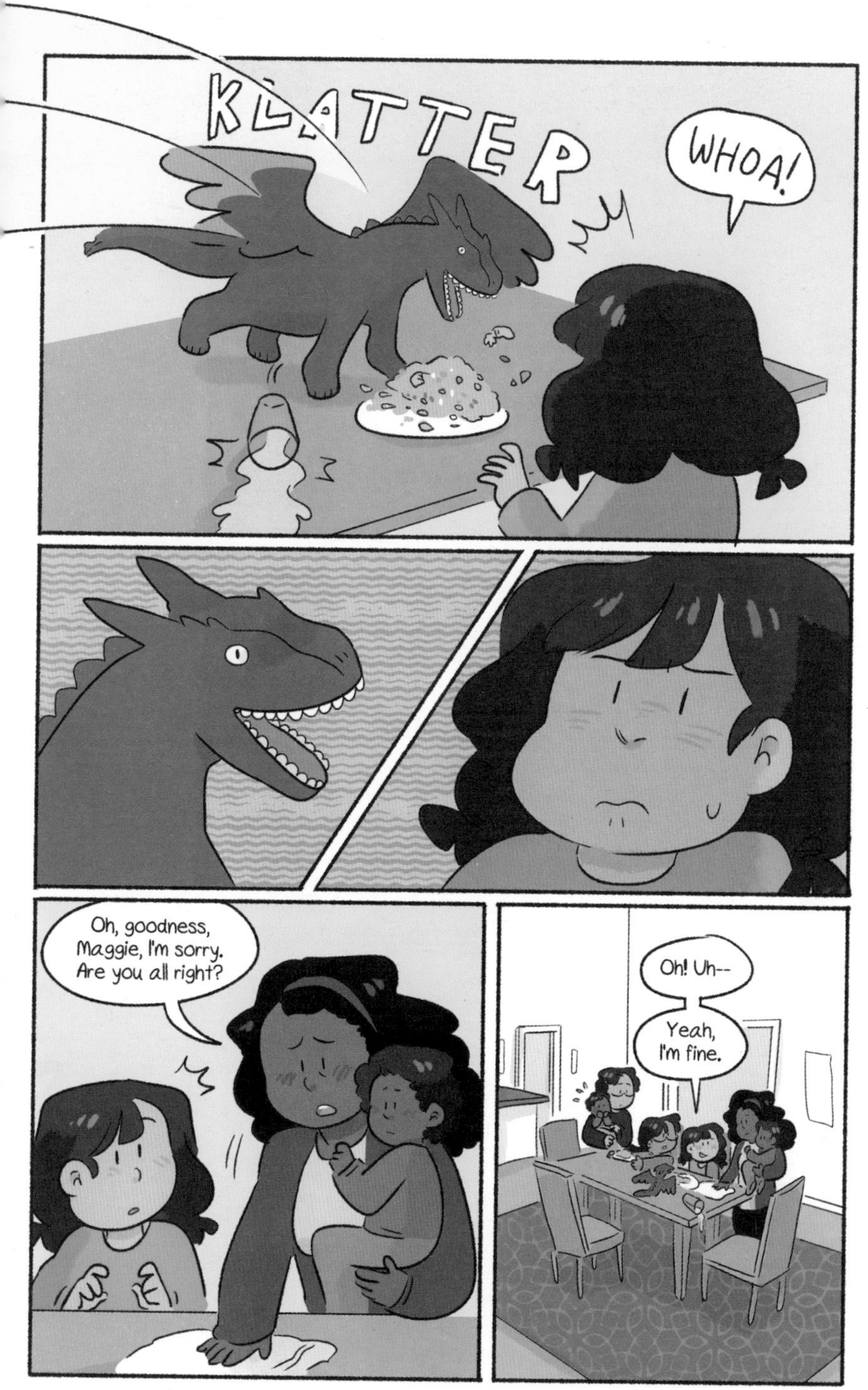
KLATTER
WHOA!
Oh, goodness, Maggie, I'm sorry. Are you all right?
Oh! Uh--
Yeah, I'm fine.

klak
klak

GUMBALL SEARCH

Q OCD

SEARCH   HELP

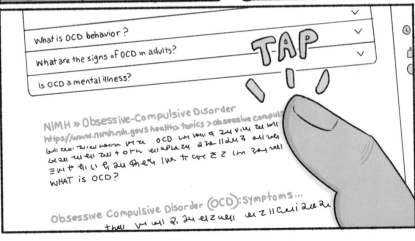

What is OCD behavior?

What are the signs of OCD in adults?

Is OCD a mental illness?

TAP

NIMH » Obsessive-Compulsive Disorder
https://www.nimh.nih.gov>health>topics>obsessive compul...
WHAT is OCD?

Obsessive Compulsive Disorder (OCD): symptoms...

OCD is a treatable, though chronic, disorder characterized by involuntary intrusive . . .

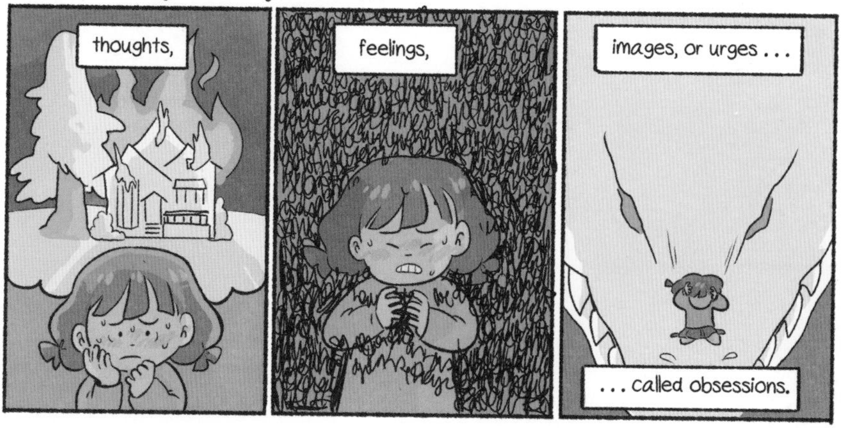
thoughts,
feelings,
images, or urges . . .
. . . called obsessions.

These are only relieved upon acting out certain rituals . . .

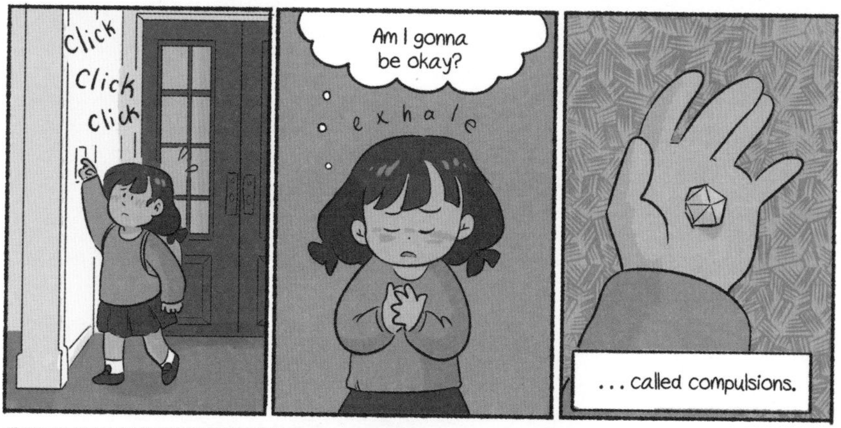
Click
Click
Click
Am I gonna be okay?
exhale
. . . called compulsions.

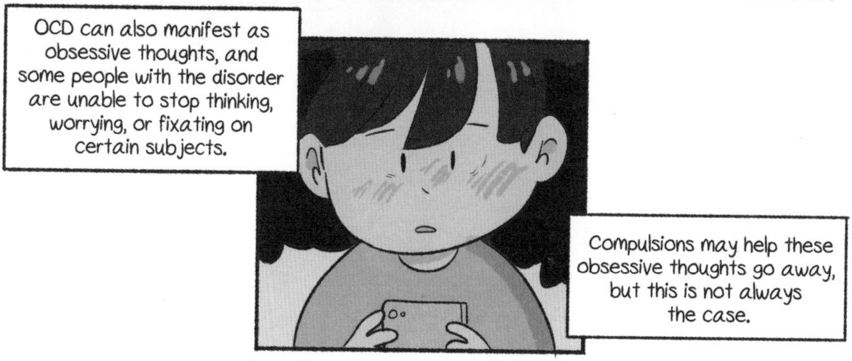
OCD can also manifest as obsessive thoughts, and some people with the disorder are unable to stop thinking, worrying, or fixating on certain subjects.
Compulsions may help these obsessive thoughts go away, but this is not always the case.

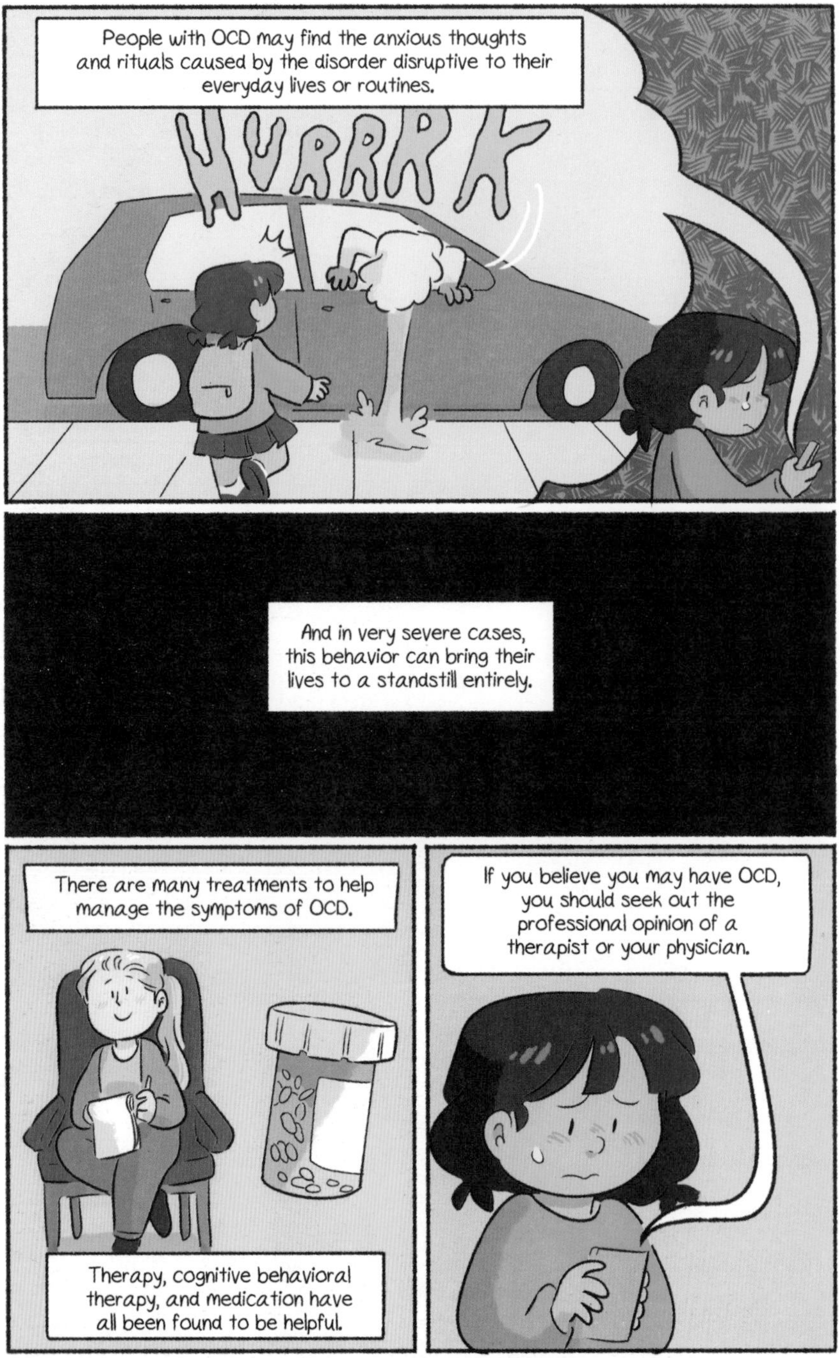
People with OCD may find the anxious thoughts and rituals caused by the disorder disruptive to their everyday lives or routines.
HURRK
And in very severe cases, this behavior can bring their lives to a standstill entirely.
There are many treatments to help manage the symptoms of OCD.
Therapy, cognitive behavioral therapy, and medication have all been found to be helpful.
If you believe you may have OCD, you should seek out the professional opinion of a therapist or your physician.

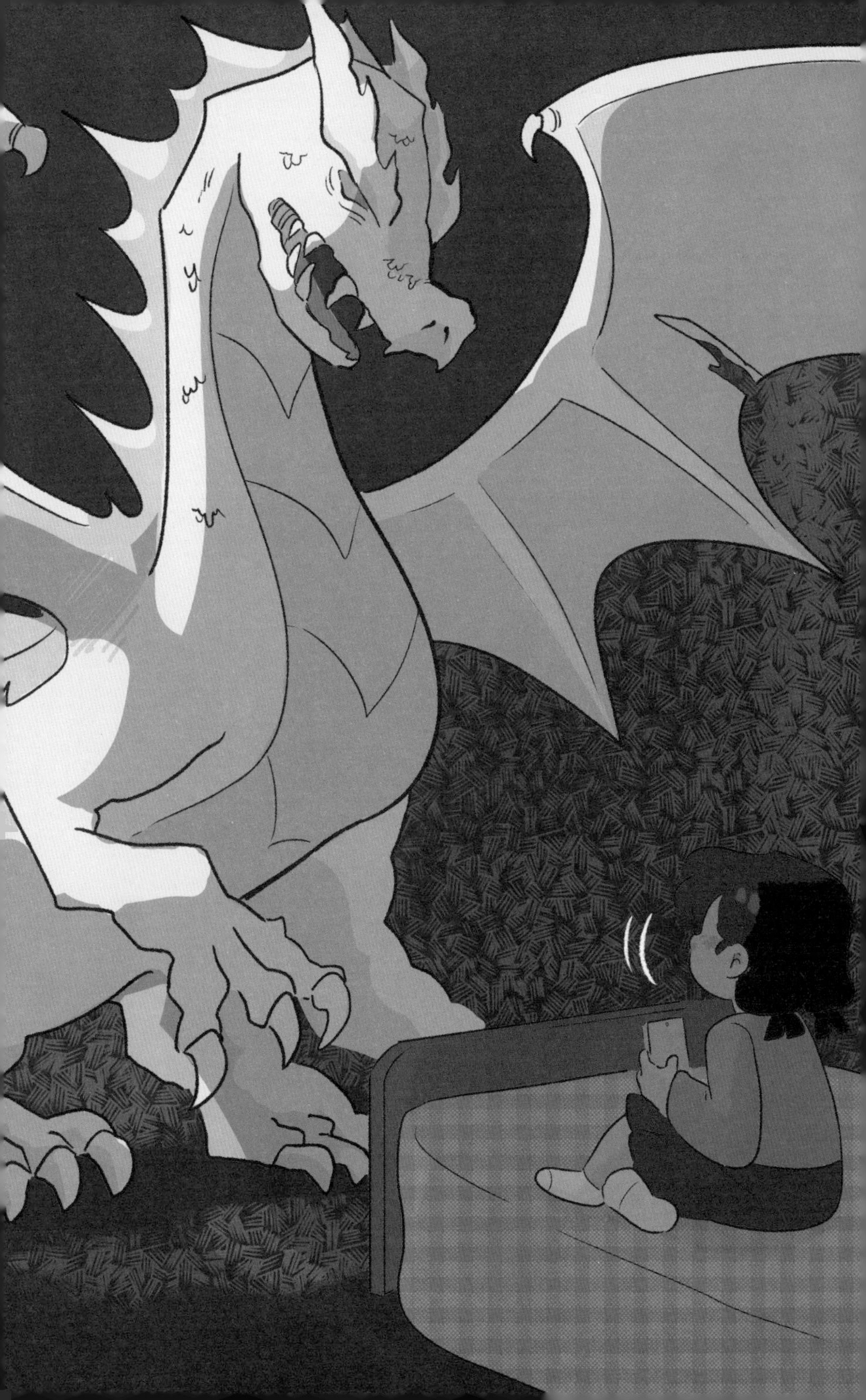

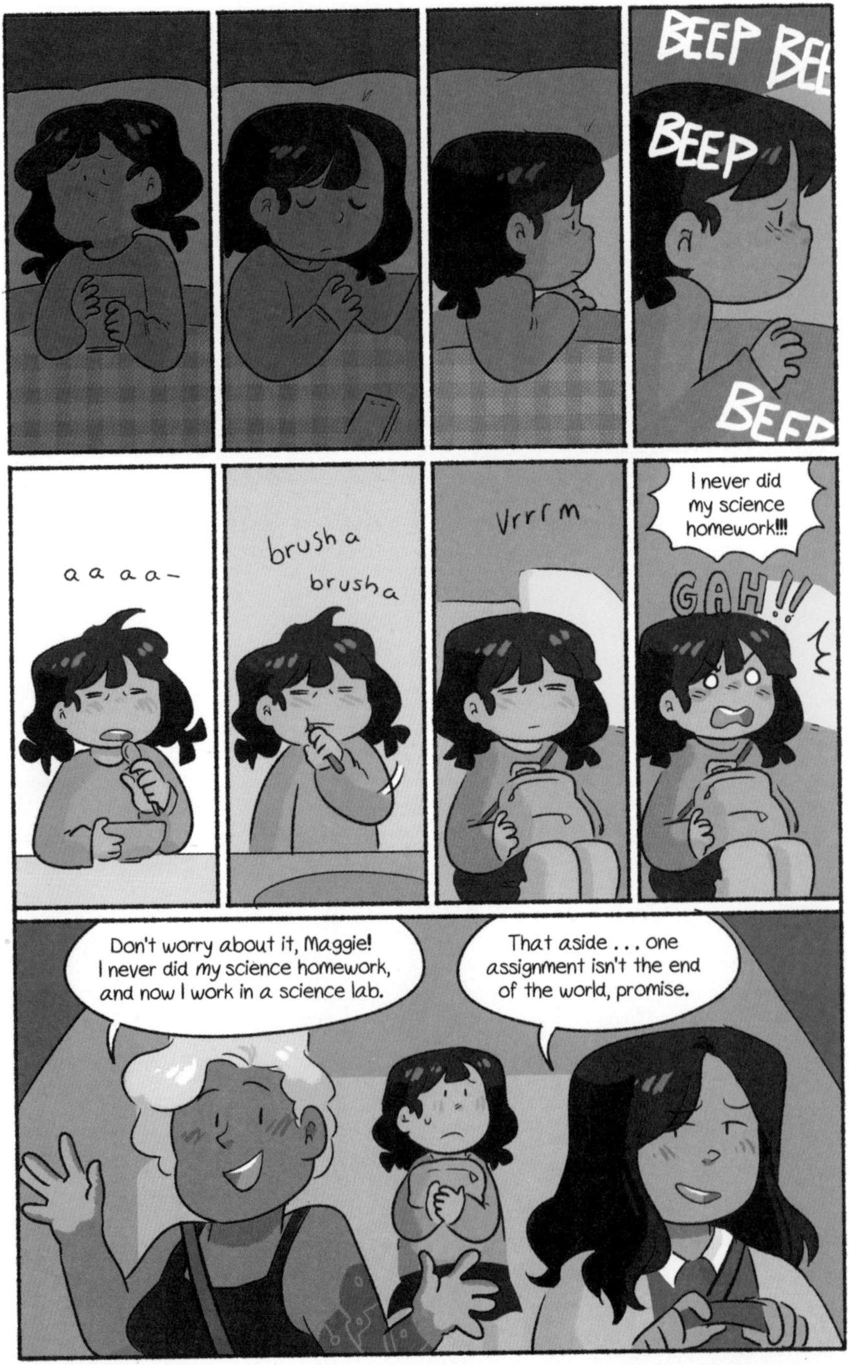
BEEP BEE
BEEP
BEEP
a a a a-
brush a
brush a
Vrrrm
I never did my science homework!!!
GAH!!
Don't worry about it, Maggie! I never did my science homework, and now I work in a science lab.
That aside . . . one assignment isn't the end of the world, promise.

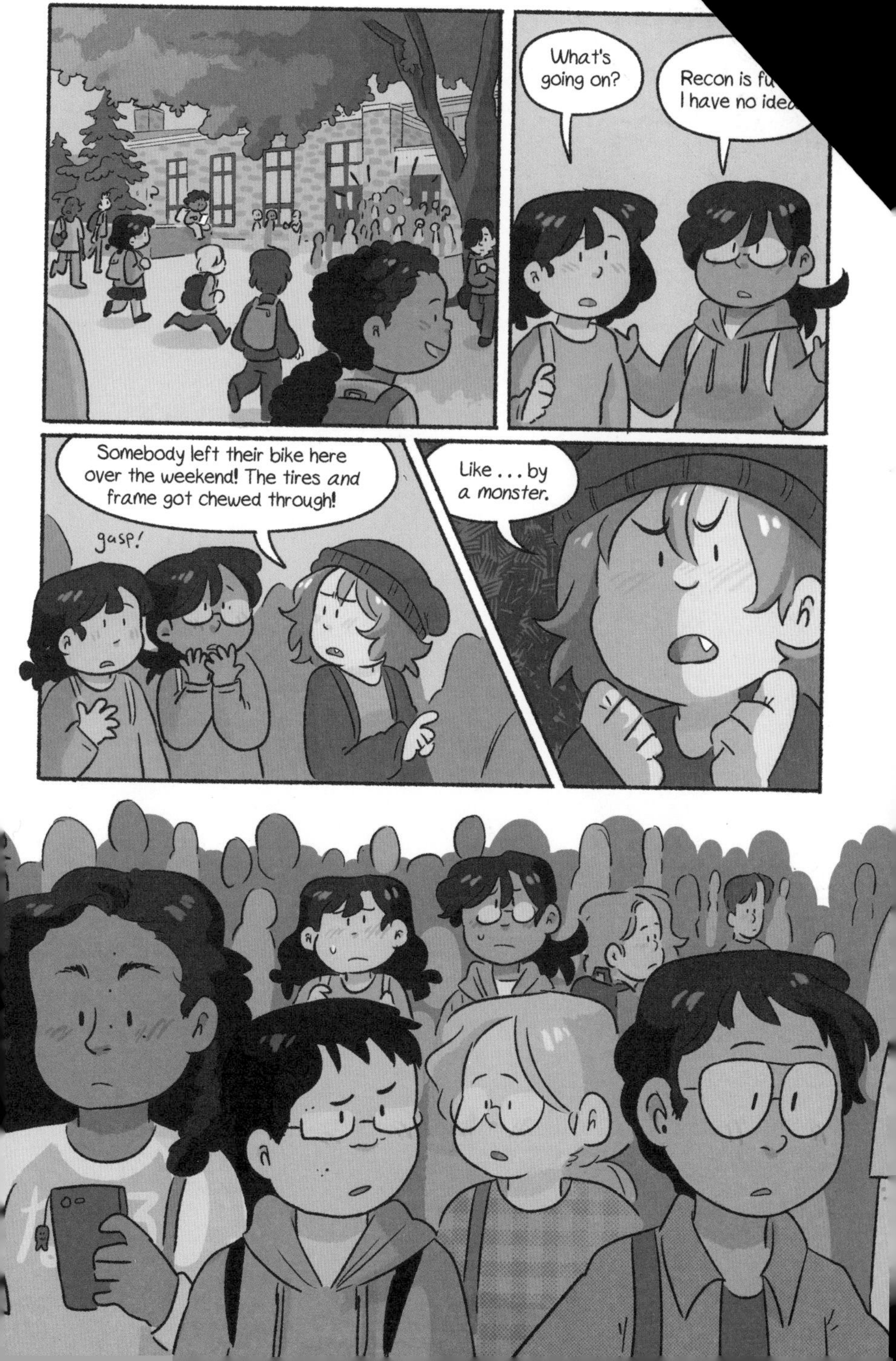
What's going on?
Recon is fu
I have no ide
Somebody left their bike here over the weekend! The tires *and* frame got chewed through!
gasp!
Like . . . by *a monster.*

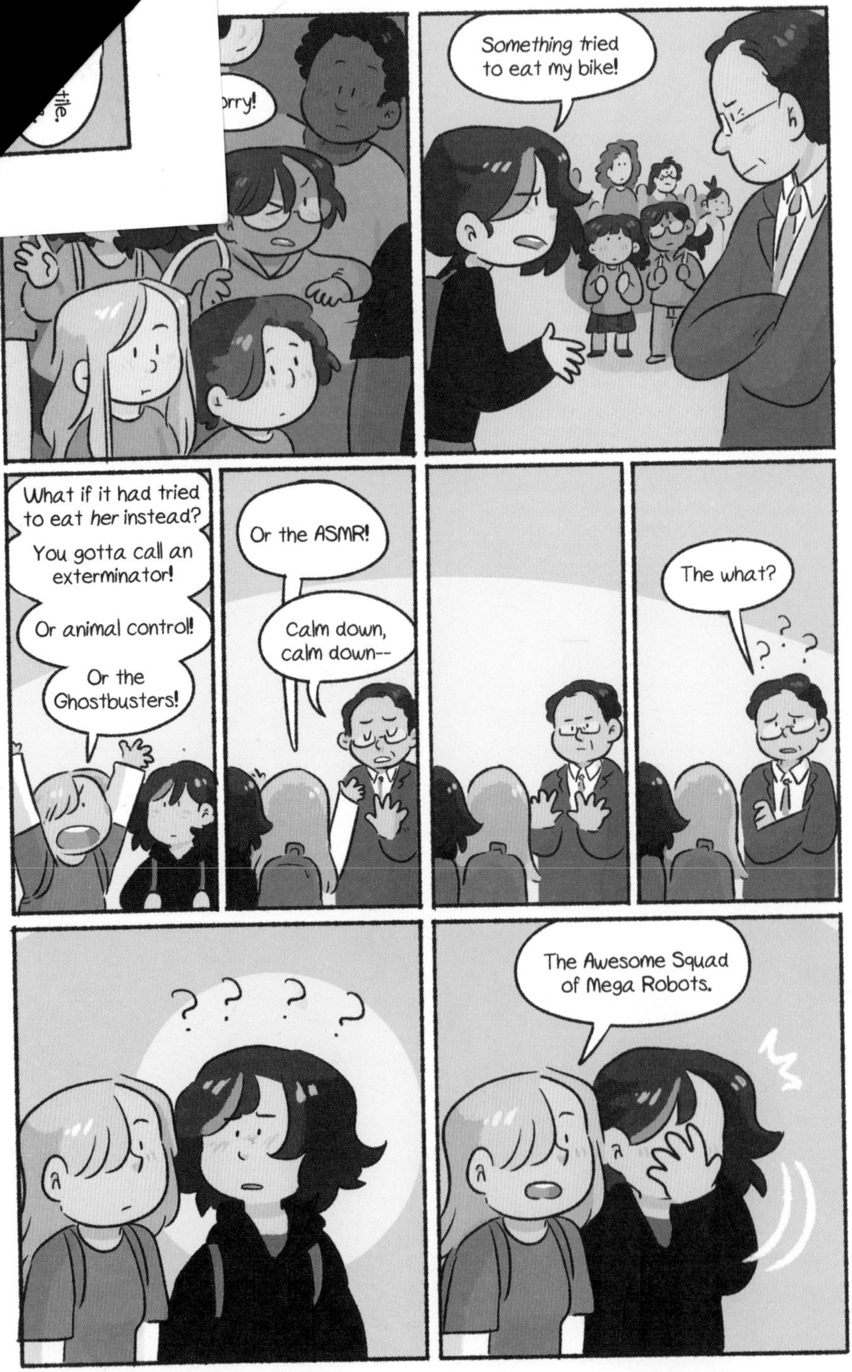
Something tried to eat my bike!
What if it had tried to eat *her* instead?
You gotta call an exterminator!
Or animal control!
Or the Ghostbusters!
Or the ASMR!
Calm down, calm down--
The what?
The Awesome Squad of Mega Robots.

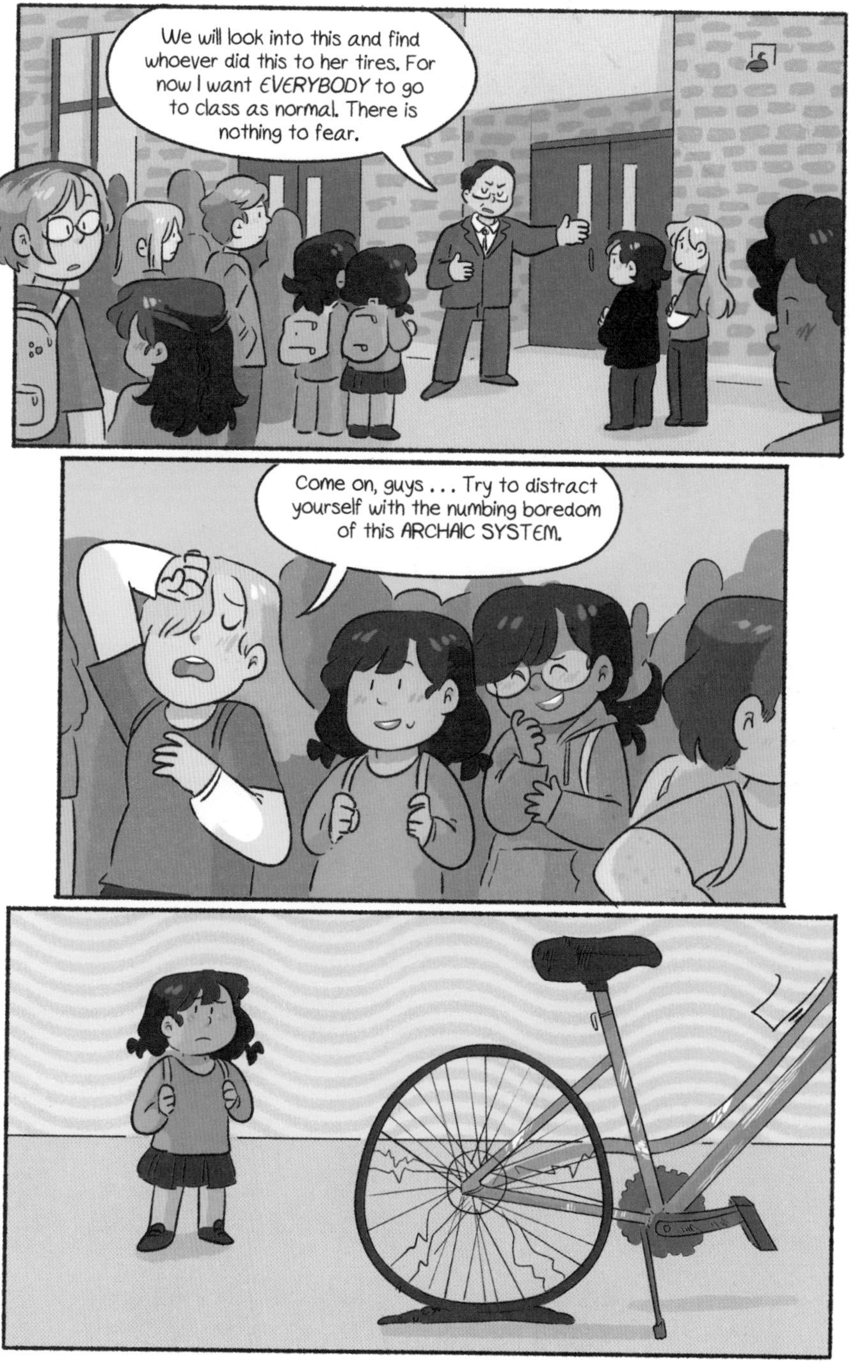
We will look into this and find whoever did this to her tires. For now I want EVERYBODY to go to class as normal. There is nothing to fear.
Come on, guys . . . Try to distract yourself with the numbing boredom of this ARCHAIC SYSTEM.

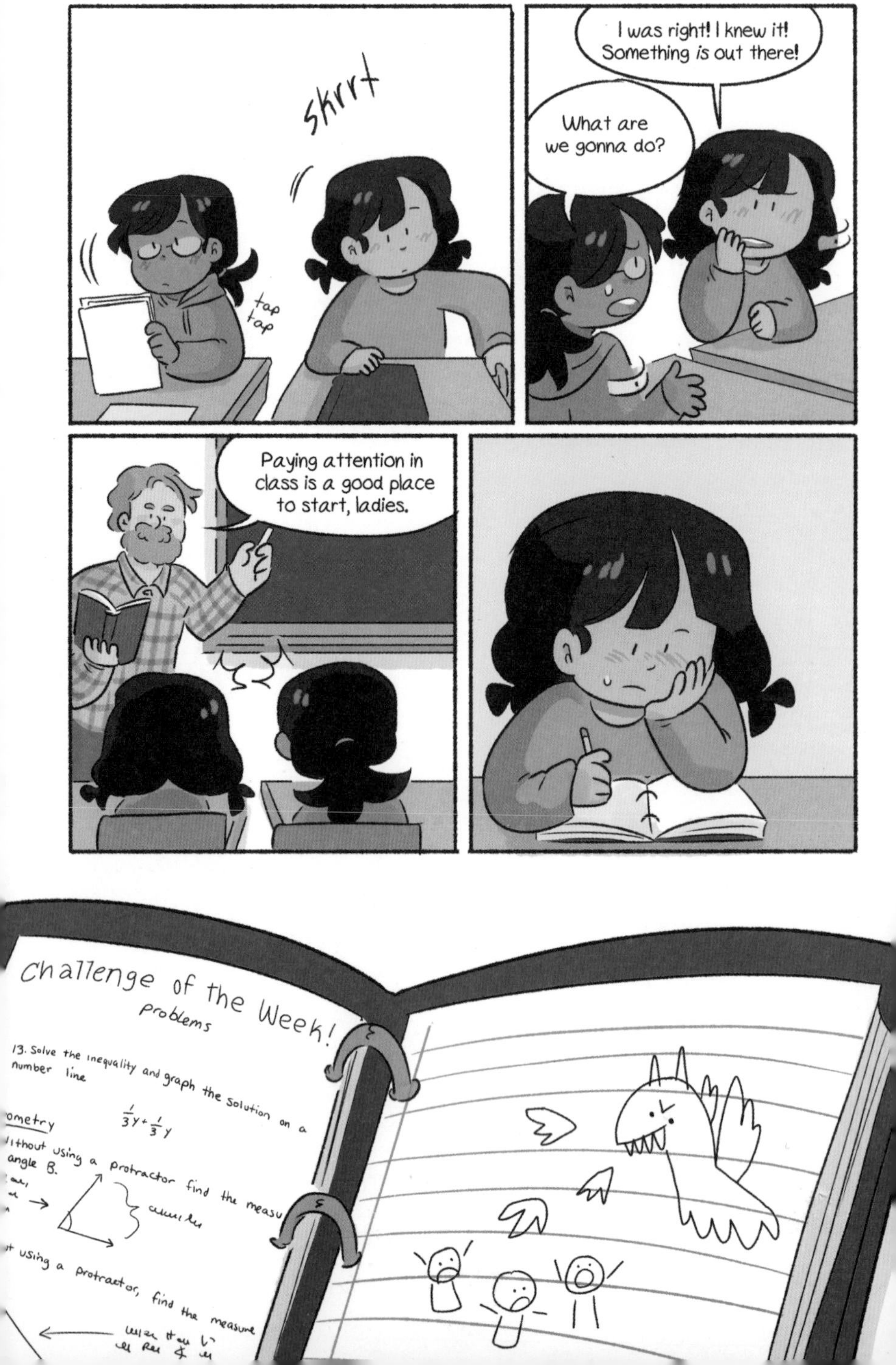
skrrt
tap tap
I was right! I knew it! Something *is* out there!
What are we gonna do?
Paying attention in class is a good place to start, ladies.
Challenge of the Week!
problems
13. Solve the inequality and graph the solution on a number line
ometry
ithout using a protractor find the measu
angle B.
t using a protractor, find the measure

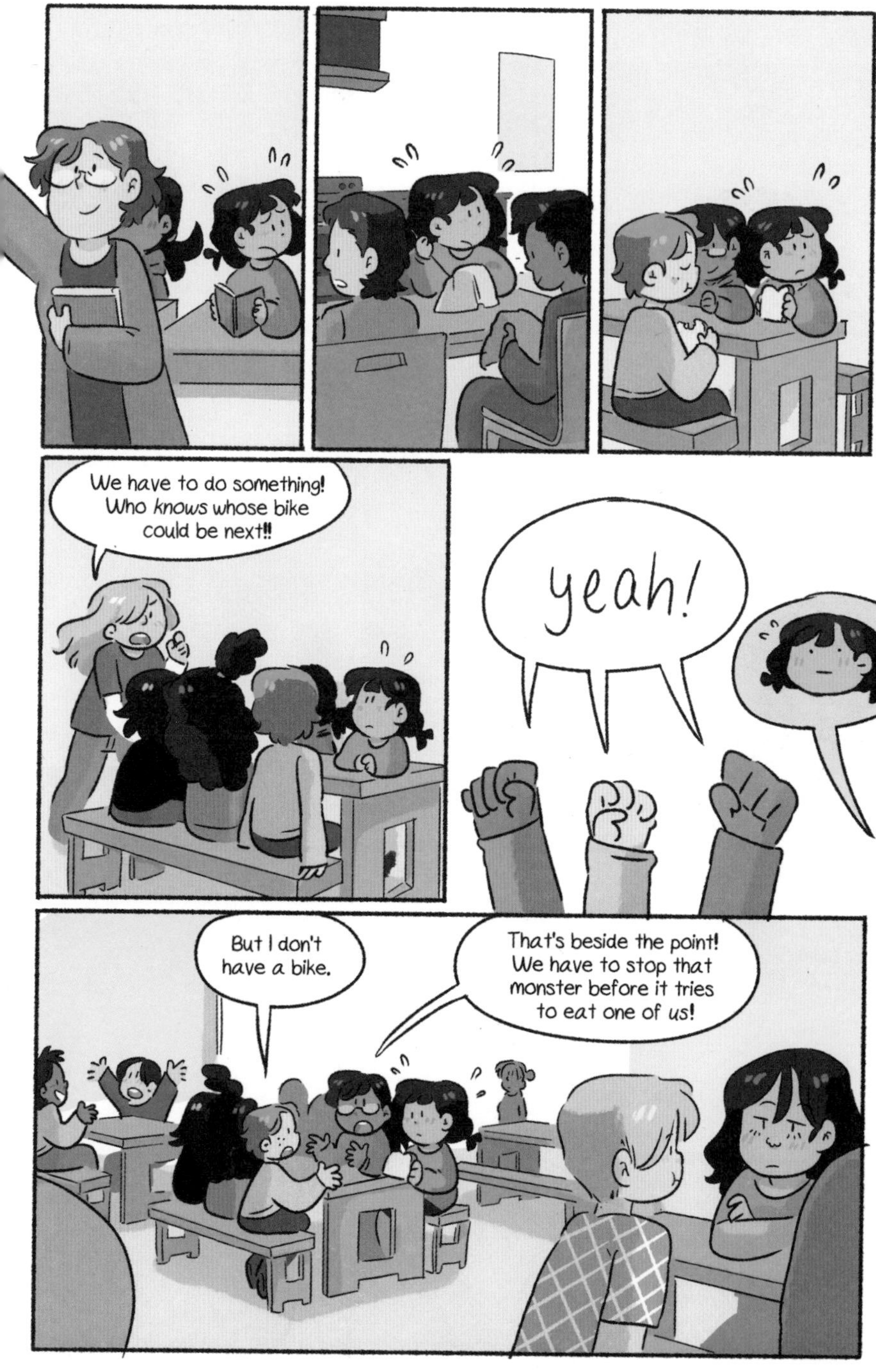
We have to do something! Who *knows* whose bike could be next!!
yeah!
But I don't have a bike.
That's beside the point! We have to stop that monster before it tries to eat one of *us*!

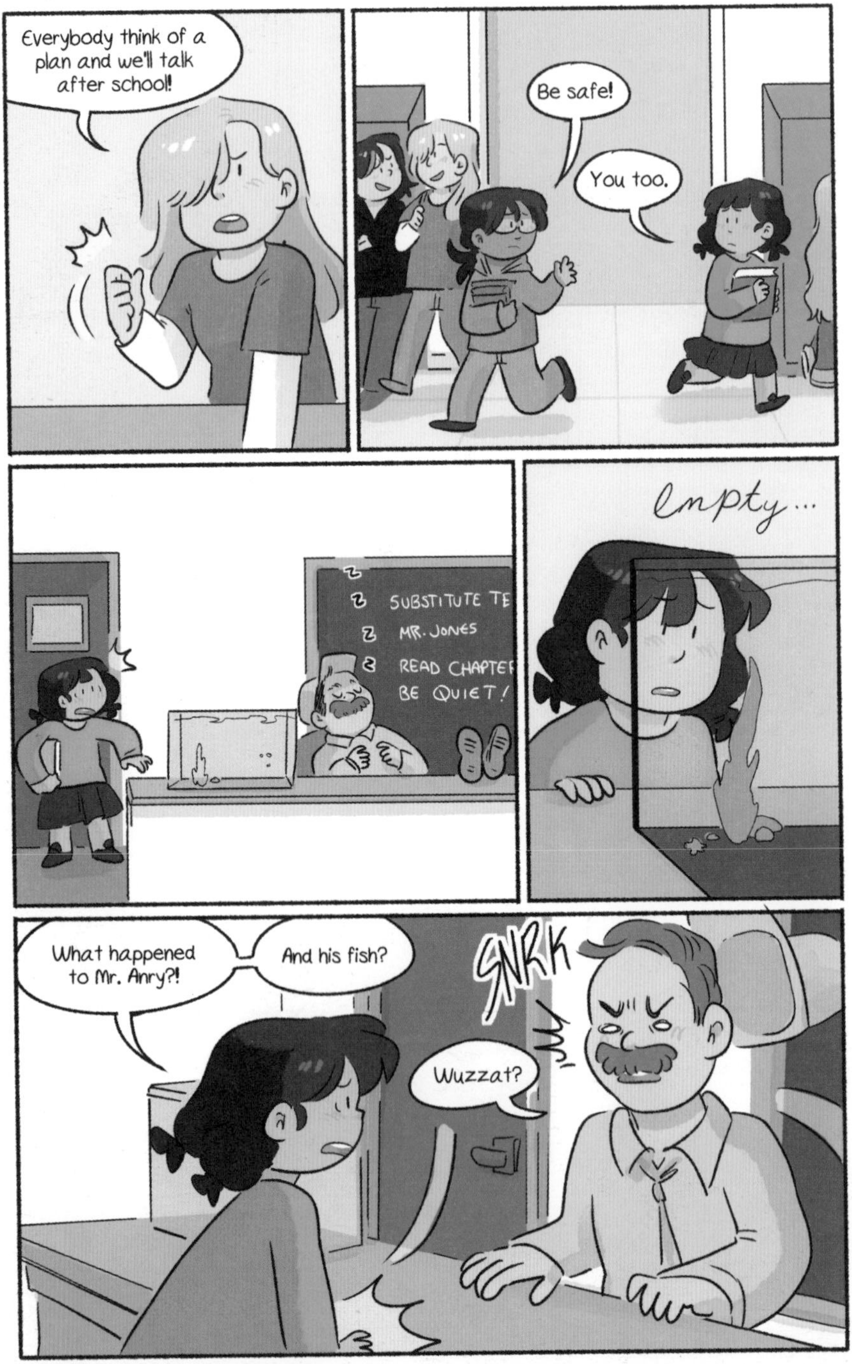
Everybody think of a plan and we'll talk after school!
Be safe!
You too.
Z
Z SUBSTITUTE TE
Z MR. JONES
Z READ CHAPTER
BE QUIET!
Empty...
What happened to Mr. Anry?!
And his fish?
SNRK
Wuzzat?

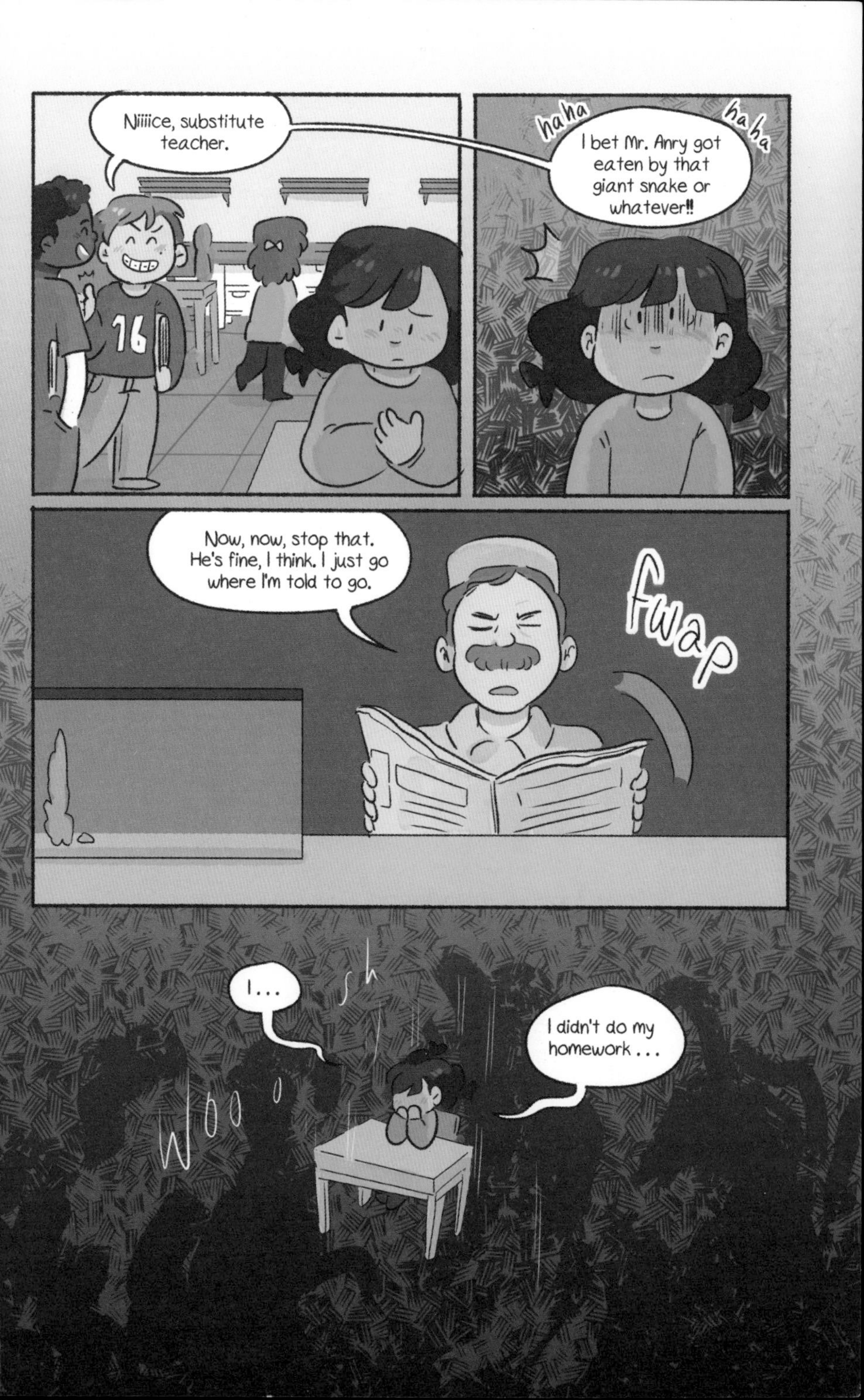
Niiiice, substitute teacher.
haha
haha
I bet Mr. Anry got eaten by that giant snake or whatever!!
Now, now, stop that. He's fine, I think. I just go where I'm told to go.
fwap
I...
sh
I didn't do my homework...
Wooo

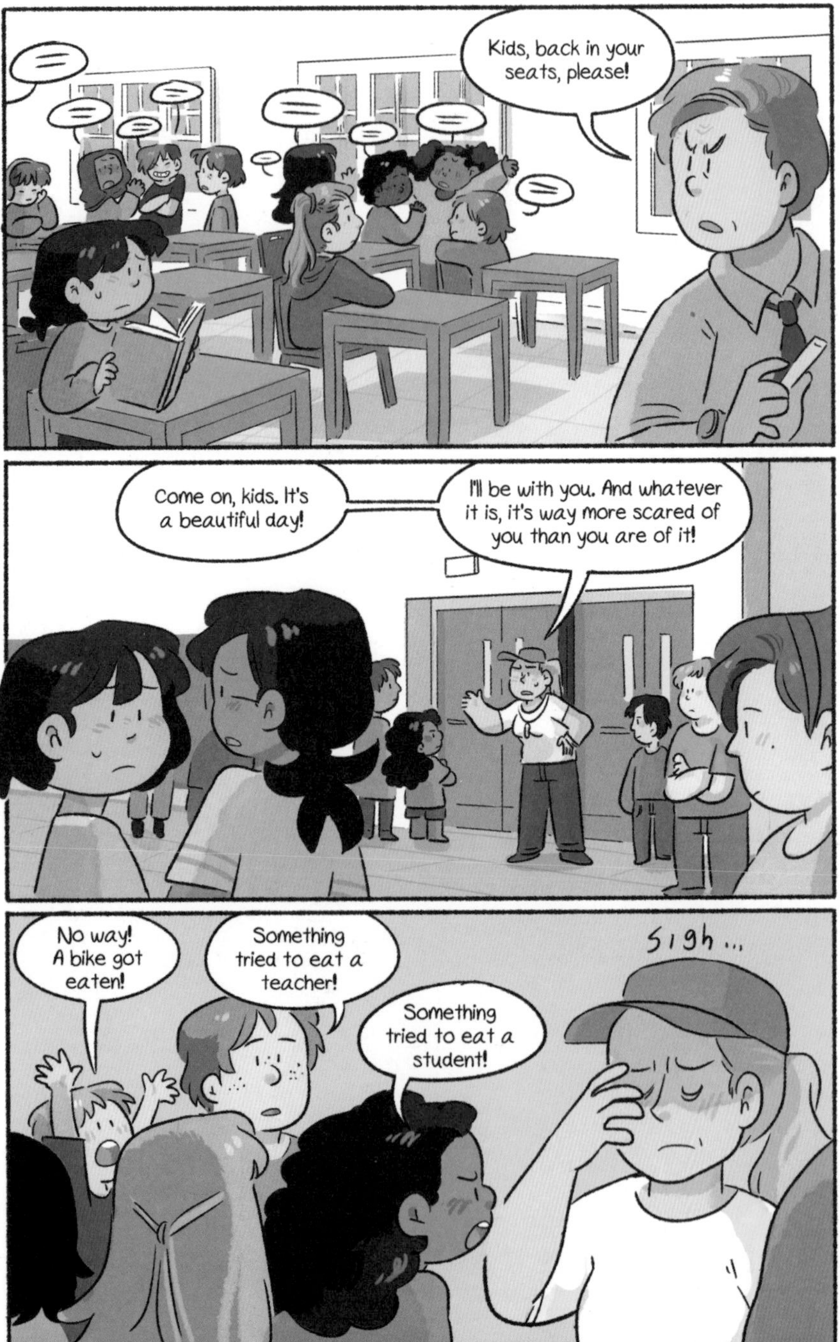

Kids, back in your seats, please!
Come on, kids. It's a beautiful day!
I'll be with you. And whatever it is, it's way more scared of you than you are of it!
No way! A bike got eaten!
Something tried to eat a teacher!
Something tried to eat a student!
Sigh...

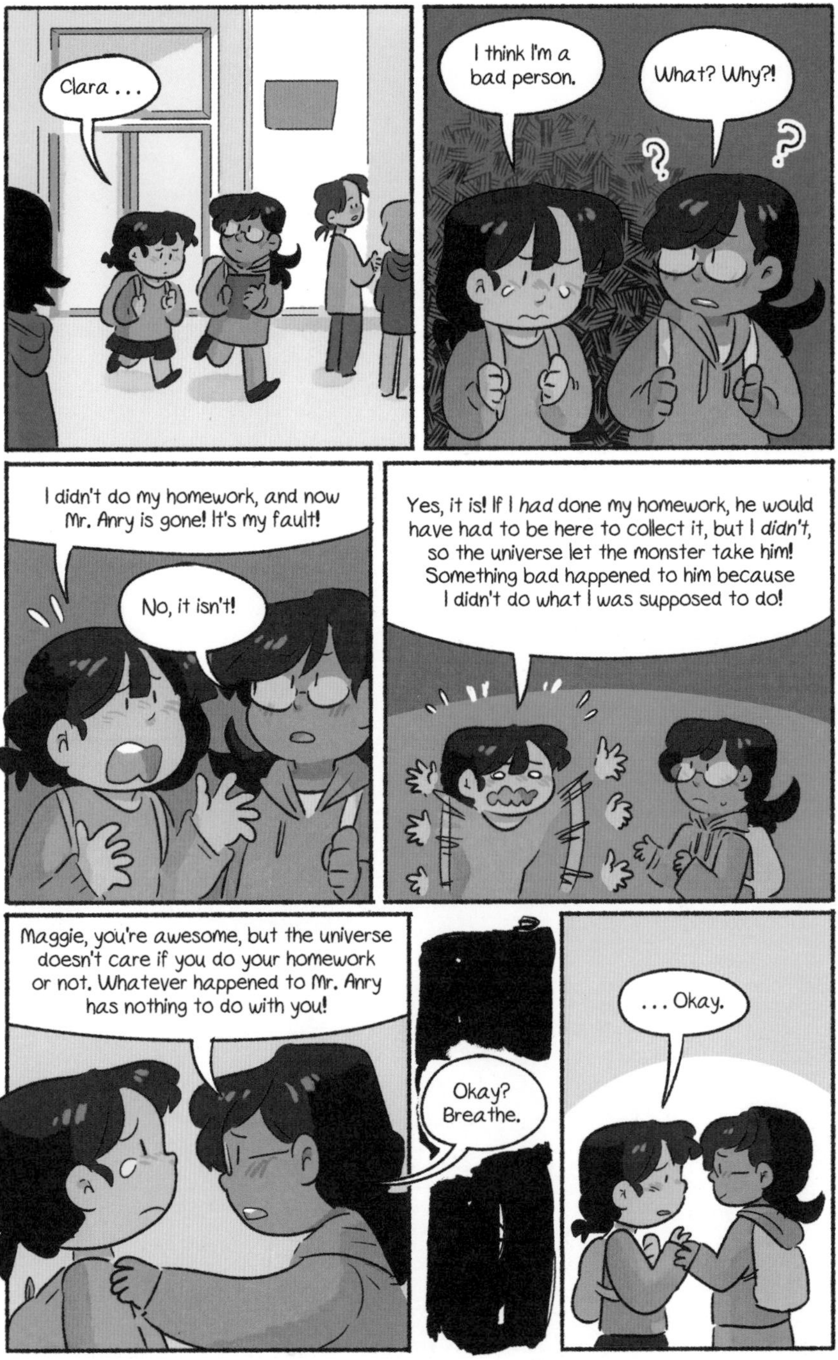
Clara . . .
I think I'm a bad person.
What? Why?!
I didn't do my homework, and now Mr. Anry is gone! It's my fault!
No, it isn't!
Yes, it is! If I *had* done my homework, he would have had to be here to collect it, but I *didn't*, so the universe let the monster take him! Something bad happened to him because I didn't do what I was supposed to do!
Maggie, you're awesome, but the universe doesn't care if you do your homework or not. Whatever happened to Mr. Anry has nothing to do with you!
Okay? Breathe.
. . . Okay.

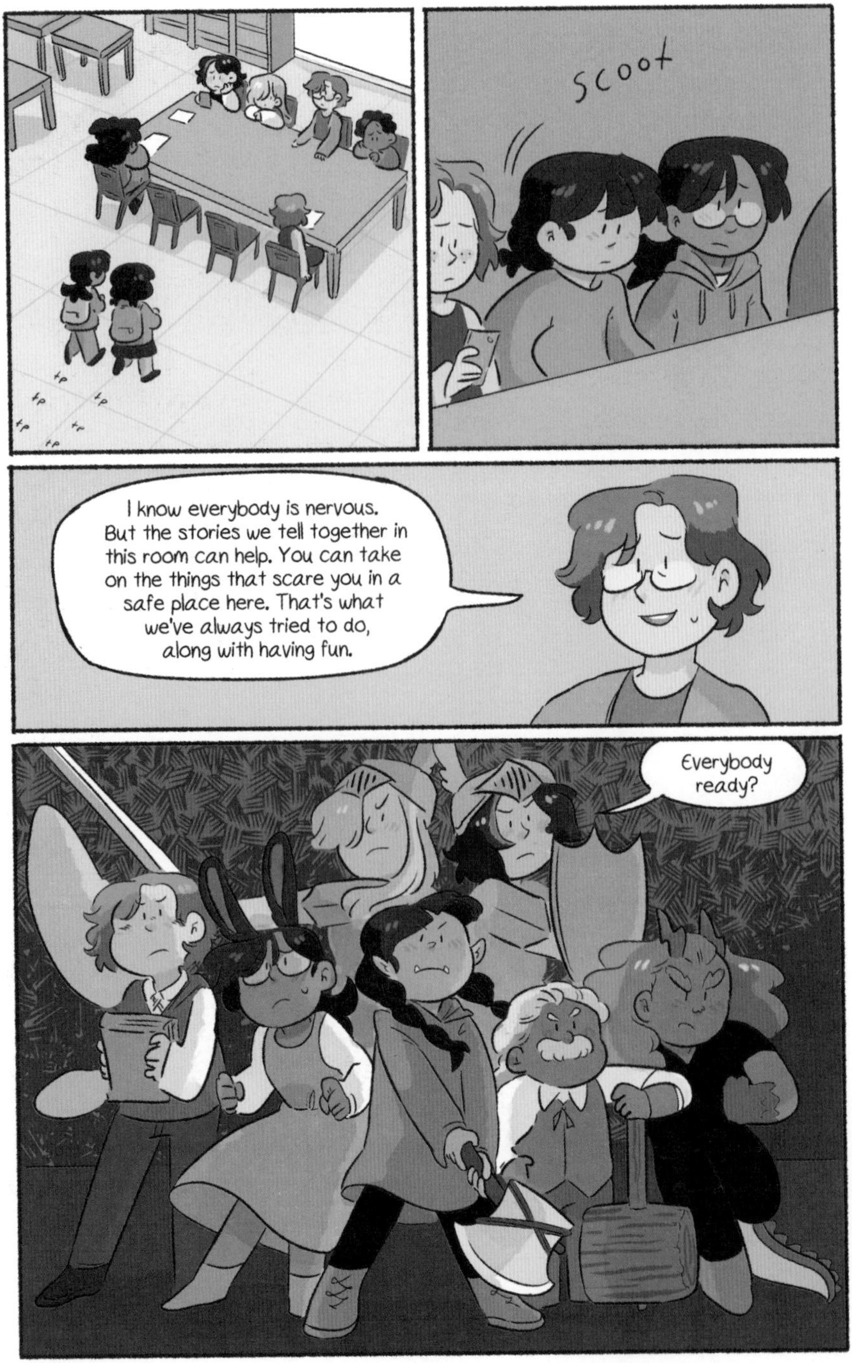

tp
tp
tp
tp
tp
tp
scoot
I know everybody is nervous. But the stories we tell together in this room can help. You can take on the things that scare you in a safe place here. That's what we've always tried to do, along with having fun.
Everybody ready?

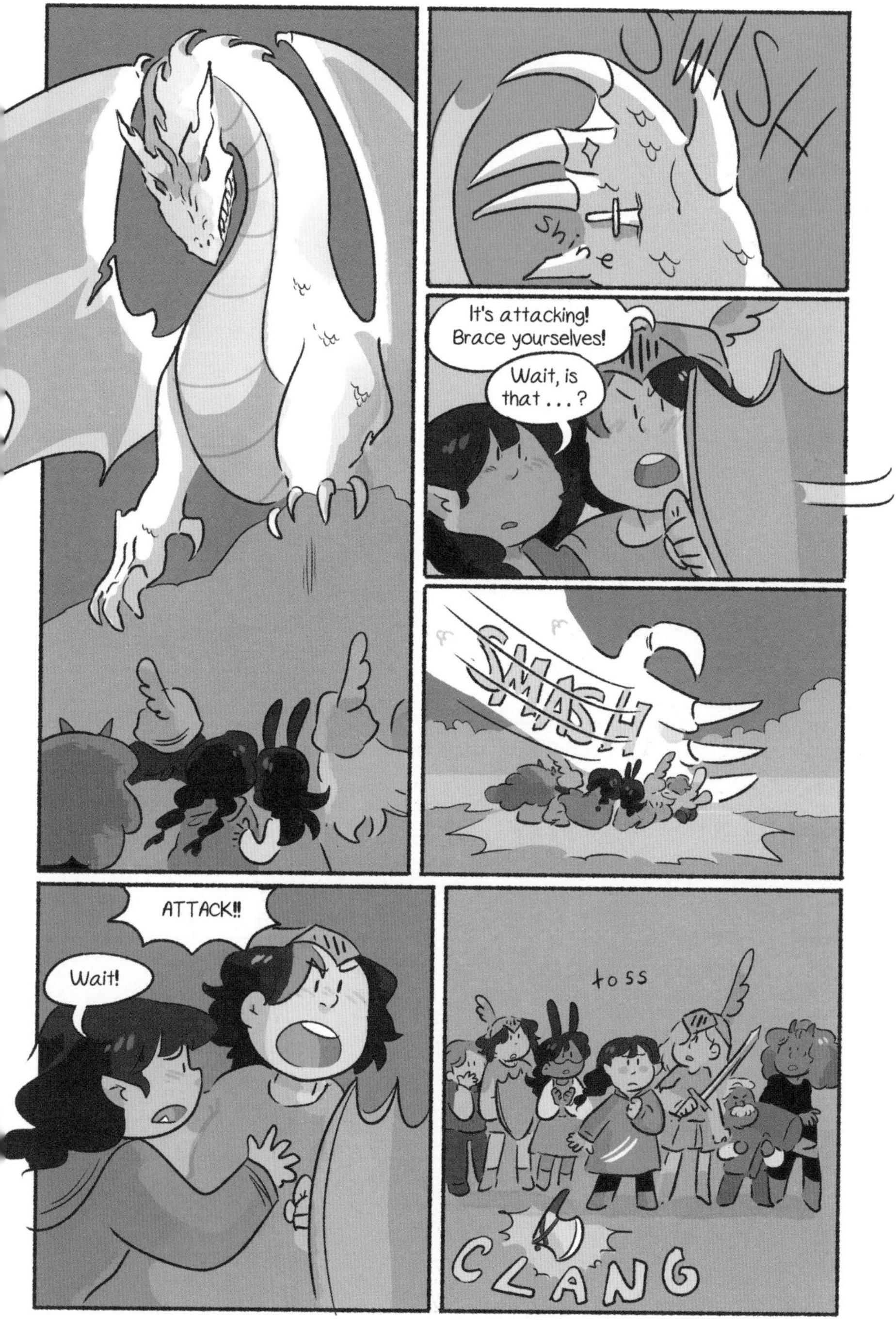
SWISH
shine
It's attacking! Brace yourselves!
Wait, is that . . . ?
SMASH
ATTACK!!
Wait!
toss
CLANG

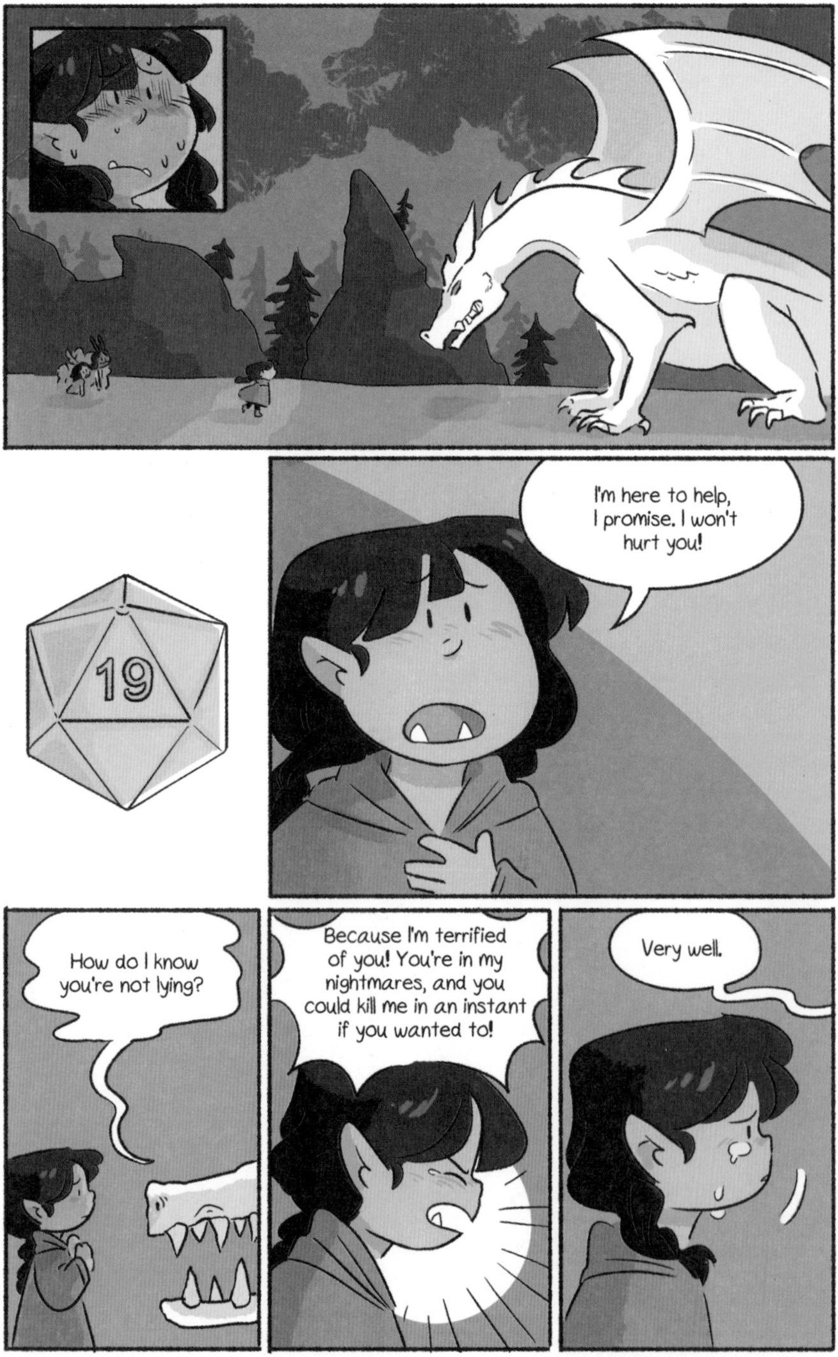
19
I'm here to help, I promise. I won't hurt you!
How do I know you're not lying?
Because I'm terrified of you! You're in my nightmares, and you could kill me in an instant if you wanted to!
Very well.

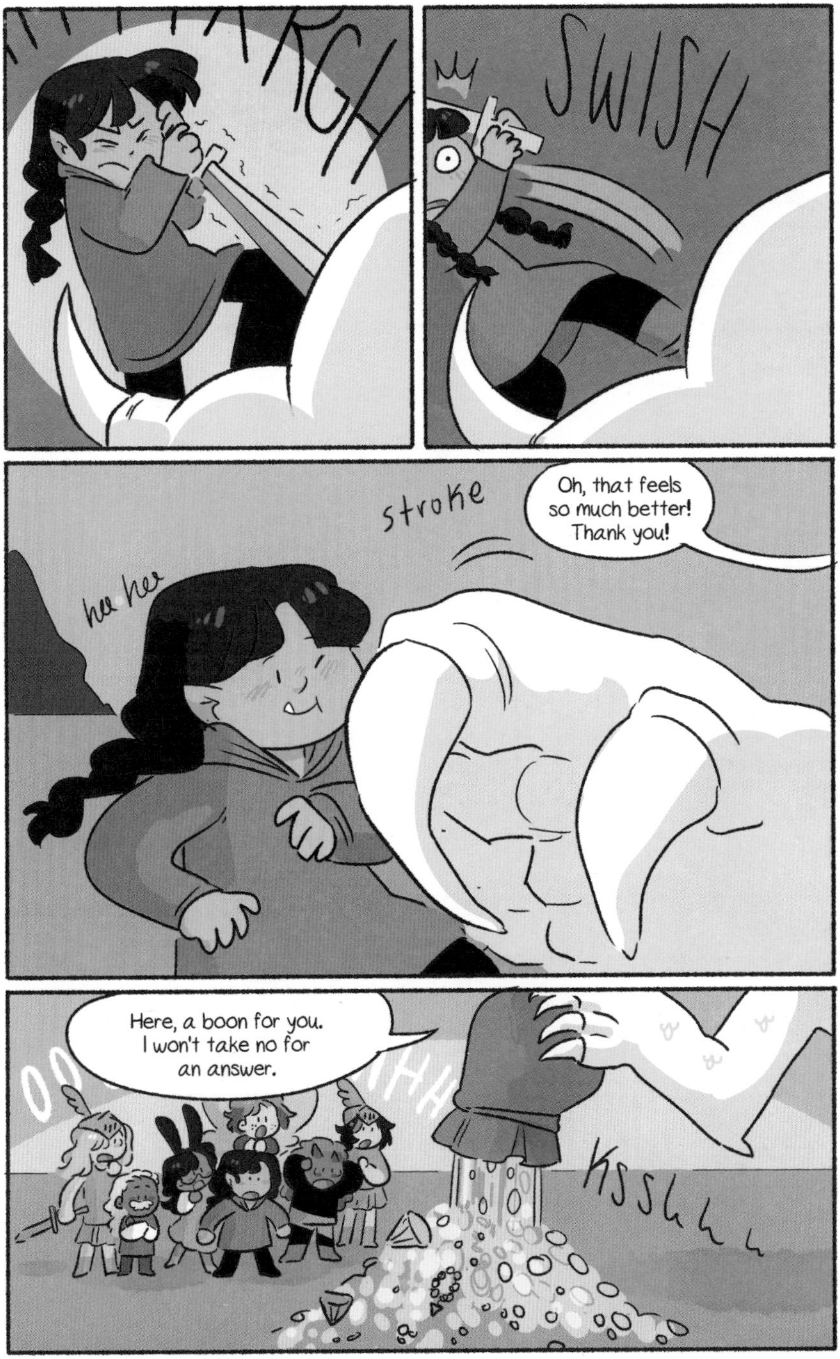

RGH
SWISH
stroke
Oh, that feels so much better! Thank you!
hee hee
Here, a boon for you. I won't take no for an answer.
Ksshhh

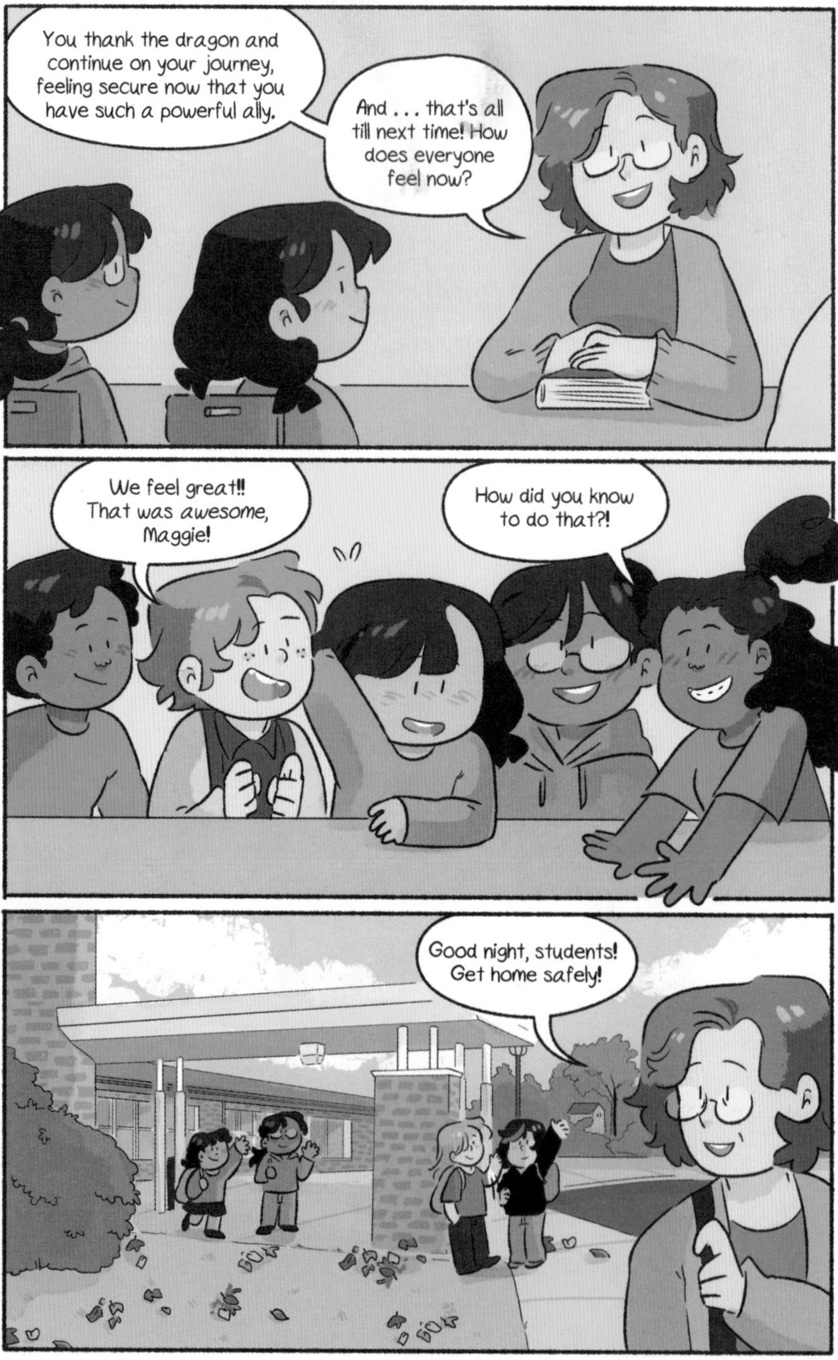
You thank the dragon and continue on your journey, feeling secure now that you have such a powerful ally.
And . . . that's all till next time! How does everyone feel now?
We feel great!! That was *awesome*, Maggie!
How did you know to do that?!
Good night, students! Get home safely!

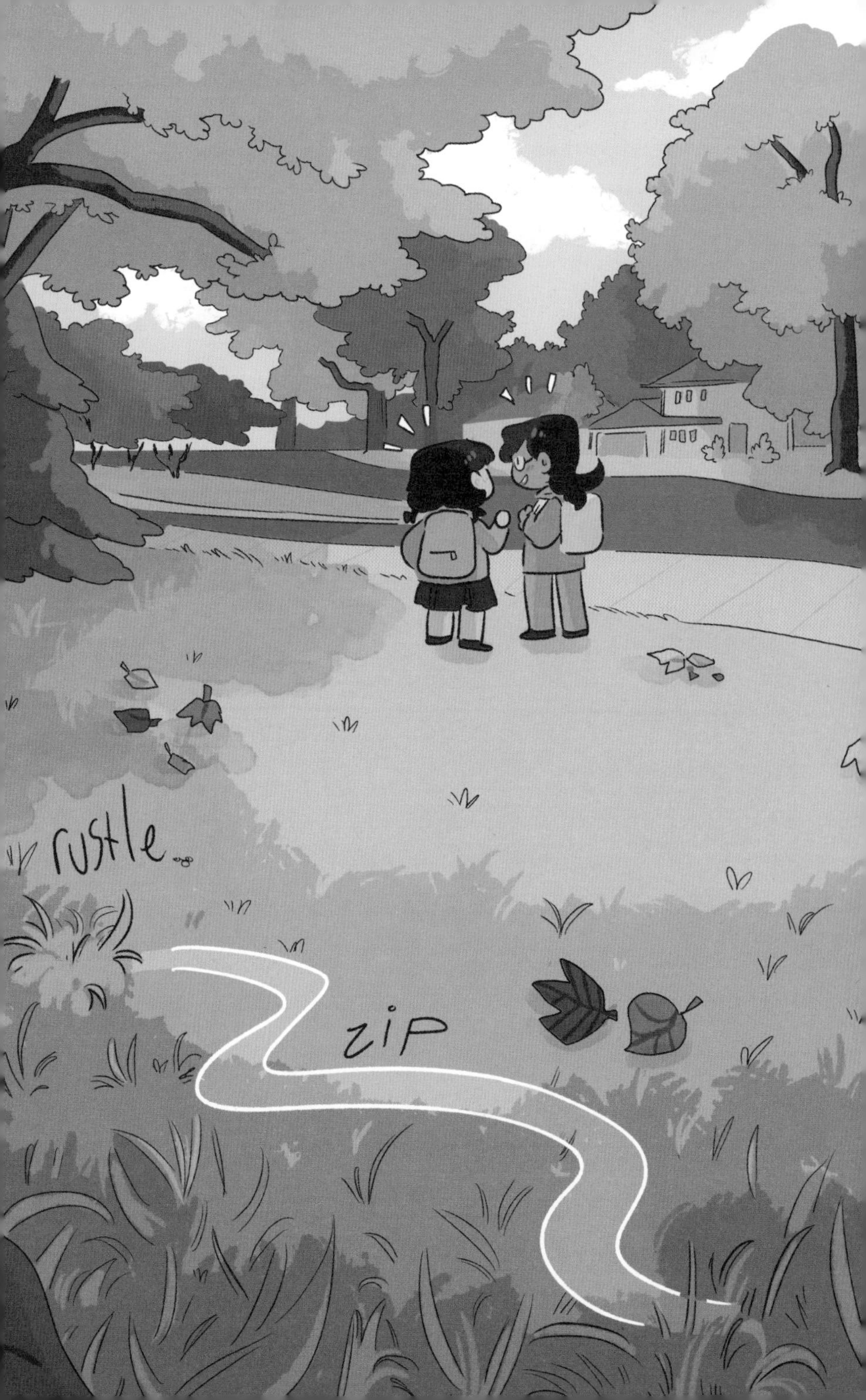
rustle...
zip

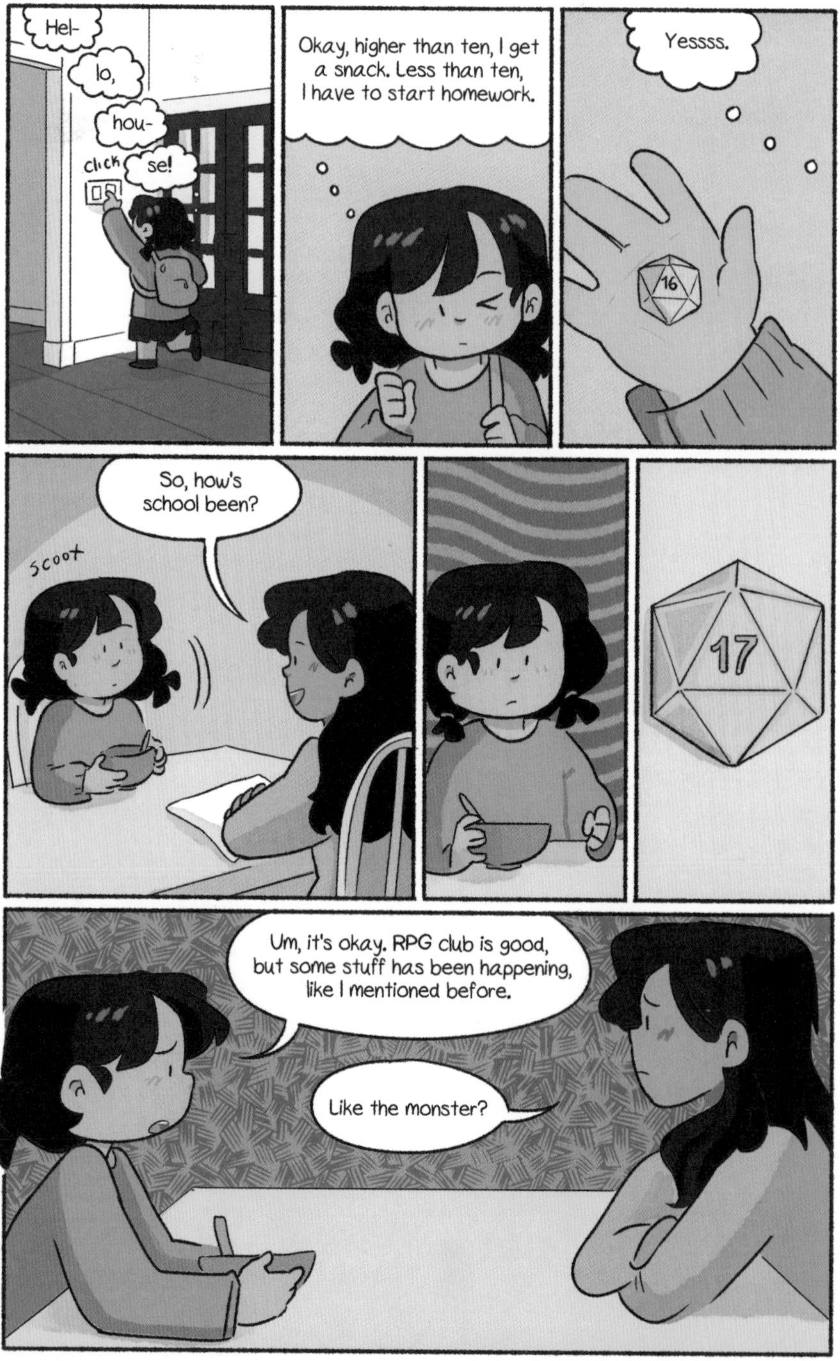
Hel-
lo,
hou-
se!
click
Okay, higher than ten, I get a snack. Less than ten, I have to start homework.
Yessss.
16
So, how's school been?
scoot
17
Um, it's okay. RPG club is good, but some stuff has been happening, like I mentioned before.
Like the monster?

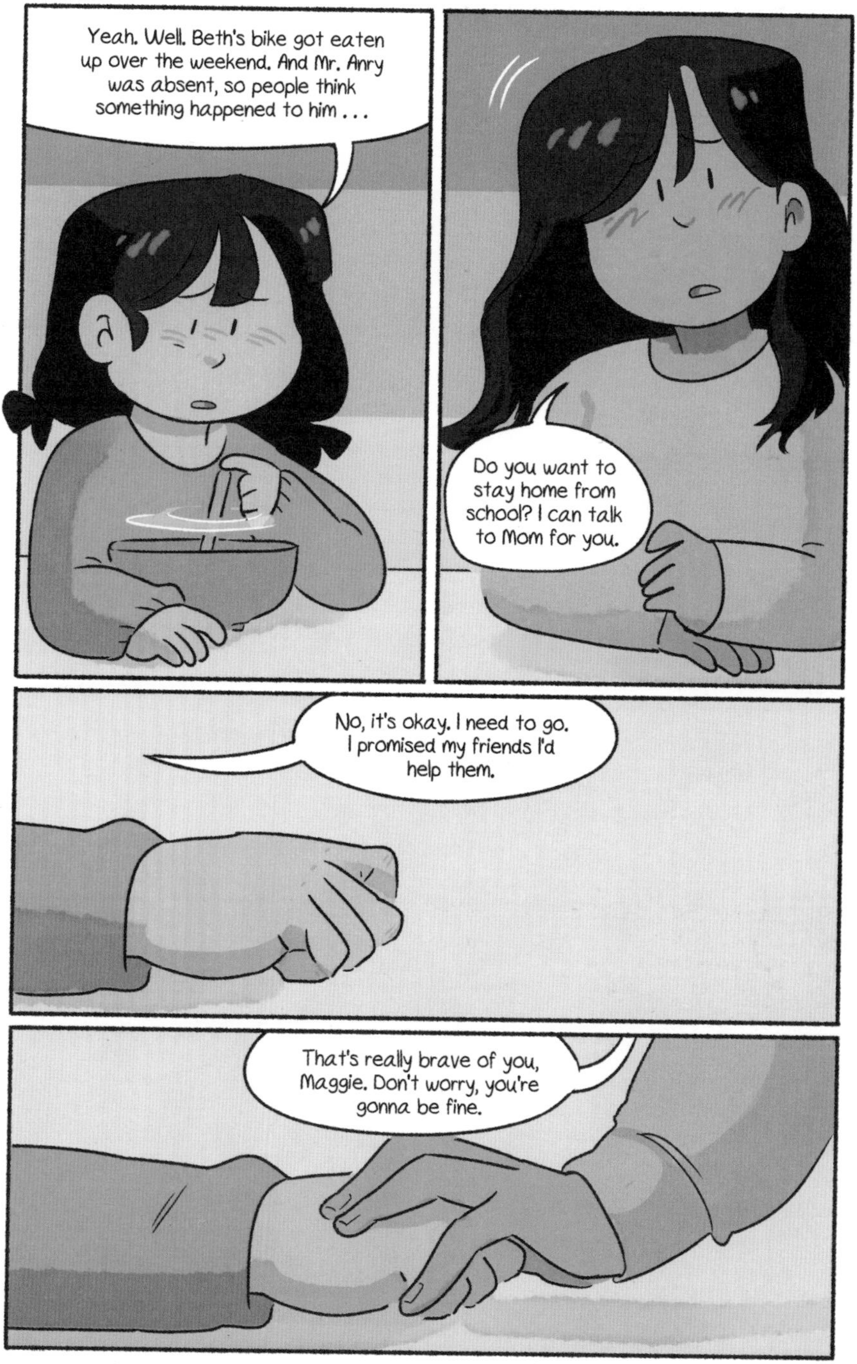
Yeah. Well. Beth's bike got eaten up over the weekend. And Mr. Anry was absent, so people think something happened to him . . .
Do you want to stay home from school? I can talk to Mom for you.
No, it's okay. I need to go. I promised my friends I'd help them.
That's really brave of you, Maggie. Don't worry, you're gonna be fine.

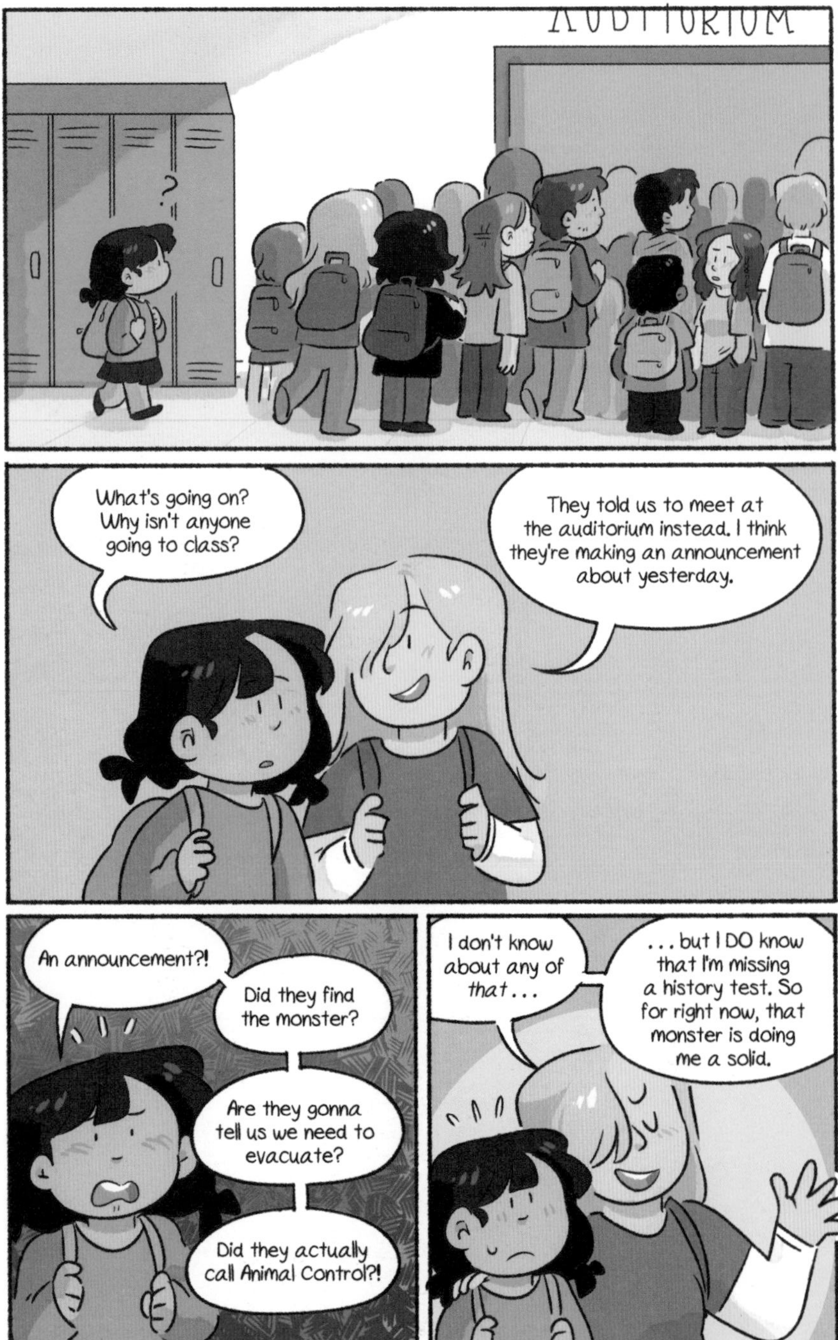
AUDITORIUM
?
What's going on? Why isn't anyone going to class?
They told us to meet at the auditorium instead. I think they're making an announcement about yesterday.
An announcement?!
Did they find the monster?
Are they gonna tell us we need to evacuate?
Did they actually call Animal Control?!
I don't know about any of *that*...
...but I DO know that I'm missing a history test. So for right now, that monster is doing me a solid.

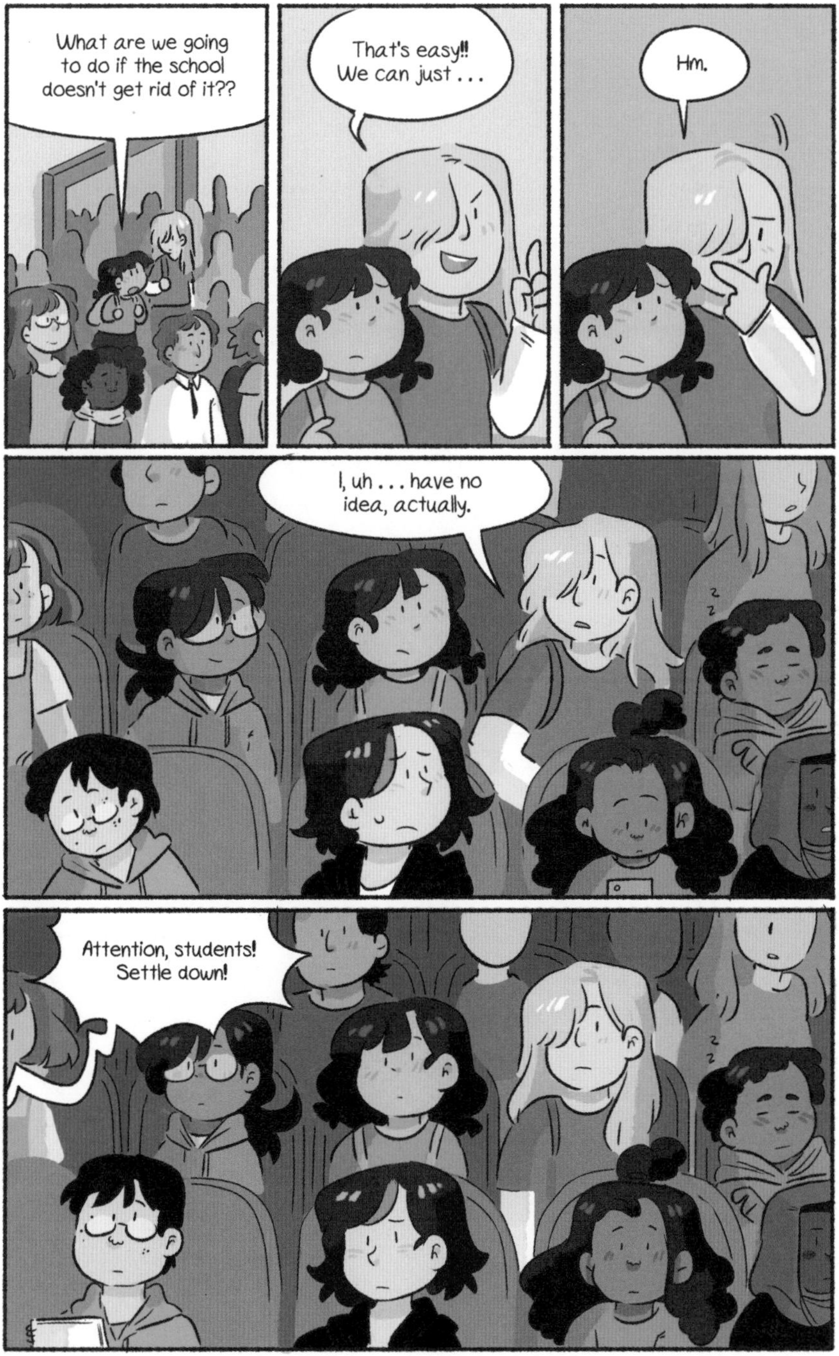
What are we going to do if the school doesn't get rid of it??
That's easy!! We can just . . .
Hm.
I, uh . . . have no idea, actually.
Attention, students! Settle down!

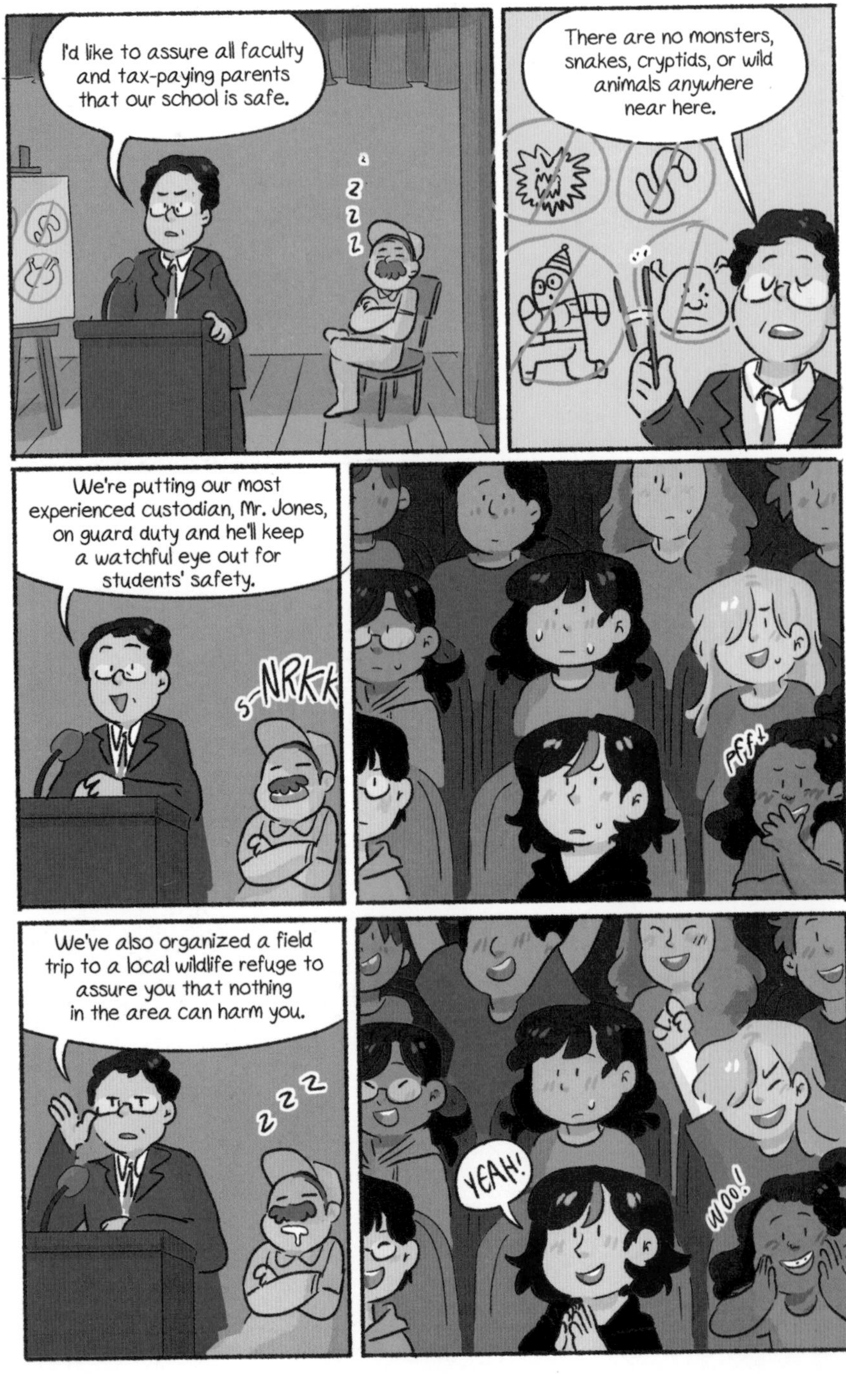

I'd like to assure all faculty and tax-paying parents that our school is safe.
Z
Z
Z
Z
There are no monsters, snakes, cryptids, or wild animals anywhere near here.
We're putting our most experienced custodian, Mr. Jones, on guard duty and he'll keep a watchful eye out for students' safety.
S-NRKK
pff!
We've also organized a field trip to a local wildlife refuge to assure you that nothing in the area can harm you.
Z Z Z
YEAH!
WOO!

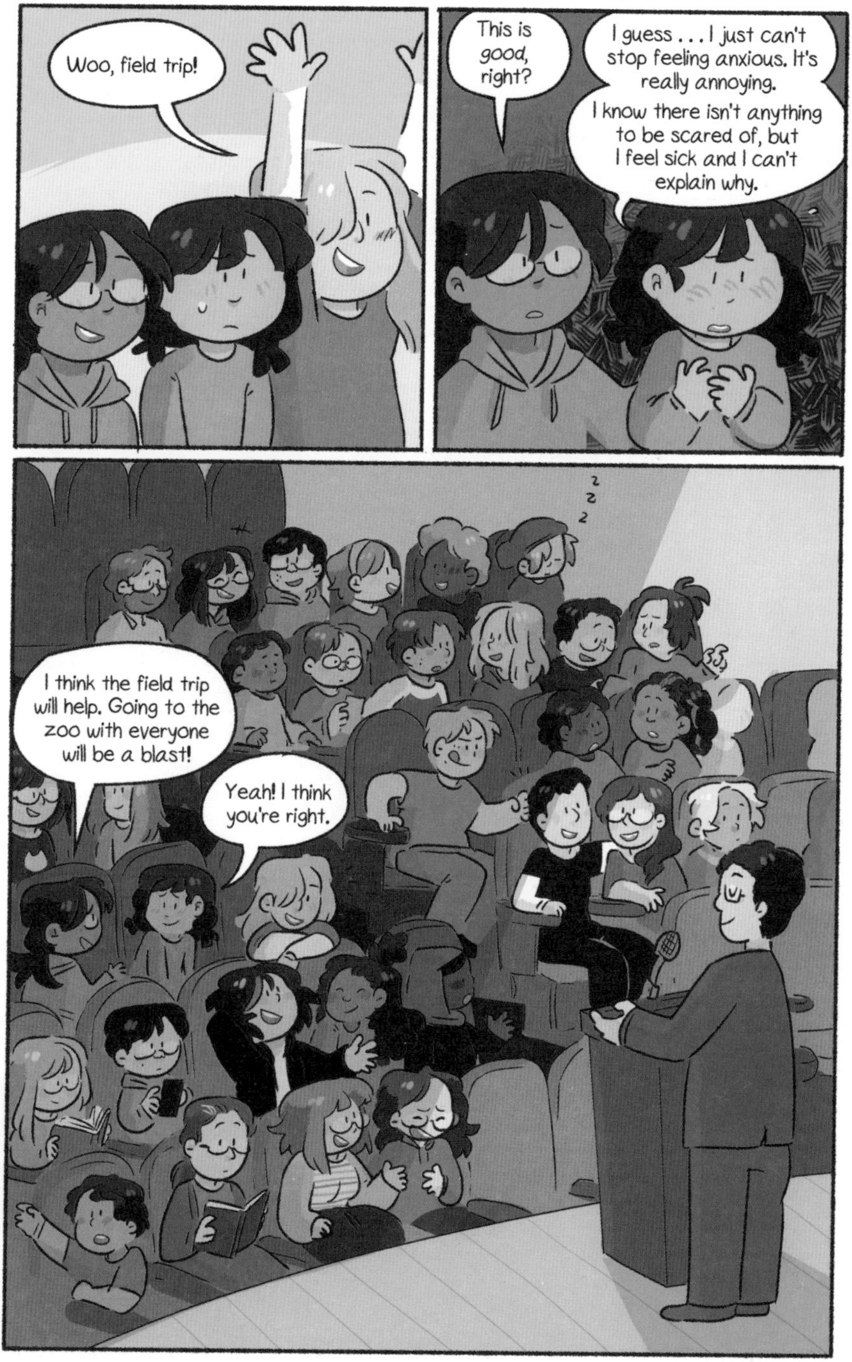
Woo, field trip!
This is good, right?
I guess . . . I just can't stop feeling anxious. It's really annoying.
I know there isn't anything to be scared of, but I feel sick and I can't explain why.
z z z
I think the field trip will help. Going to the zoo with everyone will be a blast!
Yeah! I think you're right.

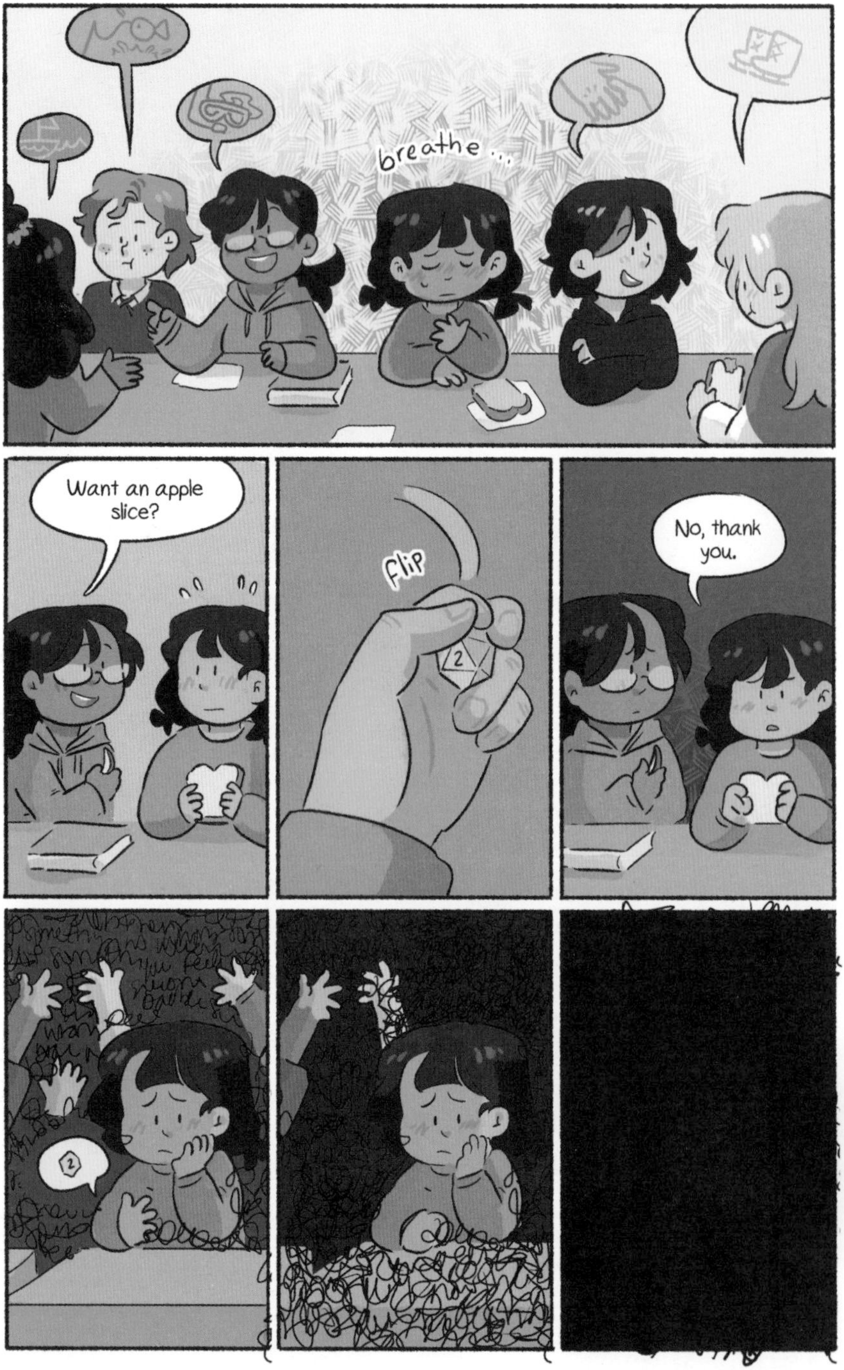
breathe...
Want an apple slice?
flip
No, thank you.

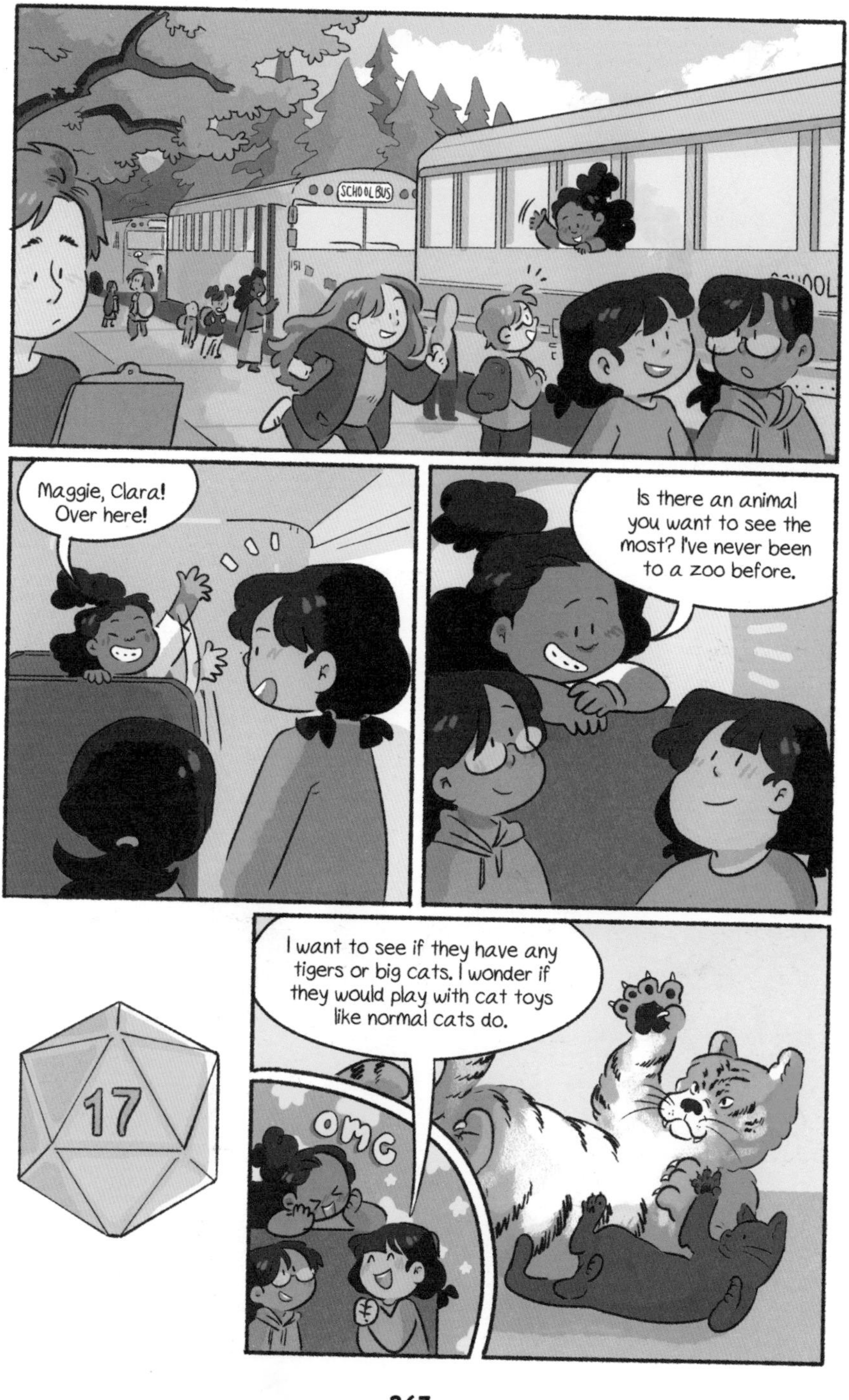
SCHOOL BUS
Maggie, Clara! Over here!
Is there an animal you want to see the most? I've never been to a zoo before.
17
I want to see if they have any tigers or big cats. I wonder if they would play with cat toys like normal cats do.
OMG

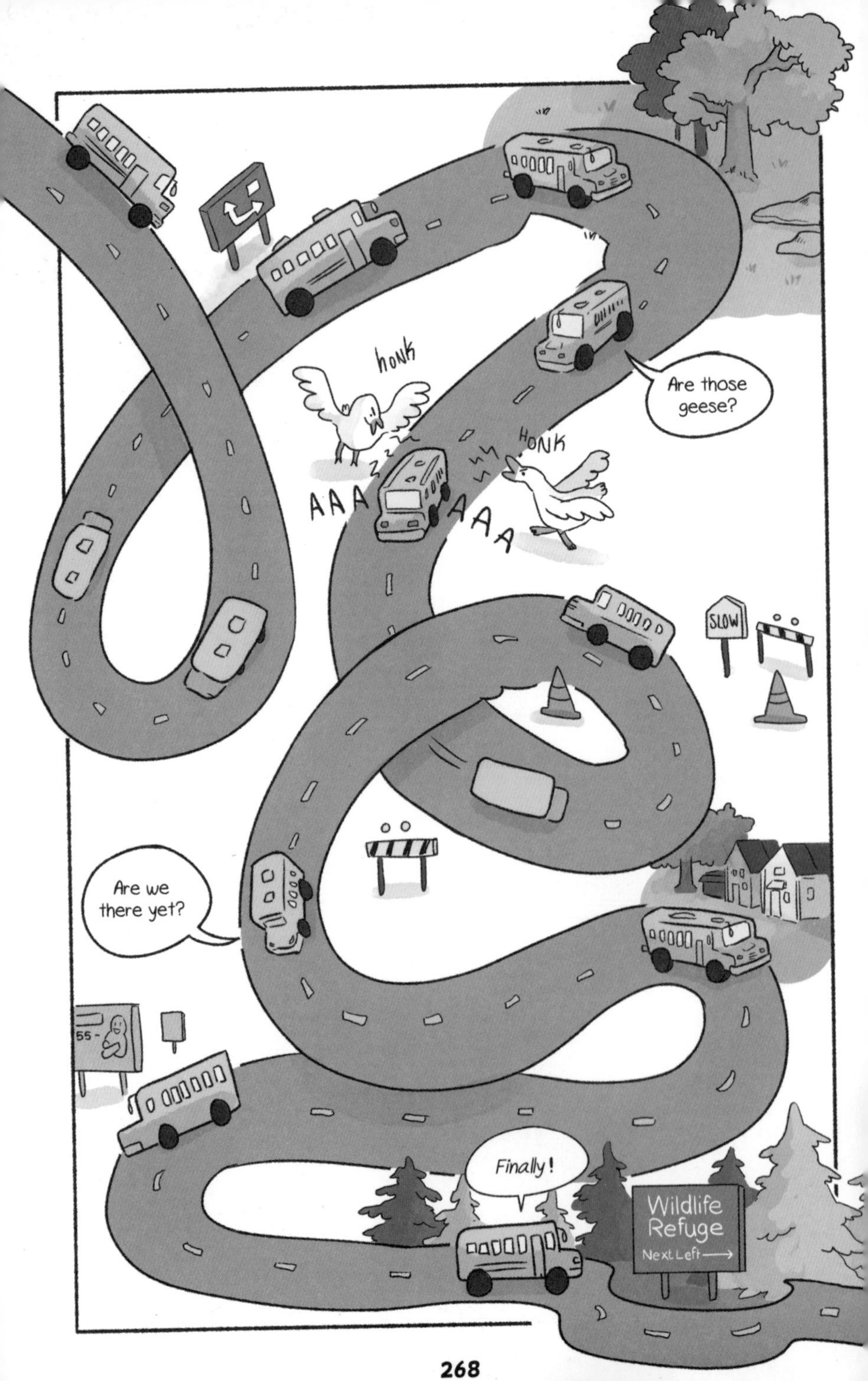
honk
Are those geese?
HONK
AAA
AAA
SLOW
Are we there yet?
55 -
Finally!
Wildlife Refuge
Next Left

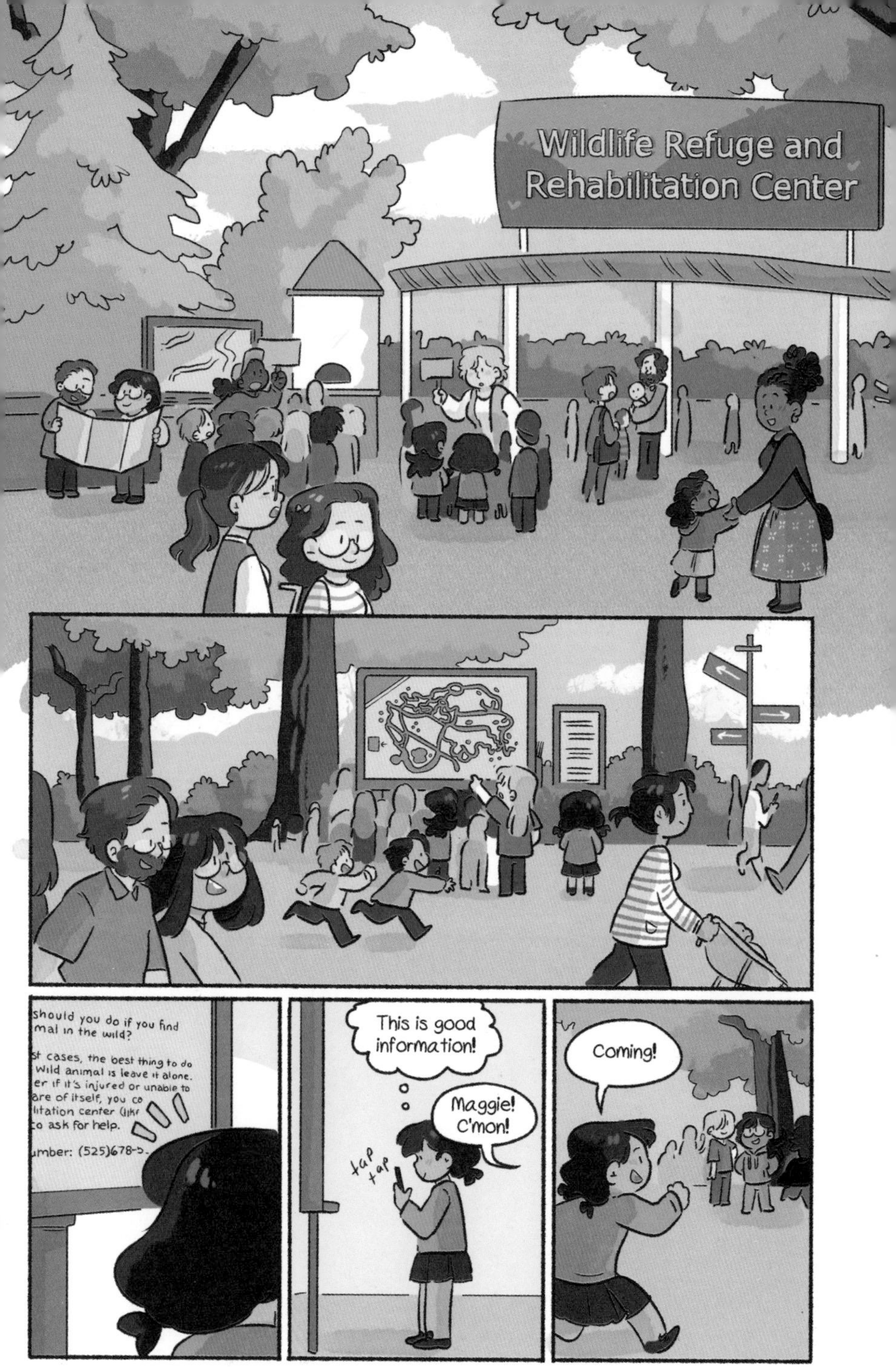
Wildlife Refuge and Rehabilitation Center
should you do if you find
mal in the wild?
st cases, the best thing to do
wild animal is leave it alone.
er if it's injured or unable to
are of itself, you co
ilitation center (like
o ask for help.
umber: (525)678-5
This is good information!
Maggie! C'mon!
tap tap
Coming!

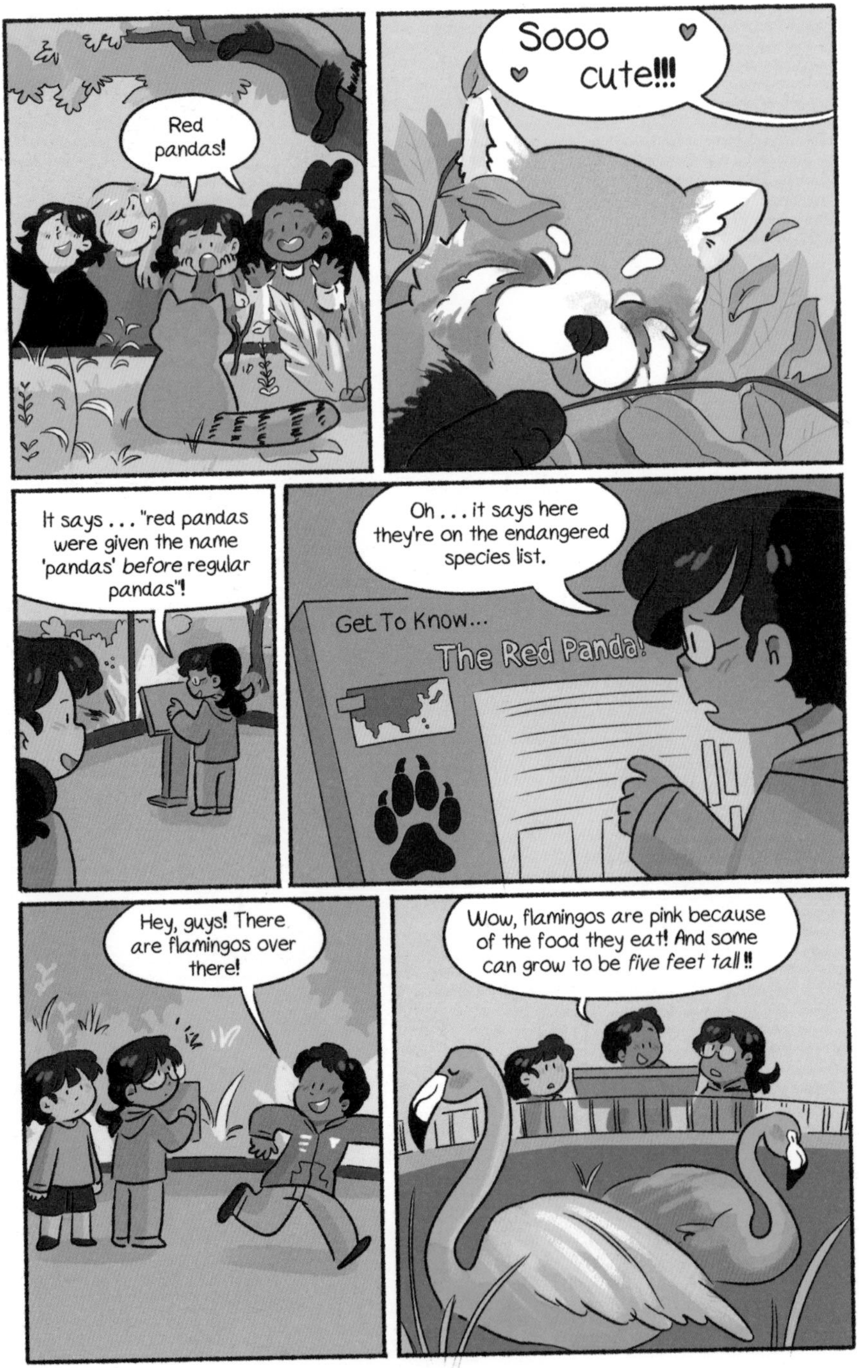
Red pandas!
Sooo cute!!!
It says ... "red pandas were given the name 'pandas' *before* regular pandas"!
Oh ... it says here they're on the endangered species list.
Get To Know...
The Red Panda!
Hey, guys! There are flamingos over there!
Wow, flamingos are pink because of the food they eat! And some can grow to be *five feet tall*!!

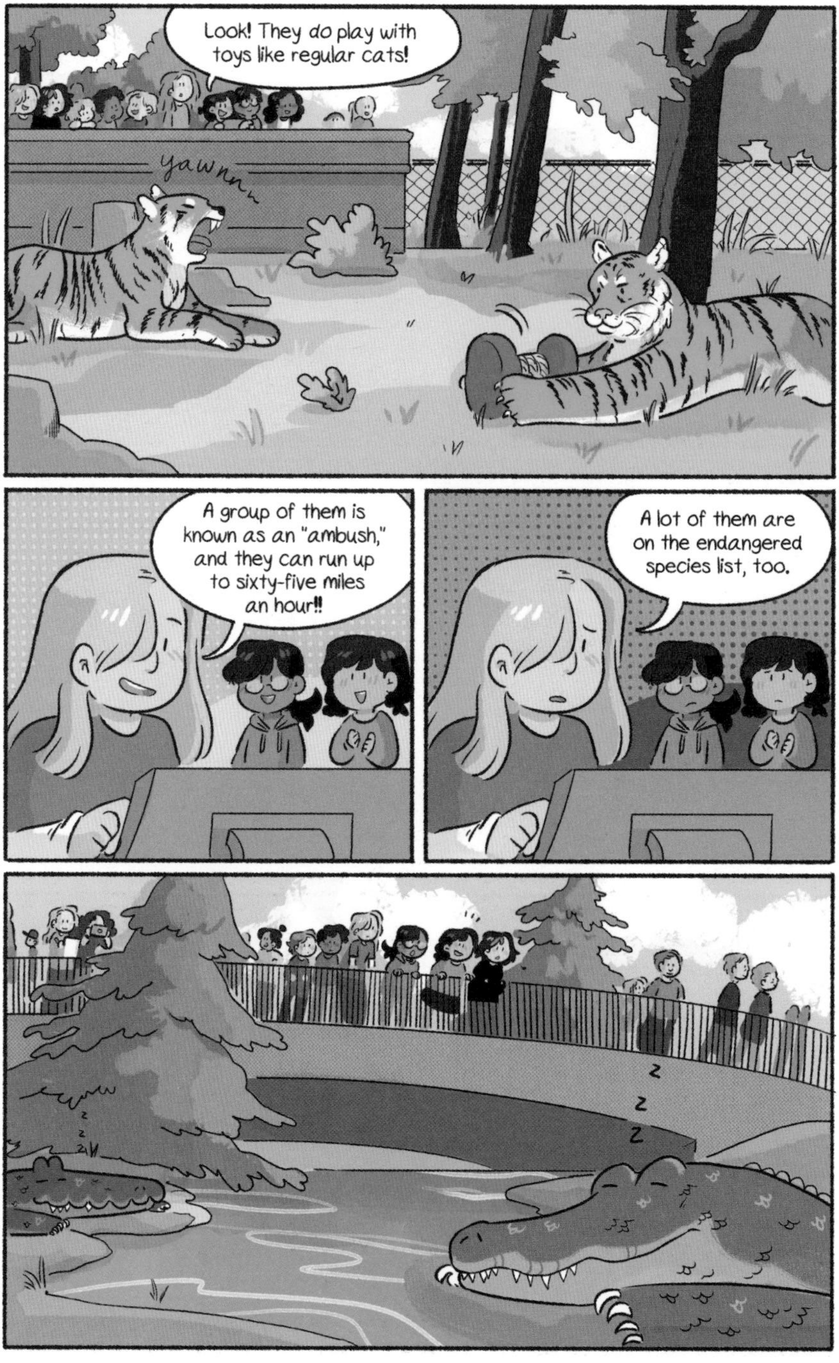
Look! They do play with toys like regular cats!
yawnnn
A group of them is known as an "ambush," and they can run up to sixty-five miles an hour!!
A lot of them are on the endangered species list, too.
z z z
z z z

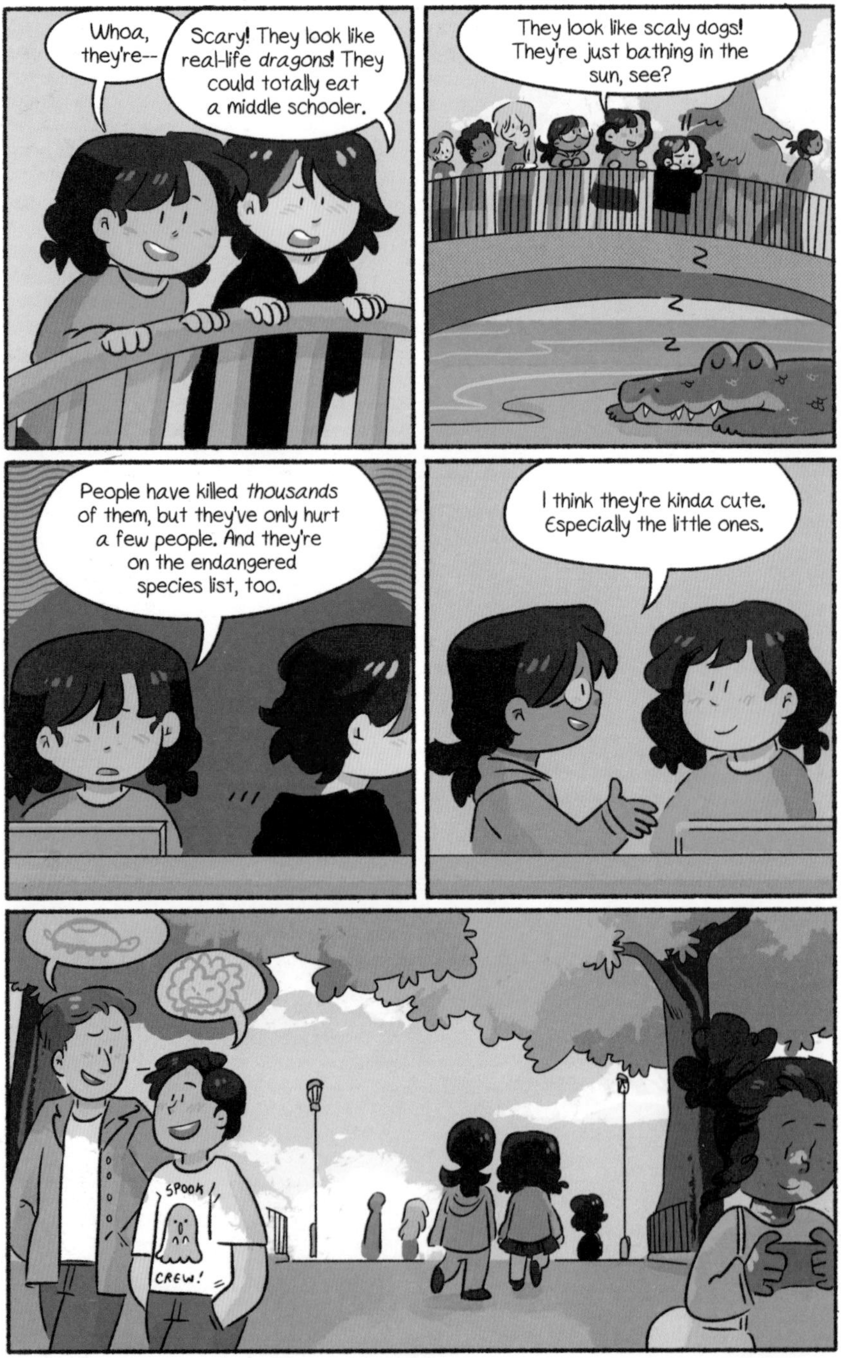
Whoa, they're--
Scary! They look like real-life *dragons*! They could totally eat a middle schooler.
They look like scaly dogs! They're just bathing in the sun, see?
Z
Z
Z
People have killed *thousands* of them, but they've only hurt a few people. And they're on the endangered species list, too.
I think they're kinda cute. Especially the little ones.
SPOOK
CREW!

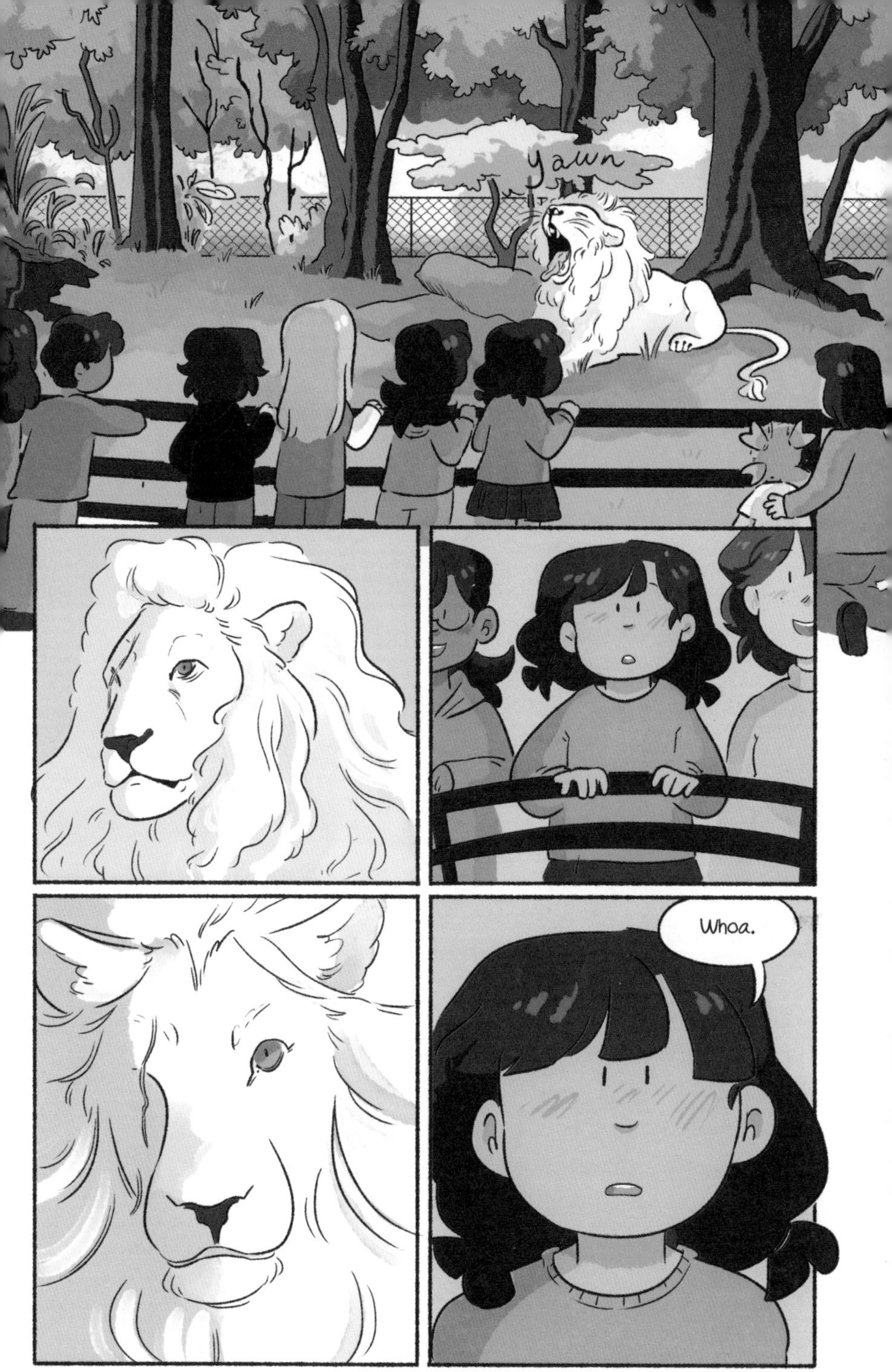
Yawn
Whoa.

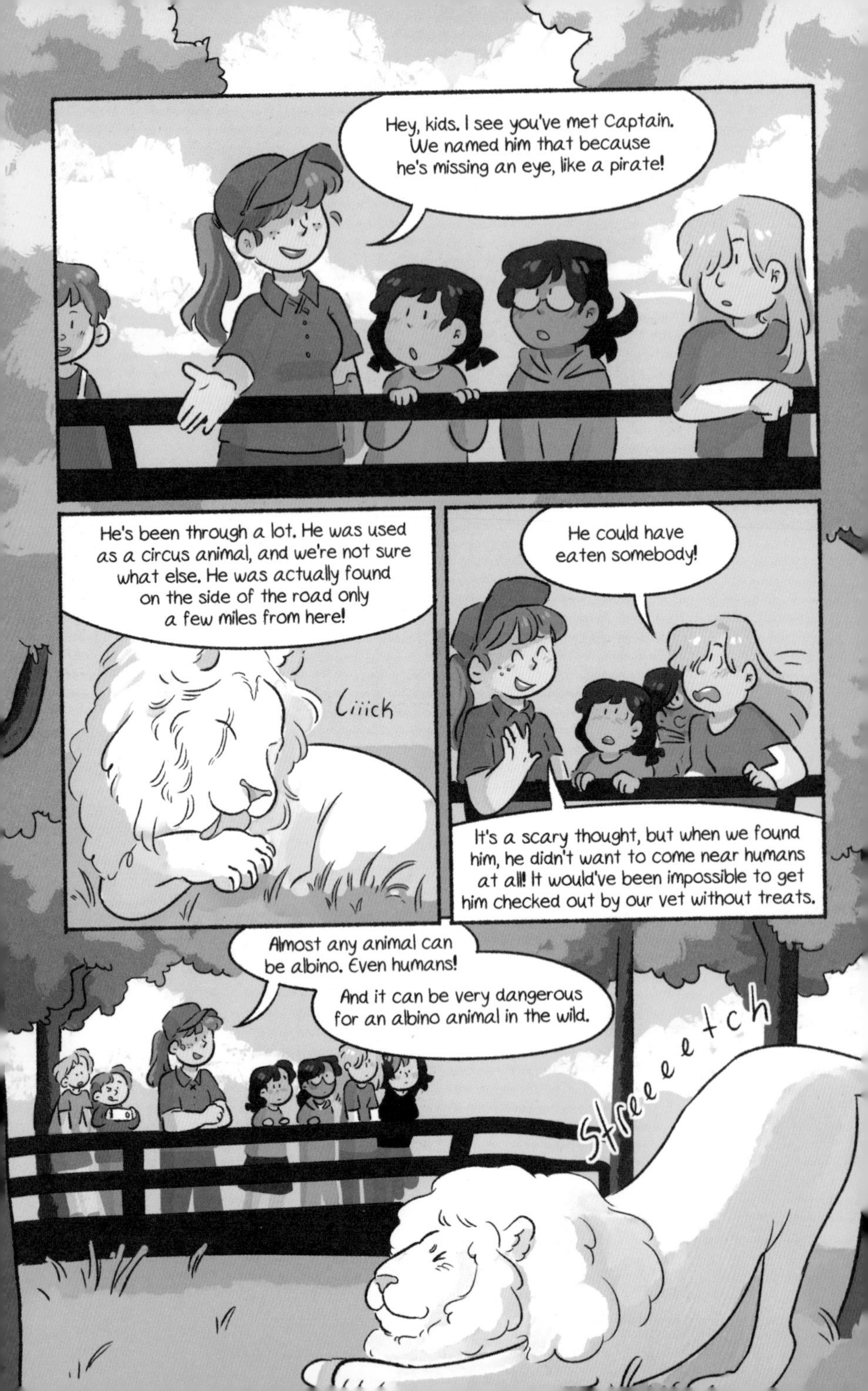
Hey, kids. I see you've met Captain. We named him that because he's missing an eye, like a pirate!
He's been through a lot. He was used as a circus animal, and we're not sure what else. He was actually found on the side of the road only a few miles from here!
Liiick
He could have eaten somebody!
It's a scary thought, but when we found him, he didn't want to come near humans at all! It would've been impossible to get him checked out by our vet without treats.
Almost any animal can be albino. Even humans!
And it can be very dangerous for an albino animal in the wild.
Streeeetch

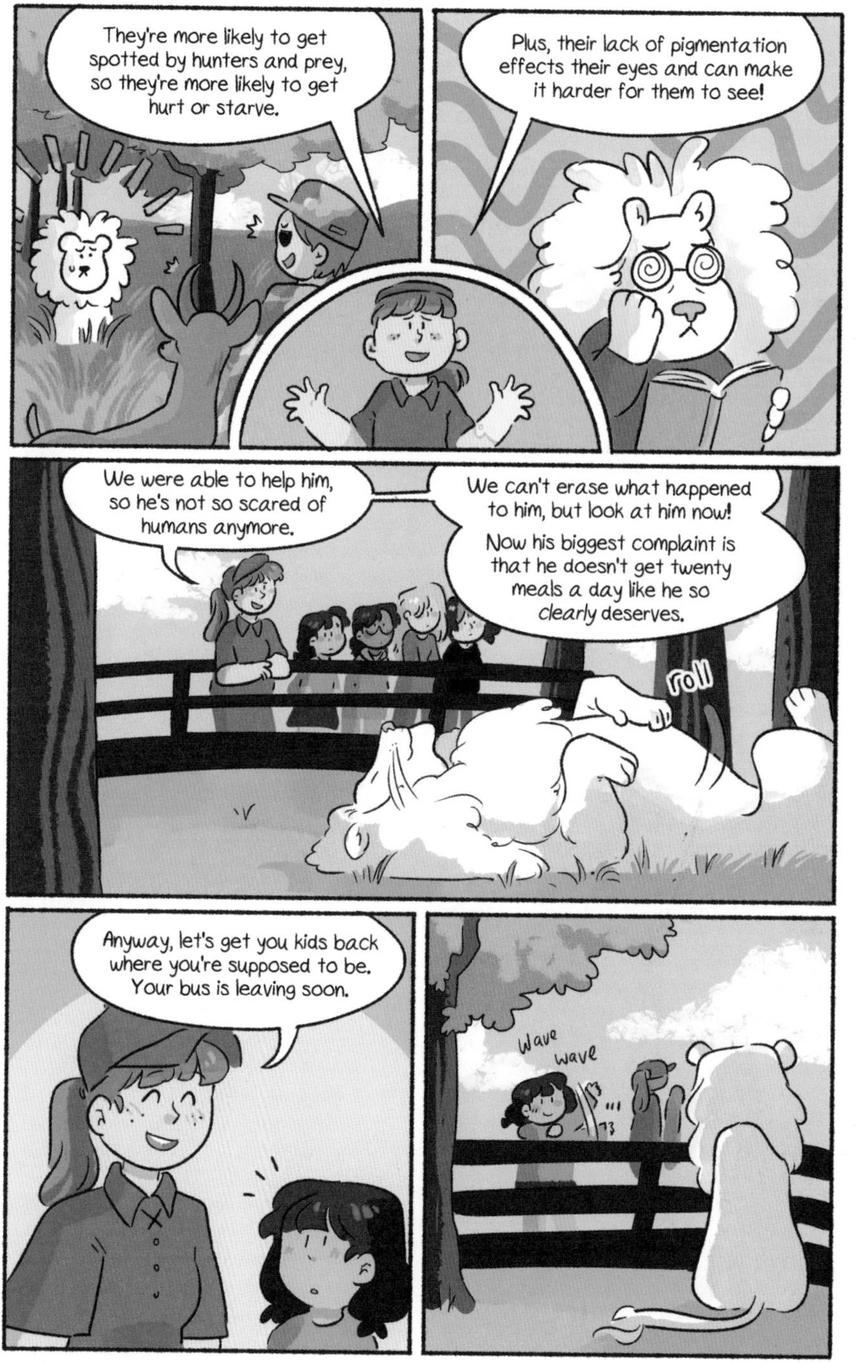
They're more likely to get spotted by hunters and prey, so they're more likely to get hurt or starve.
Plus, their lack of pigmentation effects their eyes and can make it harder for them to see!
We were able to help him, so he's not so scared of humans anymore.
We can't erase what happened to him, but look at him now!
Now his biggest complaint is that he doesn't get twenty meals a day like he so *clearly* deserves.
roll
Anyway, let's get you kids back where you're supposed to be. Your bus is leaving soon.
wave
wave

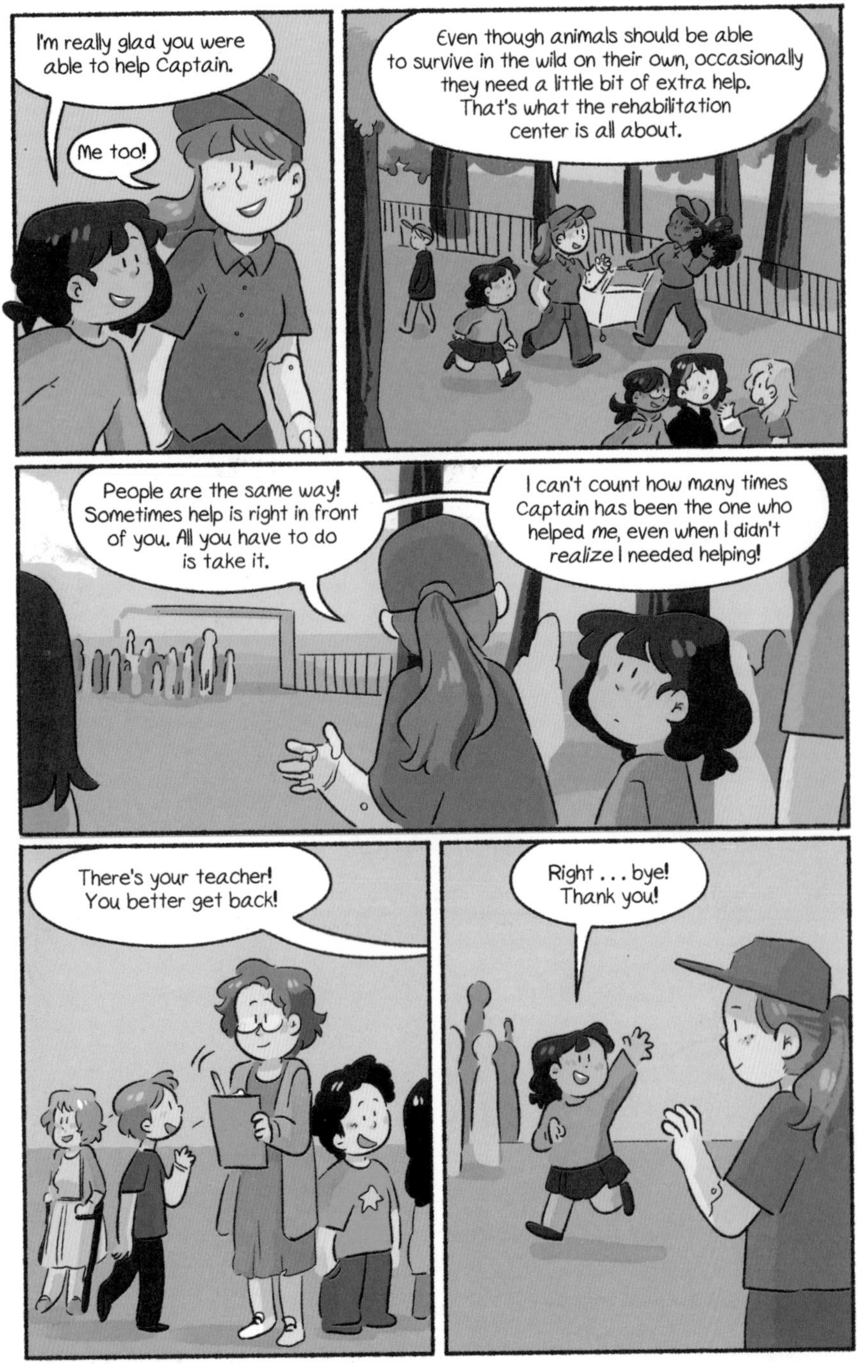
I'm really glad you were able to help Captain.
Me too!
Even though animals should be able to survive in the wild on their own, occasionally they need a little bit of extra help. That's what the rehabilitation center is all about.
People are the same way! Sometimes help is right in front of you. All you have to do is take it.
I can't count how many times Captain has been the one who helped *me*, even when I didn't *realize* I needed helping!
There's your teacher! You better get back!
Right . . . bye! Thank you!

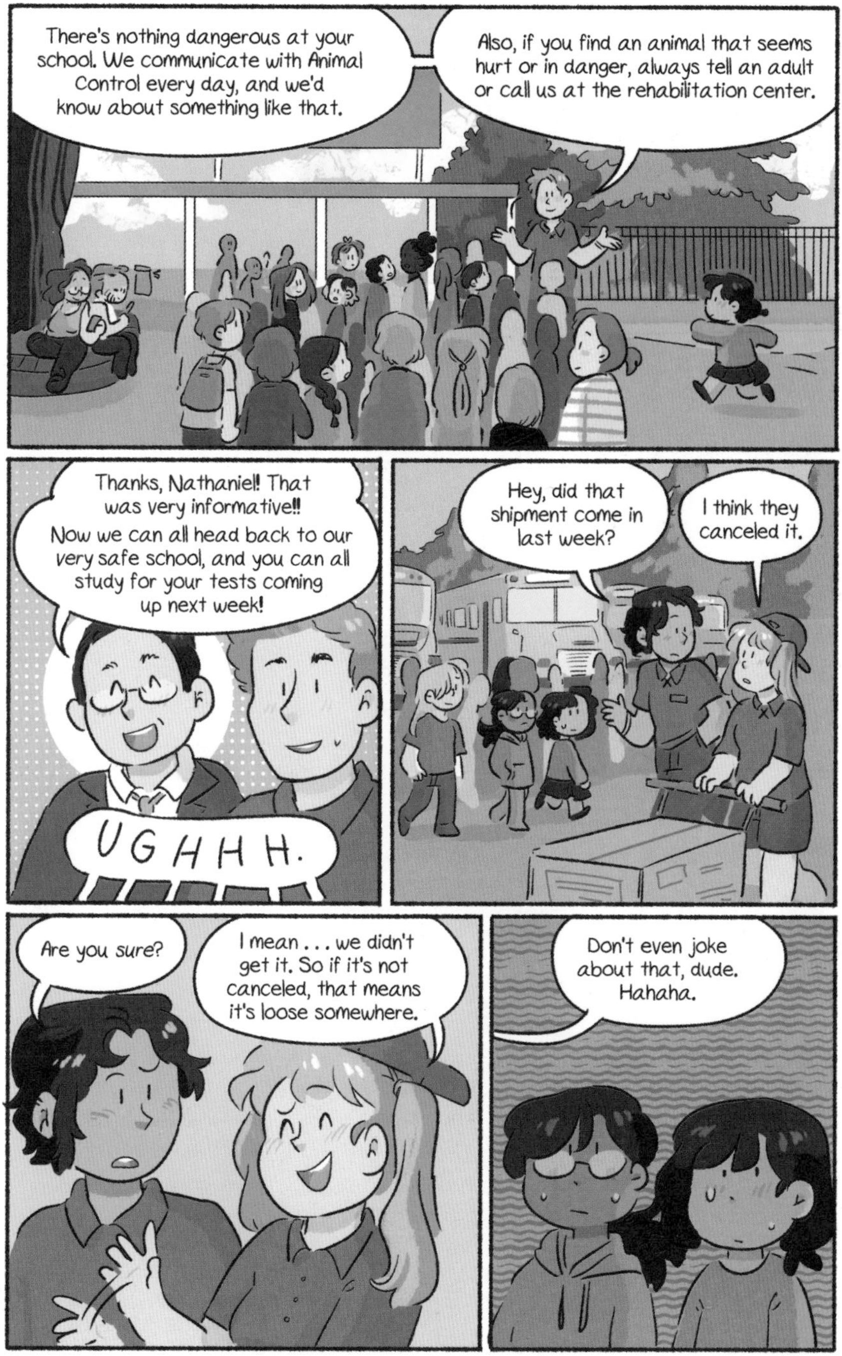
There's nothing dangerous at your school. We communicate with Animal Control every day, and we'd know about something like that.
Also, if you find an animal that seems hurt or in danger, always tell an adult or call us at the rehabilitation center.
Thanks, Nathaniel! That was very informative!! Now we can all head back to our very safe school, and you can all study for your tests coming up next week!
UGHHH.
Hey, did that shipment come in last week?
I think they canceled it.
Are you sure?
I mean . . . we didn't get it. So if it's not canceled, that means it's loose somewhere.
Don't even joke about that, dude. Hahaha.

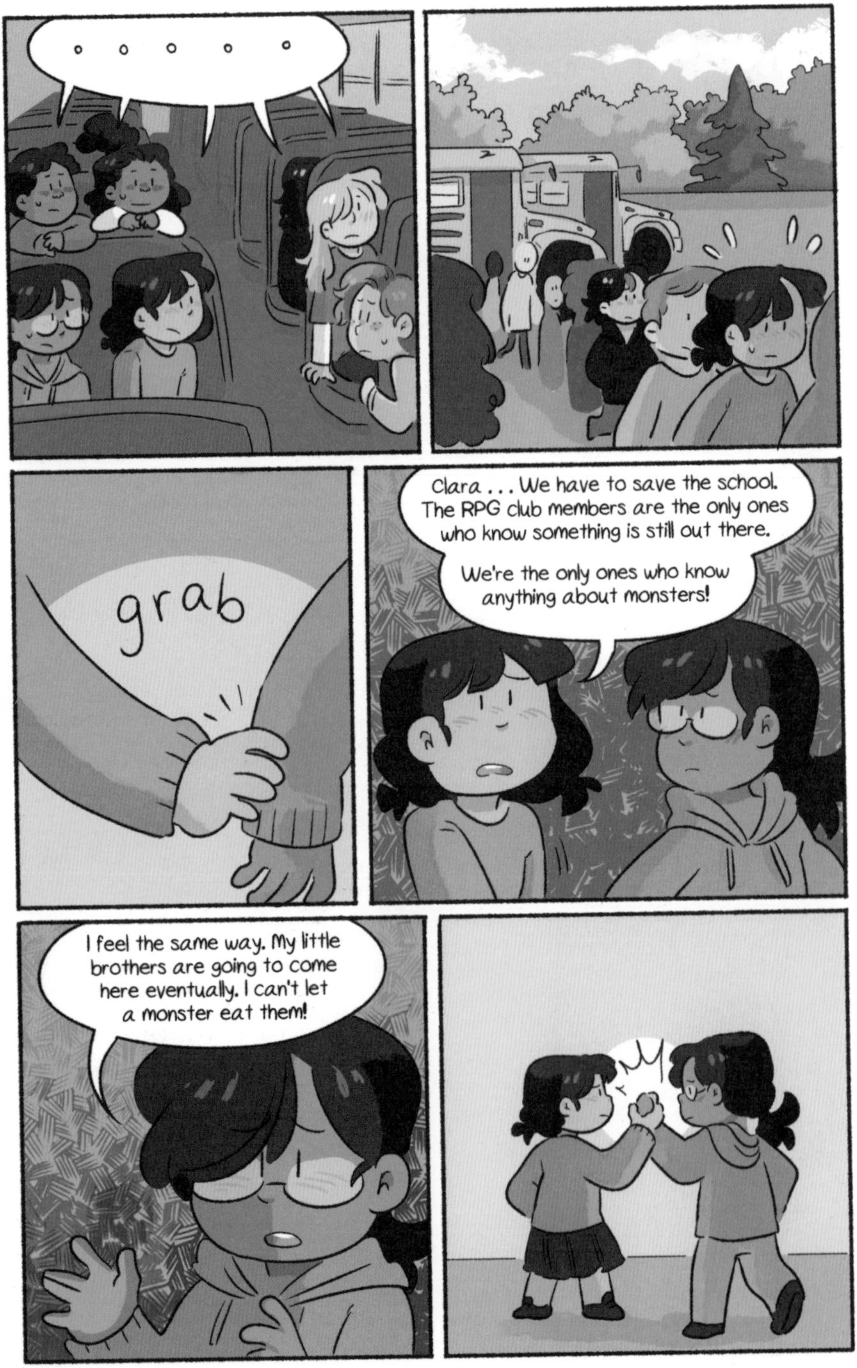

o o o o o
grab
Clara . . . We have to save the school. The RPG club members are the only ones who know something is still out there.
We're the only ones who know anything about monsters!
I feel the same way. My little brothers are going to come here eventually. I can't let a monster eat them!

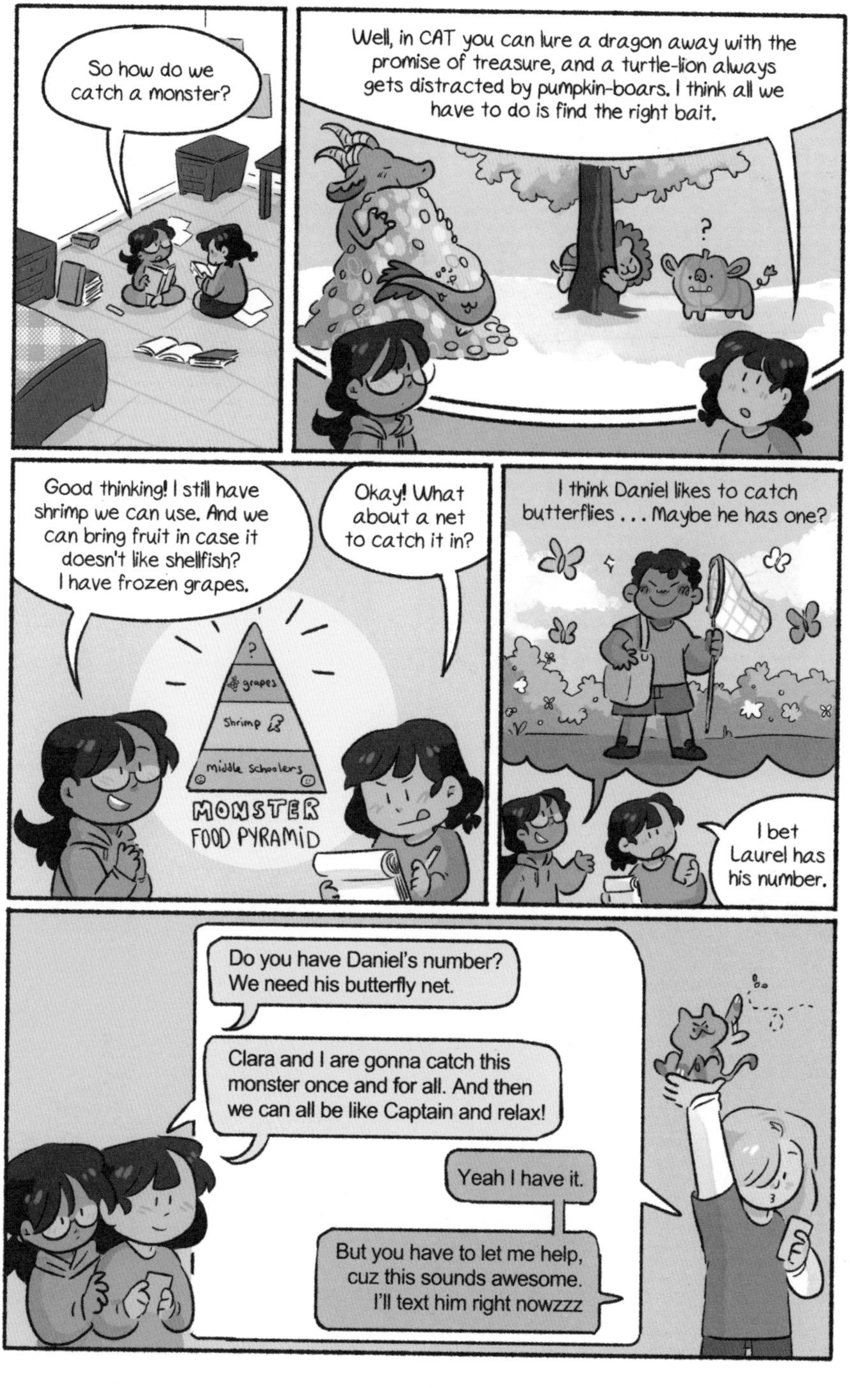
So how do we catch a monster?
Well, in CAT you can lure a dragon away with the promise of treasure, and a turtle-lion always gets distracted by pumpkin-boars. I think all we have to do is find the right bait.
?
Good thinking! I still have shrimp we can use. And we can bring fruit in case it doesn't like shellfish? I have frozen grapes.
Okay! What about a net to catch it in?
?
grapes
shrimp
middle schoolers
MONSTER FOOD PYRAMID
I think Daniel likes to catch butterflies . . . Maybe he has one?
I bet Laurel has his number.
Do you have Daniel's number? We need his butterfly net.
Clara and I are gonna catch this monster once and for all. And then we can all be like Captain and relax!
Yeah I have it.
But you have to let me help, cuz this sounds awesome. I'll text him right nowzzz

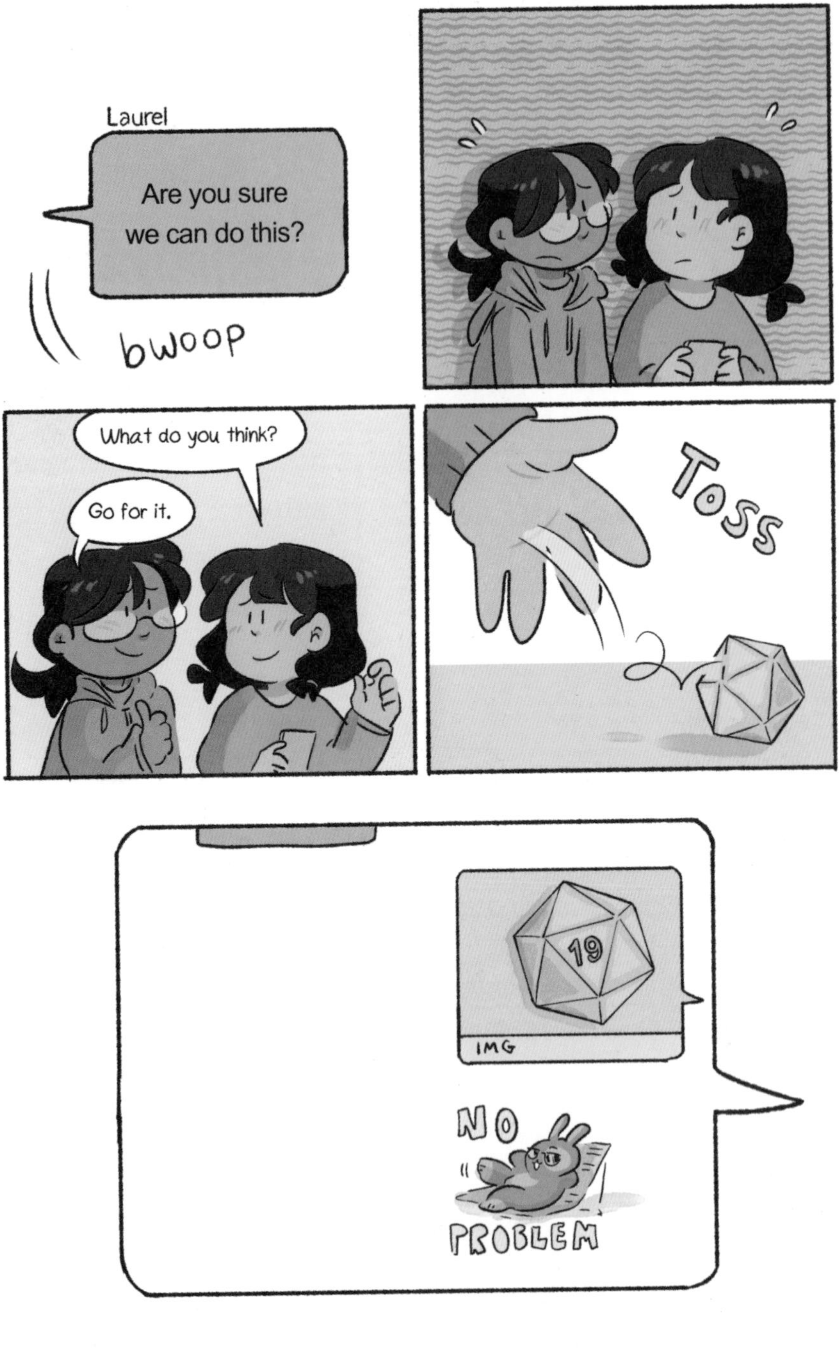
Laurel
Are you sure we can do this?
bwoop
What do you think?
Go for it.
TOSS
19
IMG
NO PROBLEM

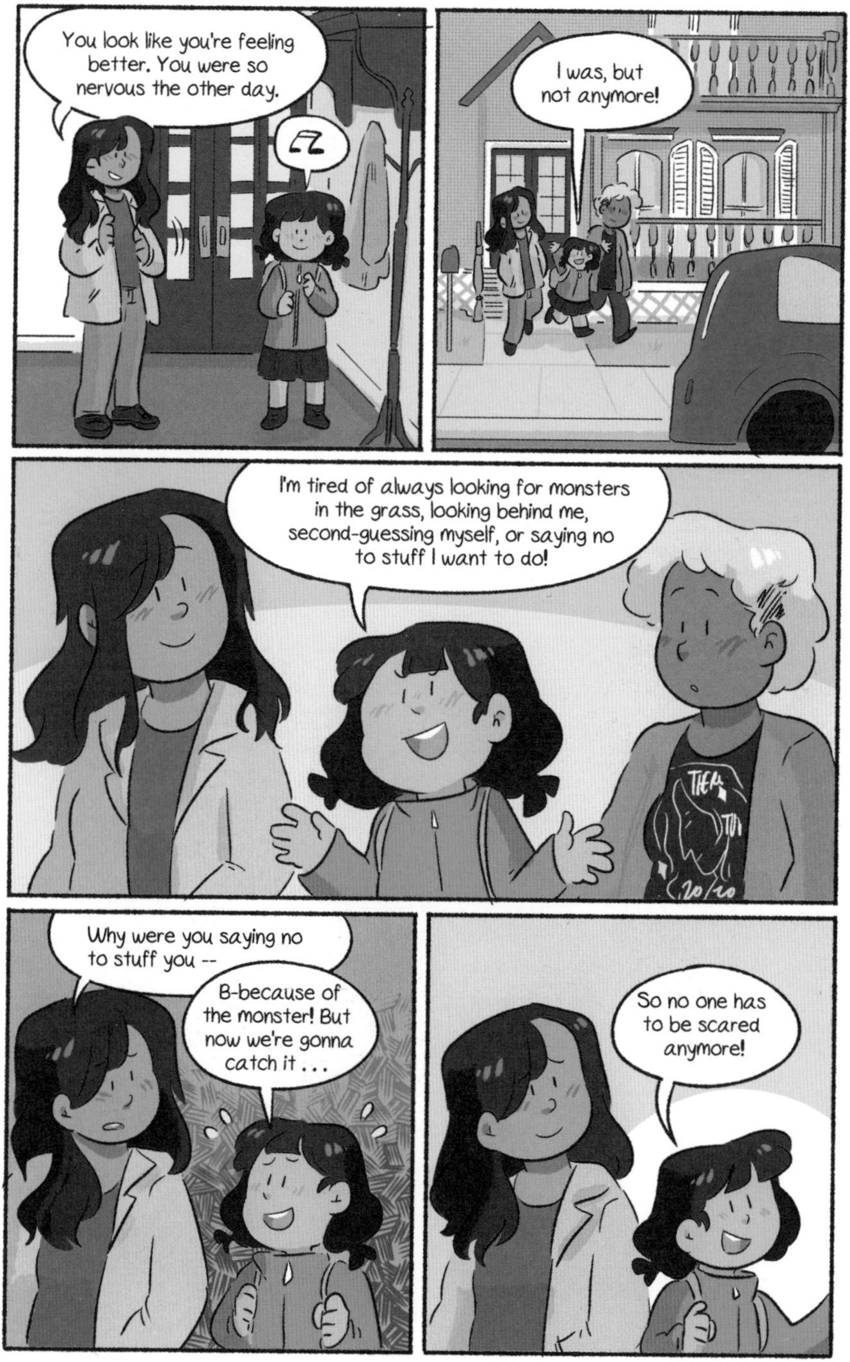
You look like you're feeling better. You were so nervous the other day.
I was, but not anymore!
I'm tired of always looking for monsters in the grass, looking behind me, second-guessing myself, or saying no to stuff I want to do!
Why were you saying no to stuff you --
B-because of the monster! But now we're gonna catch it . . .
So no one has to be scared anymore!

I can't wait until the day is over!

It better go by fast. I forgot an ice pack, and I have a lot of shrimp in my bag.

SNRK——!

$$\frac{4}{4} \times \frac{1}{2} = \frac{\square}{\square}\ ?$$

ahaha!

Shh!!

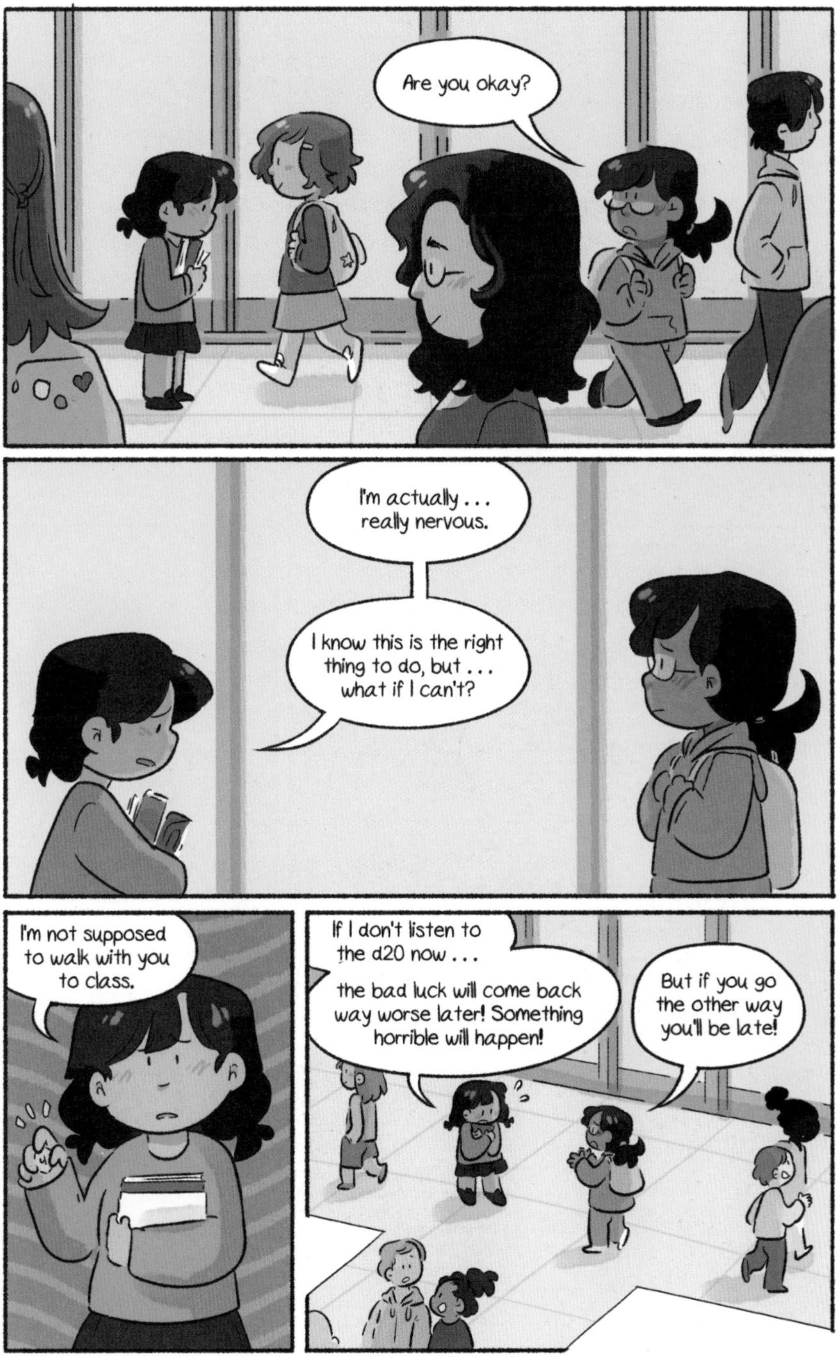
Are you okay?
I'm actually . . . really nervous.
I know this is the right thing to do, but . . . what if I can't?
I'm not supposed to walk with you to class.
If I don't listen to the d20 now . . .
the bad luck will come back way worse later! Something horrible will happen!
But if you go the other way you'll be late!

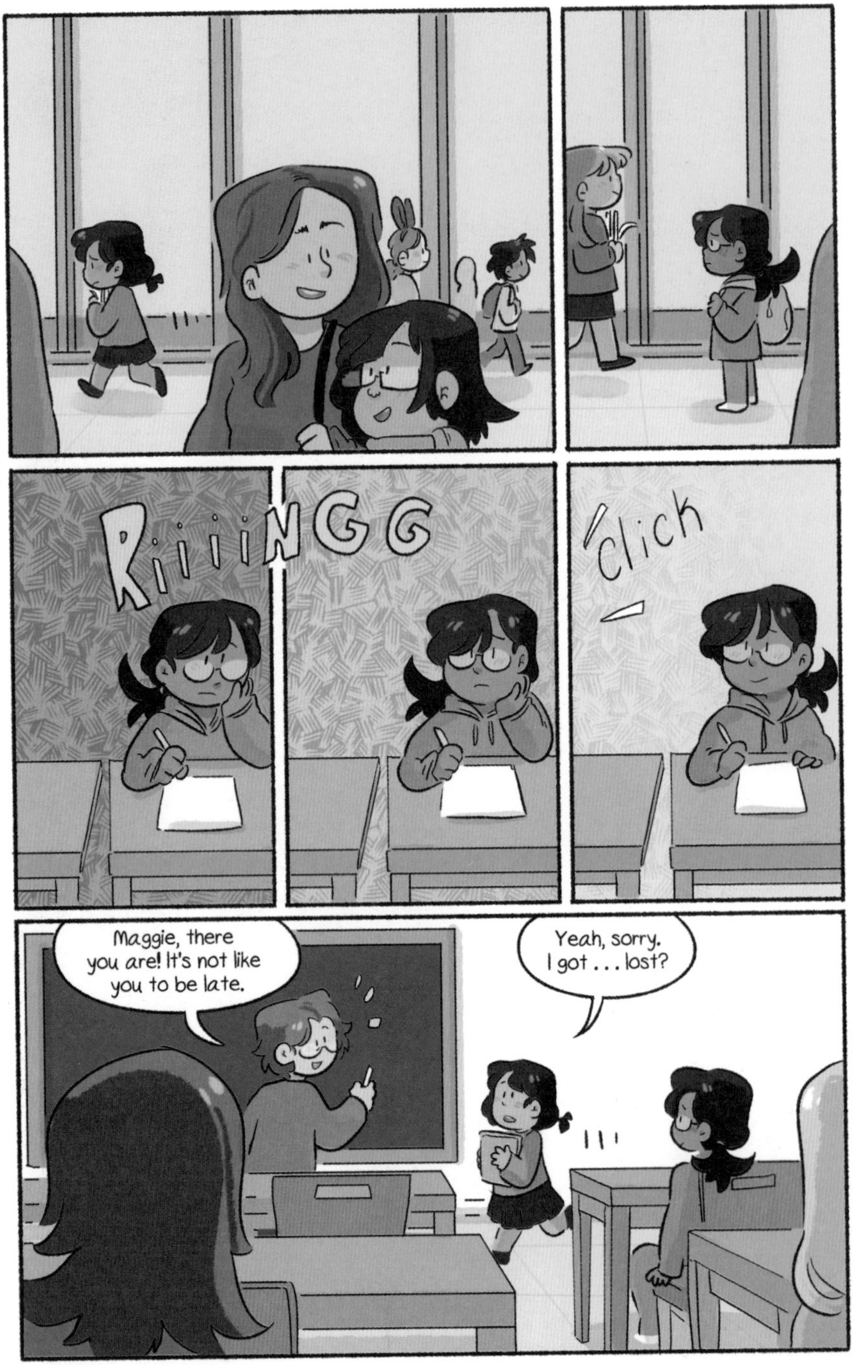
RiiiiNGG
click
Maggie, there you are! It's not like you to be late.
Yeah, sorry. I got . . . lost?

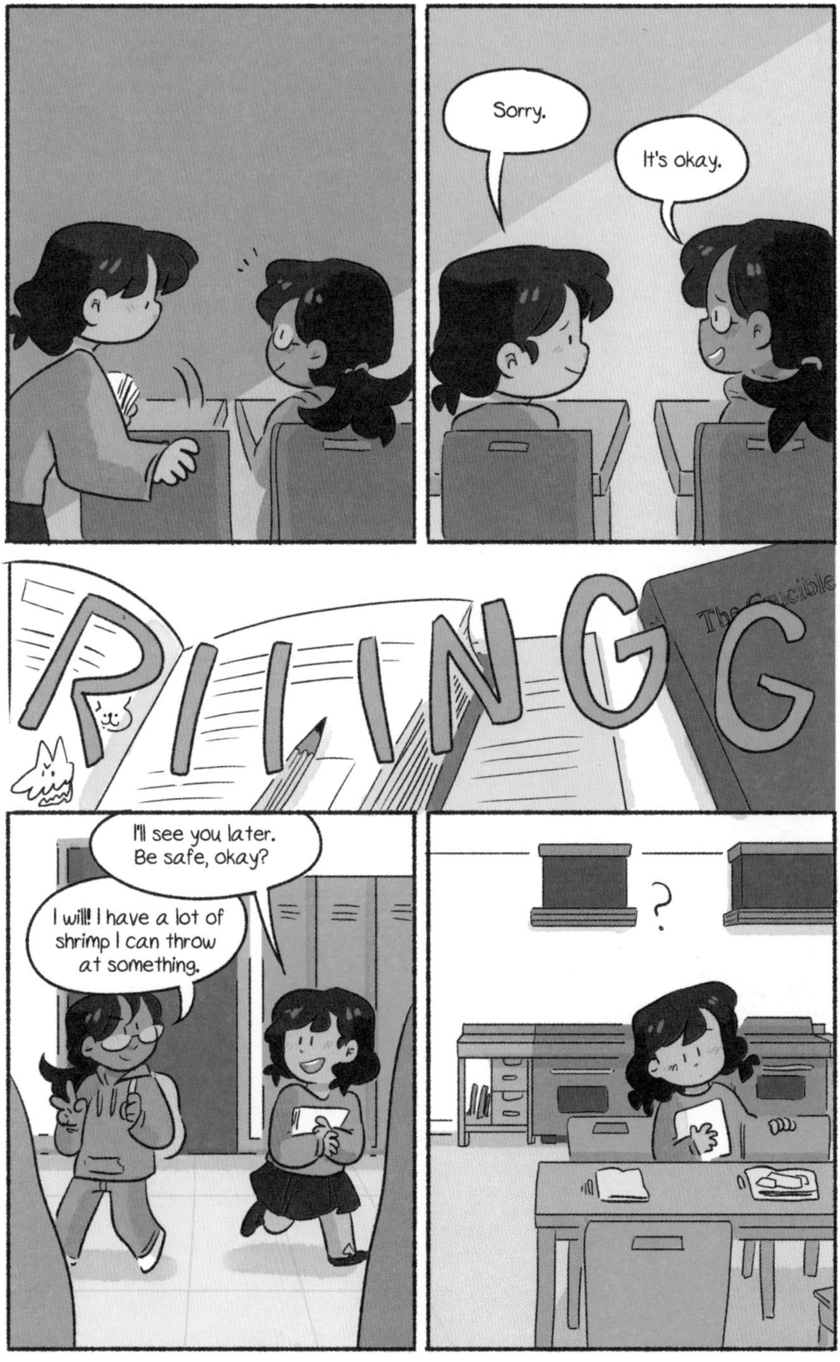
Sorry.
It's okay.
RIIING
The Crucible
I'll see you later. Be safe, okay?
I will! I have a lot of shrimp I can throw at something.
?

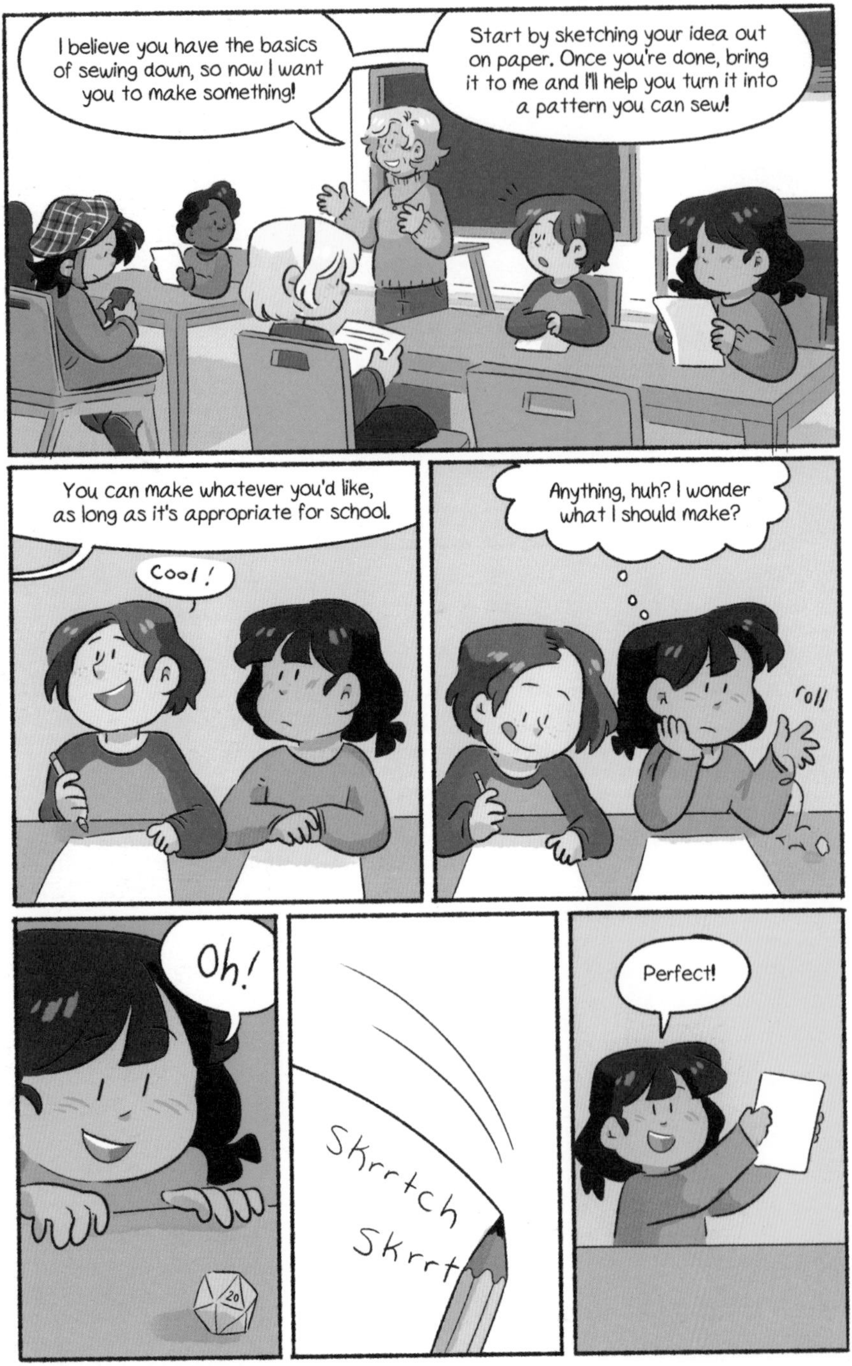
I believe you have the basics of sewing down, so now I want you to make something!
Start by sketching your idea out on paper. Once you're done, bring it to me and I'll help you turn it into a pattern you can sew!
You can make whatever you'd like, as long as it's appropriate for school.
Cool!
Anything, huh? I wonder what I should make?
roll
Oh!
20
Skrrtch
Skrrt
Perfect!

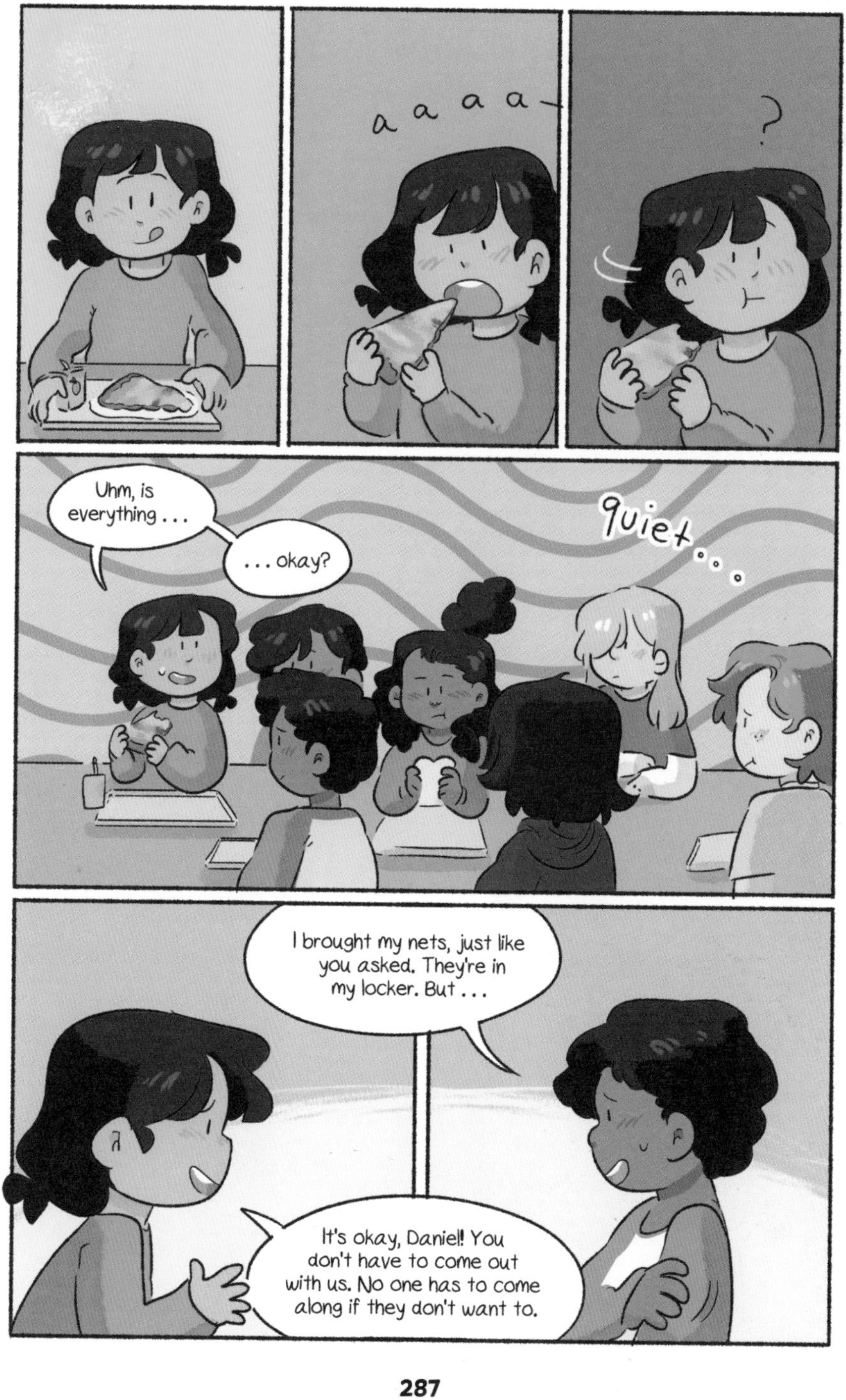
a a a a-
?
Uhm, is everything . . .
. . . okay?
quiet . . .
I brought my nets, just like you asked. They're in my locker. But . . .
It's okay, Daniel! You don't have to come out with us. No one has to come along if they don't want to.

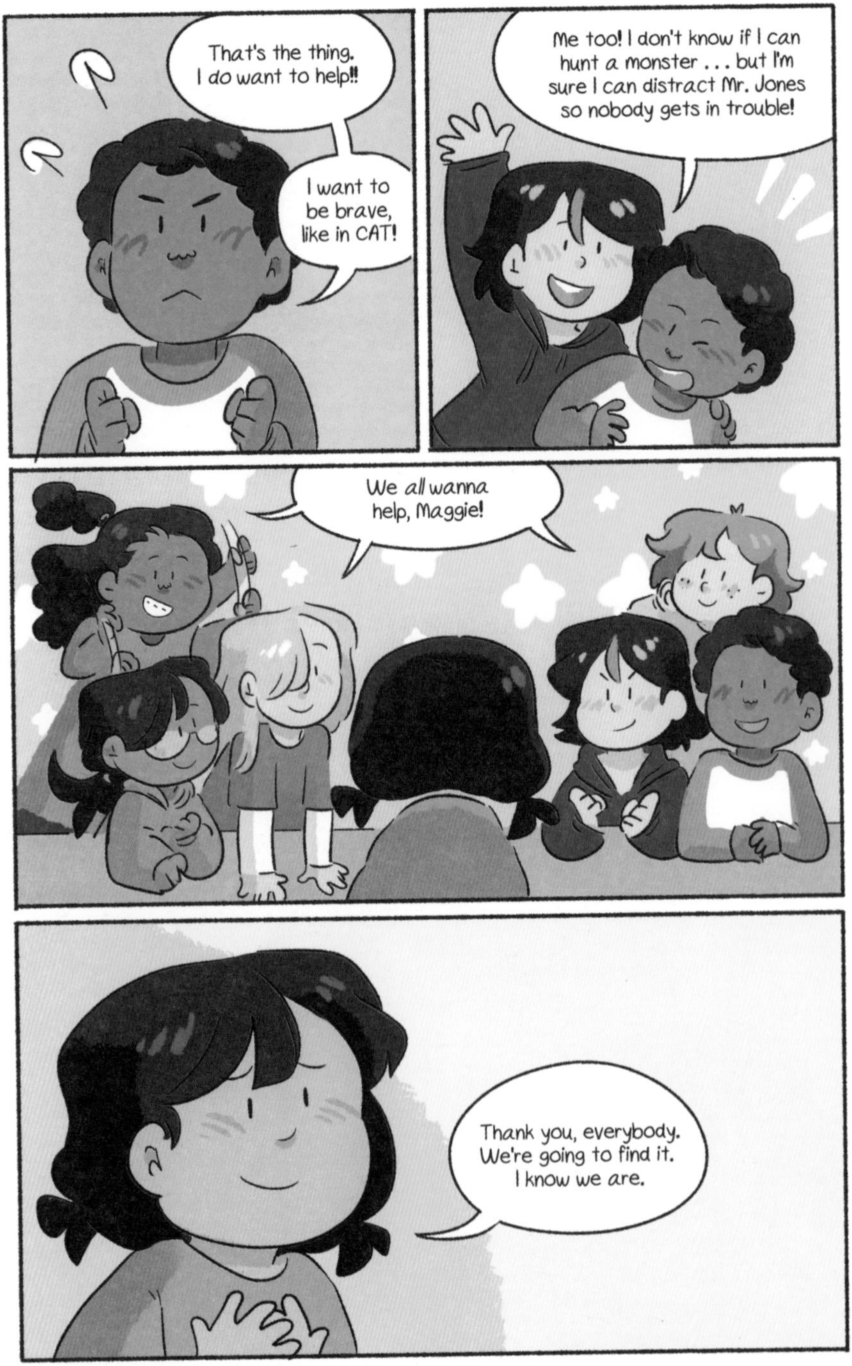
That's the thing. I *do* want to help!!
I want to be brave, like in CAT!
Me too! I don't know if I can hunt a monster . . . but I'm sure I can distract Mr. Jones so nobody gets in trouble!
We *all* wanna help, Maggie!
Thank you, everybody. We're going to find it. I know we are.

I'm going to avenge you, Mr. Anry. You *and* your fish.

Kids, settle down! No monster shenanigans in my gym class!

RAAAAAA

hahaha!

GUMBALL SEARCH

Q How to trap a wild animal safely

SEARCH   HELP

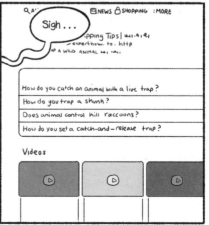

Q A⁰   📰 NEWS 🛒 SHOPPING ⋮ MORE

Sigh . . .

...pping Tips | ...
—experthow. to. http
AP A WILD ANIMAL ...

How do you catch an animal with a live trap?

How do you trap a skunk?

Does animal control kill raccoons?

How do you set a catch-and-release trap?

Videos

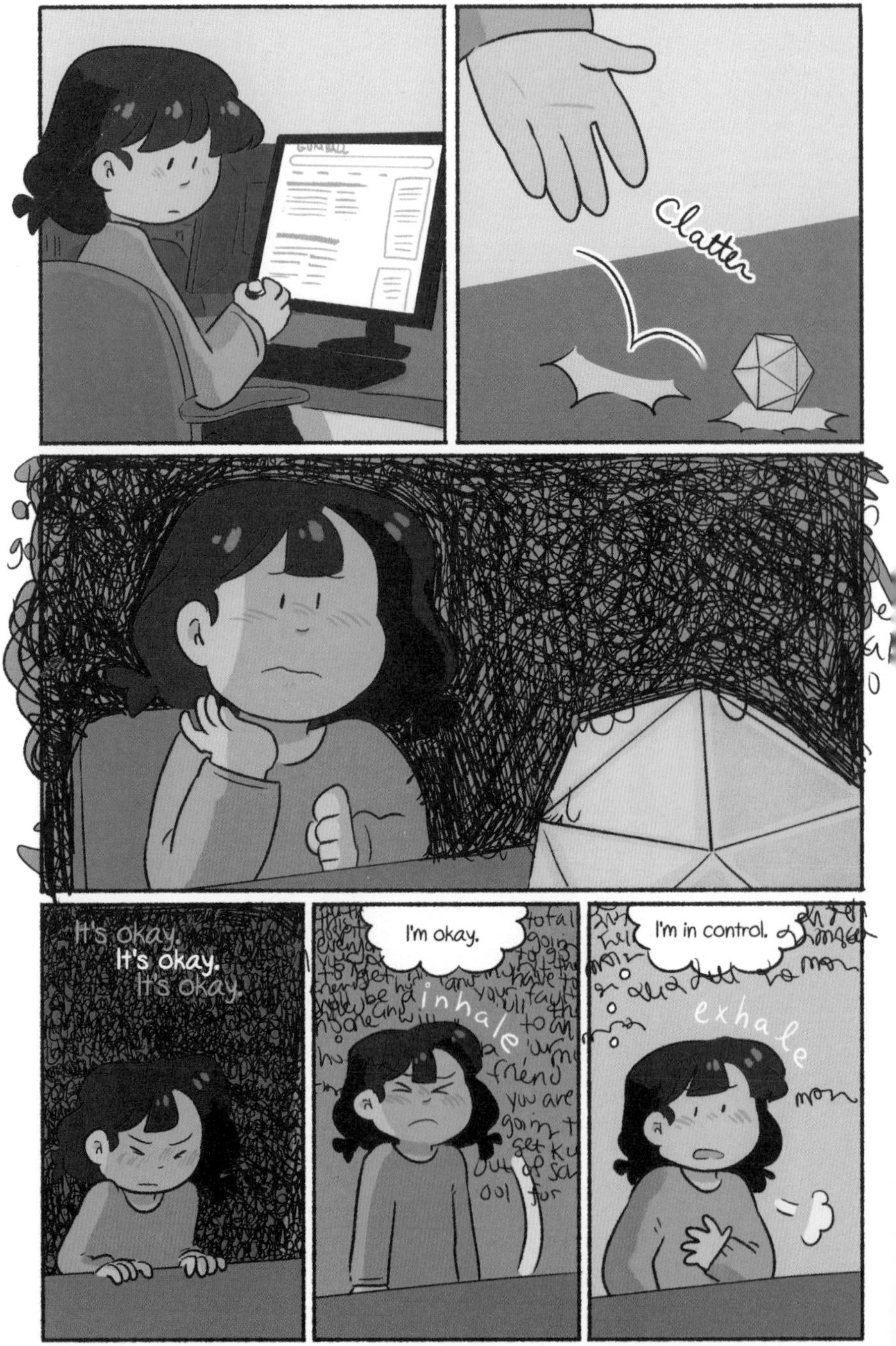
Clatter
It's okay.
It's okay.
It's okay.
I'm okay.
inhale
I'm in control.
exhale

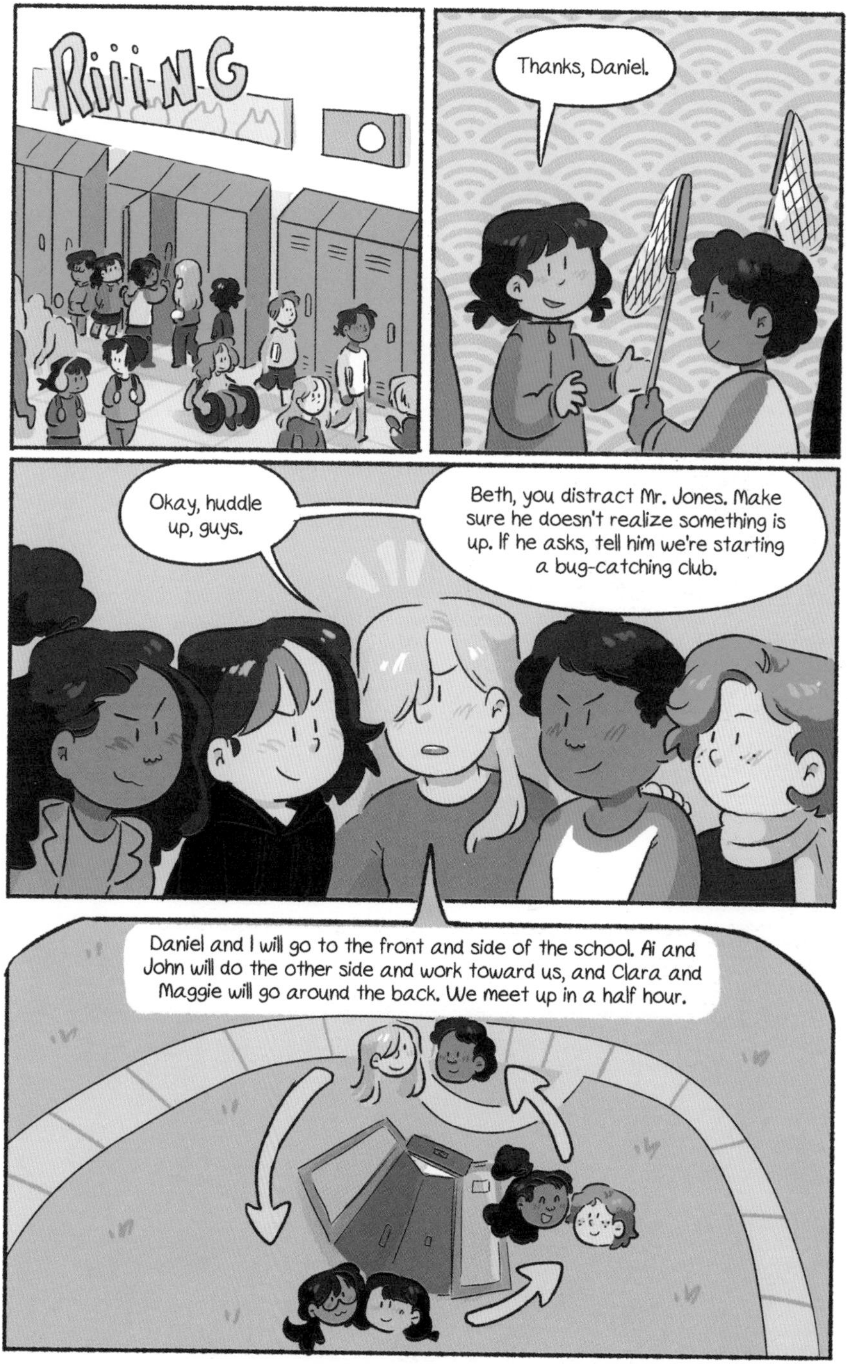
RIIING
Thanks, Daniel.
Okay, huddle up, guys.
Beth, you distract Mr. Jones. Make sure he doesn't realize something is up. If he asks, tell him we're starting a bug-catching club.
Daniel and I will go to the front and side of the school. Ai and John will do the other side and work toward us, and Clara and Maggie will go around the back. We meet up in a half hour.

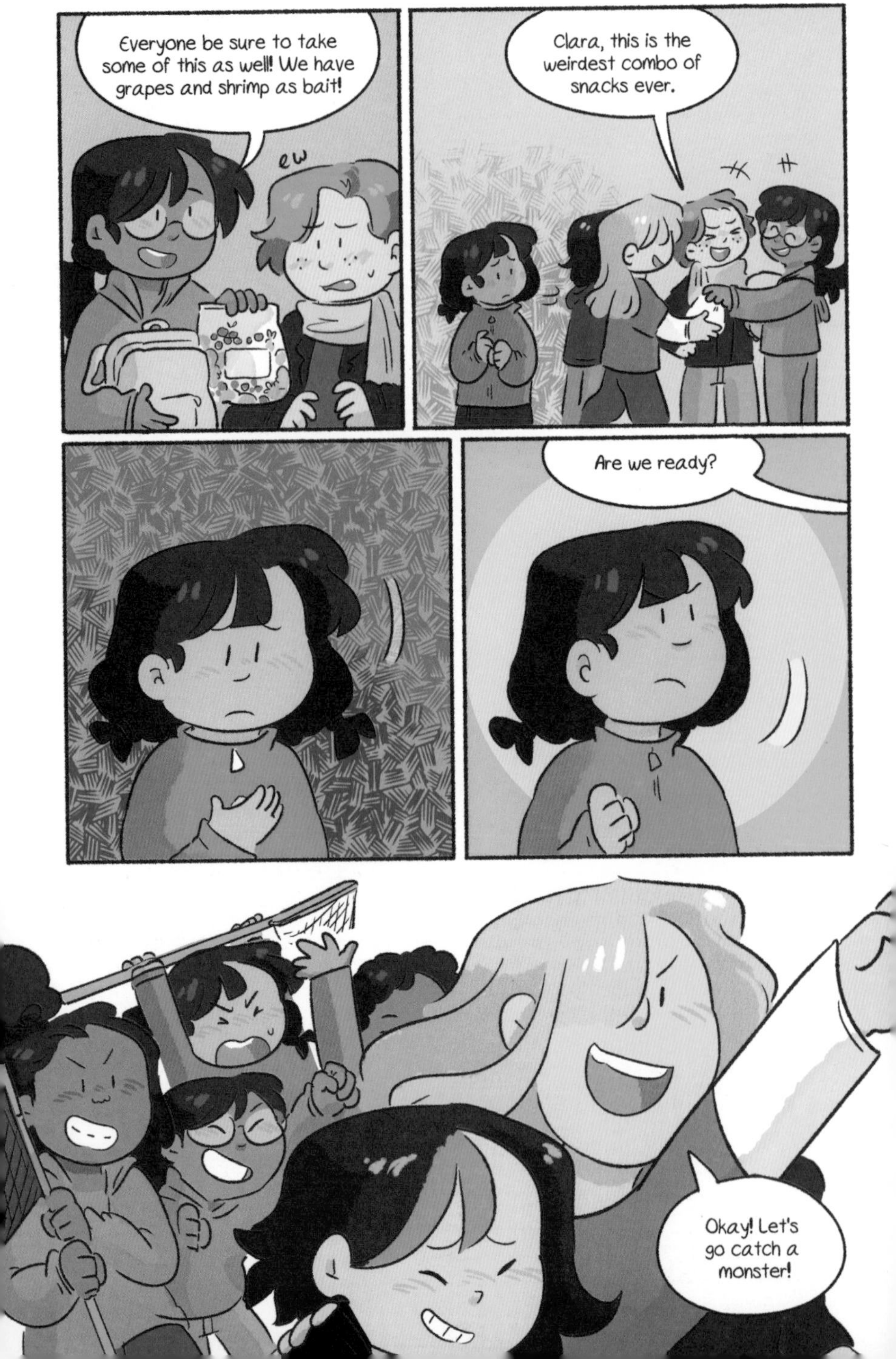
Everyone be sure to take some of this as well! We have grapes and shrimp as bait!
ew
Clara, this is the weirdest combo of snacks ever.
Are we ready?
Okay! Let's go catch a monster!

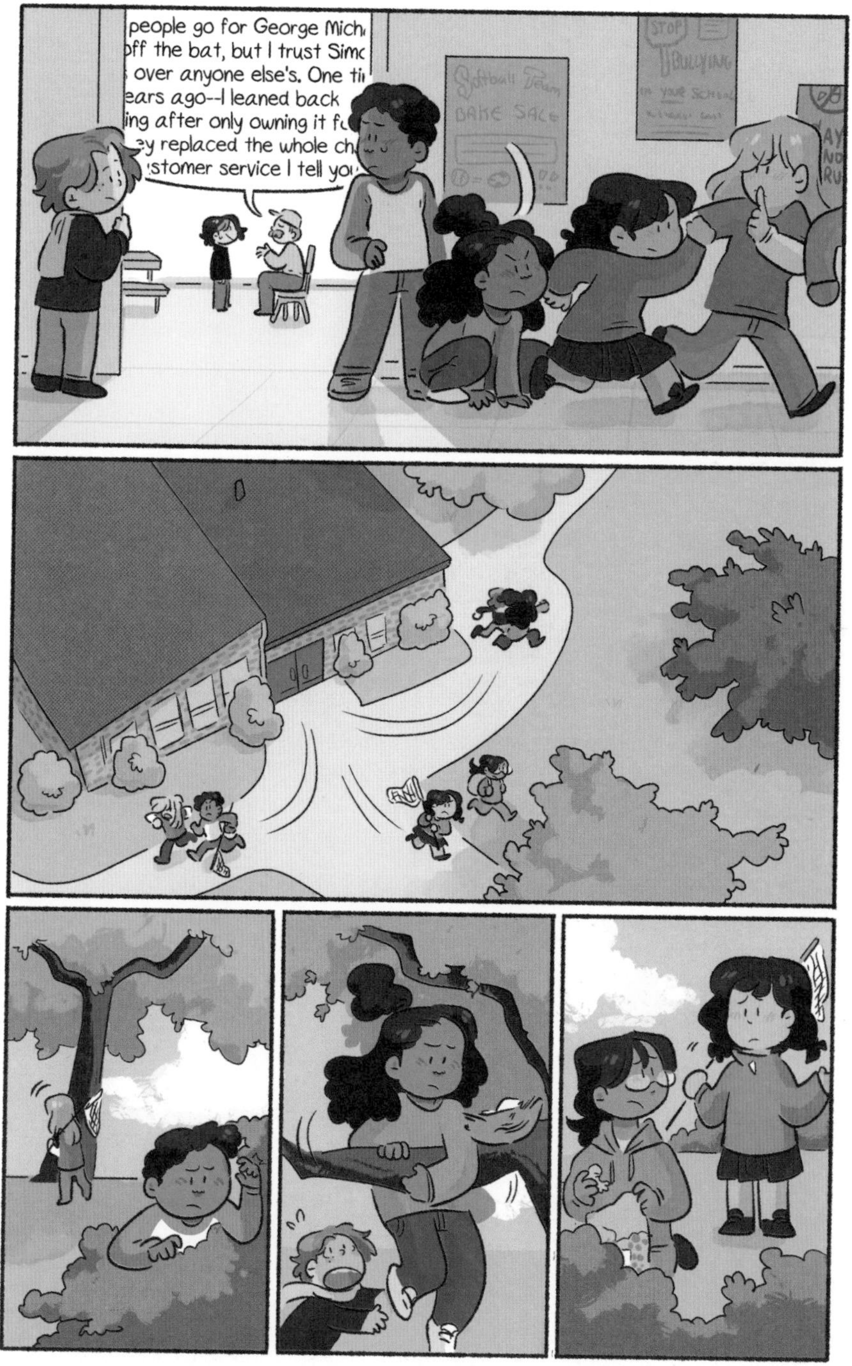
people go for George Mich
ff the bat, but I trust Sim
over anyone else's. One ti
ears ago--I leaned back
ing after only owning it f
ey replaced the whole ch
stomer service I tell you
Softball Team BAKE SALE
STOP BULLYING in your SCHOOL

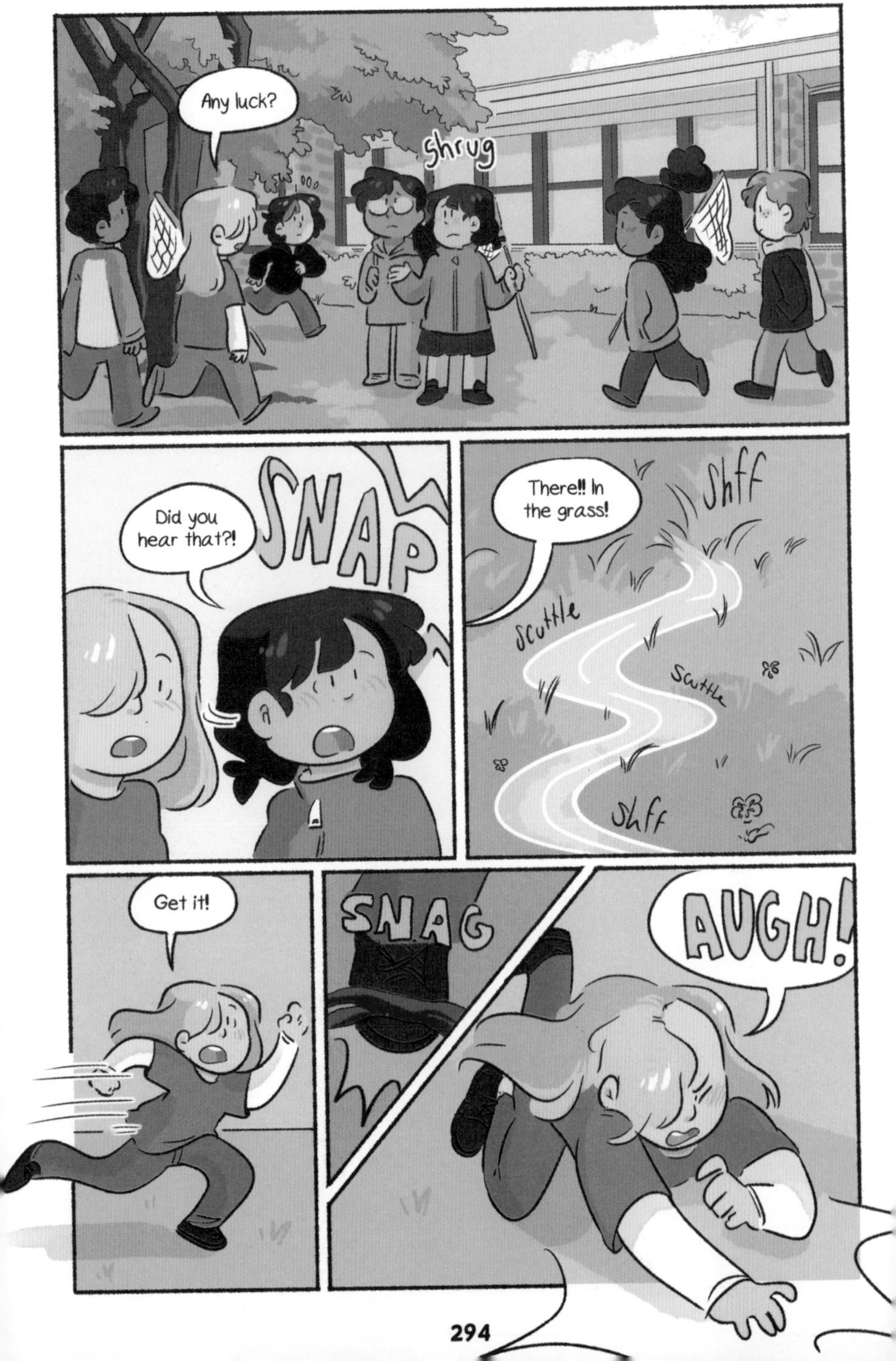
Any luck?
shrug
Did you hear that?!
SNAP
There!! In the grass!
shff
scuttle
scuttle
shff
Get it!
SNAG
AUGH!

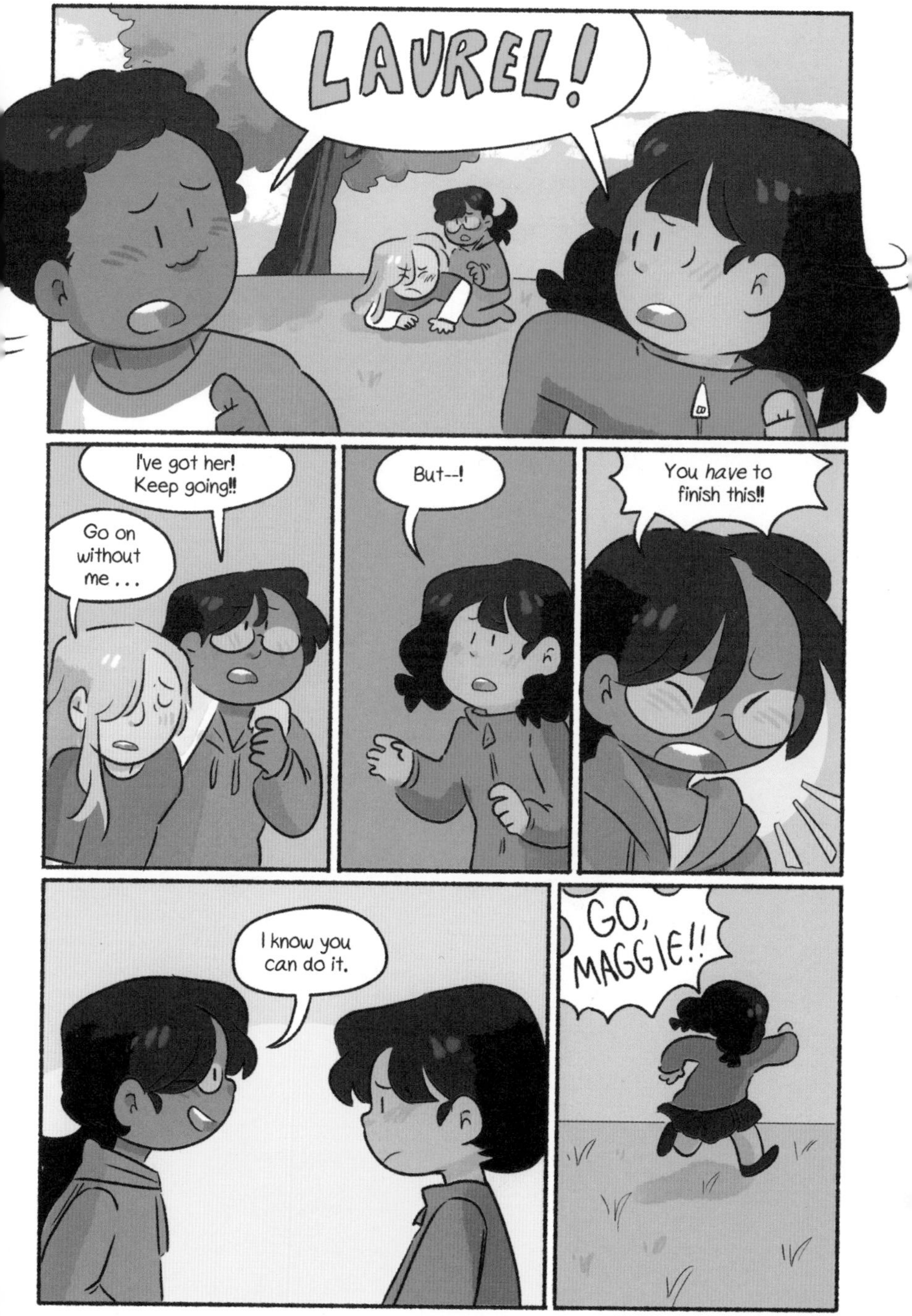
LAUREL!
I've got her! Keep going!!
Go on without me . . .
But--!
You *have* to finish this!!
I know you can do it.
GO, MAGGIE!!

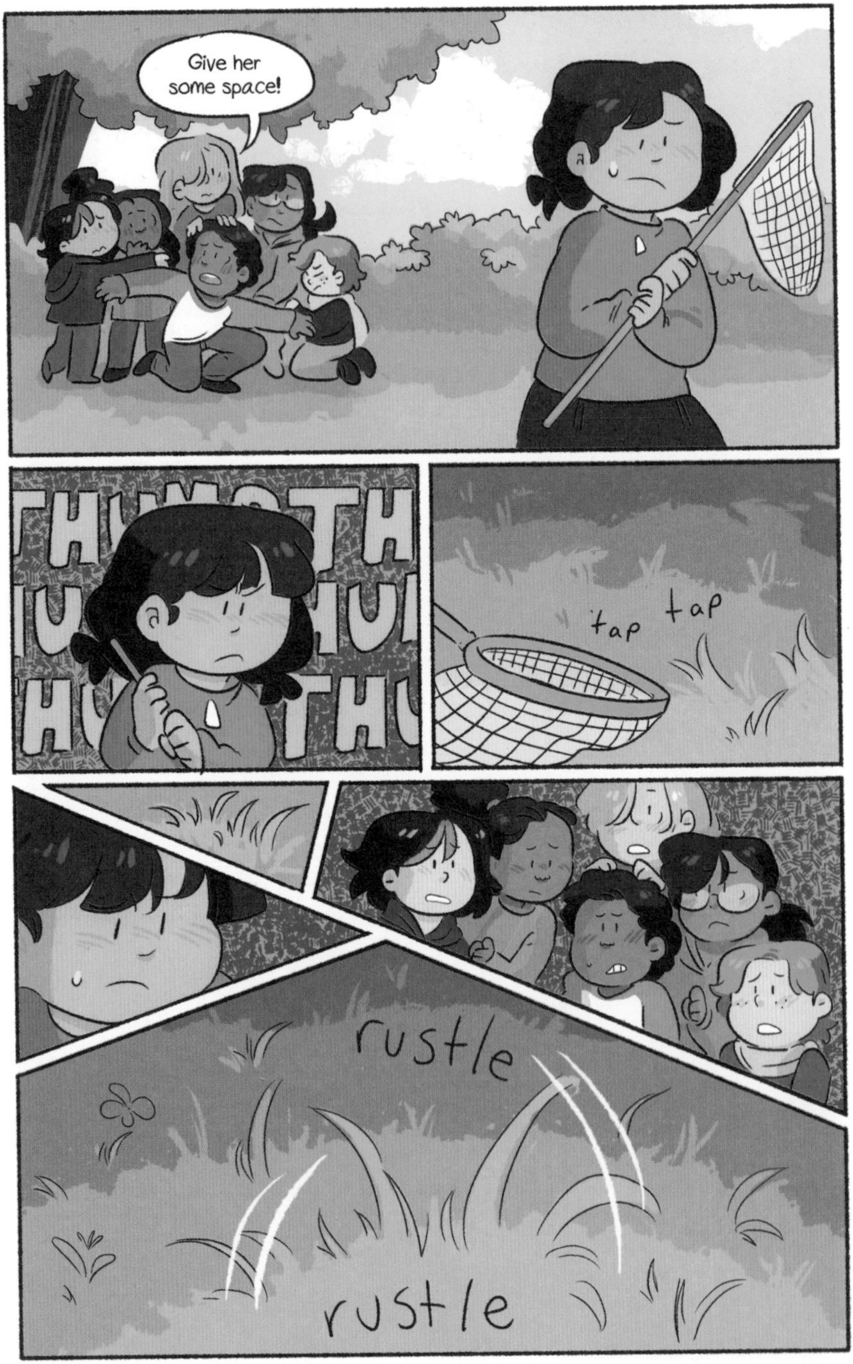
Give her some space!
THUMP THUMP THUMP
tap tap
rustle
rustle

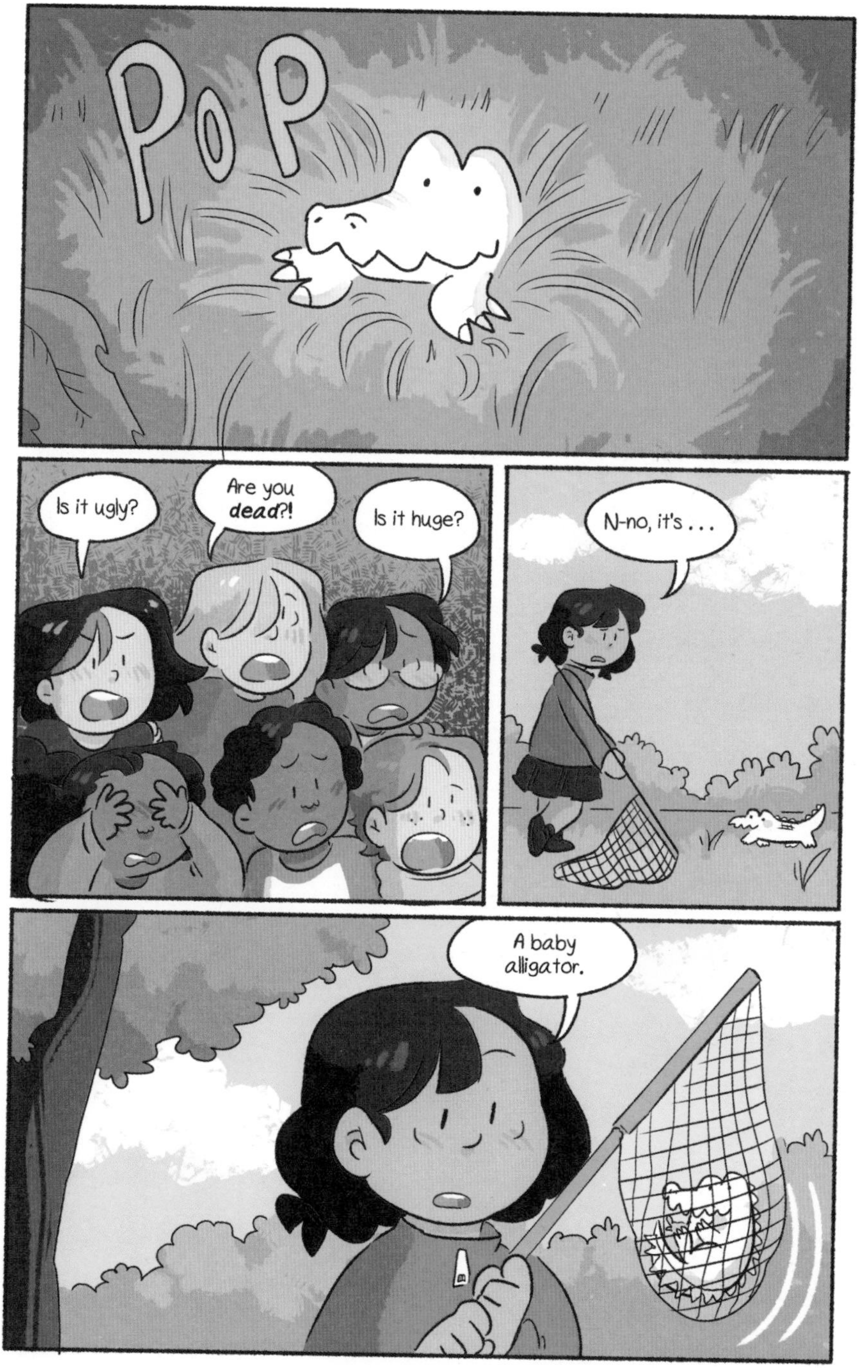
POP
Is it ugly?
Are you dead?!
Is it huge?
N-no, it's . . .
A baby alligator.

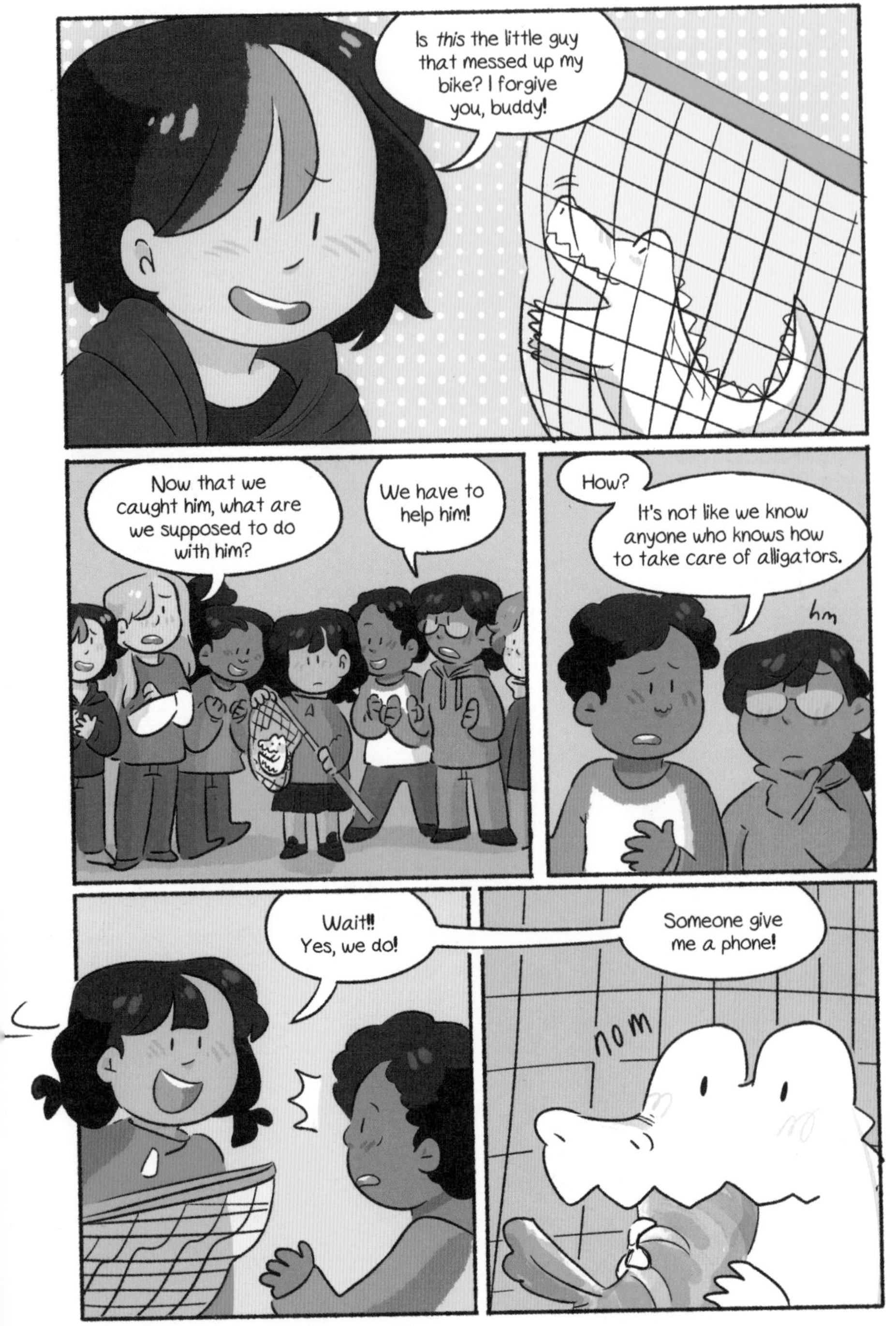
Is *this* the little guy that messed up my bike? I forgive you, buddy!
Now that we caught him, what are we supposed to do with him?
We have to help him!
How?
It's not like we know anyone who knows how to take care of alligators.
hm
Wait!! Yes, we do!
Someone give me a phone!
nom

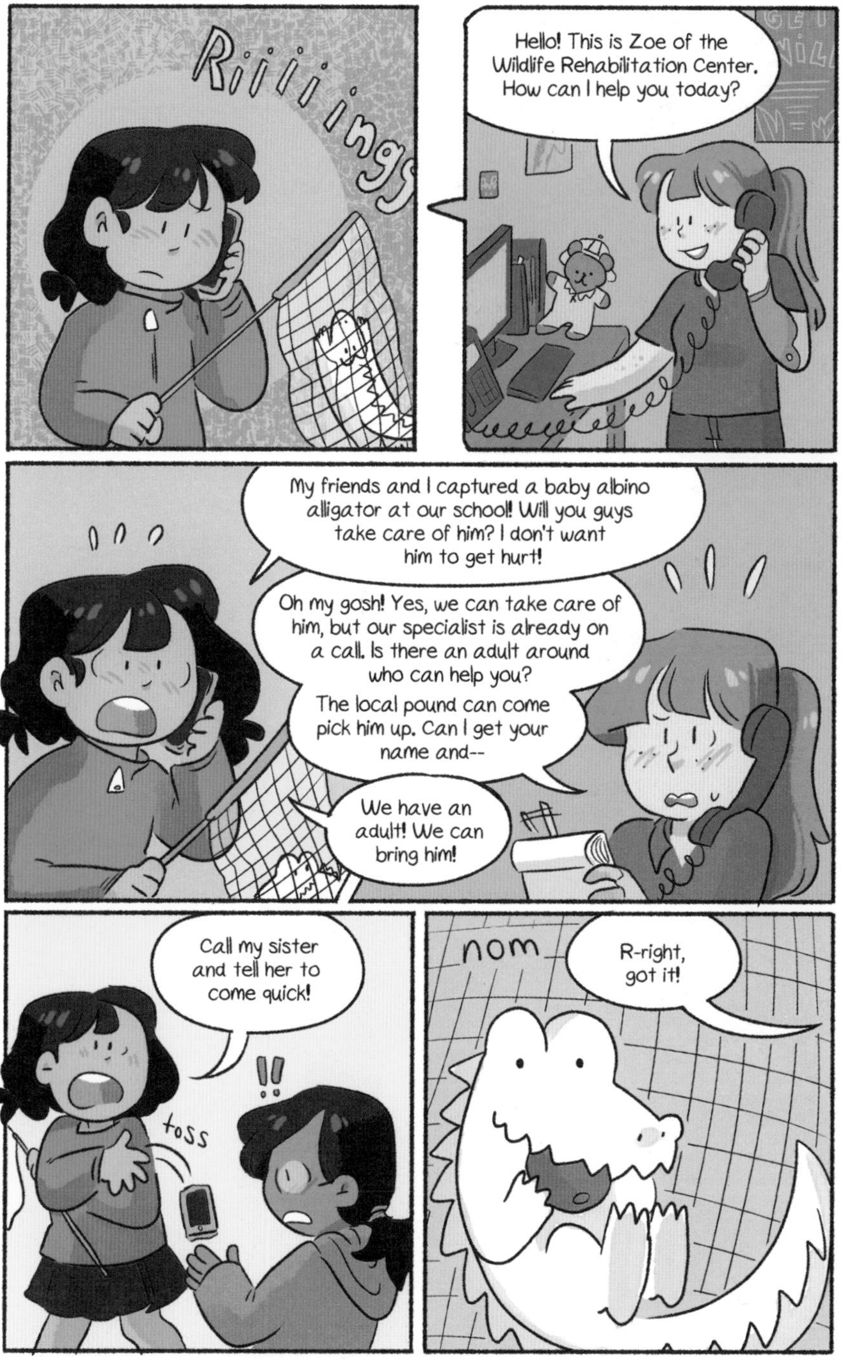
Riiiings
Hello! This is Zoe of the Wildlife Rehabilitation Center. How can I help you today?
My friends and I captured a baby albino alligator at our school! Will you guys take care of him? I don't want him to get hurt!
Oh my gosh! Yes, we can take care of him, but our specialist is already on a call. Is there an adult around who can help you?
The local pound can come pick him up. Can I get your name and--
We have an adult! We can bring him!
Call my sister and tell her to come quick!
toss
!!
nom
R-right, got it!

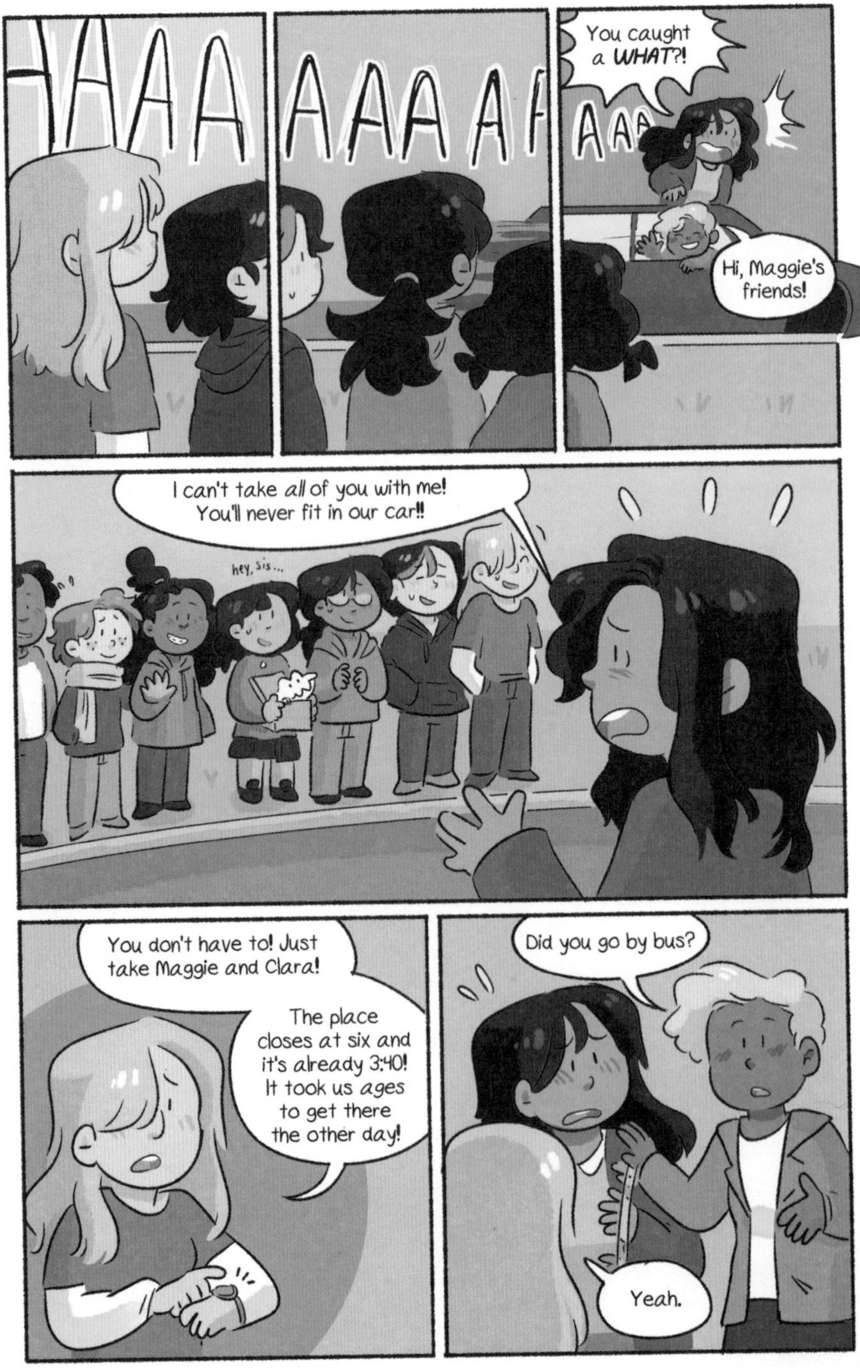
AAAA
AAAAA
You caught a WHAT?!
AAA
Hi, Maggie's friends!
I can't take all of you with me! You'll never fit in our car!!
hey, sis...
You don't have to! Just take Maggie and Clara!
The place closes at six and it's already 3:40! It took us ages to get there the other day!
Did you go by bus?
Yeah.

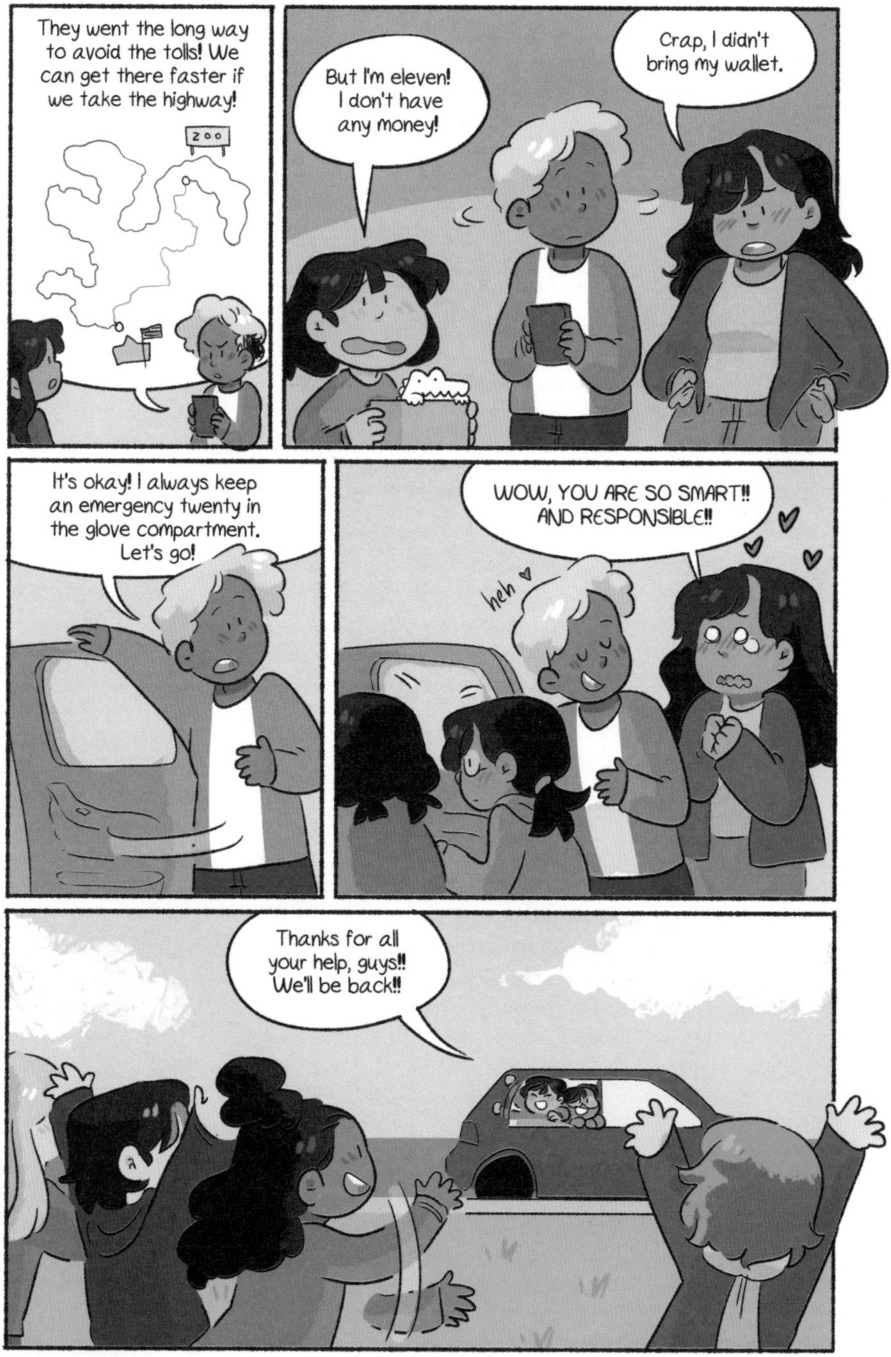
They went the long way to avoid the tolls! We can get there faster if we take the highway!
ZOO
But I'm eleven! I don't have any money!
Crap, I didn't bring my wallet.
It's okay! I always keep an emergency twenty in the glove compartment. Let's go!
WOW, YOU ARE SO SMART!! AND RESPONSIBLE!!
heh
Thanks for all your help, guys!! We'll be back!!

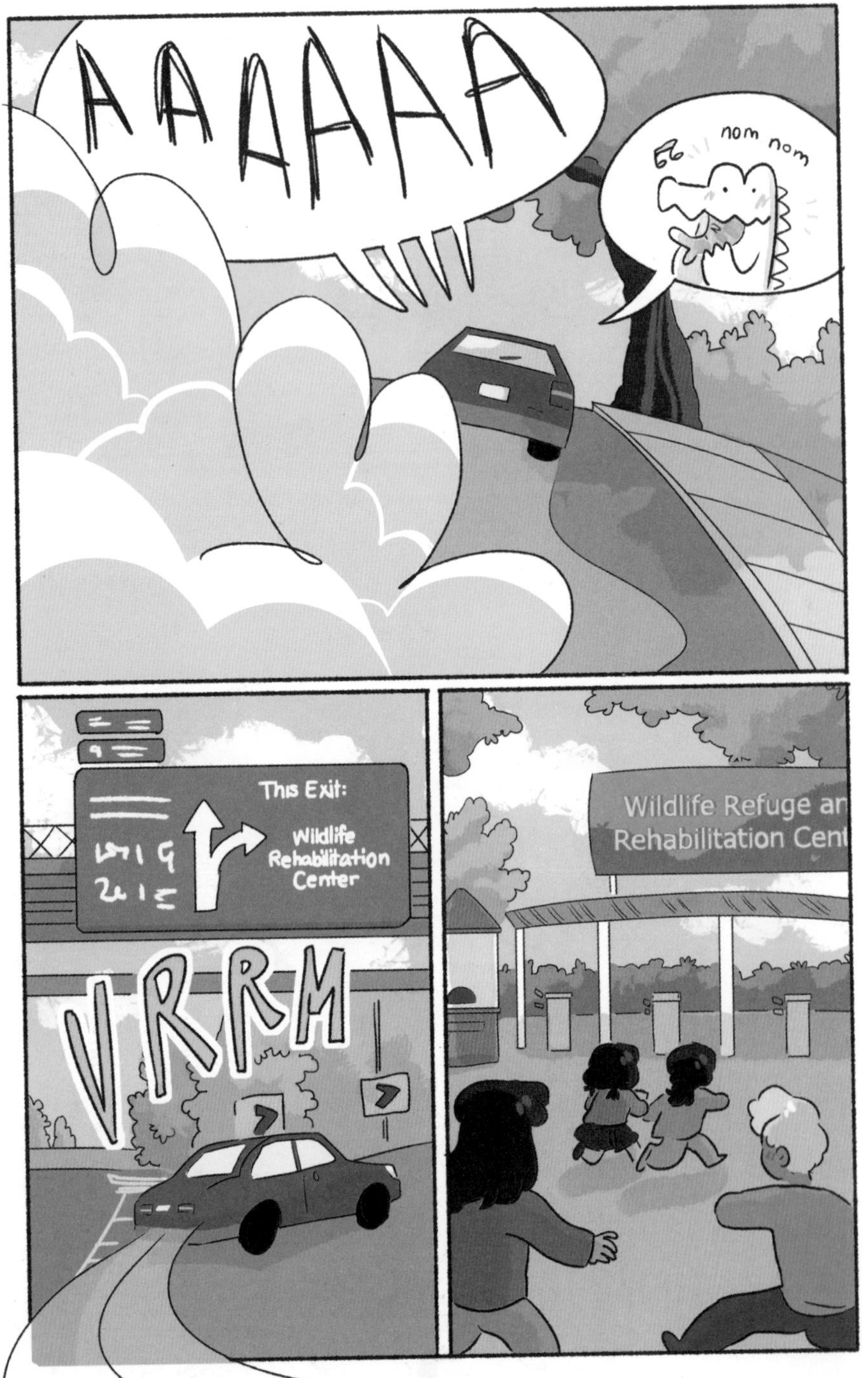
AAAAAA
nom nom
This Exit:
Wildlife Rehabilitation Center
VRRM
Wildlife Refuge an
Rehabilitation Cent

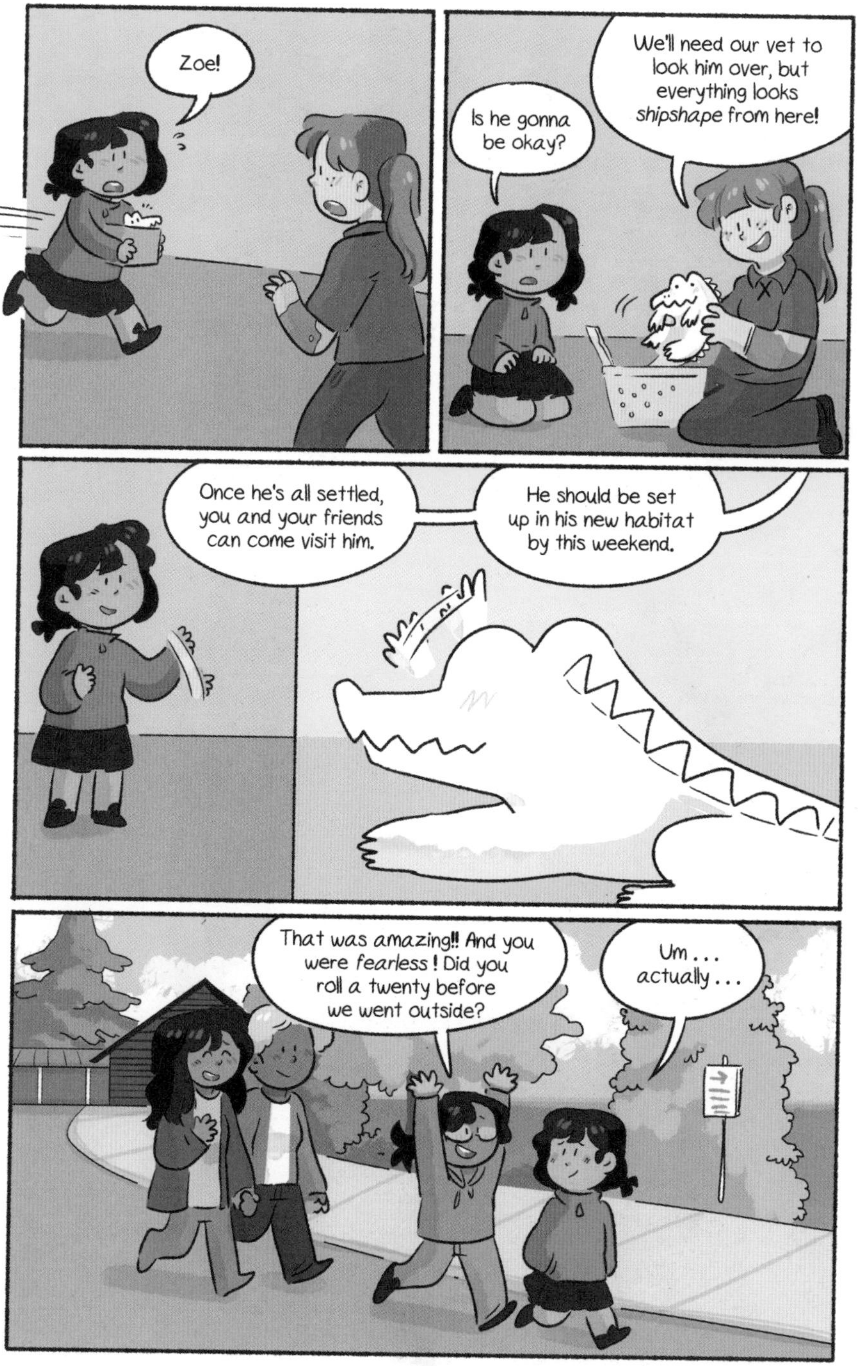
Zoe!
Is he gonna be okay?
We'll need our vet to look him over, but everything looks *shipshape* from here!
Once he's all settled, you and your friends can come visit him.
He should be set up in his new habitat by this weekend.
That was *amazing*!! And you were *fearless*! Did you roll a twenty before we went outside?
Um . . . actually . . .

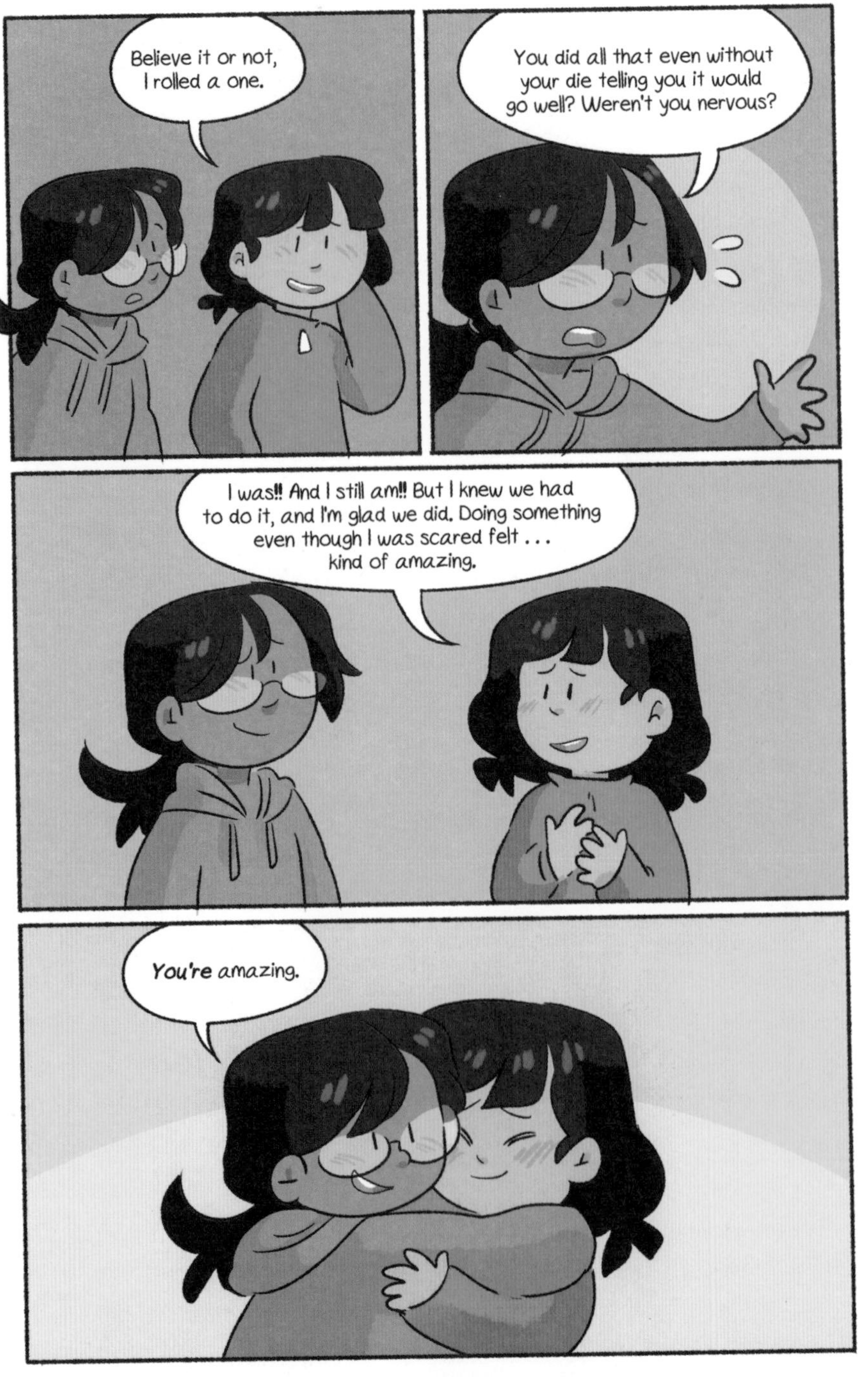
Believe it or not, I rolled a one.
You did all that even without your die telling you it would go well? Weren't you nervous?
I was!! And I still am!! But I knew we had to do it, and I'm glad we did. Doing something even though I was scared felt . . . kind of amazing.
You're amazing.

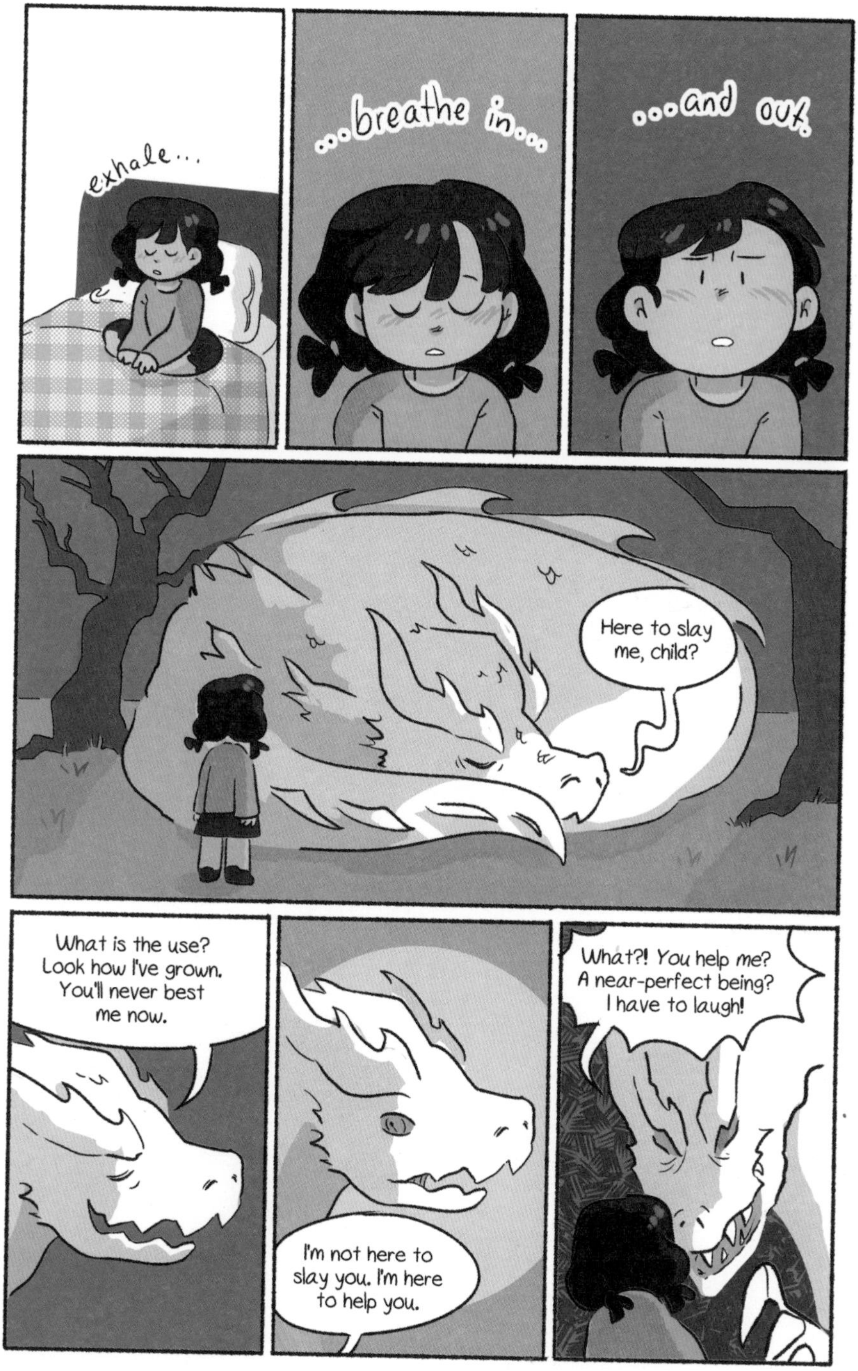
exhale...
...breathe in...
...and out.
Here to slay me, child?
What is the use? Look how I've grown. You'll never best me now.
I'm not here to slay you. I'm here to help you.
What?! You help me? A near-perfect being? I have to laugh!

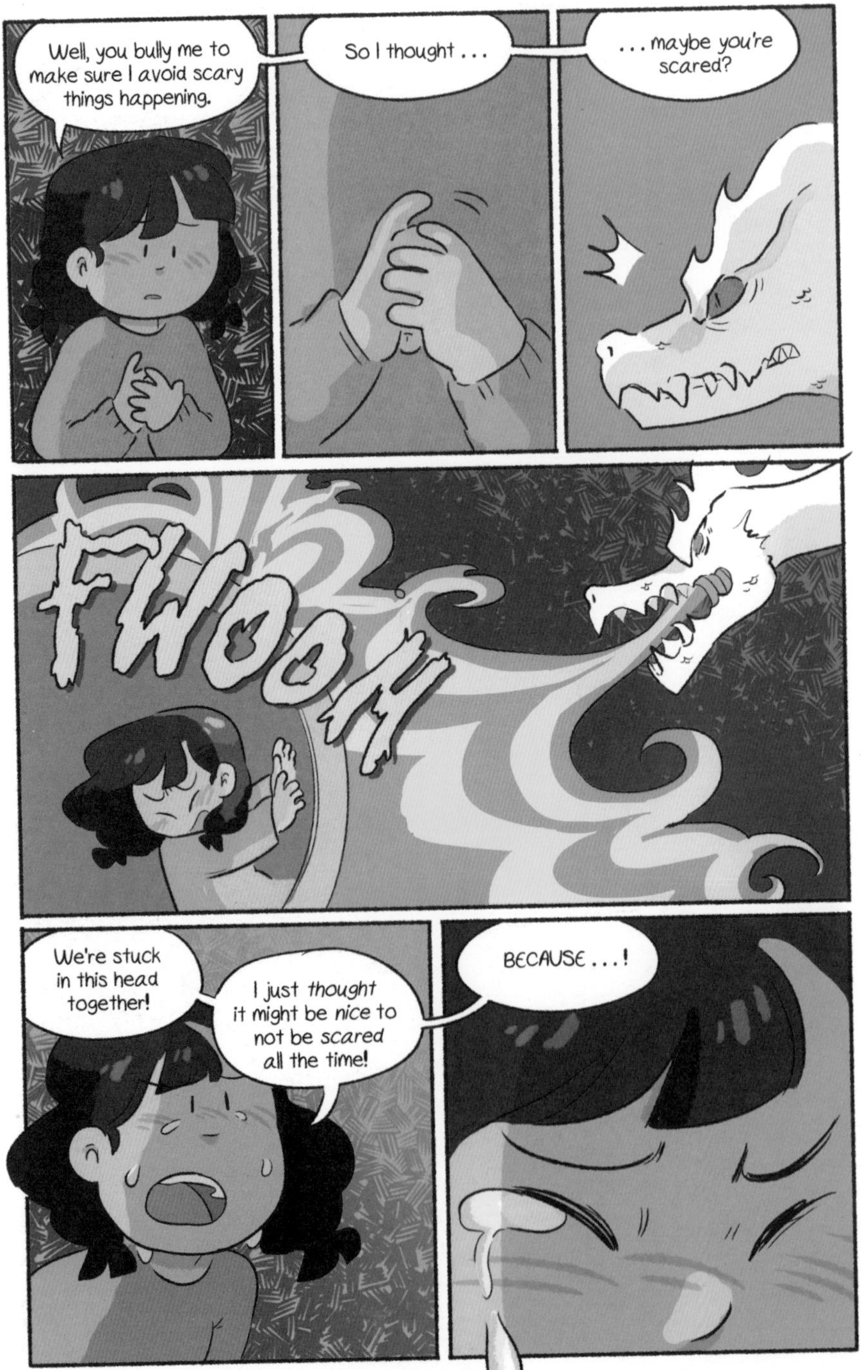
Well, you bully me to make sure I avoid scary things happening.
So I thought . . .
. . . maybe you're scared?
FWOOM
We're stuck in this head together!
I just thought it might be nice to not be scared all the time!
BECAUSE . . .!

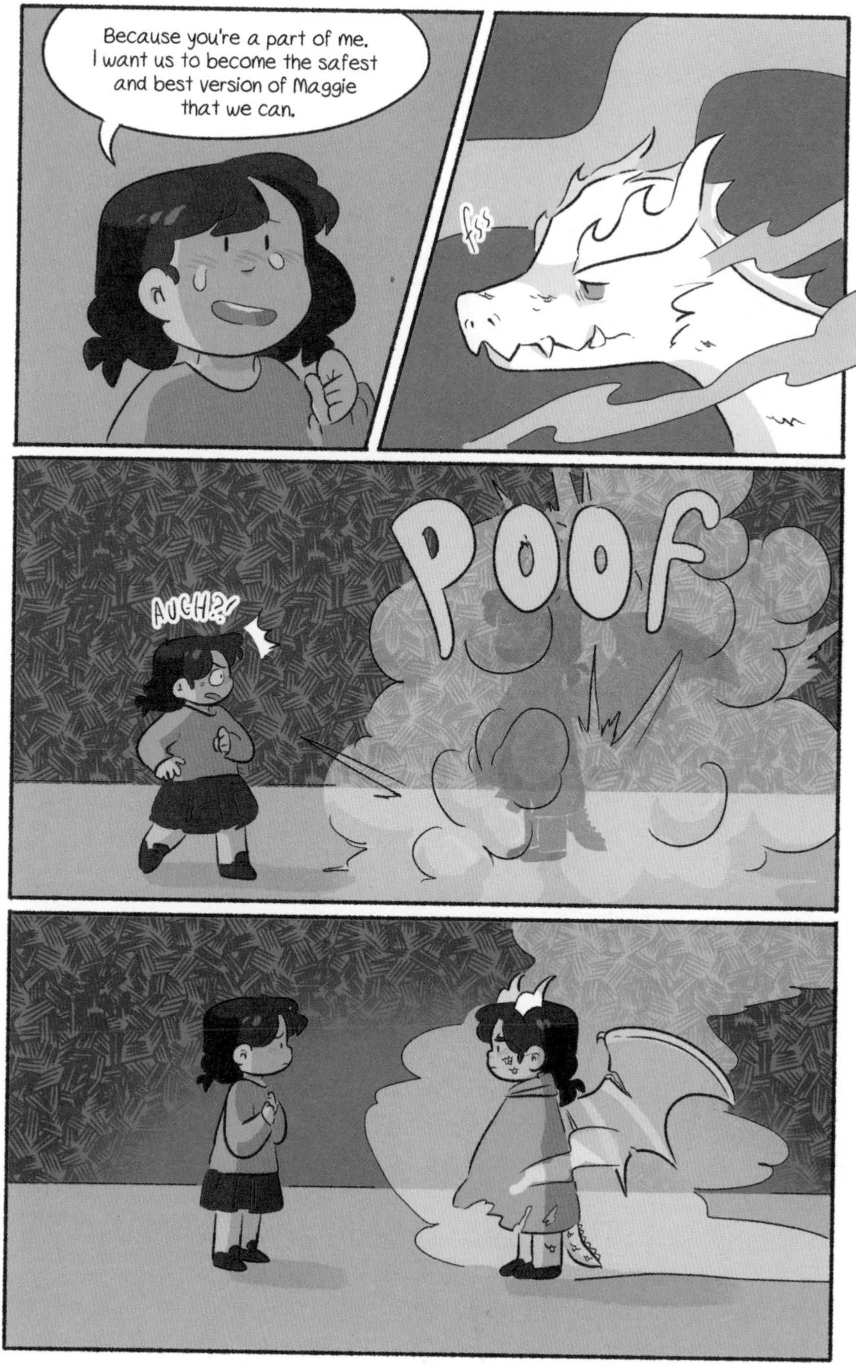
Because you're a part of me. I want us to become the safest and best version of Maggie that we can.
fss
POOF
AUGH?!

Okay.
Okay!!

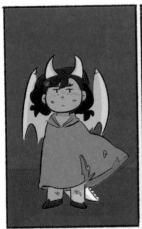

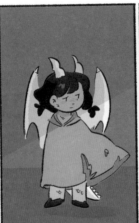

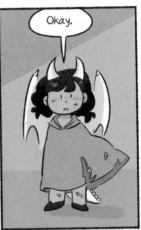

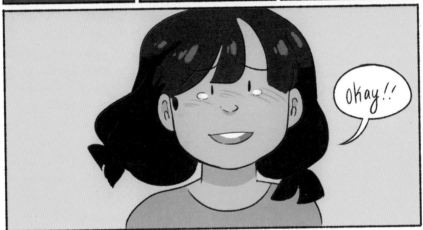

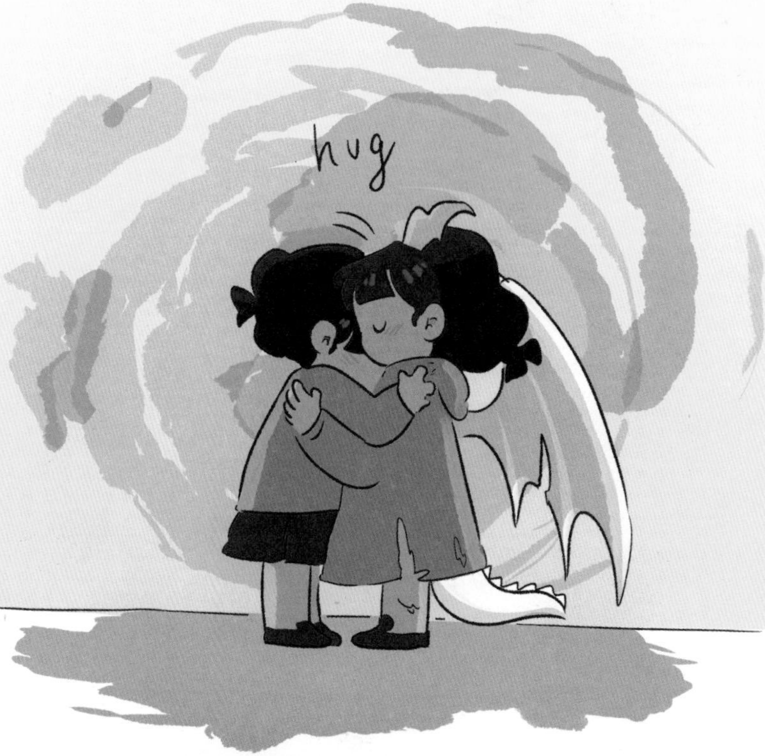
hug

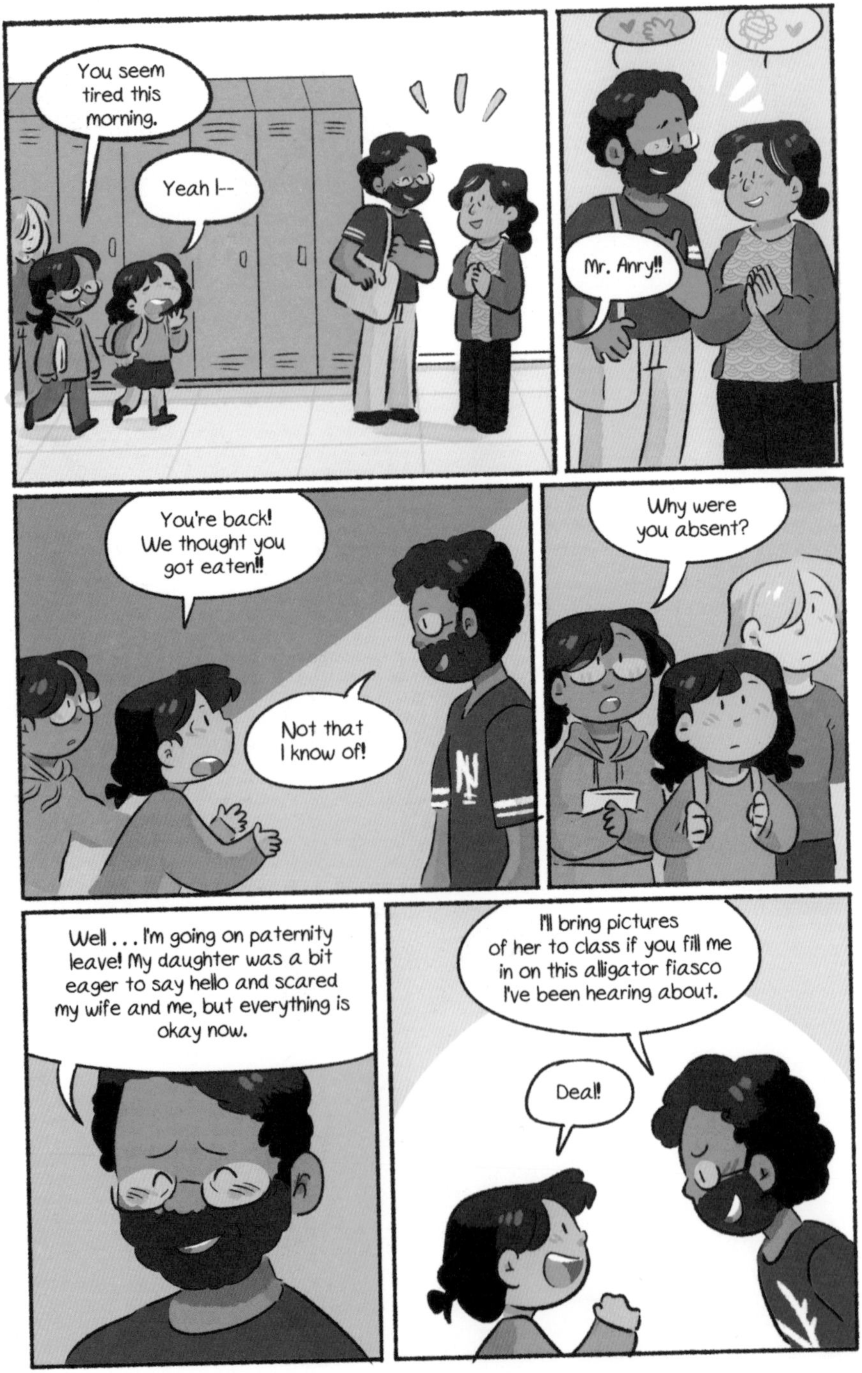
You seem tired this morning.
Yeah I--
Mr. Anry!!
You're back! We thought you got eaten!!
Not that I know of!
Why were you absent?
Well . . . I'm going on paternity leave! My daughter was a bit eager to say hello and scared my wife and me, but everything is okay now.
I'll bring pictures of her to class if you fill me in on this alligator fiasco I've been hearing about.
Deal!

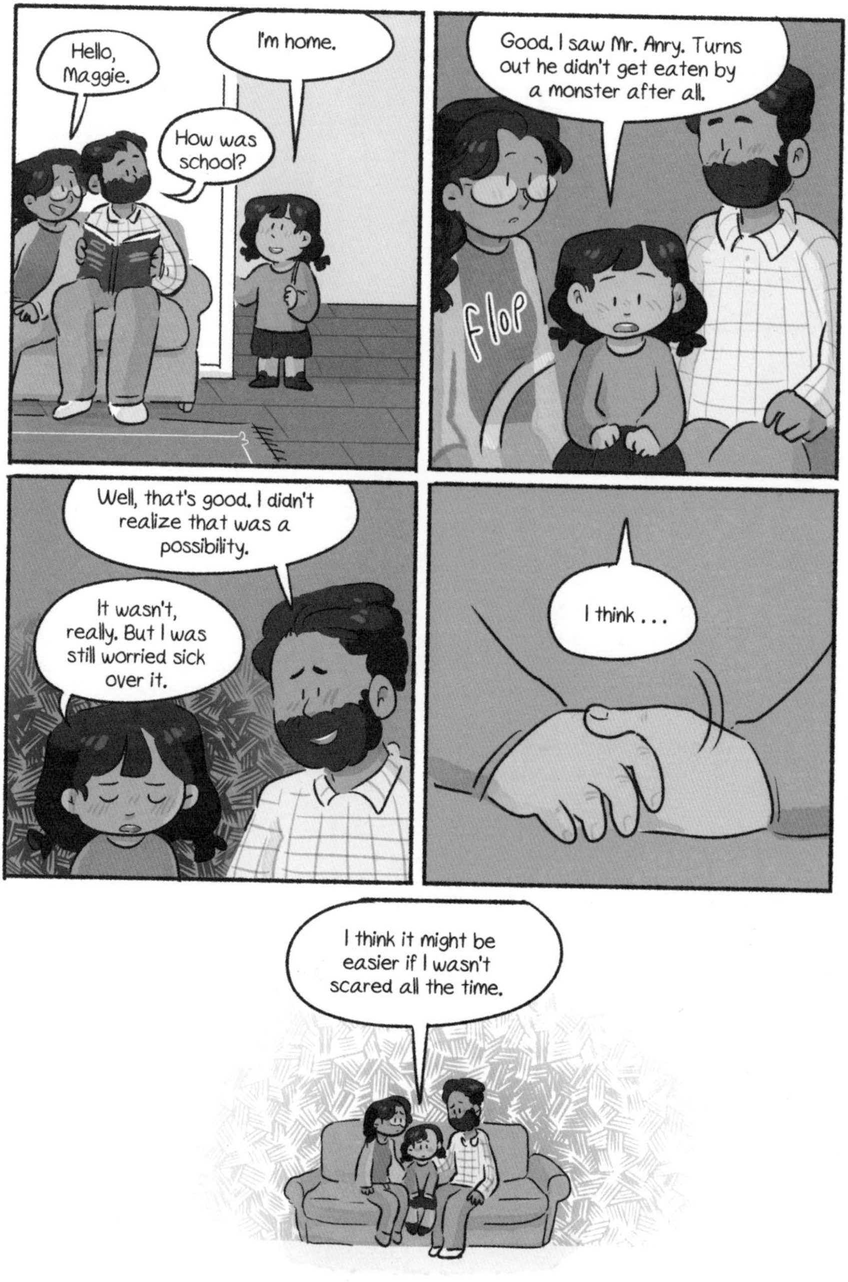
Hello, Maggie.
I'm home.
How was school?
Good. I saw Mr. Anry. Turns out he didn't get eaten by a monster after all.
flop
Well, that's good. I didn't realize that was a possibility.
It wasn't, really. But I was still worried sick over it.
I think . . .
I think it might be easier if I wasn't scared all the time.

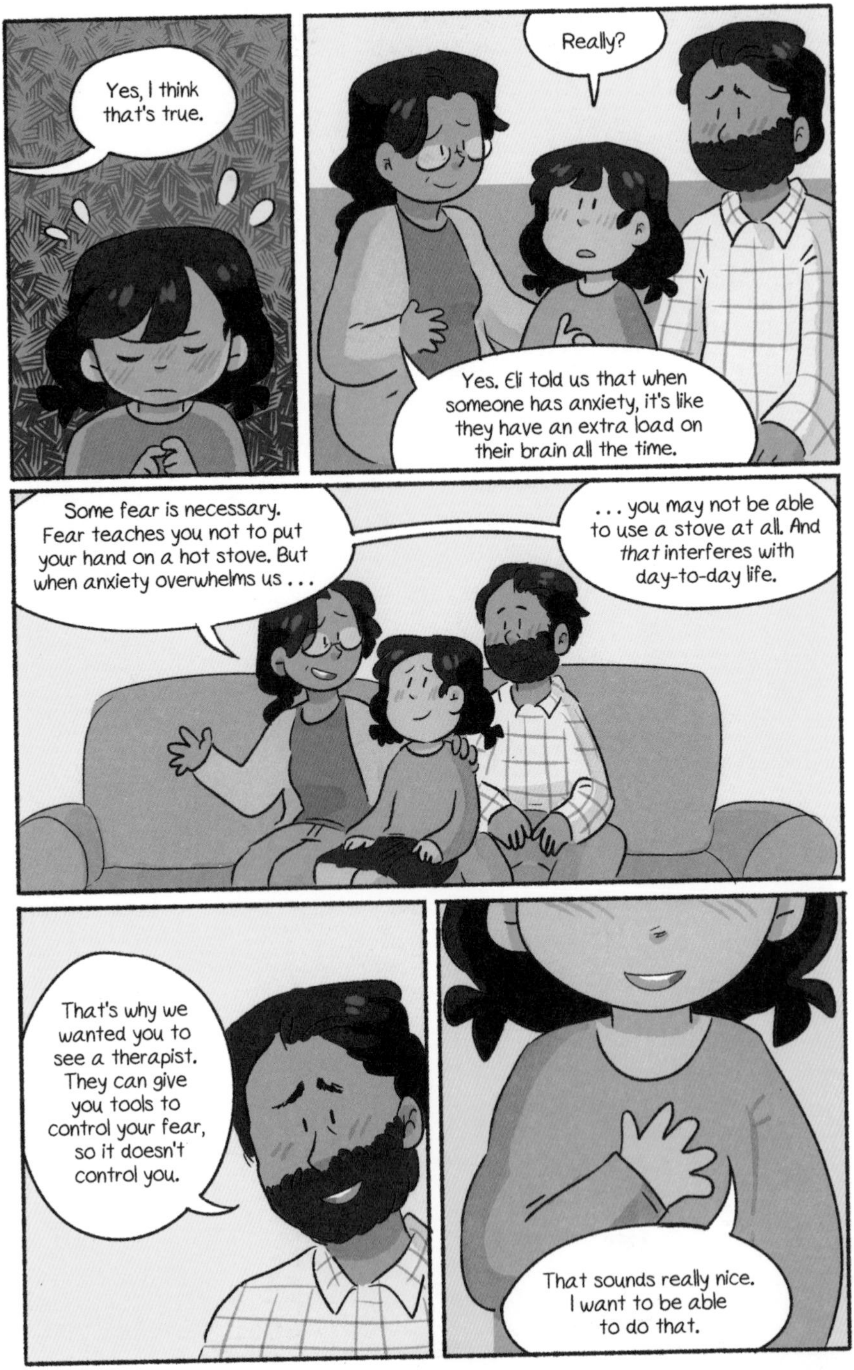
Yes, I think that's true.
Really?
Yes. Eli told us that when someone has anxiety, it's like they have an extra load on their brain all the time.
Some fear is necessary. Fear teaches you not to put your hand on a hot stove. But when anxiety overwhelms us . . .
. . . you may not be able to use a stove at all. And *that* interferes with day-to-day life.
That's why we wanted you to see a therapist. They can give you tools to control your fear, so it doesn't control you.
That sounds really nice. I want to be able to do that.

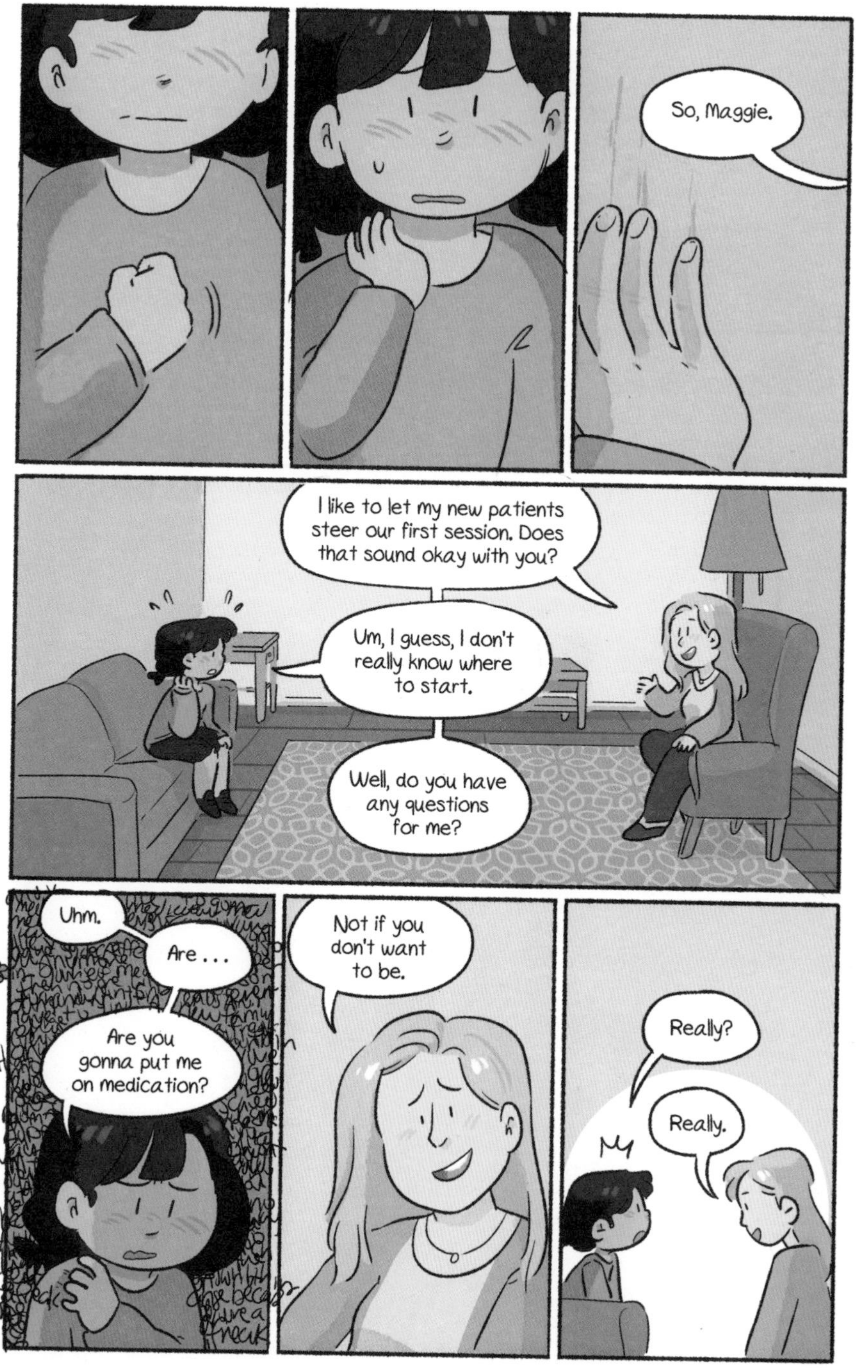
So, Maggie.
I like to let my new patients steer our first session. Does that sound okay with you?
Um, I guess, I don't really know where to start.
Well, do you have any questions for me?
Uhm.
Are . . .
Are you gonna put me on medication?
Not if you don't want to be.
Really?
Really.

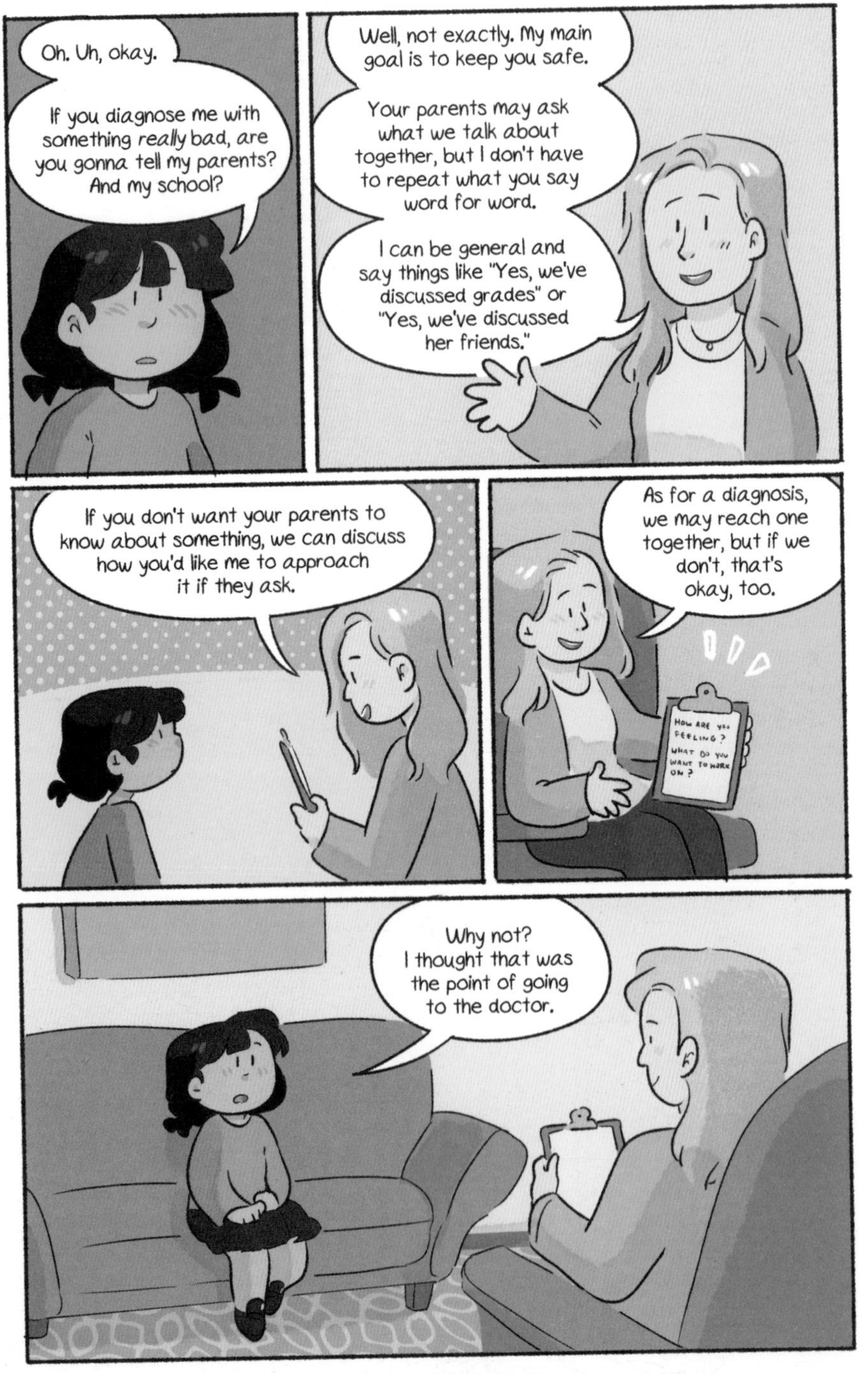
Oh. Uh, okay.
If you diagnose me with something *really* bad, are you gonna tell my parents? And my school?
Well, not exactly. My main goal is to keep you safe.
Your parents may ask what we talk about together, but I don't have to repeat what you say word for word.
I can be general and say things like "Yes, we've discussed grades" or "Yes, we've discussed her friends."
If you don't want your parents to know about something, we can discuss how you'd like me to approach it if they ask.
As for a diagnosis, we may reach one together, but if we don't, that's okay, too.
HOW ARE YOU FEELING?
WHAT DO YOU WANT TO WORK ON?
Why not? I thought that was the point of going to the doctor.

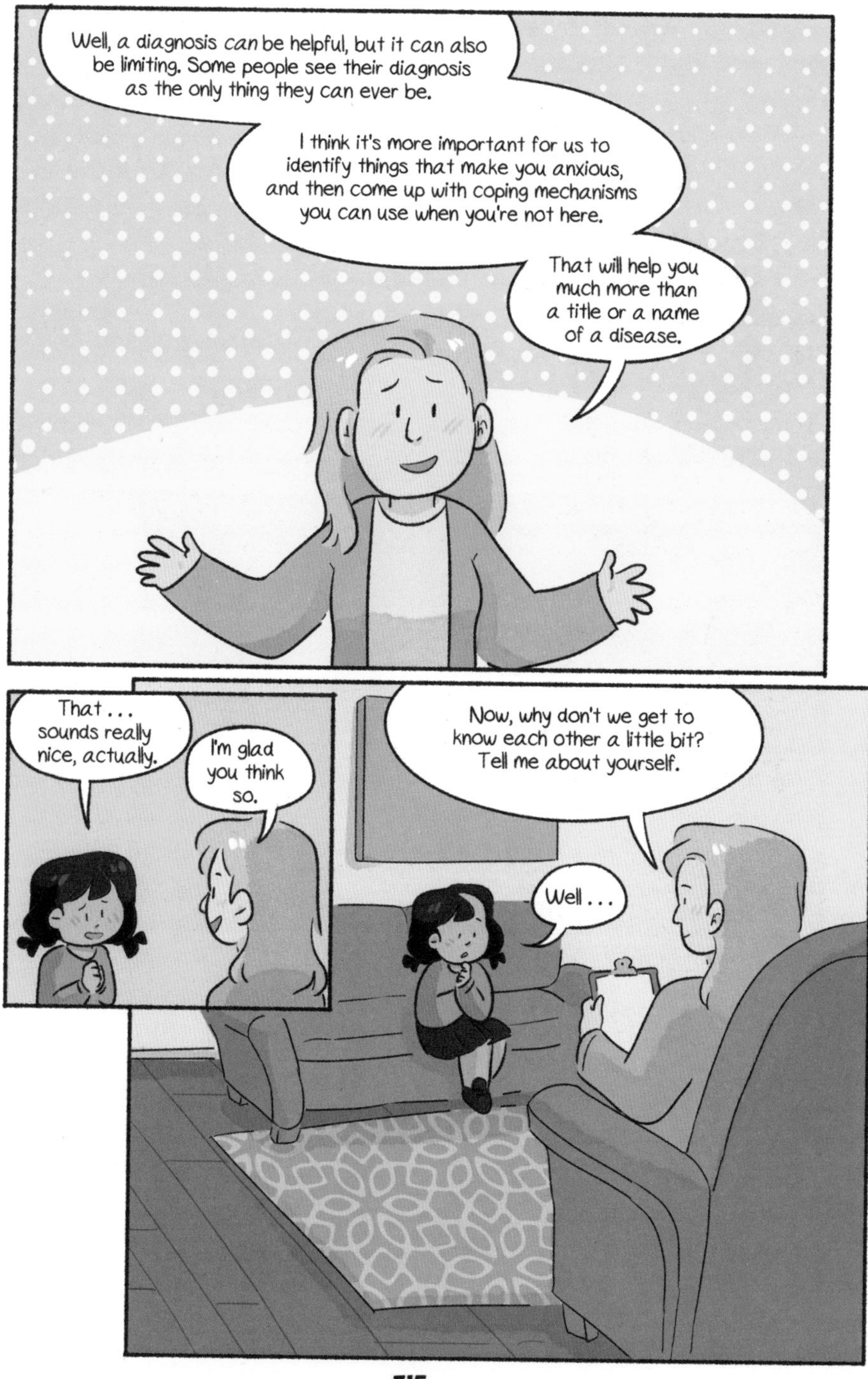
Well, a diagnosis *can* be helpful, but it can also be limiting. Some people see their diagnosis as the only thing they can ever be.
I think it's more important for us to identify things that make you anxious, and then come up with coping mechanisms you can use when you're not here.
That will help you much more than a title or a name of a disease.
That . . . sounds really nice, actually.
I'm glad you think so.
Now, why don't we get to know each other a little bit? Tell me about yourself.
Well . . .

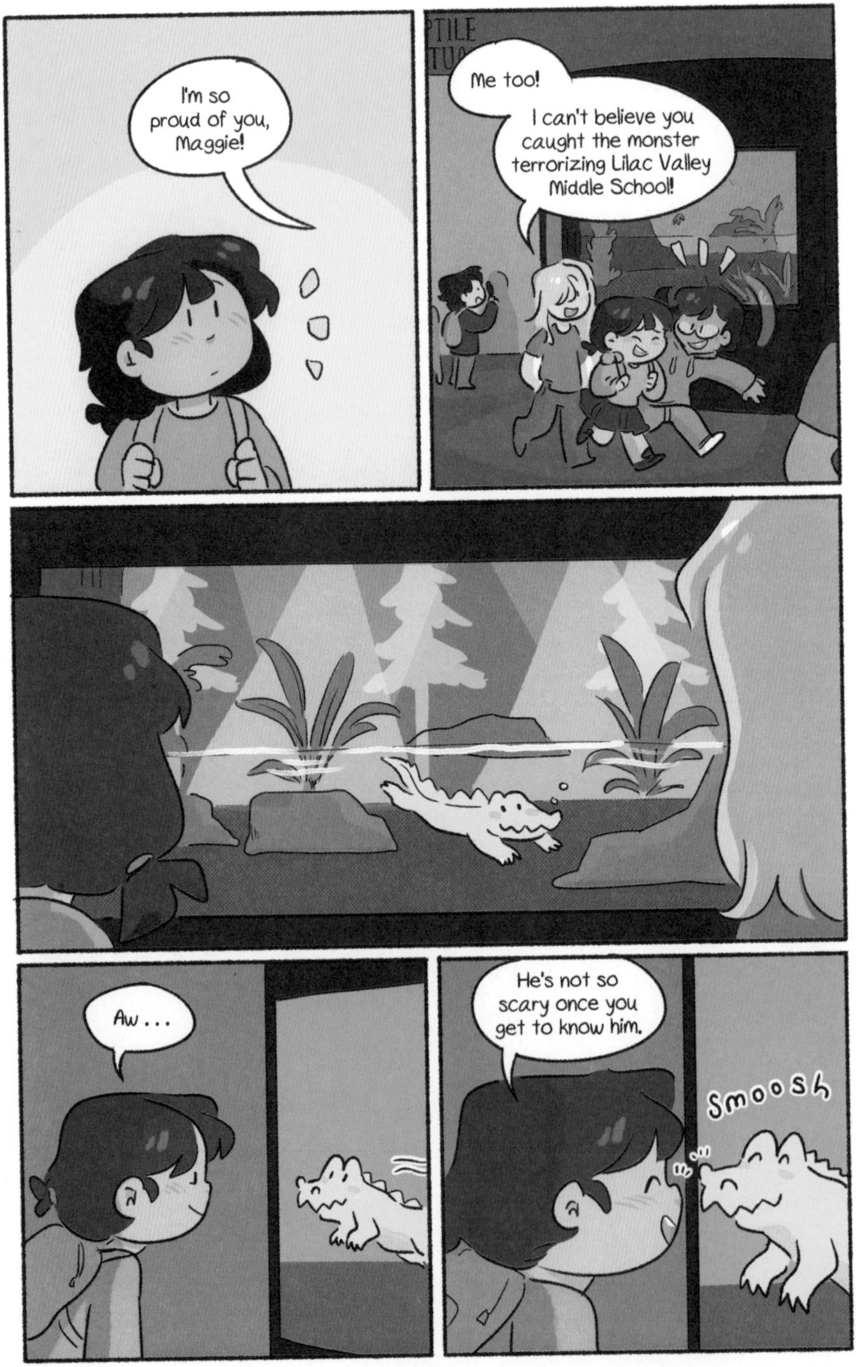
I'm so proud of you, Maggie!
PTILE
TUA
Me too!
I can't believe you caught the monster terrorizing Lilac Valley Middle School!
Aw . . .
He's not so scary once you get to know him.
Smoosh

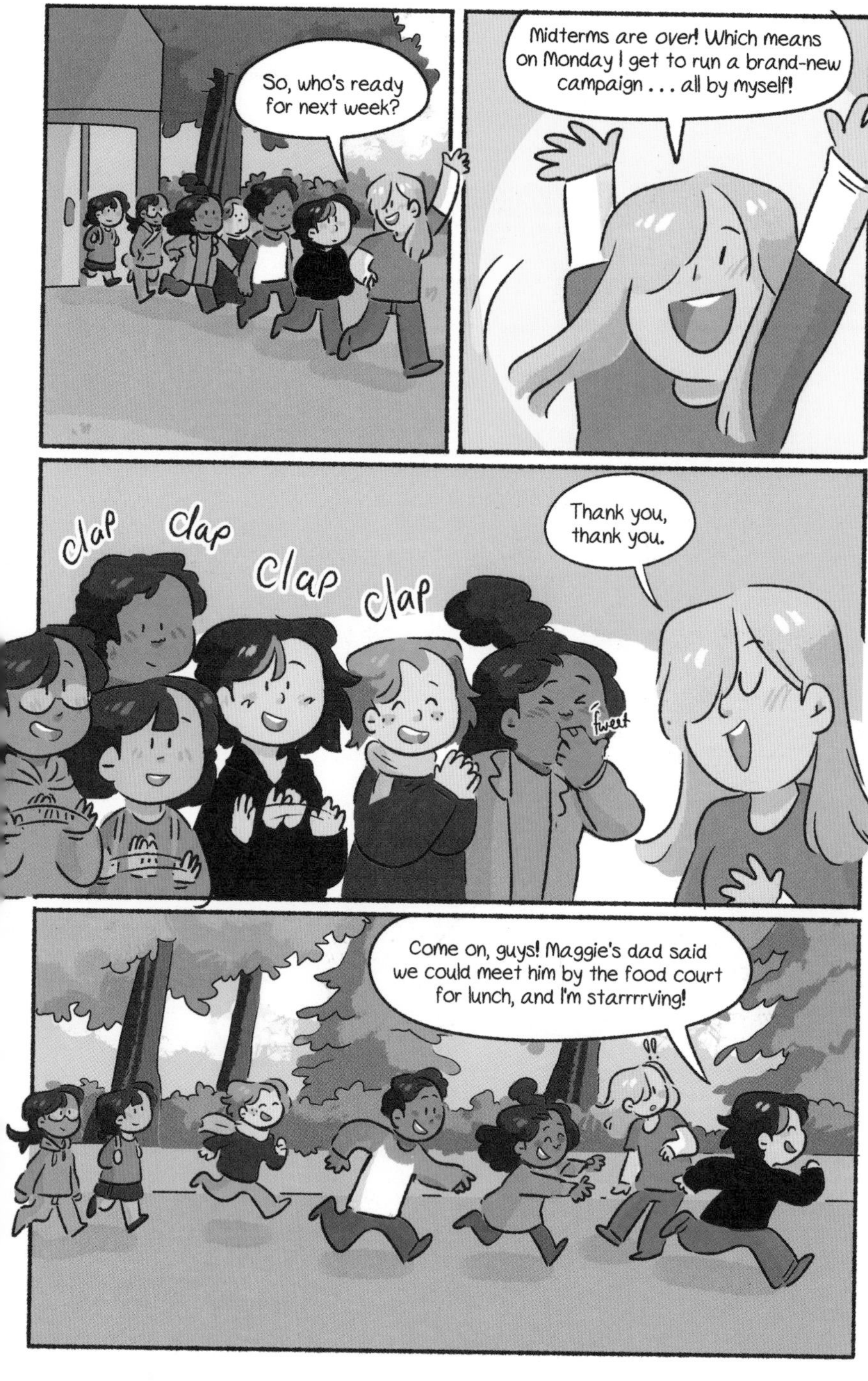
So, who's ready for next week?
Midterms are over! Which means on Monday I get to run a brand-new campaign . . . all by myself!
clap
clap
clap
clap
fweet
Thank you, thank you.
Come on, guys! Maggie's dad said we could meet him by the food court for lunch, and I'm starrrrving!
!!

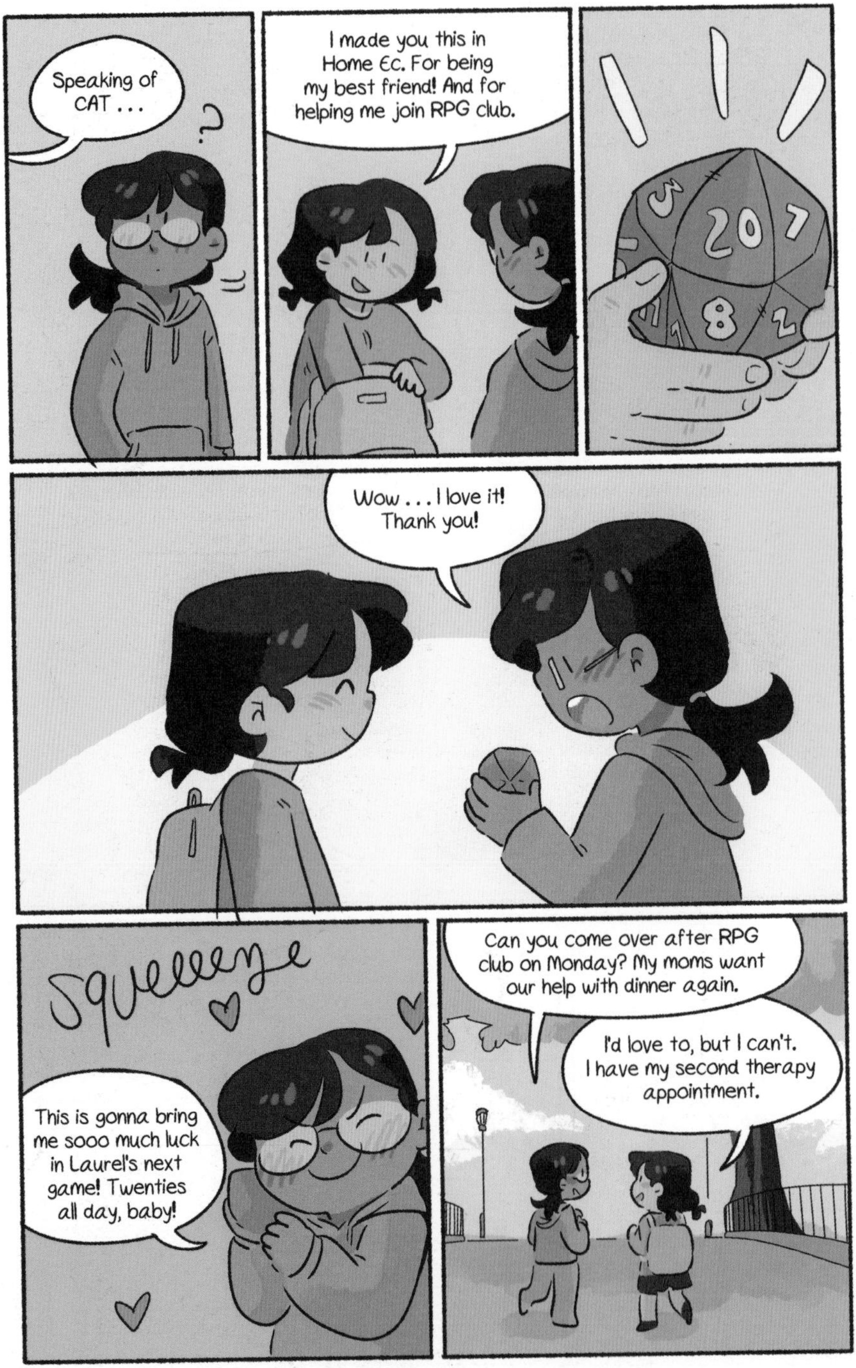
Speaking of CAT . . .
?
I made you this in Home Ec. For being my best friend! And for helping me join RPG club.
Wow . . . I love it! Thank you!
Squeeeze
This is gonna bring me sooo much luck in Laurel's next game! Twenties all day, baby!
Can you come over after RPG club on Monday? My moms want our help with dinner again.
I'd love to, but I can't. I have my second therapy appointment.

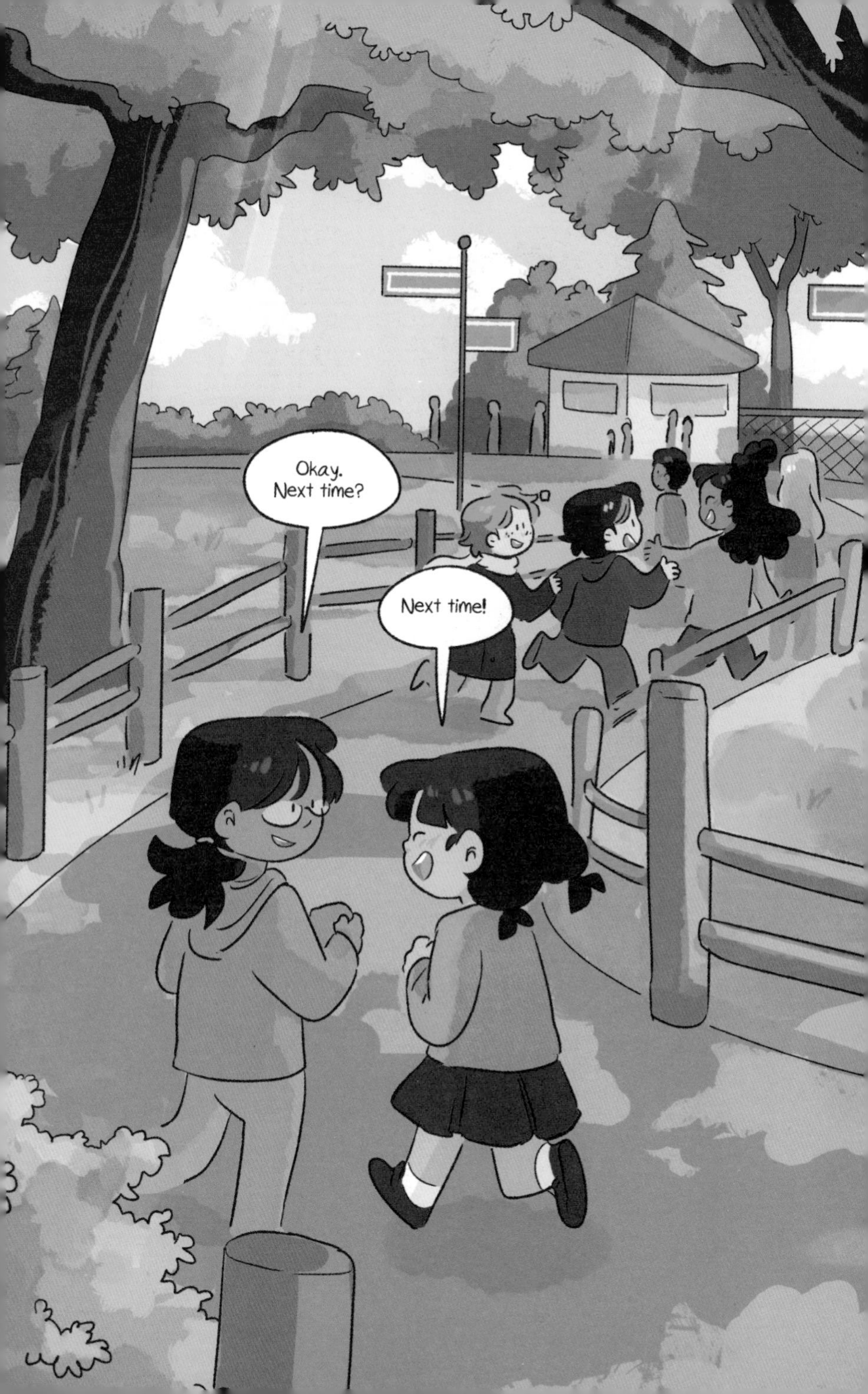
Okay.
Next time?
Next time!

ALzigorth

CHARM	PWR	HP
4	7	10

ExP

Inventory

NOTES

Likes
- Peace
- marigolds
- Her Axe
- Carliene

Dislikes
- fighting
- Evil King Leo
- Snakes
- _____

"I'm fighting for a world where no one has to be afraid!!"

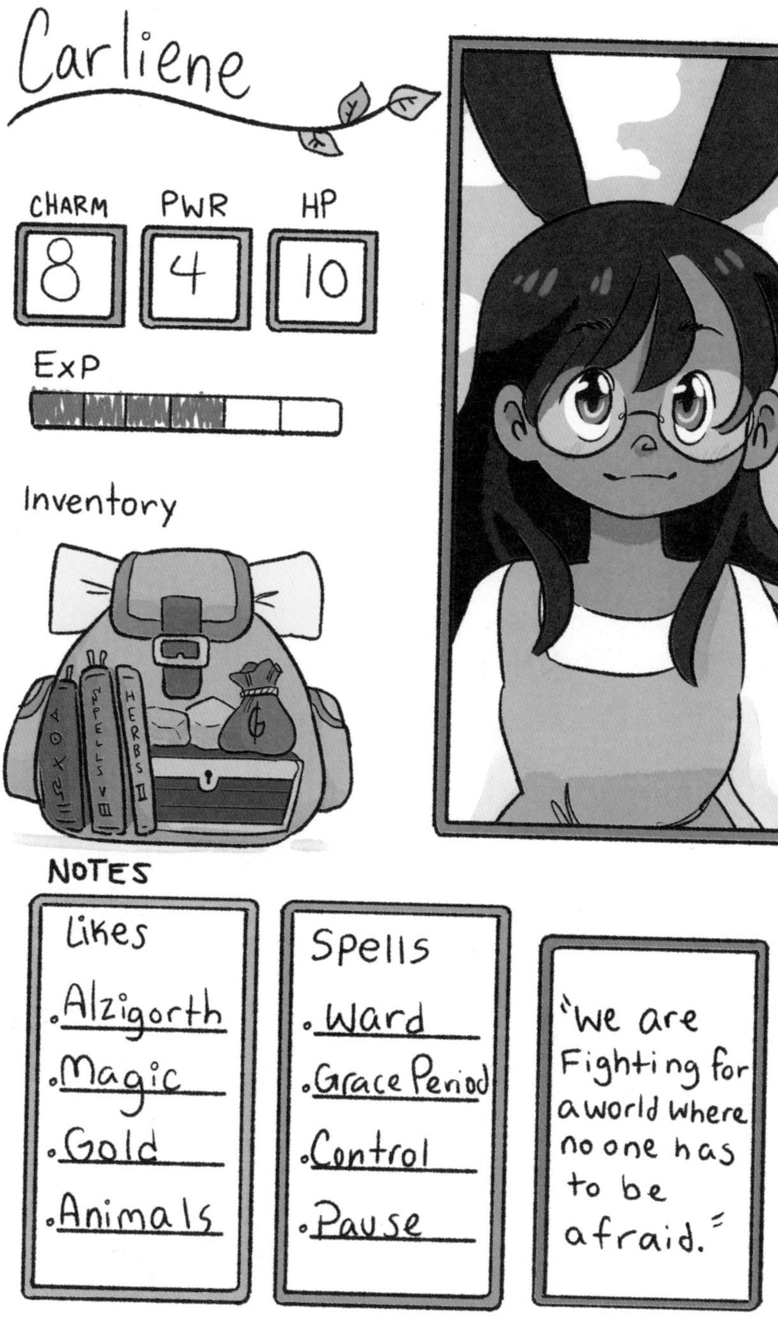
Carliene
CHARM
8
PWR
4
HP
10
ExP
Inventory
NOTES
Likes
Alzigorth
Magic
Gold
Animals
Spells
Ward
Grace Period
Control
Pause
"We are Fighting for a world where no one has to be afraid."

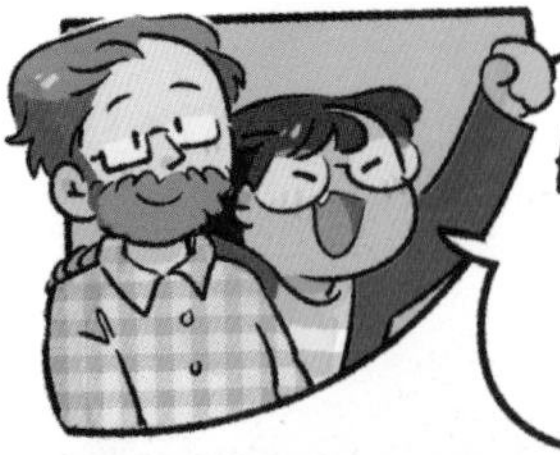

A graphic novel page from Start to Finish!!

Step 1 - Script

The script for this book was written by my partner, Lee! He wrote almost all of *Just Roll with It* using Google Docs on his phone.

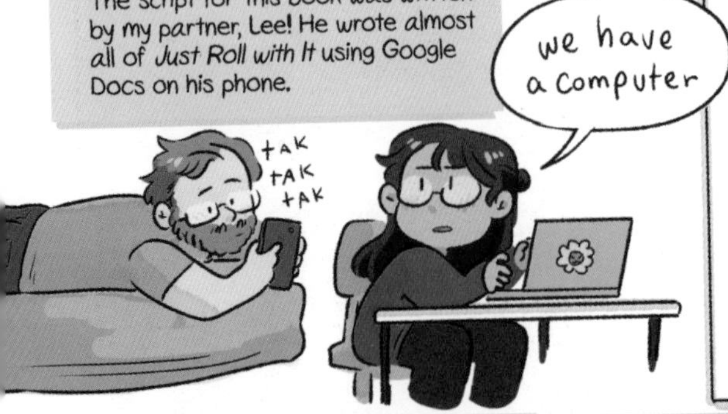

we have a computer
tak tak tak

Page 58:

1) The bell rings and Maggie is watching the grass this time as she walks to her sisters car.

2) The grass is moving and above and around it we see the whispers of some of the things she's overheard so far: 'six feet long', 'red eyes', a 'snake' 'six legs' etc.

Maggie is frozen where she stands, eyes wide.

3) The grass shakes again and she takes a step back, pulling out her d20.

4) She looks down at the d20 and it shows a four.
Maggie (outloud): What can I do? Can I run?

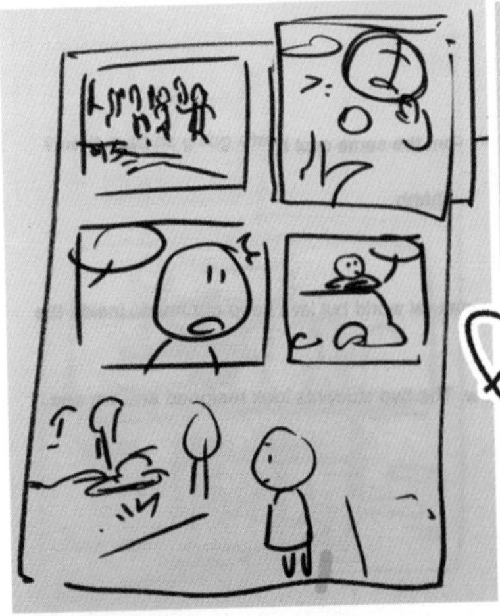

Step 2 - Thumbnails

After Lee is done with the script, I print it out and put all the pages in a huge binder. I draw thumbnails directly on the script pages using a 1.5 Faber-Castell marker!

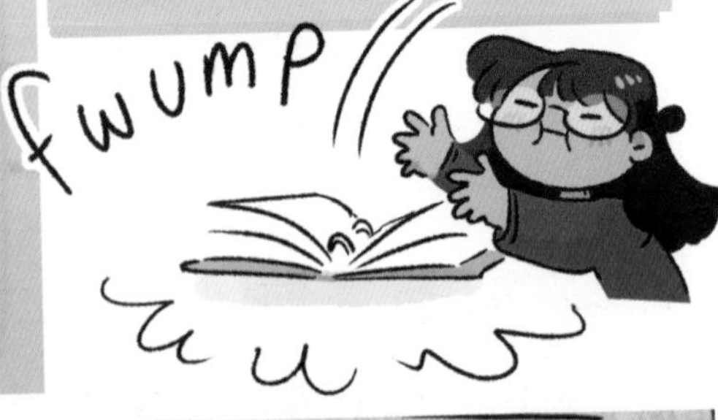

fwump

It's my favorite for thumbnailing because it helps me stay loose.

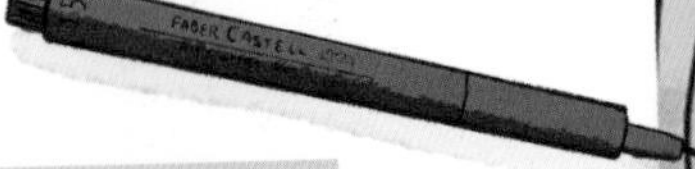

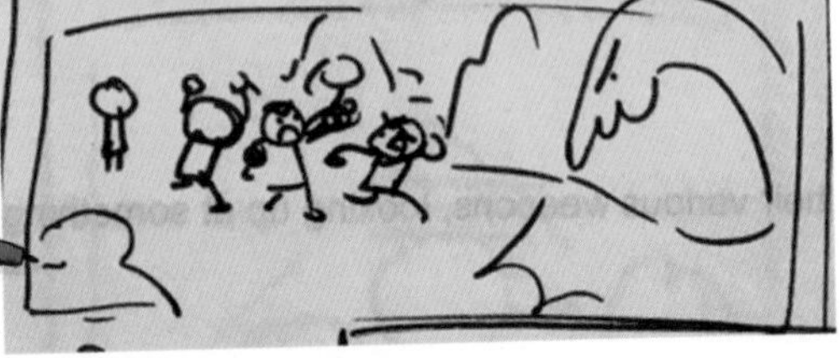

Like, *really* loose.

Step 2.5 - Get References

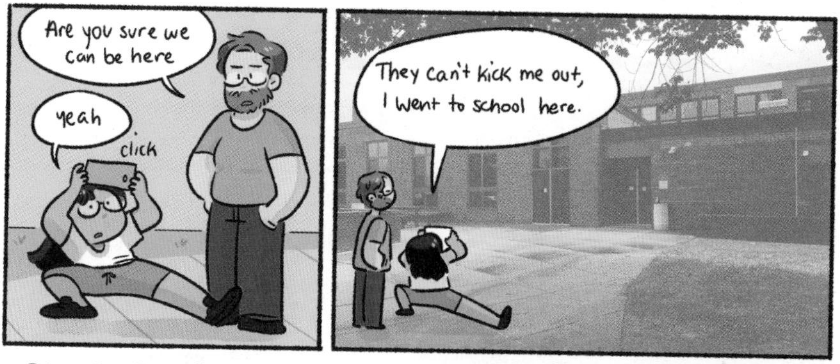
Are you sure we can be here
yeah
click
They can't kick me out, I went to school here.

Step 3 - Pencils

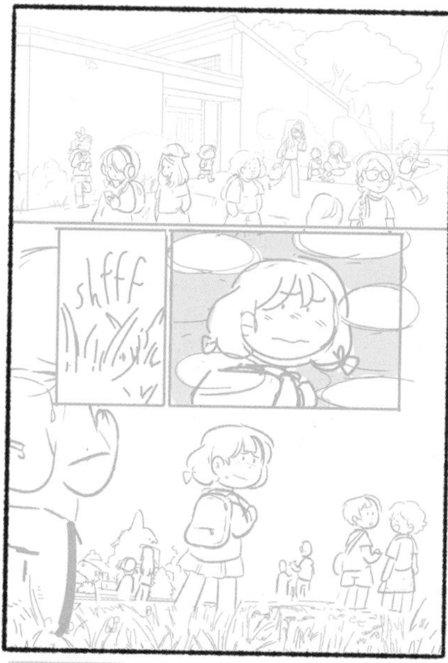
shfff

The majority of the heavy lifting is done during this stage, but penciling is a lot of fun even so!

I do a lot of problem solving here, but thankfully things are pretty forgiving.

I love using Photoshop and working digitally because I'm able to resize pieces if they don't fit right, move them around, etc.

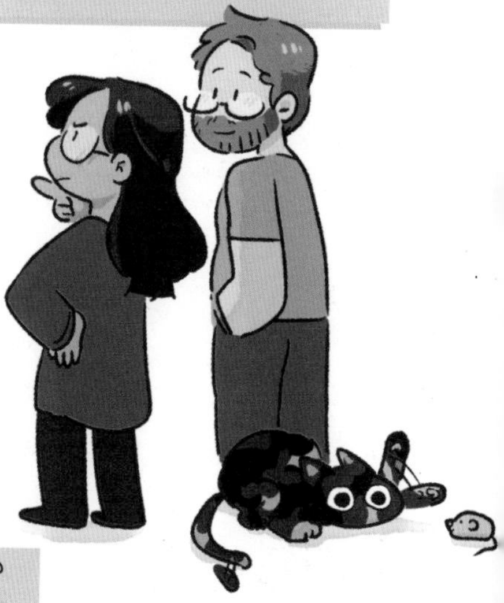

Tools

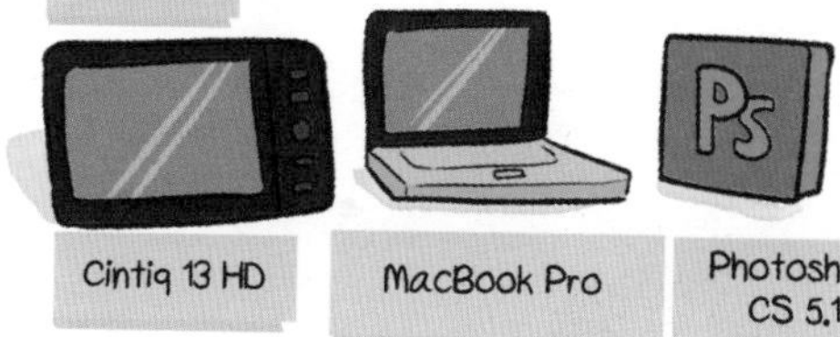

Cintiq 13 HD

MacBook Pro

Photoshop CS 5.1

Step 4 - Inks

At this point I've already decided line widths for everything, so inking is pretty mindless in the best way. I like to put on Let's Plays, anime, cartoons, or music and just chill when I ink.

For the most part, it's pretty smooth sailing. Though I do run into the occasional *blob-of-unknown-intent*, and I have to puzzle out what pencil-me was thinking when she drew it.

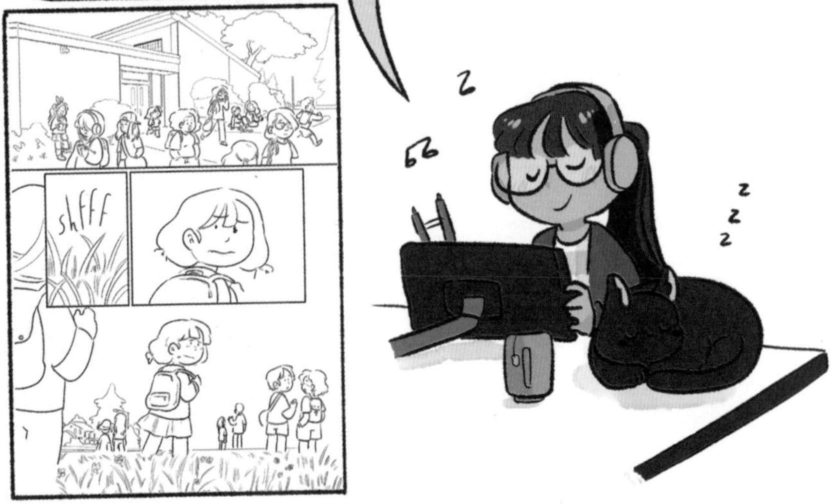

shfff
z
z
z
z

Step 5 - Color

Almost done! I flat the entire page before going in for coloring. Flatting is the first pass to make coloring easier. My best friends in the whole world, Alex and Wren, were a huge help with this!

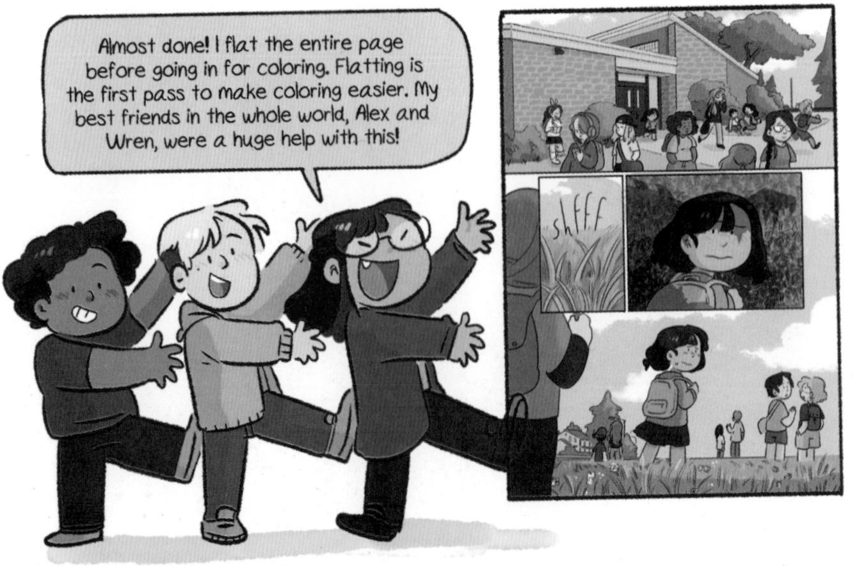

shfff

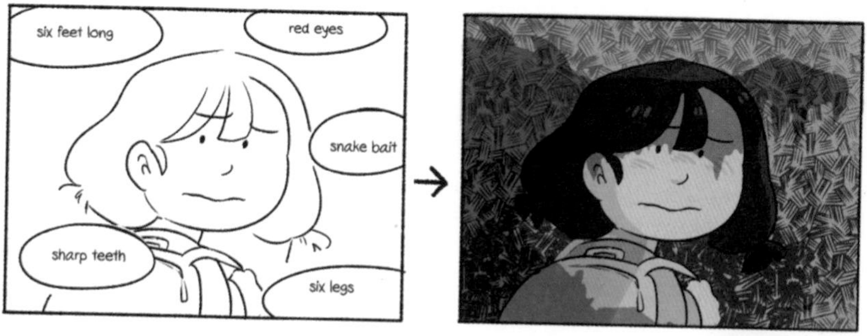
six feet long
red eyes
snake bait
sharp teeth
six legs

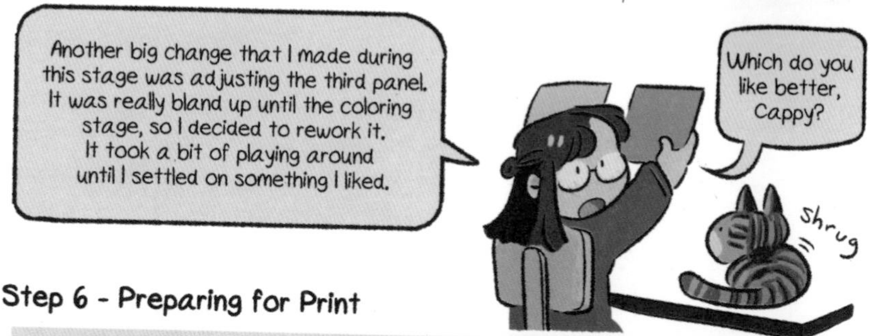
Another big change that I made during this stage was adjusting the third panel. It was really bland up until the coloring stage, so I decided to rework it. It took a bit of playing around until I settled on something I liked.
Which do you like better, Cappy?
shrug

Step 6 - Preparing for Print

The last step is focused on prepping the book for print. This includes resizing the pages, making sure they're formatted for CMYK printing and any other requirements! The requirements can differ from publisher to publisher.

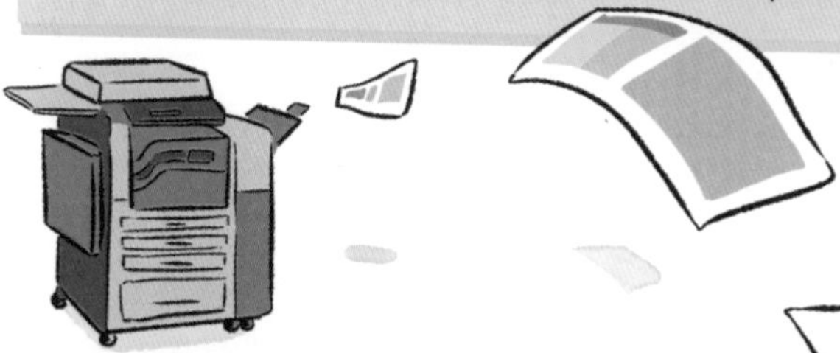

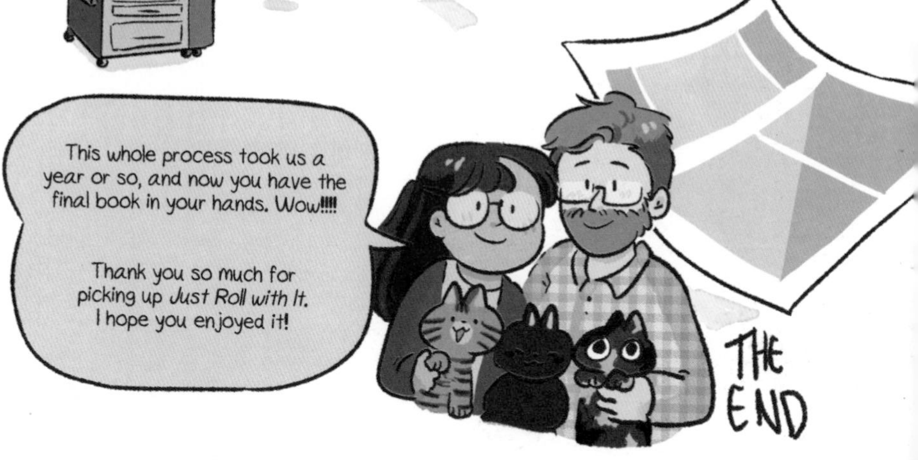
This whole process took us a year or so, and now you have the final book in your hands. Wow!!!!
Thank you so much for picking up *Just Roll with It.* I hope you enjoyed it!
THE END

Authors' Notes

In 2017, I brought up the possibility of me having OCD with my therapist of several years. After we started discussing it, a lot of things began to make sense. Previous depictions I had seen or things I had read about obsessive compulsive disorder involved physical tics, repetitive actions, counting, or cleaning. But as I learned more about the disorder and how it presents, I realized that things in my everyday life—things I had grown accustomed to and deliberately worked around—could all be traced back to obsessive thinking and compulsions: my tendency to be very picky about food, my meticulous overplanning in order to avoid being uncomfortable in any situation, my fear of dying and death . . . and my rituals to keep it at bay.

Once I gave it a name, I started to identify the different ways it had a hold on me. I wanted Maggie's story to highlight how OCD can take you hostage. Over the course of developing this story, I was worried Lee and I weren't showing enough types of symptoms. But, in truth, there was no way we were going to be able to represent every possible OCD manifestation and condense it into one story. My hope is that Maggie can help someone else's light bulb go off and give them the first push they need to look deeper if their anxiety is limiting their quality of life.

The advice that Maggie's therapist gives her at the end is taken directly from my own therapist, Debbie. I want to reiterate that what's most important is your own journey to mental well-being and not necessarily "fitting" a diagnosis perfectly. I also want to take the time in this author's note to encourage you to shop around for therapists, if you're interested in seeing one. It may take a bit of time until you find someone who is a good fit for you.

Thank you for reading *Just Roll with It* and this author's note. I hope that reading this story has given you as much as it has given me to create it.

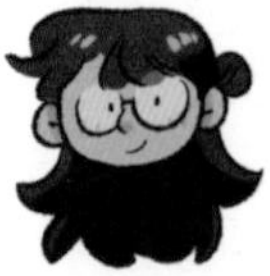

Veronica Agarwal

For me this book was inspired by being miserable in middle school. I went undiagnosed with depression, anxiety, and ADHD for a really long time, and it made certain parts of growing up incredibly difficult. My deepest hope is that this book, and Maggie's story, can help someone feel even just a little bit better about going through that sea of seemingly unending awkwardness and fear.

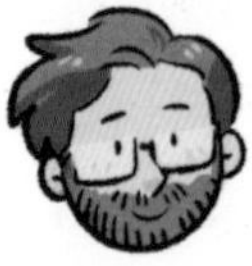

Lee Durfey-Lavoie

About the Authors

Veronica Agarwal (she/her) is a cartoonist and an illustrator from New York. She lives with her partner, Lee, and their three cats. She graduated from the School of Visual Arts with a BFA in cartooning. She's been featured in *Elements: Fire, Power & Magic: The Queer Witch Comics Anthology, Electrum,* and *When the Rules Aren't Right* by Leslie Tolf. She also illustrated *Alexis vs. Summer Vacation,* written by Sarah Jamila Stevenson. Her work aims to normalize talking about mental health through stories that are enjoyable and uplifting. She loves sunflowers, summertime, and dogs! wisbafolio.com 🐦@anuanew

Lee Durfey-Lavoie (he/they) grew up in Rhode Island but now lives in New York. Along for the journey are his three cats (Captain, Natasha, and Sammy), who both drive him up the wall and keep him sane. A proud college dropout, this is his debut graphic novel. He likes folk music, cats, and coffee. 🐦@DurfeyLee

Acknowledgments

I acknowledge that this was written and drawn on land stolen from Native Americans, specifically from the Merrick tribe.

I want to thank my entire family—Mom, Dad, Lee, Grandma Dadi, Grandma Nana, Aunt Fran, Aunt Theri, Aunt Tracy, Uncle Andy, Uncle Ted, Matt, Steve, Mary, and Amanda—for being the best family I could possibly ask for. From when we're serious to when we're silly, being a part of this family is always a blessing. To Lee's family, for welcoming me with open arms and hearts and incredibly comforting hugs.

To Alex and Wren, for being my best friends and helping me flat this book during crunch time. To Anthony, for inspiring me to be passionate without remorse. To Paloma, for her laser-focused critique and for being a friendly ball of energy. To Alisa, for inspiring the title of this book, and to Krav, for their assistance on backgrounds. To everyone in Sunflower Station, it should probably be considered a hazard to have this much talent and kindness condensed into one Discord server. Starting Sunflower Station will always be my proudest achievement.

To my agent, Susan Graham, thank you for your hard work, knowledge, and kindness. This book exists in huge part because of you. I'm so proud of being your client. Thank you for having me!

To Gina Gagliano, who saw potential in Lee and me and gave us this opportunity. To Whitney, Patrick, and everyone at Random House Graphic, thank you for allowing us to stand among a lineup of such beautiful books.

To my cats, Natasha, Captain, and Sammy, thank you for keeping me company while I worked on this book. Sometimes you yelled, sometimes you demanded attention, and you walked all over my keyboard, but I wouldn't have had it any other way.

And finally to Lee, writer, partner, and love of my life. When I was a kid, there was a huge swath of media that told me that relationships were supposed to be work, but being with you has been the easiest thing I've ever done. I always assumed I would have to sacrifice parts of who I was if I wanted to find a long-term partner. You have never made me feel like you love me for anything less than what I truly am, and for that I thank you.

—V.A.

Acknowledgments

Firstly I'd like to acknowledge that this book was written on stolen Merrick land.

Secondly I'd like to say thank you to the team at Random House Graphic who was with us every step of the way, encouraging us and helping this book be the best it could be: Whitney Leopard, our wonderful editor, who has been inspiring and supportive since day one; Gina Gagliano, who took a chance on us and let us add to RHG's wonderful mission of getting a graphic novel on every shelf; Patrick Crotty; Nicole Valdez; and everybody else at Random House and Random House Graphic.

I'd like to thank, of course, Susan Graham, who is the best agent and friend one could ask for. They guided us and made this book possible, helped give it life and a solid foundation. They helped not just the book get off the ground but me as well, and I would not be where I am without their help. My deepest and never-ending thanks and gratitude.

To my family, who, if I named everyone, this would go on for way too long. But to my mom, especially, for being the kindest, gentlest, and most hardworking person I know and who taught me to be strong and kind and compassionate. To my siblings, who, while I don't talk to them often enough, inspire me daily and were the driving force behind this book. To my grandparents and dad for always being there when I needed them. To Veronica's whole side of the family, who accepted and loved me from the beginning, I literally wouldn't have survived without you. I love you all so much. To everybody else: thank you so much. I appreciate you more than words can say.

To my friends in Sunflower Station and beyond, for being the nicest, funniest, weirdest people in the world.

And finally to Veronica, my artist, co-author, and partner, and the love of my life. The well of love, support, and encouragement you offer me has transformed my entire life and made me a better person. I can't begin to describe how much you mean to me, but this book, this career, and everything else would never be possible without you by my side. I love you.

—L.D.-L.

FIND YOUR VOICE

WITH ONE OF THESE EXCITING GRAPHIC NOVELS

CHAD SELL
CREATOR OF THE CARDBOARD KINGDOM
Doodleville
THE CARDBOARD KINGDOM
CHAD SELL
THE CARDBOARD KINGDOM
ROAR OF THE BEAST
CHAD SELL
LUCY KNISLEY
STEPPING STONES
JUST ROLL WITH IT
VERONICA AGARWALL & LEE DURFEY-LAVOIE
TURTLE IN PARADISE
The Graphic Novel
JENNIFER L. HOLM
SAVANNA GANUCHEAU
KATIE THE CATSITTER
Colleen AF Venable
Stephanie Yue

PRESENTED BY RH GRAPHIC

@RHKIDSGRAPHIC

A GRAPHIC NOVEL ON EVERY BOOKSHELF